MW00712433

Also by Linda Ashour
Speaking in Tongues

Linda Phillips Ashour

Simon & Schuster
New York   London
Toronto   Sydney   Tokyo   Singapore

Joy
Baby

a ◄ novel

July 24, 1992
For George Riley,
So glad) to finally
meet you.
Enjoy Joy Baby... Best—
Linda

SIMON & SCHUSTER
Simon & Schuster Building
Rockefeller Center
1230 Avenue of the Americas
New York, New York 10020

SIMON & SCHUSTER and colophon are registered trademarks
of Simon & Schuster Inc.

Designed by Levavi and Levavi/Nina D'Amario
Manufactured in the United States of America

1   3   5   7   9   10   8   6   4   2

Library of Congress Cataloging in Publication Data
Ashour, Linda.
Joy Baby: a novel/Linda Phillips Ashour.
p.   cm.
I. Title.
PS3551. S416J6   1992
813'.54—dc20   92-3530
CIP
ISBN 0-671-68331-4

Acknowledgments

This novel is, in part, based on my great-grandfather's life. I let fact and fantasy collide here in the hope that pure story would emerge. In the effort to keep characters and events psychologically true, I've had help from many sources.

Historical research for this book was naturally conducted by scouring books and documents, riffling through old photographs and artifacts. But it was also, and perhaps most important, enlivened by stories shared with me by those who knew Frank and Jane Phillips. I can't thank these people enough: Bob Finney, historian for Phillips Petroleum, and Paul Endacott, who was president of the corporation for eleven years, are both able raconteurs. Bob Landsdown welcomed me at Woolaroc and led me through my great-grandfather's museum on several occasions.

Frank Phillips had a long and complex relationship with the Osage Indian tribe. My fascination with this aspect of his business and personal life led me to call on many people in both Pawhuska, Oklahoma, and here in California. Among those who welcomed me, I would especially like to thank Angela Robinson for her kindness. I am grateful to Geoffrey Mongrain Standing Bear for taking time out of a frantic schedule for me. Our talks have helped me understand the immediacy of certain tribal issues. An inadvertent meeting with Mary Jo Metcalf offered insights that would shape this book. And Ray Walker's scholarship helped me find a focus on the enormous body of Osage literature.

Oil Man, a diligent biography of my great-grandfather by Michael Wallis, was of immense help during the writing of this novel. *The Osage Oil Boom*, by Kenny A. Franks, appeared on bookshelves in the nick of time. A portion of the text, the pipeline chant, appears verbatim in the novel, for it could not have been improved upon. The same is true of the passage lifted from a Cherokee outlaw's autobiography. Henry Starr's words are his own. So are those of his Aunt Belle.

I would like to thank the Corporation of Yaddo for three weeks spent in such grand quarters. I also wish to thank Denison University for the Beck Fund, and Paul Bennett for his encouragement and continued interest in a former writing student.

I am grateful to Bob Asahina, my key believer for the second time. The structure of the book reflects his scrupulous editing. Thanks to my agent, Suzanne Gluck, for taking on a newcomer. All that long distance energy has been a great boon.

Enduring friendships are a writer's real sustenance. I would like to thank the Marinoffs for fifteen years of listening, and Mamdouh, father of our two children, for giving me the conditions to write this book.

This book is dedicated to my father,
the real storyteller in the family.

To George —

Thanks for coming
down to meet my
"little girl" — also
for the great support
and encouragement you've
given her "old man"
for all these many
years —

Bob

Laydelle

chapter 1

1991

Sally Marble would give her the shirt off her back and had, on occasion. They wore exactly the same size, and something about this delighted sisterless Sally. She liked lending her clothing, liked watching Laydelle Hanks work a roomful of people in her funny, halting way dressed in Sally Marble's perfect outfits.

"Now will this do or won't it?"

Sally held up a black sheath dress and slowly turned it front to back. The dress fluttered on the hanger. Laydelle narrowed her eyes, trying to read the tag.

"My, aren't we designer-conscious. It's a Valentino. Wear a simple low heel. You do have a simple low heel, don't you? Oh, here. You're a seven and a half, too. Take these, Laydelle. You'll look perfect."

Sally paused, still offering the dress.

"What's the matter? What are you staring at?"

Laydelle let one hand drag slowly over the tangle of hangers in Sally's closet. She spun around, pivoting on frayed Keds.

"Look how these metal hangers screw up the shoulders on a blouse. You ought to buy a bunch of those wooden hangers so everything would be uniform in here. You've got such gorgeous stuff."

Sally lightly beat the side of her leg with a riding crop she used on the dogs. The early morning walk had left her out of sorts. They weren't ready for the show next month. It was becoming more and more clear. She looked squarely at Laydelle Hanks, ecru silk now dangling from her hands, and beat her leg a bit harder.

"I don't care about all the hangers in my closet matching, Laydelle. That's the first thing. Also, I like a hundred percent down on my chair, and I don't care whether your mother always bought down mixed with foam to retain the shape. She hasn't lived here for nearly twenty years."

Sally flung herself into the chair, ready for the retort that was coming.

"Hey, I didn't want to go to this thing in the first place. So don't expect me to give a rat's ass about what I wear."

Laydelle played the scene over again in her mind. She had set her alarm to meet Sally's demand that they meet upstairs at ten sharp, risen hurriedly from a bad sleep, then found all the doors locked and no one home. So she'd gotten down on hands and knees, held her breath and squeezed through the doggy door, scraping the hell out of her back as she did it.

"You're just mad about me forgetting to get that key made. You could have waited outside for me to get back. I just took the dogs down to the river."

"Waited? Waited to get into . . ."

"*My* house. Yes, Laydelle. Waited to get in my house. Or gone back to your own place."

Laydelle thought for a moment. She thought about her "own place," the bungalow that stood next to Sally Marble's dog pens. She thought about the leaky faucet and the smell of dog shit that floated through her bedroom whenever she opened a window. She also thought about her rent, which Larry Marble had just raised again. She pulled her hair up off her shoulders and rolled it into a knot, then grabbed a lacquered chopstick from Sally's dressing table and stabbed the thick round of hair.

"It must be a hundred degrees in here. What's the matter, Sally? Trouble with the dogs?"

"No. Trouble with your attitude, sweet thing. I come in here to find you plumping the pillows. My perfume bottles are lined up like they're spices in a kitchen cabinet! You know I hate that. I hate when you come in and rearrange my things."

Larry Marble appeared at the other end of the dressing room, the generous closet-filled corridor with a mirrored alcove that held an elaborate vanity. The niche where Sally sat was designed for the right settee or a generous armchair. He had just stepped out of the shower and held a black Chinese dressing gown closed with one hand. He couldn't find the belt. An embroidered dragon snaked up the side of the robe.

"Now that's all I need. All I need on a day like today is for the two of you to start going at it. Are you both on PMS?"

Sally Marble glared at her husband. How could anyone be *on* PMS?

"It's a beautiful day, ladies."

"It's one hundred and three degrees outside."

"Laydelle, darling, you're testing my patience. I'll start again. It's a beautiful day. We're on our way to a gala at Buffabrook big as all—"

Laydelle snorted with laughter. Even Sally looked amused. She slid her hand quickly over her mouth. Larry Marble was starting to drip. His dressing gown slipped open slightly.

"—get-out. A fund-raising event to end all fund-raising events, and yours truly is scheduled to speak. In a couple of hours we'll be heading toward your grandfather's ranch, Laydelle, and here you are still in sneakers and bluejeans. You look like something the cat dragged in. And you, Sally! Do you think you're going to hop on the company jet dressed like that?"

He looked at the two women. At least they weren't fighting anymore. Laydelle stopped inspecting her nails and waited for him to go on.

"Now then. I want my two gals to kiss and make up."

"Lambie?"

His wife was the only woman he knew who could speak softly and still shout. Sally Marble never modulated anything. It was one of her creeds.

"Shut up and get dressed. Your manhood's showing."

He scuttled off down the hall, and she and Laydelle turned to each other, laughing.

"I'm sorry. I didn't mean to yell at you."

"Me, too."

"Adobe Blue's got a bald spot on her rump. I can't get her to quit scratching that same patch of skin. My dogs look bad, real bad. You look a little under the weather yourself. You want an aspirin or something, Laydelle?"

Laydelle turned to study herself in the mirror. She thought briefly about the night before and the man from Broken Arrow. She had started out selling security systems, only they'd gotten diverted. She'd forgotten to talk about Pedigree Protection and how important it was to install a dependable system since his ranch was so isolated. He forgot to appear interested. The evening had gotten hazy at some point. When it came back into focus, she was tiredly climbing back into her clothes at a Motel Six and looking for her car keys. He hadn't even seen her to the parking lot. Sally ran one finger over the tip of her crop.

"Get in late last night?"

"Yeah. And a big party at Buffabrook is just what I need. Sweaty palms. Cleavage. Bourbon and beans, yuck."

"Buck up. Larry wants us *all* looking good. God. I just finished this unbelievable article in *Cosmo* about what single women do with their boyfriends these days. That stuff wasn't even invented when I was single. Tell me—"

A horn began honking frantically outside. They heard the crunch of gravel underfoot and loud, incessant chatter. Sally Marble's glowing eyes dulled slightly.

"Those twins have the combined sense of a French poodle. Tennis, on such a hot day. Do you want the dress or not?"

"It's great, Sally. But the neckline's too bare. I'm so damn bony. I'll find something in my closet that'll work."

Sally opened a rosewood box and recklessly tossed her a necklace. Laydelle caught it, barely.

"Try this."

"You sure?"

"Absolutely. Look at the time! I'd better light a fire under the girls."

Sally tucked her hair decisively behind her ears and stalked out of the room. Laydelle smiled, hearing her bark out orders to the twins, who were probably plunked down in front of the television already. She sat forward slightly, her gaze fixed on Sally's outline, which still depressed the plump down chair. That was where she'd been able to trap her mother, Mary Hanks, right there in a similar chair, at the end of long, helter-skelter days. Instead of growing dimmer, the image of her mother and a little girl playing beside her on a footstool grew brighter and brighter, until the glow filled the whole room. Then Clifford Marble spoke her name, his voice running down her back like a cold finger.

"Laydelle?"

She turned her head, chin still cupped in her hand, to see what a few months away from home had done for the oldest Marble child. Clifford was molting, boy struggling to become man. But instead of being sharpened, toned by the hard collegiate experience, Laydelle saw, he looked more formless. His body, a sad, abandoned cage, was softly spreading. He had begun drinking at thirteen, less and less furtively as he grew older. But Cliffie had been aristocratic about self-destruction, and his overt disdain for hard drugs and hard drug users saved him from the summer treatment programs of less lucky fellows. Saving Cliffie was the sole subject on which Sally and Larry Marble agreed. They simply wouldn't.

"Cliffie, you're drunk."

"I am not!"

His voice squeaked. He swayed lightly, his eyes big and blurry, fixed on her. Laydelle's mind wouldn't behave. She guessed it was the bad night, the bad day this was bound to be. She saw the two of them, just as Cliffie once confessed *he* had. His white, flabby flesh folding over hers in a corner of the room where she had once played with Barbie dolls. A corner of her mother's old dressing room given over to this? All Cliffie Marble had to do was look at her with that creepy leer, and her mind began to scream.

She could hear Larry down the hall. He had stopped whistling. He was goddamning the maid, that constant guilty party, for hiding his cuff links and pairing a black sock with a gray one.

"How'm I supposed to give a speech looking like a bum?"

He paused as he passed through the hall, mopping his brow. He hiked his pants up, which sent everything shaking. He battled constantly with his weight. Larry brightened, seeing his son, and stuck out his hand.

"Gimme the handshake, son. Atta boy. Christ, freshman year and a Pike at that! You believe that, Laydelle? Finest fraternity on the campus! Glad to see you two have patched things up. I can't stand any more dissent in this house. Sally?"

He began to bellow, moving off down the stairs.

"Sally, where in the holy hell are my shirt tabs?"

Clifford smirked and moved steadily closer. Laydelle stood up to go.

"Why are you in her dressing room? Oh, I get it! You're going to borrow her stuff again, right?"

Cliffie thrust his pelvis forward emphatically and reached for her hand. She held Sally's dress high up off the ground.

"Move. Get out of my way, Cliffie."

"Uh, I was reading this article. About what happens when women live alone too long?"

She could smell his dusty breath and his hair, still wet with some fruit-scented shampoo. She shut her eyes and pushed, squeezing past him.

As she made her way down the staircase, she fingered the edge of the man's shirt she had slapped on that morning. The twins, Holly and Molly, flanked Larry Marble near the front door. They wore tennis dresses that matched, matched, matched. Sally had probably given up. The twins had become more intractable than ever.

"What time does the plane take off, Daddy?"

"We leave at four o'clock, babies."

Larry held his round belly and addressed one twin as if she were two, like always. Holly spoke up. She had established herself in the last year as the leader.

"*What* is your problem? Where is the company plane going to go without us anyhow? This is worse than when we went to *Europe*."

Molly, not to be outdone by Holly, began.

"I really think this is the most boring thing in the world. Picture it. The Buffabrook Museum again! Like I really care about cruddy old pots and all the other junk they think is so precious."

She caught sight of Laydelle and shrugged her shoulders.

"No offense, Laydelle, but really . . . And that creepy old Paddy Mahoney: I suppose he'll be there."

Larry Marble closed his fist.

"Let Laydelle by, girls. I want you both upstairs under that shower by the time I count three. One, two . . ." As he spoke, one finger shot up, then another.

"He's a *lech*, Daddy! Ask Molly what he did to her last year in the basement. Go on, ask."

Laydelle closed the front door behind her and let her back rest against it for a moment. The sun struck Sally's heavy necklace, which hung from her neck like gold mail. She looked straight ahead. Her own father, Hubbell Hanks, had set this simple white house squarely in the center of the largest piece of property inside Tulsa city limits. The front lawn made it all worthwhile, she de-

cided. Those twenty-five deep-green acres never stopped being
mowed and picked over for weeds. The enormous space was a
caricature of a front lawn, a shock of tended, idle green that led
the eye on and on until it reached the Arkansas River. The water
snaked slow and silvery just beyond the property. She could see
the lawn and even the river from her dilapidated bungalow in back.
She could see it as it was today or as it was then, when she was a
child. She could fill its emptiness with scenes of her choice, tam-
pering with time as present melted to past. Laydelle blinked and
re-created Mary Hanks, surrounded by a squad of powerful
women. Women who could sponsor symphonies, build museums,
raise money as easily as their husbands seemed to earn it. The
women she had wooed and won years ago came back to fill the
lawn, to flap their hands and tug at the brims of their hats, delight-
ing in such a lovely garden party. Or she could banish the ladies
and introduce boys, poor, sad boys whose energy flashed over the
lawn in races and contests, anything Hubbell Hanks invented to
amuse them and make their bleak lives gay for one charitable day
every year. No one held this power but Laydelle. The view belonged strictly to her, and it made the shrieking Marbles a more
tolerable misfortune. Time. She glanced at her watch. She could
still do a facial mask if she hurried.

They made it to the airport by four o'clock. The young pilot had
been on the job only a few weeks. He laughed as he saw them
tumble out of the long black car, the twins still squawking. He
blinked at the dark-haired woman in the back seat and stuck a Life
Saver under his tongue. The fat man making his way toward him
must be Mr. Marble.

"Say, hate to make you wait like this. Larry Marble."

"I'm Neil Harris. No problem, Mr. Marble. She's ready to go
when you are."

The Marbles all shook hands with him and began to climb
aboard. The twins dropped their complaints and even Cliffie
brightened as they clambered inside. Laydelle hung back for a
moment, biting her lip. She looked hard at the jet, tapping her
fingers over Sally Marble's beaded handbag. She moved toward
the nose of the aircraft, touching it lightly before joining the rest of
the group. Neil Harris pulled on the tip of his hat.

"My name's Neil Harris. Do I detect a little nervousness?"

"No, I don't think nervousness would describe it."

"Then why don't you step aboard, Miss . . . I don't believe you gave me your name."

"It's Hanks. Laydelle Hanks."

"This is your . . . ah, I mean is, uh . . . Hanks, you said."

"Yep. Hanks."

She took a seat inside and didn't seem nervous at all. In fact, as she buckled up and leaned her head back on the seat of the plane, Laydelle Hanks seemed perfectly at home.

chapter 2

For the next twenty minutes, all it took to fly to Lovely, Laydelle *was* at home. Trains and boats and planes, her father at one time embraced them all. The grim restrictions of commercial transportation were never for Hubbell Hanks. No Smoking signs and a line for the toilet? I'd just as soon stay home, he would repeat to his wife, who wanted to see Rome. You want a foreign language, Mary? Hell, let's fly down to Baja. So in 1953 he contacted his pilot friend, the one who had flown in the war, and they had done just that, with tiny Laydelle, a dog and a cat, and the perpetual bodyguard to protect them, over Mary's loud objections. That trip had done it, convinced Hubbell that the family ought really to own their own little twin-engine. One Cessna led to another through the years, until Hubbell began to collect magazine articles on Bill Lear. He just wouldn't rest until he had one himself, though he was still stuck with certain flight regulations. Mary made him wear a tie on board his own aircraft. She insisted they dress appropriately, that husband, wife and child look at least as well as the rest of America, lining up in front of ticket counters. She didn't give a damn that they were only flying down to San Antonio to see some Remingtons. She made Hubbell polish his shoes and thought long and

hard in her cozy dressing room about which hat would best set off
her new turquoise suit.

Larry Marble erased something on his notepad and looked up at
Laydelle as they taxied down the airstrip.

"What am I sweating this out for? Hell, I've got my own resource
library right in front of me. What was it the Osage called your
grandfather? I'm talking about Nelson's official name when they
voted him into the tribe."

"Let's see. It was Hulah Kihekah."

"Right. Once more, but in plain English."

"Eagle Chief. They called him Eagle Chief."

Larry scribbled frantically, and one of the twins came back to
life.

"How come you want to know?"

"Just because, sweeties. We're going to have quite a ceremony
this evening. I'll bet even you two sophisticates will get emotional.
History! Whoever says it has to stay between the dusty covers of a
book has got it all wrong. History isn't hangdog in Oklahoma.
History holds its head up, looks you straight in the eye. Hell,
history'll knock you down if it has to."

The twins rolled their eyes in unison, and Molly motioned to her
sister.

"Pass me a barf bag, Hol. I feel like I'm gonna throw up." She
pointed toward her open mouth with her index finger.

The waiting limousine looked almost feral as they walked across
the little airstrip. Laydelle wondered if the darkened windows gave
it that forbidding look and shrugged off her apprehension as silly.
Her mother had always vetoed them. Limousines had made Mary
Hanks think of funerals. The heat glistened, rising in waves from
the cement. It might be good to sit in a cool, dark car for the drive
out to the ranch.

The driver didn't hurry to meet them. He was tall, well over six
feet, and seemed indolent somehow. Inclined to put his foot on the
accelerator when and only if he felt like it. Something in Laydelle
rose to meet this, the sight of him lounging by the side of the car.
The Marbles milled about the plane. One of the twins had lost a

pearl earring. This was her third pair, and Sally was fit to be tied. Laydelle reached the car before the others.

"Hello."

Be nice, she thought to herself. She knew she was moving a certain way in her dress. He gave her a bare nod. That was all, that plus the smile.

"My name's Laydelle Hanks."

He took her hand and gave it a languid shake.

"My name's Nelson. Nelson junior."

So that was it. Another Nelson Hanks namesake. She wanted to laugh and didn't by digging a nail into the palm of her hand.

"Well, I'm pleased to meet any citizen of Lovely."

"Why? Why would anybody be? This place is a ghost town, and I bet you think I'm kidding."

He looked at her accusingly.

"Of course, you wouldn't know. You don't live here. In fact, none of the Hanks family live here. Once I save enough money I'm outa here."

"You'll get out. You're right to want to move on."

She saw he was sore about the cap, the gloves and the whole dumb job of opening doors and driving oil company big shots (as he saw them) past hotels and motels named for a dead oil man and fields filled with motionless pumps. Past a town that had gone from boom to just barely. Maybe he would even change his name once he escaped, since Nelson seemed to hang about his neck like an albatross. She wondered if it was his father or his grandfather who had once worked for Hanks Petroleum and where that smooth Depression dollar was now, the one her grandfather handed out to every Lovely kid willing to line up for it at Christmas. Who still kept it in a special safety-deposit box down at Citizens Bank or maybe stowed away in a closet or under a mattress. Nelson, this Nelson, had said all he cared to. He puckered his lips and turned his wrist over to look at the face of a watch. The Marbles, fussing again, smoothed out wrinkles and examined one another for lint and stray hairs.

"If you want new earrings, you'll have to purchase them yourself. Perhaps that will teach you to toy with your earlobes. Pierced ears were supposed to save us this particular headache."

"God, Mom, as if you never lost *anything.*"

Cliffie slid in beside Laydelle. He scooted closer as they passed a billboard announcing buffalo and brooks, a thousand wild animals roaming the greatest family attraction in Oklahoma.

The little town of Lovely clung to the petroleum company like a sturdy barnacle. Without Hanks Petroleum it wouldn't exist. It would be a ghost town all right. Citizens knew it, and to ward off the possibility of disappearance, they worked hard on collective consciousness. Reminders were slogans and posters and namesakes that swung from every commercial corner in town. HANKS PETROLEUM—MAKES ANY CAR RUN BETTER! A cowboy wielding not a six-shooter but a gasoline nozzle offered HANKS BLEND—THE GASOLINE THAT WON THE WEST! Laydelle's head had begun to pound lightly, from the inside of one temple. It was hard to breathe inside the limo. It wasn't cool enough or dark enough to blot out everything. Cliffie began to hum along with a jingle on the radio. PUT HANKS IN YOUR TANK. They passed the Black Gold Motel, the Boom Town Dry Cleaner and Lavinia Lingerie. Lovely was small, thank God. Leaving Lovely was a snap, so what was her problem? she wondered. The speedometer pushed up toward sixty. They were on the open road to the ranch.

Nelson junior turned right toward the heavy stone arch announcing Buffabrook Ranch. Uniformed personnel smiled and waved as the car drove through the entrance, that single break in eleven solid miles of fencing that enclosed the northern boundary of the ranch. The tires thundered over a set of cattle guards. The low rumble announced the first break with the familiar world. Isolated clumps of buffalo stared at them vengefully; at least it seemed that way to the Marbles. Sally wondered if it was their beards that made them so horrible to see.

"Laydelle, doesn't anybody feed these poor animals? I swear they're skinnier than they were the last time we were out here, don't you think, Mol? How'd you like riding bareback on that one?"

The backbone looked sharp as a knife and the animal's distended belly looked full not of food but of bitter air, so severe were all the other planes and angles of its body. Laydelle crossed her legs quickly. Holly had asked her the same question before and now she was out of patience. "They get plenty to eat; don't let them fool you."

Nelson Hanks had carefully orchestrated the views at the ranch. They developed gradually in that so slow climb over the smooth road to the summit overlooking a lake. The highest knoll offered welcome relief from the green, leafy screen that both hid and revealed what the eye could see at every twist and turn. Hanks had imported the exotic animals, but he'd left topography alone. The hills at the core of the property, thickly coated with bluestem grass, were native to the land. They rose suddenly, seeming out of nowhere, and broke the fact of such flat, nearly featureless oil country beyond Buffabrook. There was no oil on the Hanks ranch, though motionless derricks could be seen from the road. Slow streams and ragged gullies etched the gently rising, falling land. The sight of sudden vistas was jarring and reinforced by such strange animals. Peering out from rock-strewn meadows or standing spread-legged, shooting rank piss into a thin stream, animals stridently marked the land. Species from Africa, Australia, New Zealand and Japan chomped and chewed their way through Nelson's pastures, their improvised habitat. The oil man had been fond of naming things. A name etched into a plain pine board seemed to intrude at every point. An iron sculpture frolicked in the middle of a clear, cold shallow. POOL OF THE WATER BABIES. The discovery of a trail was dampened slightly by knowing where it led. INDIAN PRINCESS CASCADES. The imagination didn't wander at Buffabrook. It was directed.

The car inched along, obeying the posted sign that cautioned visitors to reduce their speed as they approached the lodge. Larry Marble rolled down the window of the limousine.

"Think of it, Holly and Molly. Cliffie, you listening back there? A thousand wild animals are grazing inside this fence right now."

"Fantastic. All we need is for them to stampede."

"And that's not all, kids."

The sigh, barely audible, issued from identically contoured lips. They knew this preamble, the part about bandits. Nelson junior took another turn in the road, and they could see Spencer Spring below, just under the ledge of a cliff, named for notorious Al Spencer. They weren't far from Outlaw Gulch, the steep ravine that had once hidden scores of desperadoes.

"This land was as rich in bandits, bank robbers and moonshiners as it was in oil. They were here well before he was, and he was too damn smart to try to run them off. So he made them—"

"—part of the corporation. Daddy, we know that already. You don't have to repeat something a million times for us to hear."

Larry continued as if his daughter hadn't spoken.

"Yes, he took them all under his wing. The scoundrels, the desperadoes, the Osage that held the land and its mineral rights. He didn't run over them, and that was his secret. The man embraced them, took them all under his wing. Eagle Chief, shoot. Nelson Hanks had to be an eagle with that kind of wing span."

An ostrich standing by the dusty road chewed something slowly, elaborately, with great round rotations. It gazed at the car as they approached. A Brahman bull standing farther uphill suddenly parted a bush with its head. The lodge was barely in view, the rustic country home Nelson Hanks had positioned just above the lake. They could see the back porch from the car and the tin buckets that seemed to tack it all down. Tin buckets that once dropped into a well on a twelve-foot line now held ordinary red geraniums. The museum, constructed of sandstone quarried on the ranch, stood above the lodge, crowning the top of the hill. A dun-colored stone plaza spread before it, and they could just make out the bright-red flag of Buffabrook beating back and forth in the scorching wind. Cliffie leaned over Laydelle's lap to roll down the window. He tossed something toward the ostrich.

"Hey! Don't feed the animals, okay?"

Nelson junior adjusted the rearview mirror. Cliffie looked as if he had something to say and then swallowed it whole. He stuck out his chin instead and tried to stare down the eyes in the mirror. It didn't work. Cliffie offered a kind of apology.

"It was only a corn nut."

"You're not supposed to feed these animals anything. Ranch regulation."

Cliffie muttered something under his breath as they pulled around the loop in the driveway. The square shoulders of the driver seemed tighter than ever, and Laydelle saw how Nelson junior's name worked against him, made him part of something whether he liked it or not. He was nonchalant as he opened the door for her, but a single corn nut had blown his cover. He still cared about the ranch and maybe even about the dear, dead town of Lovely, Oklahoma.

"Thanks for the ride."

"Yeah."

Larry had his hand on the small of his wife's back. Holly and Molly, sullen hostages of their parents, stood together on the sidewalk and glared at their brother. He was already loping toward the entrance, on the prowl for a drink, and Nelson the driver had drawn a toothpick from his pocket and was back to lounging on the hood of the limo. Laydelle was about to go inside when she saw a battered station wagon farther down the long road to the lodge. The car emerged from a cloud of dust and hit a speed bump hard, but that didn't seem to deter the driver. She shook her head and watched as the car screeched to a stop for a llama just then ambling across the road. While the Marbles made their way inside, she turned to face the lot, waiting for the driver of the car to emerge.

Hubbell Hanks struggled, finally throwing his shoulder into the front door to force it open. His face was rounder and redder than usual. He pressed on the back of his head, forcing a cowlick into temporary submission.

"Whew! Did you see that? That llama could have been a goner."

"You can slow down now, Daddy. You made it."

He took out a rumpled handkerchief to mop his brow.

"Is Aresta on strike?" Laydelle frowned at her father's shirt. The collar was beginning to fray.

"You could say that. She took a fall on the boat and blames me. Before that it was motion sickness."

"Your houseboat never goes anyplace."

"That's beside the point. Aresta no longer irons. Let's go inside."

Laydelle grinned and put her arm through the familiar crook Hubbell offered.

One hundred and fifty people shook hands or brushed cheeks hello inside the lodge. There were no strangers in the crowd, yet time did pass. The shrieks indicated some change, large or small, that was being announced. The jovial, continuous hollering of the handsome group meant news was just then being absorbed. Other information was being more subtly exchanged. Skin, newly stretched or otherwise treated, was ready at last for its first public display, and the Hanks fund-raiser was as good a time as any. Trips to the Golden Door, trips to hot springs and thermal baths, had all been scheduled with an eye to the big do out at Buffabrook. The men conducted unrelenting business in small groups or traded jokes, sports statistics or the latest allegations against Barry Switzer. Everyone assembled knew each corner of the place, had been spoon-fed the tales shored up in every old pine log. No one there had dressed up, lost weight, removed some small, unsightly thing, just to hear more Nelson Hanks lore. Most people present weren't even aware that the Dutch elm disease was tearing through the state again and that a research outfit in Massachusetts was dedicated to the study of this deadly fungus. They had been meeting for years in similar oblivion, not to fund another excavation in southern Ohio or an innovative literacy campaign in Appalachia. These one hundred and fifty people had never gathered to further, sponsor or protect anything. They met to fan out among members of their own species and strut their bright and showy best as the peacocks were doing now on the crisp lawn of the lodge. Ice rocked and rattled in good, heavy glassware, the kind Nelson himself had always preferred. The good-natured shouting was still under way as Hubbell and Laydelle came into the wide living room.

"Hubbell!"

The cry came from the far side of the crowd. Dottie Evans had caught sight of them first. She sweetly butted her way toward them. Her pout seemed painted on.

"Hubbell, you have *no* defense. Now I thought the next time you came into town you were going to call me and that was months ago."

She had known Hubbell Hanks for years, and it was high time the two of them got together. He was a little gun-shy since Mary up and left him, but phooey on her and phooey on her continuing hold on Hubbell Hanks, Dottie maintained.

"You know, anymore when I drive in, I've got a checklist of things to do a mile long. And I don't always get those calls made, Dottie, as much as I'd like to."

"You also said you were going to invite me down to spend a day on the boat."

She would, too. She would trap Hubbell and get him to invite her down to Catoosa on a particular day at a particular time.

"I will, I will! Just as soon as I get finished with some modifications. I'm planning a helluva party, Dot. Have to, with so many people mad at me."

Hubbell caught a passing waiter by the sleeve and began to survey what he had on his tray. Dottie continued her appeal, turning to Laydelle. One edge of a false eyelash had begun to detach itself from her eyelid.

"Well, what does he do down there all day on a houseboat that doesn't go anyplace? Do you know?"

Laydelle shrugged, and Hubbell Hanks' daughter seemed to suddenly come into the woman's range of vision.

"Look at you! You are dressed to kill, unless—unless tonight is just target practice. Where's that gorgeous man I saw you with last year? Let's see, what was his name?"

"Johnny Beaureve. He'll probably show up at some point. Dottie, will you excuse me for just one second? A friend of mine is here someplace, and I . . . ."

"Why, sure, that's right. Mingle, mingle. I'll just get your dad here to tell me why it is he keeps giving me the slip."

When she turned, she found Hubbell gone, too. There he was, in the middle of a group that held him afloat like a human inner tube. Dottie's false eyelash popped free and landed in her drink. She scurried off to the powder room, still bent on trapping Hubbell later. I'll find him after dinner, she decided as she settled down to repair work under the soft lights.

Laydelle stood alone on the terrace as dessert was being served to the guests inside. A mountain lion had briefly appeared at the edge of the lake below the lodge. It was growing bolder and bolder, approaching the foreman's little cabin on the water's edge, the place where he lived with his wife. I shoot at him all the time, the foreman once confided. Never does seem to make him bat an eye. He'll be hauling off livestock sooner than later. Laydelle felt a hand slide over her bare back and drew in her breath sharply.

"You're jumpy tonight."

It wasn't ever hard for her to get mad at Johnny Beaureve, but staying mad was almost impossible. She started to snarl at him, taking a lesson from the animal below, but saw there was no point. His physical presence obliterated her anger, as always.

"I wish you'd break out. Or gain weight. You wouldn't be such a problem if you were a fat slob."

"You wouldn't, either."

He worked his way closer and slipped one hand down inside the back of her dress.

"New dress?"

"Sally lent it to me. What do you think?"

"Nice. I like you in black."

"Let's start over again. Hi, Johnny."

They were almost the same height. She reached around his neck, feeling for the long, dark braid and its deceiving softness. His hair shone hard as metal, yet fell softer than baby fluff when loosened from its braid. She tilted her face up toward his, but he ignored this invitation.

"How come you're late?"

"There's only so much of this I can stomach. Did you get a load of my brothers in there, wolfing down ice cream?"

"What do you mean?"

"My Osage brothers. Do you think they're doing this out of their feeling for your grandfather's little foundation? They're getting paid to do this. They even called *me*, for God's sake. They actually wanted me in this ceremony."

Chairs were scraping back slightly, and Laydelle heard Larry Marble whisper, "Testing, testing."

"Let's go inside. They're ready to start."

"I think we ought to leave now. It'll be less conspicuous."

Johnny pulled gently at Sally Marble's necklace.

"I'm not going anywhere with you. You have a lousy attitude, Johnny. Let's see some Osage pride."

He tugged again, sharply. The necklace pinched the skin on her neck.

"Cut it out. This doesn't belong to me."

His hand was farther inside her dress now. It had wandered here and there as they talked.

"Of course not. It's mine. Every square inch of this is mine."

Larry Marble's voice floated through the room. Hubbell stood beside him, dressed in full regalia. He wore his father's official costume: the full headdress, moccasins, the ornate beaded shirt. A split buffalo hide behind him was lit by spots. Johnny's hand tightened on Laydelle's waist as they stood in the back of the dining room, while Larry's voice rose.

"Some people are confused about what it is we are here for. Tonight, in my capacity as an elected member of the board, I'd like to talk about the emblematic nature of our endeavors. Emblematic. Big word, big notion."

Hubbell's hand moved to his forehead. He scratched a spot underneath the band of the headdress. A woman was waving at Johnny from one of the tables.

"You know her?" Laydelle frowned.

"She certainly acts like it. Say. Just look at your girlfriend Libby. I bet anything she's sleeping with old Mahoney."

"Friendship, Johnny. Ever hear of it?"

Libby Sims beamed at Paddy, who was seated across from her. The old curator could still cite the date of the first time she had seen the Buffabrook Museum. Her unwavering interest in his idiosyncratic gathering of things had flattered him then and now. He was proprietary about her and even took credit for her job. Would she ever have become an art historian and professor without him? Hell, no!

Larry knew to change the direction of his talk when he noticed a friend of his who claimed to have beaten the nicotine habit ask a neighbor for a cigarette.

"This ability to entertain new ideas only increases our legitimacy and our independence from the corporation that Nelson Hanks founded. In fact, we may choose to fund organizations that run *counter* to oil interests. At other times, our projects seem uncannily close to home. They seem to rise up out of the very history of the corporation. What am I getting at? Just this. When the Hanks Foundation was approached for funding by a group of whiz kids up in Massachusetts aiming to find a cure for Dutch elm disease, the vote was unanimously in favor of backing these boys. Most of us in this room have a long memory. Long enough, at least, to remember the year Lovely lost the Million Dollar Elm, the year this town lost a significant reminder of its own past. The oil leases that traded hands under that massive tree changed the whole history of the state of Oklahoma. The stump that remains is a poor substitute for its spreading branches, I'm sure you'll all agree."

Libby suddenly clapped her hands. Others joined her applause out of respect for this curious woman, who got shiny-eyed over the death of an old tree. Sitting now in the Great Hall, surrounded by the paintings and memorabilia she loved, she was happily carried away. The rough pine logs of the living room, studded with boisterous symbols of the Southwest, the thirty-foot-high walls bearing handsome evidence of Nelson Hanks' passions, the massive stone fireplaces at either end of the room filled with wood that wasn't meant to be burned, huge hunks of the Million Dollar Elm itself . . . Libby had always loved it here.

Theatrics had begun in earnest. The western edge of the Great

Hall seemed to be disappearing, sliding into itself in sections. Dinner guests turned their heads to the terrace outside, where a small
Osage delegation stood. Three of the five Indians wore Stetsons,
eagle feathers springing from the hatbands. One of the men, the
one with a beaverskin cap and a necklace of animal claws, held a
pair of reins in his hand. A pony sniffed the buffed stone floors and
switched her tail nervously.

"This concludes the business of why we're all assembled here.
Let those who have labeled our project trifling judge it again, this
time in its proper context. For it is emblematic of . . ."

Outside, the pony raised her tail in a high arch, and the five
members of the delegation frowned. A thudding sound followed,
and several guests twittered. Hubbell took a sip of water as Larry
introduced him.

"It seems ridiculous to introduce Hubbell Hanks, a man whose
family continues to affect the people of Oklahoma in large and
small ways. Why, this man's mother *named* our town of Lovely as
she stepped off the train from Creston, Iowa, all those years back.
Hubbell Hanks has managed to live through the era that transformed this state from Indian Territory into what it is today. He's
lived it in the best way, too. Painlessly, through the tales of his
father, a born raconteur. I'm anxious to hand the mike over, to let
the man get on with it. And to explain that what you are about to
see duplicates in near-perfect detail a historic moment for the
Osage tribe and for Nelson Hanks. Ladies and gentlemen, if you'll
turn a few degrees in your chairs, you can reenter an age, see for
yourselves a bright moment in a dark year. My friends, it is no
longer 1989, but 1930. Nelson Hanks is about to be honored as the
first white man to be made a member of the Osage tribe."

Hubbell marched solemnly to the terrace, which suddenly came
alive with footlights and floods that hung from bordering trees.
One of the men, the one with a beaver cap, handed him a saddle.
Hubbell reeled back as the man dropped it in his outstretched
arms. Laydelle gave a low moan.

"Daddy's losing it."

"This is news?"

"I'm talking about the headdress, Johnny. Look, it's slipping
off."

Hubbell recovered and shook the saddle, letting something settle
into place. Made of animal skins and bones, it had been in Johnny
Beaureve's family until it was passed on to Nelson Hanks. Hubbell

edged toward the pony, one eye on a back leg, cocked as if ready to trigger a fierce kick.

"This is really not his forte. Poor guy."

"He should have told the foundation to hire an actor. Look at him."

"I can't."

The pony sidled off as Hubbell approached with the saddle. One of the Osage yanked hard on the bit, and she reared her head, then took several steps back, hooves scraping the stone. Hubbell looked perplexed, grinning at the audience, and made a quip about being a tenderfoot. Johnny Beaureve smirked and lit a cigarillo.

"If this whole thing makes you so sick, nobody's keeping you here."

"Why don't you knock off the high-and-mighty bit? You're not enjoying this any more than I am."

The pony was somehow saddled, and Hubbell turned to accept an eagle feather from the man with the bear-claw necklace. He held the reins gingerly in the other hand. Larry Marble provided one last footnote as the lights on the terrace began to go out, one by one.

"Now mind you. This is a simulation. Don't go thinking Hubbell is going to give up his houseboat for a tent. . . ."

"That condescending bastard."

"Sssh, Johnny. I can't hear anything."

"As our foundation activities are emblematic of a larger concern, so was this gesture, the making of an Eagle Chief. Hulah Kihekah. They found in Nelson Hanks a considerable ally, a man who—"

"—milked our tribe for everything he could with a smile on his face. A big, wide grin. They didn't call him an oil bandit for nothing."

Heads were turned, not to the pantomime on the terrace, nor to Larry Marble as he huffed and puffed, but to Johnny Beaureve and his Italian suit. Fury suited him. The woman waved again.

"What is wrong with her?"

People shifted in their seats. They wanted a conclusion. They wanted to go to the bathroom, then watch the movie they'd been promised. They'd had enough of Larry Marble for one night.

"My time's up. I'm going to turn this microphone over to the man who has been there. The man who has gone from barber to banker to oil man from the best seat in the house, a father's knee. My friends, I present our friend Hubbell Hanks. Hubbell?"

But Hubbell Hanks was preoccupied. His lifelong fear of horses and ponies was finally getting the best of him. The pinto had shown Hubbell a full set of bared teeth and was making her way toward Nelson Hanks' living heir, her ears pinned to her skull and yellow lights dancing in her eyes. Backing away from her slowly at first and then faster, Hubbell stumbled as the pony's foreleg lifted in a sharp extension. She was quickly subdued as one of the men caught hold of her bridle. Hubbell, astonished and blushing hard, came into the dining room to face his audience. He tapped the microphone diffidently, promising to make his speech short and sweet.

chapter 3

Laydelle reached for Johnny's hand as her father concluded his talk, but not quickly enough. The waving woman trotted toward them.

"Johnny! It's Johnny Beaureve, isn't it? I can't believe it—you don't recognize me. Not a good sign for a former Fulbright scholar. I wrote you your first fan letter, or so you said. That paper that told how the Osage were exploited in France, put on display like circus animals. I still remember it! Thrilling stuff."

The woman's hair and eyes held the same bronze lights. She seemed thoroughly of her own making and looked like no one Laydelle had ever seen before. Paper. She tried to remember the paper Johnny once mentioned in an offhand way. Published in a scholarly journal, but which one? She damned her own inattention. The woman stuck her hand out in greeting.

"I don't believe we've met."

"Laydelle Hanks. And you are?"

The woman released her hand.

"I'm Sheila Langhurst. Johnny described it all so remarkably. Why, it left me breathless. A little party of six Osage traveled to France, in . . . oh, boy. Some memory I have! Was it 1827, Johnny?"

"Right."

Sheila drew a deep breath and continued.

"After reading this article, I had to sit down and write a letter. It was a wonderful piece of scholarship. Just wonderful. Johnny never let his subject lead him by the nose; that's what struck me. Stately. Didn't I call the piece stately, Johnny? One thing led to another, and I finally talked Mr. Beaureve into a long lunch one afternoon. In fact, you might say I'm here tonight because of him!"

Laydelle studied her, thinking of all the possibilities. She could throw a direct punch and probably score, flattening pretty Ms. Langhurst. She wondered if there was a Mr. Langhurst and watched as people drifted outside to follow the path to the museum.

"After that article I just had to know more, and what I found is a richness that is— Oops, here I go, carried away again! I love the Osage. They're shrewd and scholarly at the same time. Jane Anderson set something in motion that's true to this day! Why, her newspaper was so erudite it put the white community to shame. Then there's the allotment issue—quite a hot topic."

Something else seemed to occur to her. She paused and bit her lip lightly.

"Say. Are you going to France in the fall with the exchange, Johnny? Don't you know? Some Osage in California have organized the first ever cultural exchange with the village of Montauban. But you *must* go. Your article revived the whole thing."

Passion was certainly blind, Laydelle saw, arms folded over her chest by now. Johnny grew more imperious the longer the woman droned on. She could tell he was deciding whether to tell his fan he didn't need to sign up for any visit to France. Johnny Beaureve lived there six months out of the year.

"Oh, studying the Osage is just one of my hobbies, you understand. But look how a hobby takes its twists and turns. Here I am, standing in Nelson Hanks' dining room just because he is a key player in Osage history. At this point, I think it's fair to say that I'd go to *any* length to further my studies. Confess Johnny. Are there others like me?"

Something seemed caught in Laydelle's throat. She snatched a glass of water from a table nearby and drank. Better, much better. She looked at Sheila Langhurst's glittering eyes and spoke.

"Sheila, there are *so* many others like you." Laydelle's lips turned up in a tight smile.

"Miss Hanks—"

"Why don't you cut the crap about the Osage and get right to the point? Now will you two excuse me for a second?"

Laydelle caught sight of Libby outside and hurried over to join her friend.

"It's enough to make you sick, isn't it?"

Libby gave her a noisy kiss on the cheek, then rubbed at the red blur.

"I thought dinner was pretty good."

"Not dinner. Her."

She turned slightly to indicate Sheila Langhurst, who was becoming more and more animated. Beaureve drew back a step, and Libby chortled.

"Look at him. He's horrified. But then Johnny Beaureve's got disdain down to a science. Why you waste your time on him is beyond me."

Libby fished an ice cube out of her glass with one finger and popped it in her mouth.

"Your dad's talk was very clever."

"It was good, wasn't it? Let's leave those two in peace and go watch the movie."

The raw, insistent smell that hung in the air meant skunk. Laydelle watched fireflies blink and glow, as goose bumps rose on her arms. The women walked cautiously, following the soft trail of lights up the hill to the Hanks museum. Lanterns hung from the trees, and bursts of laughter punctuated by periods of complete stillness boomed above them. Paddy was at it, doubtless, with some tale concocted especially for tonight. Mahoney took less care than ever, shamelessly distorting stories about the museum he and Nelson had built together. He would be having a heyday, Laydelle imagined.

"Paddy's really wound up. You should have heard him at dinner. I can't complain, though. He's on the verge of loaning a crate of stuff to a doctoral student of mine. I would have given my eyeteeth for anything like that when I was a student."

She threw her arm around Laydelle.

"See? Tonight's not so bad, is it? I caught a glimpse of you actually having fun. Don't worry, you can trust me. I won't breathe a word to anyone."

"Very funny. You know I hate this stuff. I really, really hate it."

They reached the octagonal plaza in front of the museum and

paused for a minute. Lights shone on the sky-blue entrance, filled with Indian imagery. Silver double doors gleamed in the center, framed by an alcove of bright symbols painted straight from Osage life and legend. Laydelle approached and fingered one of the onyx plaques, running her finger over the engravings before she stepped inside. She pulled hard, letting Libby enter first. As she opened the door wider, sound poured over her like the tinkling rush of notes from an opened music box. A heavyset man was lumbering toward her with a woman in tow. Laydelle had a brief vision of him dragging a child's pull-toy along by a frayed string. The woman's head was bobbing up and down as he led her firmly by the arm. Libby sped off to have a look at a painting Paddy had been crowing about over dinner.

"Miss Hanks? I'd like to introduce myself. . . . Matthew Cox, and this is my wife, Lily."

Laydelle took the woman's hand. It was like trying to revive a small, lifeless animal. She finally dropped it, and the woman looked vaguely relieved.

"I'm very pleased to meet you."

"Mrs. Cox and I flew in from New York."

The couple joined hands and let this information sink in. Laydelle shifted in Sally Marble's shoes. They were a bit snug, and a blister had formed on one heel. It seemed to be Laydelle's turn to speak.

"My, Manhattan. I didn't know Friends of the Foundation ranged so far and wide."

"Oh, we've supported Buffabrook for quite some time now. Mrs. Cox and I have followed the unabridged story of the Hanks family for . . . why, it feels like forever, doesn't it, dear?"

Mrs. Cox took a step forward. "We certainly have. We feel almost as if we're part of the story unfolding here; that's the kind of interest we have in the Hanks family."

Laydelle took a Kleenex from Sally Marble's beaded bag for diversion. She wished the couple would get to the punch line. Something was on its way, and she was losing patience with these two. Especially the woman.

"Just what might the unabridged story be?"

"Why, the ups and downs any great family is subject to. In our view, it is exactly that which denotes greatness. Why, wild swings in fortune are part and parcel of a grand heritage. Mr. Cox and I have always stood fast on that issue. When our families suffer certain reversals, we're always there for them. Even when others aren't."

Laydelle had badly misjudged her. This woman was no pull-toy. Nobody dragged her anywhere she didn't want to go.

"You see, Miss Hanks, we are quite friendly with Paddy Mahoney. In fact, we've known Paddy quite intimately for the past ten years. It was Paddy who suggested we introduce ourselves to you."

It was her turn to open her handbag. She pulled out a business card from a sleek leather pouch:

MATTHEW COX AND ASSOCIATES
Fine Estate Jewelry

BY APPOINTMENT ONLY
212/555–2975

"Mr. Cox and I didn't think it would be farfetched, under the circumstances, to approach you. We handle heirloom jewelry and only the very best pieces at that. Our clients are often amazed to discover the prices their jewelry can command."

Laydelle squinted, imagining what Mrs. Cox would look like through a kaleidoscope. Her image spun and rotated at the round bottom of a tube, along with hundreds just like it. Her tight face was quite manageable when wedged into a neat, small diamond.

"We know that these matters are very, very delicate. Mr. Cox and I understand that discretion is fundamental to our business. In the event, Miss Hanks, that you ever find yourself desirous of—"

Matthew swiped at the end of his nose with a closed fist.

"—a lot of money, come to us. Why don't we just talk frankly, Miss Hanks? My wife thinks I come on too strong sometimes, but you seem puzzled. We only mean this: If ever you consider parting with a piece of jewelry, we would certainly be at your disposal, and if that means, by the way, another trip to Lovely, we'd be the first to hop on a plane. I think you would find our prices quite, quite generous."

Laydelle began to speak, but Mrs. Cox cut her off sharply.

"We're certainly not looking for a commitment tonight. These

transactions take place over time, as Mr. Cox and I well understand. But do keep our card and think of us if ever you wish yourself free. Oh, but you're smiling! You see, Miss Hanks, we've been
in business long enough to understand that these sales often represent a kind of liberation from the past."

They retreated just as they had approached, Mrs. Cox back on
a string, with her husband charting the course. They were shortly
absorbed into the crowd. Laydelle tossed the card into a trash can
on her way toward the first exhibit hall of her grandfather's museum, glaring at the man who approached. He might have given
Johnny a run for his money if he'd been better dressed, she thought,
watching him move. He was ready to burst out of a close-fitting
shiny suit. Too bad, he was a good-looking man.

"Miss Hanks?"

He stood too close. He didn't have the sense to keep a proper
distance. She felt knocked off balance as he said her name. She
slapped Sally Marble's bag against the palm of her open hand.
She guessed Paddy had sent this one her way, too.

"That's right. Please excuse me, I need to find someone."

Laydelle hurried through the first two halls of the museum. Paddy's
voice was amplified in the vast, echoing rooms, and she followed
where it led. Straining in Sally's tight dress, she rushed past all the
artifacts and artwork she knew by heart. Sometimes the things in
here seemed to draw her in, intimate as a warm whisper. Other
times, like tonight, she was nearly immune to their power. Tonight
she was just another unaffected guest of Buffabrook.

Paddy stood with his hand resting lightly on a glass case. Outfitted in a stylish sports jacket and perfectly creased khaki pants,
Mahoney looked like a responsible academic and curator. Except
for the Band-Aids on his cheek and chin, he could even have been
mistaken for a gentleman. Paddy peeled the wrapper from a stick
of gum.

"Of course, the film you're about to see is legendary in many
respects, but here's an angle I bet you haven't heard of."

Laydelle stood at the back of the crowd. Partially lit, the rooms
looked heavy and secretive. Not all of the display cases were illuminated. She saw Paddy had been very systematic, featuring only
the collections that contributed most directly to tonight's tale. He'd
done some moving around, brought some of his favorite blankets

up from the basement. The saddles had all been reorganized, and the Colt collection now stood next to the Winchesters.

"They took the film from a book by Edna Ferber. And Ferber visited this ranch to research her book. Right?"

Paddy cleared his throat.

"So you might say her experiences here colored the movie you're about to watch."

Paddy spread his feet apart and put a hand firmly on the saddle next to him. "I hear she was none too fond of Lavinia Hanks' peacocks. None too fond of her other houseguests, either. She had quite a scuffle with . . ."

Paddy rolled the gum around loudly in his mouth and walked several steps toward a bronze by Russell. Laydelle noticed he had toned down his limp.

"There I go getting sidetracked. Folks, the film you are gonna see tonight is called *Cimarron*. It created quite a stir in its day. I'll hand it to Hollywood—those boys knew what they were looking for when they came out here. The images of Oklahoma tell the truth. They caught the grandeur of the land rush, then proceeded through the oil boom using the smallest possible aperture—one family's experience. When you think about it, this may be the only way to tell an epic story. I'm a painter and a museum director and a very, very old man, but not too old to know counterfeit from the real thing in any medium. What you're about to see is real, folks. Take my word for it. Follow me, folks, and let's roll it."

Laydelle caught him by the elbow, just as everyone began to march downstairs to the projection room. She looked at the Band-Aids on his face.

"Somebody start up with you in a bar?"

"Nah. Cut myself shaving. I'm too old for barroom brawls."

She clucked her tongue, then scowled at him.

"Come over here, Paddy."

"Uh oh."

She pulled him off to a corner. A Plains Indian war club was mounted in the case behind them. She studied it for a moment, then spoke.

"Where do you get off, telling some weird duo from New York that I'm piss poor?"

"That's not what I told them, so just calm down a minute."

"Pal around with that kind of trash if you like. But leave me out of it the next time."

Mahoney, for a fleeting moment, seemed distressed.

"I was looking to do you a favor, Laydelle. They expressed interest in your grandmother's—"

"You know I sold that ring! You're way out of line, Paddy, and I'm mad at you."

Paddy Mahoney's contrition was so novel, she almost regretted her outburst. She held his arm a moment longer.

"I have nothing left to sell but security systems, Paddy. You get so goddamn evasive every time I bring that up. But the fact is, you and I could do business. Real business, the right way. That's what I call help."

"What about Lavinia's set of—"

"And don't send me any more clowns in shiny suits, either."

"I don't know what you're talking about."

"I mean stop giving my name to complete strangers. Butt out, Paddy. I mean it."

Johnny slipped into the empty seat next to her as Ferber's settlers barreled into Oklahoma to stake their claims. Dust and dirt swirled on the screen as mules and donkeys were bullied into the race for land. Transportation became any wheel that could spin, any animal that could move. It all flew forward at the sound of gunshot.

"So?"

"Not bad for Hollywood."

"That's not what I'm talking about, and you know it. Are you and Sheila on your way to France?"

"Hardly. I finished what you started. She ran off with her tail between her legs."

They watched for several more minutes. There was brawling onscreen, and a fistfight left Ferber's hero the victor. Beaureve's arm was tossed over her shoulder. She felt his restlessness before his arm tensed and pushed her forward slightly.

"Let's get out of here. I'm in the mood to see a real film."

"I've got a ride home, thanks."

"Clever. Come on."

"No, Johnny. I've got an appointment tomorrow."

They continued to whisper. She could see Sally Marble near the front of the dark room. She turned once to look at them. The family had all dispersed. Cliffie had found new prey, she saw. He was eyeing a little blonde, edging toward her. The twins seemed to have ditched the whole scene.

"Drop it, Johnny."

"Only after you tell me what kind of no I'm dealing with. Your usual no that means yes, with a little persuasion. Or the flat no."

"The flat no. But I'll walk you outside."

She slid past the Craft family of Hominy, Oklahoma, excusing herself. Johnny followed her out of the screening room and into the hall outside. An Exit sign glowed red at the end of the corridor. She pushed through the heavy door and swallowed hard. The smell of skunk was stronger now, sickeningly close. There were no lanterns here, no bright, gay signs of a party; the lights would go back on later, when the movie finished. They would have to make their way gingerly down the dark path. Laydelle put her hand over her mouth, shaking her head.

"That skunk's going to scare everyone off."

"That's what they come here for. Polecats and nature in all her bare-assed glory. Injuns. Peekaboo with the rough-and-tumble. Your grandfather's a crowd pleaser, dead or alive."

Johnny offered her his hand, guiding her. He was careful as he helped her down the uneven path. He rattled coins in his pocket with his free hand as he walked.

"What do I have to say to get you inside?"

He had left the truck parked at the bottom of the lot. Even this far away, it looked enormous, outsized. She smirked.

"You're getting more obvious with age. Why'd you bring the truck?"

"For the same reason I always bring the truck. It gives me an incomparable ride."

She waited for the wave of revulsion to pass. It always did. He squeezed her hand, then brought her in a little closer.

"Movie time, Laydelle. I've even got some refreshments for tonight. I can almost taste them now. Can't you?"

Laydelle looked away, seeing nothing but darkness. She heard a hoot owl in the woods or imagined she did. If she were to leave the path and strike out in any direction, left or right, she'd only wind up lost in the brush. She could see herself hobbling back to the museum with a twisted ankle, in Sally's torn and tattered dress.

"Oh, you're one swell guy. You really are."

Beaureve lifted a corner of his mouth in a smile.

"I'll get you back to town tomorrow in time for your appointment. I always do. What have you got to lose?"

She wished he would put both arms around her. That he would stand holding her for the longest time under the soft lamplight. But straight-backed Johnny Beaureve would do neither of those things and she knew it.

"You're sure? Because if I miss this meeting . . ."

"You can count on me."

And she could, that was the paradox. Johnny Beaureve was fixed in place. There was no chance that he would shift direction now or ever. She led the way, suddenly in a hurry. Good thing she kept a pair of jeans and old boots at his place. Sally Marble's shoes were killing her feet. She couldn't wait to slip them off.

chapter 4

"Hurry up. Push 'Play,' Johnny."

"When you've finished pouting, I will."

He knelt in front of the television set. Videocassettes were stacked beside him in a neat pile. He waited, examining the palms of his hands for a moment.

"Okay, okay. I'm not mad anymore. Boy, if I had a nickel for every time I've said that, I'd sure be rich."

His infractions were the same as they had ever been: the disappearing act that meant Saint-Tropez or California at the drop of a hat. No note, no phone call to say goodbye, and then an unabashed return, after weeks or months. She didn't like his insouciance, though she grudgingly lived with it. Laydelle curled up on the couch. He'd surprised her a long time ago by converting all the old films her grandfather's valet had shot through his years with the Hanks family.

"I should index this stuff. You'd think a meticulous guy like Joey Fujii would have taken care of that. Here. We'll start with this."

He turned off the lights in his living room and joined her on the couch. They sat at opposite ends, each one propped up against an armrest. Laydelle squinted at the silent images on the screen.

"God, think of it. We were so . . ."

"Rich. I think of it all the time."

"It's unbelievable."

"An empire revealed. It was certainly Hankstown."

They sat mostly silent, though the quiet was punctuated every so often by Laydelle's shouts of recognition or amusement. The public and the personal were presented side by side and saved the old films from being mere home movies. They offered a look at morals and manners as Joey turned his camera on a children's party at the town house. Hubbell was seen standing aloof to one side. The focus was on the center of the wide lawn, where a miniature circus had been mounted for the Lovely children. Josephine the Snake Charmer; Torture Box and Crystal Gazer; Palace of Illusions. Children swarmed from one booth to the next. Nelson's wife, Lavinia, could occasionally be seen swooping through with a tray of sweets or iced drinks. The film broke to an aerial view of Lovely, then a shot of the pilot's head, turned grinningly at the front of the plane.

"Art Goebel! This is the best, Johnny. The guy won the Dole Derby and then became my grandfather's personal pilot. Pretty implausible."

"Anything's possible with enough money."

Art Goebel performed tricks for a sizable group gathered at the ranch. Airborne, he swooped and preened before friends, family and business associates of Nelson Hanks. Skywriting stretched like a banner across the sky, and the film spliced scene after scene of smoky messages, then cut to a shot of the cars packed into a pasture at the ranch. All the while, threaded through the ceremonies, whether private or public, solemn or gay, were Osage. They took their place, too, in gray flannel suits of the twenties and thirties. Headdresses, beaded necklaces, pipes and braids, were jarring additions to the conventional clothing they wore. Laydelle's foot went to sleep as Joey's camera ran evenly over two decades.

"Rub my foot a little, will you?"

She'd grown bored. Not Beaureve. He was living every reel of film, she saw. She yawned and didn't bother to cover her mouth with her hand.

"Hang on a while longer. This is fabulous. Not every family has the luxury of a personal archive. He even had the damn things colorized."

Beaureve got up from the couch and put on another cassette. He

moved his head round in a circle, stretching his stiff neck, stopped
and moved it in the opposite direction.

"Last one, I promise."

The film opened on a stretch of lawn by the lake. Joey began
with a panorama. The quality of the films improved with each
cassette. He swept his camera smoothly over the surface of blue,
white-tipped water. Wind whipped the tops of trees, and as the
camera turned to the dancers, wind also slapped at the bright-
colored robes and ribboned broadcloth. But the dancers remained
unperturbed. They continued their slow circle, the subtle hops and
jumps that kept them moving before the audience sitting straight-
backed in white folding chairs. Joey's camera shifted to a small boy
dancing on the outskirts of the crowd. He danced alone in a sober
frenzy. Johnny got up off the couch.

"There's my father."

"I know, Johnny. We've watched this together a million times."

The next few frames were full of rose gardens. Joey's artistry
found another focus by the mid 1930s. Shots of butterflies and
flowers steadily cemented images of air shows and family galas,
Nelson Hanks dedicating endless plaques before grave gatherings
of business and political colleagues, or Lavinia bringing a champagne bottle crashing down on the hull of a vast tanker in a bustling port. The sphere of the family's influence seemed boundless
then. A ladybug lighted on the center of a pink rose, and the scene
shifted as another sequence began. The door opened on the back
porch at the Hanks ranch, and a tall blond woman twittered and
pushed at the bottom of her hair with one hand. With the other
she waved a cigarette in a gold cigarette holder in the direction of
the camera. An Osage fashion show seemed to be in progress. She
made her entrance, then another woman and another. Johnny
Beaureve rubbed his hands together.

"White ladies making believe. Charming."

They danced, kicking up their heels in yellow moccasins. The
costumes showed up elaborately as they moved from shady porch
to sun. Joey followed each one down the steps and out to the lawn,
where they skipped and played. "I'd still like to know who these
people are."

"My grandmother had a sorority named after her, you know.
They could be part of that crowd. Or maybe these are just friends.
Johnny, these were innocent years. Why are you so furious?"

"Innocence is only appropriate for children. I've had enough. Come on."

He shut off the machine and turned on a light at his desk. He motioned for her to follow him to the bedroom. She rubbed her feet back to life and stepped queasily. Her whole body was aching and stiff.

"Choose."

Johnny Beaureve pushed "Play" for the second time. A grab bag lay in the center of his wide bed. There was a scarf from Hermès, a bottle of champagne from the Café de Paris and a set of keys to his pickup.

"Why can't we just stay here, Johnny? I don't see why we have to go through this little exercise each time we're together."

Once she'd written it out longhand two hundred times, to see how her new decision looked on paper. I WILL not. I WILL not. I WILL not. Her handwriting had begun bold and ended up botched, practically illegible by the end of the exercise.

"It's getting late, Laydelle."

Beaureve rocked back and forth on the heels of his boots.

Laydelle sighed. She knew her choice would set the tone for the evening. She took up the keys to his truck and casually dropped them into the pocket of her jeans. He smiled and seemed appeased.

"So now about the trip. I want to hear everything. Who you saw, what you ate. I want the works, Johnny."

"You want the weather report?"

"You could start there."

"Rainy and cold in Paris. Saint-Tropez was impeccable."

Laydelle had it all memorized from here. How he entered his property through another family's neighboring vineyard, then up a rutted gravel road. How he was greeted with great hugs and kisses from all the female members of the family and a gruff clap on the back from the paterfamilias. Johnny had bought the property at a good price, in part because it was nearly inaccessible. There was no reaching Beaureve once he was installed on his farm outside Saint-Tropez.

"Do they still kiss you like they used to?"

"Yeah. Don't kid yourself. Those kisses taste of stale wine from mother down to the very last daughter. They drink all day long."

Then, because this reminded him less of duty than of pleasure, Johnny finally took her in his arms. He didn't kiss her right away. He never did. He lifted her hair, feeling for the back of her neck, and traced her shoulders with the side of his hand. He knew her again after an absence by going back to the places that belonged to him. The high bony clavicle, that sharp ledge, her eyelids, which he pressed shut gently with his lips. She loosened his braid. Their dark hair fell to the same length.

"You're supposed to say you missed me. It's protocol."

She felt him stiffen.

"Oh, right. I forgot that tender nothings were never your forte."

One of his hounds had nosed his way into the room. Barred only from the bed, the dogs otherwise had the run of the place. It made straight for Laydelle. She held herself at an uncomfortable angle, straining away from the dog.

"Don't you think you're exaggerating?"

"Call him off, Johnny."

He whistled through his teeth, and the dog slunk off to a corner.

Beaureve stood up suddenly and pulled her by the hand. He reached for the car keys in the back pocket of her jeans.

"Don't forget those." He motioned toward the bed, and she gathered up the champagne bottle and scarf, then started to the kitchen for an ice bucket.

"What are you looking for?"

"A way to keep this chilled."

"It's already in the truck. Come on, Laydelle."

She wondered if they would drive far or fast, whether they would listen to the radio. She had once predicted they would get too old for this, and he covered her mouth with his hand. She embarrassed him often but could never predict what would cause him shame or chagrin. Johnny Beaureve didn't anticipate complicity. But she did. Tonight, for instance, she wanted to chat.

"This is significant. I don't see you for weeks, and look how we reunite. Sometimes this gets to me."

"Hop in."

He held the door open. She noticed again how clean the cab was, free of dog collars and fast-food trash. Even the ashtray was empty.

"Not until you promise."

"Promise what?"

"A little conversation."

She balked. She really meant it tonight, and who knew why? She thought if she had to sit next to him without a word being spoken, she would be dead by the time they got to where they were going.

She slid in and relaxed the minute she pulled herself up by the handrest. She liked riding in his truck. Her Volkswagen was nearly crippled with bad brakes and no air in the tires. The shocks needed replacement, and the windshield wipers didn't work.

There was a huge, satisfying rumble that seemed to start right under her seat when he turned on the motor. They headed south, and she supposed they'd drive out toward the bluffs. She badgered him for details of the trip.

"So. What else did you do? You must have gone to the ballet like always."

"On opening night, yes. With Rosella."

"Why don't you pull a knife out of the glove compartment and get it over with?"

"Calm down. Rosella Hightower only choreographed the piece. There was a reception for her later in Cannes."

"You went?"

"Of course. We Indians stick together."

"You always fall back on that Indian bit at the most convenient times."

"You would, too, if you were a little smarter."

He lit a cigarette and threw the match out the window. The wind grabbed it and carried it from his hand. She looked at the speedometer, which read sixty. She couldn't even feel it; the ride was that smooth. She stared at the fenced property that went on for miles.

"If I were a little smarter, I wouldn't hang out with you, now would I? Or maybe I would, but I'd insist you take me to Paris and to the ballet to see Rosella Hightower, who happens to be a hero of mine."

"Get it right. She doesn't dance."

"She doesn't dance, and neither do I. But maybe I would dance if I left you. Just maybe I would."

She slapped her forehead hard, but Johnny didn't even bat an eye. He let her go on.

"What, what am I doing here with you again?"

He pulled the truck onto an unmarked lane. They bumped and jostled down the dark side road, and they came to a clear place, or at least a stopping place inside the thick brush and scrub oak. There was space for a truck, but not much more. The sky was lit up, though. The Little Dipper could be seen from where she would lie down.

He jumped lightly out of the cab and came around to her side. The moon shone down on him, and his features frightened her for a minute. The moon carved out whole sections of him. It took great scoops from his cheeks and made black holes of his eyes. He opened his arms to help her down.

"If you were smarter, you'd claim your own headrights."

"The Osage voted in my grandfather as an honorary. I don't see you people voting me in."

"Of course not. Because there's no one pressing the issue. You never press *any* issue. You're nothing at all unless you claim it. I told you that the first time we met."

"And what would that get me? An eagle feather and a chance to give speeches, like my father? A laminated hunk of the Million Dollar Elm? Maybe I should get into the brawl over allotment. I could snap up Nelson's two measly headrights, with oil prices the way they are right now."

"That's a hell of a lot more than you have now."

She felt his hands tighten around her waist, and she gave in like any chronic spender, drinker or thief who vowed just this once and then no more. She'd be angry at him again, doubly so, but later. She let herself go down, loosening the grip on the door. She could see now; she wasn't moonblind anymore. Her eyes were adjusting to the shapes and shadows. She felt her way around the back of the truck, heard him lower it so she could climb inside. Her hand felt cold metal, then fur. Fur?

"Is this some woman's coat? I've had it, Johnny."

"It's a fur throw. You know I like nice things. What are you learning about me that you don't already know?"

"It's . . . actually it feels nice. But think of all the animals that went to line the bottom of Johnny Beaureve's flatbed truck."

"I come from a long line of trappers. The thought of all those animals doesn't bother me a bit."

She tilted her head back. Another theory was borne out again, that the best way to look at the sky was like this. To properly sense the night sky was to comprehend limits. Confinement opened onto space. Johnny Beaureve believed his own maxim and had led her to believe it in the same way. Something in her naturally shrank from wide spaces. She searched for it, too. The strictest enclosure that was freedom. They lay down on the fur rug and looked up together toward the funnel of leafy branches through which starlight fed the floor of the clearing. She itched to feel more of the fur on her skin.

A very slight breeze ruffled the trees that ringed the clearing. Though they couldn't feel it from where they lay, they could hear it. He stood and went around to the cab for champagne. She sat up as he handed her a glass.

"Tell me about the night that went with this."

"There's not that much to tell. I went to my friend who runs the cellar at the Café de Paris, to offer him some bottles."

She tried to keep her voice casual and didn't succeed.

"And?"

"We talked back and forth, then he set aside a case of this champagne for me, and the director of the hotel phoned me for lunch."

"Upstairs in the hotel?"

"Yes."

"Who was there?"

"Well, Princess Caroline walked in, and there was quite a flap."

"Johnny, Johnny."

She sighed and held her glass steady as he poured. She had decided not to wait for a toast and took a great gulp. She drank champagne as if it were soda pop, even though she knew it galled him. She drained the rest of the glass quickly and twisted her hair into a coil. She held it there and let the air cool the back of her neck.

He began to undress her, and memory went to work, leaving her rigid. She knew exactly what she was about to feel and at the same time knew absolutely nothing. She felt her boots slide off, and then she was squirming free of jeans, her skin alive to the fur that lay underneath.

His long, loose hair fell over her, and she would have loved to pull him down to her chest to hold him like a child. She'd never dared, though she'd dared many things with Beaureve. He crouched above her, allowing only his mouth to find hers. In love-making, Beaureve conducted himself with perfect selfishness and, in that way, extracted from her the most extreme pleasure. He refused to touch her between the legs in the beginning. This only came later when she was drenched with him and he could taste the two of them together. Delicately, he first sampled her with the tips of his fingers. Then he would explore soundlessly at the edge of her until he finally thrust his tongue deep inside. First came last, and they would begin again and again as he softly praised her for the wet, open spaces that welcomed him.

She lay still, one hand resting on her chest and the other by her side, the palm open and relaxed. Had she known just such a pose took Johnny's breath away and had she been more skilled in these things, Laydelle might have profited from her effect on him. But she was curiously without guile, lying captive in her own world just when the man she wished to secure was most smitten. Her legs parted, but not crudely. The angularity of her body was softened by the moonlight.

Johnny Beaureve drew an eagle feather out from under the throw. Her eyes opened wide, and she raised herself up on one elbow.

"Lie back down. This is for me."

He watched closely as she began to change all over again. He mapped a route down her body, leaning forward to see how parts of her clamored for attention. The edges of the feather barely rustled as Beaureve drew it over her bare skin.

She opened her eyes. He had become a student of her responses, squatting over her with the feather to dab here and there, lightly running it through her legs to see what quivered or remained taut, what new territories could be opened up to his advantage.

"What exactly is your complaint?" He traced the feather gently over her eyes and lips. It was damp, and he pried her mouth open easily with one forefinger, brushing it over the tip of her tongue. "Eventually I give you everything you want."

"You give me half of what I want."

He reached deep inside her as the feather passed back and forth over the top of her legs.

She drew in her breath sharply. "I want up off the floor of your truck. I want to be the one who clambers over fences with you in the south of France. I want to share your jet lag and get those damned dogs out of the bedroom."

He stopped. She could hear a single dog yapping far away. The dog was barking like mad.

"You want to be my squaw."

He pulled her up quickly to her knees and crawled around behind to straddle her. He lowered his face next to hers as he held on. She felt his breath hot and close.

"In that case, you'll have to make yourself more presentable, like the ladies in the movie we watched tonight."

His hands dug at her scalp. He pulled her hair back from her face as she crouched, and worked it quickly into a braid. She felt him at the base of her spine, hard and unmoving.

"Ouch! Johnny, you're pulling my hair."

"Nonsense. I'm initiating you into the tribe. A private ceremony. That's what you want, isn't it?"

And then the braid was thrown over her shoulder, the eagle feather pressed into the hair at the crown of her head, the sharp quill scraping her skin. He took the Hermès scarf, which had been tossed to one side, and draped it loosely over her shoulders, squeezing her breasts as he did.

"Hey. What are you doing? You promised me you'd never—"

He drove one finger inside, and she stiffened.

"You ought to know better than to trust an Indian."

"I don't like this. Cut it out, Johnny. You're hurting me."

He opened the palms of her hands and placed them, one at a time, on the edge of the truck. He was very rough and didn't stop when she cried out in real pain. He didn't stop until the single dog's howls muffled all other sounds. Beaureve then pried her hands from the truck. He held her by the neck, forcing her head down until it was nearly between her own knees.

"Say my name, Johnny. At least say my name."

He proceeded wordless through the flawed final act. The only sound was the sound of a barking dog.

Hubbell and Mary

chapter 5

1948

"Marry me, Mary."

Mary Roberts stared at herself in the mirror of the compact and thought about his name. The name she would step into as if it were a fine new dress. Then she came to her senses.

"Darn these crow's feet. Oh, Hubbell. You *are* tiresome. It's a good thing I'm so in love with you."

He met her at Ableson's. The elevator door closed, and instead of staring at the numbers on the board or the fleur-de-lis pattern in the carpet, like most people, Mary looked Hubbell straight in the eye and told him about a dark-green sweater on Three that was too marvelous. Hubbell forgot about why he had come to the store in the first place. He followed her to Three and watched as Mary purchased the marvelous sweater. Afterward they had lunch in the tearoom. Hubbell hadn't even known there was a tearoom at Ableson's. She ordered the Blue Plate Special without ever opening the menu and offered Hubbell a cigarette, as if meeting someone on an elevator were the most natural thing in the world.

Hubbell's infatuation with the fiery, wisecracking little working girl was considered peculiar. He brought her everywhere. His high-living friends stared as Mary declined a highball and ordered coffee instead, saying she had to be at work early the next day. The midnight train for Kansas City? She looked at them as if they, not she, were mad. How could she just up and go to Kansas City on a midnight train? Most puzzling of all was Mary's consistent good humor. She actually *liked* being a stenographer in an advertising firm. She licked her lips and talked of advancement. The second mystery was Hubbell's own persistence. Highballs weren't all Mary continued to decline.

"I can't marry you now, Hubbell. I don't want to be a secretary forever, you know. I've got a meeting scheduled in two weeks with a fellow I know in personnel that could change everything."

They had drunk gallons of coffee during their courtship. They were drinking it now. Mary stirred and stirred until she was sure every bit of sugar was dissolved, then turned up her nose, finding the coffee had gone cold.

"But what does a meeting have to do with us? With love?"

"Nothing, which is the point. Crazy as I am about you, I'm not going to throw away my future on your behalf."

She lifted one arm for the waitress and the check.

"Let's go to my place, and I'll make you some real coffee. I'll show you something special, Hubbell. Something that's terribly, terribly special. Secret, too. I've never shown a soul."

Mary's rooms were in perfect disorder. Hubbell settled happily into a chair and took it all in: the white blouses heaped in a basket, waiting for the hot iron, a pile of dirty breakfast dishes and a milk bottle left on the counter in haste. The radio was playing as Mary opened the sticky door; she'd left her apartment in such a hurry, she'd forgotten even that. It was thrilling. It was foreign. Hubbell wanted to burrow into the unmade bed he could see from where he sat. He had inherited his father's weakness for working women and that near-perfect mix of perspiration and perfume. The whole tired tier of typists and waitresses excited Hubbell immeasurably. He watched Mary reach for something on the highest shelf of a hall closet. Hubbell frowned and straightened his tie. The crummy shoe box didn't look worthy of containing Mary's secrets.

"Now how about that coffee?"

Mary let it perk too long. And then she set the coffeepot right on the tabletop, so that the pot left a mark that would never go away. Hubbell's hands shook, but not from the caffeine. They shook because he was astonished at his Mary and more in love than ever. Energetic ideas proved contagious.

"Let's start here." She sighed. "Everybody needs to have a hero. Why are you frowning, Hubbell? Heroes keep us from being sad and mediocre."

Mary pulled from the box the first of many newspaper clippings on Wishbone Harris. The accounts spoke of his size and shape, his notoriety and the whimsical business the brash young man had parlayed into twenty million dollars. Wishbone's daddy staked him five thousand dollars. He was grateful that the class fat boy (Yale, 1936) with an embarrassing fondness for chicken bones had finally found something to hold his attention. Wishbone bought himself a small company with the money. He supplied the beauty industry with its peculiar set of wants—hair rollers, heating pads and waving lotions. Wishbone was fond of women. He found great comfort in their company, and their netherworld of needs hardly alarmed him. He peddled his products hard and listened to the ladies, really listened as they murmured about their darned flat heads, about wanting shape and style and curl. And he watched as they dug into scuffed handbags for a crumpled ten-dollar bill. Then he did some figuring. Seventy-two million American women, half of whom had never had a permanent wave, for want of time and money. A do-it-yourself kit, then, for half the price. He would give them all the curls they wanted. When his first home wave kit fell over backward (he received six orders), he retreated to his garage at night, mixing and testing solutions until something right was ready to go. By '44 he got it straight. By '45 he was swamped with orders. Wishbone quickly sent up a flare, and his fast-talking brother arrived from California, with a marketing plan that would rattle the beauty industry.

Mary stood up suddenly and blushed.

"Six orders, do you believe it? I know plenty of people who would have just given up. You're the first person I've ever showed my file to, Hubbell! What do you think?"

It was Hubbell's turn to blush. The dilapidated shoe box filled with Mary's clippings, photos and squashed Toni cartons was like the sudden sight of silk lingerie.

"It's wonderful, Mar. But I still don't quite get it. The importance of all this, I mean."

"But there's more! You see, the Toni Twins have everybody

fooled. Nobody can tell the difference, Hubbell, not even the experts on hair."

American housewives were stumped, and the figures showed it. If they couldn't tell which twin had the Toni and which one had the beauty shop wave, it was high time they tried one of those home permanents themselves. As Wishbone's Toni company expanded, so did a secondary industry. He needed twins to fuel his promotion project. They turned up all over—in Atlanta, Los Angeles, Dublin, Ireland. Redheads and blondies, beauties and beasts, for, he was sorry to say, not all twins were created equal and some were plain plug-ugly. He opened an office in Chicago to screen look-alike office workers, waitresses and college students who had heard of his publicity stunt and wanted to cash in. He sorted through photographs shot in somebody's Idaho backyard, read birth certificates issued in Hawaii. He took to bumping his head and lighting a cigarette when he already had one burning. When doubles began to appear in his dreams at night, leaving him no peace, he hired an indefatigable headhunter, who scoured the public domain: the skating rink at Rockefeller Center, the crowds at airports and department stores; why, even the packed house at Radio City Music Hall. She could trace identical features in any mob and claimed, upon retiring from Wishbone's venture, that she'd weeded through a thousand twins. She took a job on an ocean liner and was heard to say she didn't care if she never saw another twin in her life.

Hubbell held on to his chair. His head was turning and beginning to ache at the temples. The radio in Mary's bedroom was still playing softly. She frowned and examined a sheaf of papers.

"Imagine, Hubbell. One dollar and twenty-five cents. No fuss, no bother. No beauty shop operator to tip. And all that from a fellow called Wishbone. What's wrong?"

"Never mind me. I'm thinking is all. Where is this leading us?"

"Us? Nowhere, like I've said a dozen times. But I'm not finished with my story. There's trouble on the way, but you'll see that Wishbone's glory is untarnished. He's a model for us all, Hubbell. I mean it."

Two motorcades of twins were sent out from Chicago to introduce the product to seventy-five American cities. Six sets of twins were even earmarked for an aerial tour of England and Western Europe, for Toni was ready for her first trip abroad. Wishbone's brother steamed ahead with plans for a national twin contest. Five hundred dollars' worth of layette and nursery gear would be given to each set of female twins born on New Year's Day. America was awash with identical girls, and soon Toni dolls were on the market, with hair-set solutions included. Little girls could even apply the solution, taking their dolls from straight to curly in the blink of an eye. Beleaguered beauticians claimed the salon look couldn't be wrung from a cardboard box, no matter how smart the packaging. For a finished look, there was no substitute. Beauty shop operators launched their war in earnest. Outright legislation wasn't long in coming. State after state passed laws making home-wave application illegal, should money change hands.

"Wishbone went right on! Do you think he let a little trouble with detractors slow him up? Absolutely not. He hasn't tried to sweep it under the carpet. Wishbone never tried to *wish* them away! Why, all this noise has done nothing but fan the flames. They've given him free publicity, that's all. He's wrung fortune from misfortune, Hubbell. What a man!"

Mary sagged in her chair as fatigue swept over her. Hubbell spoke firmly, closing one hand around her slim wrist.

"I have a plan, Mary. It's so good you ought to accept it unconditionally. I say you go straight to my father with this idea."

"With what idea?"

"Father can put his gasoline in Wishbone's tanks. Think of it! Hanks Motor Fuel moving sets of twins from city to city. Hanks Flight Fuel promulgating the message in Europe and points beyond."

"Hubbell, do you really think . . . ?"

". . . that Father will accept this proposition? He'll jump at the chance. He loves publicity stunts more than he loves the oil business. I can hear the theme of Father's speech now: Two men in the hair business make good. Do I think we should get married? I certainly do."

"And to think that I had no idea."

Mary's eyes were filled with tears. They took the longest time to spill over, and while she was waiting for them to drop from her eyes and rush down her cheeks, Mary looked at her fiancé through a blur.

"I never imagined you were so clever, so quick to catch an idea and turn it into reality. Oh, Hubbell, how you've had me fooled! I've loved you for the longest time, and just imagine . . . I thought you were nothing but a party boy and a rich man's son. Why have you been hiding your own fine qualities? Of course we'll marry, Hubbell."

Hubbell thought of Mary's busy office with a tinge of panic. Would the world of appointments and contracts and sales schedules pull Mary from him? Dates and deadlines, she loved it all. Well, then, he would beat Mary at her own game.

"Within the year. We'll be married within the year, come hell or high water. . . . Okay, Mar?"

Hubbell's hand still clung to her small white wrist.

"Mrs. Hubbell Hanks. What a lovely name."

1949

Nelson Hanks' fortune was wrung from a man's world. His petroleum, blasted out of rock and soil, fueled their machines and their military. All those hard-boiled years had left a softy in their wake. A man who was dead tired of hard talk and the prickly scent of men's aftershave. The oil man and banker, nearing the end of his life, preferred to think of softly curling hair and the nape of a woman's neck. Mary Hanks' proposition was gaily accepted by a man fettered less and less by his present circumstances. For his wife's recent death had freed him from minutes and hours and days, letting him go from boy to man and back as he wished. Nelson Hanks' mind roamed increasingly, freely reliving a conversation in the Climax Shaving Parlor (Creston, Iowa, 1895) or a tryst in a New York City hotel room (1920) or an oil field brawl in the Oklahoma Osage hills that turned especially mean (1908). Not senile, he was supple, moving faster and faster, often skirting the present tense altogether. What he hoped for now was a moment of pure pleasure, a wish that was alien to no man. Nelson leaned forward in his chair, straining to understand what the little blond woman before him was saying.

"Of course, Papa. We thought of that a long time ago, when we first cooked up this glorious scheme. *Naturally* a girl will be sitting in your lap. We've made sure it's in Papa's contract, haven't we, Hubbell?"

Some bit of supper remained at the corner of his father's mouth, and Hubbell wished Joey would wipe it off. There. The valet removed the mess from his father's face so deftly the old man didn't even flinch or try to dodge the linen napkin. The oil man, seventy-five years old and infirm, frowned and echoed Mary softly, wonderingly.

"Papa?"

Was this woman his daughter? No, he had no daughter. Nelson Hanks scratched his head and remembered that the woman before him was Hubbell's bride, Mary. It had all happened so fast! His wife had died and his son had married, leaving no decent space in between for a man to sort things out. It confused him so much, he often waved his hand before his eyes to sweep it all away. Hanks ventured out less and less, satisfied to live among ghosts. Sometimes even little Hank Hanks, Hubbell's dead twin, floated past his eyes. Not as often as he liked, though. The twin was scarcely more than a bit of memory stain, rubbed lighter every year. "Go out? What would I go out for? Out's in now, Joey. Everything and everyone has come right on in here with me." He argued with them, pleaded sometimes. He explained every bit of his personal history to the dead men and women who ringed the room. Defended it or revised it to their liking. And when the orator was shaken from his delivery, spilling tea down his shirtfront, soiling himself like any common old geezer, he rang furiously for Joey. But Nelson implored the ghosts today, begged them to retreat on the twenty-third day of February, 1949, so that he could be sane and sober, full of enthusiasm for this project of . . . He stopped again. Was it Mary who had thought of Wishbone and the Toni Twins, or Hubbell? His mind, his failing mind. He let Mary help him out of his chair.

"Up we go, Papa! You wouldn't want to keep all your fans waiting, now would you? Darn, I wish it wasn't raining. Today, of all days!"

Nelson's befuddled gaze fell on his daughter-in-law's hand, where it rested on his arm. She was wearing Lavinia's ring, the ring he'd brought back from New York. Nelson blinked hard. The ring looked like a gaudy piece of paste jewelry on Mary's hand, and how was that? He could still see Lavinia slip it off her finger with great ceremony, the better to shuffle a deck of cards or speed along on a piece of needlework. He could still imagine her friends buckling down to concentrate on the cards in their own hands or quiet their chattering to take up the petit point that lay forgotten in their laps. The removal of Lavinia Hanks' splendid ring functioned as a subtle call to order. Lavinia had certainly understood the power of *things;* no one had undermined her in that. Mary's hand tightened slightly on his arm, and Nelson shook off his memories.

"Let's hop along, shall we? The manager at Ableson's has already phoned twice."

The oil man managed to stand erect in the crowded department store. He smiled and pumped the warm hands that found their way into his own. It would be his last appearance in a public ceremony. Mary freed Nelson from all the warm hands, all the damp, quizzical faces that seemed too close, and led him onstage, where he sat rigidly on a pink satin cushion, with a walking stick against his knee, puffing on the cigar that had become his trademark. His eyes lightly scanned the crowd. Mary had promised him girls in exchange for a speech. Hadn't that been the agreement?

"Now, Papa, if you want to smoke that old cigar, it's fine by me. Just try not to get ashes all over your wonderful suit while we're waiting. Oh, look! Look how sweet they look."

Nelson straightened up fast, for girls were spilling out of the first Lincoln Continental. He parted his legs and strained forward. PUT HANKS IN YOUR TANK. Why, that was good! He could see it from where he sat. Black ash tippled over pink satin. The second Lincoln pulled up to the curb, and Nelson laughed out loud. The car pulled a trailer ludicrously gotten up to look like a Toni box. The store manager had grown authoritarian. He strode through the lobby, displaying some petulance.

"Let's let the ladies inside, why don't we, folks? Excuse me. Arthur, help me clear this area. Ah, nuts! Lightning on top of everything . . . Lady, you'll have to let me through. All we need now is a power failure."

Was it the misty weather? The long drive and the endless touring? The crowd pressed around the girls, anticipating exuberance and giggles. Twelve silly fillies with curly hair and cute dispositions. One of the twins had a bad cold. Her nose was red and raw. She rubbed at it with a grimy handkerchief rather than giving it a good hard blow. One girl's slip hung down below her dress. Another twin didn't know how to smile, and it showed. She stretched her lips over her teeth, and even that looked as if it put her out.

There were two showstoppers, though. Dimpled blondies who knew how to work a crowd, all right. Their noses tipped up suddenly at the end. Eager, too. They answered questions with a rush and tumble of words.

"Do my own hair? Won't tell, can't tell. Sorry; bosses' orders."

"Marry? Not until we find ourselves identical boys! Is that real lizard? Gee, bet that cost you a pretty piece."

They made it to the stage. Nelson stood up evenly, setting aside his cane. He shook hands with every one of them. He praised them for being working girls. He said there was nothing more appealing than a girl who knew how to take care of herself. A sea of features bobbed around him as he spoke and squeezed smooth hands. He saw dark eyebrows that marched straight across a clear forehead, brows that couldn't be plucked or tweezed into submission. A beauty mark, applied with black pencil but fetching anyway. And the shapes! Round or gently sloping backsides and one, no, two bottoms that were disarmingly square, riding high up on the blond girls. The twins dropped lightly onto surrounding cushioned footstools. Nelson stared and blinked, stunned by his good fortune. The store manager checked his watch and touched the old man's elbow lightly.

"It's time for that speech you promised us, Mr. Hanks."

"Speech? Oh, yes. Fine. That thing hooked up?"

He handed Joey what remained of his cigar and tapped the microphone lightly with the rim of his wedding band.

"You all hear me way back in the back? Hear me now?"

Hubbell Hanks managed to catch his father's eye. Mary had returned to his side, and he hugged his bride tighter. She wore her hair pulled back, the way she'd worn it that day in the Ableson's elevator, just to please him. He gave Nelson the thumbs-up sign, and the old man looked past him to the back of the room.

"How many people in here think I look like a damn old fool? Don't be shy. I want to know how many people in this room wonder what the hell Nelson Hanks is doing up onstage with six sets of twins and if he's lost his mind. I see a hand in the back. What's your name, son?"

"Huey Stone, sir."

"You work for me?"

"Yes, sir; down at the refinery."

"Doing what exactly?"

"I'm a janitor, sir."

"What brings you to Ableson's Department Store? Don't tell me you want to give yourself a cold wave."

"Looking to tell which twin has the Toni, sir. Got a baby due any day now, and they're giving away whole layettes."

"Check with personnel on Monday, Huey Stone. You got yourself a new job. New job and a raise."

Mary Hanks returned Hubbell's affectionate squeeze and kissed him deeply. He bent down to hear what she said.

"You see, darling? I knew he wouldn't let us down. Your father is still a crowd pleaser. We just have to be behind him each and every minute. All Nelson Hanks needs is a little guidance from his family. Of course, isn't that what everyone needs?"

"That's *precisely* what everyone needs. Mary?"

She pressed closer to her husband.

"I think you're brilliant. This is your triumph. Why, without you, none of this—"

"Sssh. Lord, look at your papa go."

"Folks, I don't have a prepared speech, and I don't need one. That's right. I see Ed Oliver from my public relations department chewing his pencil and hoping I don't lay an egg up here today."

Four police officers entered the department store lobby. It was raining in earnest now, and one of the men mopped his face with the back of his hand.

"Old men operate without a license, you know. People figure we've got one foot in the grave anyhow, so they let the lead out on old folks. They figure they might just as well coddle us. My own board of directors reasoned that way, thinking, Hell, let Nelson have his way. Could be his last hurrah."

Nelson paused and watched Mary make her way toward the police officers. She had one hand on her hip as she marched forward, and the stones in the ring flashed suddenly under the store lights. Perhaps he had been wrong about how the ring looked on her hand. One of the officers took a step back, and Mary tapped his chest lightly with her forefinger. The speech . . . where had he left off?

"Folks, Wishbone Harris caught my eye for a number of reasons. He's a young man with ambition. So was I. He got his start in the hair business. So did I. I'm proud to see the Hanks Petroleum logo stuck up on the side of that Lincoln Continental parked outside. Damn proud."

Ed Oliver relaxed slightly and stuck a peppermint under his

tongue. Here was Nelson at his finest, reheating a few old stories for the crowd as a group of Ableson's salesgirls quietly prepared a makeup table off to the side of the stage. They lined up the contents of a Toni box, checked the lights on the oval mirror, straightened the white eyelet flounce on the table.

"Wishbone Harris takes me back to my own beginnings, when I was a simple barber."

Nelson leaned forward on his cane and rubbed the bridge of his nose.

Hubbell noticed a man in the middle of the room, scribbling furiously on a notepad. He didn't look like a local fellow. He was likely a patent holder, an inventor of some unlikely thing, here to pick up a smart tip. Hubbell felt his cheeks grow warm as he watched the man study his father, hoping to soak up the Hanks formula.

"Now, mind you, I wasn't trying to *curl* hair back in those days. I was trying to *grow* it. And staring at those hogs, at the down on their backs, had me persuaded the secret was rainwater. Never saw a bald hog in my life, and I didn't reckon anybody else had, either. Guess I was a persuasive enough young man. Nobody left the Climax Shaving Parlor without buying a bottle of my hair tonic."

The manager wove through the crowd, distributing ballots to get voting under way. Winners would be named and gifts distributed. The company photographer was setting up his tripod just in front of the stage as the Ableson's salesgirls readied the demonstration table. Rotating sets of twins would be on hand all day to give tips on how to apply the waving lotion. Nelson closed his speech as people lined up to turn in their votes and claim prizes. The girls settled in around him for a picture session.

"I'm not too heavy, am I, Mr. Hanks? You tell me if I'm hurting you, now."

A twin fidgeted on Nelson's knee. She turned to face him.

"Alice, hold still. And turn your head slightly left. Mr. Hanks, if you'll lean forward just a bit . . . ."

"Say, you girls won't mind if I ask you something?"

"Of course not, Mr. Hanks."

Nelson flipped the edge of his ear with one finger.

"How do you ladies manage to tour the whole country and still keep your husbands at home?"

"Oh, none of the girls is married, Mr. Hanks. It's a stimulation."

Rita Hill's sister, Nita, jabbed her in the side with one finger.

"Stipulation, Rita. Being single is a *stipulation.*"

"Another stimulation is that we work until we're ready to drop. All I think about is putting my feet in a pail of hot water. Or drinking a cup of hot milk at the kitchen table. I'd give anything just to loaf for a day."

Nita and Rita Hill agreed on one thing. There was no place like home.

"Or play the radio. All day long, too. With the window wide open and my pussy in my lap."

Nelson turned his head slightly. The photographer raised his arm, counted to three and cursed. The flash failed.

"You left a kitten behind?"

"I sure did, Mr. Nelson. My own little pussycat. Jet black, with the sweetest disposition in the world. She used to just curl up in my lap and purr like an engine. Our kid sister's looking after her. She'll be all grown, time I get back."

"You feeling okay, Mr. Nelson?"

"Mr. Hanks, sweetie. Never better."

The innocence of their confessions made his head spin. For it was just this that had caused a much younger Nelson Hanks to repeatedly stumble and fall. A stylish, carefully composed woman left him flat as a nickel. But the sight of a jagged run in a silk stocking, a missing button or a shiny nose begging for powder, the worry lines that worked their way onto a woman's face despite every preventive measure . . . any one of these things could turn him inside out.

"You just won't listen to me."

"Not when I can help it, sis."

The photographer struggled with his equipment.

"Say 'Cheese.' Let's hear it now. One, two, three . . ."

"Who would've thought that in first-class hotels you can't get a decent . . ."

". . . pillow. I would have. So did Mama. She had two laid out, and you were too proud to take yours. Hush up, Rita."

Rita hushed, turning one shoulder seductively toward the camera.

"That's it! Last photo, Mr. Hanks. Then I reckon I'll let you down off that stage."

There were thirty-three winners. They lined up for their prizes, and Rita Hill, her neck still stiff from the comfortless pillow of the night before, took her place beside the makeup mirror. Her first customer was a self-proclaimed sore loser.

"I guessed you, and there's nothing I hate worse than losing."

"Well, you guessed wrong. I had a beauty shop wave done in Waco."

Rita Hill looked sidewise at her angry customer and continued her demonstration, showing her the trickiest part, which was getting the tips of the hair to lay down right on the roller. But she barely had the time to part the woman's hair. Rita later claimed, in a teary phone call to her mother in Jacksonville, that the officer manhandled her on top of everything.

"Hold it right there."

The policeman never bothered to remove his hat or coat. Water dripped onto Rita Hill from the top of his hat.

"Police, lady. You'll have to come with me."

Nelson Hanks saw the commotion and waved for Joey to help him down off the stage. He patted one of the twins absently on the shoulder as he stepped down. The store manager was already on the telephone in his office. Mary pushed her way through the crowd. Her voice was so shrill it caused the policeman to startle.

"What's going on here? Who are you to harass this girl?"

"Old men may be able to operate without a license, Mrs. Hanks, but this girl can't. Not unless she's a qualified beautician, that is."

"What's your name?"

"It's Officer Trill, and I don't work for Hanks Petroleum. This little lady accepted some pocket money for her services down in Waco, then she accepted a little more in Houston. Oh, she's quite an operator, this one. Excuse me, now."

"This is outrageous."

"Maybe. If you want to file a complaint, you'll have to do that down at the station."

"You bet your muddy boots I'm going to file a complaint."

Rita Hill spent an hour downtown. Nita heckled officers as they took her sister's prints and led her past cells clogged with nameless drunks and a band of car thieves apprehended the night before. Rita sat down carefully, not letting her back touch the chair, and folded her hands together to wait. A newsman took her picture like that, then called for her twin. They held hands through the bars for a photo. Rita Hill looked chaste and submissive until the very end. The female warden led her from the cell and offered her a cigarette she nearly accepted before Mary Hanks snatched it from the warden's hands. Rita and Nita sat on a cracked red leather sofa as the police captain put his hands to his forehead. Mary's voice bore into his skull like a power drill.

"Rita Hill doesn't smoke cigarettes! Rita Hill doesn't drink liquor! She is eighteen years old and planning to go to college. But that's in jeopardy now that she's got a jail record. You've shamed this poor child and her parents, and for what? Officer Trill is a moron, and this little maneuver will cost him plenty."

Mary Hanks reached inside the split sofa and tore away a handful of foam. She threw it across the waiting room.

"Cigarettes! Smokers ought to clean up after themselves. Aah, I hate this filth."

She emptied the ashtray on the coffee table, then leaned over and blew the pile of ashes all to hell. The police captain rose up out of his seat.

"That's not all! If you think for a minute that this will shut down our tour, you've got another think coming. This tour will be a smashing success, maybe even more smashing with this bit of free publicity. Come on, girls. Let's get you back in that Lincoln. On to Next Stop, America!"

The three women bustled out the door, and when Hubbell's phone rang ten minutes later, the police captain was less than cordial.

"Your wife? You bet I've seen your wife, Mr. Hanks. You better have that little cat declawed. You're damn right I said declawed. You oughta see this place."

It took Mary forever to return home. Hubbell was frantic by the time she finally let herself in the back door. He had prepared something for her to eat. He counted on the hot, spicy food she loved to get her mind off the unfortunate business with Rita Hill.

"Driving? You mean all this time you've been out, just driving around?"

"There's nothing like driving to clear out the upstairs attic, if you know what I mean."

Mary tapped her head and lifted her eyebrows. Her eyes were so bright, Hubbell wondered if she was coming down with something.

"Gee, Mar. I didn't know driving calmed you down. You don't seem out of sorts at all."

Mary spoke between bites. She hadn't known how hungry she was, with all the excitement. She helped herself to seconds.

"There's a lot you don't know, Mr. Newlywed. Why should I be out of sorts? This is all over the radio! They're going crazy reporting this. There's fortune in misfortune, all right! The tour is going to be a wild success. And so are we, Hubbell."

Hubbell watched as Mary turned her shining eyes on him and rubbed her finger, stiff from the weight of her newly acquired jewelry. She removed his mother's ruby ring.

"Now that this is over, I'll be able to give you every bit of my energy and attention. The man who saw the connection between Hanks Petroleum and the Toni Twins is capable of great things. You just need someone behind you each and every minute. In fact, that's all you've ever needed. You'll see I'm right on this, Hub."

Just then, the mind that saw the connection between Hanks Petroleum and the Toni Twins went briefly, but decidedly, dark. Hubbell thought of nothing and struggled toward nothing, but this personal power failure escaped Mary's notice. She had already started to hum a little tune.

Nelson and Lavinia

chapter 6

1884

"A man can't talk when he's dead tired, son. Now let me have some rest."

"You can be dead or else you can be tired. But how can you be dead and tired at the same time? Papa? Answer me, Papa."

That was what was wrong with farming. What eleven-year-old Nelson decided, watching his father stump into the kitchen for supper, was that tending hogs and chickens, drawing corn out of the Iowa fields . . . all these things stole your words away. So that a child with a mouthful of questions might look spitefully out the back window at the neatly manicured vegetable garden, the animals pecking and bawling in their pens or the milk cow placidly tethered to a tree stump and think *No!* Nelson dreamed of sentences as he hauled wood or collected eggs or slapped a mule's rump, raising a thick cloud of dust. He spit words out into the air just to hear them connect together. He memorized whole passages of dime novels, read the Horatio Alger stories, the biographies of American presidents, then recited them as he worked, less to relive the stories than to appease his hunger for human sound. His father had passed silence on to his other sons. They chewed stalks of hay or tree twigs, tobacco if they could get their hands on it, while they labored on the farm. They played pranks and made bets, trapped rabbits and ground squirrels or swam in a stream clotted with trout so fearless and plentiful they were a nuisance to swimmers. But talk? One brother, commanding peace at the end of a stifling-hot June day, held him pinned on the ground until he promised to hush. But it was because of talk that Nelson became the family emissary. He represented his brothers in disputes or amatory affairs, brought life onto the farm or held it at bay. The boy was blessed with prattle. There wasn't enough money for five boys to attend the traveling circus when it pitched its tent in Creston. Nor was there enough for five boys to wander through a carnival or sit straight-backed on knotty planks of wood at a Wild West show staged by Buffalo Bill Cody. There was just enough for one ticket. They could always find money enough for one. Nelson was dispatched time and again. He brought back single ticket stubs and printed programs bearing witness to fire-eaters and fortune-tellers, men and women who could shinny across a high wire, balancing monkeys and birds from South America on their shoulders. There was no rancor among the brothers, for the decision was clear. No one could tell a thing quite like Nelson. In fact, given a choice, the shy, quiet brothers preferred this sidewise participation; they trusted Nelson to polish the event, perfecting and rounding off the rude edges in his storytelling. They gathered at the kitchen table to hear all about a woman who could rope a steer with a yellow long-stemmed rose clenched between her teeth. When she'd brought the animal to a skidding halt and bound its legs, she scanned the crowd for a handsome onlooker. Then, still straddling the thrashing animal, she yanked the rose from between her teeth and tossed it lightly into his lap.

Nelson found his way off the farm by the time he was fourteen. He wasn't encouraged to talk in the barbershop, but no one could stop him from listening. He ran errands, rinsed washbowls and sharpened razors. Employees fetched cigars and freestanding brass ashtrays for their customers but were not allowed to smoke tobacco themselves. Instead, they were encouraged to stand outside the back of the building and "replenish themselves" for ten minutes in the morning, fifteen in the afternoon. Squatting next to a rain barrel, Nelson read labels during his fresh-air break. He studied what went into all the hair potions and ointments, tonics and sweet-smelling pomades that promised to prevent undue hair loss and ward off dandruff. He swept floors and scrubbed shaving mugs until he found he had risen in the ranks one day in 1891. He was eighteen years old by the time his employer let him take his place behind the chair. He waxed mustaches into thin, stiletto points or thick handlebars and shaved off the thick beards that were swiftly going out of fashion. His apprenticeship was over. He had become a full-fledged barber and found at last that he could chat it up with no reprisals, for a steady stream of vivacious conversation was all part of a fifteen-cent shave. In no time, lawyers and grocers, even the director of the local opera house, began to ask for that "Hanks boy." He snipped and trimmed, pocketed tips and advice from prosperous locals. By 1895, when he bought the Climax Shaving Parlor, it was clear that Nelson Hanks was ready to harvest some commercial notions of his own.

He went to work on his barbers. He bought elevator shoes for one and mixed a daily digestive for another, whose nervous disposition kept his stomach in a rage. He made them read a homemade eye chart, whose scale he copied carefully out of a Chicago newspaper, for he had nearly been scalped once himself by his nearsighted mother. He dressed them in bow ties and white jackets, insisted they use hand cream and put them on a commission. The lawyers and doctors couldn't waltz through the door anymore and count on a shave and a scalp rub without an appointment. For Nelson's shop had begun to change, and the money that poured into the ornate cash register began to fall from hands torn and blistered from field work. He was clever, all right. If local merchants weren't content to sit and wait their turn next to the occasional rough sort who tumbled off the Burlington railroad line, they didn't say so. Nelson still placated wealthy young lords with a row of personalized shaving mugs and select services. But now anyone would be served down at the Climax, though a printed notice barring men with head lice hung in his shop. Chances were Nelson wouldn't suggest such riffraff buy a bottle of his Mountain Sage Baldness Treatment, and sometimes a recalcitrant barber would "forget" the hot towel, but he would give any man a decent cut and shave at a fair price. It worked. In time Nelson found he had more business than he could handle. Four years later he squared his shoulders and bought a second barbershop. The Times Two Salon opened up in the basement of Central Bank. Predictably, there was grumbling in the upstairs banking suites.

"A barber? What the hell do we want with a bowlegged barber in the building? I sure hope Fancy Pants has the sense to stay in the basement, where he belongs."

"Nelson Hanks is some recommendation for that hair tonic of his. Why, the man's hairline has already slid back to the middle of his head! How old did you say he was? By God, the man looks forty. Mountain Sage, indeed!"

But the president of Central Bank finally succumbed. He excused his daughter, Lavinia, from Sunday-night haircuts, from the kitchen shears that clipped, clipped until a generous fruit bowl was filled not with plums and peaches but with the very hair from his head. He went downstairs to the basement and shyly asked Nelson Hanks for a trim. Bending over the banker and poised on the balls of his feet, Nelson began to talk. And in exercising his gift, he felt the brittleness in the man begin to give way. He talked about the incident out at the roundhouse, the switching that had gone awry, leaving the train derailed and the cows moaning, broken-legged, in an overturned boxcar. Nelson talked about the bachelor arrested on Platt Boulevard the night before. The bachelor farmer had ridden into town and, still atop his horse, filled the principal street in Creston with his maddened, lonely cries, scaring citizens nearly to death. The sheriff held him briefly, then handed his fate over to a group of church ladies, who wrung a promise from the freed prisoner. He would attend their socials. If this was impossible, they would sweep down on him each and every month, seven strong, armed with ginger cookies and lemonade, in a hired buggy to see how he was getting on.

"Proves a man can get too alone out in the middle of the blue-grass."

Nelson gave him a hand mirror and turned the swivel chair.

"Like what you see, Mr. Trappe?"

The banker laid the mirror across his knees and, looking the bowlegged barber in the eye, answered yes.

John Trappe saw the wall he had built was tumbling down. He saw he couldn't keep his daughter in a vault as if she were a property deed. He sighed. Maybe it was silly, even dangerous, to keep on as they were. "Find me a suitable suitor, daughter, and *then* we'll talk." They were all wanting. The widower found the young men who dangled about on his front porch were con artists or racketeers. If they weren't outright thieves or bandits, then they were simple or inappropriate.

"You know more about the level of interest rates than they do! Your knowledge shames them, Lavinia."

"They don't have a father who grills them every night over supper. They don't have to read aloud from a business journal every Sunday evening."

"You'll thank me one day."

Listening to him criticize her admirers, Lavinia looked down at her lap or grabbed a silver fork and tapped it sharply on her dinner plate. She took vanilla out of the cupboard and sprinkled it over a handkerchief. She parted her hair on the opposite side and took care to disagree with him on every possible issue. As they strolled through Creston in the blue evenings, she no longer slid her arm through his. She walked on his wrong side deliberately, provoking the banker's vertigo as she marched too close to the street, challenging speeding buggies and horsemen who couldn't make out her form in the dusk. Lavinia held fast to her bad humor, cursing the raging heat and the June bugs that lighted in her hair. She devoted evenings to her handwork, as always, but didn't grace Trappe's anecdotes with her usual insolence or burst of laughter. He complimented her cross-stitch.

"That certainly shows what you know. It's going every which way."

It took her eight days to rip it apart. What was to have been a stool cover for her daddy's stockinged feet wound up a misshapen piece of linen canvas spotted with blood from her pricked finger. She poked a hole through it in exasperation and threw it at the wall.

A week after John Trappe's visit to the Times Two Salon, Nelson received a supper invitation, written on the banker's onionskin business stationery. A banking directive appeared at the top of the page in golden print: PUT SOMETHING AWAY FOR OLD AGE. He saw that Lavinia's handwriting bore down heavily on the page. Her letters marched along, completely erect, without the beguiling loops and drags most women used to enhance their writing. He was expected on Tuesday. He flushed at the ease of his accomplishment. Lavinia had begun to divorce her daddy. She expected him, and not only on Tuesday. She wasn't pretty, and that was good, because Nelson preferred plain. He liked what she was and felt protected by what she was not. For Lavinia, to his relief, was not a gimme girl.

"Oh, say. Gimme a glass of your sugar tea, please."

"Can you gimme a yard of that iced cotton? That deep blue to your right."

The speech affectation had even been popularized in a song that was sung at the closing of Creston ceremonial balls or benefits at the opera house. "Gimme a gimme girl who'll gimme the rest of her life." There was nice, and by now, in the prosperous Iowa outpost, there was naughty. The bawdier edition of the song was sung with equal gusto wherever men met to smoke and drink or play a fast hand of poker. It wasn't the song that offended Nelson; it was the sloppy colloquialism. Breezy speech was hardly emancipation, but it was a small liberty, and others would follow. The gimme girls augured change. Such subtleties were lost on Nelson. With nothing but a grammar school education, he couldn't afford to be idiomatic. Not yet. Gimme wouldn't get him out of an Iowa boardinghouse.

"Why, this is succulent."

One dinner invitation led to another. Flawless Tuesdays. Double-worked roast turkey, ham baked in cider . . . the men took turns carving. Lavinia tied a starched white napkin around her father's neck one week, around Nelson's the next. He was punctual at first, and then he was early, taking his place with Lavinia on the wide front porch, where they shucked corn or freed peas from the pod. They swapped stories and in doing so gained admission to other worlds. Lavinia hounded him for "skinny." She loved man talk more than anything. Though she didn't use profanity herself, she thought cuss words could prop up a really good story and remarked to Nelson that she said one softly to herself every night before she fell asleep. The taste of a bad word in her mouth was sharper than Sen-Sen, she confided, curling a bit of hair around her middle finger. In exchange for his barbershop tales, she told him how woman talk went, how the ends of stories became the beginnings of others, how it drifted through a room with its own gentle insistence, like a draft of warm air through a leaky window. And how women seemed to back up and go over, again and again, worrying the same themes until she thought she would be driven mad. Mad. Nelson looked at her and proposed a ride in his buggy.

Her laughter made the mare bolt.

"Whoa, girl. What the . . . Steady now!"

Nothing seemed to make the little bay shy. Not falling leaves, not breaks in the rough road, not even the sight of a dead bull snake. The mare had sniffed and snorted, then raised her hoof and severed the head from the stiff body with one sharp blow. But

Lavinia's burst of violent laughter sent her shooting to the side of the river road with the bit between her teeth. Nelson sawed at her mouth until she slowed back down to a skittery trot.

"Oh, dear. I'm sorry, Nelson. I didn't mean to let on so soon."

"Let on what?"

"Oh, everything. How I'd sooner go fishing than sit in a roomful of simple-headed women. And the way I laugh. I hadn't wanted you to hear me really laugh, either. It just booms up out of nowhere sometimes, and there's not a thing I can do. Daddy swears one day I'll shatter all his good crystal. He worries so."

"About his sherry glasses?"

"About my intemperance."

Nelson pulled the mare to a stop. He set down his whip and let the mare have her head. She plunged into the long grasses at the edge of the path, ripping out mouthfuls until green foam oozed from the sides of the bit. Lavinia removed her hat and bet Nelson could never guess how many buttons there were on her walking shoes. She raised her skirts slightly.

"Don't count. Guess."

"Thirty-five."

"Well, you've guessed wrong. There are fifty. How long do you suppose it takes me to lean over in the morning and button them up?"

"All depends."

"On what?"

"On whether you've got that corset of yours on or off."

The mare flattened her ears and lunged forward at the sound of Lavinia's laughter. She stepped hard on a lead rein and panicked as she found her head forced to the ground. Nelson jumped from the buggy and lifted her hoof to free her, rubbing his hands down her foreleg until she let her head drop back down into the grass.

"Oh, see what I've done? I guess I'd best marry that skinny preacher or the undertaker. Some old gloomy Gus so sober I'll never laugh again."

Nelson watched the little mare graze and remarked a tingling at the back of his neck. He thought suddenly of how a dog's hackles lifted in apprehension. He noted a swollen tick on the left side of the horse's mane, and the gully, which was filling with shadows, then a hawk that hauled a field mouse from its nest with a precision that took his breath away. He turned to Lavinia, to see if she was listening to the rodent's frightened shrieks overhead as it was carted off. He wondered if he should propose marriage now, before a preacher or undertaker beat him to it.

Lavinia set her hat back on top of her head and asked him what time it was getting to be. He read her the time from his pocket watch, and she announced what a good thing *that* was. That a man and a woman could keep still for such a long time was a very good sign.

"There's more to life than jibber-jabber."

On the way back to town, Lavinia exacted her first promise from Nelson Hanks. He hitched his mare to a post in front of the Climax. He fiddled with the lock on the door.

"I swear, Nelson. You'd think you'd never done this before."

"I haven't. Lavinia, are you sure?"

"Oh, dead sure!"

It was Nelson who lifted her hat off this time. He helped her onto a chair and grinned as he cranked her up to the proper height. He unwound curls and felt his knees tremble as he loosened the mass of hair gently, extracting pins to free it little by little. He emptied it into the bowl, and she cried out loud when he opened his scissors.

"Eeeh, I'm scared. Promise me I'll be pretty. Promise."

He drafted his promise carefully, stating she would have beautiful hair. Not rosy cheeks on a complexion that seemed oddly dun-colored, as bleached out as Iowa plains in summer. He cut moderately, trimming just the frayed ends. He bit his lip nervously as he touched the base of her neck.

"What's the matter with you, Nelson? You're as nervous as a lost house cat."

"A girl's first haircut is a mother's task, Lavinia. I've got no business here with you."

The slip, his first, drew real tears. He soothed her gently and quietly in a dusky corner of the Climax. He wondered, as he felt hot tears soak through his shirt, if he held a sweetheart in his arms or a bereaved child.

chapter 7

1900

The two men sat where they sat most Tuesdays, in front of the globe in the parlor. Trappe had deliberately chosen the placement of the enormous sphere that whirled in the mahogany stand. With it he found that he could dominate most any discussion and turn it into some form of instruction, just as he found that by placing an open Bible conspicuously by the entrance to the large room he could infect guests with a bit of propriety. Men with little but business on their minds instinctively straightened their ties or lifted their chins when they caught sight of the Good Book that Trappe opened mischievously to an illustrated page—Jesus furiously tipping over the table of the moneylenders gave his dinner guests pause. He delighted in their discomfiture and found, as he talked of money and empires (stabbing at the spinning globe to point out Scotland, Carnegie's birthplace; dragging a finger from Switzerland to Colorado, reverently indicating Guggenheim's trajectory), that the globe and the Bible were handy stage props. Of all the men who had sat in this room and suffered his monologues on expansion or the privilege of power, the only one who was clearly onto his shenanigans was Nelson. He smirked at the Bible and hitched up the knees of his pants as he fell into the most comfortable chair in the parlor. Trappe's temperament led him to select,

in discussions and in dreams, foreign landscapes. The Philippines!
The banker had his eye on the lumber business; he dreamed of
shearing the hardwood forests neatly, noisily. Felling the trees was
an act of pure transfiguration. Pardon? He would turn his attention
to the accountant's ledgers with regret, for he had been traipsing
through a leafy wonderland, entranced by the bickering birds
above his head and the blanket of moist shade.

"You've certainly sensed resistance on my part, Nelson. An old
man isn't always willing to let go of his only daughter."

Hanks felt something pop at the bottom of his throat. A sour
taste rose to his mouth, and he sucked down some of the banker's
port to mask it. Nelson favored a wilderness much closer to home.
The spinning globe had come to a halt once, twice, as the barber's
forefinger landed not on Trappe's beloved Philippines but decisively in the middle of Oklahoma Territory. He had pushed too far,
then. Let his chatter and his dreams get the older man's goat. Of
course Trappe wouldn't give his daughter away to someone so
wild-eyed. Couldn't he learn to keep his mouth shut? The oil stories
hit him like an infection he couldn't cast off. They put him in a kind
of nervous rage. The more he heard of both success and failure,
the more he wanted to see for himself. A land so rich in oil, it rose
to the surface of ponds and streams. The Indians valued it for its
medicinal qualities. They smeared it over ailing, aching limbs of
tribal elders, for they found it coaxed the pain from brittle bones
and joints. Otherwise the stuff was a nuisance—it sullied their
drinking water. Their ponies flared their nostrils and snorted, refusing even to bend their heads toward polluted pools.

The banker lifted his hand from the globe and stroked his forehead. He centered his glasses on the bridge of his nose and stared
down at Nelson.

"You wouldn't guess I'm an exhausted man."

He gazed through the mullioned windows in the parlor toward
rows of Queen Anne roses, straining under heavy blooms. His eyes
rested on a marble muse and a pond with one idle Siamese fighting
fish waving just under the surface of the water.

"You can't measure the kind of fatigue I'm talking about, either."

The sour taste was more pronounced now, stronger and more
bitter. Nelson sipped again.

"I've had a change of heart, Nelson. I do want you for my son-
in-law. But I will ask you one thing, Nelson."

"Sir?"

"To hold off until 1900. A few months, and we'll have ourselves a new century! In the meantime you might think about letting go of your shops."

The banker smiled slightly.

"That is, unless you plan on selling fifteen-cent haircuts for the rest of your life."

"Mr. Trappe, I haven't asked Lavinia to marry me."

"Say what?"

"I haven't asked for your daughter's hand in marriage."

"High time you did. I count forty Tuesday suppers, twenty-eight rides in a rented buggy, and the good Lord knows how many church socials and balls of the This and That Order. Forgive me, but a banking man can't help keeping records."

"She's a young girl, Mr. Trappe."

"Is that a protest?"

"It's not that; it's just—"

"You try my patience, young man. I think you'd better determine your own intentions."

The truth was that Trappe had run out of tricks. He couldn't raise his girl alone anymore. He'd said all the things he could think to say to her, and he felt he'd run dry of paternal wisdom and, more important, patience. Her tempers, her silences, were more protracted since Hanks had started coming around. She seemed to resent her father's presence somehow, though nothing had changed in his handling of her. The widower had raised her bravely and alone, unbuffered by a second marriage. He had loved and nurtured for seventeen years, supplied her with everything she needed. But what she seemed to need most acutely now was a mother, and Trappe came up sadly empty-handed.

"You strike me as an ambitious enough fellow."

"I am, sir."

"I sense a strong will."

"To a fault."

"Then may I ask you a question?"

"Of course, Mr. Trappe."

"What are you waiting for?"

"I'm waiting for your daughter to grow up."

"Well . . ."

They heard a crash from the kitchen. This was followed by a burst of excited Swedish and laughter, Lavinia's. The maid appeared briefly. They could see her from where they sat in the parlor. She pushed through the swinging door, her cheeks bright red, set an empty soup tureen in the center of the dining table and disappeared again into the kitchen.

"You're pissing into the wind, boy. Listen to me. When you were ten years old, sitting up nights at the kitchen table with a pencil behind your ear doing sums, the doctor handed me a baby girl. When you were firmly seated in a leather saddle, the baby girl was learning how to walk. Earning a wage is man-making, son. Marriage and childbearing is what turns our young girls into women. It's our modern formula! Pretty simple when you consider it. Lavinia will catch up if you'll only give her the means."

"I love your daughter, sir; otherwise I wouldn't—"

"Haven't you been listening, Nelson? I am not talking about love. I'm talking about a man's intentions. And if your intentions are not clear by the year 1900, you'll have to find another Tuesday-evening supper ticket. I prefer to come right to the point."

Maude Maker didn't allow the men in her boardinghouse to smoke, drink or stand around. "Sit if you like, boys, but if I catch a one of you standing around, you'll find your personal affairs in the side yard." When Nelson arrived home that night, he found, as he found most nights, the familiar band assembled on the front porch. They rocked or sat still until they could bear immobility no longer, then rose for a walk or a smoke in the woods at the end of the string of frame houses. Not one of them knew what offended Maude so about a standing man, why a standing man would crush the sterling reputation of her boardinghouse and a sitting man wouldn't, but they yielded to her decree and disappeared when the habit of being upright got the better of them.

"Evening, Cackler."

"What do you know, Artist?"

"Nothing more than I knew last evening."

"Which is the same thing you knew the night before. Don't reckon a fella can learn anything on this damn porch. Tell me something about hair, then."

"When you cut the stuff, it grows back. God's miracle."

"Shit."

Then came the cackle the other boarders called the idiot period. For that was how the cackler finished all his sentences. It didn't matter that the dialogue wasn't funny; the reflex earned him his nickname. He'd been living there for five years, doing the odds-and-ends work of a man who knew no skilled trade. The first year he was there, Maude swore he coaxed a curious little red fox out of the woods. The animal would appear at the end of the street, just out of sight of the first ramshackle house, tip up its nose gently, only to smell man, not chicken, before slipping back into the woods. The cackler drew him in closer and closer until a blue-eyed boy lifted his daddy's shotgun off the wall and blew him away into the air. One of the boarders found a bloody fragment of fox in the honeysuckle hedge the next day. He said it looked at first like a small furry animal caught in the middle of the hedge. Hardly seemed like it would be a piece of fox.

Nelson closed the door softly and sat on the edge of the bed. He wondered who would occupy the room when he left and suppressed the urge to carve or scribble his initials on something—to leave behind some proof of being. Then he shook his head at the notion.

"Hell, I guess it is time."

He listened as men shuffled along in the full house. The porch talk filtered through the wall and became a dull, agreeable murmur. A familiar, sleepy singsong. Once in a while it was pierced by the cackler or interrupted by Maude Maker's exclamations that came from the front room, where she sat up nights to inflict order. There was nothing in this to regret, but it was something to realize before it could be shed. Another becoming, not unlike the one he suffered on leaving the horrible stillness of his father's farm. What he felt now was delicate as shattered shell. It meant change.

He spread a hand-drawn map on the floor, just as he did most nights before he went to sleep. The map had been drawn especially for Nelson by his childhood friend Harry. It was conceived of as an enticement, and he was sure it was as inaccurate and full of lies as his clever friend could have made it. Mad Man's Curve? Panther Gulch and Dazed Indian Spring? Nor did he accept the letters that followed as any kind of truth. No. He blinked and stared at the thin blue script, wondering how a young boy, good, honest, but dull through and through, could be so transformed into the most splendid teller of tales and first-rate liar. Sometimes he stretched out a real map, a book map of Oklahoma Territory, alongside. His friend had honored the outline but had filled it with place names that told tales of bloody, seasoned conflict. *Come and see for yourself, Nelson! As Ever, Your Best Friend, Harry.* Harry called himself a crow doctor. *I have, in fact, submitted to the rigors of medical school only to find that I am called to the bedside of certain black crows. The Osage tame them, you see, and call for me when the birds fall ill. The oil derricks have spread out over the country like stands of trees. I suppose there's no place for the birds to build their nests any longer, if not in the bristly yards of certain members of the Tribe, as we call the Osage Indians here. But you must come and see for yourself, Nelson.*

"The Lord put two dark message boxes in a man's head."

"Where does it say that, Daddy? What page are you on?"

All that Nelson ever discovered about his father happened like that. Because Nelson was quicker than his brothers, lighter and faster on his feet, he caught what slipped by the other boys as his father muttered something and returned to his work, pulling harder on the cow's teat, bending more deeply over the plow, swinging an ax with the might of his whole body this time. Whack!

"What boxes, Daddy? Where's it say boxes? My page just says, 'And all my ropes are broken.' "

"And the messages never match up, ever. One day, messages will spring out of one box, making you one kind of man. The next day, the other box will pop open, making you another sort altogether. Not as if you can choose your box, either. Oh, life would be mighty simple if that were so. If we just had one box and one set of messages, there wouldn't be so many mules among men."

"What page, Daddy? I've lost my place."

"You haven't lost your place, Nelson. Read the words that are in front of you. 'I know, O Lord, that a man's way is not in himself. . . .' "

Then it was gone, forever out of earshot. That was all he had of his father, apart from stillness. Fragments of an idea, an exposure so fleet, so tangential that he imagined as a boy he had dreamed it, knew as a man that he hadn't. That he had witnessed thought itself, a process laid bare and released as swiftly as it had been taken up.

Nelson the man wanted to examine what had been held up to Nelson the boy in bad light. It was a nugget of something, but it was so small, so embedded in something else ("Stick to the Scriptures. Read what's in front of you, won't you?"), that staring at it hard as he was doing now in a scrubbed room on the first floor of a men's boardinghouse made him drowsy and dumb. Sometimes he didn't think about the conflicting message boxes inside his head for months, and sometimes, like now, he thought about them constantly. For wasn't it that, just that, that made him want to bolt, to run into the Territory his friend held before him like a carrot, and disappear forever, when there was a wedding to plan, a new century to salute and, it seemed to him more and more as he listened to Trappe's insinuating talk and watched him set the globe awhirl, a banker's dark suit to don. Nineteen hundred!

Of course word got out. It was called "Nelson's Purse," and it caused more tongues to waggle than the appearance of a young couple holding hands in broad daylight in front of the Creston post office. Nelson married Lavinia in 1900 and flushed deeply as John Trappe wrote out a check for $19,000. They shook hands in the offices of the upstairs banking suite, and though the exchange smacked of a business deal, neither man let on.

"There's moonlight on your path, Nelson Hanks. I can sense it. January first, 1900!"

It was John Trappe who left home. He struck out, light-headed, for Chicago. He was free for the first time in seventeen years. He turned to the couple standing on the wide, welcoming front porch of his home and saluted them as they waved goodbye. Then he sighed to himself, wishing they made a handsomer couple. I'll write, of course I'll write! And he did, nightly from a hotel suite in the bustling city. The banker, pleasantly jarred by the fury and roar of commerce, grew charming and avuncular. *Lovingly, Pap. My warmest embrace. Pap. Vinnie, this morning I sought advice about dress patterns. You will have a busy winter ahead clipping and snipping. My thoughts surround you. Pap.*

Not all of Pap's letters were read. They were stacked up on a dressing table or hastily pressed into a silk pouch with a black ribbon drawstring.

"Like this, Nelson? Tell me, do you like it better when I do this?"

He found in Lavinia a love partner so full of whims and enthusiasms, completely unadulterated by female advice or instruction, that he could hardly catch his breath. His legs ached. Some mornings he trembled out of bed like a sickly old man. No notion shamed her. Motherless for so many years, instructed in all matters but these by a firm, frank father, Lavinia brought to her wedding bed an enthusiasm and energy that staggered him. She clapped him on the back, wondered out loud at his skill. Sometimes she laughed at her own pleasure and it was Nelson who was shocked and slightly thrilled. His young bride loved him outright.

"I can't, Vinnie. I'm sorry, but a man tires. Let's just rest awhile and talk. Here, turn down the light."

They told each other all the secrets they could think of in the third-floor bedroom. When they ran out of them, they made up whopping stories. The Swedish maid peered through the keyhole, peeved at her loss. For she was alone in the downstairs kitchen, and the domestic chores that had seemed so light with Lavinia by her side, tickling when she had her arms full of dishes or telling her a silly story, now made her cross and angry. She tied on her apron in a huff to serve the newlyweds. Getting even meant slipping silently up the stairs to watch Vinnie through the keyhole, curved as an archer's bow and moving over this man who looked old enough to be her father. Later, ripping the sheets from the nuptial bed, she stomped her foot fiercely and wagged both braids at the bare mattress that had stolen away her best, her only friend.

Nelson read the last of the letters aloud, puzzling over its meaning: *Say, Nelson. We will shortly have our work cut out for us! Get your horse and buggy ready. The Philippines will have to wait. I have a new idea. My best to you and Vinnie. Pap.* He shook his head and was about to reread it when Vinnie snatched off his glasses and plucked the message out of his hands.

"Your father's up to something. And I have no idea what that something is."

"You'll find out soon enough, Nelson. Turn out the light now and come to bed."

Trappe returned early the following morning to explain it in person. The banker stood in the clothes he had slept in. He shook his head at the charged atmosphere.

"Smells like snow. Doesn't it, Vinnie? That same muffled, clean odor . . . funny. Why, you look lovely, Lavinia. Your hair."

"Yes, my hair . . ."

Nelson had burrowed inside with his fingers, loosening here, there. He had feminized Lavinia Hanks. The fashionable propriety was still there, but it seemed to hang by a voluptuously slender thread.

"All for me, Daddy? I'll have the smartest spring wardrobe in Creston!"

"With a little doing. Is there a window open, or isn't there? Where's that Nelson? I'm popping with good news, and he's upstairs with a shaving mug in his hand! Nelson? Nelson, come on down here."

Nelson appeared on the stairwell, pulling the belt on his dressing gown tighter, and raised his hand in greeting.

"Charles F. Gunther, A. G. Spalding . . . Nelson, we've got them!"

"Good morning, sir."

"Pap. We're going to build ourselves a coliseum. What are you waiting for?"

A dab of shaving cream still clung to his cheek. Nelson cleared his throat.

"Do I have to spell everything out? *The honeymoon is over.* You're a bond salesman now, Nelson. We're selling pieces of the Chicago Coliseum. No more hot towels. No more haircuts and please, please, no more Mountain Sage."

The coliseum was to go up on South Wabash Avenue, on the site of the existing Libby Prison Building, a dull monument to the Civil War. The Prison Building was a reconstruction of a Confederate prison in Virginia. The bricks had been hauled out from Richmond, but interest had slumped in the vigorous city. Nobody wanted to stomp through a dusty, damp building that immortalized the nation's first bad dream. Our country has a brand-new context, screamed Gunther. The candy manufacturer, fantastically sweet-toothed, reached into his coat pocket to dig up a handful of taffy bits. The former baseball star A. G. Spalding, silent and dreaming of a sports palace that would bear his name, sat up straight and proposed a golden ticket cage. It took a banker's calm to consolidate so many dreamy notions and a banker's level son-in-law to rake up investment money.

"A month? You're sending Nelson away for a month?"

"A month is optimistic, Vinnie. Several months is more like it, and I'm not sending your husband away into exile. I'm giving the two of you a brisk ride into the future. Be sensible, daughter."

"Oh, this is a war! This is just the same as a war!"

The banker gave his daughter three days to fret and worry over her soldier in the third-floor bedroom. They studied the itinerary together, and she made him recite the names of the villages on his route until she could stand it no longer. Then she would clamp her hand suddenly over his mouth and begin to wail. She removed a wedding photograph from its frame and licked the back. Then she slapped it onto his bare chest and laughed despite herself.

"Forget me not."

"I promise. One night you'll put your head on the pillow, and when you wake up I'll be back, with pockets stuffed full of promissory notes. That's how it'll be, Vinnie. That fast."

He felt knighted by his young wife's playful sorrow and her father's good faith. He swung the heavy satchel over his shoulder and returned to the world he knew by heart—boardinghouses, those turnstiles filled with a nation's temporary men. The clauses and contracts changed, but the faces, oddly, didn't. They were all of them men who feigned a future. "Just passing through." That phrase oiled the turnstile and kept the men moving, moving, lest they stop in complete despair, ruled by daily rates and, inevitably, some woman's capricious rules about men who smoked or stood or swore. He rolled up his sleeves and swallowed the same tasteless, economical fare he had endured at Maude Maker's. New England Clam Chowder? Nelson closed his eyes and swore it was Home Stew Bowl.

He liked their sharpness and their grunts that meant neither Yes nor No but Keep on telling. For he found New Englanders smart and shrewd. Selling them was flattery; his stride lengthened under the cold sun. He didn't badger or cajole, but he found that when they'd sapped him of information, even when he'd said all he'd had to about the coliseum, they wanted him to go on. To paint word pictures of a Gothic structure that would make that brash young city proud. So he painted, spoke, sang of taut black panthers culled from some golden coast, circus tigers trotting through a second ring, their bright eyes fixed horribly on, yes, children protected by the mighty spectator guardrail in the coliseum. He loaded the bases for prospective investors, invented delicious public events until they waved him to a stop and signed. One listening man fell off his porch in Vermont and another had Nelson travel to his brother in Portland, his sister in Bangor and his uncle in Augusta with the same wondrous tales.

. . . .

He stood in the shadows at first, just watching. Lavinia was down on all fours. She had tossed her hat to one side, and a pair of white cotton gloves, one streaked with red stains, lay forgotten under the willow tree. She crept stealthily toward each dandelion, crouched lower and blew hard, producing a white cottony blast. She snapped a leaf from the stem and popped it in her mouth, then puckered her lips. She brightened at the sight of the old tomcat who had appeared from the side of the house. The cat was an incorrigible fighter; there was a fresh red tear above his eye. He stopped still, cocked his tail slightly and sprang at the trunk of the tree, gaining the first limb in a fast scramble. He climbed higher, stretching and switching his tail in stiff, erratic measures.

"Sssss. Kitty, kitty."

Nelson watched as his wife removed a shoe, puffing a bit in eagerness and discomfort.

"Scoot over, Mange."

She grabbed for the lowest branch, hung suspended for a moment, paddled fitfully at the trunk with her bare feet. Then she dropped to the ground, rubbed her shoulder and slumped onto an iron bench, muttering to herself.

"Fat old frump. Can't even hoist yourself into a tree. Damnation."

She had left off her corset, and the cotton dress pulled and strained. He stepped out from behind the shadows and put his thumb and forefinger to his lips. The sharp note he produced started the dogs howling next door. Lavinia lifted her skirts and shot toward him. She hit him just below the left shoulder, knocking him slightly off balance.

"Four months and twelve days!"

"I've done it, Vinnie. I've raised all the money they'll need and then some! Let me look at you, Mrs. Hanks. Hmmm. A torn dress. Grass stains."

"Hold me, Nelson. I almost died while you were gone."

"A cholera outbreak?"

"Worse. Loneliness."

She darted around the bedroom as he unpacked, peering into his trunks and flinging herself down onto the bed as he removed the starched white shirts and bow ties, the sober dark suits he had taken care not to crease.

"I sold them, Vinnie. Ever seen such a pelican's pouch full of notes?"

He held the satchel up.

"I sold them almost *to the man.* Four months, twelve days and three noes. Mind you, they weren't real noes. Two of the men were flat broke, and the other was dying. Said to me what did a man with the Kingdom on his mind want with a piece of some coliseum? Say, did I feel bad then. Real bad."

"Nelson?"

He stood an empty trunk outside in the hall and turned. She ran her fingers over the initials in his hairbrush. Her shoulders were slightly stooped.

"Did you think to bring me a little something?"

"Why, I . . ."

"Some little something?"

"I've brought back four months of hard labor and a seventy-five-thousand-dollar commission. Seventy-five thousand dollars, Vinnie!"

"Hmmmph."

"Unless you mean this."

He drew the packet from an inside pocket. He couldn't help grinning as he held her on his lap. She gurgled with happiness, pinning the opal broach on one side of her dress, then the other.

"A star opal, Vinnie. Hold it up to the light so you can see the star."

He found, as he slyly smoothed her dress, a new round belly that suggested not fecundity but chocolate wafers and Ginger Dolly. He glanced around the upstairs bedroom, remarking a scattered picture puzzle in one corner. He noted skeins of yarn and pincushions, fabric heaped in a deep wicker basket. Chagrined, though still rocking his young wife, he saw how the signs of rich domesticity had tricked him. The dress patterns were scaled to a tiny doll's body, and the tattered yellow yarn was a plaything for Mange, who butted the door open with his bloody head and pounced on the wool in still another war maneuver.

"Scat, beast. Oh, oh, I'm Mrs. Hanks again!"

What of the modern formula? Nelson thought of the foxy banker as he stroked the inside of his wife's hand. He kissed her deeply and pressed on her soft stomach, wondering if the final answer wasn't to be found there. Since tending a man didn't make the difference, maybe tending something smaller did. She curled a finger under his chin and challenged him to a game of croquet. No? Cards, then. He saw that her sorrowing had little to do with Nelson, her husband. Rather, her close call (I almost died!) was the essential longing of a child for its best and truest playmate. He drew a long sigh.

"How am I going to do it, Lavinia?"

"Do what?"

"Take you where I'm going."

She leaped up from his lap and, standing in the middle of their room, blew the sides of her cheeks out. She swayed, using only the top of her body.

"You look like sky getting ready to blow."

She shook her head no. Bug-eyed, she started to redden.

"You're a red balloon. Nope? Then you win. What are you, Vinnie?"

"Whew! African puff adder when aroused."

She straightened her skirt from where it had slid around. Wind chimes crashed under the eaves outside. Had either of them looked out of the third-floor window, they might have seen a dog squeeze painfully under a porch. A runty mare waited for the delivery boy to return. She shifted her weight anxiously and sidled left at the sight of a dust spiral that danced a few feet, then died. Weather was making its way across the plains.

"Did you forget?"

"Not a day."

As the sky opened above them, he began to read solemnly from journal entries, giving back the four months and twelve days he had stolen from his young bride. She only interrupted him once, apologetically, just as his notes described a pair of child's shoes.

" 'There was an assortment of articles on that clothesline. Rubber fishing boots and work clothes. I saw that the child's shoes had once been blue. They seemed to have been resoled with metal, rather than a conventional material, for tin (if it was as I suspected) shone through the holes. As I walked further, I caught sight of the foundry where her father must have worked. I thought of my own barefoot days on the farm as I waited for my mother to mend my poor boots.' "

She gave him a mighty kiss, months late, for replacing that sad pair of worn shoes with another.

" 'Bluebird blue and built to last. Hanging the new shoes up on the line was strangely close to thievery, I found. My blood raced as if I were committing an act of crime.' "

He closed the journal then, for the rain was slamming the sides of the cistern, forcing him to shout. They could also hear the sounds of John Trappe, who had just entered downstairs. He swore and bellowed for his daughter, for tea, for dry clothes.

"Nelson?"

He ran his hand over her hair.

"Hear me. Being a wife is lonelier work than being a daughter. I'm going with you the next time. Even if it means a freight car to carry my affairs. Even if it means never coming back to Creston. Will you listen to that fussbudget? *I'm coming, Daddy!*"

chapter 8

1901

"Don't tell me this contraption is yours, Nelson."

"You know how to operate this buggy?"

"What a rare day this is turning out to be."

The talker eschewed his own gift of gab one afternoon in 1901. The white Daimler glistened in the sun. Nelson had swabbed it himself with scented mineral oil, patted and worried over it all morning, anticipating two o'clock and the three men he meant to woo with his own investment scheme. This time the proposal was pure Hanks. So was the presentation. The boy who loved nothing better than a circus or a rodeo had grown into a master show-man.

"Let me help you, sir."

"Pap. There, up! I've got it."

Trappe was ornamental this time. His blessings were welcome, his money was desirable, but his son-in-law had clearly abandoned the nest and was about to demonstrate his wingspan. A. G. Spal-ding stared at the Daimler and began blinking, a good sign. He blinked frenetically when pleased, and his twitching eyes now be-lied his nonchalant posture. He took a white handkerchief from his pocket and wiped the soles of his shoes, then swung into the back seat. Gunther's gaze suggested a man suffering a slight head injury. He took a place beside Trappe, sucking the inside of his mouth, and locked his legs together with delight.

"How did you come by it?"

"Conceived by a German and built by the French. Gentlemen, we're on our way."

"Nelson? I believe I asked you a question."

"I won it in a poker game, sir. I've agreed to sell it back, but not until I've had a little fun."

They set off, fittingly, from the site for the Chicago Coliseum. A crowd had gathered around the auto. They maintained a respectful distance, looked but didn't touch, and stepped back slowly, wistfully, when Nelson's mechanic bent to turn the crank to start the motor. Three boys would tag after them for several blocks. Infighting developed, for they couldn't settle on who would run closest to the Daimler. Their game dissolved into a fistfight, and Gunther wished he could smooth the dispute with a hail of hard candy. He sighed and cupped his hand, then shouted at the sensation.

"Look here! You can hold the wind in your hand. Go on, John. Have some yourself!"

Things were tossed overboard. A necktie went first, then tickets to Ringling Brothers. Trappe fed the baseball player dollar bills. He wadded them up into tight balls and, with a whoop and a holler, pitched them at dazzled pedestrians. Nelson steered with ease, then tempted an upgrade.

"We've lost every bit of our speed. Why, the mechanic is traveling faster than we are!"

"Uphill, Pap. Like swimming against a strong current."

"Yes, I see. Well, after up comes down."

When they reached the summit, Spalding found that he had stopped breathing. Trappe turned imperious, citing the rutted road and mudholes that loomed ahead. He turned to look at the mechanic, following on horseback, wondering how well he knew his trade. Nelson relaxed slightly and rubbed the back of his neck with one hand.

"Say, out of the way!"

He tooted the horn once, twice. A dog stood in the path. The harder Nelson honked, the harder the mutt wagged his tail. He approached the Daimler eagerly. Saliva fell from his mouth as Nelson waved him away. He ambled to the back of the car and sniffed tentatively. Gunther shrieked with laughter as they pulled off.

"The dog takes this automobile for a bitch in heat!"

Someone began to hum. By the time the auto rolled to a halt, they had developed a handsome four-part melody.

"What is it now?"

They were nowhere. That is, there were no children or dogs or crowds to urge out of the way. They could hear the steady droning of a mass of insects. Trappe looked worriedly at a tangle of brush. He was allergic to bee stings. The skin on the bottom of his feet began to tingle and burn at the thought of it. Water ran, but even that sound was far off and removed.

"Heat up the engine, man. My watch says quarter past."

"Gentlemen . . ."

Nelson strummed on his lower lip and turned calmly to the passengers.

"I'm afraid we've run out of gasoline."

"What! Now let's us have a look."

"Look if you like, Pap. But here we are."

"Indeed. Here we are."

Nelson let them fret. They cursed the auto for being nothing but a rich man's toy. They glared at the mechanic, who confirmed Nelson's diagnosis and then led his horse to a shade tree. Trappe looked at his shoes. Then he looked at the long road full of ruts and bumps, mudhole remnants of yesterday's rainstorm. Nelson staved off their panic just in time. For all their grumbling and dissatisfaction, no one had yet exposed himself as a fool or a coward. He gave them a discourse that they listened to because they had fallen for the Daimler mind and soul despite her capriciousness. They were attentive even though the sun was beating down and the bug buzz seemed to advance and retreat, suggesting a possible invasion. Better to listen to Nelson, even though he'd landed them in a fine mess. The mechanic would have to ride back to town for help. What the devil was he waiting for?

"The Daimler is a toy, Pap. You've hit the nail on the head. But it's a tantalizing one that every man is going to want for himself. I didn't invite you men out here today to suggest that we build these fancy buggies. I propose that we power them. That's right. Without fuel, these show horses are hamstrung. Petroleum, friends."

Later, people referred to that afternoon as if it was a symptom of something rare and wild, slightly infectious. In fact, it was just Nelson, slapping at flies with his hat, melting one story into another and talking with an authority more appropriate to a man twice his age. The three men forgot their discomfort and leaned forward. He circled the car and talked of shooting a well, the preliminary hail of rocks, sand and water that doused and dirtied onlookers. For there were always onlookers. The chamber of commerce saw to that. Picnics and ball games were organized at the opening of a well, entire families fanned out in farmers' fields like it was the Fourth of July. Oil-stained cotton bonnets were souvenirs of infancy precious as lost milk teeth. He flung a crab apple across the field. An hour passed, and the discussion grew more prosaic as Nelson sketched out his proposition. Trappe pulled softly on his ears as he studied a sheaf of papers. A gasoline wagon appeared on the road.

"Mr. Nelson, you want me to fill this thing, or don't you?"

A deal was forged in a field of stinging insects and horseflies. The driver, sullen and wishing he'd asked for twice the money, filled the tank and left the ice bucket by the front tire as arranged. If Nelson had a complaint about the staging of events, it was that only three champagne glasses made it to the site. He served his investors, then toasted the birth of an oil company with his own dirty boot.

"It's nothing more than a sluice, Nelson. *Cattle* didn't stop there, they were in such a rush to get to Kansas. Territory this, Territory that. It's not even a state!"

"It's about to be. Land's too rich to stay open."

"Oh, it's rich, all right. So rich they had to march the Indians in at gunpoint."

"The Trail of Tears is over, Vinnie."

"Over for some. A man down there sold his wife for a hundred dollars, a horse and a cow. She walked all the way to Texas, while the bridegroom rode his horse."

"An isolated fact."

"An isolated country. That's where you want to take me?"

She pushed at the cat with her feet.

"Go away, Mange. Tell me one more time why you want to go, Nelson. Only tell it better than you did before."

"I want to go because they're throwing up towns overnight. I want to go because men half my age are making fortunes by digging holes in the ground."

"And?"

"That's not enough?"

"It's enough for anybody else, but there's a bigger something behind all that. Something bigger than sinking a string of oil wells. You've got it all mixed up with some Wild West show, and don't think I don't know. Well, I wish you luck."

"What do you mean?"

"I mean you're a fool. That territory is your blind spot. All those silly maps have you tricked."

They sat still for a moment. Lavinia held a glass of lemonade to her throat.

"Then you won't go, Vinnie?"

"Of course I'll go."

"You'll . . ."

She stood up and dabbed at her forehead with a handkerchief.

"I'll need a saddle horse."

"A buckskin. A palomino. Anything you want!"

"A Tennessee walker, since I wouldn't guess there are any roads. Bouncing puts a woman in a temper, and besides, it can't be good for the babies."

Nelson was motionless.

"Lavinia, you're not . . ."

"No, I'm not, but I will be one day. Oh, and I'll need poetry books and plenty of puzzles."

She opened a drawer and unfolded a bit of yellowed newspaper to read mockingly as Nelson squirmed. A spoonful of Arkansas River bottom sand was suggested as a cure for dyspepsia.

"I won't swallow sand for you or anybody else, Nelson. We'll bring along a good stock of medicine, and when you make your money we'll bring in our own doctor. Oh. I'll want my own gun and somebody to teach me to shoot it."

"Ah, Vinnie." He reached out to hold her.

"Don't. We'd stick to each other like paste."

Lavinia sucked the tip of one finger, studied a plant that was doing poorly and guessed she'd have a nap, given the oppressive afternoon heat. He watched as his wife headed absently upstairs. She took each step slowly and turned at the top of the stairs.

"Is your mind made up?"

"Mostly."

"Then mine is, too." She took a deep breath and pushed her hair from the back of her neck.

"Truth is, we've already had this conversation."

"How's that?"

"I dreamed it, Nelson. The whole thing. Only we were sitting someplace else and I was wearing a strand of pearls. Funny, misshapen little pearls, though. Not like anything I've ever seen before."

He sat still after she'd gone, punished by the pounding heat in the room. He had planned to take her into the new country that afternoon in the same way he had been there himself, by hard imagining that split off from history books and newspaper accounts, deeds issued from still another ramshackle land office. Conflicting stories of that place spawned others, enlisting a man's dreams until he had no recourse but to bend conventional facts into private constructions. Nelson's fantastic version of the country was so personal, in fact, that the only person in the world he could safely share it with lay snoring now under a ceiling fan upstairs.

The maid passed with a dustcloth in her hand. He watched as she idled over one of Trappe's statues. She was a heavyset girl, and every swipe of the cloth made her fleshy arm wobble. Her hips moved side to side as she worked the cloth into the bronze grooves. He asked her for a glass of iced tea. She nodded, frowning slightly, and folded the dustcloth into a dirty square.

That Harry thought to rename the land, inventing his own curves and hollows in imaginary maps, that Lavinia took her turn at envisioning the place, concocting some sort of cow culvert, valuable only as a passage from one place to another, was no wonder. Descriptions of the district jutted out in all directions like spokes on a wheel. Etched first with cattle trails, then with railroad tracks, now punctured by derricks and drills, the Land of the Fair God lay trespassed and tired as an old whore. Nelson fretted in his chair, fearing all the newness would be gone by the time he got there. Had the land run in '89 and the one that followed left him anything raw and fresh, which hadn't been claimed by men seeking freedom or wealth or pure spectacle? Was there any imagining to be done, or was Nelson too late even for that? Whether Indians were sentenced to it or the soil-starved, land-grabbing "Sooners" escorted from it by the napes of their necks by government soldiers, the district bred delusions of all kinds, and perhaps that was finally its richest resource. Harry's letters. They continued to stream in, postmarked "I.T." for Indian Territory, to fatten Nelson's own rendition of the place.

Even if I had no great trade to ply, I would make this my country. For here I find, as nowhere in the States, every kind of man. Looking and listening becomes more and more a practical science.

You have no idea, Nelson. Men come to the Territory to disappear. What are they running from? One can only wonder. Bad fortune, bad debts, I would guess. I had ridden out to treat some livestock yesterday and found a man lying flat on his back in the shallows of a stream. We began a conversation which I quickly let go, seeing he hadn't come to this place for any human sound. His brain was not demented, but I supposed he had been living among the Indians. All his gestures suggested this.

Indian Territory has its strange fellows. Here is one vigilante whose greatest pleasure is not in running intruders off the land. He prefers scaring them to death with his Creek headdress and awful paint. We hear he enters a campsite just after the fire is lit and, saying no word, sits beside the by now terrified trespasser (his victims are mostly white riffraff) to consume whatever is being served up. Then he rides off in silence, to leave his hosts alone with their chattering teeth. He has been to college in the North and speaks perfect English. This form of ridicule is common and something you must witness for yourself, Nelson. Yours . . .

He stroked the top of his thigh and smiled, thinking of his passport to this country, the Daimler that had come to him fabulously after hours of cardplaying in a Chicago hotel suite. The loser was a rakehell so protected by "family interests in Rye" that as his Daimler changed hands he sighed, mentioned providence and suggested his valet find out what McKinley had eaten the week before when he had visited the city. The President's Menu was sent up at two o'clock in the morning. Pork scrapple? He sighed for the second time and handed Nelson the keys, never imagining what the evening's winnings would one day represent.

Nelson glanced at his hands. The nails were buffed, and there was something in their evenness that unnerved him. What he felt now was a boy's longing to participate. Stiffly overwhelmed by the glory of some country performance, committed only to remember and tell, he ached instead to be that small boy trained to contradict every impulse, holding stock-still as a black man flung knives at the contours of his body. Not satisfied just to witness, Nelson longed to be the one who swallowed fire, who knelt under the lion's paw

or squatted barefoot on a pony's back. How many times had he
bitten his lip or pinched himself blue just to keep seated? Sit down,
Nelson. For heaven sake's quit bumping the table! He wanted a
life bigger than just telling. For the first time he felt he was nearly
there.

"Tea, sir."

The maid had a mean bruise on her forearm. It was beginning
to heal and had gone yellow in the center. A shy farmer had proposed marriage weeks before and she angrily said yes, thinking of
Lavinia's betrayal, pressing against his arm with her head low.
She wouldn't wait for Lavinia Hanks to pack off with her husband
and leave her in the lurch! The farmer's mouth was packed with
broken teeth, and parts of him smelled of the same wild onions
that crowded the banks of his creek, but when she had suggested
that he remove his boots before entering his small, dark house he
had done that. And when she added that a looking glass would be
nice in his bedroom, a looking glass small and round as a ship
portal had gone up right over his bed. She thought of her nine
younger brothers and sisters waiting in Sweden and her mother,
cross and ill now, who appealed for her daughter's return and
leaned over each letter deliberately as she wrote so that tears
would spill onto the page. The farmer seemed to offer not freedom
but a kinder enclosure. She enjoyed teasing her fiancé's troupe of
dirty geese. She tiptoed toward the goslings, and they rushed at
her thick skirts like tiny guard dogs. She wiggled the glass now in
front of Nelson and clucked her tongue. She wondered if she were
to settle down on top of this old dreaming man, as she had watched
Lavinia do, pressing him and opening his mouth slightly with her
fingers to insert her own tongue, if she could startle him into love.
Did he imagine she didn't know of their plans? She would leave
them before they could leave her!

"Thank you. Nasty bruise you have there. You should take
care."

He crushed the sprig of mint between his teeth and watched,
amazed, as she lifted her skirts high to reveal still another bruise
she received, when, early one morning, drowsy and seeking hot
tea, she rammed her heavy thigh into a table's edge. She ran a
finger slowly over the center, where he supposed it was most
tender. He didn't lean forward to lay his cheek along the outline of
the ugly mark. He didn't run his open hands along the backs of her
legs or loosen her hair. He sat still like the old dreaming man he

appeared to be. She was interrupted not by Lavinia, deep in her own center of hot afternoon dreaming, nor by the banker, who was busily foreclosing just outside town, but by Mange, who had been a-hunting. He proudly dropped the headless corpse of a sparrow at Nelson's feet. It was a fresh kill and very neatly done. He purred and began weaving a series of hard figure eights through the maid's ankles. Unruffled, she pulled the dustcloth from her pocket and dropped the bird into the center. She folded the edges over its warm body and twisted the top as expertly as if she were preparing a pastry treat. She dropped the packet into her apron and slammed her skirts down like a weighted curtain, giving the cat a brutal kick before she left the room.

The incident amused Nelson. He declined her invitation not because she was coarse and clumsy but because he had already filled himself up with the life in this house. He heard its rumors and rustles as they rushed past, but he had already left this place for another. The exchange left him taut and exhilarated as any predator, every bit as concentrated on his leap into space as wicked Mange. He thought hard about the young, haphazard country, then blinked and slid forward in his chair. The soiled spot where the bird had lain became instead the pulsing red bloom of a buffalo heart.

chapter 9

1905

By the time the train arrived, the sweet peas had wilted and so had the violinist. He sat in the shade with his shoes unlaced, humming and plucking at strings. Nelson carried two pocket watches in case one stopped. He pulled them both out at intervals as he paced, then wiped his dusty spectacles and stared into the distance again.

"Up off your feet, man!"

The violinist laced his shoes and straightened his tie. He positioned himself next to Nelson and began to play just as the whistle sounded. Nelson wiped his eyes. The crowded Katy train finally pulled into the station, and he counted fifteen cars filled to bursting. His head pounded as he watched passengers spill onto the platform. Indians, preachers, businessmen scrambled toward friends and family.

"You'd best wipe those glasses off, seeing as you can't recognize your own wife. Are those for me?"

"Lavinia! Yes, these flowers are for you. And so is he."

He did wipe off his glasses then, even rubbed them with a bit of cleaning solution he carried. Then he looked again and saw that he had gotten his way, for there was a woman standing underneath him, not a girl. A woman so tired, so seemingly careworn, she could barely lift her lips into a smile. The violinist played with more flourish now that people stood still to listen, hushing each other like they did in church.

"We delivered a baby. He didn't live but a few minutes."

"Vinnie, wasn't there a—"

"Doctor? No. That crow-doctor friend of yours, Harry, would have been a welcome passenger. I never knew gender to be any kind of special credential, but there you are. We were the only other women traveling on that train. The baby wasn't made right. Still, when I pulled him out of her, he was alive. Pulled. That I did and with all my might, while Zoe held the poor woman's head in her lap."

"Who on earth is Zoe?"

"Zoe Simply, the new schoolmistress. If it hadn't been for her, I never would have survived the ordeal. Oh, look! There she is, just stepping down from the train. Go and help her with her things. She's carrying a load of books in that funny-looking satchel."

Lavinia didn't cry with fatigue or despair. Instead of tears there was ferocity. And pride that she had accomplished nine minutes of life. What had that too-young mother done but fight her, pushing when she said to stop and thrashing when she cried, Hold still! She had been on one train or another for two days. Two days of staring at scars and eagle feathers, gun butts, even a slingshot that its owner bragged had blinded a couple of men. Nelson pushed through the crowd of people standing on the platform.

"May I help you down, Miss Simply?"

"You may."

The young woman took in the scene before her. Amusement pierced her obvious exhaustion as she studied the wide, brawling introduction to her new life. People spilled over the platform, hoisting everything they owned to their backs or dragging poor boxes and steamer trunks along behind them with a length of rope or leather strap. They battled their glassy-eyed way through the swirling dust and the kicking, mewling horses and donkeys jamming the thoroughfare with carts and wagons. Zoe stared at the scene as the violinist sawed away, the strings screeching now. A fly inched its way up and over her dull black bonnet. A pushcart carrying chickens broke down before her, and she watched as the birds, their legs bound, fell squawking under wheels, hooves and boot heels. Two somber women batted at the swirl of white feathers and continued handing out pamphlets to anyone who would take them. Her gaze lifted to the row of oil derricks lining a bald hill that rose above the teeming street. Zoe sniffed and rubbed the end of her nose gently.

"Lovely. So this is my destiny."

Nelson looked up at her. She was one queer woman. Something told him scornful Zoe Simply would prosper here. He took the satchel from her hand and staggered slightly under its weight. She stepped down from the train and followed Nelson to where Lavinia stood.

"Zoe, dear! You must let us call you a hansom or . . ." She glanced about. ". . . something. How shall we get Zoe home, Nelson?"

Zoe Simply waved to someone just then approaching.

"I believe this man will be seeing me home. Yes, that's him. That must be Mr. Ryan, the guiding light of Lot Fifty-seven."

A burly, beet-faced man made his way to them. He plucked the cap from his head and busied himself with her things after issuing a scant introduction. He seemed embarrassed by speech.

"Mrs. Hanks, Mr. Hanks, I do hope we will see one another again."

She gave them each one firm, gloved handshake.

"But of course we will! You must come to visit us, Zoe."

Lavinia called out to the schoolmistress, now weaving through the throng behind Ryan.

"You must come to see us in our new home!"

She was home. Nelson watched and waited for awareness to take hold. She sniffed once, lifted her head high, then sniffed again. Home was something to smell first and see afterward.

"What is that odor?"

"Petroleum, Vinnie. Streets are doused with it twice a year to keep down the dust."

"Good Lord."

"Like what you see?"

"Maybe. It's a good thing I like bustle. And it's a good thing I like men."

He summoned porters for seven steamer trunks and a birdcage with a fierce cat inside, four hatboxes and a bronze statue snatched from John Trappe's living room on the day of departure. Nelson helped her into the wagon and laid a hand on her knee, seeing her frown.

"What is it, Vinnie?"

"I thought we were going to pioneer this place. Who *are* all these people?"

He laughed and flicked his whip in the air.

"I felt the same way when I first came, like I was late to the party."

He studied the street for a moment and eased his horses, a jet-black pair of geldings, toward a mule that had decided it was quitting time. The animal braced itself, front legs spread stiffly apart, until the driver jumped out of the wagon and rolled up his shirt sleeves. He slapped the side of the animal's head, waited, then slapped again.

"Durn bloody mule. Git, I said. Git!"

The animal flared its nostrils wide and yawned. Its thick tongue rose and curved into a languorous arc. Nelson touched his hat and took the stubborn mule's place in traffic.

"But the party is just beginning."

His arm swept right and left.

"This is nothing compared to what you're going to see in the next few years."

A frown pinched the space between her heavy eyebrows. She nodded carefully, for her head felt so heavy it seemed as if it might topple right off, like a bloom too heavy for its slight stem.

"Train your gaze, my love. It's too much to take in all at once."

She defied him. She defied the dizziness she felt and the weight she seemed to carry on top of her shoulders. She opened her eyes as wide as she could, looking in vain for space. For that clear place, that wide open place she had dreamed of when she dreamed of the Territory. This place was clotted with people, all kinds of people! She peered at the frantic commerce. She'd never seen people so hungry to buy: lines formed outside every shop. The pushing, the shoving. She could feel a hand on her back, pressing her forward even up where she sat next to Nelson. Cloth being measured and cut. She leaned forward and could make out hats through the white-curtained window. Hats meant gloves, and gloves meant . . . what *did* gloves mean, since she disdained them herself? Gloves meant receptions and improvement poetry, genteel card games. A shot rang out, then a second one. There was shouting, she could hear men shouting far off, but she couldn't make out the words. She slid even closer to Nelson on the seat and slipped her hand inside his pocket. Her head was spinning faster and faster now. She wouldn't tell him. He would make such a fuss.

"What's the time?"

"Two o'clock."

"Never saw such activity."

"Two o'clock light or two o'clock dark, this street's always the same. Business goes on. All sorts of business. Looking left, are you?"

She was. At the reddest lips she had ever seen. The woman snapped open a Chinese fan and slipped away down an alley. Lavinia rocked forward, nearly tearing open his pocket with the motion.

"Commonplace, I'm afraid. You'll get so that you won't even notice. Several weeks ago the sheriff rounded up a dozen such girls, handcuffed them and sat them down in church. The pastor was pleased. Church attendance was never better. Of course, this is just child's play. We'll have real law once Chris Madsen gets here. He'll tame the place in no time."

Enterprise of every kind. A sidewalk dentist operated in front of a drugstore. There were two buckets at his feet, marked Clean and Used. One sympathetic passerby stopped and laid his hand on the patient's head, but the gesture didn't still his squalling any. The dentist only stopped once. He set his drill down on a flour sack and drank long and hard from a silver flask. She saw whiskey poured and swallowed, flour and cornmeal weighed and served with a silver scoop. Squinting, she read aloud. . . .

"Ten cents a glass. For what?"

"For water. Our predicament. Believe me, a man who can locate water out here is a precious commodity. Finding him can be as tricky as finding oil. I had to learn that the hard way. There'll be plenty of time for my stories. Now that you're home."

His hand opened toward a sagging two-story wooden structure. Attention should have focused on the front-porch rocker, which meant make yourself comfy, or the crape myrtle, which meant a woman has a hand in things here, but attention didn't. Attention focused on the undertaker's handiwork, leaning up against the north wall.

"Nelson, look!"

"Meet your first dead man. The hotel owner figures it's only right to let him stay propped up like that. If someone doesn't claim him by next week, he'll lie in an unmarked grave. Our taxidermist here is a jack-of-all-trades."

She trained her gaze in earnest then and saw a handsome dark-skinned man. A man who, in life, would never be standing alone with a wall holding him up, no lady looking up at him, no cool drink in his hand. Seeing a man like that uncatered to was the primary unnatural thing. Finding out he was dead was the second.

"How did he die?"

"Shot in a gambling altercation upstairs. Let me help you, Vinnie. That's enough looking for one day."

By now she was heavy all over. Climbing down from the wagon was a mighty act. She glanced at Mange, still at the bottom of the birdcage, and wondered if he was dead, too. Movement was such a trouble. Her arm felt heavy as an anchor. If she were to lift it and let it drop on top of Nelson's head, would he fall down dead as well? She let herself be helped down from the seat and went straight to sleep on her husband's shoulder. This was misunderstood. She woke up to smelling salts and cold compresses—some woman she didn't know held up a thermometer as if it were a fairy wand.

"Poor little thing. Exhausted; she's simply exhausted."

Eiderdown, that's what she wanted, and closed windows until she said when. When was two days later. She smelled coffee this time, not petroleum, not smelling salts. She stretched one leg, but carefully, for movement felt brand-new.

"I was so afraid, Vinnie. You didn't stir, didn't make a sound. Your breathing barely ruffled a pigeon feather."

"I'm wide awake now. I dreamed of all kinds of things. That's what kept me asleep. Some dreams should never end."

"And all dreams do. Let me sit you up for your coffee. I don't know what she puts in this to make it so sharp-tasting. Don't look at the bottom of the cup when it's finished."

"Chicory, maybe. Have some with me? Come sit here."

It all came spilling out then. In between sipping hot, iron-black coffee and touching her warm shoulders and cheeks, he began the story he'd been living since he left Iowa.

"The money's gone? All the money from Daddy and whoosit with the mouth full of taffy? No, Nelson, you don't mean it."

"Most, not all. And I do mean it. I mean three dry wells. Two and a gas pocket's more accurate."

"And now what?"

"Now it's time for a gusher, my darling. There's enough money left for one more shot."

"You don't look desperate to me."

"I'm not. I leave that to other men. The wildcatters and one-shot hocus-pocus experts *are* desperate, because they believe in the way the sky looks before you shoot a well. A wood tick on a dog's spine or animal tracks that point in, and they shut down an entire operation. Plenty of men around here in a cold sweat. Only I'm not one of them, because I see there's science in all of this. Oh, right now we have to settle for doodlebugs and creekology. But the day will come when we know just where to poke for oil. I've got to stick it out until science is on our side."

They were perhaps the steeliest oil field workers of all. Men who claimed they could find oil with sticks, rubbed bare of bark until they looked like white shinbones, that veered left or right over a pool. Men who carved little oak casks and hung them around their necks, then filled them with oil that would find more oil by clanging on their chest at the appropriate moment. They stalked the Osage hills, butting aside those who said can't, won't and ain't gonna. Sometimes they knew from earaches or eye throbs, but most of the time they figured oil liked its own company best. "You'd be smart to put it in yonder," they said, pointing to an area close by an existing well. The best ones just knelt down and sniffed the ground. "That's it, sir. You drill here, and we'll both retire."

"I don't see what this has to do with losing my father's money."

"Lavinia, I'm surprised at you."

He hiked himself up on one elbow and felt convicted not only by her phrase but by his hand, open and relaxed, lying comfortably on a woman's wide hip. He listened to the commotion on the street, muffled by closed windows, and loosened his tie.

"Your father will have his money back and then some. Don't you worry. Besides, my mistake was this. This hotel. An apprentice has no business holing up in a fancy boardinghouse. Living side by side with my men is the only way I'm going to get a head start on all that's coming. I wanted to wait until I got you settled."

"And now that I'm here you intend to be there? No. You can't leave me behind so easily! Take me into the Territory."

The Territory meant blackjack oak. They armed every sandstone ridge in the country, their black lower limbs returning to earth, crisscrossed and twisted, until only screw flies and cows searching for a private place to drop their calves would bother to fight their way inside. The Territory meant plains, then plopped-down thickets of dry bramble so dense they defied entry. Yet dainty yellow flowers clambered up and over the mean, dry growth, and animals darted inside despite the thorns. Did they hollow out some cavern in the middle of it all? Lavinia wondered, biting her thumbnail. A big bone-strewn space warmed by wolf breath, lit by yellow eyes? Mountain lions shyly lapped at the clear creek water and stared at the scared-silly human community. Mange lost his nerve, pestering and hissing until Lavinia heaved him up onto her shoulders. Mixed-up nature provided other sights, too. Lavinia pulled on leather boots, a gun tucked neatly into her belt, and walked straight lines out from the camp. Toward something she could see, a stand of glistening scrub oak, or something she could hear, huge green hedge apples brought crashing to the ground by the wind. It took her days before she could tell Nelson what she saw, days before she could trust it enough, she guessed.

"A king snake?"

"Yes, I could tell by the red markings. Suckling a cow. And the cow wasn't afraid, Nelson. It went right on switching its tail at flies. Had its head down in the grass. What does it mean?"

"Means the cow knew a king snake is nonvenomous."

"Don't be funny. I witnessed something unholy."

No, she decided. Not unholy, but the opposite. A holy, God-planted sight. And it frightened her so she had to stash urine-soaked underwear behind a bush. She walked back to camp bare-bottomed under her long skirt, a yellow cat draped over her like a live stole, wishing for a more dignified response to her first spiritual experience.

They left the hotel for a tent pitched so close to other tents they seemed knit together. Camp life was contiguous, and that meant sharing everything—the sound of a neighbor's chewing and love grunts, his slaps and snores. It all passed through the thin canvas, which seemed more full of life than human membrane.

"Well days, hell days. Seems like I never get done being tired."

"Cotton picking was worser. My fingers start to bleed as soon as I remember those fields. Tired's nothing. Tired don't hurt. Besides, whatever you do, you're just bound to complain. Seems like it's in your nature. You know what I think, loafer? I think when you look at Nelson Hanks' wood rig you might just genuflect. It's a pure miracle he took you on in the first place. Quit bellyaching about tired and find that man some oil so we can stop drifting around this country! I'm nineteen years old, and it's time I had curtains. Are you gonna see to it I get some?"

"Curtains? Used to be I could sneak up on a person. I could sneak up on a person and scare the lights out of them with saying boo. Not now that I sound like a stick breaking every time I bend my knees, and she says curtains. It's that Indian store, isn't it, got you dwelling on curtains. Well, you can just stay right where you are, Miss Sassy. That's town trips for you. Town trips get me sass and— What is this? Dog meat, isn't it? Trying to poison me with bad meat. Reckon it's time for a lesson."

"You touch me with that thing and—"

Lavinia opened her eyes wider, waiting for a scream. Nothing followed but silence. Nelson's face proved there was nothing to fear. He sat at the table where he'd sat every evening for seven days. Shadows from the kerosene lamp softened his features. He studied his papers, his concentration unbroken, until she cleared her throat.

"What is it?"

"That! Haven't you been listening?"

"They want to hit pay dirt as bad as I do. They're bound to curse me, curse the well and the work until they find it. Try to sleep."

"How can I sleep? We drill tomorrow."

"Exactly. I don't want you so groggy and tired out you can't enjoy it. Good night, Vinnie."

An hour passed. Watching Nelson helped. The head-scratching, shifting sight of him took charge of her worries until she did sleep finally, lying stiff as a stake driven into place. She didn't rest that night but wandered through a dark, concentrated spiral. She woke up relieved at being back from that place that wanted so much from her. She had messages to deliver, but not now. First this repose . . . honeyed light, a silver spiderweb inches from her nose, her husband still sloped over his table. She heard his stomach rumble and guessed he'd welcome skillet bread and eggs she'd finally learned to do right.

"You chattered all night long. Never heard such a commotion from you."

"Doesn't surprise me."

She struggled up from the bedroll, shaking her boots as she'd been told to do. A centipede dropped out, its tail angry and erect. She squealed, then ground it out under the heel of her boot and asked Nelson what it would take to move an oil rig.

"What do you mean?"

"I mean how do you do it? By knocking it down and beginning again or moving it somehow?"

"Depends on the distance. I've seen it done both ways. And why this question?"

"Because you put the rig in the wrong place."

She stepped into her boots and started walking. Her hair was tangled, and her body showed up bare through the thin cotton nightgown. Never mind. The driller and the tool dresser were awake and looking, just slapping down thick sides of bacon while their wives slept or sulked. Never mind. She kept going, not even startled when she hit the cold creek water, for it took that to show Nelson.

"There's where it's supposed to be. See, where the creek pulls in over there."

Nelson roared with laughter. His hat rolled to one side of his head and fell off.

"Oh, that's good! Vinnie, darling—"

"Stop making fun of me. Can you move the rig, or can't you?"

"The shooter's on his way right now. He's hauling a load of explosives out here from town if he's not already dead."

"Explosives? Whatever for?"

"To open the well up. You have a lot to learn, Vinnie."

The soup wagon had already left town. The driver of the buckboard, drunk for days, had awakened at sunrise to say a prayer as larded with profanity as a curse (Goddamn it, Almighty Lord Jesus, I don't deserve death), then loaded the wagon with five-quart cans full of nitro to open the well. The shooter was the very best dead-in-a-hurry man to be found in the Osage hills. He tied his jaw shut with a cloth bandanna to stop his teeth from rattling on the drive north and kept his thoughts in order by counting all the times he'd opened wells and hadn't been killed. Nelson could already pick out a line of Indians on the ridge, sitting cross-legged to wait for the spectacle. The opening of a well was the best show around. His gaze returned to his wife standing in the shallows of a creek, a wet nightshirt wound through her legs. She didn't look crazy or even foolish. She looked certain. And he hadn't found certain yet, not in the maps and papers spread out on the table in his tent, nor in claims made by men with oil charms tied around their necks.

"Who is the child, Nelson?"

"What child do you mean?"

"The Indian child I saw last night in the dream. Couldn't have been more than eight or nine. And sober. Wouldn't smile for anything in the world. She was standing right over there, where your well ought to be."

Jane Anderson. An Osage girl and sober through and through. Seemed like she'd known all about sadness from the crib on. The child's melancholia was remarkable. Sisters, brothers, cousins understood that entertainment was their task. They filled their cheeks with nuts and crossed their eyes, hung upside down in trees, tickled her sides. Seeing that it had no effect, they let her go back to studious, solitary play. Now that Jane had herself a land allotment and an oil operation that was about to be launched on her property, the severity of her gaze was finally appropriate, though still unsettling.

He decided they would disassemble the rig and float the lighter pieces downstream directly to the site. The rest they would have to transport over land. He'd take on extra men to speed things up. The tool dresser winced, seeing Nelson's thoughts change direction. He'd been hired to keep the drill bits sharp as they made their way through layers of rock and hard-packed earth. He'd been hired by a man, not a woman. Grease from the frying bacon stung his face. He minded that a lot less than watching his boss listen to his wife. He addressed the cast-iron pan, the meat sizzling up too fast.

"Might as well be frying up my pay. If he expects me to . . ."

Too late. He watched with wonder as Nelson helped his crazy wife out of the water, bent down himself to wring out the ends of her nightshirt.

"Soon as that's eaten, I want you to ride toward town. Tell the shooter it won't be for today or even tomorrow. Tell him we've had a significant change of plan."

He noted the tool dresser's pinched white face, heard the driller's wife's complaints renewed inside their tent and told the lot of them to go into town.

"Kin we get back on after, Mr. Hanks?"

"You're not off, Miller. This is recess."

The man winced, and his tongue wandered back to the empty hole at the back of his mouth. Hadn't that dentist called it a recessed tooth? If he was about to be recessed himself . . .

"Are me and my wife fired, sir?"

"Hell no, Miller! When did you leave school anyway?"

"Never did go."

Nelson laid two twenty-dollar bills on the table.

"Don't drink, and keep the material sharp. I'll send for you when I'm ready."

He hired four men for the job, men who had already floated a multitude of improbable craft downstream. Not one of whom blinked when he said he wanted to float a roundhouse downstream. They were accustomed to improvisation in this place where building material was just about anything. They had already copied the Indians to turn out pirogues, canoes dug out of cottonwood logs, or transformed feed troughs into flotillas and workbenches into pleasure craft for their sons and daughters on swirling brown waterways. A wooden rig would take a bit more doing, still . . . One man poked a finger into his ear at the proposition, a sign he was about to think long and hard, and suggested an Indian be hired on.

"Be sure he knows all we want is ideas. Mention real work, and he'll set his wolfhounds on you."

The adviser, an Osage brave, took up his post alongside the creek. Pausing only occasionally, to stone one of his snarling half-breed dogs, he diagrammed plans for the launch in the dirt, explaining with mild contempt how the flatboat should be constructed. How little these men knew; had they even noted the poorest beaver dam? Large timber on top, mud, sticks and grass underneath, he said, lip curled. He used a wooden pointer stolen from Indian boarding school in Pennsylvania. Once the pride of Carlisle, he had returned to the blanket, to the director's chagrin. He had even taken up the Osage language again, something the administration had tried to correct with a spoonful of castor oil for any Indian word that slipped out of his mouth. "What is worse than this kind of turncoat, who has, in his years under the school's tutelage, been taught our excellent code, only to return to his idling life and a diet of wild potatoes and the roots of pond lilies? These people cannot be taught." The brave suggested a paste be placed between the logs. After his nap he would write out the recipe, but first sleep. He grinned and asked that water be brought up from the creek for his dogs, for they had long since lost the habit of getting it for themselves.

"Bastard's what he is."

"Don't argue. Go take care of the dogs."

One of Nelson's men traipsed down to the water's edge and brought up hatfuls for the gray dogs. Some drank, others sniffed and slunk off into the brush.

"Wish I could kick the shit out of you, little fleabite. Drink this, damn it, so I kin get paid."

Incomplete, she thought, then whispered, then said aloud.

"It's incomplete."

"It's ready to float. I wouldn't be surprised if it took off and flew downstream. It just might soar like a bird."

He scratched and hesitated, pulled the end of his nose, thinking she'd give it up. But she was already at work, bent over red cotton (ordered hastily from the Indian trader) and ripping until it came apart in long strips. Everyone looked the other way as she braided and bound the strips together. Everyone, that is, except the Osage, who was held perfectly rapt, who grunted at her lack of skill and knelt beside her, finally, to help her fix the increasingly long red cord.

"It needs a garland."

It was Nelson's turn to fret.

"Our investors aren't interested in garlands. Our investors want oil."

"They'll get it. Besides, remember the whorehouse well. If that old sot can hang strands of red lights on her well, I can hang a garland on mine."

A well pumped night and day at the bottom of a garden consisting principally of sunflowers, moony and long-legged as the young men who visited it. Despite the presence of a well, or perhaps because of it, business conditions at the whorehouse had never been better. It seemed like Christmas Eve every single night of the year, and even the most hurried customer was sure to pull back the edge of a satin curtain just to gaze out at the strand of red lights, saying, "Let's us go one more time. Hell, it's Christmas." Lavinia talked excitedly through strands of hair that had come free of her chignon. As she swung her arm this way and that, he noted a tear that opened further with each gesture to reveal cotton eyelet. The corset had long stood in a corner of the tent, an artifact from another life. There was a dirty smear on her forehead and a slight, very slight flush had fought its way through her habitual pallor. The Indian deferred and nodded as she explained. Her laugh exploded as he bent to take up the red cord with his teeth.

"Go, that's right! Straight up!"

He scaled the rig effortlessly, for this wasn't labor. It was public play. He shook his head, teeth clenching red, like one of his mongrels shaking a broken-spined wood squirrel, then waved at the people lined up on bluffs and ridges to watch Nelson Hanks sink or swim. Sentiments listed every which way. Mostly fear and wonderment at the oil man, dapper despite the dirty work and the heat, and this sweating, worthy woman who understood spectacle. There were gasps and sighs at the sight of that gliding oil rig. The planks, belts and pulleys, even the straining team of workhorses that guided it overland. The rig seemed to have a mind of its own. That it up and changed it, suddenly preferring one locale to another, only heightened the effect of the underground thunderclap that was to follow. A young woman, her mind all mixed up and thinking of Mr. Eiffel, cried "Paris!" at the sight of that regal, moving creation, Lavinia's bright cotton streamers gently slapping at the sides of prairie hardwood. Flags were raised on the bluffs, children and wind-testers lifted high, for onlookers hoped if oil blew it would blow thisaway.

"*God!*"

It was the shooter; they could hear him from even way up. Too many days spent waiting and, since dark night was twice as long, two too many nights. The only thing left was slivered nerves. Add to that prayer, prayer that was mad as hell. It had become a roar and a shout.

"*God!*"

Again. After that, God answered, or seemed to, as the bluff shimmied with the muffled blast. Up high, they overturned anything that would. That became hats, shoes, cupped hands and open mouths of the most extravagant, who wanted to taste black gold for themselves. Down below, there was stillness. Funny. They watched as Nelson Hanks slowed straight down until he looked paralyzed. The Indian locked into place, too, from where he stood. Attention turned away, even as Mrs. Nelson Hanks (her face upturned and rusty red from the spray) unbuttoned the top of her blouse as if to receive the first welcome drops of a summer rain. For something momentous had happened up on that sandstone outcropping. Jane Anderson, standing alone in her pink town dress, her child's bottom hidden by stiff petticoats, had just laughed.

Hubbell,
Mary and
Laydelle

chapter 10

1989

"Looks like we got company."

Aresta stopped right where she was, and stopping was no small thing. She was in no mood for interruptions. She squared her shoulders, rolled her sleeves tight as tourniquets and decided to give Hubbell's visitors the reception they deserved. Flour coated her forearms, and her teeth sat in a glass of foaming denture solution. With a rolling pin in one hand and a dish towel in the other, Aresta looked out the window and frowned hard. The back of the little Ford Escort stood open, and one man after another got out, until she counted five. They stood outside, smoothing their suits down over their bellies with one hand and sucking hard on cigarettes.

"Do I look like a welcome wagon?"

She addressed the single fish that drifted lazily through the aquarium.

"Too bad you're not one of them parajuanas. I'd stuff 'em all down the tank and not blink once."

Hubbell's hobby was just shaping up. Not a piranha, but a Siamese fighting fish, spent long days trailing through an improvised coral reef and underwater glade. Hubbell had begun marking down his observations in a leather notebook, dropping mirrors on a long chain to dance before the exotic fish or adjusting the lighting or the temperature of the water, to mark its effects on his new pet. She flicked the side of the aquarium with one finger, and the fish shied away. She pressed on, out of the cramped kitchen galley and the adjacent club room. Then the library, the rows of leather-bound books she didn't mind smelling. She lifted herself up the stairwell, one towel-wrapped hand on the rail, until she stood on the open deck.

"C'mon."

But they didn't. They just stood there, still talking like she wasn't standing there on the top of the boat, the top where Hubbell always stood to greet people. They just stood and stared, and it was then that Aresta got a look at who they were, besides clowns in cheap suits falling out of an orange car. Indians! Indians come with some trouble or other all the way to Catoosa on the very day Aresta was getting the houseboat ready for a party. She forgot about her collapsed, toothless mouth and her brown/white arms and no uniform. She had stopped wearing starched uniforms after coming on board the houseboat. It was pedal pushers now, nothing but pedal pushers, in all the colors of the rainbow, and bare feet since she'd taken her fall. Aresta forgot how she looked, standing at the front of the *Final Resort* with her legs spread apart and flour falling from her strong arms as she beat the open palm of her hand with a rolling pin.

"I *said* c'mon."

That did it, and they finally moved. The frown deepened as she noticed the car windows, how they were all down. Which meant that the five clowns were not only sorry but dusty. And the houseboat was clean, except for the circle of flour she herself was making as she waited for them to make their gingerly way up the plank. If they thought they were going to put their dirty behinds on her white couches, lean those dark heads against the top of her chairs, they were wrong. She would make them wait right here, standing up. Or maybe they wouldn't wait at all. Maybe they would wobble right back to that excuse for a car.

"We're looking for Hubbell Hanks."

"Mr. Hanks is asleep."

Nobody thought to offer her a name, an excuse for being there, no matter how poor. Who did they think she was? Flour was falling and time was passing on a day that resembled the old days. She had sixty *barquettes* to turn out. She had cocktail cheeses to blend with fresh herbs and a whole section of *Food and Wine* to copy in less than two hours, and she was no longer wishing for a single piranha in a tank. She was wishing for a whole school of them, right under the houseboat, to finish off five fools neat and let her get on with the first real affair on the houseboat, which meant both she and Hubbell Hanks were back from the dead. Forty people were coming here!

She took a step nearer and squinted, then put her hand quickly to her mouth, leaving a last white imprint. Had he caught himself on fire? Had he missed being scalped and come away with that? *The man had no eyebrows.* He looked out of a naked face. She stared at the otherwise bushy head and for a moment had nothing at all to say. There were footsteps behind her. Light-sleeping Hubbell had made his way upstairs.

"Where are your manners, Aresta? Get our friends something to drink."

He had his hand out and was going from one to the next, pumping like he was happy they were there. Pumping like they knew each other from somewhere.

"That would be great, Mr. Hanks."

"Hubbell."

"Anything cool. Man! It's some drive from Lovely to your place."

He waved them to deck chairs and began to apologize for his appearance. He had slept, but not long enough. This was the first party he had planned without Mary, and it had taken it out of him. The details made his head swim.

"It's certainly a nice surprise to see you all again. The last time was . . . well, wasn't it one of those foundation meetings? Out at Buffabrook?"

One of the men nodded, the man with rings on every finger of his right hand. They were massive rings, Hubbell noted. Peculiar rings, with stones set at jarring angles. Every ring was an onslaught of metal and gemstone. He didn't like to look at them. Hubbell couldn't recall a single one of their names.

"It was. Jim here mentioned to you that we would be paying you a visit in the near future. There are things we need to talk to you about, and since time is running out . . ."

"You're right. Damned if I don't have a reception scheduled for five o'clock. Otherwise I'd like nothing better than to chew the fat with you fellas all night long. Of course, you are all welcome to stay. That's it! You'll stay on for the party."

One man, the man with the shaved eyebrows, hadn't moved or spoken yet. He did then, putting a huge hand on Hubbell's knee as he did. Hubbell had seen a picture once, in one of his father's books. The Indian brave in the old black-and-white photograph had shaved his eyebrows off in the same way. An Osage fashion resurrected? he wondered. He didn't like thinking about that.

"Our time is running out. We are talking about the Osage tribe, Mr. Hanks, which is one step away from complete obliteration."

Hubbell thought about his bed, which he loved well. He couldn't imagine claustrophobia. The tight, tidy space suited him, and ordinarily, without a party to worry him, he slept the sleep of an untroubled man. He could have used fifteen minutes more in that bed. Fifteen minutes would have given him a real edge. His thoughts weren't clear. What did the man mean by obliteration?

"Obliteration? Why, Mr. . . . You know, you fellas will have to forgive me, but I have completely forgotten . . ."

Then the names. Red Dog, Tishman, White Breast and Little Eagle. Lefrancais. How would he ever keep them straight? Why would he need to? He tried hard to pay attention. Red Breast was talking—no, it was Red Dog. Jim Red Dog was talking.

"We need your support, Mr. Hanks."

"Do you fellas mean to say you're getting behind some antiwar thing? Is this some no-nuke deal we're talking about? When you say obliteration, it can only mean one thing."

"It does only mean one thing to the Osage. No, we're not talking about a threat, but a certainty. We're talking about a tribe that's scheduled to end. The end of the world, yes. The end of the Osage world."

"Ah, drinks! Aresta, you're an angel."

The fear was wearing off. She'd talked herself into looking straight down at this ghost who wasn't a ghost, but a real man, who was leaving real marks on a wooden floor she had broken her back to polish. He'd left a trail, an unfortunate set of skid marks that led straight to the browless brown man in the wicker chair. In her wicker chair.

"No angels around here, jes tired black women."

He was a coward, eyebrows or no eyebrows. He just sucked the drink she handed him, then handed back the empty glass. She took a forefinger and aimed it at the tracks.

"Mine takin' off your shoes?"

"Sure."

Lord, it was worse. The man's socks were so thin-heeled she could see the flesh of his foot. The steady pressure on the top of Aresta's head meant she might just as well sit down forever. The pressure meant she never had to get up again to make pastry boats so small they could be popped in the mouth whole, or hold a wineglass up to the light, spinning the stem between her thumb and forefinger to look for an offending spot, because what was the damn point. This wasn't any gala because how could you have a gala in such a miserable place? Catoosa. It was somebody's idea of a bad joke. The pressure meant the parajuanas might just as well swallow her, too. She left, muttering, cursing her own bad sense. Out of all the jobs she could have had, she had to choose this one.

Jim Red Dog removed his hat and tapped it softly against his knee. He glanced at the skid marks and shrugged.

"We seem to have chosen the wrong day."

"Don't take it personally. She's in a dither about the party is all. And to be fair, it is a lot to do and a small space to do it in. The refrigerator went on the blink yesterday, and I thought I'd lose her."

"Mr. Hanks, we've got serious problems."

"Hubbell. Obliteration, now that's a mighty strong term, and frankly, I don't get it. You people own more than a million acres of land. And headrights, gawdamighty! You five men sitting here must get some pretty fat oil-royalty checks in the mail. Why, Hanks is still pumping away on your land, and that's not even the only petroleum company in the Osage hills. You boys represent a small fortune, and there's no obliterating that kind of wealth. Is there?"

Hubbell sat up straighter and straighter as he talked. He surprised them, caught them off guard. He saw that in their round, disbelieving eyes. Why, they must have imagined that just because he'd left town, established a new life out on the port away from the maddening crowd, he hadn't kept up. One of the men was reaching for his wallet. Hubbell noticed his cuff was worn and thought, Sure, it's part of the con. He tossed a card down on the glass-topped table. Hubbell reached for his bifocals. C.D.I.B. The bifocals couldn't help him with that.

"Certificate of Degree of Indian Blood, Mr. Hanks. If you'll notice, I'm half Osage."

"The better half, eh? Ha! Well, sounds impressive to me. My father used to brag about his ancestors coming over on the *May-*

flower, but we mostly chalked that up to empty boasting. Nobody told a better tale than Nelson Hanks. You're one up on me, Mr. White Eagle. I'm not a card-carrying anything!"

"It's Little Eagle. Ask you something, Mr. Hanks?"

"Anything, anything."

"What do you figure that card there means?"

"Why, it means you get that fat royalty check I was talking about. Means you're just as eager to add up all the run tickets as Mr. Red Dog here."

Run tickets! He was steaming ahead. Hubbell glanced at his watch and reminded himself that he needed to wind this up. He still had to shower and shave, and how could he do that and entertain these men? Hubbell wondered if any of them really bothered with knowing how much oil was being taken out of their land, the story that run tickets told. That was it! That was why they'd come in the first place. He'd read that there was a big stink about an oil company (not Hanks, thank God) altering those run tickets, lying about how much they were taking out, even going in at night with their trucks. Farmers found the tire marks the next day and blew the whistle on the company. He was one step ahead of these men.

"No."

"No, what?"

"This card has nothing to do with owning headrights. Would it surprise you to learn that of the six men sitting here, Mr. Hanks, you are the only one who owns a headright?"

"I don't get it."

"That's okay. Most people don't. All I'm saying is that my Indian blood entitles me to shit. I can't even vote."

"What do you mean, you can't vote? You people just had your elections last month. I read all about them. In fact, my daughter was trying to get a friend of hers to run for office. Beaureve, Johnny Beaureve. Hell of a man. You must know him."

Jim Red Dog spit. Hubbell's mouth pursed slightly, then opened until a small round space appeared in front, opening and closing several times before he could stop it. Nobody had ever spit on Hubbell's boat. He wanted to speak but wasn't able to. He just stared at the spot on the shiny wooden floor.

"I know the bastard. Beaureve is exactly what I'm talking about. That little fuck lives in California and France, Lovely when he wants to get back to his roots. He don't know shit about the Osage except what he reads in books. He don't know shit about the government, how they slap down a health clinic in the middle of our land with one quack and a thousand bottles of Tylenol and call it free health care. They send us car seats from Washington and drug pamphlets 'bout ice and think the job's done. Beaureve has the right to vote because he's got four headrights. I'm half Osage and have never lived anywhere else but Lovely, and *I can't vote.* Blood's gonna spill and here's where you come in, Mr. Hanks."

"Speaking of spills, Jim, I don't mean to be rude, but I'm expecting forty people shortly, and I've got—"

"Don't jack me off, Mr. Hanks. Your party'll go on. That's what maids are for. We'll clear out in time for you to pull on your nice clothes."

"I wouldn't dream of jacking you off."

"You wouldn't? Then whose son are you? Now listen."

Someone spoke up. All the names were merged and swirling, and Hubbell couldn't listen to anything but his own heart pounding at the wall of his chest. Why had they spit on his boat after accepting his charity? Wasn't it charitable to let them sit on and on, taking up his time? Hubbell hoped he wouldn't have to call the security people. The man seemed to be a conciliator. He spoke in a nice, low voice, and Hubbell tried to rub out the tension in his neck.

"History time. Don't look scared, Mr. Hanks. I'll be brief. Flash yourself back to 1906, when your pap was alive and about to become a big shot. Well, that was the year that our Chief Bigheart made it to Washington, D.C., and made a pretty fair deal for the Osage."

"And I'm glad you see it that way! Why, you people were stinking rich with oil money."

"In the 1920s the Osage tribe was the richest nation per capita in the world. That was a long, long time ago. But forget about oil for a minute, Mr. Hanks. We're talking about something else now. In 1906 they passed the Allotment Act, which meant each member of the Osage tribe was given one hundred and sixty acres of land and his allotment. His share in collectively held mineral rights. With me so far?"

Hubbell nodded and pursued his hangnail a little more vigorously.

"All the oil was held in common by the tribe."

"Which was good."

"Yes, Mr. Hanks. It was good."

He sighed, as if he were telling a tedious story to a child.

"Now the Osage bought and sold this land as they wished. But the only way to get a headright was to inherit it from someone. Why, Scratching Wolf passed his on to your dad. And you got yours from Nelson. By the way, you got any idea what your payments amount to these days?"

"Why, I . . . to tell the truth, I let my lawyers handle all that for me."

"Do you? Well, now."

There was a bad pause, a moment when someone might choose to spit again or take one of his pretty *objets* and bring it clattering down on his face. Hubbell saw so many possibilities in that long minute or so before the man spoke again.

"How many of those original allottees do you suppose are still living?"

"Gee, they'd have to be pretty old."

"More than pretty old. They'd have to be dead or ancient. Eighty-two Osage original allottees remain, Mr. Hanks. And when they die, our tribe ceases to exist."

"But surely in the constitution there's a provision for that. For what happens when they die, I mean."

"Whose constitution?"

"Yours! The Osage."

"You mean the Osage constitution abolished by the secretary of interior in 1900 without our consent? That one? Have you got anything to eat on board this freighter, Mr. Hanks?"

He was so grateful. His legs weren't any too strong as he made his way to the galley, where Aresta fumed and shaped pastry with her blunt fingers. He didn't even ask her to stop what she was doing; he just started in with bread and mustard and all the cold cuts he could find in the tiny fridge, hoping it would be enough.

"Samwiches? You makin' them samwiches now, is that it?"

It was hot in the galley, but not as hot as it was on deck.

"Do we have beer, Aresta?"

The head jerking right meant the cupboard. He found Philippine beer and began arranging bottles on a tray in a hurry.

"You better take your shower in ten."

"Stop bossing me around, Aresta."

"Someone has to."

He returned to where they were sitting and set the tray down carefully. They didn't bother to thank him, but why would they? Oh, he wished they'd leave.

"This is no simple issue, Mr. Hanks. My friends and I are members of the Osage National Council. We're pro business, pro Conservative and pro Osage. We want our constitution back. We want to restore the voting rights to our people, and we want you at our next council meeting."

"Me? What have I got to do with any of this?"

"Everything and nothing. We want you on our side, Mr. Hanks, not theirs. Not those puppets we call our elected officials. They're nothing but pipelines from Washington. Anything the Bureau says they say. You're part of our history whether you like it or not. Having you at our next meeting just gives us that much more legitimacy."

"We're going on television with this one."

"Latvia's coming. Are you?"

Hubbell felt wobbly. It was lucky he was sitting down. He thought he'd understood for a minute or so, but not now.

"Confused? Latvia was forcibly made part of the Soviet government. And they're a separate nation in the same way that we are. Blood's gonna spill this time, Mr. Hanks, but we're ready. We're gonna fire shots. We're gonna make some noise. You're an Osage son just like us."

But Hubbell wasn't listening anymore. Rather, Hubbell was listening to someone else. It was Mary's voice, as clear as ever but speaking so far away that he couldn't hear it. He saw her, too. She was wearing a business suit, like the suits she had worn when he first met her. The squared shoulders and nipped waist of Mary's wool suit, the jaunty felt hat tipped slightly forward, made her look as tough and adorable as a little gun moll. Hubbell strained forward in his chair, blocking the sight and sound of the strange delegation so he could catch what she was saying. Mary was more and more animated. He just barely made it out and was disappointed to find it was another reprimand, like the chorus of reprimands she had issued over the years. *Pick up your ears, Hubbell Hanks! You're discarding opportunity again, and after all I've said, too. You're pissing away occasion, Hub, and then tromping on it like it's nothing but a dead leaf.* He started to argue with her, to state his case once more, but she was moving farther away and holding up one white-gloved hand to say so long. Did she mean

this? Did this vision of Mary Hanks mean he should accept their
invitation? Hubbell held stock-still, thinking maybe, if it was really
going to be televised, Mary might see it way out there in California.
Mary might see him on the TV screen with the camera moving in
for a close-up shot. She might watch him as he . . . Hubbell
stopped again, confused. As he defended Latvia? Jim Red Dog
came into focus first, then the others, one at a time.

"I take it we can count on you."

"A lifelong friend of the Osage wouldn't think twice."

"No, sir. Not twice."

There wasn't time for a response. Aresta thundered up from
below deck. Every step was heavier than the next, and each of the
men looked in her direction to see just what was coming.

"Look here. Princess Dark Cloud has had jes' about all she can
take. Princess Dark Cloud has forty people lookin' to her to be well
fed and happy. Princess Dark Cloud has a boat deck to shine again
even though she shined it before, and how can she do that with
people draped on her deck chairs. Mr. H., take your clothes off
and get showered before I take 'em off for you. You can stare. Go
on and look at me like that; don't matter. Is you is or is you ain't?"

At least they were standing, smoothing their stomachs again,
the way they had before. Aresta snorted and put weight on her
squeeze mop. It gave out a soapy little squish.

"*Leavin'*. Is you leavin', or ain't you?"

"I'll get back to you all on this."

"Not now you ain't."

"Aresta, that's enough. I certainly thank you for driving all the
way down here, and believe me, your story's safe with me."

Jim Red Dog burst out laughing, though Hubbell couldn't imagine why. He marched off, making fresh tracks as he did. Aresta
had been right on. The men smoked quietly by the side of the boat,
though a warning was posted against flammables. The sign was
as clear as day, and Hubbell wagged his head as he retreated to
the safety of a shower stall designed to hold one medium-sized
man. Hubbell took his clothes off slowly, then stood stoop-shouldered under the blistering flow of hot water that would be depleted
after exactly seven minutes. He stepped out of the shower and
grabbed a rough towel. He actually preferred them that way. His
skin felt drier, if that was possible, under a slightly abrasive bath
towel. He thought at first he imagined it. Then holding himself as
steady as he could, his feet planted solidly apart, he knew he

hadn't. The houseboat was rocking gently. He registered the first movement on board his boat with the pent-up delight of a little boy.

"Whoa."

He called out to the heavy steps he heard above his head.

"Feel that, Aresta? Must be a freighter making its way down the canal!"

He could read her expression by that voice and was glad he couldn't see Aresta's terrible face.

"Freighter nothin'. That's probably your Indian pals tryin to make us capsize. I feel sick. I . . . oh, no. Oh, no, I'm losin' my sea legs."

Hubbell smiled as he held on to the counter, his warm, pinkish body recording every single rock and roll.

c h a p t e r   1 1

1985

Citizens Bank was dwarfed by hotels and office buildings in the center of downtown Tulsa. University groups stole through the building, delightedly aghast at the excess of the Oklahoma oil man and banker. The memo to his architect, on view in the fifth-floor archivist's office, gave students of 1920 art deco a fresh take: MAKE IT SOLID. MAKE IT SHOWY. THIS PLACE IS ALL ABOUT MONEY. Existing now in the shadows of big, brawny neighbors, the building still held a charm of its own for outsiders, though tellers stared longingly out of beautiful beveled windows on their breaks. They asked aloud what good it was to work inside a gem upon which the sun never shone and wished for the sight of a slanting rod of sunlight. They wore sweaters, summer and winter, and two or three even claimed to need more sugar in their diets since coming to work at Citizens Bank, the old downtown branch.

The elevator operator knew Miss Hanks. Seeing her stride across the marble floors got her up off the tufted velvet bench where she had sat eight hours a day, five days a week, for twenty-two years. *Going up? Going down?* She brightened and got ready to tell Miss Hanks about her own daughter, drug-free at last and doing fine in a work-study pilot program. Okay, her grandson wasn't doing so good. Born underweight and, five years later, still fragile, helping himself to his mother's guilt so that he couldn't exactly be disciplined. But it didn't matter. *Going up?* They were, all of them, and she counted on Miss Hanks to ask how were things at home. Except she didn't.

She just got on and stood there. She fiddled with a button on her coat and stood there, like they'd exchanged nothing over the years. Like she was standing in a strange elevator in a strange city. Nice coat, only why'd she still have it buttoned up like she hadn't come inside but was still standing out on the street?

"Twelfth floor?"

Good morning, I'm here, take a look at me! She gripped the iron rod tightly and the latch on the metal grille she would slam shut in the next second.

"Oh, God, Estelle. How are you? Sorry. I guess I'm just preoccupied today. Yeah, take me up to twelve."

She rammed the grille into place and up they chugged, without a word. Troubles, she guessed. Troubles had taken her mind off somewhere, had let her forget the story of Estelle's life, which could have been reproduced for television, that's how close it came to being one installment of something terrible after the next.

"Twelve."

She stepped off, and the woman getting off the elevator sure wasn't the same one who got on. Estelle shook her head and returned to her tufted bench, which she shared with an old black pocketbook, filled with two magazines and a zip-locked sandwich and a chocolate candy bar lined with peanut butter. A lot could happen between twelve stories, and she had just watched it firsthand. He doesn't bite, honey! So what if he's the president; he knows your momma, your daddy, and even went to your high school graduation. He told me so when I took him down to L that afternoon! She wanted to shout it through the web of iron so fancy it could have been lace on a collar, but she didn't. Miss Hanks wasn't her daughter. Hell, she had troubles of her own. Hmmmph! Somebody on fifth was in a hurry.

Laydelle took her gloves off and put them carefully in her coat pocket. She waved at the receptionist, who gave her a big grin back and said in a carrying voice how Mr. Singleton was waiting for her. Did that mean she was late? Surely not; she'd set all her clocks fast for that very reason.

She crossed in front of the orderly desk, loving that, the precision of memos and paper clips, the always-sharpened pencils and the

five telephone lines that never elicited frenzy from Singleton's secretary, even if they were all ringing at once. She was the right kind
of secretary. She went with Singleton; they were matched articles.
Panic was rising in Laydelle, and rather than being soothed by
order, she was dismayed. She stumbled slightly, though Singleton's secretary had turned back to her typewriter. What had she
caught her heel on this time? She could trip on nothing, thin air.
She knocked on the heavy closed door and heard her stomach
growl. She put her hand on the doorknob and pushed. It was one
of those massive doorknobs that didn't turn.

"Laydelle! Good to see you. Come sit by the window. Take your
coat?"

"Yes, thanks. It's nice of you to see me on such short notice."

"Perfectly fine. Here, I'll just hang it up for you."

Today was for embroidery. That was good; she had done that
part well. This wasn't starting from scratch, she reminded herself.
She had already outlined the whole project, and Singleton knew
why she was here. All she would have to do now was . . . well,
embroidery. Her stomach was warming up now, really howling. A
combination of nerves and black coffee, because she hadn't taken
time for breakfast. She glanced briefly at his desk, which seemed
barren. Maybe bank presidents didn't really need desks. They
worked at big conference tables, that was it. Of course, very little
would happen in here.

"Laydelle, I received your outline. Very well done, I should add.
Your presentation gets very high marks indeed."

She hadn't come here for a grade card. She'd come for a loan.
Singleton didn't sit at his desk. He sat on top of it, or leaned
against it. One leg cocked slightly, his expression relaxed, he
stroked his chin and seemed to weigh each word carefully.

"I'm alarmed by several things, Laydelle."

Shit. Shit, shit, shit!

"I'm alarmed first by the group of investors. Their backgrounds
seem wobbly, and I think I'm being generous here."

"John, I know each and every one of the people involved in this
thing, and I have complete confidence in all of them."

"Friends?"

"Acquaintances. We all go back quite a few years, more than I'd
like to admit."

"Pinsky, Bellini. This Swartzberg. Where exactly did you meet
this Swartzberg, for example?"

"I was living down in Tampa when I met Mr. Swartzberg."

Guy Swartzberg. Fifty-eight years old and in mint condition, he would always say to anyone who asked. New York, you gotta be kidding. I remember the day I woke up. I'm standing on the corner of Fifty-first and Park, with my hand out for a taxi. I look good. I look real good, with a vicuña coat and wing tips. A briefcase, for chrissake. I wait and I wait, and no taxi stops though the street is swimming with cabs. Pretty soon it hits me that in every single taxicab is a lady. I'm not talking about women, no, because all the women—that is, women who work in stinking New York City—are underground, fighting off murderers on the subways. Well, Guy Swartzberg waits some more, and while he waits he thinks more about all these ladies in these cabs, their hair, their nails, the tiring shopping sprees and the drink they're going to mix for themselves the minute they walk in the door, and all at once Guy Swartzberg slowly lowers the arm he's had raised for twenty-two minutes with no results. Go on, cabbies, go on and chauffeur the ladies home. Up your ass, hear me? Guy lowers his arm and begins to walk home through miserable weather, and he's singing. Why? Because it's the last time! Guy Swartzberg's finale! The man is moving out of the city! Winter, you gotta be kidding. I'll drop dead before I see another snowflake.

"What was Mr. Swartzberg's business in Tampa?"

"Oh, personal care even back then. Guy had a salon called Nine to Five. It was brilliant! He catered to working girls, offered special rates during lunch hours, and besides a haircut, he would give a free pedicure to anyone who could prove they had a job where they were on their feet all day. I don't have to tell you how successful that was. Nine to Five still exists in about a dozen locations. Sunbelt states. I can get information on them if you like."

"Mr. Swartzberg appears to be very successful."

"He is. So is Pinsky, and Tina Bellini's story is a business case history."

Singleton was perched on the edge of his desk. Laydelle thought of that conference table vengefully. He wouldn't dangle his legs from a conference table, would he? She hadn't envisioned this kind of meeting at all. The informality was definitely working against her.

"Why do they need a fourth investor, and why, in particular, have they chosen you?"

"We're friends and—"

"Now you're friends. You just said they were acquaintances."

"No. We're . . . well, it doesn't really matter what we are. I mean, forgive me, John, but if I were simply Miss So-and-so, you wouldn't ask these questions."

"Laydelle, if you were Miss So-and-so, you'd be speaking with a loan officer right now."

She took a moment to collect her thoughts. An oil portrait of Janet Singleton hung above the fireplace. It was an unusual portrait, as if the painter had positioned himself slightly above her. It shifted the whole balance of the painting, making the observer a kind of voyeur.

"Am I going to get a loan?"

"You haven't answered my question."

She continued, but she lowered her voice slightly.

"They want to enter Oklahoma. They want to make a big deal out of the fact that Laydelle Hanks has returned to her home state to start a chain of salons called Hair Apparent. They think with a good ad campaign people will get the connection and we'll be off and running in no time."

"What connection?"

"Well, Tina thinks this *has* to work, especially with the nutty-heiress twist."

"But you're not an heiress."

"People perceive me that way. They associate my name with fortune, and it's an attractive association, according to Tina."

"Would you like to know what I think, Laydelle?"

Her cheeks were burning. Why couldn't she control her own thermostat?

"I think they want to take you for a ride. With your permission, I think we ought to run a very thorough check on these people. They seem quite professional."

"They are!"

He finally came down off the desk, sinking into the chair next to her.

"What would you suggest we use as collateral for such a sizable loan?"

"I don't have anything. You know that. All I offer you is a promise. I can work like a dog, John. I really can."

"Your capacity for hard work isn't the issue, my dear. All my instincts tell me no. Whether you want to follow my advice about investigating these people is one thing. Whether I'll risk seventy-five thousand dollars for what I consider a scam is another."

She plucked a parking violation ticket from under her windshield wiper and stuffed it in her purse. She could see the meter maid down the next block and wondered if it would do any good to argue. It didn't matter. A ticket didn't matter. She put her key in the ignition and thought about Tina, about how her pretty face would turn down around the edges when she told her the news. She began to angle out of her parking space into traffic, putting her foot suddenly on the brake when a horn blasted her from the back. She turned to see a tow truck, lights flashing, just behind her. The driver's face, clenched and angry as the fist he held raised at her, screamed soundlessly at her behind the closed windows of his cab. He leaned across the empty seat and lowered the window.

"You're asleep at the wheel!"

She shook her head, thinking herself inviolable inside a locked car. The driver finally stopped screaming and pulled away. She could see the bright-blue slogan painted on the side of the truck. HANKS ALL SERVICE. WE'RE IN BUSINESS TO STAY! She wondered if it was a hallucination. The bank, the tow truck, her stupid life. Maybe Pinsky, Bellini and Swartzberg were all part of some weird illusion. Her appetite wasn't imaginary, though. The dull ache in her stomach was real.

She drove to the old diner directly across from the depot. A man with a toothpick in his mouth held the door for her. He winked and said good morning, letting the toothpick roll along one side of his mouth as he spoke.

"One?"

"Yes. A table by the window if you have it."

"Follow me, honey."

She did, mostly past tables full of men. Working men, though. They were strict about transients. They had to be. She glanced over the menu quickly and turned her attention outside, to the street and the bus station beyond. It never changed, ever. Anything that could support a human being did. Benches, boxes, suitcases and trunks. They had stepped up the police patrol, she saw, and even added women. An officer was crouched beside a heap of old clothing and rags that contained a human being. Rags seemed to bind every extremity, hands and feet; a makeshift turban climbed above tufts of gray-brown hair. Laydelle reached for a cigarette, nervous now that the officer seemed to be losing patience.

"What'll ya have, doll?"

"Scrambled eggs and hash browns, please."

"Coffee, juice?"

"Sanka."

"Already got the shakes, have ya?"

But it was the waitress who shook, her shoulders bobbing up and down with mirth. She stuck her pencil behind her ear and looked out the window.

"Jerks. Treat the bus station like it's their private cocktail lounge. Whadda life. Thank God for cops. You can never have enough of them, and I don't care if they're guys or gals. Side of fresh applesauce? It's on the house."

"No, thanks."

"It's free."

"I don't like applesauce."

"Suit yourself."

Compotes and purees of any kind. Last-ditch food: she thought of it that way. What to do with food way past fresh? Smash it and season it, reconstitute it beyond recognition and pretend it's fun and economical. No, thanks. She let her gaze return to the officer and the woman (she saw now it was a woman), who stood up so slowly it was as if she were attached to a pulley of some kind. More, a little more . . . ah, there. The woman was finally upright and lumbering off. Where? Where did someone like that move to?

Singleton was a jerk; he'd been a patronizing asshole. Citizens wasn't the only bank on the block. She would eat and go home to call Libby or leave a lengthy message with her assistant. Libby would give her a fresh game plan. A short-term game plan, her specialty, designed to carry Laydelle over the three or four awful days after a fresh letdown. Then she'd call her father.

"Collateral. Daddy'll give him collateral."

A man in the next booth lifted his eyebrows, and she looked down at her lap. She slapped her forehead lightly, the whole situation suddenly coming into focus. Singleton would eat crow. Singleton would bow to whatever pressure Hubbell Hanks thought it best to apply. Her father would see to it she got her loan. Somehow Hubbell would ride to her rescue.

. . .

"On a clear day, you can see forever."

"What is it you see, Mr. H.?"

Hubbell stopped in the middle of his song. This was brass week. He had determined that everything that was brass on board ship would shine. When he had suggested brass week to Aresta, she changed the subject, pretending not to hear. So he had taken charge, with a special pink paste imported from England and cheesecloth.

"I will convert you yet, Aresta. Can you honestly tell me the thrill of this port eludes you?"

"Speak English."

Hubbell opened one arm grandly.

"It's pretty. Don't you think what we see is pretty and stirring?"

"Only thing stirring is my tired arms. You want to get that?"

Hubbell got up, happily straightening his shoulders. He kept a cordless telephone by his side even though there was always mild interference to endure.

"Hello?"

"Hi, Daddy."

"Hi yourself. What's up?"

Her version of the morning's events unfurled, broken only at the end by a slight waver in her voice, which Hubbell dismissed as the bad connection again. Hubbell marched down one side of the boat, then up the other, as she told her story.

"Let me get this straight. John Singleton turned down a loan for . . ."

"Hair Apparent Salons."

"Right. Hair Apparent. It sounds to me like you gave it your best shot, Laydelle. Your presentation was in order. Format was perfect, all the investors lined up and ready to go. But Singleton didn't buy it, that's all. It didn't fit into *his* agenda. So you lost, Laydelle. But by golly, you lost fair and square. No monkey business on your part or his."

"I can't believe this. I can't believe you're siding with him against me."

"Wait one second. Nobody's trying to gang up on you. This is no schoolyard, Laydelle. This is life, where hard decisions are made day after day. There is one thing that occurs to me, though."

"Great. What's that?"

"If you don't want my advice, don't call."

"Goddamn it, is that the best you can do?"

"Let me ask you about these three. Bellini, Swartzberg and Pinsky. Just exactly who are these people, and what do they stand for?"

"What do you mean by that?"

"I mean this. Up on the ranch, there's a wonderful clear stream."

She wanted to lay the phone down. She wanted to fold her arms together and lay her head on top of them, if not forever, at least for the duration of his talk. She couldn't listen to one more River Piss Address. How would he adapt it to this? she wondered. What possible application could it have here?

"Daddy, you've told me this story a hundred times. How one stream feeds another; so, if you dirty one stream you dirty them all, until you have a whole network of ruined waterways."

There is no isolated act.

"There is no isolated act."

When you piss up one stream, you're bound to piss up others, until there's nothing left to drink or swim in.

"When you piss up one stream, you're bound to piss up others, until there's nothing left to drink or swim in. These people you're involved with will contaminate your entire life if you let them. I've told you time and again that you can't compartmentalize people. You can't pretend they won't infect other, pure parts if you can only manage to keep the parts separate. I'm afraid life doesn't work that way."

Exhaustion was a blessing. She was too tired to shriek or cry or tear her hair. She would nap, and by then Libby would probably return her call. Hubbell's address was apparently completed.

"You won't believe this, but seagulls have begun building nests up here. And they say Catoosa is no port city. And clear! Why, I can see from here to heaven."

The game plan didn't come from Libby, as she imagined. It came from Mary Hanks and was issued at about seventy-five long-distance decibels.

"Mom, you're shouting. Jeez, calm down."

"You bet I'm shouting, and it's high time somebody in this family did. Laydelle, this is unconscionable. What do you mean, John Singleton turned you down for a loan? Hair Apparent was a terrific scheme."

"I mean that he turned me down. He asked me what I proposed to use as collateral and then told me no. And then Daddy told me that I lost fair and square."

"Don't tell me he dusted off the River Piss Address in honor of your latest difficulty."

"But that's exactly what he did."

"Typical. It's a wonder I stayed married to him as long as I did."

"Put down your rifle, Mom."

"Right; my marriage isn't the issue. The issue as I see it . . ."

The long pause didn't mean hesitation; it meant Mary was steaming ahead, forging a plan.

"Hey, I'm your daughter, not one of your clients."

"Is that a complaint? Because if it is, you'd better have your head examined. People pay me to do what I'm about to do for you."

"Which is?"

"Show you how to wring fortune from misfortune, which is what my business is all about, among other things. Here's our first move."

If Hubbell was predictable, his ex-wife was, too. Laydelle could hear the fingers snapping, see the light behind her mother's eyes as ideas began to ignite and catch more swiftly than dry kindling on a forest floor.

"You phone the *Trib.*"

"Mom!"

"You phone that woman who's been stapled to the city desk for years, and you suggest lunch. Don't tell her anything over the phone. That's always a big mistake, by the way. So much energy is lost. Most stories are wasted, just ruined, on the telephone. You take her to lunch and let your story slip, as if you hadn't intended to say that much."

"What story?"

"Dense. I swear that sometimes you are every bit as dense as your father. YOUR STORY—what do you think we're talking about here? The story of the granddaughter of good old Nelson Hanks, not down-and-out yet but certainly moving that way fast. I'll spell it out for you, Baby. The bank that once loaned money to outlaws and desperadoes, that Nelson Hanks created in Lovely way back when, is now refusing a loan to the granddaughter of the founding father. Wait until they sink their teeth into that! The paper will eat it up, I promise, and Singleton will phone you, begging for your business. Pinsky, Bellini and Swartzberg—are they clean?"

"What do you mean, are they clean?"

"Am I on some kind of game show? I mean it. I ask a simple question, and all I get back is another question. I mean do they have records or anything? Bad business records, criminal records, anything like that."

"You, too. I can't believe it. Singleton implied the same thing."

"Well?"

"Well, I don't know."

"Get to work. If they check out okay, then strike. And check the dates before you go in to see whatshername. Way back when won't work; you'll need the exact date he opened the bank in Lovely. Read up on it. Brush the thing in with plenty of local color. And spare nothing when it comes to your story, by the way. Tell her how you live. You know, how tight things are just now. How modest your life is."

"I wouldn't call it modest."

"I'd call it crappy, but modest will work as a euphemism. Enough on that for now. How do you feel?"

"As if I'd like to lie down and never get back up."

"Ah, just as I thought. It's a very typical response, believe it or not. I see it in my clients all the time. They come in whipped by the world. Just when you need to be standing on the absolute tips of your toes, your body wants to sink down into something soft. Well, not as long as I'm around you won't. Up and at 'em, Laydelle. I mean it. Don't suppose for one moment I'm going to just give out advice and let it go at that. I expect progress reports. I expect momentum. How do you stand on cash, Baby?"

"Reserves are a bit low at the moment."

"I'll wire you something this afternoon."

"Thanks, Mom."

"You don't have to thank me. Just do what I say. John Singleton, how dare he deny you a loan? He was in our house on at least nine occasions."

The phone was muffled. By the palm of her hand? The top of her breast, the way she'd always done it when Laydelle was growing up? She must have been talking to her assistant. She was slightly out of breath when she spoke next.

"You won't believe it. *Kenzo is here again! In person!* Not his pipsqueak spokesman, but the honest-to-God Kenzo himself! Can you believe it, Laydelle? *I am pulling this thing off!* Getaway Gear. It's real, it's real!"

She hung up before her daughter could respond. Laydelle reviewed Mary's latest coup, a perfect example of her mother's strong suit—swinging a bad situation around until it looked good. Not just good but goddamned great. The designer (some said it was after too many mediocre seasons) had come up with a new line of resort wear, and Mary Hanks Alternative Promotion had just submitted the quirkiest testimony the Kenzo people had ever heard. When singer/actress/model Lolly Pop had come dragging up the stairs of Hanks Promotion after a scary encounter on Cahuenga Boulevard, Mary listened hard.

"Could you repeat that, Lolly? Slower and take out the gum, sweetness."

"I said he tried to capture me, or . . . well, I don't know what he tried to do. He was grabbing me like he wanted to hold on bad. All I know is, Ms. Hanks, I ran like hell."

"Yes, love. But according to what you just said, you would have failed to run like hell had it not been for that little skirt you're squeezed into."

"Right. Like this. I went like this."

Lolly Pop reached for one of the silver rings at the hem of her skirt and yanked it up as far as it would go. She did the same on the other side and, legs free, demonstrated the long stride that had carried her to freedom. The former high school track star easily outran her aggressor. Easy enough to do in Kenzo Getaway Gear. Mary thought of the photographs she'd just seen of Kenzo's home in Paris. Perhaps a visit to that city was in order.

"You don't by any chance speak French, now do you, Lolly?"

"I can read French menus. And I love Julio Iglesias."

"Never mind, love. Now I want you to sit down and let me think for a minute."

"But we were going to go over my contract, Ms. Hanks."

"Something tells me we're going to write up a brand-new contract, Lolly."

Getaway Gear. But where would she, Laydelle Hanks, get away

to next? She'd already been to more places than she could count. Laydelle leaned back into a pillow propped up on the arm of the motel sofa bed. She closed her eyes. It would be okay to close them just for a minute.

chapter 12

1988

She hid her mother's red Chevrolet in a residential section of Beverly Hills, backing in carefully behind a station wagon parked on Cañon Drive. She saw a new dimple on the hood, as if the car wasn't already bad enough. She studied the parking sign and couldn't understand it. Was a permit required or wasn't it? She snapped her purse shut and let her arm slouch comfortably between the strap and the top of the bag, then set off. She talked to herself a bit on the way in, but it didn't help. She felt worse, not better, the closer she got to all those stores and, particularly, Rodeo Drive. *You look fabulous. Don't be idiotic. Look at these women . . . you're doing just fine.*

She forced herself to stroll, to look casual, as if at any moment she could wheel into one of these stores and pick out a little something on impulse. *Quit stalking. You're not walking through a pasture.* Laydelle saw herself pass in the store windows and *did* think that was someone pretty. An insider/outsider, someone interesting, someone quirky. Someone to definitely have lunch with. Those thoughts didn't stick, however. To boost her spirits, she tried reviewing her two days in Orange County. The sales conference, those two days spent in Newport Beach, had been so intense, even the most skeptical members of the Pedigree sales force were converted. Bludgeoned by two solid days of information on the horrors of theft and break-in, given round after round of national statistics, Laydelle wasn't primed to sell her clients. She was ready to deliver them from evil. But that was Newport Beach, where a grove of palm trees rose like sentinels beside the Sheraton to protect and keep her. This was Beverly Hills. She eavesdropped in earnest as she walked. This was Beverly Hills, where English was a second, cumbersome language. She was quaking by the time she reached the front door of Van Cleef & Arpels. The entrance looked like a steel trap.

To spur herself on, she thought, not of baubles and bangles, but of bills. The bills on her desk had turned into threats, and collection agencies, three different ones, were leaving messages on her answering machine. Pedigree offered a solid future, if she could figure out how to survive the present.

She pressed a button, and the first door opened. Then she found herself outside a concave set of iron doors. A security guard, not a smiling salesperson, came forward and opened the doors.

"Afternoon."

"Hello."

The foyer was filled with three massive desks, heaped high with papers and brochures but unoccupied for the moment. Laydelle, still gripping her purse, moved past the desks and into one of the showrooms. The air of a flute filled the air.

"Rampal. Nice."

"No, it's Beaureve. And you are . . . ?"

She turned fast, snagging her heel on the thick carpet as she did, and almost stumbled. She hadn't seen or heard a soul as yet, and the man's voice startled her. She'd thought she was alone in the room and was talking out loud, as usual. The man who spoke made her choke up slightly, as if someone had just put his hands around her throat. She was already blushing, but seeing him made it that much worse. He was sitting down amiably, his legs crossed at the knee, in a chair beside still another desk. He took off a pair of sunglasses slowly. Laydelle cleared her throat. She hadn't counted on meeting anyone. She was on a mission, and this was no time for fun and games.

"Are there any salespeople here? Or is the place just staffed with security guards."

"You didn't answer my question."

"I'm not sure I need to."

She pretended to look at jewelry. Pieces were displayed in isolation, every ring, every diamond collar, demanding its own low-lighted exhibit. Between showcases were photographs and text. THE DUKE AND DUCHESS OF WINDSOR, PHOTOGRAPHED AT A BALL IN THE 1930s. *Ruby and diamond clip by Van Cleef & Arpels.* Her courage was draining away, nearly gone. She forgot her own text, which she had rehearsed on her way in from Newport.

"I think I recognize that drawl."

He kept breaking in. She'd play for a minute or two, since he was so insistent. It would loosen her up until a salesperson came in. *Would* a salesperson come in, so she could just get on with it? She wandered over to where he was sitting and settled her own sunglasses on top of her head. He came into focus as she moved closer. An arrogant, gorgeous man. She noticed the long, thick braid of black hair, and she thought how lovely, then laughed, realizing she could never get free of that place. He was either quite tanned or—

"What's so funny?"

"Nothing. Okay, so my name is Laydelle."

"Do you have another name, Laydelle? Or is that all you're going to tell me right now?"

"That's all for now. Seriously, where is everybody in this joint?"

"You must be in a terrible hurry to buy something."

It was either feast or famine. Three women arrived simultaneously, one quite aflutter at discovering another person in the store. It was a bit like uncovering mice leavings in a corner of the kitchen.

"I had no idea! Why, how horrible. How long have you been here, my dear?"

"Oh, just a few minutes. I've been browsing."

"Now, how might I help you?"

She was led to a desk back near the entrance of the shop. It was over, her fear and her embarrassment. This was a woman on a salary or, worse, on commission. A woman like herself. Laydelle let down her guard.

"You can help me. My name is Laydelle Hanks, and I'm from Tulsa, Oklahoma."

"How nice. Here you are in Beverly Hills, and you decided to pay us a visit. Why, I've never been to Oklahoma, but I hear it's quite pleasant. May I show you something, my dear?"

She probably had a daughter in college. She was probably strug-

gling with bills scarier than Laydelle's own. There was a long
moment in which Laydelle wanted to cry. She wanted to confess
that a terrible car was parked outside, so terrible she was too
embarrassed to drive it into a Beverly Hills lot. She wanted to
confide that she had a mother doing very well for herself, in this
very city, even though her daughter wasn't. The saleswoman
hadn't had a facelift. Her forehead was filled with fine lines that
mapped out an entire life she had decided not to abandon with
cosmetic surgery. She wore a very smart sports jacket and sensible
shoes.

"No, but there is something *I* would like to show *you.*"

She reached deep into her bag and drew out a little black jewelry
box. The box was ancient; even the material on top was rubbed
thin.

"This ring belonged to my grandmother, Mrs. Nelson Hanks."

"Ah, I see."

The long pause contained many things. She certainly did see,
even though she was reaching for bifocals on a long velvet cord
draped around her neck. Her voice took on a new tone. Now she
held the reins, not Laydelle.

"And the ridiculous thing is that this wonderful ring just sits in a
security bank vault. I don't wear jewelry, and after all this time, I
thought I'd finally let it go. Perhaps Van Cleef might be interested."

"We're always open to offers. Now, if I could just take a look."

Laydelle took a deep breath. Thank God she hadn't confided in
her. She was so vulnerable, so stupid about things. This woman
was all business. Maybe she had a daughter, but if so, that daughter was standing on her own two feet by now.

"Just before you came, I had some time to look around. The
photographs on the wall certainly indicate Van Cleef is no ordinary
firm. The archive in Paris must be something very special indeed."

The woman had begun to drum her fingers on the desk.

"I wonder if the history of this ring would enhance its value, for
it does have a history. It certainly has a story to tell."

Brief visions, words whispered, then gone—memory was lately
her most persistent affliction. Laydelle saw her grandfather enter
the New York Van Cleef store and eye the crown once belonging
to Empress Josephine, as Joey Fujii helped him out of his coat. He
was more intent than ever on making his wife a gift fit for a queen.
A gift Lavinia Hanks would use and abuse for the rest of her life,

lifting the ring from her hand to silence others, to illustrate her own position and power.

"You see, my grandfather was quite a character."

The woman was expressionless, but she had at least stopped rapping her nails on the top of her desk. Laydelle plunged ahead.

"It happened that the day he visited your New York store, he bumped into another oil man from Oklahoma. A man named Marland. Both men were showmen. They also had rather fabulous tempers and . . ."

They slapped backs, swapped stories, then circled the showroom with a prickly awareness, not of "invisible" settings and pavé diamonds, cabochon sapphires and Burma rubies, but of mighty competition and a fresh setting for the tourney. Hanks and Marland had established an uneasy truce, which had teetered as Marland became more and more extravagant, installing a third kitchen in his two-million-dollar mansion. A third kitchen and fifteen bathrooms made the elevator in Nelson's house look like a puny achievement indeed. Their truce had all but ended after Marland's wife died. And after Marland married the twenty-eight-year-old niece of his dead wife when he himself was fifty-four. Even Nelson was scandalized. The two oil men locked horns not in the Osage fields but in a showroom in New York City. Parts of that conversation became family legend. Their words floated back to Laydelle, as she laid moist palms on the top of her skirt.

"And is Lydie well?"

They stood in front of the display case, with their legs spread apart. Both men held their hands behind their backs. They had come to rest before a ring that held a two-carat oval Burma ruby surrounded by marquise and pear-shaped diamonds. The setting was in platinum.

"Lydie is very well. And Lavinia?"

"She's having a time with her feet. They swell up to the size of viola cases once it gets hot. Otherwise fine, though. I thought a trinket from this place would cheer her."

"Seems we're out to accomplish the same thing, Nelson. The truth is, Lydie's feeling a bit blue."

"I expect it must get lonesome way out there."

"No, I don't think it's loneliness. I believe it's all the foolish talk."

When Nelson signaled for the store manager, the ante went up.

It began politely but didn't stay that way. The story of the bidding war amused the saleswoman, Laydelle saw. Her professional demeanor slipped a little as she listened.

"My father tells me things got really out of control. After all, these were businessmen, and they had bid on oil leases in the same way. Since there was only one ring in the store that day and both men had to have it, they tried to outbid each other."

"I can't imagine such a thing. Why, Van Cleef and Arpels would never allow that sort of thing to happen."

"Van Cleef and Arpels never had a chance to intervene. It quickly turned into a circus. They had spectators, people who just drifted in to see what all the commotion was about. They doubled the price of the ring, and it just kept going. It was crazy! Finally . . ."

Outdone, Marland sank into a chair. Personal debt had him throttled, and his inevitable downfall seemed more real to him that day in 1929 than on any other day that followed. Nelson had won the ring and even the final contest, the amusing gesture that turned up in the papers the following day. *Nelson Hanks, Oklahoma oil man and banker, has a notorious fondness for spectacle. Some say the businessman nurtures a sentimental fondness for the three-ring circus. But, Mr. Hanks, our shop is no tawdry Barnum and Bailey! E. W. Marland and Nelson Hanks enjoyed a showdown in the luxurious Van Cleef & Arpels fine jewelry store yesterday. The two rowdy oil men drew from their jackets not pistols, to fire upon each other, but checkbooks! The vying businessmen went so far as to disclose the state of their personal accounts. Observers tell our bureau the men wished to see who was the richest of the two. We have reached new levels of vulgar flagrance in the city!*

"Finally the ring was purchased for my grandmother, but there was such an uproar. This very ring. Just think of it."

She did, and that brought her to her senses.

"Miss Hanks, as much as I have enjoyed your stories—and believe me I have—I'm afraid they don't pertain to our business today. I'll confide in you."

"Oh, please do!"

Hope sprang back up. Maybe she could pull it off. Laydelle folded her hands together and tried to relax.

"You see, customers don't care about the history of the jewelry they buy. A customer of mine, a very important customer, once brought this point home. I described a piece that had once hung round the neck of a Hapsburg princess, and, Miss Hanks, she couldn't have been less interested. Our customers want the right style for the right price. Your colorful stories, unfortunately, will not affect the Van Cleef decision one iota. And in fact, I don't think . . ."

She opened a drawer and took out a jeweler's lens. She fit it over her eye and looked down at the ring.

"We would naturally have to disassemble it, and with the sort of setting your grandmother's ring has, the cost would not be minimal. Then there is simply market value to consider, my dear. Pure market value. We would choose either to sell off the stones or—"

"What a magnificent ring."

He had ambled into the room behind her. It was the second time she had failed to see or hear him.

"Please pardon me for eavesdropping, but I couldn't help it. I've read about that adventure. In the twenties, wasn't it?" Beaureve rubbed his chin and smiled. "I happen to know a great deal about the Hanks family. May I see this ring, please?"

The doorbell buzzed, and several people entered at once. They were left to their own means, however. For the moment, all eyes were on Johnny Beaureve, now slipping the ring on Laydelle's finger.

"Do you mind? The lady I'm shopping for resembles you."

She stood up, not sure if he was putting on her or them. The staff was both poised and posed, ready for any move Beaureve might make. Laydelle wondered if he was one of those important customers just referred to. She wondered what lady he was shopping for and if she really looked like her. She heard his accent now, subtler than her own, as if it had been tempered either by education or by exposure to other places. Laydelle had a drawl. His soft, slow diction meted out words, making each one careful and considered. One side of his mouth turned up slightly, and he pointed at a necklace in the front room.

"I'll take that today, and I want one of you to get back to me with a price on this ring. You'll have to fax me in France. Our French postal system is erratic, I'm afraid."

Laydelle turned to look at her saleswoman, still seated.

"Unless you prefer I deal directly with the young lady."

"No, of course not. Harriet, you've taken all the information we need?"

"Yes, Mrs. Harms."

"Fine."

They busied themselves with papers. Mrs. Harms left the room, excusing herself as she did. He winked at Laydelle as the necklace was being removed from the case. Was this a coup? If so, for whom? Did he really have an interest in her grandmother's ring? Laydelle was throbbing. All of her, not unpleasantly, seemed to have acquired a pulse, and she was beating, beating. God, was it really going to work? It was over; she would never find out what it meant. He had a shopping bag in his hand and his sunglasses on, and that braid was swinging carelessly down his long back. He turned right on the sidewalk and was gone. Mrs. Harms had returned.

"We can offer you five thousand for the piece, Miss Hanks."

"But that man is going to buy it for much more! Surely not less. He just walked out of here with a necklace at . . . well, I don't know how much. But five! Mrs. Harms, that's not even a fraction of what my grandfather paid."

"I know that. I've checked the registration number. Miss Hanks, may I advise you?"

Laydelle bit the inside of her lip. Why not? Why the hell not let her advise me, screw me, help me? *You're in a jam, baby.* Her answering machine had coughed that up just last week.

"Take the money and run. I don't think our Mr. Beaureve will be back for your ring, but he's put me in a bad position, and our New York office has instructed me to make an offer. Now what do you say?"

"May I buy you a drink?"

He was sitting on a low wall a block down from the store, the shopping bag from Van Cleef & Arpels impossibly dangling from his hand.

"Anybody could just up and grab that. I don't think you should just amble around with something so valuable. I think I should be the one buying the drink."

She fought down self-consciousness as they went into a restaurant and took their place at the bar. Heads turned their way, and she began to really see who she was with. A profile like that belonged on a coin, she thought. She tried to keep her hands from waving around in the air as she talked. He was perfectly still.

Everything about him seemed graceful and composed. He asked if she liked champagne, then ordered a bottle.

"Wait a minute. I'll never make it out of here."

"We have cause for celebration. They bought your grandmother's ring, didn't they?"

"They sure did. How can I thank you?"

"By accepting a glass or two of champagne."

"This is a first. I don't ordinarily talk to strangers."

"We're not strangers. If I'm not mistaken, we both go all the way back to Lovely, in very different ways."

"I thought you lived in France. Beaureve . . . that's a French name, isn't it?"

"It is. One that the Osage appropriated. I live in France. I also live in Oklahoma. It's a long story."

"Tell me. I love long stories."

Beaureve was an aristocrat. He had remained eerily true to certain traditions, recasting them as fit his needs, occupying whatever chambers caught his fancy in that long and rambling manse of Osage memory. His lineage led him back to France, but once there, Beaureve was a free man. His ancestors had been infiltrated by French trappers and traders. They had taken Osage brides and then used Jesuit priests to pierce them with Catholicism. Beaureve was of this thing and of another. His grandfather, pockets full of oil money, abandoned Lovely to buy land in San Diego. Other Osage scoffed and asked if he was going to grow lemons and oranges. But Beaureve's grandfather had no intention of farming. He had an aversion to tilling the soil. When he heard of an Indian uprising on the plains, how they'd taken a U.S. general's stiffened body and run it across the ground like a plow, he took this as a lesson. No, Beaureve's grandfather lived peaceably on his acreage in the county behind San Diego, content to let his dogs run and his quarterly payments stack up. That land parcel was passed on to Johnny. Subdividing it at a time when land prices soared gave Beaureve his present comfortable life. There was by now the farm in Saint-Tropez, where he hired laborers to work the vineyard, leaving him free to preside over wine tastings in town. There was his apartment on the Place des Vosges, crammed with books and papers written when he was a student at the Sorbonne. He often lunched in a café below his rooms, filled with architects and artists come to admire the sober, classic lines of the promenade.

"So let me get this straight. You studied art at the Sorbonne. You run a vineyard in France and a ranch in Lovely."

"You look alarmed."

"I guess I am. It's a pretty wild combination."

Seen from above, the Lovely land was split by timber into four strips, like fingers on a splayed hand. Most people thought the ranch was Beaureve's folly. He had few admirers in town. The Osage who remained found his arrogance mismatched with their own, calling him Mr. Sweetdream in honor of his revolving sports cars (he couldn't seem to hold on to the same one for more than a year), his fine flatbed Ford and Chevrolet trucks. His invidious life especially excited them when they considered Johnny's string of crossbred hounds. The light-eyed animals trailed him in a pack, their tails tucked between their legs. They wondered but didn't ask how in hell he got a wolf to mount a malamute, and not knowing only increased their spleen. They didn't disguise their delight when he received one too many speeding tickets and had his license revoked. Or when somebody officially registered a complaint about one of his hounds, whose howls up on the moonlit grounds kept the man's babies and mother-in-law awake long past what was a decent hour. Beaureve returned to Lovely for his own pleasure and at his own risk. There were plenty of men who wouldn't have minded his disappearance the slightest bit.

"Then in your spare time you picked up another degree. So that now you're a lawyer who doesn't practice law."

"I practice law all the time. I just don't have an office."

His eloquence at tribal council meetings miffed other members of the tribe. When he spoke, he crooned. He sized up the state of Osage affairs in a minute, cutting through specious arguments. The college boy's boredom was clear as he crossed and recrossed his legs while the elders aired their view of things. He declined running for office, only bursting in on things long enough to stir people up. That was Johnny Beaureve.

She fingered the rim of the glass. The champagne had gone down very easily.

"Sorry for interrogating you."

"I'll forgive you as long as I get a turn."

"Fine with me."

"What do you do when you're not trying to hock heirloom jewelry?"

"I'm in the security business."

"Banking?"

"Home security. Pedigree Protection Service. You can't say you haven't heard of us. We're the oldest and largest group around."

She paused and took a long drink. Well, why not mix business with pleasure? She started the pitch, the story of Dr. Eidenhour, his liaison with Thomas Edison, all the facts about the home security business worth knowing.

"So you're telling me that you consider yourself kind of a blue-blooded outfit. I mean, if the company founder started his research in the early 1900s, it makes all these other, upstart operations kind of sleazy by comparison. Doesn't it?"

"Mr. Beaureve, I believe you're pulling my leg."

"Just trying to keep the facts straight. Your life is as confusing as mine. If I'm being too intrusive, let me know."

"Go on."

"Why do you bother to work at all? After all, your grandfather is Nelson Hanks."

She burst out laughing and put her hand across her mouth. It didn't help. She had a wild, raucous laugh, and several people turned to stare. The more she drank, the longer Johnny Beaureve sat next to her, the more indistinct her surroundings became. They were pale and fine as a pen-and-ink drawing now, colored only by a wash of faint color.

"I bother to work so I don't wind up in jail. Daily bread, Mr. Beaureve. I work so I can live. Everybody has to have a formula, and that's mine."

It was five o'clock, and the place was packed. Music played here, too, but it wasn't Rampal. Laydelle and Johnny had nearly finished their bottle of champagne. She never let the sack out of her sight, though he did. She wondered how he could be so blasé and didn't know if she liked him more for that or less. She decided his eyes weren't brown but black. A bit of champagne slapped over the edge of her glass. What the hell.

"So is the trinket for your mom, Mr. Beaureve?"

He shook his head.

"Are you married?"

"No."

"Are you planning to marry?"

"No."

"That's an awfully special gift."

"I like nice things."

They were quiet for a few moments, completely free of each other in private respective worlds, but comfortably so. He was the first to talk.

"Part of a philosophy I have."

"What? Sorry, go on."

"About things. I think beautiful things give off beauty. If we can manage to live with wonderful things, it's the happiest circumstance of all. We become as mean or as magnificent as the things we touch and see and smell every day."

"So you think beauty can be transmitted. We're only as good as what we live with, is that it?"

"Exactly."

"How about if somebody lives in a real dump?"

He raised his eyebrows slightly and shrugged. "Then somebody ought to think about moving. Ready to go?"

They were moving against the current, golden fish struggling upstream. People streamed out of banks and boutiques, heading for parking lots and lively, life-giving bars and cafés. There was a universal prettiness at this hour, and Laydelle shared it. They stood shoulder-to-shoulder; she felt the knock of his bone against hers and was pleased. She wondered if he slept with his hair undone. She wondered what it would be like to be all tangled up in that dark curtain. She'd never been with a man like Johnny Beaureve. They turned on Cañon Drive, and she began to thank him.

"Johnny, were you ever really interested in the ring?"

"Not at all."

"Why'd you go to so much trouble?"

"It amused me, and it wasn't all that much trouble."

"Well, you saved my neck. You don't know how much was riding on that transaction."

They walked along a few more paces, then she stopped and stuck out her hand.

"Don't think you can get rid of me so fast."

"I'm parked way up there. I'll be fine. No one gets hurt in Beverly Hills."

"Don't be silly."

She was glad to be full of champagne and about to start something. She wanted the men in her life to become man, and maybe, despite that gift and that girl somewhere, the man would be Johnny Beaureve. She was initiated, and that girl wasn't. Lovely was under her skin, it ran in her veins the same way it did in his, and though she knew nothing about the man walking next to her, she knew everything. Her rising excitement tapered off and leveled when she saw her mother's car at the end of the block. It looked like a crushed and injured animal. The blackened tailpipe dangled like a damaged tail. She walked faster without knowing it.

"We're kind of related, you know."

He didn't answer.

"My grandfather was an honorary Osage. I guess that makes me sort of an Osage, too."

"Those things aren't automatically passed on. You're nothing at all unless you claim it."

They were cantering, really striding along now. He didn't seem to think it odd. They had almost reached her car. She began to wonder how she would make her way back to her mother's place after all she'd had to drink.

"Does this run?"

He looked like the Fourth of July to her, the angel on top of the tree. Every good thing was shining in his face. Had her luck changed, finally? Maybe you had to exhaust the bad, she decided. Bad faith, bad men, bad luck. Maybe you just had to empty out the place where these things had been, so good things could occupy the space.

"It crossed the desert. It came all the way here from Oklahoma on my mother's maiden voyage, and she refuses to sell it. She's very superstitious. The thing is like an amulet."

"It could stand a new roof."

"Uh uh. She won't touch it."

Pick me up. Don't bother hugging and kissing me. Just pick me up and take me home, please. If he believed in transmitting beauty, she believed in transmitting thoughts, mental messages that would mean happily ever after if he would just pay attention.

"I've had quite a lot to drink, but . . ."

Johnny Beaureve kept his hands to himself. Marvelously, she thought, he just stood there watching her. For it was a marvel that he could keep from touching her after all that had happened. Why weren't his hands in her hair, his cheek pressing hers? Why was she standing with one hand on the car door, about to leave him?

"Go on, Laydelle. I'm listening."

But nothing. She backed down and opened the creaky door of her mother's Chevy. The front seat was littered with paper and pamphlets from Pedigree Protection.

"But I think I can make it back to my mother's place just fine."

She checked the rearview mirror in disbelief when she got to the stop sign. She couldn't believe Johnny Beaureve had let her fly away. She couldn't believe she had flown.

~~Nelson and Lavinia~~

chapter 13

1905

"Ugh. The transformation is complete, and right before my eyes, too."

"Is this a private joke, Lavinia?"

"Do you see me laughing? Barber, oil man, now—presto—a banker. If I'd wanted to marry my own daddy, guess I would have done it. You've even started to *look* like him."

She knew nothing could sabotage Nelson Hanks now. So she laid all his former costumes on the big, wide bed to taunt him. It was his first day at the bank. The striped pants she'd hidden away for all these years, next the red bandanna and Stetson he wore in the fields, even the mucky boots that would never go clean again.

"I've been just one Lavinia all these years. Why can't you be just one Nelson?"

"I'm the very same man you married."

He turned and looked at his own conservative image in the mirror.

"This is business and nothing more."

"I lived with a tally sheet for years. All those years I spent sewing at Daddy's knee while he held forth on business and banking theory."

"I'm an oil man, Vinnie. And I can't grow if they won't finance my operations. Banks court cattlemen, not wildcatters like me. Nobody sees the bigger picture."

"Can we move a cot into your office?"

"Catnaps make me groggy."

"The cot is for your dearly beloved. I don't see you as it is, and I wonder if I'll ever, ever see you again now that you've gone and opened a *bank*."

It sounded like a curse the way she said it, and maybe it was. It wasn't the clothing strung out all over the bed that worried him; it was the sight of his wife's arms folded and closed over her chest. Since the opening of the Jane Anderson, he had grown properly superstitious. Lavinia's instincts were paramount since the well had blown open. Her intuition was the charm around his neck. If her gaze fell darkly upon the bank, perhaps he'd best think twice.

"What's wrong, Nelson?"

"You spend an hour lambasting me, and then you ask me what's wrong. Well, my dear, you've given me a pain in the gut."

He sat down on the crowded bed and realized how ill he felt, as if he'd eaten something rancid. Lavinia did an about-face, marching to the medicine cabinet. She grew almost solicitous, even though the sight of him in this banker's monkey suit galled her.

"Do you know how many people want me to fail? I can't understand it. They applaud the Jane Anderson and the run of good luck that followed. Their arguments are all the same. 'It looks like nothing is good enough for Nelson.' 'That Hanks is sure pushing his luck. Nibbling on his own tail like a dog.' "

"Oh, shush. Here, drink this to settle your stomach. If you think I'm going to apologize, you're dead wrong. You're about to open the doors on a two-story building at the corner of the busiest intersection in Indian Territory. Nobody has ever seen such an opulent bank. Philippine mahogany from Daddy's sacred lumber mills and marble countertops, for heaven's sake. Are you going to let yourself be stopped by a few competitors?"

"These people aren't my competitors."

"The hell they're not. You're naive and you always will be. The same thing happened to Daddy in Creston. Other bankers paid people to disappear that first day he started out, and believe me, their pockets were deep. They stayed gone for the longest time, but nothing could deter my father. Are you going to let these people give you the jitters? They won't stand in your way any more than a fussy, shortsighted woman would."

Nelson thought of the story he'd heard on the Katy train years ago. A true one, it was sworn, about a man who stood out in the field with his team, the sun shining so hot that one of his horses collapsed and died. As the farmer removed the harness from the dead horse, the wind direction shifted to the north. By the time he'd finished his work, his remaining horse was frozen stiff. Nelson's wife had become a real child of the Territory, fickle as weather.

"Whose side are you on, Vinnie?"

"Your side. I get to missing you is all."

She sat down heavily beside him, slightly out of breath.

"Sometimes I think neither of us knows half of what's on the way. And I have the awful sense that our best time is behind us. In that wild place beside the creek or in that little hotel with a rope ladder for a fire escape and a dead man in the garden. Our best time could even have been there. Nelson, I've had myself another dream. Not a dream, but a view. This time it's a dilly."

Fear hit him at the back of the neck. Or anticipation. It turned cold there suddenly and spread all the way down his back.

"You got yourself an entire town somehow. Not that it was named Nelsontown or Hanksville. No, nothing that foolish. But you were raised up over this feudal city—"

"Say what?"

"Feudal, Nelson. Like you were a lord or something. Don't worry, you weren't dressed like one. In fact, you were covered with grime. But the point was, everything and everyone belonged to you."

"What a delightful dream."

"View. Only it wasn't. It wasn't the least bit delightful, Nelson. I woke up feverish and panting like a hound."

She looked at the clock.

"Is your stomach better now?"

"Slightly."

"Good. Let's get you a hot breakfast. You'll need it. There were thirty-odd assembled on the sidewalk by seven-thirty."

"How do you know?"

"My milkman is worse than a telegraph wire."

"Thirty?"

"Odd."

And they were odd, Nelson thought, squinting as he approached the bank. It seemed to him they had marched straight in from the oil field, and he didn't frown as they traipsed through his elegant lobby all morning long, tracking his Persian carpets up, and plunked down pay in front of tellers' windows. Some of them used his brass spittoons, and others didn't bother. There were all kinds of surprises that first morning. Citizens lined up who never much held with the idea of putting money in a bank. But they'd seen Nelson at one well or another. They'd seen him tired and soiled as the most common roustabout. Howard Sims waited in line and heard talk of a pay telephone located on the second story, smack in front of the president's office. He set down his paycheck, made his way upstairs and, disconcerted, told the operator he didn't know anybody with a telephone but would she mind talking to him until his five minutes was up. She guessed she wouldn't, and at the end of those five minutes, she even agreed to have supper with Howard Sims at the Lovely Café. Some Indians came over toward noon, and not just a few. Nelson was working the second window himself, and he wondered if his bank passed inspection. The delegation circled the lobby, running their hands over the polished marble. They counted openly: vaults, teller windows, brass light fixtures.

"Good afternoon, Mr. Bigheart. Help you, sir?"

The chief's campaign was wearing him down. Washington senators and journalists, Bigheart was convinced, sucked the air from his lungs. Bigheart had spent everything, spoken away his long and entire life. Though still imperious, he had become a trembly old man, a bone-china chief, since Washington. He began to hear Nelson's question, though it had been asked some time before.

"Presidents should not sit in cages."

"And chiefs should not stand in lobbies. Will you join me upstairs, sir?"

They abandoned the delegation, the dogs growling at mirrors, and the delicate, drooping ferns. Bigheart sighed as he entered.

"This is good. Now I am not hearing my feet."

Nelson saw he meant the deep carpets. He made a quick note and watched as the chief straightened. Bigheart said that they should eat.

"Sir, if I may . . ."

The Osage chief watched, nodding his approval, as the president opened a hole in the wall. Nelson leaned way inside, fiddling with the dumbwaiter and the pulleys.

"The maiden voyage. I'm delighted, *delighted*, that my first lun-

cheon guest is Chief James Bigheart. Let's see now, I'll ring up
Rosie with our lunch order. I could do with some good, crisp fried
chicken and mashed . . .''

Bigheart stared out the window.

"We'll just have ourselves some beef and beans. I hope fried
bread strikes your fancy."

As they ate, the chief spoke of divisive young men, saying how
they would lead to his personal downfall. He caught what was left
on his plate between the edges of bread and felt stronger. The chief
asked for coffee and mentioned a camper's pie he had once tasted,
made with peaches and sugar, beef fat, he thought. Sunlight fell
through the windows, and Bigheart stroked the tops of his long
legs, which recently ached so much it seemed to him he had walked
all the way to the capital. When Lavinia's daybed arrived, the chief
grunted his approval, marched toward it on wobbly legs. The de-
liverymen stuck cigarettes between their lips and grinned at the
sight of an Indian chief suddenly stretched out and snoring.

"Beats all, don't it? Sign here, Mr. Hanks. Lee, set the package
down on top of the desk. Oh, card from your wife, sir."

Nelson signed and shook his head, drowsy himself with the
heavy meal. The chief rustled slightly in his sleep, muttered a few
syllables and drew his knees suddenly to his chest. Nelson read the
card aloud after the men had gone.

"Dear Nelson,

Look here. I told you way back in Creston I didn't intend to be left
alone, and that's just what I meant. Whether I wind up on this
daybed or not is beside the point. The pharaohs loved symbols,
and I guess I do, too. Even if it's not the actual me curled up next
to your desk when you're working, why, the other me, the invisible
one, will be. Just like she has been since Iowa. Please don't scoff at
this note. I feel things.

Your loving Vinnie

P.S. Open up the package. It should 'man' things up."

The package contained a buckskin throw, soft as butter. Nelson let
his hands just rest on it for a minute as he wondered what to think
of next. The honorable napper, who so far, despite the grand reception, had not uttered a word about his tribe's business transactions? His wife's sentiments, or the continuing traffic, which he

could see from his window and hear beneath his feet, even though the carpet had been chosen to muffle the buzzing below? No, attention would now turn to the frantic knocking on his door.

"Sssss. Sss. Mi-mister . . ."

"Yes; what is it?"

"It's-it's . . . sss."

Impossible. He saw it would be the stuttering clerk's first and last day. The man changed colors in his frustration. Marks like red fingers appeared around his neck. The chief gulped and choked slightly, though he slept on.

"Sing it, Mr. Clary. Try singing what's on your mind."

The clerk pulled on his sleeves and sang his message. He had a surprisingly clear voice.

"Mr. Hanks, there is someone downstairs I think you should see."

He paused, staring down at his hands.

"He wants a loan."

"Wonderful. What's his work?"

"An outlaw, sir. An outlaw, sir."

The clerk's voice rose in a slight trill at the end.

"Get his name?"

"Henry Starr."

"Well, it's high time. You have a splendid voice. A warbler like you should be in a quartet. Tell Mr. Starr I'll be right with him."

"A half-breed Cherokee, sir. Parker's sentenced him tw-tw-twice!"

"Does our half-breed outlaw have someone to go the note with him?"

"He's shot and *killed*, Mr. Hanks."

The song had turned miraculously to plain speech.

"Then we'd best not rile him. I'm a banker, Clary. And money is money. Shall we go downstairs and greet Mr. Starr?"

"Why, if you say so, sir. Mr. Hanks, what did you mean when you said it was high time?"

"Just what I said. I knew of the boy's aunt and admired her. Now let's get to work, shall we?"

Nelson draped the buckskin throw over James Bigheart, whose struggles had subsided. A smile flashed over his face, and he chewed in his sleep. Then Nelson stepped over to his young clerk, intelligible though still round-eyed, and moved downstairs to write up his first set of loan papers.

chapter 14

The *Police Gazette* had disseminated manners and morals for over forty years; underneath the stories lay a strict format for manhood. The *Gazette* claimed it was appropriate to knock a man down when he said anything more profane than "shucks" in the presence of a lady. A man who cheated at cards deserved to "be shot down like a dog," and a gentleman walking his lady ought always to walk nearest the curb so that tobacco spat toward the gutter wouldn't sully her bow. Finer points of etiquette were outlined. If a man's mustache hung over the lower lip, it should be carefully parted before he drank coffee from a saucer. The holiest word in the English language? Mother, anyone's mother.

Reading it was living it; written in direct English, the *Gazette* suggested more than vicarious entertainment. In '89, when the publisher printed the news of Belle Starr's death, American men lost their fierce, lawless lover. The Petticoat Terror of the Plains, the first woman ever to be brought before Judge Parker, smoked wood chips out of a corncob pipe and sported a Stetson with an ostrich plume. No fan of her own sex, Belle wrote: "So long had I been estranged from the society of women (whom I thoroughly detest) that I thought I would find it irksome to live in their midst." Women chortled and retaliated, claiming they'd heard her skin was

as tough as a saddle, that she subdued the horses she stole with
her deadly halitosis. Nelson had read of the burial privately in the
alley behind the barbershop. It was a subdued affair, with no
hymns and no chanting, just Cherokees, who each placed a piece
of cornbread in her coffin. He returned to a watered-down world,
where male heads required cutting and female horse thieves no
longer roamed. Nelson read on into adulthood, his passionate appetite for outlaw lore still unappeased. "The Dalton Brothers,"
written by "An Eye Witness." There would be "Hands Up!" and
"Triggernometry." He didn't mind the hysterical writing, which
transformed ordinary criminals into high-minded heroes.

"Stand up straight, Clary. You're a banking representative. Just
where is our man?"

"There, sir. By the door."

Of course he would stay by the door, Nelson thought. He
couldn't stop the names of towns that kept popping open in his
mind. Towns where Belle's nephew Henry Starr and his crew had
knocked over one bank, occasionally two. Nelson glanced at the
man's chest and smiled. Country people! They claimed the outlaw
wore a steel breastplate, pocked with bullet holes, which hung
from the horn of his saddle at night while he slept.

"Mr. Starr, I'm Nelson Hanks. I'm the president of Citizens
Bank and Trust. Won't you come this way?"

He started up the steps, remembered Bigheart snoring upstairs
and stepped behind the second teller's window.

"Now how may I help you?"

The man was all one tone. Eyes, hair, nothing glittered, shone
or strayed from the single shade of dusk that he was. One color
had been poured on top of him, with no pale provision for that scar
on his forehead, no wash of red for the cheekbones.

"I need five hundred dollars."

"I see. A loan, then."

Monochromatic Henry had a voice that soared out of a colorless
self. Nelson scooted forward on his chair, wanting more. What lay
behind that sonorous voice? Holdups and an infamous aunt finally
brought down by a shot in the back . . . Nelson's overworked
imagination demanded there be even more to Henry Starr than
that.

"You do work around here, Mr. Starr?"

"Most of my affairs are local. You could say that."

"We would need something to guarantee the security of the loan."

Starr was silent.

"Someone to sign the note with you, then."

"I'm good for it."

"Mr. Starr, this establishment has been open for exactly five and a half hours, which just barely makes me a banker. We're under Arkansas law here, and these are their questions, not mine. But all these things will eventually make it easier on both of us. Like chewing before you swallow."

Starr scratched his head, looked over Nelson's head for a minute. He seemed satisfied.

"All right. Put down R. L. Drumwright. He'll back me for five hundred."

"Did Mr. Clary mention that we have a pay telephone on the second floor? I'll just be a few minutes drawing up some papers, so if there's anyone you'd like to contact, please be our guest."

There was an uncomfortable pause, and both men suddenly burst out laughing.

"Well, anyway, just so you know. I'll try to hurry. I know you're a busy man."

And who would he telephone? Chris Madsen? Maybe, just to get the old lawman's goat. Nelson smiled, filling out the papers, as he invented a conversation for those two. The immigrant, long the pride of the "enforcement business," had trouble making himself understood with his heavy Scandinavian accent and lack of teeth. He had survived his share of gunfights in this, his adopted territory. He had gunned down the required number of desperadoes and at last attained the post of U.S. marshal, only to be felled by a swaybacked brood mare, who kicked out every tooth in his head as he bent to deliver her foal. And now, struggling with speech, he explained to a pale lady refusing his advances or to an outlaw, cussing and hands-upped in his own rocky backyard: "I have no teat in the mout." Or maybe he would use the phone to taunt Judge Parker himself. "Hello, this is Henry Starr. Just so you know, I'm still free as a bird, henchman." Nelson chuckled, stared at the bank seal and returned to the world.

Starr chewed his lower lip as he wrote out his name. It was a clear signature.

"That does it. Seems we're in business, Mr. Starr."

It was a deal Hanks would never regret. Word got out that Nelson Hanks was okay. That at Citizens Bank and Trust, money was money. Bob Wells, the bank and train robber who had cut his sharp teeth in Missouri, waltzed in from his hideout on Lost Creek with a stack of bills wrapped in butcher paper. He warmed to Nelson's fancy lobby, his clerks who kept their terror in check. The Daltons remained gun-shy and never did make a legitimate appearance, though Nelson's philosophy paid off even in their case. They never touched the first bank nor the others that it eventually spawned, though the region was plagued by crime despite the efforts of Madsen and others. It was believed that local outlaws robbed other banks, then deposited their loot at Citizens. In public he denied it. In private, Nelson liked to brag he'd known it all along.

"I cultivated those fellas on purpose. For a purpose. Wild West show, my eye. Vinnie, give me credit for once."

"I *am* giving you credit. I'm saying your avocation finally paid off."

"What avocation is that?"

"Bang, bang. Shoot 'em up. All those silly books. You're no different than that little boy in Creston wanting to be center stage. Well, to thine own self be true. Are you pouting? Come give me a kiss. There's still nothing like a kiss. Even when you're courting thieves and red men."

She pulled him down to her, for lately that was what it took. The bank, she figured. Grabbing up those leases and operating the wells that almost always followed. The sheer weight of what he wanted most. She drew away from him and forgot to say it sweetly or pleadingly.

"Leave your eyes open. You squeeze them shut like you're doing a chore."

His head rested on her belly, where it should have been all along. She stroked his cheek, felt a living twinge inside and dismissed that as hocus-pocus, because there was nothing living in her womb. And that was why she couldn't stop her own husband from spinning away from her in the ordinary way a woman stops a man. By creating a minute image of him. A little Nelson to lift sky-high, to struggle out a swollen breast for. He slept riveted to his side of the bed after it was over, because there was no small someone to stumble through the night for, no cries to quell. Lavinia believed potentates (business, political or just plain barroom) were

busybodies of the first order, had to be. Men turned into comman-
dants because of their fathering side. They had to meddle, and if
they didn't have children of their own, it was that much worse. She
shuddered, thinking of Nelson and the Anderson girl. Good thing
Jane stood up to him.

Their loving had grown harsh and dry. Over in minutes, pain
and pleasure in equal parts. Of course. Her husband entered a
rock quarry night after night, for she guessed her insides had grown
hard as granite. Sometimes she dabbed at herself with mineral oil,
thinking, Poor Nelson. Much later, her mouth open into the pillow
that swallowed her cries, she thought, Poor Vinnie.

She wished she hadn't had the view of Nelson on high, borrowed, she later realized, from that Flemish painter in one of her
father's books. It was more real than the man in front of her,
struggling to prove affection and desire. Lavinia's views and
dreams, her plain and simple instincts, rarely lied. One occasion
after another proved it.

"Vinnie, come out a minute, will you?"

"Where's the fire?"

"Right here. Right here on the front page."

"Well, hold on, then. Let me just rinse my face."

She emerged from the washroom, her skin moist and pink. Nelson was slapping his leg with the folded paper. He grinned.

"Listen. 'Nelson Hanks, oil man and banker, is expected to
arrive in Guthrie near the end of the week. Our Denny Richards
says he is anxious to shake the hand of the man who has looked
into the eyes of Henry Starr and such likes, that his daddy called
Nelson Hanks the potentate of the Osage hills. This reporter asked young Denny just what was a potentate. The boy replied a potentate was kinda like a king, only bigger.' Doesn't that just beat
all?"

"First I've heard about any Guthrie trip."

"Didn't I mention Guthrie? Potentate, Vinnie! You look like the
cat who ate the mouse."

"Well, after all, I did tell you so. Can I get back to the sink now?
The girls are expecting me."

It was all falling so fast. She couldn't keep track of the man's
movements any more than she could a landslide. It was a futile
business; the rocks were falling too swiftly to count or classify. She
shook her head no.

"No, what?"

"Why, you're falling up, Nelson. Not down. And nature doesn't allow that to happen. Sometimes I think I've lost my sense of what this is about. Now shoo. I'll be late to my meeting."

"I just wish I had those wrists of yours, Lavinia. How you whip along! In and out, in and out, until you're done in no time. That's how I do everything, I guess. Slower than an ox. Oopsy daisy!"

The glass of tea went, but it was four-thirty and no one cared. There were seven women, who gathered each week for whist or embroidery. Low Ladies was a splinter group of the Book Club. The group was born when the Book Club denounced dime novels, for the majority of its members felt these novels appealed to a region of "the lower mind." Mary Taft, blunt as a bad knife, favored open revolt. "Will all those in favor of the lower mind please respond with a show of hands." Seven hands shot up, and the Low Ladies marched out of the parlor.

"I sometimes think needlework got started as an excuse."

Mary Taft examined her handiwork. She had chosen a Chinese motif and was bedeviled by her cross-stitched coolies.

"How's that, Mary?"

"You've got three children, same as me. Not counting when nature calls, how often do you sit down?"

Ellen Biggs had been to a women's academy in Virginia. She had assumed that the academy was the world. That Latin and croquet would figure largely in her destiny. Indian Territory had thrown her sorely off guard.

"Jeeps, I don't know. I sit down to read to them, then—"

"That doesn't count."

"Then I guess I really don't sit down until after supper. When I settle down with my tatting."

"There, I win! Lavinia, how about you?"

"None of your grand business how many times I go to the toilet. You've won, Mary, so don't harp. Women began stitching because they were tired and had to have an excuse to sit down."

Sometimes, especially in the winter, they quarreled. They would purge themselves with French or A Cause, easy enough to find though the Low Ladies proved only marginally effective in civic affairs. They were difficult women, temperamental by nature and full of yearning. They longed for company, got it, then found it chafed. Life had, in some cases, gotten to be a long and testy season.

"What's so interesting out there, Lorette?"

"Nothing. That's just it."

"Well, why stare out the window at nothing? Just makes you morose. I would love to eat something with ginger on it. I can just taste it now."

"Ginger!" Her eyes narrowed.

She was so young, Lavinia thought. Lorette was the darling of the group. They admired her curls, her sweet pink lips. Never mind if her attention wandered and she asked too many questions. Her husband had encouraged her to join a women's club, hoping it would settle her down. She made a fatal choice. The Low Ladies loved her impudence and wouldn't spay her for anything in the world.

"I specifically asked him *not* to buy me a sidesaddle. That I was fine with my pa's old one. And here he comes home with a sidesaddle, expecting me to jump on him with kisses. Well, he can just go someplace else for his kisses."

"Lorette, shame on you. Most towns have ladies of the night, while our girls work around the clock. I just hope you don't have to eat your words one day."

"I'm not likely to. I learned to ride on a horse's bare back when I was no bigger than a minute. It was hard enough to use an ordinary saddle. Now my husband says he doesn't take kindly to having me part my legs for all the world to see."

"Oh, my."

"As if riding a horse were—"

"Lorette!"

They stopped her before she got in trouble. Lavinia thought her frankness was fresh as a field of daisies.

"You know what I see out the window anyway?"

"Pray tell."

"Mud. Miles and miles of mud."

"Of course weather does get a person down."

"Here we all are, living right in the middle of a pig trough, and not a one of us is dirty."

"My, but you're a funny one. You want to change places with the men, is it? Go slogging around outside while they sit by the fire doing handwork? Go on ahead, then. Otherwise, stop this hypocrisy!"

"Ellen Biggs, you just hush. A woman can't hardly think around you. Once her thoughts wander off the slightest bit, you're standing there ready to hack her to pieces."

"You know what I think?"

They stopped to listen. Her opinions, because she was so parsimonious with them, were valued. At least here, in this warm parlor.

"I think we're all on edge with statehood around the bend."

Mary Taft let her coolies fall to the floor.

"Hell with it. What do you mean, Lavinia?"

"I mean our lives are going to change and soon. The nation has let us off the hook for all these years. We're like toddlers who've been given the run of the household. Well, toddlers have to be taught to sit correctly at the table. They have to learn how to use sharp knives and beg pardon. That's all ahead. Our husbands are going to have to toe the line, and so are we. Otherwise we won't have a minute's peace."

"I don't like what you're implying, Lavinia. It's as if we're savages. What a portrait you paint!"

"Perhaps I should be more direct."

"Please."

Lavinia looked down at her own work. Mary was right; she had a gift. She sped along on a piece of canvas, often inattentive, yet it always came out beautifully.

"This pig trough, as you call it, contains mineral wealth we can't even guess at. Some of us sitting in this room are going to be very rich one day. And when you have money, you're going to be scrutinized. So far we've been able to do whatever we pleased, and all that is going to change."

Ellen Biggs was ravished by the news. Mary Taft gazed sadly into the fire, wondering if all this meant they would have to join forces with the damned Book Club again. Lorette remained incorrigible.

"Know what I'd like to do?"

"Lord knows. What *now*, Lorette?"

"I'd like to get hold of a jar of bang head."

There was appropriate head-shaking. Eyes rolled up, and Ellen made that sound with her mouth, like she always did.

"I mean it. Just to see what it's like. I've got a moonshiner living right next door to my house. Night and day the man has customers. Sometimes they knock on our door, thinking we're him."

"Pig trough, all right. You just won't be content, will you? Well, help yourself. Ride screaming through town, full of bootleg whiskey. Ride like you please while you're at it. Just don't say you're a friend of mine's all. Oh, no."

Ellen sniffed and pulled a dime novel out of her deep pocket. The clamor died down, and so did the fire. Only when it got too cold in the room to sit still anymore did they all guess it was time to go home. As much as they struggled and fussed, the Low Ladies loved each other deeply. They returned home and knew that they'd been living that afternoon. And that living felt good.

Was it the weather? Or certain grievances that, after one had been in the company of free women, just clung to the skull tight as ticks?

"Why, Lavinia! You act as if I've just tried to break your nose. I've only said we have more than enough money for fine pillows. I don't like to see my wife hunched over, sewing."

"You buzzard."

She stared woefully at her plate of eggs. It was a shame she had broken the yolks before this all began. The congealed yellow mess took away her hunger.

"And what else don't you like about me? One louse means a whole headful. A former barber wouldn't argue that."

He found her anger dazzling. It attracted and repelled him, kept him afloat when he failed to remember the facts that really counted. She was Trappe's daughter. Evermore. Marriage and geography hardly changed that at all.

"There's nothing else, Lavinia. Funny that you should think of this as so grandiose."

"What else don't you like? My belly? It *is* gross. My hair? Tumbling out. Cascades, cascades! Just see."

It was true. Her hair lay scattered on the white pillow every morning. She had once said a jay could have made a fine nest of it. Determined not to lose it altogether, she gathered it dutifully every morning, hiding it in a corner of a hatbox until she had enough to form a hairpiece.

"This has nothing to do with needlepoint."

He had lost all conviction, and she knew it.

"What else don't you like? What inadvertent little tics and tacs do you fail to love, Nelson? Or is it my childless self you've begun to dislike? Well, I will stitch on. Privately, away from the critical gaze

of my insensitive husband. I am sorry handwork reminds you of
the patches and making do of your hard early life. But believe me,
I will stitch. Hang Creston, Iowa, and your poor old mother."

It was over. It was a shame about breakfast, but there was no
time now. She was the first to leave the table. Nelson sat on, lost
in admiration. No one waged war quite like Lavinia.

chapter 15

1907

Two cattle-minding boys, one scared and one lazy, heard her cry. They fell into an argument about who would fetch the doctor.

"Likely it'll be dead time he gets there."

"That ain't no it. That's a woman crying, Buckie."

"Livin' alone out in nowhere. Who does she think's gonna come running to her side out in nowhere. I don't hear nuthin. Must be she's dead by now."

Buckie rolled up his jacket and lay back resolutely. His eyes were shut. He couldn't keep them that way when the second set of screams started. He'd seen his share of distressed cows, heads stuck in barbed wire and mewling. A woman, though. It didn't seem to Buckie that a woman would get her head stuck where it shouldn't be.

"Let's draw straws for who goes."

"Don't have any straws."

"Grass'll do. Shortest piece goes and gets the crow doctor."

Buckie rolled over on his side, and his brother nudged him with the toe of his boot.

"I'll tell."

"Tell who?"

"Ma. She'll take up for her own kind. If you don't get the doc fast, you'll have to sleep in the yard. It'll be weeks and weeks before she flips a griddle cake for the likes of you, Buckie Bucka-roo.''

Buckie's piece of grass came up short. He didn't quite know how you could whimper loud, but she was doing it. Those sounds were like a river flowing now, winding this way and that. Her howling misery stole toward him and lapped at him from all sides. He crossed the meadow flush with Johnny-jump-ups and monarch but-terflies, cows pushing their muzzles slowly through a field filled with batting wings and shimmers of purple and yellow.

"Hurry, Buck. If you dawdle she's gonna die. Run!"

Well, he ran. He ran hard, thinking, What if the crow doctor isn't there? Or what if he's there and so busy taking care of birds he won't come for a sick woman? He thought all these things. In fact, with every quick step, ten new thoughts seemed to pound the top of his head. He nearly didn't stop when he reached the doctor's place. He nearly crashed through the front door without waiting for it to be opened.

"You gotta come, Doc. Me and my brother heard a woman cryin' in the hills up over where we graze our cows."

The doctor's shirt was open in front. It looked like it was either coming off or going on. He was already putting a hat on and reach-ing for a small bag on the floor behind the door. The doctor's place was bare as a bald head, Buck saw. Why, Buck and his family had more in the way of things than he did. There was just an old cot and a big desk stacked high with papers. The crow doctor had a lot of books, though. Books to last into the next life.

"Take a drink from the well, or I'll be treating both of you. Drink deep. What is your name?"

It did taste good. He dipped his head in the trough alongside the house and lifted his wet, sputtering face.

"Buck, sir."

"I'll need you to come with me up the hill. Never mind those cows of yours."

He led the way. They marched steadily, not stopping once. The splash of cold water on his face was soon far behind. Gone, too, the taste of sweet spring water. His tongue felt dry enough to fall off. Toward the end, he could move only by thinking of his own mama's rewards for his perseverance, which would be griddle cakes and maple syrup, ordinarily reserved for Christmas. He crept toward the hut and thought of dusting off a dozen. He crept toward the hut behind the doctor's stiff back. As he watched him push open the door, maple sap sweetened his tongue.

"And what have we here?"

She'd tied herself apart, so the first thing they greeted wasn't a woman's face at all. Buckie blushed and looked down at his own nasty boots (nasty, but not as nasty as guess who's). Somehow he shuffled forward. Griddle cakes? This would win him a tender piece of the cow he was keeping. Now it was beef fat mingled with sweet. He came close enough to see.

"We'll need to build a fire, Buck. Have you the presence of mind to gather wood?"

"Yes, sir. I'm present, sir."

"Then go fetch some kindling, boy. But before you do, there is one thing."

And then, because he was that close, Buck Evans began to see. And once he began to see, he began to think. It looked to him that she was a full-blood. He thought, Damned if they don't stay dark even when they're hurting. For her face was darkening in front of him, fast. He saw how her dog had come up to where she was lying. It had its paws in her hair, and he couldn't see if they were caught in that dark, matty tangle or just resting there for the plea-sure of it. Beside where she lay was an open paper sack. Her eyes kept going back to that sack, and she didn't talk. She just lay still, except for her eyes, inside bright, smelly blankets. And everything was covered by blankets except what they should never have seen in the first place.

The doctor smelled the contents of the sack, then licked the tip of one finger for a taste. Not beef fat, Buckie guessed, not butter and syrup, but burning and bitter from the look on his face. Then the crow doctor shook his head and studied the situation in a way that got Buckie to thinking harder. He saw she bulged in the stom-ach, though she was thin. He saw she was tied apart with ropes and waiting. He saw there was blood and a clear-as-day plan for something. Then he took a liberty, which he figured later wasn't a liberty but an order issued by his own clear thoughts. Buck Evans looked for the second time and saw a woman's private parts. In-tervened in, messed with, as he later whispered to his mother, his head hidden in her lap.

"Jesus, God! Jesus, sir. It's the first of July! She tried to blow the baby out of her own self, didn't she?"

Her lips were dusty, he saw that now. He watched the doctor

try to give her some water, but it was like she was already sealed up tight. The water just stood on her mouth like it was a stagnant pond.

"It is, and you are a bright young man. Yes, our friend swallowed down gunpowder to try to hurry her baby along. Our little mother here decided not to let nature take its course, with so much at stake. The gunpowder technique is as shrewd as any I've seen in these parts. She may not survive, and the baby may be dead, but by God, it will be born on time to become an allotted Osage. Now, Buck, besides building a fire, I have another task for you."

"Sir."

Buckie Evans thought of the happy, grazing cows in the meadow below. His brother was probably asleep by now. Asleep with the sun on his face. Buckie was fourteen years old and didn't want to see any babies delivered, living or dead.

"I can't work like this. You must take the dog off and shoot it. One clean bullet through the head. Can you do that, son?"

"I think so."

He cried, couldn't help but, as he lashed the dog to a tree. He cried not because of the animal, for creature death was something he knew. But baby death and lady death were new acquaintances. He made a clucking sound with his tongue, and the mongrel turned its head. Buckie scored a bull's-eye and left the dog tied to the tree, its dripping head still held up by the taut rope. He struck out to gather wood, taking as much time as he could. The woods were not chattering or alive, but silent, as he scouted for fallen sticks and branches. The only noise was the noise he produced. Big crashing boot sounds filled his ears.

When he returned it was born already. It lay huge on her belly, not squallingly alive like he would have thought. But free. The doctor wasn't bent over them. He was bent over his own lap and writing. Buckie had never seen anyone write so much. The doctor filled up one page, then started on another. The woman's eyes were closed.

"Is she dead, sir?"

The man must not have heard him, so he asked again.

"Is she dead, sir?"

"She is not. She is alive, and she is rich. So is the baby boy, who I assume will bear your name."

. . .

It didn't get him pancakes.

"You didn't ask her for money, Buck? How could you not ask for a little something? You saved her life and put her baby on the rolls, and you settled for namesake. Everybody around here is getting rich except us. I bet that drunken crow doctor put something in his pocket, all right. Well, congratulations . . . Buck Coming Through The Trees. Beats all. I'll never get past cows, never."

They had to draw the line somewhere, so they drew it straight across July 1, 1907. Babies born before or on the day were allotted. Any boy or girl coming after got excluded from the rolls, and that was that. If the government was going to be that cold, the Osage would be colder. It looked as though the line on the government document was painted bright red, for there was so much blood. Physicians performed special services, and tiny Caesarean babies turned up all over the Nation. Odds were placed on which ones would make it and which wouldn't. The ones that didn't were buried quick, and not in any casket. Osage babies of every size and shape were put on the rolls, even dead babies, and mamas of the small ghosts collected oil-royalty payments until they were found out. Babies born too late were found strapped securely to trees just outside town, with toys hung from the lowest branches. The foundlings were placed in loving homes, and Lovely society ladies were given a brand-new cause now that there was an Osage underclass to nurture and tend to.

Buck Coming Through The Trees lived, one of many born mostly by hook or by crook, to grow up stunted, blind and rich. Buck's mother, driven past what any sentient human being could tolerate, spent her final days on a sloped wooden porch. Her lap, once a kind, welcoming place, now held a pile of rocks she chucked at the roadway in front of her place. She damned her luck as chauffeur-driven tin lizzies and Hupmobiles swerved out of range. The Osage took the hail of stones in stride. Occasionally the old woman marked a point, denting a fender or knocking a driver soundly on the head. There was only one route to town, and Buckie's old mother became a conventional road hazard, commonplace as a pothole. Chauffeurs were calmly instructed to put on the speed. By the time Buck Evans achieved manhood, he'd learned the hard way about being a good samaritan. It didn't get you a hallowed place at the table, and it might even get you this, a crazed mother and a seven-year-old namesake who owned twenty-three pairs of shoes. Buck Coming Through The Trees and his mother wouldn't leave

the hut for finer quarters, but a grand piano was ultimately purchased with oil-royalty payments. Too large for the doorframe, it
stood outside, under a massive oak tree. Chickens roosted comfortably inside the Steinway by 1924, and the warped, blistered
wood was lousy with bugs.

Maybe Jane Anderson was prescient and not just solemn. Maybe
somewhere in back of her conventional dark eyes she had a second
set, in steel blue, which could pierce the future and know that none
of what lay ahead was a laughing matter. Maybe the stalwart child
disregarded her cousins' comic antics because they were so pitifully
beside the point. She was a child only once, on the day when
Nelson Hanks (Lavinia, really) struck oil. She laughed uncontrol-
lably as spectators rushed to town with news and a civilian alert.
The well blew furiously; it was a full five days before people in
town were allowed to strike a match. Black drops spattered cars
up to eleven miles away as Jane filled a straw hat with oil and, still
feverish at the feel of a belly laugh, set it on her glossy head.
Nelson was delighted to become her guardian. Her seriousness
brought out his helium-filled side, and nothing pleased him more
than to hear that Jane would be coming into town. Jane and her
black carriage, drawn by roan geldings, not palominos as Nelson
suggested. It was for Jane that Nelson perfected the monkey face,
made rabbit ears appear in silhouette against a back wall in his
dim private office and approved the list of purchases she wished to
make. He tried to extract laughter long after it was appropriate.
When Jane was sixteen and Nelson himself established as oil man
and banker, he was still playing the clown unsuccessfully.
    "What on earth do you want a French tapestry for, Jane? What's
on the thing anyway? Hunting scenes, I'll bet, antique birds and
bees. Men in stockings and slippers. What's the use?"
    "I need it for my mother's drawing room. I've begun hosting a
salon on Thursday evenings."
    "I see. Up to you, young lady. Of course, if I were in your place,
I'd outfit my whole home like an Indian palace. Medicine bundles,
buffalo robes. Why I'd . . . after all, it is your mother's drawing
room. Might as well create a place where she can be comfortable.
She doesn't even—"
    He stopped midway. Jane's hands, softly folded in her lap, now
gripped the arms of the chair.

"—speak English, Mr. Hanks. Finish your sentence."

"It's not your taste I'm attacking. You have marvelous taste. I just don't understand traipsing about the world for a richness you have at home. If I hear one more word about the Continent, I'm going to go up in smoke! You people have more culture at your immediate disposal than kings and queens."

"Your signature, Mr. Hanks. I just need your signature."

Nelson gave it, grunting. He scratched his head.

"I must be getting old. Run along, Jane. What about inviting me to tea, now that you've got yourself a tapestry? Tea does go with a tapestry, doesn't it?"

"It does, Mr. Hanks. I will invite you for tea and for our readings of Homer and Cicero. If pure language studies interest you, we also meet on—"

"What, no young men? No dancing? Don't look so fierce, Jane Anderson. You're a pretty young woman who spends entirely too much time fretting. These are the best years of your life."

"You are right about that. And I'm putting them to excellent use with your help."

"You can't fool me with that smooth talk, Jane. You keep yourself cooped up all day with books and music. That—what is that thing you play?"

"Oboe, sir."

"You pass time with an oboe, when you ought to be laughing and living! Homer and Cicero, names that suggest nothing but dust and dry rot, young lady. Why, when I was young . . . Jane, are you listening to a word I'm saying?"

"Excuse me, Mr. Hanks. I'm late to an appointment. But I'll be back to see you next week, once I have the information I need."

"Not another tapestry, I hope."

"No. This is a larger venture. And modern, sir. I'm sure you'll see my plan has nothing to do with either dust or dry rot. Learning will be our salvation."

He showed her to the door, closed it gently and wandered to the window. The simplicity of the carriage always surprised him. Palominos, Jane! Their coats shine like newly minted gold. And what had she chosen, despite his advice? Roan geldings. He raised the window.

"Jane! Forgive me. I'm nothing but a meddling old fool. Do what you want with your money. Play that instrument to your heart's content."

She turned toward him, emphatically using the whole of her upper body. She called up to him in a clear voice.

"I'll do just as I please, Mr. Hanks. I always have, haven't I?"

He saw a group of reedy, cigarette-smoking boys on the corner and realized her performance was for them. He thought of Trappe all those years ago, his blanket disapproval of Vinnie's suitors. Were bankers all destined to turn into bothersome old men? He stuck a finger inside the front of his collar, then removed it entirely. It felt tight enough to choke him. Her carriage had started off down the street. She kept her horses shod, and they made a pleasant clatter as she urged them into a trot. Jane turned, still regal, and gave him one brilliant smile, which wasn't laughter or fondness but truce. He watched as she rattled past the boys, every one of them weak-kneed for his ward. His hand moved up to his heart. It was knocking furiously against his chest, as if he'd just sprinted a mile. He let himself down easy into a smooth chair and checked his watch. Nelson gave himself exactly twelve minutes to dream, then he would have to change for a meeting with investors. He frowned, seeing the black suit that hung in the corner, then lit his pipe and told his secretary to hold all calls. Nelson Hanks, free for the moment of stiff white collars and humorless Osage girls, reached for a pink-paged issue of the old *National Police Gazette*.

chapter 16

1922

"Look at the colonel. Proud as a peacock, isn't he? I don't know that I could take to a man with a ring, though. There's something womany about a gem that size."

"You'd best hush about womany. You're sitting real pretty because of that man and his hammer."

"It's a gavel."

"And every time it bangs, those Indians and you just get richer and richer. Look who just signed a land lease. Look who's got more gentlemen visitors than she knows what to do with. Who are you calling womany, Electra Sims?"

"Maybe the only jewelry worth having is the kind you can see from a mile off. Still . . ."

"Sssh!"

"Would you two ladies mind taking that chat off someplace else? This here's business!"

"This here is a elm tree. And I'm going to sit underneath it so long as it pleases me, sir."

He was just the sort the spinster couldn't stand. A kind of squire who stepped sniffing off a special Pullman in a leather jacket, khaki pants and boots that laced up to the knee. It was because of him and others like him that her quiet little village of Lovely had lately been called the Osage Monte Carlo. The fields had been thrown wide open to all comers, and the auctions for oil leases took place outside the Osage Council House under this tree, now called the Million Dollar Elm. Colonel Walters had earned his old ring, she guessed. After a stunning month in which Walters had sold $6,056,950 worth of leases, the tribe had proudly placed the ring on his finger. It looked like the fast talker from Skeedee had gone and got himself married.

There was little talk of the war. Now that horses and cavalry were bygone, what had fueled the American efforts was fuel. Soldiers' wives and children didn't forget the Great War for a minute. But for the others, who hadn't lost their daddy or brand-new husband, there was so much world right here, spread out under the giant elm. So much engaging, fractious, multicolored world that it obliterated all others. The spinster studied it all.

"That colonel. He doesn't miss a trick, does he? Every oil man has his own secret sign, seems like. Hanks pulls his left ear, and it means go. Willis takes off his hat, and the Osage are suddenly a million dollars richer. All this sign language does seem a trifle— Look, there's Emma Lou Bowden!"

"Sold to Electra Sims!"

The widow's spine struck the back of the elm. There was a big crackling sound as spectators reopened printed programs. Several men were making their way over to her with congratulations.

"Isn't that just like you, Electra, to parlay that money of yours into still more? Well, my hat is certainly off to you, dear woman."

"Why, I didn't move a—"

"Muscle? You didn't have to! I find that the gestures, the subtle signals Colonel Walters reads, has made these auctions high-caliber. The Lord knows this could all turn crass as a gambling den."

Electra let him sputter on for a minute more and then excused herself. She strode past the chief of the Osage, not honoring him with a glance. Past the spectators, to whom Colonel Walters, with his big ring, his crooning and calling out, his bing-banging of that hammer—yes, hammer—was mere show.

"What is the meaning of this?"

"Congratulations are in order, Electra. It takes bravery and acumen to—"

"Hold it there, Walters. I didn't bid on any oil lease!"

"But your hand, dear Electra. Waving hoo-hoo for me to stop the bidding."

"I was waving 'hoo-hoo,' as you put it, at my acquaintance seated quite the other direction and out of harm's way."

"One hundred thousand dollars brilliantly invested."

"I'm a seamstress!"

"You've just become a wildcatter. Get Huck Helm to speed up the transfer, so we don't have to wait so long for the money."

"You wait. This kind of shenanigan will ultimately be punished, Walters. Colonel! As if an old goat like you had ever seen conflict."

The auctioneer from Skeedee mopped his forehead with a plain cotton handkerchief. Lights danced inside the diamond. Womany. She'd been right all along.

Nelson stood in the cold, wet middle of Lovely and blew on his hands to warm them. He cussed the rain. It fell so hard, some of his men fashioned head gutters out of salvaged metal. Work in the oil field didn't stop for weather or fatigue. One of Nelson's roust-abouts, too tired to find a latrine, pissed in his pants and went right on working. He griped that the only way to win a little time off was to die. The Oklahoma boom was on, and Lavinia was partly correct. They hadn't known half of what was coming. The partly wrong was her sense that their good times were behind them. Nelson and Lavinia discovered plenty to distract and delight them in the tumultuous little towns that bloomed and died in a single decade. Just plenty.

He squinted and made out Billy, the old man who ran the pipe-laying crew. He swatted at the downpour as if he was batting aside a swarm of horseflies.

"Give me fifteen more men, Mr. Hanks. I'm short by fifteen."

"Go find 'em, Billy. Just so you get me piped and flowing by Thursday."

Billy's nose bled, but in the rain it hardly figured.

"Ain't no more room inside that bunkhouse, sir."

"Sleep 'em in the powerhouse."

"Already got five boys in there."

"Sleep 'em stacked up, then. Think an extra dollar a day would help morale?"

"Sir!"

Nelson lifted his heel, listening to it slowly suck its way free of the mud. Sometimes it seemed he was just as busy thinking about mud as he was thinking about oil. Workers believed when wells

came in, creating a boom and a town to go with it, rain automatically fell and mud soon got to be a way of life. Horses and mules
collapsed in it, dying of exhaustion, as they struggled to transport
materials to the drilling site. Trucks and cars got rooted in it, same
as trees. Double-dealing mud could be costly. A Lovely resident,
full of liquor and a week's salary, paid a quarter to be transported
out of the saloon and across the mucky street on a plank of wood.
Someone shot him off his plank and into heaven before he reached
the other side. Nelson put his hand on his stomach, pressed hard
and started walking. He couldn't remember when he'd last eaten,
and worse, he couldn't remember what he'd eaten. A deadline was
a deadline. Where would he put fifteen new men? His bunkhouses
and shotgun shacks were full, and finding lumber for housing was
out of the question; it was fed directly to new rigs. Oil workers
slept in boxcars and the cabs of grocery trucks when the cot houses
ran out of space. Newcomers announced they were Nelson Hanks'
company men, thinking it would help. The lucky ones (with wives
or children) were handed surplus tents, broom handles and a piece
of cloth to subdivide precious space. The women sewed gunny-
sacks together to cover the ground.

Billy came up with his fifteen extra men that afternoon. They
stood outside the powerhouse, waiting for work orders.

"Who'd you turn up with?"

"Fifteen first names."

"Any of 'em experienced?"

"They say as much, but you can't tell anymore. Wouldn't pay to
ask too many questions. Besides, it don't take a genius to lay
pipe."

"Get them going, then. We'll be out of daylight in a few hours."

"One of 'em claims to know you. Sorriest-lookin' son of a bitch
among them. Still, he says he's your friend. Calls himself Harry."

He could have crossed him a dozen times on the street without
recognizing him. Nelson scanned the bony man standing before
him and hesitated before clapping him on the back, at first not
daring anything so boisterous. Harry's appearance pointed to
more than whiskey or disease: too many years spent pinned under
pure sky.

"My Lord, Harry!"

"Shocking, isn't it?"

"You look just . . ."

". . . like a cadaver. Don't forget, Nelson, I did go to medical school."

"Let's move off from all this for a minute. Come get out of the rain."

"As you say. You're the boss, after all."

They had to shout because of the rain. It had flattened out now and drove down with so much force it seemed a riveter worked the metal roof of the powerhouse. At least it was dry inside. Two exhausted mechanics lifted themselves from the lazy bench to make way for them. Nelson slid his hand inside a coat pocket and offered the flask to his old friend.

"Have a little dip, Harry. Don't be shy."

"I'm not shy. I'm disbelieving. I haven't had the occasion to drink good whiskey with a friend in years."

"Drink again, Harry. Drink as much as you like."

He looked slightly better for the whiskey.

"Don't fool yourself, Nelson. We've both got what we want."

Harry laughed or seemed to. His shoulders shook under his coat, and the mad grin must have been mirth.

"Why do you think you never won any bets as a kid? You never could keep your thoughts off your face. You look appalled, my old friend. Positively appalled."

He stood up and gave him back the fancy flask.

"That Roosevelt certainly was a clever man. The quintessential symbolist. I suppose he thought that by using an eagle's quill to sign those statehood papers, he could soften the blow. The Indians were bereaved, but others were touched, too."

He buttoned his coat up to his chin.

"I'm a lost man, Nelson. I never wanted it otherwise. I've signed on field after field—Whizzbang, Carter Nine, now Lovely. A man can still disappear in the Osage hills, though he may have to work harder at it now that we're officially part of the United States."

"What kind of trouble are you in?"

Harry laughed and sputtered softly to a stop.

"What stuff. Nothing can cure you of romance, Nelson! You take me for one of your beloved outlaws, perhaps? I'm not running from or toward anything. Close your face. You look horrified. I hear you have a wife."

"For several years now."

"And children, I suppose."

"Not yet."

Harry said something else, but the rain drowned him out. Nelson watched the ghoulish old man leave the powerhouse. He shifted his weight suddenly at a gruesome image of his friend set upon by the very crows he once healed. Tame no longer, they fed on his flesh matter-of-factly. Were crows like vultures, or was he getting it all mixed up in his mind? He took a long pull from his flask and wondered if Harry could do a lick of work in his poor condition. He glanced at the mechanics, heavily shifting their weight.

"You boys have a sit. You look good and wrung out."

"I'd best lay off smokin' that stuff."

"That ain't no vision, Tommy Linwood. That there's Mrs. Nelson Hanks."

"Under that hat?"

"You bet. Say a word against her, and you'll get your butt canned. I hear he's sensitive on the subject of his wife."

"Guess I'd be, too. Can't he keep her home?"

"Don't reckon."

Even a dope addict could be reasonable if he had to be. Tommy Linwood, simplest of pipeliners, went back to his work and his song, led by the superintendent. Cold sunlight sure beat rain; he had a piece of cake hidden under his hat and a little marijuana he'd kept over to smoke on his birthday. He had an exceptional voice, and most of the time it didn't matter that the pipeline cats were digging ditches or clearing brush or backfilling to cover up the line of pipe, so long as they could be near Tommy Linwood when he decided to open up his throat. Oh, they all thought Tommy was some boy. He kept his pocket full of sugar, he said, so when he got to thinking hard about women he didn't have a conniption. He could just lick the tip of his finger, dip it in his pocket, and the sugar let him go right on working. Nobody guessed he didn't know the first thing about women. He just made it up to glorify his sugar habit. But he was nearly eighteen and coming into his time. And of course, there was his voice.

None of it eluded Lavinia. Not Tommy, not the pipeline argot, rhythm and song that lent the dirty world a little romance. Nelson had made good on his promise. She got her horse, for it looked like she'd made up her mind to leave town on an occasional "jaunt" out to the neighboring Lovely fields. Conscious of her age (he'd promised the horse to a young girl, not a matron) and her jiggling insides, he bought a Tennessee walker. Three thousand dollars guaranteed that the smooth, low stride wouldn't dismount a feather, let alone his wife. "If she trotted any lower, this mare would scrape off the top of her belly," the owner insisted as Nelson wrote out his check.

When Lavinia wanted panorama, she rode the mare out to the knoll at the southern tip of the Lovely fields. From there she could watch everything through the nervous walker's ears, tipped up and quivering. More often, though, she slipped straight down the hill to where the work was going on. She didn't need to coax the mare, three years old and full of vinegar.

"Her stockings ain't white no more, Miz Hanks."

"Afternoon, Billy. Neither are mine."

They weren't, either. Mud splattered her heavy skirt. Contrary to Lorette, Lavinia preferred a sidesaddle. She liked the rocking back and forth, even though she always wound up at the baths afterward on account of back pain.

"Don't mind me."

"We don't, Mrs. Hanks. We don't."

It was true. She became a familiar sight in the fields. Her spyglasses, the big hat, the cigarettes she'd stop to light even though Nelson gave her hell every time he caught her—none of it wrinkled a single shirt. Work went on, and singing. Only cokeheads like Tommy, too doped up to remember Lavinia from her last visit, seemed to take note anymore. She pulled gently on her horse's reins.

"Could I skin you for a cigarette, Ray?"

"Sure could. Don't tell anybody it was me, though."

"Our secret. Oh, isn't it nice out here in these fields?"

Nelson occasionally objected, saying she had no business eavesdropping on vulgar with a whole town watching. What is vulgar about fitting pipe? she would ask. They're chanting that music so they won't keel over piping your precious oil out of the state. I wouldn't miss it for the world.

"All right, cats, let's get going and roll some pipe. You pipe-hustlers, bring up the next joint. Come on, get the lead out. Catch her there, Jack. She's loose as a goose. Wrap your tails around her, cats, and give her an honest roll. Hit her like you live. Hard. High like a tree and down to the velvet. Bounce, you cats, bounce.

Load up on them hooks, you snappers. That's high. Ring her off,
collar-pecker."

She was eavesdropping, but not just on vulgar. She left the field
workers, to weave through camp. She stayed aboard her sidesaddle until she was embarrassedly invited to beef tea or boiled coffee
by a pretty common-law wife.

"Wouldn't you like something hot, Mrs. Hanks? On a day like
this?"

"I'm just waiting to be asked."

"I reckon we can tie up your horse to the washtub here. My,
she's fine. Eeeh!"

The girl backed off quickly, stumbling over a pile of rope by the
tent.

"Reckon I'm nervous. I got myself good and bit when I was jest
a kid. She's snuffin' me like I was a carrot."

"We'll just tie her up here. She won't bite. In fact, neither of us
will. Now what about that something hot?"

"Oh, why . . . won't you come in? I'm afraid you'll have to squat
your way inside. Course I can jest bring you that little something
right here."

Lavinia was already folded up inside, next to three kids and a
straw pallet they played next to. Wasn't it play? She'd thought it
was a game, but it happened that they weren't counting or juggling
those pecans they held mounded in their laps. It was certain they
weren't betting them. As she leaned forward to count the younger
boy's pile, he removed them to another corner of the tent.

"Right here's your tea, Mrs. Hanks. Watch you don't burn your
hands."

Heat from the wood stove made it seem grand inside. A single
light bulb dangled from the center of the tent. She sipped from the
metal cup and surveyed what lay around her. She'd seen worse.
The girl had pieced together a wooden floor out of salvaged shipping cartons. Three bars of Lava soap were displayed on a store
box. She saw there was only one cup, though. And she was using
it. The children watched her as she drank her tea.

"How old are your babies, dear?"

"Will here's seven, Eddie is five and Sarah's nearly four."

"Eddie, how many pecans have you got there?"

The boy answered by sucking his thumb furiously. He crouched
lower and rocked on thin ankles.

"He don't know any numbers yet."

"He may not know numbers, but he certainly knows pecans. Eddie, show me how many you have with your fingers."

Eddie frowned and let his thumb drop out of his mouth.

"How can I give you more of those nice big nuts the next time I visit if I don't know how many you have to begin with?"

Nine fingers wiggled in the air. The other children chirped and raised their hands. The youngest knocked over a bottle of Lysol and shrank back from her mother's raised hand.

"Why don't we put these children in school, dear?"

"I tried asking when we first come, but the schoolteacher is clear out of space."

"We'll find the space. Have them there Monday morning. This tea is just what I needed."

The first time Lavinia came through on her white-stockinged horse, with her field glasses and huge hat, one woman called her Miz Goddamn Lady Bountiful. She said it low, to her immediate neighbor hanging wash from the limb of the same tree, but she said it all the same. The next and only time she brought it up again, she got her shins kicked. By then, Lavinia Hanks had dismounted. She'd brought a doctor into camp for the typhoid introduced on account of men shitting up the fields and contaminating the ground water. Only the women could bear the privies, the awfulness of doing daily business in such a horrid, smelling place. They tried to sanitize them, even sloshing them with petroleum to kill the germs. Still, the men took to the out-of-doors, and it brought disease. If Nelson Hanks' wife was dismayed by the smells, she didn't show it. She took the kids' plight straight to her big heart. When she found out some boys were pooling money to get a whore or playing hooky to see Rudolph Valentino, who was in Lovely for one afternoon in the middle of his regional tour, she'd march right up to the door of a boxcar or shotgun house and pound until she got them back into her school. Her school. She formed a board of education herself, finding men and women who'd gotten a little schooling somewhere to serve on it. She laughed at the oath they wrote for the president, but by God, Lovely had itself a real school board. The oath?

"I hereby solemnly swear that I have never fought a duel, that I will never fight a duel. That I have never served as a second at a duel and that I will not serve as a second at a duel. So help me God."

The schoolmistress, the second one, stepped down off the train and was handed a chalkboard sign that read District 26. They photographed her in front of the town drinking well to make it official, then mentioned where she'd be spending that first Lovely night.

"A saloon? My contract forbids me to play cards or dance. I am obliged, *in writing*, not to bob my hair like a flapper, not to marry and to go to church on Sunday, then you people sleep me in a saloon? I've never heard of such a—"

She saw a big hat coming through the crowd. Then she saw the most beautiful chocolate-brown riding boots she'd ever glimpsed and field glasses that suggested army personnel.

"And there you are. I'm Lavinia Hanks, dear. Come, a table is waiting for us at the restaurant. I'm sure you'll find it provincial, nothing at all like what you've left behind in Neosho. But remember, you've come to an Oklahoma boom town. There's much in store for you here. I plan to introduce you to my Low Ladies, naturally, and there's a women's choir that just may interest you with your background. But let's get you some dinner, why don't we? You must be fairly starved."

"Lavinia Hanks, I'm pleased to meet you. But whoever named this place Lovely must have had a very keen sense of humor. I am taking the very next train home. I will not sleep in a saloon."

"Of course not, my dear. You'll stay with my husband and me until more suitable quarters are available."

Lavinia held her hand securely as she spoke. The field glasses rose and fell on her breast as she gently led the schoolmistress toward the restaurant.

"You see, something quite alarming has happened here. The ideals of scholarship have been embraced by some but not all members of the community, until it's become quite an embarrassment! Why, one of our Osage girls has purchased a *printing press* with the proceeds from her royalty payments. She is now turning out a delightful little newspaper, called the *WaShaShe Chronicle*. Oh, really quite delightful!"

The red-haired schoolmistress tried and failed to step gracefully over a puddle. She sighed and dropped her lifted skirts, then fell in beside her stalwart companion, who seemed undaunted by slop and squalor. She watched as her supervisor (was Mrs. Hanks her supervisor?) worked a coin into a little boy's shirt pocket and kissed the top of his dirty head. Lavinia raised her chin even higher as she spoke.

"But what distresses me so is the fact that most Lovely citizens, those who can read at all, are completely put off by Miss Anderson's sophistication. When Jane Anderson covers affairs in Egypt or the cuisine of Australian cannibals or even the social customs in France, it simply falls on deaf ears. We must certainly produce writers and readers who come up to the level of certain Osage, don't you see? You'll be happy in Lovely. In fact, I'll see to it that you are. Have a sweet?"

The new teacher carefully put one thin white disk on her tongue and followed the trail of Lavinia Hanks' deep footsteps.

"I've lost one schoolmistress, and I certainly don't intend to lose another."

chapter 17

1923

The Body of Knowledge wasn't huddled next to a bootlegger. There was no dark alley to negotiate, no curious neighbors to dodge. Miss Simply's establishment was perched on high stilts near a shallow creek that had never been known to flood. The kerosene lamp barely lit the way. Clients scaled the birch ladder slowly, for occasionally a man would misjudge a rung in the ladder, landing on his back before Miss Simply so much as opened her door. Mallard ducks nested underneath the house. Their squawking brought Zoe Simply to the front window.

"Who's calling?"

"Nelson Hanks."

He stayed poised where he was on that third rung, listening to the thin door scrape its way open.

"Again, please."

"It's Nelson Hanks."

"Come right up, Mr. Hanks."

New York City pleased him, Chicago. He'd been introduced to both Twin Cities now, but nothing came close to crawling up this birch ladder next to the Caney River. What would he find upstairs? Miss Simply, resolute and plain-faced, with her perfect pitch. A veteran of poor acoustics and the squirming inattention of oil field kids, the renegade schoolmarm could send her voice anywhere. She sent it, clear and deep, down her own ladder, until it covered him like a warm wrap.

"Is the light sufficient?"

"Adequate; oh, very adequate."

He panted a little and wished he didn't. His chin finally rested on Zoe Simply's front porch. He'd heard the whole structure was raped from a tornado site several miles south. That she'd gone there herself with an idle young boy in a liveried wagon and pointed toward the demolished house. The family had long fled the scene, scorning the tainted lumber, for the storm had claimed their youngest child. Nelson clambered up the rest of the way and waited for a moment, to be formally asked in. There was no sound, so he stepped deliberately toward the front door.

"May I come in?"

"Please do."

He'd been tricked by New York and Chicago, he saw. In his mind, Chinese paper lanterns swayed, silk dressing gowns fell open to lace and black stockings. Delightful hooks and clasps begged to be sprung open. He peered through the door, seeking these things and other tools of the trade. There was no dusty lilac odor, no sharp French perfume smacking his senses as he pushed into the room. Miss Simply was boiling a vat of vegetables. Turnips bobbed on the surface of the rolling water. Was she arranged like a tempting coquette on a pink settee or fat puff cushion, her legs tucked disingenuously underneath? No, Zoe Simply was sitting straight-backed in a wooden chair, reading a book.

"You're in luck, Mr. Hanks. A striking little lady from Texas has just joined my establishment. I'm sure you would spend a delightful evening with our young roan."

Her eyes didn't leave the page. He would have called it theater, but he saw that she was actually reading, not just scanning the pages. Her eyes raced left and right; she frowned in occasional disbelief. Maybe it was one of those bawdy serial books, like the ones Vinnie hid under her corset. Nelson squinted and scratched his head, seeing "Alexander the Great" printed on the leather spine.

"Or Elizabeth. She's been with me longer, though I don't know why I keep her on. She's so naughty. And impudent. There's nothing the girl won't say."

Nelson smiled. Miss Simply's wordplay was pure elixir.

"We struggle with the same problem. A company man is liable to say just about anything. And no matter that a lady is present."

Zoe continued reading. Nelson noticed that the table wasn't set, though the pot continued to boil. He heard a shriek come from the back of the house, then laughter. A woman's laughter. No, several women were laughing.

"No doubt that women today prefer lives of greater risk. I wonder if it isn't the issue of emancipation."

The "retired" schoolteacher shifted slowly in the chair, and it gave a bit under her weight. Miss Simply's face blurred under close inspection. There was nothing uneven to treasure in it. Her nondescript features were jolted only by a thick, heavy mouth. Clambering down the ladder after an evening at the Body of Knowledge, a man might still her frantic mallards with a shower of stale bread crusts and try to remember one single thing about her face. Even in that immediate moment, standing hot and sticky under her long-legged whorehouse, all most men could recall was Zoe Simply's large, loose mouth.

"I came to call on you, Miss Simply."

She lifted her eyes up off the page. She saw a tiny, foolish carnation poking through a lapel, a shining bald pate and thick glasses with one dark smudge in the middle of a lens. She noted a fine suit and duck dirt on custom leather boots. And she saw that her kitchen chair had been moved closer.

"I've brought you a present."

She sat up a bit straighter in the chair and smoothed the front of her skirt. Dark blue or black, he couldn't tell which. A modest length. Miss Simply was completely unadorned, so far as Nelson could see. She raised her hand to straighten her hair. The sweater was worn clear through to the elbow. She unwrapped the paper carefully, then refolded it and put it in the pocket of her skirt. She took the lid off the small box, cocked her head quizzically. He felt his neck tighten.

"Why, of course. You *would* think of that, Mr. Hanks. Very kind of you."

She let her hand cup the pink bulb of the atomizer, then gave it a gentle squeeze. There was nothing inside the crystal jar, and it let off a short, dry gasp.

"How good of you."

She set it on the table beside her chair. He saw the gift would take its place among other silly, insignificant offerings. That it had no more effect on her than a gnat would upon an elephant. She let her eyes drop back down to the page.

"He was dead by the time he was thirty-two. Just try to imagine it!"

Nelson thought about touching her mouth. He thought about laying the whole flat of his hand against it first, then running a single finger up and over it. Stroking it softly until she tightened it into a pout. He bet she didn't like her mouth one bit. That she had no idea what an indolent air it gave her. Then Nelson remembered that he was seated in the front room of the most unlikely whorehouse in town. She knew, all right.

"Do you know that he had himself lowered into the sea inside a glass barrel? And that he used underwater divers in his siege upon Tyre? All this before the birth of Christ."

He heard a man call out for someone named Lucinda and thought maybe he recognized the voice. He moved his chair closer still and allowed one knee to touch Miss Simply. She seemed unconcerned. Her eyes moved faster across the page now, and he wondered if anything could wrench her from that book.

"Mr. Hanks? I want to ask a special favor of you."

He let himself loosen his tie. He remembered he hadn't taken off his hat. He tossed it lightly to the floor. His breath came a little faster as he thought about that favor.

"Would you mind terribly taking that kettle off the fire? Those vegetables are certainly cooked by now."

He stood up and set the pot to one side of the fireplace. She was right. They looked tender.

"Miss Simply, I haven't come here to eat turnips."

"I don't suppose you have."

"And I don't give a good goddamn about Alexander the Great."

"I would guess not."

He couldn't move the chair any closer. Then he noticed that Miss Simply had changed positions. Her legs were no longer sealed shut. In fact, they lagged open at the knee. She licked the tip of one finger and set it firmly on top of a page.

"No self-respecting oil man would bother about such things."

She took Nelson's hand and slowly fed it between her legs. He laid his head on top of the book. She was bare-legged. There was no silk panty to wrestle with, no stocking to slide over a white knee. She let his hand rove and linger where it would, then slid forward slightly until his fingers reached the folds of her hidden skin. He worried petals of skin gently until he felt them change, ripple softly and flatten. Miss Simply brought herself to the edge of her chair, and he was driven all the way inside. She stood wide open for him.

"It's unbecoming of me, I know. After all, you're the gentleman paying for certain services. Ah, there!"

The heavy book crashed to the floor. She pressed him down gently, slid something soft under his head and removed his glasses. Miss Simply, blurry enough before, now vanished altogether. He touched her waist and found a thin, girlish reed. Then he caught her smell, a delight no atomizer could ever contain.

"The truth is, I've become a bit of an administrator."

He closed his eyes and felt her legs open across his chest. Her skirt brushed his cheek.

"I don't often get to handle customers myself. And though I do love to read, I don't consider it my primary passion. If you wouldn't mind? There, yes. Oh, my, yes."

The Body of Knowledge prospered, despite the steady influx of fine, free women. They erected dance halls in town. The new arrivals drove, fur-clad and jeweled, through oil fields to announce still another joint. What kept Miss Simply alive and well in such a competitive market was her fine eye and fair shake. A pretty young girl, gone from home and heading toward the lights, could find a situation with her. If they made it up the ladder, agreed not to drink and to eat her plain, boiled meals, she gave them a bed and an overnight profession. She taught them all how to read. She even coaxed two of her brightest girls into the classics, muttering, "Satin for Latin; how far you've fallen, Zoe." The girls made it through an old primer and were rewarded with ivory satin bedclothes. More than one steady customer, muttering *mea culpa* in his sleep, was routed from bed with a wife's kitchen fork. But mostly it was Zoe herself who drew in the customers. Her funny ideas, that sturdy delinquent drive, was only half of what kept them coming. It was Zoe Simply's own huge hunger that eventually got to be a habit.

. . .

He ate her vegetables afterward.

"Damn it, these are good! What's in them?"

"Absolutely nothing. What could be in them, for that matter? They were in the soil an hour ago. Maybe that's what you're tasting."

"Fresh garden vegetables. Haven't had the likes of these since Creston. Everything I eat these days has an accent."

"What do you mean, Mr. Hanks?"

"French this, French that. Sauces. This is delightful. I wouldn't mind a piece of salt pork to one side. Zoe?"

"Yes?"

"After what we've done tonight, don't you think you could call me Nelson? It's so much friendlier that way."

"Friendlier. I hadn't thought of it, but you may be right. It sounds to me that prosperity has brought you a pretty case of indigestion. Seconds, Nelson?"

Zoe Simply spoke the truth. The Hanks home on Seminole Drive had begun to take on trappings. Lavinia crisscrossed Lovely oil fields and plush hotel lobbies with the same determined stride. Shopping trips to New York were at first carried out grimly, according to the silent mandate that work, more and more, be brought home and served drinks and dinner. "Big shots need big chairs, Nelson. You can't ask a former governor of Texas to sit on *this*. I leave for New York day after tomorrow." Lavinia's resignation was quickly eroded by Manhattan. She discovered a suite at the Ambassador eased her mission considerably. That, to one sequestered by a discreet and understanding European staff and a coterie of excellent new friends, New York City could be euphoric. Vinnie's middle-aged education began on Park Avenue. She rushed home, when home was the Ambassador, to write Nelson about her field trips through the city.

Dearest Nelson,
You mustn't tease me when I tell you of the grand time I am having. Oklahoma is my first love, and I wouldn't dream of infidelity. But to think I have discovered a second amour. Me, so well past my prime! I return home late each day, wrung out from lunch and shopping for just the right thing. I find that I am wrapped

in the *odor* of this mad city. It's made up of cigar smoke and
ermine, and that new chippie cologne even the most prominent
women in town insist on wearing. And that I am reluctant to slip
into my hot bath and wash it off.

I'm having the dining room suite shipped on Thursday. Our
Texan should be quite at ease. I was aided and abetted by the
most charming interior decorator. "The first thing you must learn,
Mrs. Hanks, is to distrust your instincts." The becomes *zee*,
naturally, with his elegant accent.

Bitsy Smith and her quiet husband accompanied me to a
speakeasy last night. It was Bitsy who was to whisper the
password, and of course, in her excitement, she got it quite tangled
up. They let us in all the same, and what a night we had! Bitsy's
quiet husband went on a real toot, and it was all we could do to
get him into a taxi.

I am bringing home quite a surprise. This is,

Your Loving Vinnie

The Low Ladies winked and praised Lavinia for being so cagey,
though wider consensus was that success had finally gone to her
head. That foolishness, born of prosperity, had wormed its way
into her system like some Peruvian parasite. What next? She
brought a Japanese valet back from New York City. Joey Fujii had
bumped around America for fifteen years. He had trimmed cloth
for a Brooklyn tailor and rosebushes for a dowager in Rhode Island. He spent years in shipping yards, then moved to the rail-
roads. He laid miles of track through California, until he realized
that Joey Fujii, though constantly moving, was going nowhere.
Unattached, a bachelor still, Joey wanted to come in out of the
weather. He slid on white cotton gloves. His uncle mailed him
shoes from Kyoto so light he glided soundlessly over varnished
floors. He found a position with an asthmatic widower who grew
petulant at the sight of an open window. He studied the future
carefully, smoothed a wrinkle out of his black belt and accepted
the invitation to leave Park Avenue for Oklahoma. He didn't expect
to live very much longer, for what were jujitsu skills next to a
smoking pistol? He preferred a wild, ignoble American death to
this—the frantic dinging of a porcelain bell, a cantankerous old
man's raking cough.

Joey Fujii served her quail on toast the first morning. Then he uncovered a scam in the household accounts. An Irish maid had been keeping the change for years. He waited three weeks, then proposed a greenhouse. He rubbed the lightly sweating palms of his hands against his serving coat and spoke of the temperamental hothouse plants he wished to cultivate.

"That's it. Moved and seconded."

Fujii was a Buddhist. He wondered if this might enhance or hinder his brand-new future, which, he saw by now, had nothing to do with guns or tomahawks. Lavinia had taken her place in the back seat of a new Pierce-Arrow, with Joey behind the wheel. He would perish in a fiery crash, spinning over and over in a thousand turns. The Tennessee walker was now overlooked, a wind-up toy lost in December's surplus.

"I name you chairman of this house. I want you to do it all for me, Joey. You're better and faster at it than I am. Hire more staff if you're stretched too thin. And show me a picture once in a while. Yes, I'd like that. Glossy pictures now and then of things ladies might like for luncheon, or a formal dinner table set for eighteen. Make me a house my husband will be proud of."

He did. And Lorette, older and subtler now, got it right. She remarked on how clever it was that a household appeared more careful while its mistress grew increasingly careless.

"What are you up to, Lavinia Hanks? Joey makes the house turn like a top. Trust me! Let me be the one to know!"

"What am I up to? I'm up to the Lovely Board of Education or some small civic thing. When I'm not—you're quite right—I don't stay in the house a minute longer than I have to. I'm out looking and learning. That turgid imagination of yours."

"What's turgid?"

"Look it up, Low Lady. Shame on you."

"You can't shame me. That's just it. I'm the one you should tell about your secret life."

Lavinia laughed so hard her cheeks wobbled.

"A secret life in Lovely? Oh, that's rich!"

For she'd studied it. And concluded Nelson's secrets made him accountable. They made him tell her where he'd been and with whom, when she hadn't even asked. Secrets brought red roses to her house and rounds of "Let me call you sweetheart," played late at night on the piano downstairs, or an after-dinner audience she'd never been offered and now had to think twice about wanting. Let's sit awhile, Vinnie. Just sit? she answered, her voice incredulous. She'd considered his gallery of secrets and decided that without them and only without them could she remain free. Lavinia wondered briefly if he had one girl or ten, if she cut her hair short and whether she liked the taste of gin. She even had Joey pull the grand car to a stop one day when they were touring. She said "perfect" out loud and startled herself so, she ordered the outing complete.

"Let's get home, Joey. Fast."

For she'd got a glimpse of a young woman idling on a corner, her head held a certain way, and knew Nelson had been with her. Or if not with her, then with someone just like that. A girl slightly saddened by not being an out-and-out beauty but going ahead with it anyway.

The figuring helped to a certain point. Beyond that, the banker's daughter, the banker's wife, figured too much pondering gave a pretty meager yield. Nelson's meanderings might be triggered by her childless state. But maybe not. She lost interest and no longer lay awake. When her husband shuffled into her darkened bedroom and muttered excuses into her back, she yawned and returned to her dreams. Sometimes, the downstairs grandfather clock sounding two or three o'clock in the morning, he asked for her, his hand searching through bedclothes, and she obliged. Holy night, she cried, unused to his desire. She fell open for him and wondered where, oh, where he'd been. Sophisticated, the whole town said. Eroded, she thought, tumbling into a deep bedroom chair that cradled her gently, her clear eyes fixed on her husband, who was trying to hide a blue mark on his neck. I'm like a stone under water, she thought. And stones don't get mad; they get tired.

She saw Lorette to the door, and they both stepped over the slumbering heap of yellow fur. The scruffy cat, a stray Lavinia had taken in, jarred the beauty of the entry.

"You and your cats. Each one is as horrible as the next."

"I know, I know. Take your hat, dear."

She kissed her friend goodbye, then wandered to another room. She picked up her handwork, pierced a robin's red breast with her needle, and worked her stockinged feet into worn slippers she hid in her sewing basket. She thought about looking and listening in perfect safety from the back seat of a Pierce-Arrow. She wondered if the places they toured meant she had a secret life or simply wanted one. A foul smell enveloped her, cutting short her thoughts, and she threw one high-heeled pump at the old cat, who hissed and slouched off.

"A person can't even think without being *gassed* to death."

The air slowly cleared, and so did her thoughts. They settled like maggots on the body of poor Chris Madsen.

chapter 18

Nelson Hanks put himself squarely ahead of the game, most people thought, when he hired Madsen. He set law down in the middle of his operations when he saw rough-and-ready go to dangerous. The fields had changed with the good times, lost all innocence. Money invited elements, as they were called, lured in by good times and anonymity. It hadn't taken a murder, observers praised God, for Hanks to act. Maybe he was just plain tired of sending the company physician from here to hell for the cuts and concussions of oil field scuffles. The retired lawman appeared one day on a soup line, as if he was just another first name on the Hanks payroll. The crumb boss had been feeding oil workers for as long as he could remember. He recognized the toothless old fighter and ladled extra black-eyed peas onto his plate, honored him with a greasy ham hock. The foreman began to breathe easier. He eyed night from his bunkhouse window. The tiny bursts of light signaled his men coming in from town. They lit matches all the long walk home, checking to see if someone tailed them or waited in the dark ahead. There was thievery and more, a change in the temper of men who toiled steadily through exhaustion and pain. He'd seen it happen in streets and in fields. It didn't matter that the sun was up and the boss was nearby; one man knocked over another one, and for what? Just to see him fall, the foreman had been told. I just wanted to watch that ugly bastard drop over. He saw that Madsen's huge hands bled from the weather. He handed him a pair of driving gloves, saying he didn't need them anyways. Madsen gave him one bare pink grin that tightened into a grimace as he slid the gloves over hurting hands.

"When *aren't* you in New York, Nelson? Of course I'm happy you telephoned."

Lavinia hung up the phone, stretched and glanced at her calling cards. The Low Ladies had ceased to exist officially, just as she had once darkly predicted. Individual friendships remained, but there were no more meetings damning piety and narrow minds. Every ilk of charity or society woman lifted the heavy brass knocker on the door of the Hanks home, now that Oklahoma was growing just as earnest as she predicted it would. She loved the wildness of boom towns and feared a string of cities more careful than Creston. She frowned, thinking of the church bazaar coming up later in the week and the hours she stood to piddle away in a Methodist basement.

"World without end. Joey, Joey!"

Fujii was studying samples of damask in the kitchen, sipping coffee. June bugs clung to the screen door. They hung together in a lacquered brown cluster until he knocked them off from inside. The buzzer rang in the foyer, but it might as well have rung inside his skull. He ached all over tonight and thought perhaps he'd taken cold.

"I could do with some night air. And refreshments. Make me up one of your picnic baskets. I'll be down in twenty minutes."

"Will we be out long, Mrs. Hanks?"

"Why, I hope so. I feel like I'm sentenced to this house. A long drive would put me in such a nice frame of mind."

Fujii didn't sleep in the servants' quarters over the garage. His rooms were on top of the house, off a third-floor landing. He was given Lavinia's own childhood bed, the once-upon-a-time bed, she called it. Shipped out from Creston, it had been unused for years. Joey read at night, struggling to wedge his own head into the worn spot she herself had impressed on the mahogany headboard. When he discovered that he slept in a cast-off child's bed, he mentioned to Mrs. Nelson Hanks that he possessed a black belt, hoping she would notice that he was a man. She told him she had half a dozen black belts and wondered why he'd brought it up at all.

He dusted her hard-boiled eggs with paprika and placed two Cornish hens together in one corner. Then he pierced them with a long metal skewer so they wouldn't be dislodged by bumpy roads. There was ample fruit and soda crackers and a thick paste he made from fish eggs. He prepared a thermos of coffee for both of them, as they would be driving all night. He rubbed the back of his neck, then ran a check on doors and windows.

She began eating before they left the driveway. She snapped open the linen napkin and tucked it into the collar of her dress.

"Did you remember to pack black pepper?" Her mouth was full.

"On the right side of the hamper, Mrs. Hanks. Inside the elastic pocket."

He stayed away from the elegant section of town because that was never what Mrs. Nelson Hanks wanted to see. He once pulled up to the Constantine Theater, thinking she would enjoy the handsome people spilling over the sidewalk when the Gish sisters came to town. Peacocks, she had cried. We could go to the zoo and see exactly the same thing. She liked clots of men and the derricks, the way they were lit up at night. She liked dog fights and pool halls and pressed his chauffeur's cap down over his eyes when Joey Fujii objected to her enthusiasms.

"Your husband wouldn't like this one bit. I'm going to lose my job."

"Turn right at the next stop. Don't be a fool." Lavinia licked her lips.

"This is the best little chicken I believe I've ever tasted. You might speed up, Joey. These empty fields give me the heebie-jeebies. Left at the fork."

He thought longingly of his kitchen, the cold white tile counters, topped with finished or beginning tasks. Two pies cooling, for he always made two, apple-scented steam escaping from a slit. Cutlery lined up for him to sharpen, or the silver he never let darken, that he would slowly rub with chamois cloth. He loved every inch of the Hanks home and suspected that houses gave love in return. That the house, not the people in it, would somehow reward him one day for his careful attention and insistence that dust and decay go elsewhere. He thought of the solid front door, the reassuring jerk it required to open it at all. He watched that massive front door for fissures and buffed the brass fixtures until his arm throbbed. How could she be "sentenced" to this house? Was she such a fool as to confuse a prison and a home? He pressed on the accelerator, wishing he were plumping up the pillows on a bed or making up a grocery list. He sped along empty roads.

Lavinia let her head rest on the window. The weight on her chest had lifted. She thought of a trip she and Joey had made to a town named for old Chief Bigheart. They stopped for lunch, and midway through her pot pie, Lavinia heard a quartet pipe up down the street. She gobbled what was left on her plate and headed toward the sound of such music, as Joey slowly followed alongside in the car. You don't mean that boy's an oil field worker! What's his name? she asked someone in the crowd outside a drugstore. Name's Clark Gable. Pretty young buck, ain't he? Maybe tonight would produce a first-order surprise, another handsome roustabout with a fairy-tale name. Lavinia stroked the fringe on her shawl, suddenly fearing the sight of so many tangled black trees. Joey cried out suddenly.

"Hold on!"

The car swung around in the rear as he braked. Men and cars, their headlights crisscrossed but trained on the same thing, stood smack in the middle of the uneven road. She recognized some of the faces that turned around to greet them. Company men. One, the fellow with the pregnant wife and pregnant daughter, turned his big eyes to the ground and shielded his face from her.

Joey's heart raced. She was out of the car before he could lift his fingers from the steering wheel. He should have hung on to her wrists, protected her from whatever was out there, causing men and cars to assemble in the dead middle of a county road. Instead, he sat shaking, soaked by the water that ran from his forehead.

"Why, it's Mrs. Hanks!"

"Ma'am, don't come a step further. You wouldn't want to—"

"What's wrong out here? Why are all you people—oh, oh."

It seeped out. Her "oh" seemed so small next to the sight of old Chris Madsen, dead so long and maggoty now. Madsen's mouth was held open. His toothless gums were clamped down on something. She fought the men who blocked her path and her revulsion, which was nearing an end. In minutes, she knew, she would be retching inside that wall of spiky trees. But not before she saw, not before she forced herself to see.

"Let me through. What's that in his mouth? Poor man. Oh, poor man. Move, Mr. Stanley."

She examined it in the bleached light of so many garbled head-lights, covering her mouth with a handkerchief. It seemed to be, but surely wasn't . . . She looked up at the men for confirmation.

Jammed in, crammed in, a cow's teat held Madsen's mouth ajar. Lavinia's mind caved in on all but certain details. The way insects assumed dominion, for example. They took over Madsen's body in no time and even became its own proper feature. She headed un-steadily out of the circle of men, making for the scrub oaks. Holding on to trunks and vines, she let sickness take her completely. Talk penetrated, though. She held on to trees and heard.

"This here's an old feud."

"Wasn't it Madsen who opened up the strip?"

"It was. With the same pistol you see here. And a government stud. Hell, I read about him when I was just a kid."

"Vengeance killing, most likely."

"Yeah, and then the killer thought he'd go on and pull a joke, just to get even more even. Poor Madsen, always apologizing about not having any teeth in his mouth. Lord, but this thing's ugly. Swish off them bugs, Daniel."

"I, for one, got exactly what I wanted." A newspaperman had got him to talk, despite the immigrant's notorious shyness about his crippled speech, the accent that would keep him barely under-stood for an entire lifetime. Underneath the shyness basked a for-eigner's zeal, a certainty that his chosen country would offer him whatever he had the courage and decision to grab for himself. The marshal was allowed not only to officiate the run but to participate in it. He staked out his claim and found a man under some bushes near his creek. He woke the intruder and found the man had fallen asleep while waiting for the land run to start. Madsen kicked him swiftly in the ribs and ran him off the property. Had he bumped into the same fellow here, years later? And been issued a final property stake in the center of a lonely back road? Someone found a gunnysack. The smell was rising now and carrying. Lavinia heard him being pulled off, that awful drag. She wiped her mouth. She was empty without being lighter and wondered if a human spirit could be disinfected, like sickroom sheets or a kitchen floor.

She opened the car door herself, seeing that Joey was in worse shape than she was.

"Time we went home, Joey. That's enough looking for one night."

She wondered who to call first. Nelson, to tell him he was minus a lawman? Or Dr. Janus, to plead for more sleeping powder? Each of the Low Ladies, to whom she would explain that an end had come to their wild days, just as she had once predicted? No, she would ring up Lorette, to tell her how age and station would now have to suffice. And how a secret life had ended before it had even begun.

"I've got to expand the operation, Vinnie."

She telephoned his secretary now for luncheon appointments. He forgot otherwise.

"You're mad."

Trade magazines lay at their feet. Telegrams had begun arriving since nine that morning, congratulating Nelson personally on his company's victory over Union Carbide. LOOKS LIKE DAVID AND GOLIATH ALL OVER AGAIN. THANKS FOR AN IMPRESSIVE VICTORY. Delighted shareholders reveled in the outcome of a long legal battle. It was ruled that Hanks Petroleum violated no patent in its method of processing natural gas. Nelson had gone on national radio to protest. "Those fellas at Union Carbide might as well sue Egypt, as far as we're concerned. This is an ancient process we're talking about. We're using it to create natural gas, while they were turning out Egyptian hooch. Hell, if my men are guilty, then so are the pharaohs!" Vinnie smiled, listening. His drawl was becoming. The announcer sounded too clipped and brisk beside him.

"How large would you like to be, Nelson? You're already the largest supplier of natural gas in the country. Says so here." She tapped the top of a petroleum journal with her foot. "Watch out you don't bump your head on the sky."

"Which is exactly why I need to expand the operation. I've scoured New York. Been run through those estates on Long Island till I'm carsick, trying to find a larger operation."

"Operation? Some people call them homes."

"I've got big ideas, Vinnie."

"Don't I know it."

"We're still not half of what we could be. What separates the men from the boys, after all, isn't money."

"Then what does?"

"Spectacle. A generous public life."

"You have something on your chin."

"Have you heard a single word?"

"Each and every. You'd be surprised how familiar they all are by now. Not that there isn't comfort in that. But this is no revelation, if you must know."

"I haven't ever discussed this with you."

"You don't have to. How do you intend to expand your operation?"

"With land. With a ranch. I've outgrown this, Vinnie."

His arm indicated not only the sunroom where they sat lolling, but the grounds, too. An acre and a half. A green dream, now that Joey had complete control. His greenhouse functioned as floral library and laboratory. No one objected when he began discussing a gazebo. It was soon constructed, downwind of his night-blooming jasmine. Single-color flower beds, formal by local standards, studded the expanse.

"I want to woo 'em, Vinnie. And I can't do the job of it that I want on board some oversized tuna boat. They've had their fill of yachts and resort hotels. I want to do what I'm best at."

"Have you found it yet? The operation, I mean."

"Prettiest country you ever saw. And about fifteen miles from this sunroom."

"I take it you've already signed the papers."

"Nothing but a preliminary set."

"Any buildings on this paradise of yours?"

"Not a one. Just wood, lakes and rocks. Perfect spot for a lodge, too. Right next to Spencer Spring."

"Al Spencer Spring? Marvelous. You'll have to stage the Okesa holdup for your East Coast visitors."

"Say, there's an idea."

People liked the idea of Frank Nash and Al Spencer joining up on a job. Stories of their train robbery were told and retold, sleepy-eyed kids hanging on at the dinner table until the very end, their favorite part, where the outlaws made off with twenty thousand dollars' worth of Liberty Bonds. Al Spencer lit out for the Osage hills, and someone swore the campsite next to the little creek had been his. Spencer Spring stuck.

Nelson watched her spread a layer of butter on her biscuit. She then added a blanket of jam, even finished by popping the spoon into her mouth. Newspaper articles, reporting on the wide swath of her civic activities, described her as a "handsome woman," a phrase he regretted. She continued to build her own hairpieces out of what she found on pillows and between boar bristles. The heavy coil of hair acquired more mass every day, and he found it unbe-coming. His wife would soon be forty. Despite their age difference, she seemed to be gaining on him.

He cleared his throat and felt ashamed of how quickly large ideas were crowded out. He had an increasingly shorter focus, and he wondered who would be around for his first slip. The first indi-cation that eminent Nelson Hanks wasn't always paying strict at-tention.

"So the answer is yes."

"What was the question?"

"Whether you approve of my scheme. Whether you think it's half-baked. If in your dreams—"

"When will you forget all that? Those were a younger woman's dreams. A woman who was all wrapped up in a country exploding in front of her eyes. I don't believe I've had one of those dreams for years. Years. When I sleep now, I'm dead to the world. And hap-pier for it, I should add."

Nelson watched as she reached for her third biscuit. How much did she intend to eat?

"If you're asking me whether you're ready for a show palace, the answer is yes. If you're asking whether you should give in, once and for all, to showmanship, the answer is yes. Hiring Madsen was a start. Those weeks he strutted across your fields gave the most ordinary work another dimension. Murder brought him in even closer. I overheard two men talk about the way he stroked the top of his gun as if he were still doing it. And in *your* oil fields! Calling yourself Uncle Nelson—another beau geste they simply lap up. Uncle Nelson! What corporation would tolerate such a contriv-ance? Yours. Hanks Petroleum. You've already begun, and now it's time to move full steam ahead. You're big enough and bored enough, my dear."

"I beg your pardon?"

"Quite obviously bored. Not three weeks ago I watched you cut Eugene Du Pont off right in the middle of what he was saying to quote Will Rogers. You interrupted a magnate! And with nothing but a quip from a simpleminded, star-studded cowboy."

"That Du Pont. Never met such a stuffed shirt in my entire life."

"Your mind is wandering, and it shows. It's high time you had a proper forum. Give those Nelson boys the backyard they deserve."

There were five of them so far. Five sturdy boys who carried the name Nelson. Touched at first and slightly starry-eyed, Hanks of-

fered each proud parent a U.S. bond in honor of the little namesake. He smiled for the camera and peered inside the rough
blankets. He was still smiling for the camera by the time the fifth
boy appeared, but fatigue was evident. And consternation.

"A wailing fatso. And he doesn't look a bit like me."

"Why should he? You're not his father."

He reddened before his wife and faltered, for there it was. He
forgot, little by little, that he wasn't. By the time the fifth infant
appeared, he allowed himself gentle inquiries about a Nelson boy's
test scores or baseball standing. Road conditions on the way out
to Colorado, when family vacations took a little Nelson traveling,
or the possibility of Boy Scout Den 54 taking on a latecomer in
time for the regatta. The wailing fatso beat his fists in the air and
took his place beside the others.

"Live in Lovely, do you?" He eyed the woman who stood in front
of him.

"That's right, sir. We come up from Louisiana. My husband's
brother's been telling us for years Hanks Petroleum is the only
company in the world worth working for. My Jack loaded us all in
the truck last June and wouldn't tell us where we was driving until
we got to the state line. Baby here was conceived around about
then, and we figured, why not name him for the boss of things? Oh,
say now, little Nelson! Wish, wish, wish. There's my boy. Lie still
now. It's been our pleasure, Mr. Hanks. Thank you so much for
little Nelson's bond. He'll treasure it when he's a man. Wish, wish,
my best baby."

The granny installed in the cab of the truck opened her arms for
the child. Nelson watched as the mother climbed in beside her.
Her eyes had a funny dull cast, and he wondered if she was liter-
ate. And if she wasn't, how would she read him bedtime stories or
help with his homework or . . . Wish, wish, wish, that nursery coo
of hers. Was she stupider or smarter than the others in just calling
it out loud and clear? Because, of course, the others wished, too.
For good fortune and luck. For prowess and horse sense. They
wanted sons and leaders. They named their boys accordingly,
never guessing that the gesture left Nelson Hanks honored and
stricken, charged once more with being an honorary daddy. Their
tire struck the curb. He watched them rumble off, holding his panic
for the baby's safety in check.

"Go ahead and clear, Joey."

She broke a rosebud from a stem and slipped it into his lapel.

"Damn it, you've spotted my coat."

"Water dries. There, you look very dapper."

"Those boys already have backyards."

"You were certainly never at home with a metaphor. I'll speak plainly. I think the ranch idea is perfect and, moreover, the road leading there is wide open. We've got clubs full of millionaires, and one more old moneybag isn't going to make a single bit of difference. Pay attention to your own inattention. It means you're ready to go on to something else."

"I'm going to be late. I didn't come home for this talk that goes around and round in circles."

He watched as Lavinia rubbed the knuckles on her left hand. She had begun to complain of arthritis.

"Be, Nelson."

"What the devil are you talking about?"

"Be a story."

"Oh, Lavinia, you wear a man down. How can I be a story when I'm only a man?"

He had his hat on.

"For the sake of your new child."

"Lord, Lord. That's it. I've already taken it up with that new public relations fella. We're going to discourage it somehow. Discreetly. He's a helluva writer, and he plans to do a piece in the company bulletin about this rash of Nelson boys. Worse than the smallpox. Well, who's gone and done it now?"

"I have."

He mouthed *You what*, and then he collapsed in disbelief, hitting the chair with a thud. He looked at her hands, folded chastely over her stomach. Nelson thought of John Trappe's modern formula with a crooked smile.

"Holy Night, Lavinia!"

"It certainly was."

Hubbell and Mary

chapter 19

1957

"Lock your door."

"Mommy, I'm sleepy. I don't want to take a drive. I want to go back to bed."

"Shut your eyes, Baby. I'll let you know when we get to where we're going."

"Can we at least listen to the radio?"

"What a question."

"I don't think Daddy would like this."

"Daddy's in Chicago. Close those eyes."

They took the errand car for night drives. The car was always parked in the driveway, the key in the ignition. In her last recorded drive in the errand car, Aresta, pumped the accelerator furiously when the car stalled, finally pushing it over to the shoulder of the road to wait for the mechanic, with her arms folded over her chest. While she waited for help, it rained (she said) inside the car, without a cloud in the sky. There was no longer a mileage gauge, and the speedometer was stuck at sixty. It had been rammed so many times that the chrome fenders front and back curved into soft, graceful folds. Passengers complained that a permanent smell of wet wool permeated the car. Battered oranges sometimes rolled out from under the driver's seat.

Laydelle's slippered feet rested on the dashboard. She dozed, her hands tucked under her cheek, and startled at the touch of her mother's cool hand.

"We're here. Wake up, Baby."

"Let me sleep."

"Plenty of time for sleep. Sit up. There's my girl. Scoot closer. That's not so bad, is it?"

They were parked in front of the bus depot. The terminal itself was nearly empty, but outside the building, lined up on the ample wooden benches, was an assortment of men and women. Some of them linked arms to sleep, locked uneasily into place.

"Take a good look. I really want you to look. Never shrink from what is possible."

Tobacco was spat, backs slapped and bottles shared or hoarded. No enmity was in evidence, though the area was patrolled by a sleepy police officer. He strolled, checking his watch, then dug up something to eat from a pants pocket.

"I don't want to look at those dirty men."

"That could be us, Baby. Just think. Look at that poor woman asleep on her duffel bag! Are you not looking on purpose?"

"This is a bad place, Mommy. We're not like these people."

"We're not like them now, but one day we could be. You know something? Maybe that woman had a big old creaky house full of kids and animals. Maybe she put up summer vegetables in her basement, the way we do. Corn and tomatoes, anything she could coax out of the soil. Or maybe she just had a rock garden out back. With a birdbath. She just may have had a birdbath out back. Or maybe not. Maybe she wasn't domestic at all. Maybe she had a thousand ideas a minute that had nothing to do with a house and a yard. Only she didn't let her ideas out."

One of the women on the bench jerked awake and stabbed at the air with one straight forefinger.

"That's it, all right. Those ideas of hers just cracked her skull open like a farm-fresh egg."

"When is Daddy coming home?"

"I told you." She held her hands together as if gripping a megaphone. *"Your daddy will be home on Thursday.* Go to sleep now. It's time to go home."

Sleep. Her mother pressed her into bed after the drive back, tucking the sheets around her tightly. Her eyes burned first, until she couldn't shut them. Next it was her throat, which stuck shut when she tried to cool it with a glass of water. She grabbed a record, any record, and fumbled with it in the dark. She raised the volume and clicked on her Teletalk, pulling her covers up to her chin to wait for her mother. She didn't have long to wait.

"Turn off that noise."

"It's not noise, it's music."

"It's noise to me. Laydelle, I was sound asleep."

"So was I. Why'd you wake me up to go for a ride?"

"Everything I do is for your own good. Turn that thing off and come on."

"If she did have a house and a vegetable garden, if she had kids and animals, she must have had a husband, too."

"Must have."

"Why did he let her leave the house and sleep like that, all crumpled up on a bench? Daddy would never let that happen to us."

"Daddy, Daddy, Daddy. I'd wish you'd stop repeating that! Daddies aren't bricks or dams or bomb shelters. They're just men, for heaven's sake. Life is stuffed with possibilities that daddies have nothing to do with. About time you learned, too. Life is crouched out there like a giant cat, Baby, coming at us. Life is always ready to pounce whether we know it or not. Come on to bed."

Mary paused.

"Promise you won't ever turn the music up like that again. It *hurts* me. I've said that a dozen times."

They lay together in a tangle. A trespasser in Mary's warm bed, Laydelle sought her mother's bushy hair and heartbeat. She even knocked up against her on purpose, triggering kicks and punches, hot, sour sighs. She slept fitfully and was the first to hear Aresta's outburst in the morning. She was giving the new girl a piece of her mind, for her work was slipshod, lamentable. Mr. Hanks had raised her too soon, and the extra twenty dollars went straight to her head. Aresta waved a list of infractions in her face (chipped teacup, dust on the stairwell, tangled fringe on Persian rug), and then, right then on the driveway, in front of the lawn boy and the neighbor's gardener, who happened to be standing on the corner, the emergency brake slipped on the errand car. It rolled over Aresta's foot. The new girl pulled her apron over her head to hide her laughter. The lawn boy disappeared into the greenhouse, to see about his violets. The neighbor's gardener studied the whole situation from the corner and decided to eat lunch right then and there. He set upon a turkey wing, watching as the Hanks' cook and head housekeeper pummeled the hood of the errand car with her fists.

Laydelle's mother joined her at the window where she watched.

"Looks like we're on our own for breakfast. Lord, I hope her foot's not broken. How does oatmeal sound?"

"Maypo. I know how to make Maypo."

Aresta pushed at her cereal with a spoon, her leg elevated on a kitchen chair.

"Eat your Maypo, Aresta. It's getting cold."

"Can't hardly eat when I'm thinking about Saint Louis."

Mary Hanks sighed and let her thoughts wander. When Aresta grieved, it could take days.

"People like working in that city. Folks are proud. Not like here."

"You want her fired?"

"If she was my own, I'd give her a good licking. Big as she is."

"Can you work with her, Aresta? Or do you want me to let her go?"

"If you ask me, it's that raise that did it. She worked fine before that little extra come her way. Ouch."

Her knee wrapped in a towel (for the pain had lodged there, darting right through her foot), her dignity restored, Aresta turned out a spate of fine food that day. When the lawn boy appeared at the back door, hungry, there was ham and gravy, hot biscuits already split open. She even coddled the new girl some, urging her to sit down for some fresh lemonade. Here, honey, take the weight off for a few minutes. She watched her drink the whole glass with her chin pulled back, her thick neck working. When Mary Hanks repealed her raise at the end of the day, the new girl stomped off, spitting into a bowl of bread batter on her way out. She slammed the door so hard the china in the cupboard rattled. Aresta, calm and vindicated, threw the batter out, reaching for more flour, to begin again.

"Nasty! Good riddance to bad rubbish. Try help for four across."

Help didn't fit. Laydelle put her head down, pushing the cross-word puzzle away. She would work her mind's eye instead, learn-ing to keep every bit of it. Aresta's broad back, the china trembling behind golden oak doors. Even the tired lawn boy working his way up the path with tiger lilies for the dinner table. She stored it all in that way, every worthy sight and sound, hoarding detail in an invulnerable inside place, against the time when it would all, as her mother promised, disappear.

"Isn't this fun? Just the three of us for once. No Aresta in the kitchen, no William in the flower beds, no new girl putting us all in a bad temper. Now who wants seconds?"

Hubbell Hanks peered at something on his plate.

"Mary, what was this?"

"Don't you mean what is this?"

"No. I mean what was this. This is the same leftover you gave us last night, with something else done to it."

Mary Hanks lifted her eyebrows and shrugged, then smirked at her accomplice.

"Laydelle and I thought we'd have a little fun in the kitchen, didn't we, Baby? You have no sense of adventure, Hubb. None. Coffee?"

"You picked a terrific moment to play house. Just marvelous."

Mary Hanks decided periodically she could manage just fine, thanks. Her house, her gardens. She decided to cook, clean and shop for provisions, just like any other American housewife. She wanted to talk to herself in her own kitchen without someone chiming in with an answer or a beg your pardon. She wanted to pay her own bills or just let them stack up. Most of all, Mary Hanks wanted to carpool. She phoned women she knew vaguely through the PTA, disrupting their driving schedules until, exhausted, she heaved up the whole silly idea, letting William drive her daughter to school as he'd always done. Aresta took all of Mary Hanks' notions in stride, buying a round-trip ticket for Saint Louis, where people still knew how to conduct themselves. William took his banishment less well, minding greatly the death of a tropical plant or the sudden arrival of hardy perennials Mary Hanks planted in his absence. They didn't see eye to eye, never had. He left pointers for Mrs. Hanks, notes on the temperature control in his precious greenhouse. That this information was destined to be ignored consumed him completely.

It generally took three weeks. Three weeks before she wired Aresta and drove over herself to fetch William from his place in the country, for he had no telephone service. She took her defeat in stride, saying she could have done it, could certainly have done it.

Only she was one person, not three. And this Lovely house, these
gardens she toyed with replanting, sapped her so that she had
nothing left for a finer cause. Complete freedom from domestic
cares meant Mary could focus on her real work in progress, Hubbell Hanks.

"It's you, Hubb. This is *so right.*"

Hubbell stood suited up in a costume from L. L. Bean. He was
khaki-coated from head to foot, and the jacket Mary had mail-
ordered involved, as promised in the catalogue, fourteen pockets,
some hidden and others exposed. The jacket sported snaps, buttons and zippers in three locations. On the bed, waiting for Hubbell's approving acceptance, lay an assortment of cashmere
turtlenecks in muted colors and crisp, sky-blue button-down shirts.
More khaki, this time cuffed and pleated.

"I don't know, Mary. I feel kind of silly. I don't hunt, after all."

"That's completely insignificant, darling. You don't have to hunt
to enjoy the Bean look. Why, I bet half the men who order from
their catalogue wouldn't know a moose from a goose."

Hubbell stared at the image in the footed mirror. He looked like
a fool. Still, he didn't want to hurt Mary's feelings. She had gone
to a lot of trouble. And she was so avid that he look right.

"Close your eyes, Hubb. Don't cheat now. Promise you can't
see?"

"They're closed."

"Ta da!"

She held a porkpie hat in both hands. Hubbell shook his head
fiercely. As much as he loved his beautiful, brainy little Mar, he
wouldn't go around with that thing on his head.

"What are you shaking your head for?"

"I don't like hats. Never have, never will."

"Mommy?"

Laydelle appeared in her parents' doorway. A teddy bear
dragged at one side. She was having a tea party with her bedrag-
gled brown bear, and this constituted play. Except when her bear
refused to drink. The muzzle was soaking wet, and so was the
front of her dress.

"My tea is too hot, I think."

"Not now."

She sucked the nose of the bear, extracting fuzz and some sugar.

She had emptied the entire sugar bowl into the pot of tea while Aresta napped.

"On second thought . . . come here, Baby. Come see how Daddy looks with his handsome new hat and jacket. Isn't he handsome? Isn't your daddy the handsomest man in Lovely, Oklahoma, and maybe even the handsomest man alive?"

The child frowned into the image reflected in the mirror, and Mary brushed her bangs from her face, pulling the wrinkles back with the gesture.

"Ow."

"Tell Daddy what you think."

Laydelle held the bear tight, still dear though he wouldn't drink tea, and began examining the jacket, buttoning and unbuttoning, sliding her finger inside tiny, hidden spaces just big enough for a fish hook, a compass or a little girl's forefinger. Mary snatched the bear from her hands and continued talking.

"What did I tell you? You're too old to play with stuffed animals. Now tell Daddy what you think."

Laydelle burst into giggles, and Hubbell tipped his head to one side.

"You see? Mary, face facts. I look downright foolish. Now I know they'll honor returns, so there's no need to get in a huff. It's hard to buy clothing for someone else. Damned hard."

Uh oh. Hubbell thought he might have diverted her by involving Laydelle, but he saw that had only made matters worse. He felt sideswiped by Mary's fury, though she hadn't even raised her voice. Her cheeks were the approximate color of eggplant.

"You bet it's hard, Hubbell Hanks. After all, I can't exactly set a London Fog in the crook of your arm and give you a peck on the cheek as you walk out the door to work. I can't shop for tastefully sober suits and white shirts with just the right tie, because you don't need them."

"Why, Mary, you surprise me!"

"Is that so?"

"You sound as if you want me to look like all the other working stiffs in America."

Mary's eyes sparkled, and Laydelle tucked her head under Hubbell's chin, giving the bear's sweetened muzzle one last suck.

"Wrong again, Hubb. I never was one to kid myself. I married a man of leisure. So what do I do? I take three full days to define appropriate clothing for a man of leisure. I order the goods and instead of thanks I get lip. Look like a slump, Hubbell Hanks. Look like a slump and just see if I care."

Mary threw herself on the bed and began to wail. Laydelle, seeing her mother dissolve, did the same. Hubbell jostled her lightly, shushing her, but it did no good. His wife cried and cried, in the midst of all the careful, creased new clothing spread out on their bed. Hubbell set the child down, for his bouncing had only increased her chagrin. He patted his wife. He smoothed her hair. He handed her a linen hankie.

"Mar, Mar. What a lout I am! Hey there, I'm sorry. Mary, stop crying, won't you please? I'll wear the stuff. Maybe not the hat— oh, okay, I'll wear the hat but only when it's wet out. I'll try to look better. Mary, can you hear me?"

Her reply, issued deep inside one of Lavinia Hanks' needlepoint pillows, should have been muffled. But Mary's answer rang out like a clarion.

"It's no use!"

"No, no, Mary. You're absolutely right. Look at me, Mary. I'm wearing your hat."

Mary turned her red face right side up and burst into tears a second time.

"You're the one who's right, Hubbell Hanks. You look like a fool in that hat. I'm sending it all back tomorrow, every last thing."

The packages went out the next day, but she didn't despair. No one could keep Mary Hanks down for long. She trusted both the nature and the inexhaustible number of her own instincts. As soon as one experiment to showcase her husband failed, another surfaced. Something would come along, and she would seize it with both hands when it did.

Mary and Laydelle were cutting up a fruit salad in a fever. The fruit was bruised and going, just about to turn.

"These strawberries. Oh, these strawberries absolutely break my heart. See what happens when our eyes are bigger than our stomachs?"

Laydelle yanked hard on a stem. Most of the fruit came off with it. Mary Hanks slapped her hand lightly, and the slap surprised the child so, she fell off the footstool. Casually, without apology, Mary helped her climb back on top.

"Shame on you. I said to salvage what we can for the salad."

The fruit salad that night was a soggy, tasteless composition. Laydelle mashed it into pulp as her mother drummed her nails on the table. Hubbell Hanks had begged off after nights of his wife's home cooking. He would "have something" at the club after his golf game.

"Mommy?"

"Don't hunch over like that, Baby. You're going to grow into a C. What?"

"Are we poor pretending to be rich, or rich pretending to be poor?"

Mary Hanks brightened, thinking of that.

"I don't think we're one or the other. I think we're smack in the middle and waiting. That's it. We're waiting."

"Then how come we live in such a big house if we need to be scared all the time?"

"Why, this isn't OUR house, Baby. It's your daddy's house. And your daddy's house used to be his daddy's house. The Dominion was and still is Nelson Hanks' place. Oh, but don't you worry. I'll get us out of here. Hubbell won't be content to stay here forever, I'll see to that. Once I get your daddy off and running, we won't have to be scared all the time. Your father's half of what he could be, but once I light a fire under him—why, you just wait! We need to keep our heads on straight is all."

Laydelle dropped her head lower and bent more accurately into a C. Her mother's words beaded up and rolled away, as she struggled to hold everything in place. The bell pull, the grand piano, the secret passage built into the library wall. Lavinia Hanks' handmade pillows, which splashed the house with cross-stitched Queen Anne roses and symbols of the Orient and homilies (*Waste Not, Want Not*) transported all the way from Creston, Iowa. She could summon up anything, singly or massed together in a larger frame like a crowded portrait, and this recall was pure victory.

Mary Hanks tickled her daughter under the chin, coaxing a smile. She outlined a heart in the air with one finger.

"You really are, you know."

"What?"

"My Baby. My Joy Baby."

c h a p t e r   2 0

1958

When Hubbell agreed to move to Tulsa, Mary whistled for weeks. He heard her on the steps, in the bath, downstairs in the kitchen, free melody squeezing through her pursed lips. She had been delighted to leave The Dominion, the Lovely house they acquired when Nelson died, the house Mary declared was so full of ghosts there was no room for them. He was sure buying this new home of their own guaranteed happiness. He had been glad to leave, too. Those lonely months he had spent in Lovely just waiting for Mary to return from the Joy Baby campaign had been revealing. The walls closed in on him after her departure, until, late at night and many drinks later, they stopped just short of squeezing the breath from him. The pack of goons (as Mary dubbed them) hired to watch over his wife and child after the campaign ended, and finally Amos Sweet, Jr., had been as much about the brand of awfulness and fear he suffered there as the letters addressed to Mrs. Joy Baby. They both fled Lovely, really, though this new house would prove as much a public display as The Dominion. Just what *kind* of public display was a question that tormented Mary so much that all the show tunes, all the sweet, formless melodies pouring from her buoyant soul, dried up and disappeared, practically overnight.

"We were too rash. Oh, I see it all so clearly, Hubb. We moved too fast on this thing."

"We both decided on this place. We bought it together."

"Yes."

"Then what? Good God, Mary, what now? Are you telling me you don't like your new house?"

"It isn't that. It's very comfortable and pretty and everything a house should be, except . . ."

The house irked people. It irked them because it suggested an outrageous duality in its owner, who seemed to talk out of both sides of his mouth. When the sign went up that read Private Property, passersby wondered why the hell he didn't put up a fence if that was how he felt. And most people didn't see that the pretty but relatively modest house stacked up to that carpeted spread in front. Oh, they didn't know. But mostly, because it was riverfront, because Hubbell and his strange wife had refused to go with a stone fence or any kind of fence at all, they felt invited and excluded all at once. Plus they knew he was the Hanks boy, that he could have thrown a French château up on the place, as oil people did in Houston, and nobody would have batted an eye. The house wasn't even satisfyingly tacky. One thing they did enjoy, though, the fishermen who worked the Arkansas River for carp and catfish or the adventurers who struggled through the wilds along the banks before the parks department decided they needed to spruce things up, or the drivers out for a Sunday jaunt on Riverview Road. That was the sight of the little one coming out of the white house. The sudden appearing dot of a girl would come most days toward four o'clock and press the automatic awning button they could see from where they sat or sauntered. And it would lower, regal as a palm fan in a Tarzan movie, to cool her and shade her from the killing sun. They could see her neat white stockings moving back and forth in the swing. Too far to know if she was having a cold drink or some ice cream, but it didn't matter. They'd seen the automatic awning dropping, and that was enough.

". . . except it doesn't stand for anything."

"It stands for beauty, Mary, because it is beautiful. It also stands for shelter and protection, which both strike me as good things unless you've decided they're not."

"When people drive by, they have no idea who we are."

Mary held Laydelle tighter than ever. She was sitting pretty indeed in her mother's lap. They were dressed in matching pink

skirts and blouses, and by Mary's reckoning, it was the last year
they could. When a mother-daughter team reached a certain point,
she felt, their similarities were all too apparent, and too much
became too much. The two of them were just about there.

"An oil well wouldn't be bad. In miniature, of course. Perfectly
re-created, down to the last detail. We could have it built by one
of the old-timers. Heavens, Lovely is full of them, and it won't be
forever. Having a teensy, tasteful monument to the industry out
front would kill several birds with one stone."

Hubbell turned his head to see if his wife was joking. But there
was no grin on her face. Her eyes were not turned up at the edges
but wide and staring off into middle space, the way they did when
she was thinking hard.

"People driving by should know you're Hubbell Hanks."

"Why should they?"

She kissed Laydelle lightly on top of her head and pushed her off
the swing.

"Go play, Baby. Daddy and I need to have a little talk."

Laydelle sucked the inside of her cheek and dusted her forehead
with the end of one braid. She studied the empty green space in
front of her for a few seconds, then turned to go inside.

"Play in the front yard, honey. Go on, run and have fun. Take
your puppy with you; he's getting all fat from sitting."

She got down on all fours to coax the bone away from her new
dog, who lay curled in a basket. The puppy made a terrible fuss,
growling and clawing as she wrestled it from its mouth.

"He doesn't want to walk, Mommy."

"Of course he does."

"No, he doesn't, and I don't, either. It's too hot. I want to stay
under the awning."

"It's a beautiful day. I'm counting, Baby, and when I get to three
you'd better be running with your puppy. One . . . two . . ."

Laydelle pulled hard on the leash, and the white puppy bounced
down the steps on its rear end, finally breaking into a lopsided trot.
This lasted several seconds, then child and dog settled into a slow
trudge that would carry them over a lawn unmarred by a single
stickleburr or dry spot. No incline, no decline, it was a sumptuous
level stretch, tended every day of the week. Mary stood up on the
porch. She pushed her voice into a shout.

"Take off your shoes, silly. Run! Play! It's your own private patch
of velvet, for heaven's sake. Now take advantage of it!"

"Mary."

He tried to take hold of her waist, but she shrugged him off, her eyes on her now barefoot daughter.

"Mary, when will you relax? When will you just lean back and live?"

She whirled to face him. Hubbell thought that of all the sights he'd ever seen, from the Rocky Mountains to Baja and well beyond, he would never, ever see anything so marvelous as Mary-Right-This-Second, whose blond hair had come free of the tight knot, curling at the temples and the base of her neck. The water glinted behind her.

"Never, so it does no good to ask. And that may be the root of our problem. The time for relaxing is over. You can't afford to let possibilities float by anymore like a raft on that old river. And neither can I."

"Mary, we're secure. We have all the money we'll ever need."

"I'm not talking about money. I'm talking about personal enhancement. I'm talking about using your name, your family history, to its full advantage, the way you did when you fused the Toni tour with Hanks Petroleum."

"I did that so you'd marry me."

"Well, you got me. You got a woman who only stops long enough to sleep. I want to live *to the hilt*. If you don't feel the same way, stand back. I mean that from the bottom of my heart."

Hubbell bit his knuckle. He wished he understood. He wished he could see the line that led from an oil derrick model standing in his front yard for all the world to see and any of the words his wife had just used. To the hilt. Yes, yes, he was for that and had always been, but something wasn't clear. There was something Mary wanted him to seize that remained just out of reach.

"Look at her. She's slumping! Her shoes are back on her feet when I've just invited her to slip them off and run."

"Mary, you're a tyrant. Why, you're a charming, incorrigible little tyrant. It's a good thing I adore you."

"I don't need adoration. I need get-up-and-go. I need a kindred spirit. I need . . ."

"Finish your sentence. I can take it."

"I need a drink."

Hubbell jumped to his feet. The sky was in flames. Reds and oranges, fantastic remnants of a white-hot day, layered a ceiling that grew more florid by the minute. The power company, just across the river, would shortly turn into an illuminated castle. They had front-row seats to the finest theater in town, so far as he was concerned. *Carpe diem.* He had garnered that much from his studies. Not only would Hubbell Hanks seize the day, he would seal it off, secure it somehow in memory and in fact, for there would never be another one quite like it.

"Should I make us a couple of martoodies?"

"Why not? And make mine a double."

She sighed, and maybe that sigh meant he had won this round of the debate that, more and more, colored their existence. Life equaled pleasure. Mary's struggle was incomprehensible. It seemed to him she was always preparing for battle. With little or no imagining, he could see his little Mar strapping on iron leggings, slipping a sword into its scabbard. Where are the enemies, Mar? he would find himself shouting. But not now. Mary-Right-This-Second was lolling in a chair, taking it easy, with her bare feet propped on a clean white rail. He would get them martinis, but first he would kiss each tip of his wife's perfect toes. Mary's eyes, violent and blue, moved from the top of her husband's tousled head to her daughter, lying facedown in the middle of the grass, the puppy's leash held tight in her fist.

"Damned if she'll turn a cartwheel or do a somersault. She's as tough as they come."

"Mary, she's only a child."

He continued his kisses, though Mary was oblivious.

"Hmmmph. A child with a stronger will than most adults. Laydelle, get up! Will you *please* get up?"

Looking back on it, as Mary did, leaving The Dominion took forever. Months would pass, then a box would arrive at the new house, full of things they had left behind in a corner of Nelson Hanks' town house, now museum, that a kindly curator or Lavinia Hanks sorority woman would place in a box lined with old newspapers and tissue.

"Aresta, do you have any idea what they mean by this?"

She waved a yellow slip of paper in front of Aresta, who was mending a blouse and didn't bother looking up.

"The notice says we refused to accept a parcel last Tuesday."

"If you mean the parcel from Lovely, yeah, I know what they

mean. They mean we don't have no more room for this stuff, how 'bout you take this off our hands. Well, no, thank you. We don't need one more thing in this house. Way I see it, if those ladies don't know what to do with Lavinia Hanks' old sewing kit or all those movie pictures the Jap took instead of doing any real work, it sure isn't our problem."

"But it could be something important!"

"Could be. Not likely."

"Oh, Aresta. Now I have to go all the way downtown."

Sometimes the packages *were* aggravating, Mary granted. Filled with silly scraps of clothing or yellowed souvenir postcards with messages too faded to read. She blew the horn hard and muscled the errand car into congested traffic on Riverview Road. Other times . . . she thought of the box of music rolls for the player piano. How had she left them behind in the first place? All that great music from the twenties. She tapped her finger on the steering wheel, listening to the heavy ruby ring make its pleasant metal racket. That's what she'd do after dinner. She plotted out the bubble bath, could even imagine the faint smell of Wild Strawberry on Laydelle's warm skin as she joined her on the piano bench in her pajamas and robe. The two of them would sing a few of the old songs, the ones that funny little composer from New York had written in Nelson Hanks' honor. What was his name? The composer was a Russian, named somethingoff or somethingcoff. Mary accelerated and flew through the intersection, just as the light turned from yellow to red. She looked at the clock. The post office would close in fifteen minutes.

She showed the notice to a mail supervisor and was told to stand on line.

"It's just a parcel."

"I'm sorry, ma'am. You'll still have to line up."

Anybody else would fire Aresta, Mary thought, the space between her eyebrows pinching up. She did just what she pleased, when she pleased. Most of the time, that was convenient, because as Mary rushed from meeting to meeting she certainly couldn't focus on running the house. No, she could hardly chastise Aresta for taking charge when that was exactly what she wanted. Still, refusing that parcel . . . She would have a talk with her. Mary lifted one stockinged leg and rubbed it against the other at the knee.

"Next."

"Mrs. Hubbell Hanks. I'm here to pick up a package. I may need some help getting it out to the car."

The clerk disappeared for a moment, then returned with a small box.

"Think you can manage?"

Mary frowned again and signed the paper. It was heavy for such a small parcel. Whatever could they be sending now? She studied the handwriting and moved through the crowded room. It belonged to that silly, dithering secretary, who seemed to live and die for just such tasks as these. Mary could imagine her, full of purpose, carting it downstairs to the bustling mailroom of Hanks Petroleum. She would open it in the car.

"Mmmm."

She held the paperweight in the palm of her hand. The sunlight pierced the glass, sending sparks from the bronze at its center. It must have been an old seal for Hanks Petroleum, discarded for the sleek new version the company sported now. Mary liked this version infinitely better. It was highly stylized, a bit of art deco, she supposed, though she was no authority. The fluid lines of the letters formed one graceful, feminine arc, finally rendering the initials *HP*.

"I *like* this."

She cupped her hand solidly over the top of the paperweight and brought it down into the palm of the other hand, listening to the smacking sound that made. She wondered how many other artifacts were lying about besides this one. Probably a whole cellarful of them. One of those sorority women was probably sitting on them right this very moment, settled right on top, like a hen guarding eggs. Mary wheeled out of the parking lot, her tires lightly striking the curb as she turned left.

"I've never heard of such a silly thing in my whole entire life. Of course I want them to see you, Hubbell. Now are you honestly telling me you want to sit and drink tea with a bunch of women?"

"No! But you have this thing so carefully orchestrated. I feel like an actor in a stage play."

"Nothing wrong with that. And today I need you to be a bit player, not a star. Help me into this, will you?"

It was spring, and Mary was throwing a tea for key people.

Hubbell slid the zipper up and fiddled with the clasp at the top of her dress. It was a wonderful dress, full of pale pinks and yellows. The pastel drifts of color surprised him, for she never wore these colors. She had a sprig of fresh flowers pinned to one shoulder. The informality was refreshing and also unlike his Mary—here was a woman who gave in to her own mad impulse to gather wildflowers and pin them to her dress. And on a day when she was to meet thirty women she had never laid eyes on. This room was a fine idea. He saw now why she had insisted on having her own private dressing room. It gave Mary just the runway she needed to make sure every effect was as it should be. She paced up and down, now that she was zipped up and tucked in. She pivoted before the mirrors, examining the whole spectacle.

"Yes. This will be just fine."

"Aren't you nervous, Mary?"

But there was no nervousness. There was complete concentration on the task at hand. She held her head at different angles, opened her eyes wide to make sure no dark line was askew, that every lash stood separate and fine. She checked the front of her teeth for lipstick, her jawline for some flaw in the makeup.

"The second silliest thing I've ever heard. Why should I be?"

"Well . . ."

Hubbell crossed his legs and looked around for a cigarette. As long as the window stood open, she didn't mind his smoking up here.

"What if they think you're a social climber? What if they think you want to know them just so you can get ahead? After all, you don't know these women from Adam."

"You're walking backward as usual. I haven't asked these women here so that I can know them."

"But why have a party at all?"

"So that they can know me, my darling. So that they understand Mrs. Hubbell Hanks has finally moved out of The Dominion, where she was in complete and total seclusion. So we can all get moving, Hubbell. These women are in Junior League! These women build concert halls and throw charity balls. These women sponsor symphonies, help deserving underdogs and who knows what all! Do you really imagine they have the time in those busy lives of theirs to come find Mary Hanks? Of course not, which is why I must go to them. If that's social climbing, then hand me the rope and ladder so I can do a proper job of it."

He shook his head, drawing deep on a cigarette. The words vied with the soft, silky image. The dress floated as she paced back and forth.

"Now let's back up. I do want them to see you, Hubbell. But I want you bustling through the living room, shaking a few hands on your busy way out. Hubbell Hanks with scads and scads of things to do."

She turned her head slightly. Aresta's voice came over the Teletalk.

"Miz H., are you sure you want these samwiches cut in triangles? Says here 'finger samwich,' and they don't look one bit like—"

Mary rushed to the Teletalk. She bent down and lowered the volume.

"Aresta, please stop shrieking. Don't cut a thing. I'm coming down right now. Where are you on the list?"

"Twenty-one. Only goes to twenty-five."

"Good. We're right on schedule. Put down the knife."

Mary stopped for a moment to study Hubbell, framed by the window that opened to the Arkansas River, metallic today and running hard after days of rain. A ruined stocking lay beside him on the carpet. An overturned high-heeled shoe seemed lightly tossed into a still life of feminine energy and disorder. Rather than disturbing the composition, Hubbell's presence gilded it, gave it an ornate, baroque edge. His large, slack body tossed casually into a deep armchair made Mary's dressing room complete.

"This is going to work beautifully, Hubbell. They're going to march up in twos and threes, wearing hats and gloves. They're going to glance up and see . . . well, you know what they're going to see! And right away, as soon as they do, they'll see intention and energy. Oh, Hubbell, I know just how Rodin felt! When I saw that frontispiece go up over the door yesterday, it felt just like I was being stabbed in a good way. Something went straight through my heart."

For Mary had put the paperweight away in her own desk drawer that day. She knew some application of those shapely letters *HP* would occur to her and her job was only to wait for the inevitable moment. What to do with the old insignia, too grand to be trivialized in some needlepoint facsimile, some awful pillow or wall hanging. She waited, displeased that the house bore no testimony to greatness, that the stately surrounding acreage was imposing and *mute*. Inspiration would come—and when it did she jumped delightedly from the chair where she sat going over her mail. The organizers of Main Line Tours had not only given her a free five-page brochure; they had given Mary Hanks the means to live peaceably in her new home. The autumn Main Line Tour promised multicolored falling leaves and a five-mile-per-hour glimpse at fine old family homes on the Philadelphia Main Line. The tour bus would actually stop before one of those fine old family homes, stop and reverently enter the home for a ground-floor tour. Mary's fore-finger pressed hard on her cheek as she studied one glossy picture after the next. Each home on the Main Line had its own family crest. Displayed over the front door was the mark of someone born and bred and decidedly living it to the hilt. She was on the phone right away and finally hit pay dirt when she spoke with Mr. Rey-nolds of Reynolds Pottery, who had been in business for over forty years. Mary wheedled and begged. She pointed out the renewed interest in heritage. Why, hadn't he read in last week's paper about the revival of family trees. There was an agency here in town doing land-office business in family research, she'd heard. Mr. Reynolds, who had never been seduced in quite the same way, at last saw the virtue in Mary's plan. It would certainly behoove him to create a frontispiece for the Hubbell Hanks home in Tulsa, even though he'd never heard of such a thing. Other families would follow suit, and oh, the future held promise. Mr. Reynolds turned down his hearing aid, for the woman's voice on the line had risen.

"And not only that, Mr. Reynolds. Why, just think of it. You could reproduce the *HP* symbol in a line of formal dinnerware. What? Then, informal dinnerware, since you are a pottery factory. Oh, I like this more and more! Do you have children, sir? Yes? Well, tell them to buckle their seat belts, because the family firm of Reynolds Pottery is about to take off."

HP. The letters now rose in a glazed earthenware oval just atop the front doorway. It had been delivered the day before. A place setting for eighteen was in the making. Unfortunately not for to-day's tea, but the crest was enough. The lovely, lilting letters sus-pended over Mary's front door would suffice.

Her pleasure was contagious. Hubbell squirmed in his seat, sud-denly raring to go. But go where? He had forgotten to make a plan for this afternoon, but no matter. He would take Laydelle on an excursion. The two of them would bustle out the door, giving Mary's guests just one short take before they were gone. Or maybe, to give her just the leeway she needed to make it a special day, maybe Hubbell and Laydelle would just go now and stay gone. It might be much better for everyone if he wasn't in the house at all.

Nelson and Lavinia

c h a p t er 21

1923

Zoe Simply's professionalism failed her. She fell for Nelson Hanks the first time he shinnied up her ladder, and the tougher she urged herself to be, the tougher it got. She charged him for special favors just like any other customer, got him up and out when it was over and stifled the endearments that threatened to fly from her lips. She was in love with him and met this failure miserably, as if it were an enemy in her path. When she heard his wife was pregnant she broke out in hives. She painted her lips the reddest red, chanting *whore, whore, whore* into the mirror as a simple remedy for heartsickness. She greeted Nelson several times this way, her mouth smeared with color as though she'd been sucking a messy sweet, her skin stinging even with the hives long gone. He ended his visits when Zoe Simply offered him a cigar, already lit and smoking. The erotic feat, months before, would have had him bent double with laughter and longing. "For the father-to-be," she cried, her voice trembling as violently as her opened legs. Smoke drifted up lazily from between her knees.

She telephoned the office when a month passed with no word.

"Priss."

"Why, hello, Zoe. This isn't like you."

"Oh, yes it is. This is perfectly like me. You're becoming an old fuddy-duddy, Nelson. You've always liked my jokes before."

"I still like them, but they could bring me bad luck, and I have to be careful, Zoe. Everything is at stake."

She held her hand over the telephone, and he could hear her berating one of the girls.

"Would an apology for my obscene behavior change your mind?"

"Not likely."

"Reason, then. Do you actually think tasteless antics will have an effect on your unborn child? Do you believe that your wife will miscarry or bear a simpleton on account of my sorry prank?"

"No."

"Then come see me. Come visit the Simply establishment in the dead of some night. No one will be wiser. I promise. I may be a poor clown, but my discretion is beyond reproach. I wouldn't be in business without it."

"She's struggling, Zoe. I'm trying to spend more time with her. More days and more nights."

She straightened up and tapped her heels together lightly. Then she drove her pencil into the table, cocking her head in surprise as the lead snapped off.

"My, my. I don't know your wife and don't wish to. But I hope for your sake that she drops a healthy foal. I also know that, despite your aspirations, you'll make a middling choirboy. And that middling doesn't suit you one bit. Best luck, Nelson."

He hung up the phone and swiped at his forehead with a handkerchief. Nelson, for whom visions were new, watched as Zoe Simply's house waddled slowly away from him on awkward stilt legs. He woke to find his secretary standing before him, repeating something she must have said several times.

"From Zoe? She's rung up again?"

"I said the men from the *zoo* are here. They've been downstairs waiting for fifteen minutes."

"The zoo? Marvelous! Why didn't you say so, Miss Adams?"

Thirty-six hundred acres to fence. Thirty-six hundred acres to fill. His secretary rang up biologists and veterinarians, forest rangers and farmers. Animal husbandmen of all kinds who dispensed advice on what would and wouldn't prosper on Nelson's spread. After she had consulted the specialists, she turned to hobbyists

and crackpots, ostrich gurus and high priests of monkeys and ma-
caws. Nelson's ranch stretched over the Osage hills like an empty
canvas. He began by painting in wild animals.

"I want to stand here and smell buffalo dung."

He stood with his secretary on the lip of a rocky ledge. She stood
staunchly beside Uncle Nelson in a pair of forest-green lederhosen
purchased through the mail. He had mentioned yesterday the
probability of a "business hike."

"Dung, sir?"

"I want to see a flock of geese lift off that lake in the morning. I
want bobcat to prowl, yaks to yak. Kangaroos to hop!"

His secretary was still a single girl. She hadn't gotten to the
altar, but she had made it to the fitting room. Been measured for
an ivory gown, even stuck in the arm with a pin by a clumsy
seamstress. Everyone reckoned her fiancé had been scared off by
her efficiency. She handled arrangements brilliantly, phoning and
firing, decrying caterers and their scandalous prices, Miami hotels
whose hotshot bridal suites didn't even overlook the swimming
pool. When the wedding was canceled, she pulled on leather trousers and stalked through Bavaria.

"Precisely. I want this ranch to be one of a kind. Take a letter,
Miss Adams."

She spread a gingham picnic napkin on the ground and settled
down with her clipboard.

"Ready, sir."

"To Mr. Amos Hundee of Fargo, North or South Dakota. Dear
Mr. Hundee. It has been brought to my attention that you are the
proud possessor of a substantial herd of wild buffalo. This news
gladdened the heart of one Oklahoman. It has long been my wish
to see these magnificent beasts reinstalled in their native habitat.
Do I need to recapitulate the awful annihilation? Whole herds were
left to rot in the sun, one neat bullet hole piercing the left shoulder.
Over a million buffalo once roamed this region, and their obliteration took four years. While we cannot rewrite history, Mr. Hundee, we can guarantee the future for animals so ignominiously
slaughtered. I am in the process of establishing a wild-animal reserve here in Osage County. To do so, I shall need your help. You
finish, Miss Adams. Plug in the figures and flatter the old goat into
considering our offer. Get 'Pappy Buffalo' to part with a couple
hundred babies."

She sat rolled slightly to one side.

"Anything else?"

"Suggest a night freight car. Two hundred buffalo thundering off a train for an audience could be a terrible mess. Yes, this ranch is certainly going to be one of a kind."

"Aren't you forgetting the Miller Ranch, Mr. Hanks?"

The heat shimmered off the ledge, stifling even birds and insects. Nothing soared, swarmed or warbled.

"I'll give you some free advice, Miss Adams. If you don't learn discretion, you'll never get off this rock and out of those ridiculous leather shorts."

Miss Adams bit her tongue to keep from crying and wished Uncle Nelson would take a flying leap into the still lake that lay below. Here she'd gone, trying to save her boss from being a copycat, and he'd reacted like a schoolkid. She pulled her shorts down with a jerk.

"I just meant, sir, that the Miller brothers approximately did a ranch entertainment idea years ago and that their place had one hundred ten thousand—"

"I'm not talking about a *ranch entertainment idea*, my poor misguided dear. I'm talking about an animal reserve, and a *natural* introduction to Western culture that will set dandified businessmen and politicos on their ears. I'm not mounting a Wild West show here. This will be a home, a haven. I'm an oil man, not a ticket salesman."

The Millers were cattlemen and farmers first, running their operation on land leased from the Ponca Indians. They crossed a buffalo bull with a range cow, and the small herd of strange creatures prospered on their ranch. More gene-meddling came up with a tender, drought-resistant little steer that satisfied a market suddenly fussy and discontent with stringy range beef. They mixed and matched livestock, even took on plants, cross-breeding corn until they came up with White Wonder. They were at this apex when the bug bit Joe Miller. He looked out over his land and saw not a thousand pair of gleaming longhorns, not chuck wagons and cow ponies, wild turkeys and miles of silver-green corn husks. He saw movie cameras and grandstands. He saw races and Wild West sports at a dollar a head. Show biz struck the Miller 101 Ranch.

Nelson ate peanuts and popcorn with the rest of them. For those who had missed their appointment, wound up in Oklahoma too late to spot a buffalo or a land run, there was still, gloriously still, the Miller Ranch. Nelson had reveled in the spectacle of Geronimo, bowed now with old age and sprung from his jail cell to perform a last rite for the Millers. He killed and skinned his final buffalo in 1905 before a respectful crowd. There were roundups and rodeos, chamber of commerce bands, days of chain events that led to the finale. A wagon train appeared on Miller's horizon. Just as it arrived in full view of the amphitheater, an Indian raid commenced. Puzzled but well paid old men who had taken scalps of their own in earlier days painted their skins and their ponies. They coached younger Indians and swept down on the band of white settlers. Wagons were burned and scalps waved for a cheering throng; Kodaks swung from sunburned necks as they clapped and shouted. Nelson delighted in it and sat down for his chuck across from Bill Pickett. He couldn't help but stare throughout supper, the way the black cowboy meticulously dislodged bits of buffalo meat from his famous teeth with a little finger he curved into a precision instrument. It was Pickett who invented bulldogging, who swung from his pony until he held a bull's nose between his teeth. He didn't let go until the stunned animal lay lashed and still on the ground.

"I'm too proud for beholden, Miss Adams."

"I didn't mean to say that."

"Too old and stiff to turn myself into a copy of anybody."

Nelson was the first to wire his condolences when news of trouble began to spread, when it was publicized that the 101 Wild West show had long lost money, its losses spiraling once the show took to the road. Delusions of grandeur, people whispered. He and his boys shoulda stuck with White Wonder. He sent off a message to Zack. *We pray for miracles and inch toward them with hard, remedial work. I am at your disposal in this matter. Please let me know if I can help.* Nelson received an invitation to the first auction, and it seemed fortune was working both sides of the street. The Miller public sale was the beginning of a Western collection that would grace Nelson's own show palace, just then in the making. His lodge built of Arkansas pine was going up next to Spencer Spring. The Miller 101 show saddle, trimmed in gold and silver, pocked with precious stones, was crated and would be delivered later by armed security guards. Nelson staggered away from the auction under a pile of buffalo skins. He held the first breech-loading gun to be brought into the Territory respectfully in his lap as Joey turned the car toward Lovely, past fields that had known every kind of spectacle. Even this: Joe Miller, standing on the porch of his white house, kneading his fists and defying eviction.

. . .

"Do you swim, Miss Adams?"

"I crawl."

"Ever felt mud between your toes?"

"Not since I was a little girl."

"Ever wanted to since?"

Miss Adams knew a trap, all right. But what kind was this? She shook her head, and drops of water dappled the rock ledge. She was toasting inside her shorts and didn't dare raise her arms. She hated shields worse than she hated perspiration.

"Think you could make it down to the water's edge from here?"

"I guess I'll have to."

They clambered down the overgrown path, Nelson leading. Brambles scratched the side of the secretary's briefcase, and she struggled to keep her breathing light and effortless. Why anybody would want to buy land out in the middle of this—She spotted poison oak and shrieked. There was no poison oak in Bavaria. She put her memory to work on Alpine sights and sounds, every window a tended garden, glossy cows burdened with bells. She rarely questioned her good judgment, but she did now. Slipping and sliding behind a multimillionaire who dreamed of smelling buffalo . . .

"At ease, Miss Adams."

She stared at the water, wondering where the shine had gone. The lake, viewed from a distance, seemed set with a thousand diamonds. It was dull and opaque now, full of snakes and snapping secrets. The secretary practiced her crawl once a week at the public pool. But all water knowledge failed her as she watched the lake lap at a sandbar, persistent as a cat's tongue on milk. She thought of mud creatures and bottom varmints, a lake filled not with gems but with glittering eyes. All of them rolled up and fixed on the surface.

"Take off your shoes, Miss Adams."

When did you tell your uncle no? When did you tell him you weren't *that* hot, to please mind his own sweet business? She hugged her briefcase and thought of home, now ennobled by this wild place owned by a wild man. Home, even though it contained an invalid, aging parent, was the kindest spot on earth. She set her eyes on the center of the lake and dreamed it away, all the water sucked down in a great spiral starting there. She kept her eyes on that sight, even after Uncle Nelson rolled his pants up to his knees and waded in first. His legs were skimpy and horrid; she wished them gone. She bent over to unlace her boots and decided it was punishment. He was making her wade because she'd brought up the Millers. She would draft a letter of resignation. Sinclair wouldn't do this to his secretary. Neither would Skelly. She had skills, and this old coot wasn't the only oil man around.

"Marvelous, isn't it? Miss Adams, unless your briefcase contains a flotation device, I'd suggest you leave it ashore."

She closed her eyes and stepped in. She shivered at the sensation: the mud was unexpectedly kind. A soft, perfect fit rose to cover her foot. She felt no resistance and stepped farther inside the lake. No jagged rock, no mean jaws slamming shut. She lowered her arms and let her fingertips lie on the surface of the water.

She tentatively scraped the water with the flat of her hand.

"You only work through Friday, Miss Adams. How do you keep yourself busy otherwise?"

"Oh, there's plenty to do. You see, I live with my mother, and she isn't well."

"I see."

And he did. He saw Miss Adams free of her leather shorts and gotten up in something finer. Nurse's white from head almost to toe. He was chaste for the moment, thanks to Vinnie. He didn't rue his condition. It felt like Lent, and Nelson, lover of Ash Wednesday and long, repentant days, genuinely missed its celebration. He was sworn off women, and his baby would be born firm and whole because of his abstinence. The proof was his swollen wife, sweeping through rooms with her beautiful belly. He spent whole evenings now rubbing her aching feet and legs. He added features as her pregnancy advanced. . . . Hair and nails this month, Lavinia. Can you beat that? She couldn't and laughed, pushing him away as he struggled to put his head in her lap. She had no lap left, he'd seen to that. He was bemused by her attention to diet and exercise. She'd cut back on cigarettes and grown wary of red meat, though he didn't see why. His wife and unborn baby gathered strength and size every month because Nelson didn't. Didn't run off to find a more accommodating lap. Didn't sniff around, seeking red meat elsewhere since it was no longer served at home. He stuck to his own yard like a dog.

But his mind wouldn't mind since he'd stopped seeing Zoe. It was working now, stripping his secretary of her foolish costume and supplying her with another. The nurse's white didn't wash.

Well, it washed but not entirely. He saw Miss Adams bending over
her ailing mama's bed with a tray, wearing nothing but a perky
nurse's bonnet. Nelson dwelt on that for moments, thinking out
every line, every darling crevasse. He hadn't dreamed for a moment that a hidden country lay so bright and lush under the sharp
pleated skirts she favored for the office. He looked almost troubled
as he considered the larger picture: corridors and water coolers,
coat closets and crowded elevators filled with leagues of Hanks
Petroleum secretaries. His secretaries, weren't they? A country became countries of swirling, shimmering women. And all of them
cloaked and clothed. Practically hooded, when he thought of it. He
imagined the romp they were entitled to, that the entire family was
entitled to, for wasn't his company this, a gossamer familial web
of workers and friends? Sweat leaked from his head. Not even knee-
deep water could adjust his thermostat. He watched the whole
event spread out before him. He saw every tiny pinpoint, the
sheaths and streamers, the gay banners and all the other contest
froth that would delight and honor Miss Petroleum, whoever she
was.

"Take a letter, Miss Adams. No, better yet, take a bulletin."

She backed out of the water, her eyes round and wet with excitement.

"I'm ready, Mr. Hanks."

Sweet, sweet Miss Adams. How was it he hadn't seen her before? Nelson sighed and guessed she would keep.

" 'To All Hanks Employees: Well, Uncle Nelson has gone and
done it. Gone and bought a big old spread of land outside Lovely.
Some of you men and women are asking yourselves what I'm going
to do with it. Build myself a castle and a moat so nobody can get
to me? Not on your lives. Engineer a pleasure park for myself and
my family? That's more like it, but let's define family. There's myself and Lavinia, our baby-to-be, of course. And there's you, each
and every Hanks employee. That means all of you from custodian
to roustabout to financial manager or personnel director. I figure a
great big hardworking family like ours needs to relax from time to
time. We'll barbecue and jump in the swimming hole, plus plenty
more. I'm appointing Dobey Grave my head of festivities. He'll be
informing each and every one of you of the date and the doings.
High time this industry had itself a Petroleum Queen. So, ladies,
practice your dips and spins, shake off those extra pounds for our

beauty contest. The winner will receive—hell, I don't know yet what she'll receive. But I promise my family a day to remember.'

"That's all, Miss Adams."

He sloshed toward her, grinning. He removed his hat and stroked the top of his bare head with water.

"You'll need to make yourself some travel arrangements. There's a store I want you to visit in New York—Abercrombie and Fitch. I want a diving board for this little lake. Order bows and arrows and fifty of every kind of ball they sell. Now where on earth do you find firecrackers for that number of people? You've got your work cut out for you. Go out and investigate fun. I want to set up the biggest damn playpen Lovely ever saw. And, Miss Adams, I didn't mean that about your hiking shorts. They suit you. Why, I'd climb into them myself if I could."

She twittered and drew her knees up to her chest. On the long drive home she plotted pin curls and cold cream, intensified use of witch hazel. The right shade of pink for her toenails would be essential. She didn't know the first thing about dips and spins, but she would learn. She forgave Uncle Nelson for every one of his misdemeanors and mentioned as she drove (he always insisted she take the wheel) that Miss Petroleum would certainly be tickled with a bouquet of flowers, but she'd probably faint with pleasure if he honored her with some stock shares. He patted the top of her knee, and she pulled her shorts down with a jerk for the second time that day.

"Who asked him?"

Señora Alvarez from Mexico City peered through her lorgnette. The gaunt and ragged man who had just appeared was her excuse to remove the ivory antique from her handbag and slowly raise it to her eye for a better look.

"Oh, that. He won't bite. He won't bite you, at any rate. Harry is here for the grub, Señora. He's an old friend of Nelson's."

"Grub is what?"

"Grub is all the food he can eat before this party ends."

Señora returned her attention to the party. She noted that American women danced like mules and risked everything by looking directly into their partners' eyes. But they were animated and brave, talking to whomever they pleased without being approached first. Clumps of men broken up like sod. And by women! She wished she could preserve the sound of their loud laughter and take it back to Mexico City.

Lavinia complained that Harry had no right calling that way. He was a Saturday-evening affliction, turning up in the midst of anything he pleased. Nelson, delighted by the presence of his old pal, bellowed at him to start singing where it read "Ain't it sensational. Bet this temptation'll. Get the best of me. Oh, but you'll get the best of me." He turned back to the player piano, but Lavinia didn't. She huffed and puffed, furious at this panhandler and his power over her husband.

Sharp pains felled her in the middle of the hootenanny. She narrowed her eyes at the platters of fried chicken, thinking perhaps . . . Then another pain struck her back. The jolt deadened the top of her right leg. She excused herself to the few guests who noticed her unsteady departure from the garden. She hobbled through the profusion of footlights, glaring at the hillbilly singers and the dancers who crowded the wooden dance pavilion Nelson had designed for the affair. There was her husband, with a banjo and bandanna, sitting next to Señora Alvarez. He led a sing-along. He looked perfectly ridiculous, and she would tell him so as soon as she settled this. She wanted to spit at the smell of oily perfume released by hundreds of gardenia blossoms. It was too strong, too thick. Men's aftershave hung draped over all of this. She lurched through a doorway and straight into Harry, who held drinks in both hands. The drinks left the glasses. Punch and hot coffee flew straight into his shirt and unkempt beard, but he didn't flinch.

"Damn the prohibitionists. They've reduced us to dreary nights of citrus punch when we long for another sort of refreshment."

He gathered her gently up in his arms and led her to a settee, then closed the sitting room door firmly. She couldn't object, for everything was faltering and all at once. She'd taken such care, such care. Self-pity swept over her as forcefully as the pains that beat against her rib cage and continued in her back. The concert roared outside, but inside her there was another kind of din, which deafened everything.

"You mustn't be afraid. I've assisted at births of all kinds."

"I'm not giving birth. I—oh!"

"My dear Mrs. Hanks."

Lavinia's eyes darkened. He smelled the way she imagined a man would if he left himself alone except for the most occasional bath. The smell of untended flesh wasn't bad, but it was sharp. And unfamiliar.

"As a young man I preferred animals. Their birthing, I mean. Sturdy and simple. Those great blank eyes. A heifer has precious little memory, I can tell you that. The scrawny beast beside her, struggling to stand, is pure coincidence. Oh, there's nuzzling, of course. She'll lick the little thing down. But the birth event is over and done. A younger man was fond of this curious sangfroid. I want you to breathe from the top of your diaphragm, Mrs. Hanks. Light puffs of air . . . that's it. Don't be afraid."

She responded to his hands. The pains continued, but she wouldn't die from them as long as his hands slipped over her softly. She arched her back once and cried. He laid his head on a low part of her and listened. The intimacy offered comfort. His odor mounted and enveloped her; she rode inside its unctuous lining and was less afraid.

"But a much older man wants his birth human. And perhaps this will be my salvation. Human drama draws me closer and closer. This bloody clutch holds us all, down to the coldest man. Your sons are very clever indeed. Hide-and-seek for months, then when they meet, clap! A great uproar."

For he thought he found a second heartbeat. Faint, and that was worrying, but he held his ear against the spot and could make out the small second tap that echoed underneath the first.

"This baby isn't due. I'm not near ready."

"Baby might be babies. Your readiness has nothing to do with it, I fear."

"Oh, Lord!"

She tilted her pelvis up to meet the blow. At least the pains now struck the same spot. Knowing where the center lay, she began riding each spasm in like a wave. A fierce rap at the base of her spine had awakened her early in the morning, before it was light out. She hadn't even heard Joey lightly padding about in the room upstairs. There had been intermittent thuds and thrusts inside her all day long. She believed in agendas and contracts, promises kept. To believe otherwise was to concede that a baby, now two, would be born this night in her home. And that she would have to appeal to an oddity, a crafty doctor (hadn't Nelson said?) of *crows!*

He left her side only once, returning with Nelson, who stood posted outside the door, stiff as a wooden totem. He thought of stopping the party, of rousing the dozing chauffeurs and phoning

for the taxis and hired cars necessary to sweep them all away.
There would be an hour of bidding departing guests farewell and
paying caterers, waiters and musicians. And this hour would take
him away. Joey moved past him with a stack of white towels. Next
he brought a great brass bowl covered with muslin cloth. The door
opened to heat, as if it were not a parlor but a boiler room or
smithy shop. A column of warm air slapped his cheek, and the
door clicked shut again. Did babies give off heat, or was it the
women who bore them? He had turned his head as Joey entered
and seen his wife's bare knees and hair, unlocked at last from its
coil. Then Harry's elbows, crooked at a right angle above her. He
didn't need to imagine bellows in that stifling room; he'd seen them
in those lowering arms.

The party was lit up with bootleg by midnight. He heard one
glass shatter, then several, and figured Jud Simpson had begun
four-legging it, with guests taking bets on his progress. Simpson
could barely do it sober or drunk, but revelers still loved to see him
on all fours with a dozen crystal glasses balanced on his broad
back. He claimed to have traveled the entire length of Saint Mark's
thus, risking a set of hand-blown Venetian goblets, then a square
in Montmartre the next spring, with cheaper café ware donated by
a league of artists and students. There was applause outside, and
he guessed Jud had made it to the end of the garden, lifting his
trousers as he always did to reveal bruised, sometimes bleeding
knees. He passed a hat to collect his winnings; he would swallow
the coins by the end of the night. The hootenanny recommenced,
the musicians working harder now that they were competing with
whiskey.

He pressed his back to the door, and that was his work. To hold
that door shut against all the odds. He heard her call out for Daddy
and a doctor. She turned her voice into a stinging whip. Did she
free herself from pain with fury as she goddamned Joey, who did
nothing but stand and stare? She shrieked at Harry, crying that she
wasn't a brood mare and how dared he. Then the condemnations
subsided, and the silence scared him worse than all that. He
rapped on the door, and there was no answer. He tried saying
Vinnie, Lavinia, sweet and low, then louder, but no one heeded
him. Not the party inside or the party out. He checked his watch
and tried the knob. Locked. He wondered what it would mean to
bear a child one month early, what features would be unfinished
or forgotten altogether. His clothing was soaked through, and he

tasted fear on his tongue. He coughed, and it was worse, more bitter than a root.

He tried the door again. It turned this time.

"Come this way, Nelson. It's over."

She slept, and why was that? In every version he'd ever seen, women were tired but gazing at the newborn. In this case it was Harry who looked serene. His face, still weathered and yellow as sandstone, nevertheless threw off a kind of light.

"My friend, come spend a moment with your son. This one."

Two babies mewled inside a blanket. Two small, uneven twins, unrecognizable as proper children with their awful violet cast. Nelson held his breath and moved in closer, a sleeve across his open mouth. One was lifted gently from this cradle. Too still and curled like a worm teased into a tight coil with a stick.

"He's alive."

But it was a question, and the three men knew it. Nelson was grateful she slept.

"The other one's a scrapper. Had a hell of a time digging him out of his mother. He'll have to spend time in an incubator, but he'll be fine, just fine. Hold on to your son. Hold on for both of you."

Nelson couldn't very well rock in a wingback chair, but he eventually found a spot in the middle of his shoulder that suited the two of them. He took all he could of his son this way, feeling the shape of his curved spine and the base of his skull with the tip of his finger. The room was still hot, and after some time passed, he let the soft cover drop from the baby's body. He unbuttoned his shirt, tears streaming now that the child was growing cold, and slipped him inside right next to his heart.

"You have another son to raise, Nelson. A son to pick up and praise and welcome."

Nelson might not have heard, for he had begun to sing. It wasn't the song that roared outside on the wooden pavilion that was tipping, tipping under the weight of so many dancers. He couldn't complete the song, he could only begin it—that little was left. *Baby's going bye-bye, Mama's going to cry, cry.* Harry's shadow fell across him, and he felt his friend's hand on his shoulder.

"Have you thought of a name for him?"

Nelson didn't raise his head.

"For your son. Your living son."

"Hubbell Hanks. Vinnie liked that name."

"Nice. Let go now, Nelson. You must let go."

It was early morning by then. A chauffeur had backed into a sycamore and was fired. A wife threatened divorce, and Jud Simpson threatened to shit quarters if somebody didn't get him another drink. There was weary talk of eggs and ham at the club on Tulsa Road. Some guests were calling for coats and hats. Others were calling for order, a proper farewell to the host and hostess.

Story of the birth would spill across the headlines of the evening newspaper. OIL MAN'S WIFE BEARS HEIR IN THE NIGHT! Nelson rose, bone weary, from the wingback chair. He kissed his sleeping wife's pasty forehead and clapped his friend roughly on the back. He didn't look inside the soft folds of the blanket but moved to quell the frantic rapping on the door.

"Settle with the hired people, Joey. I want a private burial service for Hank. Keep this out of the papers. I'm going upstairs to bed."

Nicknames had become the pastime of the prominent. President Harding rekindled the fad, tagging friends Winky or Sip; even the scoundrel up for indictment was treated to a sobriquet. So no one blinked when little Hubbell Hanks became Half. Half was thought to be far more distinctive than Nelson Hanks, Jr., and most people thought there were too damn many Nelsons around anyhow. Half Nelson, though. Now *that* name had a ring to it.

chapter 22

1927

"Henry Starr, photodrama ruined you. That was years ago! Hell, you're a thief who acts as temperamental as a film star. Now do we have a deal, or don't we?"

"We have a deal to pull off something *lifelike*. I always did things simple. What would I be doing with a pack of fifteen men? My work is swift and clean, and fifteen men would trip over themselves. You ought to know that. You, of all people."

"I want to scare the daylights out of 'em."

"All you need is one concentrated son of a bitch to scare your pals. You're looking at him."

"Listen here, prima donna. I have respect for your talent, always have, but that temperament of yours could get you in trouble."

Starr, out on parole again, jeered. It was true that he loved a solo performance, though he didn't think this meant he was ruined or any worse than he was years before, starting out green and tender as a blade of winter rye. He was just what he claimed to be —concentrated. Distilled down to a deeply colored self after years spent in a cold jail cell with no company but an ink pen. He wrote down a few facts of his life during the idle afternoons, and receiving little more than derision from penitentiary officials, he whispered a curse and wrote down more. *Thrilling Events*, Starr's autobiography, was published in 1914. Detractors said it had been ghostwritten, for no Cherokee half-breed outlaw could ever have such thoughts or write such words. *Am I a child of misfortune, or is it just plain "damn bad luck"? Privately, I don't believe completely in anything that has or ever will happen; only in the inexorable law of total obliteration and nothingness.* A history professor wrote him his first fan letter, expressing particular delight in Henry's philosophical passages, his charming digressions. *There may be a few good step-parents (I have seen a few myself) but I hold it does not pay to examine a snake's tail to see if it has rattlers.*

Later, they let him out of jail to reenact on film his most popular bank holdup, the one that proved a heart of gold beat beneath the legendary bullet shield. Spying a child sitting on a chair, Starr made his grumbling assistants put away their guns. The bank heist was conducted with no bloodshed because of the small girl's presence. Years after the act, hand-held cameras turned as he poured pennies into the lap of a young actress, bidding her to wait quietly and he would return to buy her ice cream. Starr found his performance wanting and asked that the scene be reshot once, then twice. He shared the playbill for *The Passing of the Oklahoma Outlaw* with Bill Doolin and the Dalton brothers, even Al Jennings. He believed he had a cameo role but realized he'd been doubled-crossed when he saw the theater marquee. "See the Jean Valjean of American history!" The publicized Jean Valjean turned out to be Al Jennings. It was the first and last time Henry would play second to somebody else.

"So you want me to lift their wallets and purses. Then I shoot off a couple of rounds and disappear."

"Exactly. Then you return to the lodge for some supper. By the way, Henry, you return *with* the loot."

"Not even a keepsake or two? Those bankers' wives will be sporting a lot of fine jewelry."

"Word of honor."

"You've got it."

They returned their attention to the card game. Doves moaned outside under the eaves as they smoked and slapped down spades. A bad windstorm was on its way. He laid his cards facedown and relit the stub of his cigar, looking at his friend's guarded face. Starr was right to demand the leading role.

The private railroad car, loaded with Hanks Petroleum shareholders and investors, was to leave Grand Central and wind its way west. Nelson planned to introduce his secret weapon in the war against competitors on board the train. Exhibit A was Eddy Bleam, the newest addition to the Hanks Petroleum Company. The slight but confident geologist sparked a conflict that raged like a well on fire. College boys who turned up in an oil field were always suspect, but this Bleam was worse, for he signaled the final act. Bleam came equipped with a gravity meter and a seismograph. Members of the old school spat when they saw his bag of rock samples and ever after called him a pebble pup. "That mud smeller! You see that? Spends his days eating dirt and sniffing mud, trying to track down oil. Hell, I guess it *is* time to retire." There would be no derision, however, on Nelson's private car. Bleam would woo his guests with colored maps and pointers. His job was to stuff them with science. Hanks Petroleum was a competitive outfit, clearly at the modern forefront of the industry. Ed Bleam was just one case in point.

Nelson would oversee every detail, register every response. Nearing Lovely, the final destination, spectacle would unfold on schedule. Oil wells would miraculously come in on Hanks leases: "gushers," existing wells capped for days, would blow just within sight of the Hanks Pullman. He planted cowboys and Indians along the way, whetting his guests' appetites for the Wild West. When the train finally pulled into the station, passengers would be ushered into the stagecoaches Nelson now collected as casually as arrowheads. They would bump and rattle toward the lodge in the genuine article. His guests would be ambushed as they crested the hill behind the lodge. But just Henry Starr, when Nelson could so handily collect a whole pack of badmen?

"You're playing your hand like a schoolkid, Nelson. I just won five hundred dollars with my eyes shut."

"I want you to ride with Bob Wells."

"Man's a horse's ass. I wouldn't ride with suchlike."

"For me you would."

And it was true. For all the years Nelson had accepted his money down at the bank, no questions asked, inviting him upstairs afterward as if he was a gentleman . . . in honor of those years he would say yes. Nelson had always treated him like the hero he believed he was. Thieves and murderers sat out sentences, growing harder, more thoughtless, with days. But a hero slept with his head propped on a dictionary, so fresh words could seep in all night long. And when they did, one by one, until there was a whole assembly of words, a hero made sense of them, made thoughts of them, until they became stories he could tell with a pen and paper. He would ride with Wells and play badman if Nelson wanted.

"Quit pouting, you bastard. I'll ride with old Buttercup if that's what you need. I'll ride with him and go bang bang and lift a lady's skirt with the tip of my stick if that's what you want. Don't see what that's gotta do with the oil business, but I'll do it anyways. Gin."

"You'll be rewarded, Henry. And not just with a paycheck. I'm going to have a party like this state has never seen."

"You're one smooth son of a bitch, Nelson Hanks. Here you have everyone fooled into thinking you're an oil man. Hell, you're one of us. You're a bandit. You're an oil bandit."

Nelson forfeited the card game with a laugh. After all, he was the real winner. Bob Wells and Henry Starr riding together in a mock holdup . . . His dark alliances were finally paying off.

"Shortchanging him? What do you mean, I'm shortchanging him? If that isn't the biggest bunch of bull I've ever heard."

"You ought to give Hubbell a *real* birthday party. He's four years old and—"

"—and his father's about to give him the grandest party any little boy could hope for. You might think about giving up drink, Lavinia. Your logic gets cloudier by the day."

"My logic is sharp as a pin, and you're fussing because it sticks you right where it hurts. You're not preparing a birthday party for Hubb. You're giving yourself a party. You didn't even bother to include him in the invitation."

She held the scroll in front of her, then read.

" 'Nelson Hanks and his family would be right proud if you could join us for our first Cow Thieves and Outlaws Reunion.' And on and on. I don't need to read any further. There's no mention of a son's birthday. Well, you're safe for the moment because he's only four and commotion is commotion. Have you at least included a birthday cake with candles?"

"That's a vindictive question."

"Well, did you?"

"Of course."

"And is it chocolate?"

"Would I order rum cake for my son? Why, there's Half now! Ahoy, matey."

The boy was got up as a minute mariner, in dark blues and gold. Nelson spread his arms to him and flapped them in a gesture intended to invite him in. Hubbell sucked the edge of his collar and hesitated, for a cigar stood in his father's teeth and he had been burned once before. Finally, unable to stop himself, the small sailor ran, flew to his father. The edge of the rug stopped him in midflight. His cries increased, moving from shame to anger, as Lavinia ran to soothe him and lift him up from where he'd fallen.

"It's the way you dress him, Vinnie. I've told you time and again. A boy can't move when he's bound by fussy clothes. When I was a boy in Creston—"

"Your family didn't have a pot to piss in. Your mother would have given you exquisite clothing if she could have. Don't talk to me about Creston and raggedy clothes. Come to me, Hubbell. That's the way."

Nelson, studying the two of them on the floor, strained hard to remember and understand. She rocked and caressed him for the slightest mishap. She seemed constantly poised for any potential incident. Poised with such a store of love, it seemed to connote much more than simple maternity. Maybe she'd just had to wait too long for this precious presence. Nelson shook his head, thinking of his own exhausted mother, obliged to break up still another dogfight between her sons with a shovel.

"The two of you planning a big day?"

Lulled by his mother's lap, Hubbell lifted pudgy legs into the air. He studied shoelaces and socks, snapping elastic until Lavinia released him.

"I'm going to Nora's for a committee luncheon. Joey's taking him out for a ride in the car, and we're due at the photographer by three o'clock. Right, Hubb? Watch, Nelson. Hubbell, remember pretty picture smile?"

Hubbell did remember. He clambered into a chair and pulled a wide grin, tickling his own stomach for good measure.

"Well, I'll be. That'll come in handy when you're in the limelight one day."

Lavinia set a hat on her son's head and kissed his chin.

"Think about what I said, Nelson. It's not my idea of a four-year-old's celebration. Buffalo meat and bourbon! After all, Nelson . . ."

"Well, it's damn sure mine. If you want to give your son a tea party for his birthday, that's your business. So long, Half. Christ, Vinnie. Tell him the photo session's over."

For Hubbell sat on, the grin painfully painted on his face. He squirmed fitfully on the leather chair.

"Hubb? Do you have to make number two?"

He watched the two of them fly down the hall, Lavinia half-pulling, half-carrying the boy.

"God save his fancy trousers! Back at eight, Vinnie."

He headed down the hall, passing the new maid, who was smoothing his son's bed linen with a methodical series of slaps. She made a great show of her labor, puffing noisily as she worked.

"G'morning, Mr. Hanks."

"Janie, is it?"

"Jane Maloney."

"Welcome on board, Jane Maloney."

"Thank you, sir."

He found Joey downstairs, watering a potted plant.

"Say, Joey."

One of Joey's eyes was bloodshot. An angry network of red capillaries shot out from the corner.

"We'll need to order a birthday cake for Half. A real whopper, too. Hell, why don't we put four stories on it? There'll be more than enough guests to finish it off. Make sure all the Nelsons are there, too. That way we'll give him a real party with other kids."

"Chocolate, Mr. Hanks?"

"Right. Does he like cherries?"

"He likes to throw them, sir."

"Then give him a barrelful of cherries. You're only four once. You look like hell, Joey. Take a week off after this bash. Tell Lavinia she'll have to borrow one of her girlfriends' drivers or take a taxi. Call my secretary and get her to make you an appointment with Doc Hammond for your eye. You're no good to me blind."

There were one hundred guests at the first annual Cow Thieves and Outlaws Reunion. In later years the number of invited and uninvited would swell to over a thousand.

"He musta dug purdy deep in his pocket for this one. Yessir. Who d'ya pay to call off the law?"

"That's not the proper question. The proper question is who

don't you pay for a day like this? Course by now Nelson Hanks stretches all the way to Washington and then some beyond. Look at that, will ya?"

Predator and prey found themselves strangely dislocated that day in 1927, for Hanks had bought his guests a day of immunity. Cattle ranchers and cowboys, ex-marshals and bandits, left their weapons with Big Amos Sweet, Nelson's ranch manager. Sweet groused about being a glorified hatcheck boy and laid the guns on a picnic table covered with a sheet of red oilcloth. He predicted trouble regardless of whether or not guests were armed.

"Bob Wells, you carryin' lead?"

"You serious? This here's a party."

"What's that pokin' out from your boot?"

"That? No bigger than a teaspoon. Fact is, I use it to stir my coffee."

"Let's have it, Bob. Look left, old friend."

Bob Wells looked his old enemy straight in the eye. The ex-lawman had made a genteel career from the fact that he'd once shot a horse out from under Bob Wells. He spoke to business groups and civic leaders now, had become a rather grandly paid storyteller and fabulist. His lower lip trembled slightly as he moved toward Wells, extending his hand.

"Gotta hand it to you, Bob."

"No, it's me gotta hand it to you. You shot the finest quarter horse I ever owned and *missed.* I can forgive anything but lying. You bastard. Yeah, you plugged her, but in the foreleg! I had to finish her off myself, and then you dragged my ass into jail on a false charge."

"A case of miscarried justice, for which I'm deeply sorry."

"Yeah? Just how deep? Deep enough to send me a cut of your speaking fee? Word has it you get five hundred dollars every time you shoot off your fat mouth. If I didn't think so much of Nelson Hanks, I'd straighten out that nose of yours. Durn thing's crook-eder than the old Chisholm Trail. Ah, what the hell. Where do you get a drink around here? And somethin' to eat."

"Right this way, Bob. Pickled buffalo, barbecued buffalo, boiled eggs and baked beans. Smoothest bourbon you ever drank."

"My Gawd, speaking of mouth-watering, just look at that little maiden. Now that's what I'd love to put in my mouth."

Wells sighed heavily. The Indian dancers and fiddlers, the square dancing and assorted festivities, muffled nearly everything;

the old feuds fizzled like a dampened fuse. Playing hooky for a day freed Nelson's guests. Even Ray Boy, a bleary con man from Kansas, let up slightly.

"Senseless murder? Hell, there is no senseless murder. A man puts somethin' in yer wife that don't belong there, and you plug him. That makes sense. A man makes water on your property when you ast him nice not to. Course he's gonna get hisself shot. Me, I haven't ever killed anybody yet, but I can think of a hundred and one occasions when I might just need to. Times when it would make perfect sense. Well, looky there. If it isn't Mr. Dunne. You fellas excuse me."

The banker knew how to tell a good story. He was in the middle of one just then, telling a group of cowpokes how he'd been held up by Ray Boy but good. He'd lifted four thousand dollars off him in the bright light of day. Last he'd heard, Boy was up at the state prison on a five-year—

"Howdy do, Mr. Dunne. I been meaning to ask you this."

"Why, Ray. I mean Mr. Boy! What are you doing— Welcome, I mean. Welcome."

"Nelson posted bail so I could get myself a breath of fresh air. I gotta go back to the slammer tomorrow. But like I said, Mr. Dunne. That day you was just now talking about, I only took you fer four thousand. You told the examiners I took much more. Twenty thousand, seems like. Now who robbed who, Mr. Dunne, is what I was lookin' to ask. Damn if these ain't the best beans I ever ate."

"Hey, cut it out! You're gonna hurt him."

"I'm not doing it to hurt him. I want to show him something is all."

"You told his daddy you were going to look after him. That's not looking after him."

Surrounded by four Nelsons on a grassy knoll, Hubbell shivered, for they blotted out the sun. One of the boys stood taller than the others, and this one, the big one, had told him to put one arm behind his back. He was so cold up on this high spot that he was grateful when a Nelson reached for him, weaving his own arm through Hubbell's, to affect a wrestling hold. His back hurt, and his arm was pinched and not moving. Still, the feel of warm flesh was welcome. He had promised not to cry or tell, because now he was four years old.

"High time he learned what a half nelson felt like. His daddy asked for it, didn't he? Made him a sitting duck with a stupid name like that."

"Hey, I guess you didn't hear me the first time. He's just a little guy. What do you want to go and do that to him for?"

Hubbell's guardian angel was an Eagle Scout. He didn't fear venomous snakes or rock slides, but he was unprepared for malice. He didn't know any handy antidote for bullying. He looked at his fists, clenched from nervousness, and wished he knew how to use them. Hunched over the smaller boy, the other Nelson couldn't answer. For he didn't know, really, why he'd started trouble. He just knew it felt good to hold the smaller child this way, to watch the fragile cords stand out in his neck and feel the bones, so slight and so negotiable. The crude power he enjoyed up on the knoll blotted out filial responsibility. For wasn't this boy his brother? Kind of?

"Half?"

Hubbell didn't answer, for he was tracking his own tear. Detained momentarily in this painful hold and leaning forward deeply, he felt a teardrop travel backward through his scalp. That this wet drop had moved up rather than down held his attention.

"Half, you hear me?"

"Uh huh."

"What'd you get for being four?"

"A fort."

"You already have one."

"I got a bigger one this year so when I get a friend my friend and I can sleep in the fort at night."

"And what else?"

"A pony."

He straightened Hubbell up slowly, carefully. His eyes opened wide when he saw how red he'd become. There was a long, empty moment that the older boy didn't hurry to fill. He thought about the old fort, which could easily have slept two, and about the pony. His feelings blurred as he thought about his own fourth birthday. He'd been awarded a bed, and that was fine because it meant he didn't have to sleep with his older sister anymore. But he'd never had a fort, and he never would have a pony, that was sure. Free for the moment, Hubbell knelt down to examine a grasshopper. It leaped up, knocking him in the face, and he jumped back in fright. That leap back, the look of pure fear and surprise that swept over Hubbell's face, provoked in his tormentor not remorse but recognition. Boy addressed boy again, and the long moment ended.

"Hey, that's nothing, Half. They might spit at you, but they don't bite. I'll beat every one of y'all to the bridge. On your marks, get set, go!"

"Cheater! Wait up, Nelson. No fair."

"Not my fault if you run like a girl. Shit, look down there. Get a move on, Half. They're bringing your birthday cake on in, and it looks like . . . hell, the thing's so big they're using a wheelbarrow. Race you down!"

Not even the Eagle Scout tarried. They slipped and slid down the hill, braking just before they toppled other guests, who were ogling the grand cake, an iced four-story wonder the European baker had mounted like a stage set. His shop was popular with sweet-toothed locals, but he had his mind set on empire. Leaping at the exposure the birthday cake provided, he launched a wild and woolly western theme. Miniature sheriff's badges replaced typical candied rosettes. He laced the cake not with traditional pastel swirls but with sugary figments made up to resemble hemp rope appropriate for a hanging. The shoot-out the baker replicated at the top of the cake was not for the faint of heart. The towering fourth story was littered with tiny dead desperadoes, and some of the women covered their mouths, seeing the melee. Nelson shouted into a megaphone, his back turned to the hill.

"I'd like to introduce the creator of this marvel and ask him to take a bow."

The baker blushed deeply, happily accepting the applause and the business that would ensue.

Lavinia stood to one side of Tom Mix, who was smiling for photographers. He hadn't returned to Oklahoma for years, but his agent urged him to accept the invitation to the Reunion. And to lay off the booze for a couple of weeks, take a cure down at Mineral Wells while he was at it. Personal debts led him to be less and less selective about the roles he accepted. Ex-wives circled his remaining assets like vultures, and his image had lately taken a beating. Dropping in on solid citizens wouldn't hurt. Cool your heels for a while on that ranch, Moe Sisley urged. Mix squawked, having long gone Hollywood, but accepted Lavinia's invitation to come down.

A bed at the Hanks place invoked images of a hospice: early to bed, early to rise, *and* he'd heard the place was dry as a desert. The photo session completed, Lavinia turned to her husband and glared.

"I bet Hubbell would just love a look at his own birthday cake, don't you?"

Nelson turned, feeling himself contract slightly as he did. He squinted hard, searching the hillside for spurs glinting under sunlight or a red bandanna waving for help. He started to chastise one of the Nelsons, the one charged with watching his son, then changed his mind.

"I'll be damned."

For there he was. Instead of clambering down the hill with the others, Hubbell had fashioned a hasty bunker under a slab of limestone. Leafy branches safeguarded the entrance. Nelson could just barely make out the child inside. Crouched low, half his face hidden under a cowboy hat, Hubbell was nobody's mark. He'd gotten hold of a Colt .45 and held it braced on top of his knees. Nelson started, seeing that the gun was leveled at his own head.

chapter 23

Art Goebel had never guessed that a single wire strand would become the most important piece of equipment on the monoplane, soaring now at 4,000 feet somewhere over the Pacific Ocean. He was separated from his navigator by a tank that held several hundred gallons of Hanks Cold Point Flight Fuel. The two communicated by scribbled messages attached to the pulley with a clothespin. There was an oil drum on board, hot coffee, ample fruit and sandwiches. An inflatable lifeboat and other requisites. But a hastily scribbled message came to mean more than any of the provisions in the small hold. His copilot was younger by several years. It showed in the final lines he sent to Goebel as darkness set in. He read the words aloud, even though they couldn't be heard over the rumble of the engines, the rushing wind. They had gotten their speed up to l00 mph.

"What will Dole do with his $25,000 if there is no winner?"

They had set off from Oakland just after noon. Only eight aircraft were lined up to begin the race. Two planes had crashed on takeoff, five had withdrawn and another was disqualified. The Dole pineapple heir, contacted in Honolulu at each development, wondered if his contest would take place at all.

The Hollywood stunt pilot had the proper temperament for an

air race. His flight partner, with his years of military training, surpassed him in technical skills. But the loop-the-loops and swift low swoops over movie lots in Culver City proved Goebel had the nerves for the endeavor. He penned a reply, carefully folding the edge of the note over the pulley.

> Lay off the coffee. It's giving you the shakes. Do you mean winner or do you mean survivor? Hey, buddy, you're on leave. This is no war, friend, this is a race. Once we win it , we're going for a swim. Waikiki Beach, here I come.

Goebel shrugged at the hollow note. Maybe jocularity would calm the other man. Goebel had passed his hands over every inch of the aircraft. Any modification he had suggested was dutifully carried out before the race. He had flown down to Wichita himself for the final stages of the aircraft's construction. That Nelson Hanks sponsored the flight was a final benediction. Goebel knew members of the research department from student days. He had followed the development of the aviation fuel with avidity. The completion of a formula for a light, highly combustible gasoline in time for the race meant Goebel got a shot at the ring. He listened as the radio signals came in with clean regularity. It wasn't loss of faith the men were suffering now. It was loss of light and an intimation of the solitude they would endure for the next few hours. He pulled a note off the wire. He read it and smiled. Mickey Dane had decided to suck in his gut.

> Wind drift negligible so far. Will release one more smoke bomb for a final reading before nightfall. You'll have the beach all to yourself, boob. I'll be on the lookout for my first Hawaiian lei.

As the last bit of light leaked from the sky, Goebel felt fears rise unobstructed to the surface. All kinds of fears. He tried not to think of Lindbergh, who had been invited to enter the race and declined. In his mind, he could see the jubilant face of the pilot. He had been the king of Paris that day, as sure a monarch as Louis XIV. Lindbergh's refusal to enter the race could mean any number of things. His public statement was that the risk was too great. That trying to land on the island, a so small fragment, was beyond the measure of his powers. But maybe Lindbergh was satisfied and wanted nothing more. Goebel cursed his nerves.

He set to work on his night vision. The eye refused training at first. Saw in passing cloud banks not clouds but omens. The icy, vaporous forms were full of menacing signals that could shatter the concentration of even the steeliest Hollywood stunt pilot. He thought of New Mexico. He had gone up there with his newly licensed friend, who had a letter from the aviation board in his pocket. He was the thirtieth registered pilot in the United States of America and planned a private air show for the man who'd inspired him in the first place. Goebel stayed on the ground, prepared to picnic after his airborne buddy's short performance. He'd been hungry, so hungry that day, and he started a sandwich just as his friend turned a wingtip toward him in a mock salute. The food turned to grit in his teeth as he watched the little plane start a series of bucks and rolls that ended in roaring flames just short of a mesa. To think of that now just because it was black and Art Goebel was alone or almost. Life was nothing but tight spots. He tried to think of the sand on the beach.

He did for a while, and he thought of northeast winds, which would have them there in good time. Then he thought of Nelson Hanks, whom he hadn't started out liking particularly. Of course, he'd wound up in the palm of his hand, just like everybody else. But first off, he'd found him a hard man. Too hard for Goebel, who had gotten into film work with skill but also with good looks and a wide, brilliant smile. A public relations man offered invaluable advice when Nelson left the room.

"Personalize it. Tell him it's high time he got his name up in lights."

Goebel dropped the talk about his belief in the Travel Lite operation and his competence as a pilot.

"There are millions of cars out there, Mr. Hanks. And I wonder whether the drivers of all those cars associate your name with the petroleum you sell. Since they buy their gas under a trade name, I mean. You independent producers deserve better, if you ask me."

It was something Hanks knew, of course, but repeating those things brought Art Goebel into focus.

"You're young, Mr. Goebel. How young are you?"

"Thirty-one. And the entire nation is busy craning its neck, just looking for what's going to cross the skies next. Why, it'd be ideal, Mr. Hanks. News of your flight fuel will be splashed all over the papers! That race, once I win it, will be like a coming-out ball for you."

"Interesting thought. What makes you think you're going to win it?"

"I've got a great machine, and you've got great gasoline. I could land that baby on a camel's hump. There's nothing to it, Mr. Hanks. Nothing."

Hours rolled past slowly. He was in a curious suspended state. It was like being stretched out on ice, and he wondered whether, if a calamity arose, he would be able to act at all. After several hours he imagined a texture change in the darkness and realized it wasn't imagining, that light was being let in again. He turned around to see the thinnest blade rising from underneath, as if working its way into a room with a closed door. Fear had made parts of him clammy and tender. He welcomed his physical changes as these symptoms disappeared. Goebel felt a tinge of cockiness return as black gave way to gray. He began to swallow coffee and wolf down sandwiches with a demented appetite. His watch read 6:20. The flight was far from over. He touched the tiny window. Still brittle cold. He poured a second cup of coffee, staring down at the glassy ocean. He pulled a note off the pulley.

Rise and shine. Never felt better. How about yourself?

Goebel smiled and began a smart-ass reply. He wondered if Dane had been as shaken by the night passage as he had been. He kneaded the back of his stiff neck as he planned thoughts, mind adventures that would carry him across the rest of the long morning.

Whazat?!

He slid the note across on the wire, sure Dane already had the spot in his sights. He looked at the control panel, then tapped nervously at his watch. Maui lay ahead. Maui and Diamond Head, all the leis young Mickey Dane could collect. Goebel rocked in his seat like a kid. It was all behind him. Months of nervous planning, all the worry melted away, just plain dissolved in a single moment, like sugar. He hollered and heard his own voice for the first time in (he checked his watch again) twenty-six hours and seventeen minutes. An army plane appeared at their side. Goebel could see the pilot laughing, mouthing his congratulations. They were the winners.

The monoplane, initials N.H.P. still gleamingly intact, touched down on the Honolulu airfield, light as an island butterfly. The two men blinked, not believing the size of the crowd. Over twenty thousand people mobbed the field. Most of the crowd had spent the night in the fields surrounding the airport, but sleeplessness didn't dampen their enthusiasm. They wanted to squeeze the Hollywood pilot's hand and carry away his autograph, but they settled for words issued from a high platform. Goebel would eventually give his speech, a speech honoring Nelson Hanks and his oil company, the company that had now secured its spot on the cutting edge of the industry. "The finest aviation fuel available . . . why, Mickey Dane and I wouldn't be standing here before you without top-quality fuel." Afterward he stayed on for over two hours, his eyes trained on the sky above the airfield. Only one other plane followed him in. When Art Goebel finally stepped into the surf of Waikiki, he sobered up fast. The aviator miscalculated the speed of a wave and caught it at the wrong moment. He was churned up inside the fierce white curl for what seemed like an eternity, then spat out on the beach. He pulled himself up on his hands and knees, panting like a dog. When he recovered, he pulled on a hooded white robe and headed heavily toward his hotel, his thinking untrammeled and focused. Art Goebel read the news of his own mortality loud and clear. He was ashamed at his own weak knees.

And what if they hadn't won the race? What would Nelson Hanks and his celebrants have done with the Hawaiian dancers, standing ready with garlands of flowers? What would he have done at the news that his monoplane was afloat in the Pacific or, worse, had simply vanished? Shipped one thousand Dole pineapples back to Hawaii? Ground as many hibiscus blossoms into powder? Journalists stood ready to record an event that could turn funereal at the receipt of a telegram. Nelson had his long night, just as Art Goebel had his. But the prospect of several hundred guests awaiting uncertain news wasn't what kept him awake. Hanks was stirring again, planning and plotting again, as he once had. If it worked

. . . He rolled his eyes. If it worked, it meant winning a much larger race.

Researchers worked in a series of ramshackle buildings outside Lovely. Art Goebel's buddies and others worked not only on aviation gasoline but on a new auto fuel combining natural gas and naphtha. The results were tested at the unimposing site on a number of American makes and models. Results were impressive. A gasoline that ensured a smooth start and a livelier run, even in cold-weather regions—gas customized to fit harsh weather implied a wider market than Nelson had ever dreamed of. No knock, no slow early-morning start and considerably higher speeds. It would be the ideal moment to introduce a revolutionary auto fuel if Goebel managed this tribute to his company. He rolled over and sighed.

"Nelson, who are you thinking about?"

"Me."

"No surprise. Well, try to get some sleep. You have a big day to host tomorrow."

"I'm not only going to make it, Vinnie. I'm going to pump it."

"Mmmm. Pump what, dear?"

"The new gas my boys have been mixing up for the last year. Haven't you been listening?"

"I don't understand why you're thinking about this tonight, when right now two young men are out over the Pacific with nothing but the stars and a little flying contraption to count on. And *your* aviation fuel. I pray God it's worth something."

"You bet it's worth something. Much more than you think."

"You're overwrought Nelson. Get up and have Joey make you a grog."

She seemed to doze off but then turned to him with a start.

"You don't have any gas pumps. What are you up to now?"

He would get them, and that was what kept him up way into the night. His plans to enter the retail business. He had a great deal riding on that Hollywood stunt pilot. Nelson was keyed up, renewed by ambition and already dreaming of a woman in an aviation costume. Above her flew the winning monoplane, and behind her was a four-pump filling station. He got up, more agitated than ever, but not to fetch Joey and grog. He got up to phone Zoe, for they were back in business, too.

"That you, Nelson?"

Her voice on the line was deep and controlled, even though she was only partially awake.

"Question for you, sleepyhead. Would you be willing to pump gas for a living?"

"You mean if I weren't earning a handsome living at my present trade?"

"Right."

"I'm afraid I wouldn't know the rear end of a car from a sow's ear. Someone would have to teach me how to do it. That is, show me which hole to put that long hose in and what buttons to push, et cetera."

"There are no buttons, Zoe."

"No matter. I'm educable. Pump gas? Yes, I suppose I'd do it. One satisfied customer is like another. Can I go back to sleep now, Nelson?"

"Good night, my darling."

"Good night, Nelson."

He blessed Zoe in his mind. Initially, to reinforce the connection between the Dole Derby and his filling stations, he would dress female service station attendants in aviation costumes. Of course, there would be a fuss and stir ahead of him, a corporate assembly to convince and financiers to court again. He could hear the din from where he sat. Women pumping gas? Enter marketing, Mr. Hanks, but honor convention for the sake of your corporation.

Zoe Simply had accepted Nelson after his long absence. If she teased him at first about his foolish superstitions, his failure to keep a complicated life with conflicting loves and loyalties properly compartmentalized, that was fine. For she'd had him back. She gave him a genuinely warm welcome in her fancy new quarters, a two-story brick "coffeehouse." Zoe had treated herself to several European tours during their sabbatical. What she found charming in the Place Pigalle, for example, or certain bustling streets in a Dutch love district, was sociability. Even the poorest prostitute was offered a drink at the local bar. She'd seen it dozens of times; the transaction was so civilized by the simple gesture. The idea smarted, and she returned to Oklahoma ready to level the Body of Knowledge in favor of something more sophisticated. When Nelson knocked at the new address, after nearly two years, he found that bygones were indeed bygones. He accepted a cup of rich coffee and took a seat at a bistro table for two, placed inside a recessed nook. A panel of brocade fabric eclipsed them from others. "Like the lace napkins, Nelson? Have a sweet. Don't stare, my dear. You're all here for the same reason."

"I missed you, Zoe."

Zoe munched a pecan cookie.

"As I was saying, you're all here for the same reason. Which is why there will always be room in this town for a business like mine. Like ours."

Nelson blinked hard.

"Yes, darling. Ours. I need a little capital to manage this place properly. And all of my friends have helped me but you."

"This beats all. I knock on your door after two years with my heart in my throat. I tell you I miss you, and you hit me up for money."

He shook his head.

"Have a cookie, Nelson. Fifty thousand dollars, and I could really spruce things up. Fifty thousand dollars, and you could become a limited partner in—"

"—a whorehouse."

"No, Nelson. In an adventure."

Hanks gazed at the telephone, then at the clock standing on the library mantel. It was four-thirty in the morning, and he pulled back the drapes for a look at the skies. He felt profoundly peaceful, though tired. Nelson heard a light cough at the end of the library. He turned to find his son, standing wide-eyed and sleepless in the doorway. He dismissed the aggravation he felt. It was just the late hour.

"There are bears in my room."

"What kind?"

"Black ones. They tried to eat me, but I ran under their legs."

"Come over here, Half."

The child's hair was dusty, and he wondered why. He was given a bath every night. He supposed that included shampoo.

"Do you know what I do when the bears come into my room?"

"They don't come to your room. You're a grownup."

"Nonsense. They come to my room most nights. Most of the time I sleep straight through their visits. Other times, like tonight, I have to address them directly."

He wondered at a child who would pull on a robe and slippers in the middle of the night. He'd risen from nightmares screaming bloody murder for his mother and brothers, demanding that an entire household gather round his bed until he was comforted and sent back to sleep.

"I say, 'Bear, come clean. Are you here for polite conversation or a meal?' "

A smile slipped up on Hubbell's face. He was quick to cover it with his hand.

" 'Because if it's a conversation you want, we can talk about all kinds of things. Where you go when you hibernate. How it is that you move so fast, being so big and clumsy-looking. However, Mr. Bear, if you're looking for a good meal, I must warn you. I am not the man for you. I'm a skinny man, a tough man, full of bones that are going to stick in your throat and make you cough and choke. Better to look for a round, soft man, of which there are plenty, just plenty. A tasty, chewy man would make a far better meal for a fine bear like you.' And I'll tell you, son, not a single bear has ever been tempted by the likes of scrawny old me. It's not likely that they'd go after you, either."

He was comforted, but this wouldn't be finished by words. Nelson could see what the boy wanted as plain as the day that was coming. If he did it, it would be worse. And that constituted the only sorrow in Nelson's life. A grudge (though it didn't seem possible) or something like that, which he couldn't seem to lick. Maybe it was simple memory he couldn't cover over with six feet of dirt and gravel. His dead son refused to be forgotten, no matter that he hadn't known him for over ten minutes or so. Hadn't done anything but stuff him inside his shirt. He hadn't been able to repeal death by that gesture. His living son was a grim reminder of his own failure, and when the racket was over, a ranch paradise complete, fabulous gifts opened and forgotten, a clever discourse on bears delivered, there was this terrible moment. His son ached to be held. Soon it would be over, for he could claim that Hubbell was too big for such things. But for now he had to take the child onto his lap and try his best to enfold and comfort him. He fought down a revulsion that rose from the bottom of his stomach and wondered that the boy didn't run from his stiff, unbending self. He fought shame, and lost.

"Better?"

For he would stay only a minute in the awful, false pose. Hubbell cinched the belt on his robe even tighter and put the silk tassel in his mouth.

"Would you like to sleep over there?"

"Over there" needed no amplification. Mama needs her rest was an undisputed concept. "Over there" had long been the sole and abiding alternative. He nodded violently, and Nelson dialed for Hilda or Betsy. His son would spend the night over the garage with one of the servant girls. Soon, Nelson knew, he would cross over on his own. With a flashlight or a candle, he would learn to seek out comfort alone, without a permission slip from his father. He would scurry over the dark driveway to nestle against one broad back or another. Perhaps it wouldn't even rouse them, exhausted as they were from a long day spent dusting and waxing or from a dinner party that had raged too long.

"Betsy, that you? Sorry to bother you, but I have a little boy here who can't seem to sleep. Right; thanks."

He put one finger on the side of his cheek, figuring. Yes, it would probably take another two years. It was a question of age. Then he'd be able to treat him as if he were one of the Nelsons. For those boys were . . . he searched for the words. What was it that made those fellows so attractive? He was made for many; maybe that was what it was. Why were the Nelsons so much easier for him, even when they fought and struggled for his admiration, than one small boy wrapped in a dressing gown, needing nothing more than bear stories and a warm lap? He wished he could stop his own questions from coming.

"You know what we're going to do on Monday morning? First thing Monday morning, in fact."

"No."

"We're going to buy you a pony!"

"I have a pony, Father."

Nelson scratched his head. Right, of course. They had bought him a pony two years ago. Black as coal and already trained to stretch out in the most beautiful goddamned show pose he'd ever seen. Why didn't he ride it, then? He tried to remember if he'd ever seen his son on top of that animal. He wrote down *Talk to Sweet* on a piece of paper at his desk.

"Then it's time for a horse. On Monday you and I are going to buy your first horse. That and some glue for your riding pants. You'll be too far off the ground to risk a tumble. Not as far off the ground as those boys in the flying machine. You do know about the flying machine. Don't you, Half? Have you heard about your daddy's flying machine?"

He heard footsteps outside and saw the back porch light come on. Relief flooded over him. It was nearly five o'clock. Time, he saw, to give up any notion of sleep. Joey would be stirring soon, and the barber would arrive before he knew it.

"Remember, Half. Remember Monday. Night now, son."

He couldn't blame him. At least he wasn't a sniveler, and he was less a mama's boy today than he was a year ago, before Vinnie had . . . well, before the change. The hatred in Hubbell's stony little face meant he had a healthy kick inside. The child calmly held out his hand for the maid and followed her through the door.

chapter 24

1928

The pilgrimage to Buffabrook backfired. Lavinia Hanks' graciousness, the kid's birthday bash, the calm and peace of the ranch itself—it was all supposed to put Tom Mix back on the right path. But as it turned out, he'd gotten more tangled up than ever.

Moe Sisley reread the article in the *New York Post* several times in total disbelief. No doubt about it; he had badly miscalculated.

"She's having the time of her life at your expense, Tommy. We're going to court on this one."

Mix sat slouched in his chair. He wore the same purple dinner suit he had slept in, for he hadn't bothered to change when the phone rang fiercely at 6:00 A.M. that morning. Moe Sisley never slept, it seemed.

"If you'd ever listen to my advice . . ."

"Shoot, I went to Mineral Wells like you told me and then I went to the Hanks ranch for a week."

"Why did you tangle with Edna Ferber, Tommy?"

"I *didn't* tangle with her! I didn't, and that's why she pulled her pen on me!"

Mix's interpretation of events was cloudy. When he had learned that the winner of the Pulitzer Prize was due at the ranch, he began to come undone. He tossed in a comfortless bed, unraveled and sleepless by dreams of *Show Boat*, its wild commercial success. Edna Ferber now turned to Oklahoma for material, her sights set on a romantic rendering of state history, and Tom Mix was already in line for a leading role.

"Wait a minute. Let me get this straight, Tommy. You're saying this Ferber broad wanted you between her legs, and when you didn't she went to town on you?"

"Right!"

Moe reached excitedly for his pen.

"Now we're talking. Okay, Tommy. Let's you and me go over this deal before we meet with the lawyer. She said what exactly?"

Tom Mix wanted a drink. Moe's face looked terrible and flabby in the morning light. He didn't like his dull office, and he didn't like the way Moe traced the outline of his lips with the tip of his tongue.

"She told me she liked my white hat."

"Sure she did, Tommy. But what did she say to tip you off? You know, did she come right out and *ask* you for it, or did she do something? Come into your room or something at night?"

"Yeah. She came into my room."

Lavinia Hanks had put her up in the bedroom next door. So Tom, sitting pretty in a silk dressing gown, took care to leave his door ajar. She appeared, toward midnight, just as he imagined she would. But things had taken a funny turn. She'd pushed open the door with her shoulder and just come on in without asking.

"What'd she say?"

"She said, 'Those fucking peacocks.' Then she opened a bottle and poured us both a drink."

"Oh, this is hot! The peacocks were doing it?"

"Doing what?"

"Fucking, Tommy. You just spelled it out. This lady writer, over-heated by Nelson Hanks' barnyard, comes into your room with a bottle of . . ."

". . . Scotch."

"Yeah, and a proposition."

Tom scratched his head.

"Moe, the peacocks were screeching. Those birds make a terrible racket, and they roosted outside her window. Edna Ferber couldn't sleep."

Sisley shrugged and waved the pencil in the air.

"Oh. Okay, so then what happened?"

"We drank. She kept her glasses on."

"What was she wearing?"

"Trousers."

"You mean pajamas."

"No, I mean men's trousers. I told you she couldn't sleep."

"Then . . ."

She took a look around. Oh, they'd kept up a light conversation, but Tom could see she was talking with only half her brain. The other half wandered like a butterfly, flitting over his dressing trunk, his fan letters neatly stacked by his bed. He never left home without at least fifty fresh letters his butler selected and bound with satin ribbon. He read them before going to bed, and they rocked him to sleep like lullabies. Her gaze fell on his medicine chest, and he made his fatal error.

"I let her open it up."

"The bitch!"

Moe got the picture. She was clearly a professional. She knocked off work for a week or so to have a little romp with his Tommy. The article was a lark, a clean exposé of a fading film star's fragility. Maybe there was another angle.

"Stay with me for a sec, Tom. Did she write stuff down?"

"No; we talked a little while she looked is all."

"Okay. So lemme know if there's something on this list that doesn't stack up. 'Oil of wintergreen, essence of peppermint, ginger, glycerin, cholera mix, smelling salts, mosquito lotion, chloroform liniment, castor oil, witch hazel, gargle, cold cream, headache tablets, toothache tablets . . . Christ, Tommy, stop me, will ya?"

"I can't. It was all there in my chest."

"Why did you take it to an oil man's fancy guest ranch?"

"I take it with me everywhere."

Moe droned on, and Mix nodded in his chair, giving way to his hangover. Ferber's slight article, though resembling an inventory sheet, produced a guffaw in New York and Hollywood. She described the former Texas Ranger's dressing gown as being "luminous as a spawning salmon."

"Tom, wake up! What am I, reading to myself?"

"One thing, though."

He thought of how she looked, that half-turn she made in her stockinged feet. She wanted to know not about trick roping or prizefighting, all those years bartending before his true calling became clear. Ferber wanted to know about his Wonder Horse.

"She asked me if Tony was a gelding or a stud."

"Aah, Tommy."

"But I'll tell you, Moe, by the look in that woman's eyes—"

"Go back to bed, darling. I'll call you."

Tom Mix and Edna Ferber were certainly the most celebrated houseguests to feud. But they weren't the first. Nelson's quirky western montage was impressive, but it put modern visitors on edge. Nelson had sat slumped over blueprints, making notes on a scratch pad that would rein in the architect, whose vision was emerging. . . . Guest rooms on the second set of plans had grown more elaborate. He provided niches for muddy boots, a spacious sunroom here, and there a screened-in sleeping porch with space for twenty narrow beds—perfect for muggy nights. The architect proudly noted he had admired the like in ranchers' homesteads on his first tour of the West. Nelson replied by handwritten note: *Hang the guests. Where am I supposed to play poker?* All of Nelson's preoccupations were eventually given full rein. Guests tossed and turned, listening to field mice racing through the walls of the lodge. Plaster between the logs? Never heard of such a thing back in Creston. The space between unchinked logs was threaded with sharp black field snakes. That they dined on fat mice at odd hours, triggering gruesome squeals of protest, didn't bother Nelson one whit. Peacocks multiplied and were not routed; departing guests were too exhausted to collect feathers that lay scattered under the birds' favorite haunts. Pigs made their way up the garden path at nightfall—Nelson liked the sight of them gathered round the back door for table leavings. The tribute to Iowa eluded everyone but Nelson.

No one dreamed that a showcase would bear such a personal stamp. But Nelson had turned his impaired attention span to things. Curios and art objects, furnishings and even taxidermy consumed him. He discovered in trappings a neglected frontier, a new world he could dominate with complete authority. When an animal failed in the Oklahoma climate and knelt down to die on the banks of one of his creeks or streams, he had Big Amos saddle up his favorite mare. The mare didn't fear the dead and would nuzzle a fallen water buffalo, a stiffening heap in a pile of brush. If he let her, she'd lift a hoof to pummel the fine head of a giraffe to see for herself what the curious mound was about. Many of the failed experiments in adaptation ended up on the living room wall of Nelson's lodge. But not without commotion. He went through three taxidermists before he found one that suited him. His complaint was always the same.

"What do you mean?"

"I mean you sanitized him and mounted him. While you were at it, you made the king of the beasts look like a stuffed toy. You're fired."

He appropriated every fallen carcass. When the walls of the living room could accommodate no more trophies, he had odd parts integrated into furniture and accessories. A fir gun cabinet with tinted glass stood in one corner. It was decorated with the snarling head of a cougar, its door designed to open with one slight tug on a deer-hoof pull. The antlers from elk and reindeer were not preserved as mere artifact. They were transformed into ashtrays or the base for a low coffee table. Beaded leather curtains were fringed with the braided hair from a mustang's tail. Polished bear teeth and stiff zebra tail, a minute monkey's paw . . . it was all converted to some implausible household use. If the less fortunate members of Nelson's wild-game reserve were not embalmed, their forms were honored in an iron fire screen or in a metal chandelier Nelson's welder had coaxed into a scene from a buffalo hunt. The animals circled a rawhide tepee set into the middle of a five-foot-wide carousel. That light actually fell from the chandelier, that the door on the gun case could be opened, was pure coincidence. His crude enthusiasms didn't always incorporate comfort and utility. If eastern guests or dignitaries new to the parts scoffed, then hang them. For Nelson had discovered burl.

But burl and brocade didn't mix. Lavinia and Joey had their bright, burnished domestic interiors completed in town. Nelson sensed she was restive and knew it wouldn't be long before she challenged the look of his country retreat. His world required defense, like any frontier. The initial attack was launched at 6:00 A.M. He could hear it coming, rustling outside. Lavinia's voice pierced the locked bathroom door.

"If anyone can talk sense to him, you can."

Herbert Bard, of Hot Springs, Arkansas, came just to the top of her breast. He was quite at home with his size and managed by his own grace to make larger men seem hopelessly clumsy. He

spoke well and learnedly on many subjects. When Herbert Bard
saw that a discussion of passementerie or the treasures buried with
Tutankhamen would lead no further, he adroitly skipped to trout
fishing or a Negro baseball team that held particular promise. If
necessary, he called himself Herb.

"Stop that whispering, Vinnie. You have something to say, say
it!"

"Just remember, Herbert, keep it straight and keep it American.
If he hears the phrase 'on the Continent,' he's liable to go up in
smoke."

"I understand perfectly, Mrs. Hanks."

"Good luck."

Herbert shook his head. He felt affable this morning, as if everything were possible. He had liked the Hanks ranch. It was shapely,
unlike much of the land in this part of the country, and had lain
especially revealed in the early-morning hours. With the sun just
rising, the hills around Spencer Spring rose gentle and unprovoked
in a light mist. The art dealer from Hot Springs enjoyed his trade,
every aspect of it. He bought and sold now but hadn't always.
Restoration had been his first love. To a trained eye, dirt and
disrepair meant nothing. He applied principles of restitution to the
animate world as well.

"Does your husband always receive callers in the . . ."

". . . toilet? Often enough. He's at his best in there. Don't forget
to mention Hearst."

Herbert rapped twice on the door.

"Mr. Bard, come this way."

He was ushered in by a butler. Herbert noted the crisp white
jacket and a generous stack of linen towels, the quantity more
appropriate for commercial use. Here in the town house he could
see Mrs. Hanks' influence. There was ample use of rose marble,
beautifully veined, and water spilled from gold-plated fixtures,
arched fashionably to suggest a swan's neck. Her self-restraint was
apparent in the dressing room and bath; Lavinia had clearly teetered toward the out-and-out. Herbert nodded approvingly at her
taste, which she had managed somehow to stop just in time. Most
oil people didn't. He eyed a partition, rather stark in contrast to
the rest of the room. He imagined a fresco in place of the muted
gray, or a silk wallpaper hung with engravings of scenes from
Greek myth.

"Pour you a drink, sir?"

He moved toward the partition, toward the gruff voice—"Bard, is it?"—at odds with the rose-and-gold decor. He could smell liquor.

Nelson didn't even open his eyes but continued to enjoy his hot towel, which the Lovely barber had just applied. The daily haircut and shave, the unfailing shoeshine: an appointment that had stood for years. Nelson started each day with a shot of whiskey and a spit shine, come what may. The barber chair, straight from the Climax, stood behind the partition. Herbert thought of the throne room at Versailles and chided himself, remembering her admonition. Keep it American.

"Pleased to know you, Mr. Hanks. Yes, Bard. Herb Bard."

"You're an emissary, it seems."

It had been years since Herbert had questioned his abilities. He knew the tabula rasa perfectly well. He'd often been called in to etch on smooth, blank stone. To offer artistic impressions and sensibilities when there were none. Then, as tastes formed, likes and dislikes developed (never mind that they weren't his own), he could begin a treasure hunt for acquisitions. He eyed Nelson Hanks' cuff links. They held some kind of rough composite stone. Unusual. Ugly.

"Your wife seemed to feel that now, as you move into the final stage out at the ranch, perhaps the two of you might profit from a second opinion."

"A third, since Vinnie has hers and I have mine."

"Perhaps."

"Time, Jessie?"

The shoeshine boy rotated his wrist slowly. He didn't stop moving his cloth across gleaming leather.

" 'Round six forty-five now."

"What's your pitch, Mr. Bard? Time's wasting."

He studiously avoided pitches, prepared talks. He threw himself out into empty space, loving that risk. His accent thickened. None of his refined gab for Nelson Hanks.

"I grew up on corn pone, Mr. Hanks. My mother raised eight kids by herself. The only art we had in our home was a religious calendar my brother stole from a traveling salesman."

Nelson lifted the towel from his face and raised himself slightly to puff at his cigar. Bard talked on.

"It's part of me, but not all of me. I can turn it off and I can turn it on."

"So I see."

"You've amassed a great fortune, Mr. Hanks. And you've come around an important bend in the road. The decision to buy a ranch and build a guest lodge suitable for film stars and politicians—"

"Don't forget certain pals that go way, way back."

"I haven't, Mr. Hanks. Nor have I forgotten that they might sit next to Mr. Kaiser or Amon Carter at the dinner table. Monsignor Spellman might ask one of your pals to pass the peas. My opinion is that you've plotted out a brilliant design. Just brilliant. You've got big-city newspapers buzzing about your cowboy-and-Indian mixers. All your notorious acquaintances. You have a unique vision, and your generosity in sharing it has been—"

"Get to the point, Mr. Bard. I'm a busy man."

"My point? That you don't have to play the rube any longer than necessary. It worked."

Nelson's eyes sparkled behind the thick spectacles. He finished his drink and began to blow his nose.

"So you reckon, Herb, it's time to move on to other things."

"Exactly! All of Europe waits to be—"

He remembered Mrs. Hanks' interdiction with a stab, just as Nelson interrupted.

"Raped? Ransacked?"

"Discovered."

"I get the picture. A man of means has no business dressing up like it's Halloween, expecting his sophisticated guests to do the same. We should move into the first-class cabin is what you're saying."

"Yes, yes! I'll give you just one example of the possibilities open to you. I have had my eyes on a thirteenth-century monastery for some time now. It's located on a private property right outside Bordeaux, and the owner is completely disinterested. It's a shambles, Mr. Hanks. His grandchildren have claimed it as a fortress. Otherwise it stands empty and abandoned. He is open to discussion."

"About?"

"Why, about a sale. A man of means can do anything. And that is my point. What is being accomplished at San Simeon can be done on a somewhat smaller scale anywhere, anywhere. There simply are no limits."

"Oh, but there are, Mr. Bard."

Nelson rose from the barber chair and handed a five-dollar bill to the grinning shoeshine boy. It was coming, and good.

"There are limits to patience. Limits to what is healthful to listen to. Vinnie, come fetch this little toad!"

Herbert's impromptu method had drawbacks. Things seemed perilously out of his hands now as he heard himself speak.

"Mr. Hanks, if I can offer some free advice. Your gothic animal mausoleum may hold charm for you, but believe me, there are others, friends and well-wishers among them, who are genuinely appalled. Mr. Hanks, you've just had a mahogany Steinway covered with bark veneer."

"Arkansas *pine* bark veneer."

"A hair ball, sir!"

"Not just any hair ball, friend. It was extracted from the belly of a longhorn. I defy you to find *that* in France. Now you'd best toddle back to Hot Springs before I lose my temper. Vinnie!"

For Nelson's western collection had grown since his purchases at the Miller 101 Ranch. The embryonic collection was amorphous and unwieldy as the many gifts and donations that came his way. Tokens of appreciation such as the hair ball were housed momentarily in apartments over the six-car garage in town. Ninety-five million years old, Nelson whispered, pointing to his prize: portions of a dinosaur egg lay protected in a glass case. University funding had led Nelson to a banquet table in Austin. The administration threw the spotlight on the anthropology department as the main speaker turned to Nelson with sincere thanks for his donations and a memento of his expedition to the Gobi Desert. Inquisitive friends coughed lightly, recoiling at the sight of shrunken heads sent to the oil man by an admiring rancher in Ecuador. Nelson spoke evenly of the Jivaro Indians. Their craft, if one had the stomach for it, could easily be admired. He pointed to the skeleton sweetly napping on a serape, going on to discuss Choctaw burial, the meaning of the small collection of objects heaped next to the deceased. The remains had been dug up in a remote corner of the state and driven to him in the back of a farmer's produce truck.

Nelson was content with his oddments. It was enough, for the moment, to follow the uneven path that led to an oxcart and a peyote fan, a war club that had once belonged to the Plains Indians. Emma Sweet recorded appropriate data in a file box ordinarily reserved for family recipes. He held no disdain for serious paintings and sculptures, but he was in no hurry. For now, he was happy to test his skill on this broken trail, following one strange scent after another. But a new course was being determined for Nelson. He was not to be influenced by the machinations of a foxy antique dealer and his wife, and certainly not by the artistic ambitions of leading industrialists. Work would begin as the 1920s ended on a structure to house Buffalo Bill's revolvers, the hair balls and shrunken heads, Nelson's stagecoaches and stuffed bongos. But the museum configuration was most affected by Nelson's latest procurement: a Travel Air monoplane, which had turned the faintly disinterested founding father of Hanks Petroleum into the doting daddy he had once been.

chapter 25

1933

It was early morning, and Joey Fujii was drenched in dreams. The shrill ringing of the service bell woke him up, and he shook his head until the dream was knocked loose. No woman ducked her head when he passed. He held on to the flamboyantly dressed man of moments before, turned over in his bed and cursed. The only scarf he owned was used to cover his lamp at night.

He passed Nelson's bedroom and heard his heavy snoring through the door. He tucked his chin into his chest, remembering his posture in the dream. It often took him hours to dilute the richness of his nights, only skimming off what was pertinent to *this*. He knocked softly and swung the door open, not shrinking from her wide, angry eyes.

"Get Eddie Cantor out of my bedroom."

She lifted her bedcovers and swung her legs to one side, dangling her bare feet over the bear rug. He bent down to place her slippers on her feet.

"If he thinks he can dupe Lavinia Hanks, he's dead wrong. You heard me, Joey. I want him out."

He looked up at her from where he knelt on the rug and knew he was capable of everything. He borrowed all his power from the man he'd been in the dream.

"Why, it's you who belongs on my bedroom wall, Joey. You look positively imperial."

She stood up suddenly, and the front part of her nearly bumped his face. He hopped back in surprise.

"He had no business saying those things, Joey. I invited him here! I fed him that awful lumpfish he likes, and we made him cups of Darjeeling tea with honey and lemon juice. Didn't we, Joey? Didn't the two of us take good care of him?"

He found Cantor's picture on the third row from the bottom. He carefully removed it, rereading the signature that slashed the top corner. "To Mrs. Nelson Hanks, with hopes that I can one day return her kindness." He could barely remember the face in the picture. There had been so many guests, and this man had done nothing to distinguish himself, aside from demanding lumpfish. He set the picture down on her bureau, hoping Lavinia Hanks didn't remember Eddie Cantor was also captured in moving pictures. Cantor was present in one or two home-movie reels, but so far her wrath was confined to what hung on the four walls of this bedroom.

"There, Mrs. Hanks. He won't bother you again. Now you must rest."

"How can I rest when I am pursued by traitors? All I do is think, think, think. And when I do, I get so angry I could burst. What day is it?"

"The twelfth of June. You aren't pursued by traitors, Mrs. Hanks. You're pursued by family and friends. And people who admire you. One of them arrives today by train. Have you forgotten?"

He saw by her expression, that change from bewilderment to anticipation, that she had. Harriet Store would arrive at noon. Joey would have uninterrupted nights once Mrs. Store got to the ranch. He forgave the two in advance. For the shrieks, for the havoc, for the complete abandonment of the boy, who was home on holiday, in favor of card games and cigarette smoke they would send wafting through open windows in wobbly, uneven O's. He breathed deeply, pleased at his choice. For he hadn't killed Mrs. Hanks when he might have, raw as he was from his dream and its authority. She crawled back into bed, forgetting Eddie Cantor's defection and never guessing the effect she had on Fujii. What right did she have to awaken him so rudely, prying him from a better world?

"Thank God I have you, Joey. You're better for me than any sedative Doc Janus could prescribe. May I have a glass of water, please?"

I have you. He smiled at the phrase. Lavinia's assumption that she owned not only the objects but the people surrounding her lent him complete freedom. So long as he maintained his own polished surface he would elude scrutiny. She wiped her wet lips with the back of her hand and pulled the covers clear up to her chin, her eyes already closed. With the exception of hapless Eddie Cantor, all her men would smile down on her while she slept.

With the photograph gallery, Lavinia Hanks took her first giant step backward. She insisted that visitors to the ranch succumb to the photographer's bright white flash. "Anything. Write down anything. Would you mind terribly signing it with love?" Over the years, the glossy photographs of visitors to the ranch increased, filling first one wall of her bedroom and then another, until the entire room was loaded with black-and-white prints of great and famous men. Where were the women?

"Oh, that. Never mind the women. I sleep better with my boyfriends around me, that's all."

When they ceased to please her, their photos were solemnly removed, an empty space indicating a quarrel or some imagined slight to Mrs. Hanks. They were hidden but never thrown away. For many of her boyfriends, Cantor included, worked their way back into her favor. New faces and old gleamed on her wall. The collection fueled the local rumor mill. Those who knew her assumed it was just her petulance again, that Trappe side of her fussing and fighting. Others blushed with shame or envy and whispered, *Imagine, at her age. Why, I hear she's taken every one of them to bed, and when they don't please her, off goes the picture. With a little boy, to boot!* Only her husband and her valet read into this fickle demonstration the beginning of another new passage, one that wound back to an unfinished time—a girlhood so unsatisfactory, it had returned to impose its own demands. Joey removed photographs dutifully, smothering laughter at this rich, foolish woman's preoccupations. Picture puzzles and phonograph records, long lazy mornings in bed and the most curious resolution of all: She released her only son suddenly, with apparent nonchalance. She had sent him to military school as casually as if she were applying lipstick. Joey remembered the night of the boy's birth, the stench of the crow doctor. Had he planted in this woman

an animal's detachment? Her most constant companion now
wasn't husband or son, or even one of her favored "girlfriends." It
was Joey Fujii.

Nelson, swimming in sensation, forgot he would shortly have to
get on an airplane. He forgot the dark field stretched before the
car, feeling not his own terror but Zoe, who lay still and peaceful
beside him.

"I love this."

He might have meant the soft parts of her where his hand still
lingered. Or he might have meant the warm, fragrant night so full
of perfume it seeped right into the locked car where they lay. Zoe
tickled him gently.

"Say, it must almost be time."

"My whole life. I am grateful for my whole life. How many men
can say that?"

"You sap. How many men have what you have? Your whole
existence, with only the slightest exception, is like an answered
prayer."

"I don't pray."

"You just did. Giving thanks doesn't always have to be liturgical.
Here, clean yourself up."

She handed him a handkerchief and pushed him away. Zoe
sometimes loved him in a great hurry. It didn't happen often, but
it amused and satisfied him when it did occur. She would hoist
herself up, as she had tonight, needing nothing from him but the
simplest, most urgent thing. She didn't want his tenderness and
folderol; there wasn't time. Her stockings were rolled down at her
ankles. She leaned forward and worked them up expertly, taking
care not to puncture them with a fingernail.

"Art ought to be here any minute now."

"I can taste it now. What did you say we're having for dinner?"

"I'm having duck. You're a big boy. You know how to read a
menu."

She stretched her arms and sighed, listening to the wind stir the
trees.

"Flight. Why, we've always imagined it, ages before it was ever
possible. Makes me think of a painting I once saw in Holland. That
was years ago, back when you were watching your p's and q's for

Hubbell's sake. This painting had Alexander preparing for flight in a basket carried by griffins."

She adjusted her hat and reached for his hand.

"Sorry, Zoe. I was just thinking about these damned takeoffs. They set my teeth on edge."

"Now, as I was explaining before, Alexander was thought of as—"

"Alexander the Great? I thought we left him at the Body of Knowledge."

"May I finish? We're talking about Alexander the Great because we're about to thumb our nose at gravity. We're going to lift off the earth just as man has always dreamed of doing! Who wouldn't sit up and take note? But back to what I was saying. Myths were grafted on through the ages, so that by the thirteenth century, artists depicted him as having absolute *dominion* of land, sea and air. Of course, Alexander's exploits were imaginary, whereas— What's the matter, Nelson? You look as if a bee just stung you."

"Dominion, that word. Why, it's got a ring to it. The Dominion! Congratulations, Zoe. You've just given me a name for my town house. Lavinia's been racking her brains for two years. The Dominion. Now that's smart. That's classy."

"Wonderful. I'm delighted to be of service to your wife."

On this night full of sweet, swelling odors, Zoe Simply succeeded where Lavinia hadn't. Nelson's freethinking mistress had proceeded to give his home a name. He held on to the sides of his head, thinking. Then he looked up at her.

"You're too smart for that dirty little business of yours. Why don't you come to work for me?"

She closed her eyes and smiled.

"Not on your life. I'm happier than I've been in years."

"I'll give you an office on the top floor. You'll have a staff."

"I have an office. And as you and half the men in town know, I also have a staff."

She had come to her senses when Nelson turned his back on her. Now he wasn't the only one who could count his blessings. Her coffeehouse was thriving; she had investments that granted her both security and a degree of respect. Nelson Hanks wasn't her sole friend. Not by a long shot. She had allies who remembered her with more than candy on Valentine's Day. She held the title to a summer cabin in Maine and a strip of undeveloped land along

the Florida coast. She owned a stud in Kentucky that once earned
her an invitation to the governor's box when a three-year-old descendant of Deliberate Spirit ran at the Derby. She glanced down
at her hand, which Nelson held cupped in his own.

"We've come a long way, haven't we?"

Certainly they had, though he couldn't answer. Bad nerves made
him rigid as a bird dog. She cocked her head, thinking of dominion,
that queer and appropriate word. The two women in Nelson
Hanks' life sustained independent claims to Nelson Hanks. She
was on this night flight because his wife, the more convenient companion, had chosen anagrams or charades, an evening of laughter
and female gossip, instead. People talked about Nelson's exploits
incessantly and with good reason. He had grown so incautious
that Zoe chided him sometimes ("Leave her *something*, for heav-
en's sake, Nelson"), and she was sure his wife knew of his infidel-
ities. And that they suited her somehow. The boy, now off at
Stauffer, seemed more fiction than fact. Who had chosen to discard
the child? She squirmed as she thought of him, for the schoolmistress in her was still alive. Nelson's grip tightened, and she slid her
hand free of his. She had great fondness for him, though these days
it was cut with condescension. Zoe leaned closer to tease him.

"Did you see that ad in the paper for aircraft collision insurance?"

"I bought some. Why, if an airplane came crashing into the top
floor of Hanks Petroleum or the Great Hall at Buffabrook—"

"Heavens, yes. By all means protect the Great Hall."

He'd done some investigating and found that the farmer had a
new complaint to add to his list of woes. If it wasn't the weather
or pests that threatened to run him out of business, then it was a
biplane that had just flattened his cowshed. A dazed pilot sometimes managed to pull free of the wreckage, but not the farmer
unprotected by airplane insurance. The ad spoke to Nelson's greatest fears. He had his secretary call for information the day the ad
ran.

"Look over there. Isn't that Art? Quick, Nelson, light up the
runway! Chicago, here we come."

He turned on the headlights, then switched to the highest beam
to light up the landing strip. A raccoon scuttled across the dim
runway before them just as a wing sloped to make a wide circle
over the open field. Every time he stepped into an airplane, Nelson
grew sharp and tense. Seeing the blinking red lights above him

didn't make him think of Chicago and a swanky restaurant where a table was waiting for them. It made him think of his New York attorney's office, where he had gone to make out his will. Before stepping into a plane, any plane, Nelson would turn on his heels to feign some forgotten detail. Only Art Goebel knew he lightly patted the nose of the company plane for good luck before each and every flight. He wouldn't have flown at this hour for anyone but Zoe.

"Well, I hope dinner's good. Getting Nelson Hanks to Chicago without his having a breakdown may be the greatest stunt Art Goebel's ever performed."

"That him?"
"Sure is. Got his whore with him, too."
"She don't look like a whore to me."
"How do you mean?"
"I mean she looks more like his wife than his whore. He *talks* to her, for God's sake. Look at that, how she holds her menu. For cryin' out loud, now he's askin' her what he should eat! I've seen everything."

"These days you can't tell women apart. Used to you could, but not anymore. But hell, we're not here to get a look at her. He's our man. That son of a bitch flies to Chicago for something to eat and a roll in the hay. Then they fly back home in the morning. It's like gettin' up outa bed for a glass of water. I say we make the ransom five hundred thousand. I can taste it, Bird. Honest to God, it's gettin' so I can taste money."

Nelson Hanks was expected at The Blue Tower. The maître d'hotel had been standing by since nine o'clock. The chef had been alerted well in advance. He knew about Hanks' aversion to flying and was prepared to coax his appetite back with anything, from the simplest dish to the most elaborate, *aiguillettes de canard aux cerises*, *gâteau de foie de volaille* or a clear beef consommé followed by . . . He scratched his head under the toque, seeing the oil man's gray complexion. He'd heard the man had ordered milk toast at a reception given for him by the French government at the Waldorf.

George Birdwell let his eyes rest on the woman. He knew he was stubbing his toe on a stupid detail, but he let himself look, all the same. A whore? He had to defer to his partner, for wasn't it a

whore who had dubbed him Pretty Boy in the first place? Floyd may
have been born in Sallisaw, Oklahoma, but he'd since roamed far
and wide. It was a pleasure to think how different things were
these days than back when they both started out. That they could
waltz into a snooty place like this when the whole town was crawling with G-men was really something. A night like this figured in
the payoff. Floyd didn't need to sit in the same room with the oil
man he intended to hit and his little friend. He didn't need to follow
him into the toilet or see how much he left the busboy or whether
he slipped a fat wad into the headwaiter's fist. He didn't have to
watch how the two of them were together, whether she touched
him under the table or let him touch her. Pretty Boy Floyd never
let anyone inside his head. But Bird knew these exercises made the
real work sweeter. He saw how Floyd would rather hurt a man he
knew than one he didn't.

"Nah."

"What's up? Don't like your meat? Send the plate back and make
the chef eat it."

"The steak's fine. I'm not gonna do Hanks, and I'm not gonna
do his little piece, either."

"What are you talking about? We've been working on this for
months. Four trips to Lovely, and you change your mind?"

"I didn't say I changed my mind. I said I'm not gonna take him
is all. There's an easier way."

Birdwell swallowed, and it was difficult. He helped the food
down with all that was left in his glass. He figured it was their last
job, which they cut too close. The Kansas City Massacre was
imperfect. They'd missed a beat, and neither man could say exactly
where. They'd pulled off the job, but it hadn't been smooth. They'd
been slightly out of step since, too.

"We're gonna nab the kid."

"I don't see any kid."

"Of course you don't. He's in his bed, asleep. Christmas we
move. It'll be fast and clean. We'll have the money in a week. Wait
and see."

"Maybe you've got something there. Hey, hang on. He's not a
baby, right? 'Cause when babies cry I go nuts. I'm likely to go nuts
on you."

"He's no baby, but something's wrong with him. Ever seen a
sand crab?"

"You mean those things that crawl kind of sidewise?"

"Yeah. Well, that's how he moves. Never seen anything like it. It'll be like picking an apple off a tree."

Bird's coffee was cooling, and it didn't matter. He looked at Floyd with wonder. They'd never attempted a kid before, and now, with their troubles since Kansas City, how had his partner understood that an easy target was just what the doctor ordered?

"That man's nothing but a lapdog. Look at him. Woof woof."

Nelson had taken off his eyeglasses to clean them, but instead of putting them back on right away, he folded them and put them on the table for a moment. The room swam before his bad eyes, and he rested in the blur of soft colors.

"I've never had a night like this."

"Neither of us has."

"I wish it would never end."

"Put your glasses back on, Nelson."

"What?"

"You heard me. Put them on."

He did it, though rather sheepishly.

"I care for you as much as I ever did, but you're getting silly with age. Look at me closely, Nelson."

He did and wasn't displeased. Zoe had become more mindful of her appearance. She had her hair colored, and it glinted with a red rinse. Spit curls teased just under her cheekbones, and the lipstick she had earlier smeared in careless swipes was now meticulously applied, deepening her thick, rich mouth. She had adopted a tailored style that suited though it didn't soften her.

"Sorry to tell you I like what I see."

"But do you know what it is you see? A mouth that, God knows, has chirped up appallingly and not just with news concerning Alexander the Great. I love my ledgers, Nelson, and my temperamental girls and my men, who are poets and rotters and politicians. And I love it when, instead of reaching for one of my young beauties, they shuffle and stammer and ask for me! I love taking off fine shoes at night and sitting raggedy with books in a nest I have feathered myself."

"Shush, Zoe."

"I will not shush. I will make you listen, and in listening, you will not suppose that this night will or should go on forever and ever. You are grateful because this mouth has given you a fine name for your home, though quite by accident. You are happy because you are a wealthy man sitting in a smart restaurant, and as the chatelain gazes down on his lady, he is well pleased. But don't you dare insult me."

"Insult you? You are the queerest woman I've ever met in my life."

"I am a prostitute and a businesswoman. You insult me with love. Waiter!"

When they finally got up, Nelson guessed it was just his dread of the flight home and the late hour. Or Zoe's insistence that no fleeting happiness could be multiplied until it lay in a wide arc over everything. But he sensed as he began to leave the restaurant that something bad could well up out of nowhere. Something bad and so punishing it could eclipse everything around it. He watched as she tightened the belt on her raincoat, for it had begun to drizzle lightly. The evening had already been marred by Zoe's unrelenting horse sense. He damned her, not the imbecile who stuck his leg out into the middle of his path.

"Sorry, buddy."

Bird watched the grin that started up too early on his partner's face. He hadn't been able to control his mirth, and that was a mistake. Christ. The oil man paused and squinted at him. That was it, all they needed. For Hanks to recognize him and flag down a cop. Pretty Boy Floyd's face switched over to remorse just in time. He drew his leg back in and repeated his apology.

"Say, I'm really sorry about that. I guess I've had one too many."

George Birdwell shoved his hands deep down into his pockets and stood up.

"Guess I better get my friend home. Come on, pal of mine. Time for some shut-eye."

Birdwell watched from the restaurant window as the two hailed a cab. It was really raining out now. He noticed the woman made it to the cab in two long strides.

"Man, look at those legs."

He cursed such a lucky stiff. His breath made a foggy circle in the window, and he quickly rubbed it out with his sleeve.

"It makes the hair on your arms funny."

Floyd looked at him out of the corner of his eye. This was the hardest part. Listening to Birdwell's blathering. They'd driven straight for the last three hours, and most of those three hours Bird had managed to fill with junk like this. Stupid observations from a stupid man. He didn't bother to answer. Instead, he laid on his horn long and hard at an old man whose blinker signaled for nothing.

"It's the damn electricity in the air out here. I learned all about that in science when I was a kid. About how electricity can make the nerve endings in your hair tingle."

Floyd growled low in his throat, and Birdwell changed the radio station.

"Listen up, dumb butt. You don't have nerve endings in your hair. How do you think we get a haircut without bawling like babies? How about shutting up for the next mile or so."

They rode on without speaking. The radio forecaster predicted a remarkably warm Christmas. Somebody would think this was May, not December, he said. Birdwell piped up, he couldn't help it. He glanced at the mileage and guessed it was okay.

"What's he mean, May not December? All he has to do is look at the trees, for Christ sake. And you're calling *me* a dumb butt?"

Now, since they were twenty miles out of Lovely, it didn't matter. Floyd's mind had a home stretch, where things were varnished bright and clear. He had reached that place, and details like Birdwell had no further importance. He was going over what he already knew. The rest would come later, when he met Starr at the appointed time and place. He had to see him first. There was no use predicting what he would say to him before he laid eyes on the man.

A boy sat on a folding chair at the first stop sign they came to in Lovely. Soapsuds slopped over the edge of the bucket he carried. He knocked at Birdwell's window until he rolled it down.

"Wash your windows for a nickel? Front and back. No charge for the headlamps."

"Sure, kid. G'head."

"You mean it?"

"Yeah, but make it fast. We got an appointment to keep."

He started in back, whistling one note hard. Floyd watched him from the rearview mirror. The kid's shirt was too small, and every time he reached over the windshield it slipped further out of his pants.

"Tell him to step on it. Get a load of this town. Like living in a saucer."

He meant the gentle rise that lifted the edges of Lovely slightly at its rim. Floyd rolled down his window, seeing the boy still hadn't finished the back window.

"Hey, kid. We didn't ask for a spit shine. Come get your nickel."

He pulled two dollars from his wallet and waved them out the window. The boy approached warily.

"That's no nickel, mister."

"You want it or doncha?"

"Sure, but I don't want to cheat anybody."

"Then plan to spend the rest of your life at this stop sign. Which way's the Dollar Hotel?"

The boy pointed straight ahead.

"See that For Sale sign down there? Okay. Turn left there, and two miles later on your left is the Dollar. Thank you, sir."

They followed his directions to the hotel. It had seen better days and was now advertising residential rates, slightly higher with a hot plate and a phone hookup. Three cats fed from a plate on the porch, their tails erect and twitching. Birdwell got out first. He felt jumpy now that his partner had stopped talking. Had gone into that goddamned trance of his. He studied the trees, shaking his head, while Floyd gently closed his car door.

"Figure we'll recognize Henry Starr?"

Floyd was past words. But Birdwell saw it register in his eyes. Damn baboon. You are a damn baboon, Bird. So he pondered it alone and thought back to the newspaper clippings they'd both studied months before. Bird wondered as they marched up the path to the entrance if a photograph told the truth about a face. He followed Floyd through the lobby, pulling his hat down slightly out of habit. The clerk was busy working the phones, and they made their way to the taproom. The bartender had his back turned, but he saw them in the mirror. He didn't bother to turn around.

"What'll it be?"

"Bourbon and water."

"Two?"

"Yeah."

Henry Starr sat next to a jukebox. Birdwell spotted his black braid and nudged his partner gently.

"Sit here. Don't get up till I tell you to, and keep your eye on the door."

They were partners again. Birdwell was relieved at the orders and nursed his drink, watching the bartender talk with the other men at the bar. He glanced calmly at the door. The murky room was stocked with country boys. No problem, he thought, letting the bourbon slowly lick the back of his throat.

"Afternoon."

"Afternoon, Henry. You look good."

"I ought to. I'm livin' right."

Floyd knew Starr had taken partial retirement. That his last stint in prison hadn't won him any friends. He was doing his best to keep his nose clean.

"I need your help."

He had no leverage, and that bothered him. No old friendship to dust off like a piece of furniture stuck away in an attic. No debt to repay or loan that had finally come due. What he had was fraternal but only to a point. Nelson Hanks carried on with rascals and outlaws, but he liked them homogenized. Pretty Boy Floyd was not his type. The Indian's face was like a slab of Sheetrock. He saw nothing there.

"Birdwell and I are going to move in on Nelson Hanks' kid next week. We're asking five hundred thousand. We can split the money two ways or three."

There. Now there was something crossing his eyes.

"It's easy money, Henry. All we need is a little dope. You know. Their habits. How they're likely to spend the holidays. The easiest pickup spot. The kid and his pals, where they play, or where his mother takes him for ice cream and candy. That driver, the Jap. He anything to watch for? The easiest job in the world, and you can make it even simpler."

"Nelson Hanks got a lot of friends around here."

"Which is why I'm calling on you."

"The Osage initiated him into the tribe. First white man ever."

Pretty Boy Floyd closed two fingers and waggled them at Starr's braid.

"There are Indians and there are Indians, I reckon. Well, Henry?"

"Not for less than two hundred thousand."

"You greedy sucker."

Starr shrugged and moved his chair back from the table.

"Aah, stay where you are. You'll get what you want. When do we move?"

"Next Thursday. There's a big flap up at the house. Nelson's giving away a sack of candy and a silver dollar to all his kids. He'll have Amos Sweet with him. But no city police."

"Didn't know he had more than one kid."

Henry Starr smiled. Even in the dark Floyd could see his mouth was an aching black hole.

"Man's got a whole townful."

"You one of 'em?"

"Was. But now I'm grown."

Pretty Boy Floyd laughed right out loud. For there it was again, just like he said. It wasn't the taste of whiskey mash that slipped over his tongue, but the dull, dirty taste of metal. This time the taste of money was oddly mingled with flesh, as if it had just fallen from another man's hand.

Hubbell,

Mary and

Laydelle

chapter 26

1951

"She says she won't leave until you see her."

"Tell her the office opens tomorrow at nine o'clock."

"She's been on a train since yesterday, sir. And that's not all. She's got a little baby with her."

"What the devil does she want?"

"She won't tell me. Says it concerns the future of Procter and Gamble."

"Get her to telegram the president. She's got the wrong guy."

"She's very insistent. That baby looks all—"

"Oh, boy. Call my wife and tell her I'll be late getting home. What's her name?"

"Mrs. Hubbell Hanks of Oklahoma."

"Go tell Mrs. Hubbell Hanks of Oklahoma that Mr. Dick Shore of Ohio has exactly ten minutes, so it'd better be snappy. The boss is gonna decorate me for this one."

He stood up quickly, less out of courtesy than from genuine surprise. Mrs. Hubbell Hanks marched across his office and sat down without being asked. She wore a black fur stole and didn't look like she'd spent the night on any train. She took a gold cigarette case out of her purse and offered him a Pall Mall. He accepted one even though he didn't smoke and wondered in an idle way where she'd stuck the kid.

"I bet you think I'm indecent, don't you?"

Dick Shore bit his cigarette inadvertently. He picked the tobacco leaves from his tongue and leaned forward in his chair. Mrs. Hubbell Hanks arched her back slightly and removed her stole.

"Who am I to come bursting in here without an appointment anyway? I'm probably keeping you from all kinds of things."

She pulled off a glove, plucking at one fingertip at a time, then the other, and tossed them into her purse.

"Truth is, if I hadn't just this minute finished a gin fizz, if I hadn't spent all night long jiggling and joggling on a wretched train, keeping one eye open because of all the *military men*, I wouldn't be in your office. Can you keep a big secret, Mr. Shore?"

She didn't wait for an answer.

"I'm in a frenzy. And if your secretary hadn't let me in to see you, I have no idea what I might have done. The way I feel this minute, I could just . . . well, I could just do anything!"

Dick Shore heard a baby yip. It didn't sound like a cry, more like an animal's chirrup.

"How long have you been doing public relations for this company, Dick?"

He felt his stomach rumble. He grabbed his letter opener. Sometimes objects suddenly spun out of his hands and onto the floor, leaving him with the impression that he was, in fact, the clumsy boob his wife claimed he was. He had momentarily lost the center of things and sensed that he ought to ask a question to regain control. Any question.

"My secretary tells me you've brought a baby along?"

"We'll get to that. Fifteen years, twenty?"

"It'll be seventeen years in May."

"Ah, wonderful. To think of it. How someone, probably fresh out of college, can make a career choice and go right along. Just go right along for years and years."

He heard his secretary laugh. Far off, muffled by the closed door, he heard her begin "The Eensy-Weensy Spider . . ."

"I've come to your office with a whole lot more than a baby and a railroad ticket, Dick. I've come to your office with a plan."

Mary Hanks lifted herself lightly out of the chair and called to his secretary. She entered his office with a rattle between her teeth and Mrs. Hanks' baby balanced in her arms. His secretary was flushed. She bent her head right and left, kicking up a round of excitement in the baby. The baby tugged on the rattle, making that noise again. That chirrup. Dick Shore scratched his head.

"Mrs. Hanks—"

"Not a word! I know, I know. Babies and this housewife, for heaven's sake, who's likely got a screw loose somewhere. Well, *take a look.*"

She set the baby on his desk. He blinked and, startled, felt the solid edges of a paperweight in his hand. With a letter opener clenched in one hand, the glass dome in the other, Dick Shore stood poised like a man ready to strike. Yet what was there in that office but two women and a baby?

"Mrs. Hanks, your baby could catch cold! Or—"

The baby's clothes were off in an instant. She batted the air with her legs, delighted.

"—make a mess on your desk? Not this baby. Not the Procter and Gamble *Joy Baby.*"

His stomach had left off rumbling. It emitted wheezes and whirs, like firecrackers being shot off. He suspected nerves, for he wasn't hungry at all. Comprehension failed him. One thought, then another, fizzled out like a blackened fuse.

"I don't understand, Mrs. Hanks."

"Of course you don't. Not yet anyhow. Touch."

She took his hand and guided it along her baby's cheek, then down the plump, round arms toward the tiny feet. Had he ever been this small? Dick Shore felt something indescribable as the baby girl wiggled under his touch. Saliva ran from the side of her mouth. It fell in a rivulet down the folds of fat in her neck.

"This baby's skin is so soft, so smooth. Anybody would think this baby'd known nothing but lanolin soap, petroleum jelly and talcum powder. Not true!"

She grabbed his arm, and for the first time he noticed the size of her ring. The fiery lozenge dominated her small hand.

"I wash this child in detergent! But not just any old detergent. *Joy* liquid nearly from the minute I brought her home from the hospital. Happiest mishap of my life!"

She slipped a tiny pair of booties over the baby's feet.

"What's her name?"

Mrs. Hanks frowned and rolled her eyes up to the ceiling. Was it the triviality of his question? He wondered fleetingly if she was really this child's mother. She stuck the baby's fist in her mouth and drew it out with a smart pop. The child's mirth was immeasurable. She laughed and shook, pulling on Mrs. Hanks' lips, evidently wanting more.

"Laydelle."

"Nice name."

"We like it. I say we go national with this thing."

"With what thing?"

She swung her head around toward him. Her conclusion about him was etched into that dead stare.

"In six months, if you listen to me, Joy liquid detergent is going to dominate the market. When women find out there's a baby whose mother finds your product so gentle and mild that she actually *bathes* her firstborn with it, they're going to run over each other in a rush to buy it. I'll tell my story on television. My baby and I'll do the store circuit. You people can put us in a booth in parking lots all over the country. Let's put it this way: I'll do whatever you want."

His secretary cleared her throat discreetly and took Laydelle up in her arms for a little bounce. Mrs. Hanks' eyes shone as furiously as the enormous stone on her left hand.

"I'll give you Joy, all right, Dick Shore."

In 1951, in a hospital chamber choked with white orchids, Mary took charge of matters in an uncommon way. What didn't come naturally, she'd already looked up in a book. So that when a nurse crossed her, or her own husband, she'd be able to reply, "Says so right here," or, "Spock claims." Laydelle's temper had a pitch as fierce as an ocean squall. When her crying spun out of control, it was Mary herself who thought to swaddle her, even though it was old-timey and the RN gave her an ugly look. She breast-fed though Hubbell feared it might change her lovely shape. Eventually everyone gave way under her authority, thinking she was certainly a plucky little thing. She didn't ask questions, like most new mothers. She seemed to know her baby right off, too. Slightly reckless but sure, like a nipping, nuzzling animal. So they let her alone.

Hubbell just plain stared. He told himself as he looked on how he ought to feel. Words went up in his mind like kites, so high up and far away, he could hardly pursue them. Protect? Defend? Instead, what Hubbell Hanks felt was an arousal so profound, he sat down and crossed his legs. Then he took his wife's hand and laid it on top of his lap. She shrieked, but it pleased her all the same.

"Hubbell Hanks, I swear! Shame on you!"

He wondered how long it took to, well, heal. He wondered if the doctor wrote that out on a prescription pad or if it was another thing Mary just knew, since she seemed suddenly to know so many things.

"Hand me a cotton pad, Hubb. Look at me. I'm as bad as one of your daddy's wells!"

She had too much milk. Watching the baby search for her breast, then struggle slightly and cough, Hubbell longed for admittance. To his wife, to his baby girl. To the brand-new synthesis that had suddenly become his life. In this state of longing or passionate confusion he would have agreed to anything.

"I can't stand thinking of how they're all going to be there. Ogling me. Ogling this little baby. And that old nurse is probably full of beans, too. She looks like a mean one. Just give me a little time, Hubb. I want an empty house for the first few weeks. Okay, honey? Then they can all come back. I won't make a fuss, promise."

"Aren't you exhausted, Mary? I'd think you'd want a little help right at first. Having a baby is—"

"Of course I am. Of course it is. But I want to slump around in my old comfy bathrobe. I want to make myself a cup of something in my kitchen without someone rushing to do it for me. And especially I want to feed my baby anywhere I feel like it without having a spectator gallery."

"I was only thinking of you, Mary."

"Of course you were, you sweet thing. Come give me a kiss."

The baby had fallen asleep. Mary lifted her off gently and laid her on her side, the way she seemed to sleep best. A thin, bluish stream of Mary's milk ran down the baby's cheek. He leaned over his wife and kissed her forehead. Her skin was burning.

"Put down those orchids and crawl in next to us. You look so forlorn standing there."

He hesitated, then sidled in next to her, his legs dangling from the side of the bed.

"Big galoot. Here, taste."

Mary Hanks inserted her forefinger in his mouth suddenly. As surprising as a sweet drop of honeysuckle nectar, the taste of his wife's milk spread slowly, deliciously through his mouth. Hubbell blinked at the infant wrapped tightly in the hospital blanket, amazed that the sweet potion alone could sustain another life.

They remained like that for quite some time, Hubbell's ankles demurely crossed over the side of the bed. He found he could fit them both in the curve of one arm. He ambled lightly over his wife's body, his free hand stroking her softly under the hospital gown. He laid his cheek on her, not daring, and reached for her hand.

"Go on, Hubb. I don't mind."

In that way Mary Hanks ministered to both husband and child. She touched the back of his ears as he settled his mouth over her breast. She felt her stomach cramp and tighten, then she let herself sink into pleasure, watching the light strike the white wall in front of the bed.

The door clanged open. Mary Hanks cocked her head straight back at the interruption, waking the baby. Hubbell scrambled to his feet.

"Suppertime, Mrs. Hanks. Oh, I didn't . . . Say, excuse me!" The nurse's aide let something clatter and fall from her hands. She backed out, apologizing with each step.

Mary Hanks won her empty house. Her right to rise at twelve and three and six, to open her comfy bathrobe when she pleased and, indeed, to whom she pleased. Her cloudy gaze fixed on something other than the mounting dirt and disorder, Mary rocked and sang loony tunes of her own invention. She ate something heated from a can as Hubbell held the shrieking infant. The milkman delivered and the paper boy pitched the *Trib* into the same azalea bush every morning at six-thirty. She phoned for diaper service; otherwise their hermetic existence continued, undisturbed, for weeks after Laydelle was born. "I feel like I'm living in a love bubble. I've never been so happy, Hubb." The events that followed were, perhaps, an effort to hang on to her own turf just a bit longer.

"I say we tell them how the whole thing started. Any housewife would understand my plight. An empty house, a sour-smelling, colicky baby. What was I supposed to do?"

There was no soap. She scouted the storage closets and the utility room, all the guest bathrooms, where even an ivory scallop might be found. Nothing. She'd flat forgotten to put it on the shopping list. Laydelle fussed and hollered, spitting up, it seemed, every time she turned around. Mary thought of the good a bath would do her. How she'd settle down and relax in the Bathinette. She thought of calling Hubbell, downtown, but that, even that, seemed to intrude upon the perfect solitude.

"So I just reached for the bottle of Joy. One little squirt, and so many bubbles! Economical as all get-out, too. You're certainly a man of few words, Dick Shore. What do you think of my angle?"

Mary Hanks snapped her hip to one side and jostled her baby. Happy time was over. The child's temper flared, and she flailed at her mother's face, then reached decisively for her strand of pearls.

"Now quit, Laydelle. Just when I'm bragging on you, too. Sleep on it, Dick. Why don't you give me a ring tomorrow morning, after you've had a little time to sort out your thoughts? Laydelle and I are staying at the Alameda Plaza for the next couple of days. Give me a jingle. I ought to warn you, I'm not one to take no for an answer."

It took some doing. Mary Hanks extended her stay, ten days becoming three weeks. She sobered up and modified her presentation, wheeling Laydelle regally into corporate headquarters. Instead of plopping a naked baby down on top of the conference table, she lovingly placed her child in the arms of the company president. Then she took her place beside Dick Shore while he talked about sales trends and statistics. About revitalization and a thing he kept calling product dynamics. She wore a hat with a short net veil. She kept her cigarettes in her purse. Dick phoned her at the hotel each night to advise her of the derision or excitement they had generated during the day. When it seemed that ill winds were blowing ("They're dragging their heels, Mary. I know all the signs"), she took matters into her own hands and phoned the Cincinnati newsroom.

"Don't blow a gasket, Dick. I had no choice. Besides . . ."

She winked at Dick.

"It worked, just like I knew it would."

He pounded the top of his desk with the rolled newspaper.

" 'In Search of Joy: From Black Gold to Detergent.' You nailed them, Mary. With all the attention you've attracted by pulling this stunt, they can't say no. Well, congratulations. You'll have to settle for regional at first. They're planning a five-state sweep. Why didn't you tell me you were *that* Mary Hanks?"

"I was saving the best for last."

"I would have put you on your husband's plane and sent you back to Oklahoma. You're married to millions."

"Wrong. I'm married to a man."

Mary pursed her lips and continued.

"By the by, that kind of thinking will get you nowhere fast. I've made the most of my name in a practical, efficient—"

Dick Shore cut her off in midsentence.

"Cut the crap, Mrs. Hanks. Mrs. Hubbell Hanks of Oklahoma."

Laydelle took her first halting steps in Prescott, Arizona. She said "Bow wow" and pointed to a ten-gallon hat in Golden, Colorado. Her first haircut was administered in Santa Fe. By the time the five-state sweep foundered, both mother and daughter had done a lot of growing up. The Joy Baby knew better than to shrink from strangers. She grabbed a bottle of detergent when it was proffered and smiled. The Joy Baby became coy, and photographers shook their heads, remarking they'd never met a more professional baby. "Professional baby? Oh, Mary, please come home. That's enough now." Hubbell's speech was slurred on the telephone, and she wondered in a remote way just why that was. Mary Hanks was learning about professionalism, too. She found out how to think on her feet, how to answer appropriate questions and fence the others without ruffling feathers. She taught herself to deflect female envy, discovering that the energy it required could be completely re-routed with surprisingly little doing. Mary Hanks wasn't modest. But she did believe in giving credit where credit was due. Fessing up was part of her ingenuity.

"Did I cook this scheme up myself? Just between us, if I hadn't been standing in a certain department store a mere two years ago, I'm not sure any of this could have developed. *That* was when I learned you can't afford to throw away experience. *That* was when I learned how to wring fortune from misfortune. Now that day, the day I discovered there was no soap in the house . . . you want me to go slower? Wring fortune from misfortune."

Mary Hanks was quoted in trade magazines, and Laydelle's doings received vigorous newspaper attention. In fact, Mary had begun to book independent speaking engagements, when she received an ominous wire from Dick Shore. She phoned him right away.

"Over? What do you mean, over? You can't close this down.

We're going great guns out here. *Inventory problems*, Dick. They can't stock enough Joy!"

"*I'm* not closing anything down, Mary. Tim Tinker says we're in business to sell dishwashing detergent, not bubble bath. He doesn't buy the Joy Baby idea at all."

"And you're going to listen to him?"

"Tinker's the new product manager. I don't think I have any choice. Tinker doesn't think women care about their dishes; he thinks they want to be beautiful and rich with Joy Babies of their own, and once they find out they can't buy *that* with a bottle of detergent, we'll be up shit creek. He could be right, too. Mary?"

"What?"

"I may lose my job over this."

"Want to know what I think, Dick?" Mary didn't wait for an answer. "I think you'd *better* lose that job. After seventeen years of working for boneheads, you're beginning to sound like one yourself."

The campaign was dismantled more efficiently than a stage set. Mary Hanks took what she had learned about professionalism and went home. She rode the train across country and accepted a drink from a stranger. She passed Laydelle into the arms of an admiring schoolteacher from El Paso and smiled when the woman said she looked so familiar it was eerie. She decided that not now, but later, she would prepare herself a feast out of experience alone. She looked out the window and watched the train unzip the whole countryside, exposing it in great, deep waves. Mary Hanks paused and lit a cigarette.

"Boo!"

Laydelle blinked at her mother and didn't start. It was as if nothing could surprise her now. Nothing. She rubbed her eyes, which were irritated by the smoke.

"You old baby, you. Listen up. The two of us are going to have to lie low, fallow as these fields, for the next few years. But one day we're going to claim what's already ours."

Mary Hanks locked the door of her compartment and smoked her cigarette right down to the butt. She strung up the Zozo Man in front of the baby seat and jammed a bottle of apricot juice into the corner. Then she fished Laydelle's favorite blanket out of her suitcase.

"Hanks! The day we decide to go on the road with *that*, nobody'll be able to stop us. Not Procter and Gamble. Not corporate idiots who can't understand their own sales figures. Now then. Naptime, you hear?"

Mary Hanks fell asleep promptly. Laydelle poked the Zozo Man with one finger and rocked herself back and forth in the baby seat as the train rolled along.

"Da?"

The Joy Baby resisted sleep, rocking herself into a fever and glaring at the Zozo Man. In a significant act of defiance, she lobbed the empty juice bottle across the car, striking her sleeping mother in the forehead, just as the train pierced the Great Plains.

chapter 27

She bounced Laydelle so hard her rosy cheeks looked as if they might wobble right off.

"Who's the goon, Hubbell?"

"He's not a goon. Be fair. His name is Little Amos Sweet."

"Little? That man looks like a mountain. What's he doing under the shade tree?"

"Maintaining a discreet distance. He's a bodyguard, Mary."

"Well, you can take him right back to the store. This minute, Hubb. You try my patience so."

Hubbell saw that his baby had opened her fist for his nose. Glad that she remembered their old trick, he tipped his head forward and let her have a squeeze.

"A sound advertising campaign has just dissolved because one damn fool can't read a sales report. I have been traveling and thinking until I'm cross-eyed from fatigue, and I come home to more fool behavior."

Hubbell handed her a stack of mail he had held behind his back. The first, written in an elegant hand, was addressed to Mrs. Joy Baby.

"And there's more of the same at home. Some of it's fan mail and some of it's not. You've put yourself in the public eye, Mary

Hanks, and I've heard all I want to hear about fool behavior. Sweet stays."

"Sweet. Sweet. Why does that name sound so familiar to me?"

"His grandfather was guardian at the ranch."

"Figures. I've been out on the road with my baby for months. And not for one minute did I stop going and blowing. It's your turn now, Hubb. Here."

She passed the baby to her husband and stalked off to do her lips.

Mary Hanks had ordered eggs benedict and a dictionary on the second day of her honeymoon. She drained her glass of champagne, smiled at her sleepy-eyed husband and looked up "scion" in the tattered Webster's the bellhop brought to their room. Five newspapers had covered the wedding, and four out of five made the same claim. That she had wed oil scion Hubbell Hanks. She thought hard about that, wondering if being a scion added to or subtracted from the man you were in the first place. Mary didn't know much in the beginning. Just that people were never quite what they seemed. The man she'd nearly written off as a handsome playboy had taken over her own raw schemes and given them a professional finish. He had seen something she hadn't and acted on it. But Mary was precocious. It didn't take her long to discover that being a scion meant you lived with reflexes. That nothing could deliver you from memories when you were lucky or washed-up notions when you weren't. If Sweet angered Mary (and he did), it wasn't because of the long shadow he cast. It was because of the other, the greater presence of Nelson Hanks that Mary discovered at every turn.

Sweet didn't last. Mary gently subverted him by suggesting, not that he maintain a discreet distance, but that he join right in. Why, Little Amos, you feel like part of the family! She took one look at his enormous hands (they hung down the sides of his legs like wooden paddles) and decided to really put him to work. She called him out of doorways and made him change diapers. Laydelle, skilled now and frisky, rolled and kicked, dodging his huge flapping hands. When Mary took over the kitchen she called him to her side, teaching him to transform radishes into flowers or to curl carrots until they looked like birthday wrap. Sweet distrusted words and women, having learned that both tended toward treachery. His sheer size made Mary Hanks' demands the more ridiculous.

"Here, Little Amos. You push the stroller."

Following Mary, who marched ahead with a package or two, Amos longed for mayhem. He didn't see why anyone would want to menace such a pretty baby, and he didn't think anyone could menace Mary Hanks. His posture took a turn for the worse. Sweet started slumping. Then one day it happened. Someone giggled. They were standing in line at the Drug Shoppe and someone flat out giggled at him. He looked down and saw that he was holding a box of sanitary napkins in his great strong hands. Mary looked up at him as she wrote out a check. She had the prettiest eyes he'd ever seen, really. Oh, he'd had a collie who'd come close, but she had the prettiest woman eyes he'd ever seen. And they'd sabotaged him completely.

"Something wrong, Amos?"

"Yes, ma'am. I reckon there is."

She stuck the cap back on her pen and thanked the cashier. They went outside to find a tree to stand under.

"What do you measure? Tell me again."

"Just under six foot three, Mrs. Hanks."

"There's your problem. A big man like you tucked into a little tiny job like guarding me and Laydelle. You need the wide-open ranges, don't you, Little Amos?"

"Well . . ."

"And *real* danger! Not toodling around after a woman and her baby. Not in this town anyhow."

"I see it that way, Mrs. Hanks."

"There are no hard feelings. You and your grandfather have certainly served this family well. And I understand that need of yours. Why, you want a man's job, don't you? I'll tell Hubbell you gave notice, and that's the end of it."

But that wasn't the end of it. Her husband didn't give up without a struggle. He "sensed danger" for almost four months after their return home and hired a string of worthless hulks who were swiftly fired for stealing, lying or snoring in the hot back seat of the car. The last one hailed from Arkansas. He held a dubious employment history in one hand and a shattered lollipop for the baby in the other. When he smiled, it was discovered that he had one tooth remaining in his head. Laydelle opened her mouth and shrieked, then turned and flew straight into a wooden table leg. As a knot

rose on his daughter's forehead, Hubbell telephoned for a sophisticated security system. He devised a checklist for Mary. She
obliged him for a while, following the hysterical instructions his
secretary typed out on a piece of paper. When the security system
jammed for the third time, when Hubbell suggested she shop at a
different supermarket or change her old familiar driving route to
divert potential kidnappers, Mary Hanks gave in. Little Amos
Sweet was rehired and given both a larger salary and a renewable
seven-year contract. What did it mean? Mary got right to work,
roaming through the archives at Hanks Petroleum. She flipped
through old family scrapbooks at Buffabrook until she had the
proof she needed. Saddened but satisfied, Mary found that Nelson
dead was as powerful as Nelson alive.

"Tell me, Hubbell. Is this nervousness all because of one little
old kidnapping attempt when you were home from Stauffer?"

"I can still hear the sound of those shots."

"What's done is done. You were a child. Besides, Hubbell, I
don't see how—"

"The mastermind behind that 'one little old kidnapping attempt'
was Pretty Boy Floyd. Did you discover that in all your research?"

"One thug is another to me. I can't believe that for the next few
years this Sweet monster is going to tail me and Laydelle around
town. Did you remember to put the words 'discreet distance' in his
contract, Hubbell?"

She wasn't one to dawdle over a conclusion. That Hubbell
lacked originality was the most disappointing discovery Mary
made in the years she spent tracking him down.

"Yes, you flew us all down to Baja, and I loved it. But now, with a
plane of our own, the only limit is imagination."

"And fuel capacity, Mary."

"Oh, don't think you can pull the wool over my eyes so easily!
We refuel and press on. The only limit to travel is our own imagi-
nation. It's time we left the country, for ourselves and for Laydelle.
Exposing her to a new language is crucial."

"Mary, she's a baby! She can barely speak her own language."

"Quibbler. Oh, look at these pictures, Hubbell!"

The first travel agent Mary contacted quit unexpectedly in the
middle of their vacation research. The second mysteriously
stopped returning her phone calls, leaving all the legwork to Mary,

so that it became clear she would have to plan their very first significant family trip alone. That was fine, since Mary, freed from her detergent campaign, claimed to have ants in her pants.

"Why, these beaches are blond as almonds. Hubbell, it takes my breath away."

Mary lay on the floor in the middle of the bedroom. They'd gotten a fire going against the cold rain and sleet that fell outside. Hubbell sat in a wide armchair above his wife and watched the firelight throw her shadows along the wall. She never stopped moving. The wall was the blank screen, and nonstop Mary was the film. She wiggled, pointed bare toes from time to time in excitement or threw her head back as she leafed through the travel brochures accumulated since she had decided it was time for their first big trip. She lay with her fanny pointing toward the fire, bare under one of Hubbell's shirts.

"You know . . ."

She rolled over on her side to look at him, abandoning her investigations for the moment.

"We could use a second honeymoon. There are times when you and I are sitting in the same room, someone's reading and someone's not. And, Hubbell, I can be not three feet away from you and miss you like crazy. Why, it's as if you're not there at all."

He slid down beside her and slipped one hand up inside his own shirt. The flames from the fire seemed to have landed on her back.

"Mary, you're burning up!"

"Leave your hand there, Hubb. Let's not move for a minute, okay?"

Hubbell obliged her, leaving his hand flat to one side of her spine. He resisted the urge to lift the shirt up and check on her skin. He was growing uncomfortable with the heat, but feeling Mary still and calm was worth it. The fire hissed and popped. It was the only sound in the house, for it was Sunday. Cook's night off, Sweet's night off. Even the baby nurse had been dismissed for the evening, for Laydelle had gone down early. Content, he looked over Mary's shoulder at the wall. They were frozen inside a single frame of film. She flipped suddenly onto her back, teasing him. His hand slipped naturally over one breast.

"Oh, no you don't. Back to work!"

"But we're planning a vacation. Since when is that work?"

"You really don't get my message, do you, lover? You don't

work, and neither do I. That leaves free time and plenty of idle hours. If all we have is leisure, then how we conduct that leisure becomes essential. Vacation equals *oeuvre*. Now it seems to me that Barbados wins hands down. The island functions, number one. None of this silly business about the hotel being out of hot water or the telephone lines shut down. It photographs well, too. Look at how these island blooms show up on the page. Then, of course, there's the whole charming Anglo-Scot business."

He kissed the back of her neck, for she'd flip-flopped again and was turning down pages with listings of hotels and services. He laid his hand beside her spine again, but the moment for that had passed.

"You're a funny one. You act as if this is all another public relations exercise."

She stood up and shrugged off Hubbell's big, soft shirt. She lit a cigarette, then turned in a slow circle.

"Am I fat? Be honest, Hubb. If my own husband won't tell me the truth, who will? These breasts, they're all out of proportion, ridiculous. Oh, you were right. I should never have nursed her in the first place."

The firelight was kind, but Hubbell was even kinder.

"You have a beautiful figure, Mary. I love every curve."

"Curve? Which curve, where? Good God, that's the last thing I want. Look at me, Hubbell! Where do I need to take it off? Here? Over here?"

She slapped and pulled at her flesh, pinched until she was covered with angry red marks. She would not rest until Hubbell came clean.

"Mary, if you lost five pounds you'd be slim as a bean. Ten and you would disappear entirely."

Hubbell tried pulling her down to the floor again, but she wouldn't come.

"Five pounds? Don't try to spare my feelings, darling. Remember, you didn't marry a woman. You married a little rock. Are you sure all I need to take off is five?"

Mary spent the next ten days on a stationary bicycle. The steady grind of her pedaling set Hubbell's teeth on edge. If she wasn't astride the bicycle, she was jumping rope or doing sit-ups and leg-ups on a bright-pink exercise mat in the living room. Sweat poured from her brow. She both weighed and measured at the end of every grueling day. She didn't dare confirm hotel reservations until she was sure of results. Hubbell had finished bathing Laydelle when she called out the news. Father and daughter were covered with talcum powder.

"One little piggy went to market, one little piggy stayed home."

"Hubb, I'm down to one-oh-five! Call the Coral Reef Hotel in Saint James. The number is on the notepad by my phone. Tell them to go ahead and book those rooms."

He poked his head into the bathroom minutes later and shouted. Mary's upper torso was coated with slick green slime.

"My God, Mary! What have you done now?"

"After weight loss comes the real work. What is it you wanted?"

"Oh, right. They've made some kind of mistake. They're holding too many rooms."

Hubbell held up his fist, and fingers sprang up to match the names.

"A suite for us. Miss Hardesty. Little Amos. One night for the pilot, but they say you wanted an extra room. I've still got 'em on the line."

He looked nervously at Mary's vanity. Green liquid was bubbling in a hot pot. There was a whole array of jars and brushes he'd never seen before. The slime was hardening and turning brown as it did. He wondered if he would have to take a mallet and free Mary by force.

"There's no mistake. The extra room is for Miss Peterson. Now hang up the phone, Hubbell. It's our nickel."

Hubbell greeted the tall brunette rather sheepishly. She was at least five inches taller than he was. He was sure he had met Miss Peterson before. Before Mary. At a party, at parties. But work was work and play was play, she asserted in a husky voice.

"And the two should never be confused. Isn't that right, Mrs. Hanks?"

The two women certainly saw eye to eye on things. Hubbell and Little Amos Sweet stood to one side of the new Cessna. The plane's metallic gleam nearly blinded Hubbell. He'd made a foolish mistake and left his sunglasses at home. The nurse chased Laydelle round and round inside the plane. He could hear them thundering up and down the short aisle.

"I'm going to record each and every aspect of your trip, Mr. Hanks. That's what all this means."

Miss Peterson spread her big hand and motioned to the cartons and to the metal trunks that gleamed as fiercely as the plane itself.

"Don't worry, Mr. Hanks. This is a painless procedure. You'll barely hear or see me. Why, most of the time I'll just be a fly on the wall."

He doubted that. Amos swung to one side to let her pass. She diminished even enormous Little Amos Sweet. Her generous hips were squeezed into a contoured straight skirt with a slit in the back. Hubbell made out just a hint of lace, at the top of the slit. Mary sighed deeply.

"Class. That woman is pure class. She does all the great families, Hubb. And she is so professional, she can't even give out their names. Naturally she showed me samples of her work. But she could hardly expose the greats. Their private islands. Their suites at the Café de Paris, their châteaux in the Dordogne. African safaris. Mmmm, gives me the goose bumps just to think of all that woman has witnessed."

"What is she, Mary?"

"She'll document every moment of our vacation, catch it all on film or still photographs. Written coverage, too. We get to choose the form."

Hubbell stared.

"We *choose*. For the same price, we can have our vacation captured either in verse or in prose. For a little extra, she'll even imitate Chaucer."

Mary lowered her voice to a whisper.

"*Apparently* she did the Rockefellers for years."

"You didn't answer my question. Is she a newspaper woman or a public relations gal?"

"She's a portfolio specialist."

Hubbell rolled his eyes and blew air into his cheeks.

"I told you, Hubb. Vacation is *oeuvre*. Now aren't you glad you wore a necktie?"

They were some threesome. Mary, Hubbell and Miss Peterson danced to dawn, although work was still work and play still play. The prim capital had its Friday nights. Song and dance infected Baxter Road once night fell, and Hubbell, flanked by the two women, wandered in and out of rum shops with Bridgetown's finest.

"Barbados, I marvel at your marvels."

Miss Peterson sampled flying fish and pig's head, salt-fish cakes and black-eyed peas. She swigged rum and claimed her camera gear was growing lighter by the day.

"Your Friday-night children, Bajans, I embrace them!"

Miss Peterson knelt to inspect a citizen, slumped inside a doorway with his sleeping head to one side. Mary pulled on Hubbell as Miss Peterson struggled with her camera.

"Isn't she marvelous? Barbados has seeped into her soul. To think that woman, that poet, is actually going to translate this experience for us! Not only translate but turn a transitory moment into something of lasting and potentially commercial value."

Hubbell didn't love rum. It made his tongue curl. He longed for solid drinks and plain meat, unadulterated by cassava root or lime juice. Barbados eluded him, and so did Miss Peterson. She was snapping pictures of a drunk in a doorway, and tomorrow there would be fish for breakfast.

"There is absolutely no reason why we shouldn't enjoy a little press coverage. I've been speaking with Miss Peterson, and she's all but promised a piece in both the morning and the evening editions of the *Trib*. Happy, Hubb? I am. Oh, I am!"

She nestled inside his shoulder and, yes, held still. Hubbell stroked her head gently.

"Then I am, too. Only . . ."

Miss Peterson was walking unsteadily up the steps to still another rum shop.

"Chapati, chapati. Staff of life, I love thee."

"Mar, I have this feeling about Miss Peterson."

Mary tipped her happy face up toward Hubbell.

"I have the feeling she is not all she seems. I'm dead sure I've met her before, though where I can't remember. And that's not all, Mar. I think she's eating and drinking up one whale of a bill in exchange for a few pictures and a lot of bad poetry."

"Hubbell!"

"My gut feelings are she's not the kind of professional you think. Where's the family angle, Mar? We've been here eight days, and you'd never know we were traveling with a baby girl."

"She's saving her strength. Don't underestimate Miss Peterson. The best will come last, just wait and see."

. . .

"Coochie, coochie. Say cheese."

Miss Peterson plopped a straw hat on her head. Laydelle snatched it off. She handed her a wild orchid, which Laydelle squashed, frowning with concentration.

"Hey, there. What kind of behavior is this from the one and only Joy Baby? I see the baby, now give me the joy, sweetness. Cheese."

Clear water licked the edge of the beach, and Miss Peterson took a deep breath. She smeared fresh sun cream on her nose and blew a very few grains of sand from the camera lens. She counted to ten and tried to think of another pose, one that might please mom and dad and baby, too. She glanced over her shoulder toward the Hanks suite. The shutters were still closed, and Miss Peterson smirked.

"Come on now, kid. The sooner you cooperate, the sooner we clear out of here for something more interesting."

She picked the baby up, surprised to find she was as heavy as her equipment.

"Gee, kid. You're some load."

She trotted gingerly over the sand. It burned the soles of her feet.

"Lookit. I want you to make nice with the sand. I want baby to make nice for the camera. When I tell you to hit the button, smile, okay?"

Miss Peterson had slipped the baby nurse a ten and pointed her in the direction of a cake shop. Laydelle had done nothing but cling to her, and that didn't make much sense photographically. No one wanted shots of a baby girl and an overweight nanny. Miss Peterson's wide-brimmed hat took care of the sun, but it was no defense against the headache that split her skull into two throbbing parts. She'd sent Sweet off for an aspirin. She blinked, her eyes fixed on the group of rooms above, dark and shuttered close at midday.

"So. Just the two of us. Pattycake, kid, and no monkey business."

Laydelle stooped over, spying something moving in the sand. She laughed, she sputtered, as she saw the same something scuttle off.

"Now you're talking! Joy Baby! One more time, big smile for big Miss Peterson. One, two . . ."

Three. Laydelle caught the movement under her fingertips and squeezed. The squeeze was returned in earnest. Pincers were applied to the baby's fingers and even her wrist. The crab fought back and was joined by a mate. The horrified child lifted her hand up with one still clinging and screamed. The screams rang clear across the beach, and several vacationers, Brits mostly, turned heads toward the sight of the child and the other. The other was big and screaming, too.

"Ugh! Good God, sea monsters! Oh, someone please help me. Please."

She couldn't, she later claimed, move to help the child. She was that paralyzed by fear and loathing. Phobic, she had said, but fiercely. I'm a trifle phobic, and that's why the child was more or less on its own.

"Help! Oh, please, please." Miss Peterson tried it again, in French. *"Au secours*, goddamn it!"

A man with a newspaper on his head finally came round to help the child. Sweet came running next; even the baby nurse, with a bag full of pumpkin fritters. The wailing caravan exited to the hotel lobby, where management applied antiseptic to the baby's poor wrist, which had begun its swell. Miss Peterson was momentarily left to her own devices. She wept, then wobbled to her room on long, unsteady legs.

"Hubba-Hubba."

He thought at first he imagined it. The old nickname rang in his ears, eliciting conga lines and soldiers' bars in the gay, thoughtless days before Mary. He stirred his coffee, watching Dream Cream turn it from black to brown.

"You keep my secrets, Hubbell Hanks, and I'll keep yours."

Miss Peterson hadn't been the same after her unpleasant brush with marine life. The island had been much more than she'd ever bargained for. Her headaches multiplied, and Miss Peterson un-apologetically took to her bed. The portfolio is done, Mrs. Hanks. And so am I, she added weakly, an ice cube held to her temple. You and Mr. Hanks must carry on without me. But now that they were homeward bound, in the sky two hundred miles out from Holetown and Bridgetown, all the Saint villages forming the western wall of the island, Miss Peterson was coming back to life. She poured herself a cup of coffee at the back of the plane and sipped, one eye on Hubbell, one eye on Mary and Laydelle. Mary was performing a Mother Goose medley for her delighted audience.

"Hubba-Hubba. You were really something back then. Just about the best dancer I'd ever seen. And boy, I'd seen my share!"

Hubbell kept on stirring, and while he did, he erased Miss Peterson's laugh lines and those two worry creases between her eyes, which made him think of quotation marks. He subtracted years, added a blond wig and black peekaboo lingerie. Then he put Miss Peterson in a gargantuan birthday cake at the Ribacher Hotel in Kansas City and had her leap forth from the sugary tower at his old friend Spikey Adams on his twentieth-birthday blast. She gave startled Spikey a big wet kiss and started a dance on the crystal tabletop. He couldn't remember the tune, but he could remember every single step of Miss Peterson's dance.

"You were our birthday surprise to old Spikey Adams! That was you, wasn't it?"

"It sure was. In my prime, I jumped out of thirty-two birthday cakes. I did a grand total of forty bachelor parties before I changed my line of work. Most of those faces I've forgotten, but not yours, Hubba-Hubba. You were one of the sweet ones. You were one of those men who said things like 'May I get your wrap?' or 'Allow me.' I was dead right about you, too."

Hubbell couldn't recall saying any of those things. He didn't remember fetching a coat for Miss Peterson or lighting her cigarettes. He mostly remembered signing checks and tipping waiters.

"Yep. My predictions were all right on target. I said you were too nice for your own good. That all those pals of yours knew a red-hot deal when they saw one. Where are they now, all those guys with the same first name?"

"I'm a family man now. I have no time for shenanigans."

"Maybe you don't have time for shenanigans, but you must have time for old friends."

So it was a continuum. Hubbell thought of all the Lovely Nelsons, those boys who seemed to have formed the substance of his childhood. The continuum proceeded straight through military school. The boys he met there later became the recuperating soldiers Hubbell took under his wing after the war. The boys, the men, were all the same, and he hadn't known that until now. Funny that Miss Peterson should bring them all back on board his plane, when they'd been gone from his life for so many years.

"Too bad I wasn't in the portfolio racket, uh, business back then. You would have had some fancy pictures and limericks to boot. Boy, what I could invent about *those* years!"

And thus began a second medley, one that had nothing whatsoever to do with Mother Goose. Miss Peterson, full of strong coffee and vitality now that they were flying home, struck up a ditty so naughty that Hubbell spilled his entire dream-creamed cup down his shirtfront. Mary looked up from where she sat. Laydelle stared from Mary's lap, her precious wrist bound in white gauze. That was his life now. Not soldiers, raw from the war, not parasitic sons of men as rich as or richer than his own father. The Nelsons no longer ruled his life. Hubbell shushed Miss Peterson so violently, a bit of spittle flew into her face. She recovered gracefully, wiping off the spray with a fresh hankie.

"Boy, your wife sure clipped your wings. I hope it's worth it, Hubba-Hubba."

Miss Peterson winked and returned to her seat. Hubbell breathed somewhat easier as he watched her move deliberately to the front of the cabin. Little Amos had fallen asleep, and the baby nurse got out of her seat to spell Mary. He had all the life he needed, right here in this pressurized cabin. Memories were for old men, not men smack in the vigorous middle of their lives. Hubbell peeked out the window and watched the wingtip pierce a patchy white cloud.

chapter 28

1958

"You call this a party?" Mary didn't like his guest list. "Is this charity?" She didn't think it qualified, not by a long shot. Charity was written up in the Sunday paper, and who cared to read about forty dreary boys pitching horseshoes and running gunnysack races? She questioned who the afternoon was meant to serve and shrank from the answer Hubbell gave. The picnic was for the boys, of course, and their leader, poor, depleted Father Ed. Then Hubbell would grow mystical. He saw things in a new light as the boys fanned out over the wide lawn. After all, what did the land yield? It had absolutely no purpose beyond what its own beauty suggested. Unleashing these trying, unhappy boys each year revitalized it; didn't she feel it, too? No, Mary didn't. She didn't feel it at all. She withdrew to the English rock garden she fought to keep alive. But Oklahoma was not England, and she lost her Living Beauties, her single Shady Rose-tipped Venus, to fungus and pests. A whole host of inhospitable conditions stymied Mary's efforts. He accepted her bad temper and let her retreat into a garden that wouldn't grow. Perhaps Laydelle, then. He tried and tried to generate enthusiasm for the event, but she was clearly her mother's daughter.

"And just think, your grandfather used to throw parties all the time on his ranch. Sometimes the parties were for all the boys in town named after him. The little Nelsons would then invite their friends, until practically all of Lovely turned out. Other times he'd invite outlaws and Indians. Lawmen, too, only on the day he gave the party, everybody had to behave like proper ladies and gentlemen. No fighting, no shooting; just a great big party, honey. And now it's our turn to have a big party, just like your grandfather."

She swallowed Coke thoughtfully and held her belch inside.

"I don't like those boys, Daddy."

"You don't know them, Laydelle. They're nice boys with hard lives. It does them good to come to our place. They don't get a chance to stretch their legs and play like you see them do. Or even loll around. This could be the best meal they've had in months. You can bet your grandfather's guests sometimes had hard lives, too. Why, most of those little Nelsons had it pretty darn tough. Besides, this is fun. Is that Coke good, honey?"

She didn't bother to answer him but sucked harder on the straw to make that noise at the bottom.

"They don't look like the boys in my school, and one of them was petting Mineown."

I can't eat it because it doesn't taste good. I can't wear it because it isn't pretty. I can't sit on your lap because I don't like you. Mary was working on developing tact in the girl, and Hubbell was sorry to see her untroubled honesty go. His daughter would never be as pure as she was now, aged seven and mad that ugly boys had overrun her home and touched her puppy. "This is mineown puppy." She had baptized the sweet-tempered little animal herself. Hubbell thought of her school, the sailor-top uniforms for girls and the obligatory saddle shoes. The discreet dark slacks and white shirts for boys and a campus wide and welcoming as the lawn at the state capital. No, Father Ed's boys didn't look like the boys at her school.

"And, Daddy . . . ?"

"If you want more Coke you can have it."

That made her happy. Mary didn't trust carbonation. The bubbles worried her. If they do that in the glass, she once said, pointing at a fizzy drink, just imagine what they do in your stomach.

"What is bit o' honey?"

Her attention strayed. She plunged her straw into the top of an anthill and started to move it around in small circles. As she continued to gyrate it round and round, ants poured out of the tiny hole on top. They gushed from the opening, and she laughed delightedly.

"Candy, I think. Laydelle?"

"Icky. They're coming and coming."

"Why, sweetie? Should we have had that kind of candy for our guests?"

She looked at him. Her eyelashes lifted in a long, thick curve.

"They already have it. One of those boys asked me if I'd let him give me my very first bit o' honey."

Hubbell wanted to fall. He wanted to fall into a deep wide ditch and lie still in a world where man and nature were mute. Where he could hear nothing, see nothing and feel only darkness and damp. Oh, his little girl.

"And what did you do?"

"I threw a rock at him and ran away."

She returned to her play, forgetting the original issue, the ugly boys who spoiled her home.

"Shall we go and find that boy, Laydelle, so I can give him a talking to?"

"I can't. I promised Mommy I would help plant her garden. Daddy?"

She stood up to face him. Her shorts were caught inside the line of her buttocks. She didn't notice, but he did. Hubbell tugged slightly on the bottom of her shorts, and they came free.

"You said I could have another Coke."

"Sure, Baby. Then I want you to go help your mommy dig, just like you said. Later, when it's almost dark, you're going to see something very, very pretty."

"Tell me!"

"I can't. You know your daddy keeps the best secrets in town. Come on, Baby."

Her hand inside his was the smallest thing in the world. He held it gently, with wonder and sorrow, worried about how easy it would be to lead such a little hand anywhere. He lined up with Laydelle, for there was a queue for drinks. He felt frosty as the shaved ice that lay shaped and cold in a firm white mound. She reached deliberately for a can of Coke, and he watched as she set off to find Mary. He felt alone among strangers until he caught sight of the preacher, who balanced a plate loaded with food on his knee. Seeing him reassured Hubbell. The old man clearly loved a full belly and the feel of the warm sun on his face.

Father Ed's teeth were studded with nuggets of gold corn. He smiled as he ate, smiled and talked excitedly, for he was in the middle of the best day of the year. There was nothing pleasant about running Pleasant Hill, unless he computed the Hanks picnic, treated the event as if it were part of his salary or some quantitative job benefit. He loved Buffabrook. He knew and loved it, down to the last wooded acre. But this vast, manicured lawn was much more to his liking. He could supervise the boys without having to ford hill and dale. The preacher was nearly sixty-three.

Father Ed had no delusions about Pleasant Hill. Not quite a reform school, it was a last chance for forty boys who needed one. Boys whose trouble warranted a set of barracks inserted between two hills that rose like bare knees near the airport road. Often boys used this stopover at Father Ed's to blueprint a larger escapade. The preacher laid on hands and books and vo-tech training, mostly to no avail. Father Ed was eternally broke. He shaded literal meaning into his location off the airport road. The rich were flying elsewhere. His cause, caught between two nude hills, wasn't heartrending enough for them. His boys were too old to hold their attention. As juveniles, they weren't quite bad enough, either. Their missing teeth and poor grammar, their dull hair and eyes, made them unattractive as a civic cause. Their potential connection to a criminal class was too obscure to attract the Republicans, and Democrats wanted something darker, closer to the bone than his boys. He turned to heaven and found no answer. Sometimes his despair was so deep, he prayed in limericks or ballads, hoping God would hear something novel and lend an ear. At least his position as director bought him a ticket to the finest garden party in town.

He nibbled the rest of the corn and got a jolt of pleasure seeing the pretty Hanks child pass, even though this one seemed set in steel. She was clearly displeased at having her home overrun with boys. Father Ed had heard she'd once been called Joy Baby. A nickname of some kind? he wondered. He slid over to make room for her on the bench, but she glared at him and moved on. This slight was shortly forgotten. . . . Father Ed caught sight of a cotton candy machine. He could already imagine the spinning sugar dissolving on his tongue.

Hubbell wrangled a loan from the museum's board of directors and had his father's creaky chuck wagon purchased from the Miller Ranch brought out at the foundation's expense. Trays of baked beans and barbecued beef lay stacked inside the wagon. He hired caterers to keep the food and drink coming but insisted on constructing the Sloppy Joes himself. He ordered slabs of yellow corn bread iced with sweet butter, any food so particular to summer that it would be extinct in another month. Hand-cranked peach ice cream perched on waffle cones . . . Hubbell had ordered whatever he imagined a boy would want. For it was Hubbell who did the imagining for the event. The fishing contests, the stone skipping, the scavenger hunts in which every boy was a winner. He watched as the boys wolfed down the food. Scowls or direct threats from Father Ed failed as they failed every year. They ate too much too fast. He shook his head and savored the sight of their gluttony, this known, familiar peccadillo. It was a wonder one of them didn't choke. Hubbell took his lemonade to the porch swing.

The clamor and glad yells of forty free boys seemed far away up here. They didn't approach the front porch, didn't peer in a window to see who lay napping on a wide chintz sofa or crane their necks to see who turned out tunes at the player piano or who lay sprawled on the deep area rug before the fireplace. Even free boys, Hubbell still thought, understood there are limits. He heard his wife's voice from where he sat in the swing. Faint as it was, her voice was thin and irritated. He finished his drink with a grimace. It needed more sugar, and a piece of pulp had gone down the wrong way. He walked through the house, loving the ordered interior and the generous drafts of air from the river. The heightened sense of well-being the special day gave him had returned. Over the Dutch door in the kitchen, he could see Mary on her hands and knees. She and Laydelle were tunneling through the soil, avid as moles. Everything would be fine, just as it always had been, and Hubbell wondered how he could have made such a thing of an adolescent joke. Mary swiped at her cheek with the back of her hand, and she handed Laydelle a trowel.

"The two of you come around front in about thirty minutes. Don't miss my show."

"Whose show? If it were truly yours, you wouldn't toss the microphone to that religious bag of wind."

"Mary!"

He knew relinquishing her brand-new home to his uneven cause took it out of Mary, and he was doubly grateful for the concession. It had been only ten months, after all, since they'd moved to Tulsa. It was like asking a child to share a brand-new toy.

. . .

It wasn't church. These weren't votive candles. Still, the Pleasant Hill boys were quiet as they strapped a leather harness over the carapace of each box turtle. It was as close to reverence as some of them would ever come. Hubbell bent among the boys, his fears forgotten, and named the concave male bellies, the flat and solid planes of the females. He was hot and excited, perspiring as he explained to the boys, each of whom held a turtle in midair. Father Ed offered to lift Laydelle up so she could see her daddy better, an offer she glumly refused. Mary had gone off to get drinks.

"Set them down gently and watch they don't get away until you're ready. This part under here is called the plastron. You can tell whether you've got hold of a male or a female by the shape of it. The turtle shell is called the carapace. Tough name, isn't it? Careful they don't wiggle out from under you when you strap on the harness. Bill, you need a hand there?"

The boys each completed their task as the streaked sky let go of reds and golds, succumbing to dusk. They fixed the candles on the top of each harness. They were handed matches, something strictly forbidden at Pleasant Hill, and they lit the candles carefully, dreaming of cigarettes and reefers. Forty turtles began to lumber away. Hubbell smiled. He would have settled for extravaganza alone, the slow, flickering sight of them. But forty boys needed more. It took a preacher to translate this experience, a front lawn filled with moving light. Father Ed's voice carried. The boys were used to it and wouldn't have listened, but the extraordinary day had tranquilized them.

"This is living, boys. What do you say we give Hubbell Hanks a big round of applause? It isn't every day we get a treat like this."

Hubbell's face flushed. He felt his ears burn and tingle.

"Hubbell Hanks deserves praise for many things. His generosity, his patience in letting our rough-and-tumble crew come and invade his territory again. Not everyone is ready and willing to give in the same way. But I also want to thank Hubbell for the range of his imagination. He is an extraordinary man who hasn't sealed off the boy in himself. The boy in Hubbell greets the boy in each of you. I thank God for putting such a man in our midst."

They knew they would have to pay for it somehow. The marvel began to fade as individual flames burned out. One candle toppled altogether, and someone ran to extinguish the flame. Old Windbag. Some of them grumbled under their breath. He has to put his two cents in, just like all the other times.

"I think of this, boys, as I watch these animals circle this wide and open space. I think of these lumbering animals and how ungainly they are. How their movement is sometimes less than graceful, often laughable. Yet how tonight, through a simple act, they are transformed into Messengers of Light."

Some of the turtles had already disappeared into the woods, and one headed into traffic. A child streaked off toward Riverview Road, the busy street in front of the Hanks property, now shining with spotlights. Father Ed watched as he swooped down on a turtle. They moved faster than he imagined. The preacher looked around for Hubbell, to let him know he was organizing a roundup. He spotted him, holding a turtle and talking to his wife. The turtle worked its legs methodically, stranded in midair. Father Ed thought this all might have been a bit better organized, then reprimanded himself for the uncharitable thought.

"This is a beautiful display, Hubbell. You've come up with quite a mesmerizing image."

Mary Hanks' upper lip was twitching wildly. The old preacher didn't realize he was staring until she covered it with her hand. He had walked into a marital struggle of some sort.

"I hope the boys enjoyed it. I was quite moved by your talk, Father Ed."

"Thank you. I'm afraid my audience was paralyzed by boredom. They much preferred learning a male plastron was curved, the better to mount the . . . Excuse me, Mrs. Hanks. What salacious little minds they have at this age."

"Boys will be boys."

Mary set off for the house and Father Ed considered Hubbell for an instant, how unlike his wife he was. There was something of an overgrown Scout in the man. It was quite unaccountable in a man who stood to command so much.

"But especially at this age and especially with the kind of boy who comes to Pleasant Hill. It's the hardest struggle I have, containing that, hmmm, energy they have. Yes. Containing that peculiar energy and imagination. Well, shall we make use of some of it to round up the remaining turtles? I'll just line them up, then."

He blew hard on his whistle, and boys began to appear from behind the house or from the southern side of the property, bordering the dark woods. The woods, ten acres of it, lounged untended and wild. A stream flowed there, and the matted trees hosted not only sparrows and robins but redbirds and hummingbirds, drawn to the trumpet vines that climbed the scaly spines of stunted oak trees. Hubbell would eventually get around to cleaning up the woods. He dawdled without knowing why.

"Form two lines! No shoving, now. Ned, you head up this line." He blew twice on his whistle, short, hard blasts that got their attention. "Count off."

They had to count over. Somebody screwed up, they figured, because they only came up with thirty-nine. But the second count came up the same.

"It's Cab, Father Ed."

Father Ed's throat tightened. Cab Edwards was seventeen, too old for Pleasant Hill. And too clearly hellbound. He had refused to take him at first, but his mother was too sad and weak to turn away that easily. So Father Ed accepted him with great reluctance. The boy had a man's experience already. There was no line to take with him. He knew too much, had seen too much. Father Ed read the Bible to seek instruction. But he also read for recognition. He discovered Cab Edwards in Exodus, in the punishing flies, boils and hail God rained down on his people, for the boy was a blight on his very soul. But Cab wasn't the only one missing. Mary was running toward them from the house.

"She's nowhere! I looked in every room."

Father Ed turned dull and hopelessly stupid when he was afraid. He could bluff to a certain point, but not when there was too much at stake. He opened his mouth to say something firm to the two lines of boys standing perfectly still. But he was too slow; she saw through his skull to where his brains lay coddled as eggs. Mary stabbed the air with bright-red nails.

"You get this."

She spoke as if someone had a hand around her neck. The tight voice barely leaked from her throat, but they still heard.

"My daughter is in there with one of you. Not one of you is any different from him. You would hide where he's hiding if you'd thought of it first. Those woods contain ten acres, and there are thirty-nine of you. It's a scavenger hunt, and my daughter is the only thing on the list. Go get her. Go get my Joy Baby."

They beat the hell out of there. Not one boy was tempted to linger and see if she cried.

"Man, that broad is a jackhammer."

"We better come back with her girl is all. Fucking Cab. What's he gotta steal a little girl for?"

They ran in a jagged line and hit a formation once they were inside the trees. Cab's best friend, ashamed now for the affiliation, panted and said not to talk. Not to try to suck up to him, because Cab wasn't like that. So they entered the woods noiselessly, with sour air in the gut because of being scared. They were too scared to take Mary Hanks' advice. Their minds and instincts were split down the middle. The part of them that might have been stealthy and clever wasn't. Twigs cracked underfoot, and instead of dodging thorny plants, they made straight for them, yelping with dismay. The formation began to fall apart, and boys struck out on their own, but dark was darker still inside the trees. Only a few of them had watches, and it was too dim to see anything, certainly not the tiny face on a watch. Mick Thatcher started yelling he had them when he didn't. It turned out to be part of a shirt or sack, something caught on a bush that wasn't a kid at all.

"Dumb fuck. You went and alerted him for nothing."

"Who you calling dumb fuck?"

"You, asshole."

They went down in a pile of fists. They were good fighters, so it took several boys to pull them apart. A whistle was blowing far off. Shit! It was harder to breathe, now that they saw familiar red lights pulsing. She had called the cops, and they were in for it now, but good.

"Settle down now. Y'all tried your best. Now just set here and think where your pal might be. That's right, I want you just to think hard."

They spread out miserably on Hubbell Hanks' front lawn, after thinking like the officer had told them to, kissing it all so long. The right to be plain boys with no trouble tagging along after them for one day a year. Come hot weather, they couldn't help thinking about it. Wondering about the food and what Hubbell Hanks would think up this year that was different than last. Damn that Cab was what they mostly thought now. Damn his magazines he hides, the ones with girls' legs spread open wider than Texas. Damn the condoms, too. Which he said he'd sell at a very good price when the time came for one of the Pleasant Hill playboys to have a playmate. Cab was a high-priced good. He had cost them this. One of the boys knew the big cop. He'd driven him out to Pleasant Hill three years before, when his own daddy wouldn't.

It got to be ten o'clock, and the buses had all come. When Mrs. Hanks saw those buses pull into her driveway, it was like she got electrocuted or something. She went kind of nuts. It turned out Hubbell Hanks got a little nuts, too. Mary Hanks hit her husband on the chest several times with her fists, and he raised his voice until they could hear him from where they sat on the dark buses waiting for Father Ed.

"What has this got to do with Amos Sweet? That clumsy lout is a fool who can't walk ten paces without tripping over his own big feet. Why you ever invited this caravan out here in the first place beats me. Hubbell, you're a fool. I knew it the day I married you!"

"If you hadn't given Amos Sweet the night off without my permission, we would have our daughter, wouldn't we? You're a careless bitch who can't see the forest for the trees. I know how she feels right this minute! I remember crouching underneath my own father, scared to death that Pretty Boy Floyd was going to gun me down!"

"Oh, it's forest, is it? Look who's mentioning forest. If you'd listened to me, she wouldn't be in there now. Mutilated by some brain-damaged punk you decided to feed and entertain. Mr. Big Shot, oh . . . oh!"

An officer hurried toward her as the storm wore itself out. But she didn't faint or fall. She began to move, even though it was hard. And then it was easier, because she was sure that what she saw wasn't a mirage. She pushed Hubbell roughly to one side, since the big galoot stood between her and her girl, now moving up from the base of the lawn. She could see her because of the power company, which threw out its sweet and showy lights. Mary ran hard and kicked up bits of soil as she did. Not even Hubbell could catch her when she ran that hard.

"Baby! Oh, Laydelle."

The child let go of Cab's big hand and stared at him wide-eyed, over her mother's tousled head. Mary had sunk down on her knees to sniff and hold her baby girl. How could she even begin to check for what ailed her? For all the things the thick lug had surely done. She rubbed her arms so hard it started hurting. Laydelle pushed back slightly from her mother.

"What's the matter, Mommy?"

"Just tell Mommy nice and slow where you've been all this time and what you've done. Tell Mommy as much as you can tell."

"That's a cinch. First I got a new name. Cab thinks Lady is much better than being called Laydelle. I think it's better, too. Then Cab and I went shoe fishing for a little while. And then when we found too many old shoes and got tired of that, I showed him how to make reed bracelets, and then we got busy with fireflies. See?"

The boy, silent so far, held up a glass jar. As they blinked she could see his face. And see lights of another kind exploding in his eyes. All right, Mary, she managed to say to herself. Keep your hat on, now. What did this confusion mean? It only lasted a minute, but it was the longest minute of her life. She wanted to throw herself into the strong arms of this man, for the fireflies showed that, too: Cab Edwards was certainly no boy. What for? To thank him for returning Laydelle safe and sound? But how could she thank him when what he'd done was steal her in the first place? She was thinking about all this and looking for a way out, when he gave her one.

"Messenger of Light at your service, Mrs. Hanks."

Cab Edwards was off the hook. She had spent her huge store of anger and fear on Hubbell. Her reply wasn't half of what it could have been.

"I don't know what it is you're dispatching, young man. But any fool can see it sure isn't light."

She held on and on to her little girl, for there was nothing left inside her now but joy.

Nelson,

Lavinia

and

Hubbell

c h a p t e r 29

1931

"Renovating a town house now is not only inappropriate. Why, it's immoral."

Nelson's hand trembled slightly under the table. Judge Tucker was overweight, and a band of flesh, pinched by a tight starched collar, rolled up and over the edge.

"Told you once and it looks like I'm going to have to tell you twice, Judge. New York sent you here to oversee corporate financial matters. If you continue to interfere in my personal affairs, I'll have to send you home."

Judge Tucker took it in stride. He knew what it cost Hanks to have an outsider there day after day, taking part in meetings that would determine the future of the oil company. He figured the man's drinking would subside when he had his house in order once again. Tucker had been a legal counselor for years, and he'd seen this behavior in all its forms. Watched whining and pleading whiplash into fury. At least Hanks was consistent, countering every one of Tucker's proposed controls with the meanest insult. He had done it, seen his company through its worst hour. But he'd wound up with enormous debt. He'd wound up with Tucker. The counselor continued to speak.

"The ballast is gone. We don't— Sweet Jesus, Nelson! Women

aren't sending their children off to school anymore. They're sending them into the streets to hunt for food or some scrap of work that might bring home a nickel or a dime. What gives you the right, Nelson? In times like these, what kind of man adds a new floor to his corporate headquarters and freshens up his town house to the tune of half a million dollars?"

Nelson's voice dropped to a whisper.

"I've staved it off so far, haven't I?"

Tucker had to hand it to him. The series of maneuvers over the past three years had delayed the worst, though Nelson's scheming had put him under the control of bankers and New York financiers.

"I've always given my men and women a show."

Nelson coughed hard into a handkerchief and took another swallow of Scotch.

"If I falter now, the game's over, Tucker. You know that. If that means I build a basketball court for my employees at my personal expense and gussy up the town house to celebrate an upcoming wedding anniversary and send skywriters up in the air with a message about Hanks Petroleum, then you'll have to figure I know what I'm doing."

Nelson turned to look out the window, and the other man studied his profile.

"You go ahead and do your job. I'm beholden to you, and you know it. But style is still my strong suit. Don't meddle in something that you don't understand."

Tucker ceded. What else could he do? Hanks had taken an annual salary of one dollar that year. If he wanted to spend his personal fortune on these gestures, it was his business. He was right about style, though. The tough leader had guided his corporation through the worst years. Personal telegrams from Uncle Nelson hand-delivered at the darkest hour had been the first coup. DON'T DROP YOUR SHARES IN HANKS PETROLEUM. WE WILL ALL GET THROUGH THIS TOGETHER. YOU HAVE UNCLE NELSON'S WORD ON THAT. The shareholders hadn't let the bottom drop out in '29. Nor did they the next year, when the employees themselves embarked on a wild stock-selling campaign. The plan to keep the company afloat left them shamefaced when the value of a share dropped to three dollars months later. Employees had gone on to job sharing, one Hanks Petroleum employee per family, submitting to salary cuts and dried-up dividends if not with good humor, with good faith. Nelson had partially buffered Lovely from the full brunt of the nation's ills. Judge Tucker had valuable business skills, but the plump, efficient adviser shared nothing of the older man's rage and brilliance. He thought back to the first time he met the oil man. Nelson was cornered up on the roof at the Waldorf, surrounded by finance men. They might as well have been wolves, snapping at his heels.

"I'm just stating the facts, gentlemen. With oil prices the way they are, I can't afford to ship a gallon of gas to my own mother. We need a pipeline to get my products to Illinois."

"The economy is collapsing, and you want to expand your operation. Think, Nelson. Think."

"Whose economy? Mine or theirs?"

"Ours. My poor fellow, you are part of a community. You can't suddenly secede, no matter how much you would like to. Your plan is unfeasible. We won't approve a loan of this size."

"If I can't run my company the way I see fit, then I resign. I'll draft my letter this afternoon and have it on your desk by nine o'clock tomorrow morning."

"I won't accept your resignation."

"You'll have to. There are two candidates for my job; both of 'em have grown up in the company. Good men. You have a tough choice to make."

Nelson stood up. No one spoke immediately. His eyes glinted in the sun, and he took another drink of water.

"Please sit down."

On the roof, there were no gaunt faces, no outstretched hands. The banker's life had become a holy terror, like most others. But for the moment, the Depression was going on far below, a negligible war, conducted out of earshot. A pigeon started up, then another. That such ordinary birds could produce this soft and sobering chorus was an amazement. He paused for a minute before returning to his task. He faced his own kind and felt no discomfort.

"You're a banker, Nelson. The same as I am."

Tucker had wondered at the synchrony. They appeared to know the piece by heart. Was Hanks bluffing? Did the other men know it?

"So you'll recognize the validity of my proposal. I need a wider territory. And I can't haul my petroleum to the Midwest on back of a mule, Mr. Shrader."

"You'll have your loan, Nelson, because you're forcing my hand.

The people's eyes are always on you. They line up in front of a Hanks station not only for your product but for your personal image. You've been clever in that respect, Nelson. You're indispensable, and if you weren't . . ."

"An incontrovertible fact, eh, Judge?" Nelson smiled at the pink-faced counselor.

"I can't dispense with you, Nelson. Your company would founder tomorrow without you. Half of me thinks you're going to pull this preposterous project off. The other half thinks you're whistling in the dark. You'll have your financing."

Shrader shook his head.

"Seven hundred miles of pipe and a thousand men to do it. And once you get it in the ground, you'll have union men waiting to club you at the other end, in East Saint Louis. This could be the damnedest decision I've ever made in my life."

Nelson hadn't sat down. A breeze lifted the napkin up off his chest. The other men were finally relaxed, lifting a hand for more coffee. Only Tucker saw it coming. Watched his thin film of control lift off and vanish. Nothing was clear in 1931. Honest men who had once held whole families together, toiling away at jobs, awoke to find those jobs gone. Gone forever, and so swiftly that having once had a job at all felt like magic, the most impossible thing. *Sir, I wonder if you have any spare change.* Their wives didn't accuse them and neither did the children, but they felt sentenced to hunger and need. And the sentence implied some crime, an awful collective crime they had committed without even knowing it. Nineteen thirty-one. The meeting had taken a great toll. Nelson didn't like pleading. He let his breath out slowly.

"You won't regret your choice."

He rubbed his hands together slowly.

"You've certainly had me jumping through your hoops today, Mr. Shrader. One day I'll see to it you kiss my ass in like measure. Gentlemen."

He decided to walk forty blocks. Forty blocks would rinse him of this day and help settle his thoughts, which were flitting left and right. He gave along the way to women and children, but mostly to the men, saddest spectacle of all. The press of people tired him more than the exercise. He bought what he could: a week-old newspaper, potholders made of cast-off clothing, a child's high, off-key song. And when he could no longer carry his purchases, he placed them neatly on a curb and continued walking. He'd gone thirty blocks now and was nearing exhaustion.

He noticed a man who seemed supported by the archway where he stood. He was Nelson's size, though his stoop-shouldered posture belied it. There was nothing on his face to indicate his age. He could have been any age at all. He held his hands folded under his armpits. Nelson reached into his pocket and brought up all that was left.

"Those are fine shoes you have. Must have cost you."

The man didn't thank him for the money or for the shoes, which slipped off easily. They weren't the same size, after all. He walked to a trash can and brought up a sheet of newspaper, then rolled it into a tight wad he wedged at the bottom of Nelson's shoes. He grinned at his feet.

"I used to have charge accounts in three department stores. A house at the shore and a car. My name was Harry Beecher."

He left the doorway, the shoes gleaming and ridiculous in contrast to his shabby clothing. Nelson watched until he disappeared. The walk back to the hotel was easier without shoes, though the pavement had worn holes in his socks by the time he reached Fifth Avenue. He caught sight of a male bulldog, unleashed and moving toward a fire hydrant. Instead of lifting a leg to spray the plug, the dog squatted weakly to one side, urinating like a bitch.

"Pitiful."

The kick was badly placed, brushing the animal's flank. The dog gazed at Nelson and continued to pee. The animal lumbered off slowly, leaving a dark, ragged trail.

"Miserable, just miserable."

He nodded to the doorman.

"Evening, Sam. Any rain up there?"

"Just might be, Mr. Hanks. Though lately it's tough to predict anything. From weather on down."

Sam held the door wide open and didn't flinch at the sight of the unshod oil man. He wouldn't kick a stray dog, but he understood the impulse. Sam had worked the door for twelve years and imagined he'd seen everything. Banks of dark clouds did ride in that evening. Nelson sat up sleepless all night, anticipating a thunderstorm. But by dawn the clouds had skimmed over Manhattan, leaving the city hot and muggy, poised for relief that clearly wasn't coming.

• • •

"Is that big enough for five people?"

"It could take five. Yes."

"Put a phone line through. I want cupboards in there and provisions for a long stay. A modicum of comfort. Bookshelves inside bookshelves. I like that. And certainly space for a chaise longue for my wife."

"You'll have it, Mr. Hanks. Would you like for this, uh, area to be connected to your intercom system?"

"Goes without saying."

Renovation was going on inside and out. Rumor was that Mrs. Hanks was going batty trying to think of names. Because, of course, once the work was done, the grand new house deserved a grand new name. Somebody even said Mrs. Hanks was thinking of staging a contest! She'd let the winner figure out what to call her new home since she couldn't. The work crew out at the Hanks place didn't exasperate Lovely citizens, as Tucker predicted. They saw it as fitting, a nick-of-time move, for who needed one more symbol of despair? Not that Mrs. Hanks had ever allowed her home to fall into disrepair, but it hadn't *beamed* out at the town, as it had years before. Her servants worked tirelessly, the gardens were scrupulously maintained, but where was that little extra? That something new, that curiosity that made your head turn and your eyes hold? A pair of urns you'd never noticed, set there on the porch simply to please the passerby, who, God knew, could stand a moment's diversion. Or the sight of a new side path being laid, one that wound through that houseboy's lily pond at the bottom of the lawn, then up again past the waterfall and under the trellis bearing up somehow under a wisteria bough, such a grand, purple blind. Well, that hardworking construction crew, made up of Lovely men and boys bare to the waist and turning copper under the scorching sun, was a welcome sight. When talk turned to money, how much was being spent, how much more was *likely* to be spent, spite was remarkably absent. Enlarged servants' quarters with, no kidding, extra space for the servants' families, who came visiting from Japan and such. Excited observers counted on extravagance and hoped like hell for lush. All this meant that things were tough but not hopeless. The Hankses wouldn't shut down and turn their backs on so many people who counted on them. They were widening the entry, preparing for more, not less. The removal of that massive door, leaning wondrous and unhinged against the front of the house, sent out an uncomplicated signal. The Hankses were home, and that was that.

But there was more to the renovation than civic reassurance. The discretion of the architect was assumed. It wouldn't do for anyone to know of Nelson's premonitions, his new sense of vulnerability. The project meant not only damask and marble, a Turkish bath and mirrors, mirrors on the walls, but underground passages and bookshelves that fell open to hidden rooms, blessed air pockets that would sustain one or five when it came time.

"Who would want to hurt us?"

"Who would want to hurt them?"

Nelson meant the five men who did business in New York and Florida, one in Minnesota. Men who earned their livings the same way he did, with skill and flamboyance. Men who made an earnest attempt to give the public their money's worth. The kidnappings had been bloodless so far, the work neat and tidy. But that could change anytime, when amateurs got into the act.

"Mere prudence, Lavinia. I'm acting in the interest of my family is all."

"This is more of that affliction of yours. The frontier follies have returned. I'll tell you one thing: If you expect me to remain hidden inside our bookshelves for long, you're flat wrong. To play hide-and-seek at my age does seem a bit foolish."

"You prefer being kidnapped by Machine Gun Kelly?"

Lavinia let her head drop to the back of the chair where she sat.

"Machine Gun Kelly wouldn't last a minute with me. I know exactly how to drive a man out of his mind, and you can attest to that. So go on and build your hidden cabinets, Nelson, if they make you feel any better. Just so you know I'd be a goner either way."

The phone rang, and it sent her straight up out of her chair. Her calm was a ruse.

"Of course. Put him through, operator."

She held one hand over the receiver and whispered *Hubbell.*

"Darling, yes, it's me. Why, you sound so small and far away! There, that's better. Speak straight into the telephone so I can hear you better."

She settled down again. He thought of an air cushion as he watched her. How, after having been punched down by a fist or a behind, it slowly rose again to its proper dimensions. She chatted with Hubbell lazily, as she would with a friend. She wore high-heeled house shoes and flapped them back and forth as they chatted. One pom-pom was loose and about to wobble off.

"Tell me again where that friend's from. I can't keep them all straight. Alabama. Now, there's a place!"

Nelson thought about what it would mean to lose this. Not just his wife and his child, but indolence, a pink bedroom slipper slap-slapping, and the assumption that life stretched out as long and unhindered as you pleased. He reached for a roll of peppermint lozenges he kept in the pocket of his shirt. She handed him the telephone.

"That you, Half? What's that? Not until you tell me why."

They talked for several minutes, until Lavinia finally rose, impatient with the pauses and unfinished sentences. She walked to the window, her hands on her hips. She watched three young men crouched on the roof of the gazebo. They were putting on a new roof. All three worked furiously, with towels wrapped around their heads against the sun. She bit down on her cigarette holder, watching four other workers pass with paint buckets and ladders. One carried a large marble basin. She could see the veins standing out on his neck.

"If this isn't like living in the middle of an anthill. There is no peace in this world."

She hadn't noticed the end of Nelson's phone conversation. She hadn't noticed how his voice dropped off at the end and how he massaged the back of his neck after he hung up.

"Vinnie?" He paused and frowned at something on the mantel. Some spot, some flaw she couldn't see.

"Does Half like candy?"

"As well as any boy."

"How much of it could he eat in a month?"

"Enough to make him good and sick. Well, if you're planning on sending him candy, be sure it's not the kind he can choke on. Send him a box of those Atlas bars. I hear the boys love them."

"But why would I send him candy when he can buy it for himself?"

"That's just it. You *can't* buy candy at Stauffer, which is why he's wheedling you for some."

She returned her attention to the spectacle outside, the digging, the doing, the hauling.

"I'm going out to the ranch tomorrow, Nelson. Millie's coming in to keep me company and do my hair besides. You'll be all right?"

But her back was turned and she was leaving as she said it, so he didn't bother to answer. She was suddenly in a hurry. He didn't have a chance to ask what a boy would buy with so much money if he wasn't buying a month's supply of candy, like he said. And why he needed it by Monday.

chapter 30

1933

"Let me look at you. Oh, Hubbell! Mama's so proud of you."

She asked to see it all assembled at the foot of her bed. The steamer trunk and miniaturized greatcoat she had had copied from a men's fashion magazine, a new suitcase from Paris for weekend and holiday visits. Nelson fretted that the leather case was too fine a thing for such a young child. That other boys were bound to tease him. Last of all, there was Hubbell, dressed in full regalia, who sidled oddly into his mother's bedroom. Ten-year-old Hubbell was setting off again for military school.

"To think you'll be a lieutenant one day. But why settle for lieutenant? You'll be a captain or a major, Hubbell. Oh, you're a sight. Remember our promise now, that you'll try to eat more. You're way too thin, Hubb."

Hubbell pulled at his glove and bit his lip.

"They give us dog food, Mama. They try to hide it with the sauce."

"That's nothing but silly nonsense."

His mother's eyes rested contentedly on the steamer trunk, packed to the brim with new purchases. She'd made a special buying trip to New York just for him. Hubbell watched his mother's face. He wished many things, but mostly he wished she were dressed. Why, when he had to meet his train in thirty minutes, was she in a nightgown, with her hair still tangled and a spot of jam from breakfast yet on her chin? Then slowly, with amazement, he realized she wasn't taking him to the train. That it would be his father, since he was pulling on his overcoat.

"Mama?"

She smiled at him.

"Why can't I just go to school here, Mama?"

The smile didn't go away, and he saw he would have to remember her like this until Christmas holiday. Sitting in an unmade bed in a nightgown so skinny he could see the top of her.

"Oh, pooh! Lovely will always be here. It's important for you to be around older boys and men who will make you strong and give you courage."

He watched her sink back into pillows. She looked at her nails and clucked her tongue. Hubbell thought about bad dreams and the long halls he had already walked down that stayed lit all night. His mother hummed her favorite song, lightly rolling a stray lock of hair between her fingers. When Hubbell approached to kiss her goodbye, she started slightly. Did she believe he was already gone? By now he had many tricks for bad times. He decided to disappear a word by repeating it to himself so many times it lost all meaning. By the time his father slapped him amicably on the back, saying it was time to leave, the word "home" was as strange on his tongue as a strand of sour grass. He turned his thoughts instead to those boys his mother promised would make him strong and give him courage. Hubbell thought of Tom Anderson.

That younger boys veered toward Tom Anderson in their first uncertain years at Stauffer was no surprise. By day he was a paradigm of excellence, pursuing sports and studies with equal intensity. By evening he turned dramatist, slipping them stories in which Tom himself stood firmly front and center. He was the proof that pain passed and long nights ended. Tonight he told of the hoot owl perched outside his bedroom in Alabama, its talons dug into a tree limb next to Tom's upstairs window.

"Didn't give up one night, not one, until I turned twelve. Every midnight he hoo-hooed till I liked to piss my own pajamas with fear."

"Why didn't your father shoo him off?"

"Nobody could shoo him off. That bird claimed his limb. That was my trouble. But I claimed my bedroom. That was his trouble. Nope, nothing fathers can do in that case. It was meant to be a showdown. The owl versus Tom Anderson."

Tom's stories padded the space between living and dreaming. The hero, sitting cross-legged on the dormitory floor, lined that awful moment before sleep came. A letter from home couldn't protect them; neither could a photograph. The only thing to ward off the creature stalking peace was a fresh story of contest. Tom sneaked in one night each week, sometimes two.

"So then what happened?"

One boy turned his flashlight on the ceiling and made it dance. He made it rotate first in small concentric circles, then let it grow until a trail of light grew wide enough to touch the four corners of the room.

"Then I turned twelve and decided things had gone on long enough between you-know-whooooo and me."

Hubbell drew his knees up closer, even stuck his hand between his knees for extra comfort. He thought of the battery of ghost stories the Nelson boys told, the kind that made him so scared he couldn't sleep afterward. He wondered if Tom Anderson stories qualified as ghost stories, then decided no. A story that left you better off than you were before couldn't be a ghost story exactly. He wished the flashlight were turned off.

"The clock struck twelve, and up he started. I could see his bright eyes from where I was lying in my bed. I threw back my covers, because I'd got hot. Almost like I had a fever or something. The floorboards creaked as I went toward the window."

One of the beds was jiggling. Hubbell could hear it. He didn't know if the kid meant it to be like the floorboards or if he was just shaking so bad it couldn't be helped. He held still, even though it was hard.

"I slid open my window, but not fast. I didn't want him to just fly away, see. I wanted the thing between us to end once and for all. So I slid the window up and up until it was standing wide open. Until there was nothing at all between me and that awful bird. God, he looked meaner by moonlight. But I went on anyhow, struck up a conversation with him—"

"Birds can't talk."

"They can in Alabama. I struck up a conversation with him

about him getting up and off that limb, so I could sleep. But I didn't get a chance to finish what I was saying. Because he slipped off that limb before I could blink my eyes. Guess where to?"

They couldn't or didn't dare to. No one made a sound.

"He flew into my room. Past me but not all the way. I felt his wings brush my cheek, and I saw his claws come way out and his beak, the way it was part open, ready for something. He flew directly to my desk. Now had I been thinking at all, I would've known all along what he wanted and how he'd stop at nothing to get it."

"What was he after, Tom? Tell us."

"Why, my white mice. He'd been watching 'em year in, year out from where they turned on their merry-go-round. That had just about driven him crazy, watching them from the tree. I had four of them in that cage. I say had."

The author, hero, actor rose from the floor and took the flashlight out of the boy's hand. He made figure eights that whirled fast and faster until the form was gone and the light sheered straight across the whole ceiling.

"He grabbed that cage in his talons and lifted it up in one motion. Perfection. He knew what he wanted and nabbed it. Not a second's hesitation. I could hear the mice shrieking as that owl carted them off. They must've known they'd be swallowed whole. One by one."

They knew he hadn't finished.

"I'll tell you what. Those mice were a small price to pay. That owl never came back. Just goes to show."

"Show what, Tom?"

"How sometimes you got to give a strong animal its due. I coulda let it go on, see. But I wouldn't have been free that way, because the bird wouldn't get off his limb. Or maybe one day he would've lost all patience and come crashing through my bedroom window to get what he wanted. Then there would have been hell to pay."

They let the epilogue sink in, watching Tom as he got up from the floor and dusted the seat of his pants.

"Time you muchachos got some sleep."

"Stay!"

"Tell us one more story. Just one."

"Over's over. I'll be back, don't you worry."

Those who dared watched him leave. The others burrowed

deeper into their blankets or turned to face the wall. Hubbell chose to watch. He studied the top half of Tom Anderson and vowed one day to transform himself into the same upside-down pyramid. He had already memorized his lopsided smile and his chipped tooth and the way he bolted suddenly from the room like a dog dodging a car.

The seventh boy born to Mary Louise Anderson achieved what the others hadn't. Studies came easily to him, and his brothers looked on with disbelief. Special provisions were made for Tom from the time he was very small. When he learned to read by hanging on to the knees of various brothers and sounding out for himself the symbols they struggled so hard to understand, artful Mary Louise went into high gear. She took in other people's laundry, and with that extra money, Tom had his own reading light by the time he was six. They ate supper early so that the kitchen table could be cleared and ready for Tom and his library books. Mary Louise cajoled the driver of the bookmobile to come through town not once, but twice a month, in honor of her young reader. He sucked sweet tea through a plastic straw and flipped pages while his mother sighed contentedly, seeing his eyes widen or his hand move suddenly to his mouth during the good parts. She watched him nights and thought about his forearms, how he always leaned so hard on the wooden table to keep the book propped up and open. She suffered the derision of her truck-driving husband and six other boys. She sewed him little cushions attached to an elastic loop to protect his forearms and slipped them up and over his hands. When he won the county spelling bee two years in a row and all the achievement awards his little country school could offer, when he was awarded a full scholarship to Stauffer Academy, Mary Louise Anderson was not only proud, she was vindicated.

Storytelling came naturally to him. In all the tales, conflict was elemental. Tom was pitted against a hoot owl or a migrant worker, a tornado that dropped down out of the sky into central Alabama. The hero never once vanquished the enemy. According to Anderson's stories, the new breed of man chose dignified subjugation. Defeat, by virtue of its having been conducted wisely and with grace, came to be a form of victory.

Hubbell struggled to find his slippers. It was regulation. They couldn't walk barefoot except when they were leaving the locker room for the showers. He could still see Tom, though he was way off down the hall. The other boys were quiet, maybe sleeping already or just wishing they were.

"Tom, wait up!"

Hubbell hated making any noise. He didn't like having to call out to stop him. He would be leaving in the spring. This was Tom Anderson's very last year at Stauffer.

"Father said yes."

"Did he?"

"Well, not exactly yes, but 'we'll see' is the same thing."

"Maybe in your house, little fella. That's not how it is in mine. Yes is yes and no's what it always is."

"No, it'll be okay. You'll see, Tom. We'll get the money on Monday, just like you wanted."

"Hold on, Hubbell. I didn't want the money. You wanted the money, right?"

"Yes. But I want it so I can give it to you."

"Okay. But that's not the same thing as me wanting it. Remember that. Hey, listen, get back to bed. They hear us talking, and they'll shoot us. Remember, kiddo, this is a military academy."

He let his eyes rest for a minute on the boy. He wondered if, with skin like that, this Hanks kid felt hot and cold faster. Hubbell was pale as a white cotton sail.

"Goodbye, Tom."

"Goodbye? You're only going to sleep."

A strange, prayer-filled boy, Hubbell believed the words *If I should die before I wake*. He turned around, but not before Anderson laid a hand on his shoulder.

"Hey. You done good. I mean it now, Hubbell. Thanks a million."

What the scholarship didn't cover, the little boys did. It had started inadvertently, as most things had in Tom Anderson's life. He had begun by extorting favors first. Say, could ya give me a hand with this? Durned if these shoes couldn't stand a polish, and with this exam tomorrow . . . Really? Hey, thanks! His skills developed, and he found with just slightly more effort he could cadge gifts and, eventually, money from boys who badly needed mooring. And better him, Tom Anderson figured, than somebody else. While Tom's fictitious sagas dealt consistently with greater forces, others, the real sidewinders, told of Tom's own stark youth. For that was where the money lay.

"My dad had seven boys to feed. Ever left the dinner table with your stomach still pinching for more? No? Lucky for you."

"So your uniform scratches, does it? Poor little rich boy. Why don't you just think for a moment how it feels to split three winter coats seven ways. We took turns freezing to death."

"Hog for breakfast, hog for lunch and hog for supper. That's what we ate when the sun was shining. Otherwise it was grits or beans. Just what are you spitting into your napkin, punko?"

They grew to recognize comfort, a thing formerly unnamed, and understood that the excess in their own lives was somehow linked to the scarcity in Tom's. They ransacked their homes during holidays or, like Hubbell, hounded their parents until money was wired or small treasures boxed and shipped out first-class. Anderson netted six hundred dollars in his last, most lucrative year at Stauffer. In forking it over, the boys both toppled injustice and paid homage to their hero. For some, the exercise would be transcendent.

Hubbell knew the older boy's schedule by heart. He complained of stomach cramps in fourth period. The route to the infirmary would place him directly in Anderson's path. He had trouble spotting him at first.

"Cutting class, buddy?"

"I have something for you."

He scowled slightly, then waved him over to one side of the courtyard. Something rustled in the ivy, and a sparrow flying overhead splattered the pavement.

"Crap. Look out! You do, huh? What do you have for me?"

Hubbell plunged his hand into his pocket and drew up a hundred-dollar bill. Tom Anderson whistled low, and it sounded like the faint sigh of a firecracker before it exploded into light.

"A hundred bucks! That daddy of yours is some big shot, eh, Hubb? A hundred big ones. What's it like, anyways, having a hot dog like that for your father? Say, I gotta go to trig."

Crisp, too. He pursed his lips thoughtfully and folded the fresh bill in half. The question, apparently rhetorical, didn't require an answer. He rumpled Hubbell's hair roughly and held up the flat of his hand to say so long, another one of Tom Anderson's habits. If he saw a new expression dart over the younger boy's face, he didn't say. Hubbell watched Anderson return to the others and saw how he was jostled, lightly provoked, before being allowed to rejoin the pack. Before he claimed a bed in the nurse's bright yellow sickroom, Hubbell hung on for a few seconds longer, savoring the sight of Tom and his friends. He slowly let his hand open inside an empty pocket.

"Well, everything is in place. Just like I said it would be."

Lavinia chuckled. They stood outside on the curb, seeing themselves as others saw them. Joey had hung blue lights in every window for Christmas. They blinked softly, and she was glad they had chosen blue after all.

"Sometimes I do feel old. It's as if I'm Methuselah's female counterpart. It must be these terrible times."

They each wore their favorite set of "slumpy things," and they did look like spectators. Nelson's favorite slippers had the color rubbed out at the heel. Her shawl, once tricolored, had been washed into one slightly graded pink tone.

"Can't you get Half to buck up a little? After all, he'll be handing out the candy tomorrow, and it wouldn't do to have such a sad sack leading the festivities. What's eating him this time?"

"When will you call him by his proper name?"

"The day he asks me to. If he doesn't like it, he ought to have the pluck to say something. I hate to see melancholia in a boy so young."

"Don't be such a fool. Hubbell is sensitive beyond his years. You wouldn't know sensitive if it hit you in the face."

He turned to face her. He couldn't recognize sensitive, eh? She had a host of similar claims. They watched the house together for a little while longer, as if it would emit some message, explain away some small dissatisfaction. It didn't appear, and Lavinia pulled her shawl up closer around her neck, suggesting they go inside for a cocktail before dinner.

"We'll stand over there, then?"

She pointed to the bottom of the garden, where they would distribute the candy the following day. Mistletoe and holly lay heaped in baskets. The children would come away with more than candy and a silver dollar. Far more, if Nelson only had his way.

"Or to the right. I want them to have perfect access to me. At least on the day before Christmas."

"That's right. Line them up to touch the hem of your garment. Nelson Hanks, the patron saint of Lovely."

He couldn't concoct a retort. He followed her up the path to the house and tried to remember when he had ever felt as tired as he did that night.

The weather turned. Not full-fledged winter, but there was a cold slap to the wind. The mothers who added their children to the line that formed in front of the Hanks place that day allowed that winter, late to the party, would sure make up for lost time. They were hard on the kids; their insistence on manners and posture was lathered with shame. In some cases, cuffs that should have been hiding small wrists rode right up the arm for the second straight year, and skirts were so short as to be indecent. Here it was Christmas, and there would be no banquet at the house. The finest present would be offered not by a child's mother or father but by the town benefactor. The kids craned their necks. It was all they could do not to stampede.

"What if there's no more candy when it's my turn?"

"You wait and see, Ma. There won't be a dollar left time I get there."

"Hush! There's plenty for everyone."

Their mothers, seasoned by disappointment themselves, lied. They feared the same thing, that by the time Jill, Judy or Joe made it to the center of that lawn, the treats would have disappeared. Shoot, they should have gotten up an hour earlier! Had they known . . . had they known what? That in their lives there would be winters without heat and summers where there was nothing to put up and preserve? It was better not to know. They bit their lips and prayed that the silver dollars held.

The mood at the head of the line was euphoric. By that time they could see all the loot, wondering why they'd feared it would run out in the first place. They could also get a load of the family. Their son had grown, hadn't he? He was there, holding himself still as a stone. He wasn't the image of Nelson Hanks, no, not at all. But he was the next best thing in that cute military uniform, his cheeks high red with the wind and the excitement. And when he handed the Lovely children their Christmas cheer, he sometimes asked the boys their names. With the girls he just couldn't bring himself to, they guessed, for shyness. If he was grave, unusually solemn for such a young man, why, it was just that he took his little job seriously. Mrs. Hanks looked well, didn't she? Maybe, the women speculated, she didn't drink and carry on like people claimed.

Maybe she just needed more occasions like this one. Charity, the right kind. Not the other kind, drowned out by rich women and rich food, with flowers far too boisterous for the times imported from her greenhouse. As for Nelson Hanks . . . well, there he was, as fine a figure as ever. He'd added a cane, they saw, and it suited him.

"Father?"

"And you just enjoy that dollar however you see fit, hear? What did you tell me you're going to be when you grow up?"

"A fireman, sir. But not in Lovely. In Chicago or New York City, where fires burn every single day of the year."

"That's a fine goal, Jimmy. You're right. You'll have your hands full in Chicago or New York. Have a merry Christmas now. Why, Jack Nevil. You're looking awfully smart."

"Father?"

"Excuse me for a second."

They stepped back together, out of earshot. Lavinia continued where they left off.

"They don't need a sack of candy."

"What do you mean, Half? Every kid needs candy at Christmas."

"But they need more than candy. Their clothes don't fit, and they don't look happy at all, even though it's Christmas tomorrow."

Nelson cocked his head, suddenly inquisitive.

"Well, a philanthropist is born. All right, then. What do we do, son?"

"We let them in our house."

"To live?"

"No, Father. To take what we have."

"Like that. We just open the doors to all the cupboards. Every closet, all the cabinets and sideboards. The storeroom and your mother's armoire that little French flip of hers bought in Paris."

Hubbell looked at his father's mostly bald head, dusted here and there by a light tuft of hair.

"And then we all, the whole horde, march straight up to your room and find them clothes and toys and cuckoo clocks from Switzerland among *your* things, Hubbell."

He understood the test, which was no better or worse than any other he'd known.

"Yes, Father. That would be much better than this."

Of all the moments Nelson Hanks endured or was to endure in

his life, only one held itself perfectly erect as he edged toward death by way of a long and loitering old age. It was this one, the moment he was in now, that shot through his breast. The sudden, unexpected prick of pride for his son was amplified by the sound of an actual gunshot, which ricocheted through the basin of land that held his home, his family and nearly all of Lovely's young population. Nelson believed himself wounded and dropped to his knees. The line of people waiting to get at him had been sinuous, though orderly. It broke up now like a clot of birds pelted by gravel.

"Daddy!"

His voice broke, and he dived into his father's chest to share death. Three more shots rang out, and Nelson called to his wife.

"Hit the ground, Vinnie. Don't just stand there."

She didn't join them but dropped down alone, her hands cupping the back of her head. What shattered them next was the stillness. The silence seemed to mount, even after a minute or so. Lavinia thought of a slowly turning spit and wondered how many people could be pierced by the same bullet. Then, because of the quiet, they could hear a car speed off. The tires screamed, and one last shot sealed the event. Nelson dared to raise his head and saw that the long lines knelt too, or bowed away from the something they heard screech off. Kids were tucked into parents, he saw. Then he saw he held his own son in exactly the same way. Had him gathered up under him, as if his own curved back were invincible as armadillo armor. It didn't matter how Hubbell had gotten there. What did matter was that for once, Nelson had held on and shielded his own son.

Not everyone had closed his eyes. Versions of what had just happened began to multiply.

"Damned if he didn't. Henry Starr fired the first shot. Could've had him if he'd wanted him."

"What do you mean 'if he wanted him'? Sonny, that was Pretty Boy Floyd. He's the most wanted man in America. . . ."

"I never seed such pretty shooting. Henry, you fired direct into the gas tank. They won't make it to the county line."

Somebody asked nicely, if sheepishly, for an autograph. Pretty soon the line formed anew, this time in front of Henry Starr and Bob Wells, and they were signing boot soles and brims of hats, plus all the odd pieces of paper Lovely kids could collect. They forgot silver dollars and sacks of candy, for the Christmas rumble had grown larger and louder in an instant. The two men had sure ridden again today, hadn't they? Every Lovely kid knew the two irrepressible outlaws had long vowed never to join forces again. But they had managed today, Starr putting aside whatever beef he had against Bob Wells. They abused each other laughingly as they signed more autographs, then told the kids to git.

"Go on now. That's enough. Police'll be here in a minute. I said go on. Look out you don't lose your candy."

Starr hardly defended himself with a rush of words. He twirled his hat around and around as Nelson let him have it.

"What do you mean, you knew about it beforehand?"

"I mean he approached me on the deal. I let him think I'd go in on it with him."

"Any one of us could have been killed today. Any one of them." Nelson's voice began to tremble.

"And all because you and Wells wanted to ride the range. You wanted the Wild West to exist all over again. That time is dead, Henry! Dead and gone, like my family could have been because you and Wells tried to be big shots!"

"You're right, Nelson. Hell, I'm sorry. I figured I'd handle it my own way. Reckoned I'd need old Buttercup to do it. Damned if he's not the worst shot, though. We could have had ourselves one swell reward."

Wells jumped in.

"Worst shot now, is it? Look who's talking, will you. He claims he punctured the gas tank, Nelson. Bull. He didn't even graze a hubcap with those shots he fired."

"Cut it out, you two. What did he want here?"

"He wanted your little boy. He priced him at five hundred thousand dollars. Asked did I want a cut. You can get up now, Nelson. He won't be back anytime soon."

He let Starr help him to his feet.

"You ought to think twice about Amos Sweet, though. He lit out like a hound when he heard the first shot."

Wells filled his mouth with tobacco, then took an unauthorized spit into a hedge. He caught sight of Mrs. Hanks, where she still lay sprawled on the ground.

"Excuse me, ma'am."

"Bob Wells, you can spit anywhere you damn well please."

chapter 31

1934

"I didn't drive all the way from Spiro just to be swept off Nelson Hanks' porch like I was dirt. Now call your boss before I lose my temper."

Nelson was out walking, and Joey had to work fast. He wanted the dirty intruder off the premises before Hanks caught sight of him and invited him in for coffee. It was six-thirty in the morning, not an hour for riffraff.

"You'll have to make an appointment to see Mr. Hanks downtown."

"I'm not taking my business downtown. Now if you don't plan on letting me in the house, I'll just make myself comfortable right here. Right here's where I'll be when Mr. Hanks leaves or gets back from wherever he is. Happen to know he ain't on a business trip, so don't feed me any bull about him being in New York or the like. I could stand some coffee. Course, it's up to you."

He was just the detached, curious sort that appealed to Nelson, who wouldn't be long now; his twenty-minute constitutional was nearly over. Joey withdrew, closing the door softly. The coffee was already made, though the man would drink out of ordinary cups saved for staff. By the time Joey returned, Nelson was puffing up the path. His brisk walk cost him more each year, given the hard drink and late nights his doctor unsuccessfully implored him to give up.

"Hell of a morning, don't you think?"

He seemed delighted to find the dusty stranger sprawled on his front steps.

"I reckon, though I had hoped it would be a little cooler over your way. Name's Evan Griswold, Mr. Hanks. I'm mighty pleased to meet you."

"The pleasure's all mine. Make that two, Joey."

Evan Griswold was pleased to see that he was already spit-shined by six-thirty in the morning. He'd heard about Nelson Hanks' standing barber appointment and daily morning walk. He smelled liquor on his breath and was glad the part about the shot of whiskey each morning was true, too.

"What exactly brings you to Lovely?"

Griswold took his time. He had a long sip of coffee and studied the sun for a moment before he spoke. The truth was, he felt rather grand sitting on the oil man's porch, being waited on by a Jap, and he wanted to feel good as long as possible. This might be the single high point he and the three men had been working toward out on that barren mound near the Oklahoma-Arkansas border. And if it was, Evan didn't want to squander it by sprinting through their meeting, when he had every right to saunter.

"I got a business proposition for you, Mr. Hanks. I done brought some samples of our affair up from Spiro that I'm sure will interest you. Me and my associates head up the Pocola Mining Company; maybe you know about us already."

Nelson figured as much. As unhurried Evan Griswold drank his coffee, Nelson noticed the grime on his shoes. The man wore no hat, but he had the habit of one. His face was divided into two hemispheres. He clearly worked in the partial and imperfect shade a hat afforded. Nelson also figured the man's business had some-thing to do with the stickpin he wore, a rather grand pearl stickpin that contrasted with his worn suit and shoes. Griswold rose from the step, warming to his presentation.

"If you'll excuse me just for a minute, Mr. Hanks."

He ambled off down the driveway to the cab of the truck parked in front of a neighbor's place. He returned at the same slow pace. He had a hat in his hands, though he held it like a basket. When he got closer, Nelson saw it was filled with pearls. There must have been two, three hundred pearls in the shabby felt hat.

"And this is nothing."

He thrust the hat at Nelson, inviting him to dip into it with his hands.

"Did you and your associates roll over a jewelry concern out there in Spiro?"

Griswold grinned, and Nelson wished he hadn't. There was a kind of greenish coating to the man's teeth. Perhaps that was as particular to eastern Oklahoma as the grime on his shoes.

"Ain't no Depression in Spiro. Leastways, not out on our mounds. We leased them from niggers who didn't know any better, and this is just a sample of what we've found out there. I reckon a man like you with special interests and a museum of his own ought to get first shot at what we're hauling up every day."

Joey appeared with more coffee. He offered Griswold a sweet roll, and Nelson could see how it pained him.

"Believe I will, thank you."

The hat rested on the porch between them, and Joey's eyes widened slowly. Salt- and freshwater pearls glistened in the sun. He hoped Nelson would note the difference before he bought them.

Griswold felt better and better. The rolls were fresh, and since he had driven straight through, stopping only once to eat, out of a brown paper sack, the rolls were definitely helping him to think. And he saw he could have it any way he wanted, even though Hanks was offhand about the hatful of pearls. He knew the oil man played poker, and sitting on the porch as if it was the most natural thing in the world had everything to do with his experience at bluffing. If he could do that, Evan could do this. Dilly-dally and tell him the whole story before arriving at how much money he stood to get for the pearls.

"See, some Choctaw niggers had the land for years. They had the land and didn't do nothing with it, even though they knew they was sitting on some kind of ancient Indian burial ground. They didn't want nobody else to do nothing with it, either. That was fine until the old lady died and her son got himself into money trouble. It got so bad he figured he'd talk with us finally. Even though his mother had fed him bull all his life about how the mounds was haunted. She'd seen blue flames on the mounds, she said. Blue flames licking the top of the hill. Just a lot of nigger rot, though, 'cause me and my boys never had any misfortune, and we been digging for nearly two years now. Night and day. Of course now, the pearls aren't all we come up with. The mounds are full of all kinds of things. Pots and feathers. Cloth, too, if that suits your museum."

Nelson wiped his mouth with a napkin.

"I'll give you two thousand for the pearls."

Griswold sucked on his sore teeth. They'd started up again with the iced sugar from the rolls.

"That's pocket change. Them pearls is worth much more, and you know it, Mr. Hanks. This here is assessed at sixty dollars."

He pointed to his stickpin, poking out from a dusty yellow tie.

"Not only that, but Tiffany's valued the whole thing at something like—"

"Now, now, Evan. Do you really think Tiffany's would do business with you? You and your men are thieves. You're working in a state without an antiquities law, but the golden era for pot-hunters is coming to an end. I know about the legislation coming up. You boys are working wildly against the clock, and that's why you've driven straight through the night to come here. And you've come to the right place. I value the pearls because I value the stories."

Nelson rolled several together in his hand.

"These are freshwater pearls found in ordinary mussels. The rest are saltwater pearls. These people, whoever they were, traded with other Indians, who hauled them up out of the Gulf. Common enough, Mr. Griswold. Two thousand dollars is all you're going to see for your pearls, and it's quite a high price tag for them anyway. Look at the shape they're in."

"Some of 'em needs buffing, but any jewelry man can do that."

"Nonsense. What are you boys using to get into the site?"

"We've hired some out-of-work miners. They come with tools of their own."

"Using any dynamite?"

"Oncet."

"Take my money and run, Evan. I've made you a sound offer. Pretty soon those burial mounds of yours will be nothing but rubble."

It turned out that much of the mystery was man-made. The ancient burial mounds in LeFlore County contained riddles galore, but the Pocola Mining boys were making a hard task even harder. They'd been coached by nervous anthropologists from the University of Oklahoma, who first appealed to them in the only way that would make sense to the relic-hunters. They explained that shattered pottery fetched less than something intact. And that whatever they found would be enhanced by context. Griswold blinked hard. Stories, Mr. Griswold. People want stories to go with their pots and pipes and jewels, and your digging methods have to take that into account. They had them just about convinced to move slowly and carefully, to write down what lay next to what, when winter set in. The cedar poles once supporting the dwellings could have yielded more conclusive data about when the lower Mississippi culture flourished. But it turned out those cedar poles made handy kindling for the Pocola boys. By the time the site was released and archaeological laws were passed, gin bottles littered the abandoned site along with scattered bits of feather and fur textile. Broken pieces of pottery crunched underfoot, along with engraved shell, stone and bone beads. The professor heading the university investigation, shocked at the extent of the desecration, accidentally stepped on the tail of one of his cats. The effete bachelor owned six Siamese cats, which accompanied him on any and all expeditions. A reporter from *Time* was waiting for him on the porch of his bungalow, with a notebook and pencil carefully poised on the railing. The professor groaned and killed the motor. The younger man had been nipping at his heels for months. He no longer bothered to phone from the bureau desk. He just appeared, like a force of nature. The door of his station wagon squeaked open, and six Siamese leaped at the startled reporter.

"Back again? Well, I can tell you this—Evan Griswold didn't leave us much, but we can draw a number of conclusions about this prehistoric band. They were clever traders. We know that much from the quantity of conch-shell pieces. The engraving I found today on a gorget indicates a . . ."

The reporter hadn't yet begun to write. The professor chose another tack.

"You're here for stories of the fabulous pearls, I see. Ah, yes, the King Tut tomb of Oklahoma. I've told you, young man, these tales are wildly exaggerated. First of all, the specimens I've seen have lost their luster from being buried for the past fifteen hundred years or so. Or they have become so soft that you can grind them to powder with your fingertips."

"Those pearls represent a fortune. A good restorer could have them on the market in no time."

"Not according to the American Gemological Institute."

"My guess is that somebody struck a hell of a deal with Griswold. That man is simply too ignorant to know the value of the grave goods he's peddling."

"And you're too ignorant to know the value of the story you're trying to write. Forget this 'March of Time' poppycock and write a real account."

Nelson treated the pearls as casually as if they were marbles. He had some strung for Lavinia, reminding her of the dream she'd had as a young bride, on her way to Indian Territory. She scoffed at him but didn't toss them out. The dull necklace lay in the bottom of a lingerie drawer. Joey found the pearls everywhere: in the pocket of a jacket about to be cleaned or rolling around in the drawer of the library desk, where Nelson sat to make a phone call or dash off a personal note. It finally got the best of Joey Fujii. The valet knocked twice on the door of his study and snapped the door shut once he was inside.

"Mr. Hanks, I found these in your slipper."

He held half a dozen pearls cupped in the palm of his hand. The pearls happened to be perfect.

"I find them everywhere, in ashtrays and pants pockets. I'd like to make an offer for them, Mr. Hanks."

Nelson grinned. He could see his butler was livid. The offer to buy the pearls was a subtle reprimand, the only one he could permit himself. He decided to call his bluff.

"Go ahead, Joey. Make me an offer."

"Twenty-five hundred dollars."

"That's a fairly healthy return on my money. Where do you plan to get twenty-five hundred dollars?"

He knew about Joey's black belt and wondered if he was ever tempted to land a chop on his employer's neck.

"Forgive me, Joey. Your money's your business. Well, I'm not selling, but let me make a confession before you go. I know you're thinking my son takes better care of his things than I do. That much may be true, but here's the rest. Those pearls agitate me as much as they agitate you. I carry 'em with me all over the house, can't get the things out of my head. I've decided to buy into that little venture in Spiro."

Joey frowned, imagining a house full of Evan Griswolds.

"I'm going to fund the university dig. And then I'm going to find somebody really first-rate to transform our airplane museum. The damn thing's an eyesore. By the way, keep those pearls, Joey. You've got them coming to you for all the aggravation."

It took time, but Nelson eventually found that first-rate somebody at the University of Oklahoma. Paddy Mahoney was the youngest addition to the teaching staff in the anthropology department. The department chairman called him out of class one Tuesday.

"Nelson Hanks is sending his plane for you this afternoon. He wants to talk with you about the possibility of a job out at his museum."

"I can't. I have plans for this afternoon."

"Cancel them. Paddy, be ready at three o'clock, and no circus tricks, you hear? Hanks has just signed a check to this university for some sixty thousand dollars. And that kind of money ought to buy some civility, don't you think?"

"I'm not paid to think, it seems. I'm an anthropologist, a painter and a Democrat. And I am not going to work for that two-bit museum."

"It doesn't have to stay two-bit, Paddy, and that's the point. I proposed you for the job. Someone with your, shall we say, curious temperament and fine eye could turn that museum into a real showplace. Three o'clock. Oh, Paddy?"

Mahoney was limping away. Polio had crippled him from the age of nine. The illness threw a wrench into plans to continue in his father's footsteps. Paddy came from a family of circus performers.

"Take a nice long bath."

"So now I smell bad, do I? Well, what's good enough for my students is good enough for Nelson Hanks, and I don't give a—"

"Paddy, you're fired. If this hadn't come up, I would have suspended you anyway. Two young women have lodged complaints, and you've only been working three months."

"Now wait a minute—"

"And since you're between jobs, perhaps you'll rethink the interview I have scheduled for you with one of the most influential men in the country."

"So this is what it means to have money. It means you can push people around just by writing a check and making a phone call or two. Let me past, Mr. Meese. My students are waiting."

"Just remember, Paddy. You *are* fired. Put your best foot forward."

"And just which one would that be?"

Paddy dragged his bad leg a bit more mournfully down the hall to accentuate matters. But at three o'clock he stood on the runway, slightly impressed at the Hanks logo despite himself. He didn't like the idea of working for Hanks one bit; he'd heard the man was ornery as a bull when it came to his strange collection. But Paddy came from a family of trapeze artists and high fliers. As one propeller started up, then the second, excitement prickled the back of his damp neck. He took a long, hard pull on a silver flask he carried inside his jacket and felt some of his misgivings subside as Art Goebel gave him a wide grin. He tapped the pilot on the shoulder as they completed a deep turn and headed east.

"Say, this isn't the way to Lovely."

"Who said anything about Lovely? Uncle Nelson is in Spiro."

Art Goebel traveled with his own brand of fuel. The two men were soused by the time they set down in LeFlore County.

"Hell of a place for a job interview. This is one hell of a place."

Goebel landed the plane in a pasture, where they bounced and jostled to a stop. As he switched off the engine, a black Angus bull began its slow, sober approach to the airplane.

"Damn but that bull looks serious, doesn't he? Couldn't you have chosen a regular landing strip, Arthur?"

The bull was planted in front of the plane. They watched from the cockpit as the animal lowered its head and stopped, knees locked.

"He doesn't have horns." Paddy offered this hopefully.

"He doesn't need them."

"To the future, bright as a bubble."

"Bauble, Art. We decided the future looks bright as a bauble."

"Here goes nothing."

They jumped from the airplane, Goebel in the lead. Paddy pushed hard to stay ahead of the animal, his face contorted with the painful effort. The bull pursued them for twenty or thirty yards. Then they split, to leave it turning in furious circles, and leaped over the fence at opposite ends of the long field. The animal trotted slowly back through the dry grass, and they made their way to a dusty highway north of the pasture. Art checked his watch. A cloud of red dust appeared far off down the road. They could make out a black sedan at its center.

"Like clockwork, pal. This one's on me."

He offered Paddy a final swig, then the two men stood under a shade tree to wait for the car. Art was scheduled to take off again in an hour. Evidently Nelson Hanks didn't think it would take much time to reel in the likes of Paddy Mahoney, who suddenly remembered he'd been fired that very morning. He laughed, thinking of that bath he was supposed to have taken and hadn't.

Hanks invited him to stand beside him.

"Don't hang back, Paddy. You're the expert. I'm nothing but a charlatan."

Mahoney started. The oil man was on his hands and knees, with a tool in his hands. Paddy felt his irritation increase. The charge he had been about to level was swept away from him in a clever move. For Paddy, thoroughly drunk and raring to go, had decided to give Nelson Hanks more than a piece of his mind. A real Mahoney feared no man. His uneven swagger was unnerving, and he knew it. Hanks prattled on as Paddy got closer and closer to where he was poised at the excavation site. A skeleton lounged on a canvas cloth near where Nelson was kneeling. A female. Paddy squinted and pressed harder on the tape that held his eyeglasses together. A comb lay near her outstretched hand. Of ivory? Or bone? A hole had begun to puncture the haze of his alcoholic fury. He peered through it to see an effigy pipe and a dull red bowl with scalloped edges, miraculously saved from a stick of Evan Griswold's TNT. Through the hole he also spotted Nelson Hanks, fancy pants tucked into his boots, striking a phony pose for a photo shoot. As if this project was so close to the oil man's heart, he had to squat down in the dirt and dig. Stay bad, Paddy Mahoney, he reminded himself.

"Where I come from, Mr. Hanks, only sheep-fuckers tuck their pants in their boots."

Paddy's stomach tightened instinctively. The photographer was putting away his equipment. Fast, since all hell would be breaking loose. Nelson got up and pulled the brim of his hat lower, now that the shoot was finished. He plucked the cigar from his mouth.

"Did you learn to talk like that under the big top, young man?"

He offered him a cigar, which Paddy accepted. He had never smoked one in his life, but this seemed a good time to start. Hanks surprised him a second time. The oil man threw an arm over his shoulders.

"I have something to show you."

Paddy kept his eyes on the ground as they crossed the site and started down a path that led to the river. Better this way, he thought, still intent on warding off temptation. He tried hard not to see, not to watch, as the excavation, orderly now, continued on the burial mounds. They came to a stop under a cottonwood. Paddy listened to the river for a minute or two. He had a hard time being next to water, because he couldn't swim. But he managed to keep down the fear that kept threatening to rise up out of him like contaminated food.

"Now what exactly put that bee in your bonnet?"

Paddy noticed the driftwood, how fast it traveled once the river took hold of it.

"Getting fired for no good reason, to start."

"Anything else?"

"I don't believe I like the *idea* of you, Mr. Hanks. You might be a hell of a man, for all I know, but I don't like what you stand for."

"Which is?"

"Money."

"You have an objection to money, then, as idealistic young men do."

"No. But I object to your using it the way you do."

"I see. The issue is power."

"Maybe."

Paddy was smoking successfully now and thought it wasn't half bad so long as you paid attention to the way you smoked. One deep puff, and he would have landed on his back. He enjoyed the discussion, too, which was turning lightly Socratic. He hadn't figured Hanks to be so patient a man.

"Do you have any idea what I want from you, Paddy?"

"I can make an educated guess. You want me to dress up that half-baked museum of yours, and then you want me to dress up, too. Like Little Lord Fauntleroy, so I can have arty talks with your rich friends."

"I understand you're a painter, Paddy."

"That's right. Watercolorist."

"Visited many museums, have you?"

"Not too many. Been too busy working toward the teaching job I just lost."

"Think seeing other paintings would help you with your own work?"

"Sure."

Nelson took a fat roll of tickets from his pocket. They were pinned on a string.

"This measures seventeen feet. Some of these are tickets to every museum and art gallery east of the Mississippi, and the others are rail tickets to get there. I have letters of introduction for you in my office in town. How can the two of us put together a museum that's worth anything if neither of us knows the first thing about it? And that's really the issue, Paddy, though you don't understand that yet. You fear what you don't know. What I'm offering you isn't the circus, and it isn't the university. All your piss and vinegar is really about wondering whether you can do the job I need you to do."

Paddy turned his head away from Nelson Hanks. The driftwood was nowhere in sight now. All that was left was the sludgy brown surface of the water that hummed along at his feet.

"Does your pilot always set down like that in the middle of anywhere he damn well pleases?"

"Generally. Don't forget Art is a stunt pilot first."

"Well, if I'm signing on, you'll have to change that."

Paddy still struggled. He was so close to water.

"A gimp can't run from a bull more than once without getting crushed. And you wouldn't want me to get crushed, Mr. Hanks. Would you?"

chapter 32

1946

"I lost it, Father. Fair and square."

They stood beside a stream at the ranch. It was a crisp fall day, the first they'd had after a month of vicious, oppressive weather. Nelson was seething by now and felt cheated on two counts. The larger loss was naturally the fine brick house five blocks away from his own that Hubbell had managed to lose in a poker game. The second loss also counted in his irritation. Hubbell had undermined the first day of autumn. For aging Nelson, who found the harsh Oklahoma climate more and more difficult, this infraction was significant, too.

"Were you drunk? Of course you were. I suspected as much."

"Send me away, Father."

"I plan to. But that doesn't settle the matter of the house."

He watched the stream in silence for a few moments. Sweet had stocked it with freshwater fish, and they had multiplied beyond his expectations. Where could he send Hubbell this time? He'd been discharged from officers' training school after one too many incidents. Drinking became his sole career until his father intervened, insisting he dry out on health farms in Tennessee and Kentucky. Nelson cast about for something to occupy his son, finally capitalizing an expedition to the Andes so that Hubbell could go along, relinquishing drink for several months to comb ancient ruins in Bolivia under Paddy's direction. Nelson sighed, thinking of the notebook Hubbell produced on his return. The fastidious journal shocked his father. It showed him what his son could do when he wasn't hung over or being helped through some doorway in some public place by a goodhearted friend sadly depositing his son at his feet. The records Hubbell kept hinted at a mind whose hinges were hung on detail. Hubbell could have had a career in statistics or accounting or . . .

"Let Nelson Reeve keep the house. It doesn't matter."

"And I thought you'd sobered up. Nelson Reeve *owns* the house. You lost three acres and a solid brick house in a game of seven-card stud. You didn't offer him a toy that you can suddenly demand back!"

He shook his head in disbelief, still watching the silver shapes dart in and out of the shadows. All the Nelsons had grown up, all of them. Why, this felt just like a father's deepest sorrow, one son pitted against another. He stood up and his head spun, thinking of Nelson Reeve, his namesake, who had successfully swindled his true son, the discharged army officer, the hopeless drunk.

"If I were to stand here . . ."

Hubbell held himself wretchedly as his father clambered out on a grassy spit of land so that all around him rushed clear, cold water. He stood on a precariously slender peninsula, and Hubbell wondered what good the cane would do in the churning stream. His father seemed so fragile out there.

"Yes, here. Look at me, Hubbell. Don't turn your eyes away. If I unzipped my fly and pissed here, I'd dirty this stream, all right."

Hubbell slapped his arms, for there was that brisk wind. His father had staged all kinds of humiliations in retaliation for Hubbell's stunts, and at least out here in the woods there was no audience to witness his shame. A herd of deer grazed downstream, near the banks. Otherwise they were alone.

"But since this stream feeds others, this isolated act would hardly be isolated. When you piss up one stream, you're bound to piss up others, until there's nothing left to drink or swim in. Hear me, Hubbell?"

Hubbell wondered where his father's discourse would take them, but he was hung over, and thought was as difficult as turning his heavy, hurting head right or left. He could hear his mother's voice, though, just as it had been when he'd told her the news of his latest loss. He could hear the dismay and the sorrow, so tilted and distant that it became something closer to simple inconvenience. She wondered out loud where on earth Hubbell could possibly live, since he was much too old to come back home.

Nelson backed up slowly through the brush and ferns that flourished next to the water and met his son's gaze.

"I'm going to buy you back your house, Hubbell."

His son brightened, thinking of all his wonderful things coming back to him in a steady trail, like a line of inching ants. Here came his jade bottles, his ebony glassware, the collection of western watercolors. All edging toward him in a happy parade. On the strength of so much bourbon, Hubbell had said "my house and all its effects," upping the ante as he imagined a handful of blurry aces and wild cards. But his present delight was oddly shallow. Nelson saw this cheer was matter-of-fact. That really, once his confession had been made, his son's ordeal was over. That a grown man remained so unseasoned by greed or want or need was the most staggering disappointment of all. He was afraid to peer behind his son. What if, after fighting through the wild drinking bouts, the failures and more obvious shortcomings, Nelson Hanks was to find nothing? Nothing but his son's weightless, sunny nature (most evident after a trip to the headwaters of some restorative spa) and mild curiosity, which sometimes latched onto a thing but mostly didn't. Hubbell circled idly, circled like a lost goose cut off from its flock.

"Where are you going to send me, Father?"

"Arizona, where it's nice and dry. You want to drink, you'll have to split open a cactus plant. Your mother know about this mess?"

"I told her last night."

"Get your things ready today. Hubbell?"

He studied his son's dutiful, untroubled face. Some of his military-school training was in evidence. The young man knew how to respond to orders.

"Don't worry. I'm going to help you."

The floodgates opened as Hubbell began to weep. Nelson was wildly embarrassed and tried to mend this outburst by brisk claps on the back, an admonishment that he buck up, why, nothing was broken that couldn't be mended. But something was, something was. Hubbell sobbed into the sleeve of his own shirt and held his throbbing head with one hand. Nelson slapped his neck with water from the clear creek. After a while it seemed to help.

"You need a plan. All young men need a plan. Let's head back to the house and get cleaned up. Arizona will have you feeling better before you know it, and when you get back it won't be like before. I promise."

Help for Hubbell came from an unlikely source. Reeve sat on the other side of Nelson's wide desk. Reeve appeared perfectly at ease. The old man had lost track of most of the Nelson boys. This one, for instance. Which baby had he been all those years before? He was a finished piece of work, with none of a youth's hesitation or openness. Reeve offered him a cigarette, which the older man declined.

"What brought you back to Lovely in the first place, Mr. Reeve?"

"My father's been ill for some time."

"I know that. Your father was one of the best men that ever worked for me. Anything else?"

"Professional interests."

Pity he couldn't match this man up with the young boy he'd once been, but that was all too long ago.

"Were you ever a Scout, Reeve?"

"That was another Nelson. You never could keep us all straight. Not that it's your fault, sir. There were so many of us."

Reeve's round eyes took it all in. The view of Lovely from the fifteenth floor of the suite and the comfortable decor seemed proof of the oil man's prosperity. It was clear that he was not an interloper. He felt loose and easy, for Reeve still imagined he was on a roll. Hubbell Hanks was not the only rich man's son in town. His last poker game was scheduled for tonight, then he would head back to New Orleans to relax for a few days.

"Will you settle for seventy-five thousand dollars?"

His eyes stopped roving the room. He jiggled a cuff link, then flicked the ash on his cigarette so hard the burning end fell off. He relit the cigarette.

"I should add it's my final offer."

"You're on."

"You bet I'm on. There's a contingency, too. You clear out this afternoon. I'll get a check for you, then you disappear. No more high rolling at the country club. You and the golf pro are smooth, all right. I have a certain amount of admiration for your business skills. But you've milked enough of the boys around here. I want you gone today."

"I didn't cheat your son, Mr. Hanks."

"You didn't have to. He can't play cards sober, let alone drunk."

"I'll tell you something, Mr. Hanks."

Reeve didn't mind, really. His trip had been plenty lucrative, and he still had the silver dollar Nelson Hanks gave him that Christmas. His first silver dollar had brought him luck. Christ, he owed the old guy. He leaned forward eagerly in his chair.

"Your son's always gonna find a way to lose his money. Man oh man, the stories! There's nobody that hasn't stiffed him for a hundred bucks here, a hundred bucks there. It's like the guy loves to hand the stuff out. You've gotta know that, though. You're his father."

Reeve's father, sick as he was, knew his son inside out. The minute he walked through the door, the old man lit into him from where he lay dying on the bed. Begged him to get clean, to drop the gambling habit and all that, before he even bothered to ask if that was him, Nelson Reeve, banging through the back door. But maybe this was different. Maybe Nelson Hanks hadn't figured this out yet, the part about his son's being a patsy. He didn't feel remorse. He felt amused that he was tipping the old man off. Maybe the information was worth something to the old geezer. Jesus, it was worth a shot.

"Sir, the price is right for the house, but when you consider the—"

"Button your lip before I retract the offer. I'll see nobody buys the house, and then you'll have a permanent address, complete with property taxes. There isn't a great deal of night life in Lovely. A man like you might find time hanging heavy."

He pushed a button, and there was a knock on the door almost immediately.

"I'll need a check made out to Mr. Reeve for seventy-five thousand dollars, Miss Jacobs. You can also book him a seat on the train for . . . where is it you're going?"

"New Orleans."

The old man turned his chair toward the window, and he guessed that was all. Reeve winked at the secretary. She was a real babe. The young man had his hand on the doorknob.

"Did you manage to fight in the war, Mr. Reeve?"

"Until they sent me home. I was wounded in Germany."

Hanks nodded. Reeve had a soldier's bearing, and it didn't surprise him. He turned back to the window, and Reeve left his office,
still stepping softly on the balls of his feet.

Nelson and Lavinia strenuously agreed on one issue. They had not
seen one century end and another begin, hadn't witnessed mere
territory move toward respectable statehood, hadn't built their
long life together, to face *this* alone. They didn't grace the graceless
with discussion but provided for it, and the provision lay way out
on a ledge overlooking their favorite lake at the ranch. The same
architect who mapped out the hiding place inside the town house
library lent a hand in a greater project.

It took a year to construct the Hanks burial chamber. After its
completion, the mausoleum sank determinedly into its own back-
drop; the layer of sandstones marking the outside layered from the
floor of the ledge in a successive pile that seemed nature's design,
not the silk-shirted architect's. Native habitat quickly reclaimed it.
A skunk sprayed it, lizards and rattlers sunned on the roof, and
nothing more stately than a blackjack graced the entrance. All this
contrasted with the interior, where Nelson would one day lie next
to his wife. A thirty-square-foot room was lined with steel, water-
proofed and air-conditioned. There was even a telephone line and
a water fountain. The area fronting the burial chamber supposed
time—an eternity, for that matter—spent in reflection and repose.
A rotunda tiled in green and gold mosaic was outfitted with
benches and statuary. Lavinia asked for a variety of marble this
time, and the architect scrambled to collect samples subdued and
elegant enough to satisfy her. The architect had to reread her
memo three times. Mrs. Hanks asked for a fridge. Dismayed at
her request, he sank one just behind where the bronze doors swung
onto the rotunda. Lavinia feared hunger, even in death. Nelson,
with his telephone lines and call buttons, imagined communication
would continue in perpetuity. Their preoccupations and fears were
clear. It seemed to shatter the peace and symmetry he labored to
inject into plans for the permanent storage of his prosperous
clients.

So Nelson's goof surprised him the more. He thought he'd taken
care of everything. But he found himself as negligent as a farmer

who failed to see the hint of a whirring gray funnel, the way dark sky shifted open, suddenly coalescing into destruction. And in failing to see, he stood to lose everything even though provisions had been made, the storm cellar girded and safe, stocked with all that his family would need. Nelson rose from where he'd stumbled. Within an hour he had scheduled an appointment with three lawyers and his trust adviser. He even phoned his old pal Judge Tucker and hinted at real trouble when the judge balked.

"I've run into overtime, Counselor. I need you. I'll send the company plane tomorrow morning. Now don't disappoint me."

Tucker didn't, nor did the others. They would spend the next forty-eight hours drawing up documents that held the design for Hubbell's whole future. The legal papers were watertight, and nothing, no future contest, no pleas by braying, berating Hubbell or his attorneys, would ever break the seal on a plan that guaranteed the heir's simultaneous ruin and salvation.

When he returned from Arizona there was a plan, just as Nelson promised. He called Hubbell into his office. It seemed more fitting that the discussion take place there. Nelson fingered the papers in the pocket of his jacket. The rustle reminded him that he was acting *in a timely fashion*. This was a *judicious move*. On the papers were notes meant to joggle him into recognition of the world he was intent on saving. He had jotted down certain corporate facts and figures, as if these figures weren't engraved on his consciousness. Forty-one thousand shareholders. A net of some eighteen thousand employees. A corporation valued at $625 million. He wasn't a father about to smack a child's hand. He was governing a whole universe. Nelson's voice caught as he greeted Hubbell, peeling since Arizona.

"You look well, Father."

"You do, too. Except for that mess on your nose."

"Oh, that. You had the right idea about me going out there. I didn't even want a drink. I was on the tennis court every morning. I swam and even hiked up the mountains around Flagstaff. I feel ready to begin again."

"Begin what?"

"Well, I don't know exactly. But I feel ready. That's the point. Alert again. Sorry as hell about the house, but that's what happens when you play the pros."

Hubbell picked up a glass paperweight on Nelson's desk. A

bronze replica of the Hanks Petroleum seal was held inside. Hubbell tossed it lightly in the air and caught it with his right hand,
though he was a lefty.

"I had all the time in the world to think out there, Father."

"Good. I'd hoped that."

"Fellow up there named Sal Braverman and I hit it off like brothers. Sal's had his ups and downs, too. Nice guy and sharp. He
comes from an old Boston family; maybe you know them."

Nelson shook his head no.

"Anyway, we did nothing but talk. The thing is, Sal's got ideas
about this family business of his. About how to expand it and make
it really profitable. It's slightly undercapitalized. To really be competitive, he needs—"

"What kind of business?"

"Speedboats. Small craft. Anyway, the way Sal looks at things,
if he could just pump some money into his family firm, two, three
hundred thousand to wipe out some debts they've been struggling
with—"

"Stop, Hubbell."

"Stop what, Father?"

"All this."

Hubbell slid to the back of his chair and started tapping pockets
to find his pack of cigarettes.

"While you were away, I was thinking, too. I was thinking how
odd it is that a father and son can struggle with the same issue and
never discuss it. How, in fact, the same issues come up time and
again. Money, how we can acquire it. Then, once our pockets are
stuffed with it, what to do next."

Nelson studied his son's puzzled face.

"How many times can you eat breakfast in the morning, Hubbell?"

"Just once."

"Lunch, dinner?"

"Well, the same, Da—"

His cheeks were suddenly flushed red. He caught himself just in
time, before he'd called him Dad. He'd gotten on with Sallie Braverman. He'd even confessed how he longed to drop the formal
Father in favor of Pop or Dad. He breathed deeply, horrified by his
near misstep. Warm trade winds seemed to swirl around Nelson
as he talked. In his present kindly mood, he invited familiarity.

"A man can only eat the same meal once, Father."

There. He set it upright again, like a precious piece of porcelain.

"And once your clothes are on your back and your supper's on the table, the kids are all in bed, fed and warm—for there will be kids, Hubbell. Once all that's done, what do you do with money?"

"You give it away."

Nelson's fist slammed down on the table.

"Right! We agree, Hubbell. Which is why I've taken action."

Hubbell's tongue appeared at the corner of his mouth. Something was about to foul the moment, though he didn't know what.

"Let me tell you something, Hubbell. Inherited money is poison. Yes, you heard me. *Poison.* Nothing ruins character like a fat trust fund. Why, it's little more than a handout, and I don't care how we try to prettify it. But assume for a minute that Uncle Nelson didn't leave any money to his only son. Imagine if the press got hold of that tidbit. The public would brand me as a skinflint, wouldn't they? Why, I'd be thought of as a fraud! So I'm making an exception for you, Hubbell. I'm going against my own natural beliefs. Hubbell, do you hear me?"

Hubbell did, though it was hard. The room was too hot, and it was harder and harder to concentrate. He shook his head yes. He would try harder to act as if he understood.

"Yes, the hardest thing to do right is give away money. That's why I formed the foundation years ago. I needed a reasonable way to channel the money to others. But for me to do it in a random manner, as I once tried, is to invite chaos."

Hubbell folded his hands. His father's demeanor had changed. He'd gone on to the central issue, whatever it was. And all he had to do now was wait and listen. Something prickled the back of his neck. An angry rash crept all the way to the top of his chest.

"You're twenty-three, Hubbell."

"Next month."

"You're not a boy. You have a decision to make."

Panic started in him. He muffled it as he would a cry or curse.

"No man can have it both ways, and neither can you. I've put a great deal of money in trust for you, and in doing this, I've suppressed my best instincts. Tucker and I have made some permanent financial arrangements for you. A man could live very comfortably on the interest. Very."

Hubbell thought immediately of the graceful curves of a martini glass. The long, thin stem that supported its own saucy little dish.

An appealing green olive that turned and bobbed, revealing a round red pimento eye. He wanted another cigarette, but he knew his hands would tremble with the match.

"I've asked my lawyers to draw up papers I'm going to ask you to sign. The terms of our contract are simple, Hubbell. If you want to finance an enterprise or someone else's—this Sal, for example —you'll have to find the money elsewhere. The worst thing a man with money can do is give it away unconditionally. All I'm asking you to do is agree with my conditions."

Hubbell guessed he didn't understand. Otherwise, why would his father look as if this were a kind of death sentence?

"Can I buy a house with it?"

"You have a house."

"But another. What if I'd like another."

"If you like."

"Or land."

"All depends."

Hubbell began to sense something. He decided to forge ahead. His doctor in Arizona had spent three afternoons on objectifying fear. Hubbell hadn't quite gotten it, but it meant keeping your eye trained on the shadows until your fear emerged undisguised.

"If I just want to put my interest money, the part I don't need to live, into another bank, or, say, maybe I'd want to put my trust money in trust for someone else."

Nelson looked out the window for a moment, then at his watch. He hadn't counted on talking such a long time.

"Trust money? For your children? My God, after all I've said! I'll make it clear to you, Hubbell. Maybe that's been the trouble all along. Maybe the things you're supposed to make clear for a son, I've hopped over on my way to other things. I've arranged for you to have plenty and for the rest of your life. But in having plenty you mustn't jeopardize it. You mustn't take it up as if it were something to amuse you until you grew tired of tinkering. I'll tell you the truth, Hubbell. I can't stand the thought of you mounting a pipsqueak, throwaway business that goes bust after three years or four years and takes hundreds of thousands with it. Look around town and you'll see plenty of examples. Tie a string of these together, and you've got a real hangman's noose. Do you see, Hubbell?"

He rubbed his aching wrists. Maybe the noose started there, not around your neck, the way he always thought.

"I've arranged to give you not only money, Hubbell, but a

greater gift. The gift of guidance. Help will continue long after I'm gone, just as I promised before you left for Arizona."

"I think I see, Father."

It was clear he didn't. And Nelson wondered where the hating boy had gone. The boy who knew a masquerade when he saw it. He peered into his son's eyes and found they spared him everything. Not only hate but comprehension of a plan that would tie him up forever in a life of emotional receivership. Hubbell, to whom the world of business meant nothing, smiled and asked him about cars.

"Of course, Hubbell. Of course you can use it to buy a car. You'll be able to buy as many cars as you please."

Hubbell did sign the contract, surprised by the solemnity of the event and the number of lawyers present. It sure seemed like a funny winner's circle. His thoughts went swinging on ahead to his birthday bash that night at the club.

The conga line he led by midnight would wind through the next few years of his life. He would spend them testing the strength of his father's assurances, pausing only occasionally to look over his shoulder. The arrangement didn't snap, no matter how far Hubbell stretched it. It covered lengthy stays at the Broadmoor to study Rocky Mountain flora and fauna (the hiking boots and field glasses from Abercrombie & Fitch took Hubbell high and low) and a suite of rented rooms on Coronado Island when humpback whales were migrating nearby—what an easy hop to Baja, were Hubbell to follow the battered gray backs of the leaders. It took in riverboat parties to honor a best friend's completion of his family tree. When it was discovered that Samuel Clemens crouched way out on one of the limbs, Hubbell decided on a real celebration. Two hundred invited guests steamed mindlessly ahead for three days and nights on board a restored riverboat called the *Clarissa*, her huge paddles churning the muddy waters of the Mississippi into quite an uproar. Hubbell had such a lot to be grateful for . . . his friends, his festivities. It seemed this good world would never end.

~~Laydelle, Hubbell and Mary~~

chapter 33

1967

"Amos?"

She didn't call him Little Amos, and that was a sure sign she was up to no good. He folded his arms across his chest. She was hot and bothered about something.

"Your wife just called! Her car broke down way out on Lewis. She sounded scared to death and asked you to please hurry and get there. She was on her way to Jenks to see about an antique sale and then bingo, the breakdown. She's all alone, with her hood up, Amos."

His huge hands flew into the air, and he patted down what was left of his hair, a mannerism she knew by heart. It meant he was leaving. He continued patting, then set his hat firmly on his head.

"Lewis and what?"

"I don't know. But it's next to that awful trailer park. She was calling from a pay phone on their property."

"If your mama calls, tell her—"

"No problem, Amos. I'll cover for you."

There was a moment, just one, at the kitchen door when Little Amos Sweet wondered if he'd been hoodwinked. He turned to remind her about the security system and saw a look of smug satisfaction cross her face.

"I promised not to tell, but she was crying on the phone."

"Lord almighty."

Little Amos Sweet slept too heavily for his own good. He slept so hard he never heard his wife leave his bed to slip on red high heels and clatter out the door to meet one of her various lovers. He didn't hear dogs turning over his metal trash cans or burglars breaking the lock on his garage to cart off his power tools. He slept the impenetrable sleep of a good and innocent man every night, except for the one night every seven years that rattled his glorious existence. For every seven years Little Amos Sweet's employment contract was up for renewal and review. And every seven years Little Amos Sweet suffered a brief stab of self-doubt, wondering why a man of his size and caliber was still doing something so implausible and (the word had crossed his mind) foolish. Mary Hanks treated him like an errand boy, and her daughter treated him worse. *The incredible hulk. The bozo. My dad's pacifier.* He forgave but didn't forget. In a funny way, Little Amos couldn't blame her. She was sixteen, and he still tailed her as if she was a toddler. It didn't matter, for the end was in sight. When Laydelle turned twenty-one, Little Amos planned to light out for Colorado. He would have quite enough saved to just fish in perpetuity, with pretty Mrs. Sweet by his side. He hurried out the door, hoping she wouldn't try to walk to a filling station or something too horrid to imagine. Pretty Mrs. Sweet, with her thumb out for a ride.

Laydelle ran upstairs, two steps at a time. Leon Russell was on the radio, and she turned the volume down as she answered the phone.

"I'm leaving in five minutes. I'm scared he'll wise up and turn around. Be ready, okay? I don't want to wait."

She stuffed makeup, perfume and Kleenex in a quilted cosmetic bag and twisted her long hair into a fast chignon at the top of her head, piercing it with two long chopsticks. She tore through her drawers and pulled a black tank top over her head, then squeezed into a pair of faded cut-off jeans. Bangle bracelets, rings for every finger. She reached under her bed and drew a pack of Marlboro cigarettes from a carton.

"Blast off."

Her car was dirty and she had only half a tank of gas, but that would get them to Lovely. They could fill up there; gas was cheaper anyway. She barreled down the driveway, stopping before she joined the traffic on Riverview to adjust her rearview mirror and polish the lenses on her sunglasses. She was nervous, really nervous. She had ditched Little Amos three times in her life, and each incident had been aborted. Every time, he had figured out her scheme midway and returned to find her smoking grass or committing another sort of misdemeanor. Once he caught her upstairs with a wrestler from Enid. Her stomach hurt when she thought of how that wrestler had scrambled out of her bed and run buck naked through the hall to the bathroom, locking himself out of harm's way.

"Chickenshit, plain chickenshit. Well, not me."

She was careful about the speed limit, careful about parking across the street from her girlfriend's house, not wheeling into the driveway as usual and blowing the horn. Laydelle didn't want a discussion about safety today, not when she was in a hurry. She watched the curtains part upstairs, and minutes later, her friend walked nonchalantly out the front door. Laydelle waved at Sarah's mom, whom she could see through the kitchen window. She liked her, she liked hearing her voice on the telephone and her friendly questions about the substitute in chemistry or the genius in their class who had gotten early acceptance at Princeton.

"Look at that."

Sarah sighed disgustedly.

"She offered to pack us a lunch. Tuna fish, I'm sure."

"Oh, shut up, Sarah. Your mom's neat."

They pulled away from the curb slowly. Laydelle even put on the signal, though the street was deserted.

"Did you buy beer?"

"What do you think?"

Sarah raised the volume on the radio and held up one desultory hand as they drove away.

"Hey. She's your mom. It's not like having a bodyguard on your rear all the time."

"She still bugs me."

"Should we take the highway or back roads?"

"I don't know. Maybe the highway up so we won't miss the festivities and back roads home so we can take in the great scenery."

They burst out laughing. There was little scenery on the quiet roads back from Lovely. There were yards full of tires or hubcaps, yards full of rusting cars or one sad horse, leg cocked, with four kids on its back that were sadder still. Between the string of poor

towns lay uncultivated fields and signs that promised ultimate grat-
ification for those who endured the monotony. LEAVE IT ALL BE-
HIND. LOVELY, OKLAHOMA. 50 MILES AHEAD AT FORTUNE EXIT.

"Boy, that's for sure. So long, civilization."

Sarah passed her a can of beer, wrapped in a brown bag. Laydelle rapped her head with her knuckles, the other hand lightly on
the wheel.

"Oh, gee, a brown bag. That's intelligent. Now nobody will ever
guess. Well, cheers."

She spotted a truck up ahead and moaned.

"Pass him. He's standing still."

By the time they reached the truck they were on an incline.
Laydelle stayed behind the truck.

"What are you waiting for?" Sarah turned in the seat to face her.
She loved to drive fast. It was one of the reasons she didn't have
her own car.

Laydelle moved into the left lane, her foot flooring the accelerator. It felt as if they were standing still, but she didn't drop back.
She would be fine once they got to the top of the hill. They edged
up on the cab of the truck until the gold Camaro was pulling along
nose-to-nose. They crested the hill together, the truckdriver blasting them with his horn. Laydelle stuck her hand out the window
and waved ringed fingers in the air.

"No way. Did you see that guy? Give him the finger and see
what happens!"

"*You* do it. I already waved. He's got his brights on. He's doing that thing with his headlights. Trying to blind us so we'll
crash."

They were getting closer, and the signs grew ecstatic. LOVELY,
BYGONE BOOM TOWN. SEE IT AND BELIEVE IT. EXIT FORTUNE. . . .
VISIT BUFFABROOK! PLAYGROUND OF OKLAHOMA OIL BARON. EXIT
BUFFALO BOULEVARD.

"I don't believe we're doing this. This is nuts." Laydelle tried
again, thinking Sarah hadn't heard. "We could have gone to the
lake instead of this. I'm losing my tan."

Sarah lit one cigarette with another, tossing the butt out the
window. She looked at herself in the mirror and tightened the scarf
that held her hair back.

"You're not losing your tan; you're losing your nerve. Every time
I ask you to drive me up here, you cook up some excuse. Well, it's
not fair! I'm your best friend, and what is the big deal anyway? It's

a contest. It's a public contest, and I have as much right as anybody else to see who gets Miss Petroleum. So do you."

Laydelle pulled off into a rest stop and made a face at what she
saw in the mirror.

"I'm so pale."

"Not for long. Maybe they'll spray everybody with oil."

"Very funny, Sarah. Oooh, look at those guys. See, they're going
to the lake. But oh, no, we're going to see who wins Miss Petroleum."

One boy was sprawled in the back seat. His bare legs and bare
chest were oiled. The other two were just returning to the car,
tugging significantly at their pants.

"Pull up next to them."

Laydelle stuck the tube of black mascara back in the bag and
moved the car forward, its windows already down.

"Hi."

The boy nodded. Laydelle muttered *Hardass* under her breath,
but Sarah continued. Her voice sounded blasé.

"Excuse me, but can you tell me how far Buffabrook is?"

"Tells on the billboard."

His lips barely moved. He rolled his head up to get more sun on
his face. Sarah seemed content to do all the talking.

"Oooh. You're not using baby oil, are you? 'Cause I'll tell you, a
friend of mine used it once and she wound up toast. I'm not kidding! Plus she put iodine in it to get really good color? I guess that
made it even worse?"

"You askin' me somethin' or tellin' me somethin'?"

"Better decide."

His pals had joined him by the side of the car. Country cousins,
jokers, they played comic foil to the back-seat Marlon Brando.

"Yeah, better decide if it's a question or a answer. 'Cause if y'all
want somethin, just better go on and ask for it."

Laydelle started to drive off, but Sarah grabbed her leg. She
continued pressing it as she spoke.

"I already asked. I said I wanted to know how far Buffabrook
is."

"Tell y'all what. Nothin goin on out there today but a beauty
contest with no beauties. Why not come on with us to the lake?"

Marlon moved. Slowly and subtly, but he did move. One finger
over the top of his glistening arm, then the same finger in the air
as if checking for wind direction.

"Y'all was wantin to know about baby oil?"

"Yeah?"

Sarah still pinched her, held her in place when she wanted to be moving on. She'd probably have to pass that truck all over again.

"I tell y'all somethin. There's nowhere I don't put baby oil. That way I make sure everything gets nice and brown."

"Gross! Gross me out!"

She finally stopped pinching, and Laydelle pulled out fast, faster than she should have. A Ford pickup nearly sideswiped her. The driver, a woman with her hair in pigtails, laid on the horn.

"All right, all right. Sorry. Jeez!" Her hands shook a little, and she slowed down.

"Why did you bother with those hicks in the first place?"

"I don't know. For fun. I don't know. They were *so rude*. How come you were so quiet? You didn't say a word the whole time."

"Who could get a word in edgewise, Sarah? Look, I didn't want to come up here in the first place. This whole escapade is for you. I'm going to be in such deep shit."

Whether she defied Little Amos or endured him in cantankerous silence, he was always present. Seeking shade, dumb as a dog, he was part of everything she did. She could never shake the thought of him, even when she had succeeded in giving him the slip. He had even been back there, witness to an episode that had given her no pleasure. She hadn't found that funny at all.

"Don't worry, Laydelle. Your parents won't do anything. They never do anything. Which is also why I hate my mom, by the way. She is always on my back, whether you happen to think so or not. I'd like to know what other sixteen-year-old gets grounded for drinking."

"Plenty."

"Still. Your parents would never do that."

"They would if they knew."

"That's what I mean! They don't know anything about you and never have."

That was the advantage to the peculiar circuitry in their house. The current of information ran back and forth between Laydelle, Aresta and Little Amos Sweet. Very little actually got through to Mary and Hubbell, because the jolt (the housekeeper and the bodyguard deemed) would be to no one's advantage.

Buffalo Road was the long, narrow country road that led to Buffabrook. Billboards now advertised wildlife species and hiking trails, myriad outdoor activities and the artwork and artifacts housed in the museum. The road was surprisingly smooth. No potholes marred the blacktop stretch on the way to the ranch.

"Does the fact that we haven't seen one car on this road tell you anything about the afternoon in store for us? I can't believe this."

"You want to turn back and go to the lake with Tom, *Dick* and Harry?"

"No."

"Well, then, hush."

They turned into the entrance to the ranch and spotted several cars up ahead, which were carefully observing the speed limit. Sarah finished her beer and ground out her cigarette, spotting the No Smoking sign.

"You're a very good citizen."

"Wouldn't want to get thrown off your ranch."

"It's not mine, Sarah. I've told you that a thousand times."

"But you could make people *think* Buffabrook is yours, which is practically the same thing. Oh, look! I wish we could pet them. I used to have a real thing about zebras when I was a kid. I drew them, read every book I could get hold of. My mother and I drove out to the zoo every weekend as long as it lasted. It was like a sickness or something. Then I got a boyfriend, and I was cured."

"See? I told you your mother was neat."

"Yeah, yeah. Well, you live with her, since she's so terrific."

The parking lots were full. Laydelle waved at the attendant, and he told her to park in the space reserved for administration.

"Where you been, stranger?"

"In the library, Jerry. All I do is study."

"Well, keep up the good work, Miss Hanks. But come see us sometime. Your dad doing okay?"

"Fine, thanks."

"Good, good. Well, pull in anywhere behind the offices. Say. How come you don't run for Miss Petroleum? You're prettier than any of 'em."

They parked in the shade and rolled down the car windows. Laydelle hid the sack full of empty cans under the seat.

"Why don't you?"

"What?"

"Run for Miss Petroleum. Well, I don't mean that exactly. I mean, I guess that would be illegal. But why don't you . . . take advantage of this somehow? You won't believe this, but some people actually *don't know* this is your family. Who was I talking to the other day? Halsey Evans! He said, You are shitting me, she's not really. I mean, he couldn't believe it. If people haven't visited your house, if people haven't seen Sweet playing hide-and-seek with you, they sort of don't make the connection."

"Good."

"I mean, you look completely normal."

"Better."

"Well, I personally think that's completely stupid. If I were you, *everybody* would know it. My friends, my teachers. I'm not kidding. Everybody."

They skipped down the stone steps, stopping every once in a while to admire the glistening lake, so inviting at that distance.

"I'll tell you where you could start."

"Do you have a broken eardrum or something?"

"I'm just telling you what you could do if you wanted to . . . well, what would really be cool. You could have the graduation stuff out here. Next year when committees form, you could sign up for one and sort of casually offer your grandfather's ranch for either the dance or one of the parties. That would be totally neat! Plus I'd help you! I mean it, I'd do everything. What is there to do in Tulsa? A country club? Bo-ring."

They met other people on the path, families with picnic baskets, their elder members taking careful, mincing steps on the uneven flagstones. Children squeaked and squealed as mothers made them hold hands and march in pairs. No running! Stick to the path! Poison ivy threatened, too. Laydelle saw treacherous patches on either side. She scratched her cheek. She could smell the stuff and break out in a rash.

The contestants floated offshore. Sarah counted out loud. Thirteen contestants stood in the middle of the old swimming platform in the middle of the lake. Each contestant sported high heels and a corsage on her bathing suit.

"So what's the deal? Who are those girls anyway?"

Spectators lined the shore. Most people were eating and drinking by now, although it wasn't even noon. The mood was giddy. This seemed to infect the contestants, some of whom doubled over with laughter on the rolling platform.

"They work for the company. Or their families do. I don't know. This is all so weird."

"How'd they get out there?"

"They parachuted in. Beats me."

"Boy, you're a real help. I might as well have come by myself."

Slowly the platform began to move toward the shore, and the crowd started clapping wildly. It began with a slight jerk, and one contestant nearly fell, grabbing another girl to right herself. This produced more laughter, more applause. The motion of the platform produced a little breeze, and ribbons fluttered, hair lifted slightly. Music drifted over the area.

"Oh, brother. The fife and drum. This is so corny."

It was a rosy-cheeked crowd. The Lovely locals shouted spirited greetings at each other, which carried over the water. They even called out to the girls, called out the names of their favorites, the names of their own wives and daughters. There was strictly no littering. Everything was ceremoniously hauled to one garbage can or another. Any stray paper, cup or paper plate stained with ketchup and mustard was snatched up fiercely. Lovely people picked up after people they didn't even know, and the act of picking up held great meaning. Uncle Nelson's ranch was pristine, and this group vehemently intended for it to stay that way.

"Well, just look at what the tide has brought in."

Attention turned to the speaker, a bow-tied, shoe-shined master of ceremonies. He held a microphone, though he didn't need one.

"Ick. His voice sounds like it's squeezed out of a tube. Check his hair."

"Petroleum jelly, I'll bet. Get it? Petroleum jelly."

They smirked and settled down to enjoy the event. The girls were coming closer and closer, and the music wasn't that bad, once you got used to it. Like John Philip Sousa, it could be tolerated under certain conditions. And, Laydelle was pleased to learn, she would tan after all. She rolled her cutoffs higher up her leg, and Sarah followed suit.

"Girls, girls, girls! You know, folks, the Miss Petroleum title has always been a true title. It carries with it great privilege. It marks each and every contestant. Competing alone is an honorable attainment."

"Wake me when it's over."

The platform was just offshore now, and they got a closer look at the girls, most of whom were blushing. Two women actually seemed to shrink from the crowd. They fiddled with the edge of a bathing suit, a shoulder strap. Peacock cries sounded on the hill above the lake. The M.C. paused deliberately and held his micro-

phone in the direction of the birds. He shook his lacquered head
and eyed the crowd.

"Pretty transparent, isn't it, everybody? They're used to strutting
their stuff, spreading their marvelous plumage for everyone to ogle!
Well, not today. Sorry, peacocks. You've been outdone by these
bathing beauties. *Miss Theresa Williams!* Let's hear it for Theresa,
everyone."

One by one, each girl stepped delicately to the stationary landing
under the diving board. They were helped to shore by a blue-suited
young Cubscout. He offered each contestant a hand, then let them
march to the edge of the dock, pivot to make one full turn before
the crowd, and return to stand in a line facing the audience. As
they walked, the announcer described the prize money, the community services the winner would perform, the initial Miss Petroleum contest, just after the ranch was purchased.

"This is a big deal, Laydelle."

"If you mean the money, yeah, it does seem like a lot."

"Uh oh. Seems like everybody wants to strut some stuff today.
Look over there."

Five Indians stood at the edge of the shore. They were in uniform. Jeans, bare torsos, with some bit of costume in evidence.
They swaggered and were making their noisy way over to the
contest. Two tipped their heads back and drank from cans.

"Those aren't milk bottles."

"Uh uh. God, they're barefoot. They must be on painkillers."

They made it over the rocks with no apparent trouble. Some
shouting could be heard, but it was indistinct. Maybe they were
cheering the candidates, Laydelle thought. The thought didn't last
long.

"The members of the sixth civilized tribe would like to ask the
judges where our candidate is."

"Boys. Fellows. You'll have to . . . Gentlemen, there's a regulation here on the Hanks Ranch about drinking. I'm sure you've
read the posted notices."

"Maybe they're puffing peyote. Or swilling pedseni."

"What's that?" Sarah kept her voice at a whisper.

"Firewater. Didn't you take Oklahoma history?"

Most of the contestants had grown as pale as their white ribbons. One of the women, who had not been embarrassed as she
floated to the shoreline, turned to the detractors and shook her
finger in the air.

"You all have no business here! You all have no business coming in and mocking this contest."

There seemed to be a leader. He stepped forward, and though he was no baritone, his proud carriage made everyone sit up a little bit straighter. Many people stopped chewing, slowly let their sandwich slip back onto the plate.

"We're not mocking this contest. We're asking a legitimate question. We are curious about a judging process that systematically eliminates—"

"Us!"

He put a hand on the shoulder of the boy who had spoken up, a boy whose voice rose in an irritating whine.

"—a qualified candidate such as Leona Strike Ax. She has been a Hanks employee for the past five years, and this is the third time she's tried to enter the Miss Petroleum contest."

"Young man, is this really the moment for a political forum? We have not come here for that kind of contest. Frame your questions properly, son, and they will receive a proper answer. Now on with the show! Let's hear it for *Miss Elaine Scott.*"

"Screw you."

Here was trash they had overlooked. A stray something that landed on the shore of Uncle Nelson's gentle lake. One or two men began rolling up their sleeves to do the dirty work. It proved to be unnecessary. A police siren could already be heard on Buffalo Road. The ranch security personnel were clambering down the stone steps. Their walkie-talkies were cackling, making more noise than the peacocks and the baritone combined.

"Screw you and you and you." The boy pointed at random contestants and pulled at his belt. "If this were a legitimate contest, with legitimate representation, we would have had an Osage winner years ago. Has there ever, in the history of this ridiculous competition, been a contender, let alone winner, with anything but blue eyes and blond hair? No! And Leona Strike Ax is hardly the first Osage woman to try for the prize. Our women have been systematically overlooked. Systematically barred from what is clearly a rigged contest."

The same unembarrassed contestant shook as she spoke. Her corsage rattled right off, but she paid no attention. She forgot all about eloquence and grace, key requisites for the title of Miss Petroleum.

"Oh, bull. I am just so sick of all this bull! How about the Nelson

Hanks Scholarship Fund? How about that ticket to the Ivy League and who knows what after? I don't see any blond, blue-eyed contenders for that! That prize has gone to an Osage for the past nine years, and I don't remember who all before. We are bathing beauties! We are nothing but bathing beauties. Let us have our contest in peace!" She paused for a moment and continued.

"Don't you think we would love to go to Harvard? Talk about being systematically overlooked!"

She began to cry, and the other girls gathered around to shield her. All order had vanished. The Scout started playing with his neck scarf. He didn't know who to escort where. The Osage tirade began again.

"Screw you, you crappy imitation of Bert Parks. Screw all the people here. This is a criminal celebration."

"You're the criminal, young fella. Shut your mouth and come with us."

"Wow!"

"Man oh man!"

"Stand up, Laydelle. Introduce yourself and take a stand! God, you're right in the middle of this deal. You could be."

"You know, you're a rabble-rouser. You don't care what's going on; you just want to be in the middle of it! I wonder if they'll go to jail or just get booted off the property."

The show went on as security guards marched the boys up the stairs in a silent, sullen train. Sirens were really wailing now, several of them. The whole basin echoed. Somebody would win the contest, but neither girl wanted to stay for the outcome. They followed the crowd instead. The boys were shown into the waiting police cars. Doors were snapped shut, and one of the Osage slammed his fist into the rear window.

"What now?"

"I don't know. I don't know what I'd like to do next. Maybe we'll just drive. Any beer left?"

"Oh, yeah."

They couldn't find anything good on the radio. Laydelle was suddenly tired of talking, tired of driving. The notion of cause and effect was finally dawning, and she'd begun to think of what it would mean to face Mrs. Sweet, whose car probably hadn't even left her own driveway all day. She knew that for crime there was punishment and could only guess what form the penalty would take.

"Wanna drive?"

"Oooh, yeah. Thought you'd never ask."

Laydelle let her head lean against the window. Instead of the Sweets' combined fury and shame, she chose to consider the Osage boys. They looked too good to be true.

"You know, I've never actually seen an Indian before. Can you believe that?"

"Me, neither."

If the contest was actually rigged, who rigged it? Maybe her grandfather had made that one of the contest rules, though she couldn't guess why. Nothing put her to sleep faster than political discussions. Weird. It was all just too, too weird. She drank a little and, since they weren't doing much talking, let herself doze off just a bit. With her face exposed, she could get a touch of sun and not waste the entire day.

She didn't sleep the sleep of Little Amos. She slept a sleep that could be broken by a scream and a jolt; other sounds, too. Branches breaking and rocks landing on a metal surface. By the time she fell into the dashboard, both forearms were locked against her forehead to fend off whatever was coming. She felt giddy as Miss Petroleum herself, who was just then receiving the crown, when the Camaro finally came to a stop bottom-up inside an irrigation ditch. She grew giddier and giddier, feeling something tickle, dribbling down from her forehead to her chin. Then she fell into a second, deeper sleep.

chapter 34

Hubbell glanced up from the book he held open on his lap, just as Mary discreetly covered her yawning mouth.

"I own a Packard, Mary. As of this evening, I actually own a Standard Eight Packard convertible."

Mary did a neat imitation of the auctioneer.

" 'A hundred-point Packard. Winner of the Silverado Concours d'Élégance at Napa. Only twenty-two thousand miles, this fact verified in a detailed history of its notable owners from Coachcraft custom body shop. Steamer trunk in tip-top condition, complete with fitted luggage. The *original* tissue paper is still inside, folded in neat squares.' I was there, Hubbell. Don't forget, I did escort you to the auction."

Mary caught a glimpse of herself in the mirror over the mantel in the hotel room. The mirror held dark glass, shot through with fine gold veins, so that she could barely see her own image. She moved closer for a better look.

"Well, congratulations, Mr. Silent Bidder."

"Thank you, darling. Drink, Mary? How about a nightcap before we turn in?"

"Congratulations, Mr. Low Profile. Mr. Blend Right In. Tell me, since you're so intent on being an ordinary citizen, what exactly are you going to do with the Packard you just bought? How are you going to join the Classic Car Club for those Sunday jaunts into the country, those forty-mile parades they put on in Oklahoma City? All the Gwendolyns and Bunnys, all the Medawicks, Hollingsworths and Chads—what on earth will they make of Mr. Barely There?"

Mary cinched the belt of the hotel bathrobe tighter and plopped down into a soft, ample armchair. She burrowed into a corner of red-and-yellow chintz and tugged hard on tassels that dropped off the sides of plump pillows. She watched his back as he mixed drinks at the side table in the cozy sitting room. She thought about how a man's shoulders had no business sloping like that. She decided he was pouting and using his dumb, silent back to do it with. He did it on purpose, made it all heel over on top like that.

"You haven't answered my question."

"That's because I don't know what it is. You knew we were coming to Chicago to bid on that Packard. You knew what I wanted to pay and how I wanted to pay."

"Incognito, with your head down? Like hell I did!"

He turned with drinks in his hand, and there was no sign of a pout. Hubbell's head felt full as a fire hydrant. He could drown his wife with a single blast, just like that. One more word, one more accusation, and he would twist off whatever capped the anger of years. He set her drink down in the middle of the coffee table and made her reach for it.

"I'm sorry I brought you to the auction, Mary. You wore an ugly expression on your face and spoiled the whole thing for me. You've taken the fun out of the evening. In fact, you succeeded in ruining the entire trip. I wish you'd never come with me in the first place."

Mary leaped from the chair like a cat. She came around the coffee table to face him and beat her legs with her fists, ignoring her after-dinner drink, ignoring the thud and scuffle overhead, the occasional cries, which merely meant love. None of these things mattered just now.

"Oooh, I would like to hit you, Hubbell. I would like to pound you on the side of the head and knock you down flat. Couldn't you have done it for me? Couldn't you have worn a beautiful tux and raised your arm high, higher, then highest of all the bidders in that room as the price on that old car went up? Sold! Sold to Hubbell Hanks of Oklahoma! That's what I came to hear."

She beat her legs as she walked, as she plotted and planned, redesigned the entire failed evening. The man and woman in the suite upstairs continued to shriek and couple. Their passion might have spilled right on top of Mary's head had she allowed *that*. But she didn't. She certainly hadn't come to Chicago for *that*.

"Do you even know why you wanted that old Packard, Hubbell? Do you even understand the hold that car has on you?"

"*Christ, Mary!*"

Hubbell heard. Hubbell heard the sounds of the wonderful engaging world where love was made in fancy hotel suites. Love, simple love. Abiding or fleeting, it didn't matter. Love given, love purchased. Love adorned with words and gestures or spread-eagled, raw and ruder than bark. It didn't matter. Hubbell heard the sounds of the world where love in any context was being transacted. He roared, he bellowed out the name of his wife, who wouldn't love him now, who hadn't for years. If Mary would have liked to pound him flat, he would have liked to do the same to her. And maybe then, finally forced to stop, pounded flat as scalloped meat, Mary could be held fast, love could be pressed from her, ground out from warm, marrow-filled bones.

"I know damn well you'd never join a classics club. You'd never buy it for that. But that old car not only has fitted luggage and tissue paper in its trunk; it holds your whole life history. That car is the Japanese valet driving endlessly through Lovely, Oklahoma, with Lavinia Hanks on board. It's the same make, Hubb! The very same, and when I think of the noise this sale could have made, my head spins. It would have been the perfect piece for our portfolio. The right kind of notoriety, Hubbell. That's all I ask for, and guess what, Hubb. The right kind of notoriety is all you have to offer. It's high time I said it."

There was a fist on his heart. It was closing off valves and stopping all the blood that had been rushing through his body. There was a fist in his throat, slowly closing down on the words that wanted to fly out. His voice, when it emerged, was half of what it could have been, because of the fist.

"You've been saying it for years, Mary. And I've been listening. Believe me, I've heard it said over and over again."

She held her head with both hands because it was throbbing. She left that room and filled an enormous footed bathtub with water hot as she could stand and slipped in an inch at a time. Lowering her body into that tub, into the blistering water, took every bit of her strength and concentration. When she emerged, red and wrinkled, slightly dizzy, the headache was gone. So was Hubbell. She went to the window, examining the starry sky and the whole flirtatious city with its winking white lights and thrilling winds that licked right over the top of the lake.

"I'm on my way. Mary Hanks is coming somehow, someday. And every one of you out there had better hang on to your hats."

She went to bed. Grandly undisturbed, Mary wondered if Hubbell had gone off on a toot. She thought about praying but rolled over instead and went straight to sleep, with both hands curved under one cheek.

The staff at the Newton Arms Hotel knew all was well in room 405, so well, in fact, that several guests had called to complain about the amorous couple. They also knew there was somewhat of a scuffle in the room directly below, for the night clerk had seen Mr. Hubbell Hanks rush out of his room toward 1:35 A.M. with an overnight bag. The following morning, when the emergency call came in for Mrs. Hubbell Hanks, reception decided to send the message up personally rather than by the rude ringing of the telephone. The message announcing trouble was written out on a piece of onionskin with the hotel letterhead, a delicate tangle of leaves and vines that cradled the words *Newton Arms Hotel* like a baby. Mrs. Hubbell Hanks came to the door immediately. The bellboy was surprised to hear her cheery hello, given the circumstances. She smiled up at him as if he were the gladdest sight on earth.

"Why, good morning!"

He scratched a spot behind his ear thoughtfully, then offered her the letter that lay on the oval serving tray.

"Message for you, Mrs. Hanks."

"Thank you. You've certainly appeared like magic! I could absolutely eat a horse. Will you take my breakfast order?"

He did that, just as she was tapping the unopened letter against her chest and gazing out the window toward the lake. It held little whitecaps this morning, and he guessed that was why she kept staring out.

"Three scrambled eggs, please, and tell them downstairs I like them moist. I want a rasher of bacon, well cooked, and a pot of strong coffee. Oh, and a basket of bread. I told you I was hungry, now didn't I?"

"That be all, Mrs. Hanks?"

"Yes, that's it. What's your name?"

"Rodney."

"That's a nice name. Here, Rodney. Thanks so much."

She tucked a bill into the pocket of his jacket, still smiling, as he backed toward the door. He closed it gently, thinking of the bad news that envelope contained.

Mary looked at the letter for a long moment before she opened it. She talked to the envelope bearing the Newton Arms logo, chastising it a bit, but tenderly. Mary had slept wonderfully well and woken up with all kinds of certainties. She felt so well that morning that she had been reluctant to move at all.

"Of course you're sorry, Hubbell. You always are. But I understand slipping off like that, and I'll tell you something. If you hadn't left this room, I would have. That's how mad I was. Oh, but that's behind us now. So much is behind us now. Mary Hanks is all done with anger, believe me."

She sliced it open with a letter opener and read the two-line message. She picked up the phone, taking little stabs at the blotter as she spoke.

"Mary Hanks here. I want to know why I wasn't apprised of this message immediately. This is an emergency, and I see that a full fifteen minutes has gone by without me being given my message. You what? Give me your name, young man. Oh, never mind. Ring this number. Area code— What? Of course I want this call on my bill!"

She was all right, that was the important thing. Laydelle was all right, though terribly shaken, and the hospital would release her tomorrow. She had a broken arm and a few cuts on her face, miraculously near the hairline, so the scars wouldn't even show.

"Tell me how you are."

"I told you."

"Tell me again. Your thoughts, your memory."

"I'm only talking funny because of painkillers. Don't worry, Mom. Amos is here. Even Mrs. Sweet. She came right over the minute she heard about the accident."

Mrs. Amos Sweet's unsmiling face had been the first thing Laydelle had seen when she woke up from that second sleep. It happened she liked crossword puzzles. She just worked and worked in one corner of the hospital room until Laydelle was feeling well enough to hear what she had to say. *You spoiled brat. It isn't enough you have to humiliate my husband for years. It isn't enough you have to drag him through your orgies and your pot smoking. Oh, no. You have to scare him to death, then wreck the car and put him in a nasty situation. By the way, my car did break down, but it wasn't on Lewis at all, and of course there was no one to call, since Amos was hunting all over the wrong side of town. You little brat.*

"I'll tell you all about it when you come home. When are you all getting in?"

"I'll call Bill Simmons right this minute, Baby. We'll fly as soon as I check out of the hotel. Oh, God, Laydelle, I love you so much."

"I love you, too. Can I speak to Daddy?"

"Daddy's . . . why, he's gone. Packard this, Packard that. We bought it, by the way."

"Cool. Better go, Mom. I'm kind of sleepy."

"Do sleep. Try to sleep all you can. This is all my fault. If I hadn't decided to come up here with your dad, the two of us would have been—"

"—fighting about my curfew. I'll see you tonight, Mom."

Her mouth was really dry. When she hung up the phone, the very minute she hung up the phone, Mrs. Amos Sweet was by her side with water in a pleated paper pill cup.

"Bottoms up."

Her husband had gone down the hall to use the bathroom.

"Just between the two of us, sweet-eyes, the story had better come out in our favor. I want Amos to be the hero, not just the dumbshit who bought that story of yours, hear?"

Laydelle thought her eyeliner was the most amazing sight she had ever seen. It widened and narrowed perfectly, finishing like the upturned tail of a scorpion. A nurse was here now and Little Amos, who had to duck each time he entered the doorway to avoid hitting his head.

"Time for your medication, Miss Hanks."

"Again?"

"Again. You keep forgetting you've been in quite a scrape."

Hubbell's toot lasted four days. It consisted not of boozy days and nights but of Glenn Miller and Count Basie tunes playing on a

portable radio purchased in Galena. Hubbell's toot included a
picnic by a creek and complete surrender to a woman named Lily.
Lily cornered him at a soda pop machine in a gas station just as he
cleared Illinois. She begged him so sweetly, so insistently, that he
could hardly say no. He hitched up the leg of his trousers and
preened, posed in the warm spring sun as she clicked Instamatic
photos of Hubbell with his foot on the running board of the Packard, his straw hat rakishly tilted to one side. As she exclaimed over
the lavish car, ran her hand over the wine-red leather and opened
the glove compartment to read aloud the charming starting instructions, proud blushing Hubbell even shared the old advertising slogan with her.

"Ask the Man Who Owns One."

"Wait till my boyfriend hears about this! One more picture for
my scrapbook? Oh, please, please say yes."

But later, as he idled toward Oklahoma, following the zigzag
Triptik map furnished by his car club, he realized Mary was right.
The car made him swoon, but not because of gleaming Sungate
Ivory paint and the endless details James Ward Packard and his
brother devised to delight and astound. Hubbell rose and fell on
waves of strangest memory as he drove farther south. He floated
in the middle of this sea, his body sealed tight against all intru-
sions, buoyed by sights and sounds belonging to another time. His
mother and father took turns sitting beside him, admonishing him
about the speed limit or wishing out loud for another day of such
fine weather, waving occasionally at the kids hopping up and down
on sidewalks as they caught sight of the grand car. Hubbell drove
through Missouri amazed and unblinking, though Missouri was
not what he saw at all. He saw Nelson and Lavinia as they nested
comfortably in the Lovely sunroom among newspapers he mustn't
touch because they were dirty, among company reports he mustn't
muss because of their importance. He saw them again, far away
but approaching, only this time he was a bigger boy, waiting for
candy and the velvet comforter his mother had promised to bring
up to school since the nights were frosty and Hubbell complained
of being cold. He watched them get out of the back seat stiffly as
Joey held the door. Hubbell raced breathlessly to a makeshift airfield in a farmer's field to watch Art Goebel flip his airplane, tip it
belly-up in the blue sky until it looked like a sad, stranded animal
and not a plane at all. Then it was Hubbell himself who was rising,
grown now, in the high-speed elevator to his father's offices, where

he watched Nelson erect his whole life as if it were a kit he had only to assemble. He clambered through rooms clogged with Nelson boys, each one of them blocking his path with a muscled forearm or a surreptitious trip that sent him sprawling until he reached another room, a better room, where there was sunlight and worried soldiers sent there to heal under the spell of Hubbell's kindness. All the while he drove, he saw not Saint Louis, not the Arch at all, only a long darkness that produced one bright forgotten scene after the next. They were issued like flares over black water. His hands loosened on the wheel but only gradually.

"You feeling okay, mister? You're looking mighty pale."

He had pulled the car over to the shoulder of the road. He smelled horse manure. Strong as that odor was, the smell of his own sweat pierced that. It poured off his head and arms. It soaked through the back of his shirt.

"Have some of this. You look like you could use it."

So Hubbell drank from the flask of a stranger in . . . he read the roadside sign. He had just entered Oklahoma, sneaked in through a northeastern corner. The drink brought tears to his eyes. It was like swallowing paint thinner.

"Wife and I brew as a hobby. Like some people pitch horseshoes."

"Thank you. That was just what I needed."

"Like some more?"

"Better not. But thanks."

He sat for a moment wondering what fearful thing had made him stop his car. Then, since he had entered Oklahoma, since he was on his way home after a serious dispute, Hubbell awoke, jarred. He would break the chokehold of the past this way. He opened his Triptik deliberately and laid it on the dashboard. The dotted orange line would take him right to his doorstep, right to the center of discord that he must now work very hard to vanquish. He thought of Mary with a horrible shooting pain, for she was still his dear heart and the thing he prized most. She had said bad things, but he had done worse. He had disappeared. Vanished. Stalked out of the hotel room like a little kid in the throes of a tantrum. She would be sick with worry. Oh, he had so many things ahead of him, so many problems to tackle. But he would tackle them. Starting now. He would lay his surprise at her feet, like the hunter's trophy it was. Hubbell began to smile now. Once in a while, laughter broke through as he drove. He guessed she would clap her hands and throw herself happily around his neck when he told her. For Hubbell's surprise, so long in coming, was capitulation. *Mary, you win. Let's storm the palace, honey.* He was through resisting his wife. He chuckled, thinking of the new batch of schemes his gesture would produce. It meant he would be going up to Lovely each and every month for foundation meetings. It meant a new set of social weights and measures. It meant a brand-new calculation about how he spent his leisure time. Hell, he probably wouldn't have any more leisure time! Hubbell whistled a Basie tune, "One O'clock Jump," through his teeth. It probably meant polo.

Mary was sitting in the swing when he pulled up. She didn't rise to greet him. She didn't even stop swinging. Her shoe soles brushed the top of the porch. She looked completely at peace. He had never seen Mary Hanks so happily idle. Hubbell hopped out of the car and decided the casual pose was intentional. It indicated that his homecoming didn't matter one bit. Well, by God, Mary was right. He deserved to be punished. Hadn't he left her high and dry in Chicago and promptly disappeared for four days? He went right around to the trunk, hoisting out the steamer trunk, removing the first of several suitcases with exaggerated care. He hopped lightly up the steps and laid the suitcase down in front of her feet, which still skimmed back and forth over the floor of the porch.

"Would an apology be completely beside the point?"

She looked down at him. She'd done something new to her hair.

"Hello, Hubb. An apology for what?"

"For running off like an angry adolescent. For leaving without a word and reappearing after having been God knows where for four full days, that's what. For leaving you to settle hotel bills and fly home alone. It must have been humiliating. What did you tell Bill Simmons?"

"To make sure there was a bottle of Beefeater on the plane."

"Is that all?"

"Why, yes, Hubb. That's all."

He opened the suitcase, and that got her to stop swinging. She knelt down on the porch and examined the dresses he'd bought her, five in all. She read the tags approvingly, even stood up to see how the blue one looked. She stood on tiptoe to see her reflection better in the front window. There were scarves, too. He'd gone a little nutty over some silk scarves, and though he'd never seen her wear one, Hubbell thought scarves had everything to do with the new life they'd be living together.

"Like them, Mary?"

"Adore them. What's the occasion?"

"The occasion is love. The occasion is also regret."

He spoke slowly at first. They didn't get up from the floor of the porch for the longest time, for Hubbell at last had Mary's attention. She rubbed both eyes slightly as he talked, leaving a slight smudge of midnight-blue mascara underneath one eye. She'd been dabbling in new colors all morning. Hubbell began to talk faster and faster as his excitement grew. Her ideas weren't loony at all. They were good, they were really quite good. He had resisted because he hadn't understood how much they meant to her. Only suddenly, after Chicago, after the quarrel and the frightening four days he'd just spent "without you, Mary," he'd finally seen the light! After all, Hubbell insisted, his wife's hand in both of his, my father was a terrible bully. Like father, like son, don't you see? Maybe I was trying to be as headstrong and deliberate as my father, and this seemed the way to do it! So now . . .

"Why, we're going to live differently. We're going to go to polo matches. We'll take up skeet shooting and fly to fox hunts in Pennsylvania the way you always said we should. We'll subscribe to the Opera Ball! What's wrong, Mary? Mary. I said I was sorry, and I am. I'm desperately sorry."

"So am I, Hubb. Let's fold all this up, shall we? I wouldn't want a single sheet of this tissue paper to fly away. Isn't this luggage marvelous? Not a mark, not a blemish."

Hubbell forgot to get up. He watched his wife fold the dresses back into the suitcase, snapping it shut. He watched her fold her arms over her chest and settle into that back-and-forth, that whooshing sound her feet made on the porch as she regained her former rhythm. He watched his entire proclamation disappear as if it had never been made in the first place. He felt banished and invisible where he remained. So Hubbell tried standing. He tried standing with his legs apart, the way he would have if he had been a football player.

"Do you accept my apology, or don't you, Mary?"

"I should be the one apologizing to you, darling. For years of ranting and raving. For years of trying to fit a square peg into a round hole. But none of that matters now, Hubbell. Not one bit of that matters. Now why don't you go on upstairs and be the first to sign your daughter's cast?"

"She's home? It's so quiet, I thought . . . Her car's gone. What are you talking about?"

"Laydelle's learned a very hard lesson, but maybe the end results aren't so awful. Our baby's had her wings clipped. My guess is she'll think twice before she tries to fly again."

"She's hurt?"

"A broken arm. And quite a broken car. Amos said it was nose-down in that ditch. Amos said it made him think of an ostrich. A crushed and broken ostrich."

"My God!"

"He was there, Hubb. He was watching over our baby."

His hand was on the doorknob.

"Oh, Hubbell! I forgot to tell you. I have a new hobby."

He blinked and noticed for the first time the midnight-blue circle under his wife's eye. It looked as if someone had lost all patience and given Mary Hanks a real shiner.

"Crystals! I've begun harvesting crystals. It's mad. I simply can't make them fast enough."

chapter 35

1948

Affable, able Hubbell stood braced to gather up old friends who stumbled back from the war. It was nothing for him to put up a pal for weeks or months, for he found he could reproduce aspects of his father's life in miniature. Thus, there was a household staff (smaller) and a private airplane (single-engine). These things equipped him to set up a kind of way station for those temporarily out of luck or out of money. Old acquaintances of his that dated back to Stauffer found a phone call from the train station was all it took for a memorable and sometimes lengthy stay at Hubbell's place. He operated a luxurious veterans' outpost until Mary arrived to announce that this interlude was over. He hadn't known it was an interlude; he considered it his life. For a while, soldiers' tales were told on every landing of Hubbell's town house. Hubbell, still in his bathrobe at 11:00 A.M., drank black coffee with those returned home, glad he had finally found a way to serve his country. His years at Stauffer had been negated, practically stolen from him, with the swift kick in the pants that was his dismissal from OTS. It had taken his breath away. *You aren't officer material. Hell, you're not even war material. You're not fit to wear a uniform, and I don't care whose son you are.* Hubbell and two friends had rounded up some pigs belonging to a neighboring farmer, then pretended they were enemy troops, in a farcical war game that ended Hubbell's military career. He could barely remember the night; additional details were provided in a formal report sent to his family. *Intoxication. Vehicle theft. Deliberate destruction of property.* Hubbell had found a way of retrieving those years after the war. Later, when he had time to weigh what obtaining Mary meant, the demands she made that seemed both hideous and necessary, it was this, the "interlude," he reckoned he missed most. Mary didn't mind everything in the beginning. That came later. Hubbell didn't have to forfeit his travels and trinkets at first, the wandering to places that felt like divisions of his own imagination. No, Mary meant the men had to go. He acquiesced, and it took years before he admitted the loss. It had been a good life, why, the best life he'd ever had, sitting up nights with Al Smith and Park Thompkins to hear how they entered Paris, how the French loved them for the chocolate they carried in their duffel bags. And Al's wide feet. The women stared at his feet as if the war had been won on the strength of size E's.

"But who will lure them back into life, Mary?"

"Somebody else, Babykins. You'll have to close down the commissary if you expect me to live here."

He loved her even in his sleep. He tossed and turned, pricked and punished by a love that kept him seeking her voice, the smooth tips of her small hands, at the most inconvenient hours. At three-fifteen one morning, he rose from sleepless exhaustion and trudged up the stairs to tell Tom Anderson the sad news. Tom Anderson, golden boy at Stauffer and hero of his own tales, lay flat on his back, now a more vulnerable god. Hubbell had never known sleep to be such an undertaking; it took up the whole double bed. Tom was everywhere at once, snoring and tussling, his mouth open and rumbling with messages from some chunk of a dream. Hubbell shook and shook the slumbering lieutenant. By the time Tom woke up, Hubbell was sure it was all a mistake. That Mary didn't understand what it meant to dislodge such a man, to send him back into the world in his present state. It was too late. He was rubbing his eyes.

"Tom, look, I have some terrible news."

Here was the proof. Tom's fist flew into his face. Hubbell didn't have time to dodge the blow or prepare his jaw for what was coming. He tumbled back, striking his head on the bedside table and bringing down a lamp with him.

"I won't go. I won't!"

After his capture by the Germans, Anderson had never really been rescued. Even now, during his "visit," Tom heaved food at the wall, forgetting. His desire to be healed was often obscured as Hubbell fished him out of wading pools in summer courtyards that Anderson mistook for the Rhine, which he would ford until he was free or dead, blasted from the back by a grenade. Hubbell got up carefully, avoiding the shadows. He presented identification gently, in a whisper.

"Tom, Tom. Hang on, friend, it's me."

The soldier came to, just in time. He crawled carefully to the edge of his own bed, peering down at Hubbell.

"Oh, what have I done? Jesus, Hubb."

Maybe Mary was right, after all. Hubbell rubbed his jaw. He moved it laterally, and it popped.

"I'm going to get married, Tom. Soon, too."

Anderson looked happy for a minute, then frowned as he scratched his head.

"Not a Kraut, I hope."

"No, nothing like that. But it means you'll have to go, Tom. A woman can't live with two men."

"Who will take me in?"

"Why, your mother, of course! I've already written to her, and she's got your old bedroom spruced up and waiting."

He didn't take the news well. Anderson crawled under the bed, taking his pillow with him. When he was finally extracted the following day, he didn't thank Hubbell for two and a half months of a generous soldier's leave or the new wardrobe designed for the bathos of civilian life. He hiked his pants up, hoisted the knapsack onto his back and grabbed a banana from a fruit bowl as he marched out the door.

"Mother?"

Lavinia's mouth was tight. She held a piece of the picture puzzle in her hand that simply would not fit anywhere. It was green, the color that always gave her the most trouble. That was where the puzzle people always stopped her in her tracks. With a vast green landscape, leaves melting into grass, grass melting into pools . . .

"May I bother you for a minute?"

"You're already bothering me."

He pulled a chair up close to the table, and she fingered the piece of tricky scenery as he talked.

"Are you feeling well today?"

She rolled her eyes and lifted her hand to scratch a spot on her back. Hubbell noticed she didn't smell fresh or even bathed. It was four o'clock in the afternoon.

"I feel the same as I always feel after roaming around this house all night. Sick and tired. But that's not what you want to hear, is it? You want to hear that I'm feeling chipper, so you can get on with it. What is it, Hubbell? Don't put me through this. Just tell me what it is you want."

She set the piece of cardboard to one side. She supposed it was some detail about the wedding. That girl, that Mary. She simply couldn't wait, and that impatience (not her smile, slapped on a split second too late) hinted at greater indecencies, which would triumph later, after the wedding party was over.

"I wanted to know if—"

He didn't want to know, *she* did. As scarcely as she understood her grown son she did understand this. How he had run a fever from the first day he'd met that little working girl of his. Everything took a back seat to this, an improbable girl's caresses.

"Actually, uh, we wondered if you are sure the reception should be held at the club. We thought perhaps we could just do the reception here. Not *here*, of course, but in the garden."

He was deep red and moist, as if he were holding his breath under water. She didn't particularly feel like saving him. She'd been up and down those stairs in the night. The trips to the kitchen had increased her frenzy. When Joey had finally appeared, hearing her on the stairs, she hissed at him and told him to leave her in peace.

"She really wants it, doesn't she?"

"Wants what, Mother?"

She thought of Cardinal Spellman, her dearly beloved, her chum. He was like a dependable black trench coat lined with something sumptuous. Fur, maybe. She considered his passion for Ecclesiastes and Afghan hounds, for her peacocks and for card games that ran until midnight.

"Your fiancée wants a benediction, a big, bold public okay. Ah, my, my."

She knew she was mean enough to withhold it, but she lacked the energy. Lately she said yes to nearly everything.

"Give it to her, Hubbell."

"She doesn't want to take your garden, Mother. She just wants to *use* it. Mary wants something more comfortable and homey than the club."

"You know so little about women. Oh, you may understand how they feel under your hands, how they look and how they smell. But you haven't got the faintest clue about what's going on under those hats, do you? Or in their hearts. But you'll soon learn, Hubbell, dearest. I've given you my garden, now help me make another. Where does this damn puzzle piece go?"

She died with her dukes up. There was a letter for her husband and another, shorter, for her son. Even and clear, the letters were written as if Lavinia planned to be away for a weekend.

Dear Nelson,

I thought of leaving you something, but what? That stopwatch of Daddy's you always admired? All those maps he collected over the years? No, I told myself. Nelson already has the burden of things. Don't increase his trials. Help him.

How? I started to work on a plan to help you. Even this has been difficult, because of my tiredness, which barely lets me think, so badly do I want to close my eyes each time I start to work on an outline of this letter. Finally I had to stop all that, planning the shape of what I wanted to say. I shall just plunge ahead, then, and hope you find the solace and direction I suppose you'll need when I'm gone.

You must marry Zoe. I can just see you now, turning your head the way you do and snorting like an old bull. But you really must, Nelson. There are many things a younger man can do without appearing ludicrous. You've done them all in the past and gotten by because of your relative youth and station. But those things would be unseemly now. You can't cuddle poor, tired shopgirls and pay for their miserable rooms and little trips to that lodge at Grand Lake without appearing a simplehead who's gone around the bend in old age. And why Zoe, a woman for whom I have no affection? Because she is respectable, that's why. She's gone out in the world and made her living in a way that is both crude and pure. And done it without apology. She has also gone to great lengths to spare me humiliation, and for that I am indebted to Zoe Simply. I suspect my wishes are not hers and she'll be a tough customer. At least on this issue. But I do think your remaining years could be well spent in her company. I hear she tells an amusing story, and of course, when conversation fails, she can steal a topic from those infernal books of hers.

You will have to struggle with our future daughter-in-law on your own. I know her for what she is. She won't be long in carving her own world out of ours. Some of this is good. She must make her place alongside Hubbell by preparing her own garden plot. I urge you to let her build what is hers without destroying what was mine and what remains ours. I overheard her once with Hubb. She was going on about the Lavinia Hanks Circular, the quarterly the girls publish. She saw that as idle flattery to me, and as she spoke I could imagine her setting fire to the whole enterprise. Well, don't allow it. Those women who work for you lead small lives. This professional sorority is no different from the Low Ladies. Singly, alone, we would have drowned in the dreary horror and ennui of those days. Together, we laughed, fought and survived.

As much as I dislike her, Mary is a good thing for our Hubbell. He is lucky to have her. She has passion and energy and if she doesn't turn to plunder will do our son a world of good. I don't know Hubbell well, for I wasn't a good mother to him. But I did see one thing. And that is how he stopped at a certain age. What brought Hubbell to a halt is beyond me. He decided not to become a man at Stauffer, nor afterward. So he just stopped. He grew, of course, and became kind. But he has chosen to remain a boy, and this, though Mary doesn't know it yet, will be the content of her struggle.

I shall miss you. I often wonder if we will sense each other's presence in that cold vault on the hill. I wonder if we weren't mistaken. If, rather, we shouldn't have taken our places in the dry earth, untarnished by coffins and telephone wires and, heavens, food for the hereafter. I'll soon see, and I wonder if, when you follow me there, I will feel your slow familiar breath on my cheek, full, as in the old days, of stories and secrets you imagine I don't already know. My heart was the wisest thing, Nelson.

I shall miss you.

The second letter was composed in a great hurry. She didn't replace the bottle of ink when it ran dry, but instead took up a dull lead pencil.

Oh, Hubbell. Here's one thing I have that I wish I could pass to you. The time to construct one's own ending. I can watch from where I lie as the covers on my bed inch up slowly from my feet. Every day they continue to crawl closer and closer, but not in the fearful way you would imagine. For it is my own warm blanket that will cover me. And because I've had the time to consider it, my death will be as familiar as this blanket once it slips up over my heart and finally my head.

I am struck by the queerness of it. Any other mother would be drowning in remorse by now. For this is the moment when our life spreads out around us and we're free to examine it. All the colors stand out, all the decisions in its design. I see my shortcomings clearly and feel complete detachment from them. Is this a last bit of cleverness on my part or the true root of the poison plant? I don't know, but I could never draw in closer, Hubbell. You sensed it as a child and went round to maids and teachers for all you couldn't have from me. Why, all those Nelson boys practically raised you, didn't they? I not only allowed it, I encouraged it, hoping someone would spring into your path who would nourish you in the way mothers do. I've *wished* for goodness often, and perhaps that isn't enough. Perhaps you must simply march out and get goodness, demand it of yourself rather than merely hoping it will come to you. At any rate, the matter is closed. I can't be now what I never was. But there is something I can do yet.

Your father has cut you off from certain things, Hubbell. Not because he is mean or selfish. But because he is a good bully. A tyrant and a kind of king. He came to a free country, one that no longer exists. And he marked it as surely as the lines on the palm of his own hand. He has prevented you from even trying to do the same thing, and can we blame him? This contract he made you sign is a copyright agreement of his own life. He won't have it done again, by someone else, no matter the someone else is his own son. But there's something he forgot. I saw it first through a small peep-hole of understanding. It widened into certitude. Here, Hubbell, is who you must become once you've gotten on with babies and the rest of it. The family life, I mean to say.

You have his feel for spectacle. Your grand parties on the Missis-sippi! Why, you led packs of friends through the most enchanting days and nights before you met Mary. You are a kind of artist. But why allow it to evaporate into the folly of a social circuit? You have something Nelson doesn't. Your heart yearns, Hubbell. His never did, never. Now I don't quite know how these things in you will marry. I'm struggling with tiredness now and the rushing days. So I can't say or even think further than this. I know that you are free, though it appears otherwise. I know he didn't make you sign a paper surrendering what I've just seen through such a small bright opening.

I did love you, Hubbell, though I wasn't much good at it.

Nelson was enraged. The widower wanted angels in his house.
Joey found one in the Episcopal church the Sunday following Lavinia's death. Catha Willis nodded gravely, certain she understood.
Besides, there was college to pay for, and the extra money would
help. The soloist in the church choir began to appear midmornings,
and not with a sturdy golden halo. She pulled up in the back seat
of Nelson's black limousine. She would quietly open her hymnal in
Nelson's sunroom, smile sweetly, and sing until lunch. Catha was
an honest girl, who was engaged to be married. When Nelson
insisted that even songbirds needed supper, she demurred, citing studies or her waistline. Whatever would keep the tippling
mourner at bay. Nelson was lonelier than he ever would have
wagered, and the girl's steady resistance just made matters worse.
Hung over, his head throbbing, he fired Catha Willis one day and
screamed *Where are you, Vinnie*, as she ran out his front door. He
was enraged by his dead wife's attempt to commandeer the rest of
his days and by the partisanship in a letter to which he couldn't
reply.

Hubbell was quickly becoming realigned, not by the shadows
and mysteries of a last letter, but by the prospect of a new marriage, which would soon be ticking and under way, ominous as a
bomb. Either man could have soldered something out of those
messages and didn't. Instead, it was Joey Fujii who went immediately to work with what was left him. Joey's message was not a
memorandum, nor was it twilit by a dying woman's dim impressions. No, in fact Lavinia had risen with difficulty from her bed to
write her last letter. She had put on a silk suit, cursing the white
pearl buttons, so difficult to master, exhausted as she was. She
phoned her lawyer and a notary from the bedroom, telling them of
her intent, and then she got on with it. The last letter. The last
thing she would fight to control. She removed the heavy ring. Her
fingers were swollen, and it didn't come off without a struggle.

TO JOEY FUJII, WHO HAS WIPED THE SPITTLE FROM MY MOUTH
    And so much more, I know. I was a wretched old woman at the
end. Was I always? Spoiled, certainly, and wanting my own way
whatever time of night or day. I have no remorse, for I needed you,
and if I wasn't pretty or polite while you were in my service, surely
I wasn't the worst employer. I am not asking your forgiveness here.
Someone said that Japanese are Christians. I never asked, but if
you are, you would know the line about turning the other cheek.

Why do I bring this up? To make sure you know this is not what I am doing as I turn toward home.

I am settling my accounts. No more, no less. You have driven me from here to hell. You have taken my rage in stride, my rage and foolishness. I've learned the expressions on your face quite well, though you've worked hard to conceal everything. I know what it cost you, listening to my foul and furious arguments, never batting an eye over the numerous stupidities of an unhappy woman. I can't give you back your sleep, but I can do this.

Do seek advice. You have lived on a wage for all these years, and this money can be increased if you seek appropriate guidance.

I am sorry about one thing. The Dutch clogs. They made you look like a monkey. But believe me, they made Lavinia Hanks look far, far worse.

He sewed the letter from Lavinia Hanks inside the pocket of a black serving jacket, which would hang in whatever closet belonged to Joey then or on any day that ever followed. He put the money in a bank, not Nelson's but another, with superior interest rates. It wasn't to stay there long, but short-term interest on fifty thousand dollars wasn't a negligible amount.

Later, Hubbell guessed his mother had been correct. He didn't now, nor would he ever, know what was going on under Mary's wide hat.

"Happy, darling?"

"Mmmm."

Her eyes flashed from under the brim of rose-tinted straw. It hung so delightfully down to shield his bride's shining face from the sun. Married Mary Hanks downed glass after glass of champagne. Hubbell had been on the wagon for over a year. He sipped a Punch Royale and nibbled little cakes as Mary settled on her guests like a pollinating bee.

He was proud of her for shouldering such a burden with him. For helping him through what he regarded as his first adult sorrow with such tenderness, even expertise. For Mary went on nearly alone with the wedding plans, leaving Hubbell to care for his father and help with the necessary arrangements. It was clearheaded Mary who determined that the wedding should go on according to schedule. That a proper mourning period for Lavinia Hanks had been observed and it was time to go on with living. Mary said his mother would have wanted it that way. Hubbell was overcome by her bravery. She stood momentarily alone under a willow tree at the end of a gravel path. He made his way over to her, squeezing hands and exchanging pleasantries along the way until he got to Mary. He toyed with the brim of her hat like a child fiddling with a closed curtain. Her eyes were strangely dull, and he cursed his own stupidity. How had he ever imagined his bride was unaffected by his mother's death? Did he suppose her a robot or a silly wind-up toy? He kissed her cheek briskly.

"Thank you."

"Whatever for?"

"For being so strong and knowing so much. Thank you for marrying me."

"Silly goose."

She said that firmly, and he bent his head for the kiss he was sure would follow.

"And, Mary?"

She lifted her chin slightly.

"Thank you for knowing how to begin. I didn't. I didn't have the vaguest notion."

He meant the men, the banished soldiers. The upper rooms in Hubbell's house had been aired for days after they left, swept clean until there was no sign of sick or hobbled warriors returned home to consort with Hubbell. She had brought a halt to it, the construction of a proper ending to their war, which, they discovered through the sadness of stories, hadn't been completed by a nation's victory. Hubbell saw that now the rooms stood empty and waiting for them, Mary and Hubbell Hanks. They would fill them with small children and friends they would make together. Only their stories would end the war, making it a final and closed-off thing.

"I'll have another drink. Sweetheart."

Under the rose-colored hat loaded with silk flowers and the proper dose of satin ribbon, Mary Hanks stood hating heliotrope. She saw how mistaken she'd been not to have it ripped right out. The little clump of marigolds stood isolated at the base of a bird-bath. Wrong, she thought, tapping her foot under the willow tree and watching guests weave in and out of the throng on the wide green lawn. She thought of handing them lengths of crepe paper, for their movements suggested a gang of children about to decorate the maypole. Mary Hanks bit her lip as she waited for Hubbell to return with a glass of champagne.

Mary's triumph was incomplete. Lavinia Hanks had surrendered her garden, her green grove and scores of azaleas, just now exploding in a continuous racket of red alongside the house. And then she begged off, stood up the guest of honor in a flamboyant show of bad manners. Her heart failed, and Mary shook her head at the transparency of it. She died right on schedule, and nobody but Mary Hanks saw how this was true. How she saved up dying out of meanness. She could have done it anytime, with her picture puzzles and life of Riley. Her rich and ornery sequestration could have stretched out over years, not weeks. She didn't have to die *then*, three weeks before her son was to marry. But she did, dying in a quick and quiet spectacle designed to blot out the one that would follow, the one she never wanted in the first place. Oh, Mary knew that kind of will—the kind that would have its way, but indirectly. By twists and turns that no one saw were nasty and selfish. Mary put both hands on her hat and pushed. Thank heavens she had a focus. Thank heavens she could think of Wishbone Harris, who had responded warmly to their proposal about the Toni Twins and Hanks Petroleum. Lavinia Hanks couldn't ruin everything, then. Here came Hubbell.

Mary shifted her weight, leaned hard on her left leg. Hubbell cheered as he marched up the front path.

"Here, love. Better watch how many of these you drink. With all the excitement, it could go to your head."

Mary drank deeply and wiped her upper lip with her forefinger.

"What excitement?"

"Funny one! This . . ." He opened his arm, and just as he did, Mary saw the little Adams boy yank a ribbon from his sister's hair. She lifted her foot and would have given him a swift kick had he not pushed her off balance first.

Mary got started, and at first it was incomprehensible, low like the blurry murmur of several people talking at once. But Mary was talking all at once, and several voices, surprising ones, seemed to spill from her tight red mouth. The brim of the hat began to flutter softly as she spoke.

"Peacocks, those precious peacocks of hers! Who suggested such a thing? A death mantle of peacock feathers. Why, who decided that Lavinia Hanks should be entombed like Nefertiti in the first place, way up on the hill? Only queens have the right, Hubbell. Only queens."

Hubbell covered her shoulders with his arm.

"Please."

She swept his arm away and continued, not minding that the pattern was gone. She sensed that her thoughts were disorderly, that she was not making the proper argument she could have, if Hubbell would only, if they would only . . . oh, she didn't know exactly, but none of that was important. Mary Hanks had thick and angry things to say. She said and said, as Hubbell seemed to shrink beside her, his brand-new bride.

"That sorority of hers. Now what does that mean? She didn't start this oil company. Your daddy did, so I don't see why all the fuss. Why they all meet like that once a month, sing songs like that once a month. Oh, I swear, the way they acted at her funeral. It was shameless! I was embarrassed, and you should have been."

She paused to catch her breath and right her hat, which had been slipping all along.

"Hubbell?"

He'd never known a word, a sound, could contain such derision. That a name could become an accusation.

"We didn't get a telegram from Harry Truman."

"But, Mary, we didn't die! All we did was get married."

He was afraid she might cry, but she didn't. Instead, Mary Hanks seemed magically to coagulate out there under the sweeping tree. All her features slowly settled into an expression of pure intent.

"Why, of course, Hubbell. That's the answer to my question."

"Which one?"

"This one: What excitement? All we did was get married."

And Mary Hanks turned her back to him, heading down the path toward her guests.

chapter 36

1950

Everybody knew death was partial to pairs, so that wasn't why they were angry. They knew Nelson had to die shortly after Lavinia. But a public man had demanded a private funeral, and it galled them. Most people were infuriated by the service and came away sorry they'd gone in the first place. They arrived in fantastic numbers the morning of the funeral, and when the Lovely church filled and overflowed, they stood outside in a meek, accepting herd that only began to be otherwise at the grave site, when they realized they'd been duped. The mass of people showed up at the plot, hoping to be fed and fueled with some final message passed on by the oil man's surviving friends and family. If not, they wanted entertainment. They didn't get that, either.

Zoe Simply was in mufti. She was dressed in a matronly dark-gray wool suit. Heavy, cantilevered breasts made her look more like a piece of aging architecture than a mistress in mourning. If she cried, no one saw her tears. She didn't hang back, but she didn't approach the family. She stood near his grave while the sorry little preacher from Creston mumbled a few inane things about a man who had successfully blown life into Oklahoma for the past fifty years.

It wasn't that the right people didn't appear; it was that they didn't speak. Somebody said Nelson designed the whole thing and deposited the outline for his funeral with his lawyers the moment his wife died. "I have attended enough circuses in my lifetime," it led off. Included in the things he didn't want were eulogies. So people caught sight of celebrities and statesmen, all the important people they had hoped to see. But Nelson had issued some kind of gag order, and most people felt gypped. No speeches, no grandeur . . . just a fresh-faced preacher who presided over some church of the frozen chosen out in Iowa. Too young to have ever known Nelson, too immaculate to bless someone as big, boisterous and dead as Nelson Hanks. He was soft-spoken. Some people in the back of the crowd couldn't even hear him and left early.

The Jap was supposed to show up, but he didn't. Now that would have been worth squeezing into dress shoes for. Seeing him pull up in a big car, maybe even with a chauffeur of his own. They'd heard little about Fujii since he'd left the country for Kyoto, only that he'd built some kind of private temple to Buddha. Thinking of Fujii sitting far away in his privileged digs, doing nothing but staring at a statue or counting his money when he should have been there paying homage, so distressed certain members of the American Legion that they left early, too. Later, the sight of the private cortege passing by Legion headquarters didn't help matters any. Nelson's mourners were by then soused, and the slow black auto show only underscored their exclusion from a proper expression of sorrow. Only five cars left Lovely for the Hanks ranch, where Uncle Nelson would be solemnly, privately filed away next to his wife. Veterans of foreign wars, bow-legged roustabouts and tool dressers, geologists and crippled aviators, cowboys and Indians, duly elected presidents of bonsai clubs and town halls and tiny countries moored somewhere in the middle of the Pacific Ocean, plus all the gathered others who could have flooded the whole town with their tears, beat their hollow chests instead. A leader had not only abandoned them; he had sneaked off.

The only spectacle, if it could have been called that, was reserved for the hushed rotunda of the Hanks mausoleum. Mary Hanks had a hissy fit. It began in a low whisper, then echoed out from the dead center of that private cold-storage center. Something had just occurred to Mary as she studied the setup. The little preacher from Iowa had a few solid, simple things to say about entry into the next life. He still needed to speak up, even there in the cramped rotunda.

". . . and we must mark his passage in the only way we can."

Mary pinched her husband. She hadn't meant to do it so hard. The pinch left the tiniest blue notch on his arm.

"Who's Hank Hanks?"

"That was my twin. He died almost at birth."

"Hubbell, why didn't you *tell* me you had a baby brother? Did your dad have this thing built right away after he died?"

"No; it came years after."

"So they sort of had the baby on ice for years and then what?"

"Then they exhumed his little body."

The preacher was soft-spoken enough to be sensitive about it. It wasn't that he wouldn't raise his voice. He couldn't raise it, which meant he held people's attention any way he could. He watched Hubbell Hanks and his bride. The two of them chattered like magpies, as if he didn't exist at all.

"In keeping with Nelson Hanks' notorious modesty, he declined attention even at the end of his life."

That did it. Nelson Hanks modest? All eyes turned to him, and the assembled wondered who dug this preacher up in the first place. The Osage present were deeply ashamed and expected the lid of the coffin to fly open any minute. Surely their friend wouldn't allow this to go on much longer. A Hanks company man checked his watch pointedly. Mary got back to work.

"So there's his plaque, and there's your mother's next to the space with your father's name. I don't see one with your name."

"It's not a parking lot, Mary. It's a mausoleum. Sssh."

Hubbell's stomach was turning. There wasn't any fresh air in here, and no one had thought to leave the door ajar. A mere inch would have helped his throbbing head and rocking, rolling stomach. The weight of his legacy had begun to fall and fall heavily. The sole survivor was beginning to sense just what he had survived.

"If I were you, Hubb, I'd look into it. The mere hint of it being otherwise is a scandal."

The preacher wouldn't let up. He'd been given a journal, and Hubbell wondered who'd passed him that. One of his father's lawyers, probably. Maybe old Tucker had a whole basement full of his father's writings.

"Before we say a final goodbye to this giant of the oil industry, let me just read my favorite passage in this business journal dated

1933. Nelson begins his day as he does any other. 'Woke from a sleep deeper than death, then showered and shaved and ran for the 9:03 to Saint Louis. Art Goebel spreading the word about Hanks Petroleum by the time I arrived. Each of those letters written in the sky was reported to have been one mile high, though seen from the ground they became almost inconsequential, one letter breaking up just as Art began the next. Watching those letters of dubious dimension vanish was a good lesson for me. Every man needs to recall his own mortality so that he can *be* with more vitality and precision than ever.' "

That seemed to satisfy the preacher. He folded the paper he read from and let the pallbearers get on with it. He was pleased that the words stilled the small group of people, for he had bucked Uncle Nelson by slipping in the subtlest eulogy of all, the kind the dead assemble themselves before leaving. He could catch his plane for Des Moines, having placated both the living and the deceased. He tipped his head to the side. There was a stirring toward the back of the small room.

"Hubbell, you shouldn't have to jockey for position, at least not here. Your father did a grand job of excluding you from many things, but you should at least rest assured that your body will one day lie next to his. It's the smallest thing."

Hubbell's stomach had begun a whole series of complaints, and now his entire body pitched from side to side, though he hadn't moved an inch. There was nothing momentarily to lend him balance. Because of that, when he shouted at his little bride inside such holy quarters, it wasn't Mary who reeled back in surprise. It was Hubbell.

"Shut up, Mary! Do you hear me? Close your face, you indecent bitch, before I close it for you. *The old man is dead!*"

The Osage chief nodded his head approvingly, while Mary smoothed down the front of her dress as if she had been sitting, not standing. Her wide, clear eyes stayed that way, and she moved forward to shake hands with the preacher and thank him for coming all this long, long way. The women present in the group instantly gained a terror of Mary that would remain intact through years of clubs and tentative car pools. One woman later remarked to another inside the safety of a parked car that Mary had smoothed down the front of her dress like that to hide her balls. This comment grew to legend in Lovely, and certain women turned crimson as Mary marched into a P.T.A. meeting or crashed a schoolboard hearing, carefully stroking the front of her rumpled skirt before taking an empty chair.

1967

Mary was stirring a big pot of something over a low fire. It wasn't burning, but she was. Hot, it was so hot in the kitchen. She sighed and sank her hand into a bowl of coarse salt, pitching a fistful into the cast-iron pot. She listened to the tick of high heels coming her way.

"Who said you could borrow my stockings?"

"You haven't even looked up. How do you know what's on my legs?"

"I can hear what's on your legs. Swish, swish. You're wearing the one pair of silk stockings I own, which I have managed to safeguard for over two months. This stew needs something. Here, have a taste."

She threw in another handful of salt and continued stirring. Hubbell knew better than to get his hopes up. The kitchen had grown fragrant, but Hubbell had been tricked too many times to believe in good smells coming from Mary's concoctions.

"Not that I mind you borrowing my things, but you should ask. Where are you going, again?"

"To see the Fifth Dimension."

"What a glorious name for a group. Is there some Hollywood agency in charge of naming groups? I wonder. The Fifth Dimension. I really, really like that. Can they sing at all?"

She stopped stirring to look at her daughter. Laydelle chewed slightly at her upper lip, and her smile began to fade.

"You're so beautiful, Baby. Jeez."

The phrase was familiar by now. It was the beginning of a chant that had begun when Laydelle turned sixteen. Her mother's raw assessments embarrassed her. They contained strangely little envy. In fact, the cold measurement of her daughter's youth and beauty didn't seem maternal at all. Mary Hanks looked at her daughter as she would at anything with an intriguing shape or structure. Mary Hanks looked at her the way boys did, even smacking her lips on occasion.

"You're weird, Mother. You're just too weird for words."

She poured herself a glass of iced tea and drank it standing up.

"I'm skipping dinner. I'll just grab a bite there."

"Nonsense. You've got a nervous stomach because you're about to enter the fifth dimension. I may be weird, but I still see to it my family is nourished. Here. Hubbell, put that down. Supper's ready."

Hubbell laid the paper down, the lost-and-found section he habitually read as other men sought the sports section. He looked at the bowl Mary set in front of him, his fears confirmed. The stew was undercooked. He could tell by the neat shape of the beef cubes.

"I have ideas. God, I've got so many ideas, and that's the trouble. I'm a victim of my own expectations. This place is burning up! Dig in, everyone."

She threw open every window, while Hubbell and Laydelle chewed her meat.

"And I'll find a platform for them someday. The Fifth Dimension. How about naming a band the Brown Dwarves, now that musicians are such eggheads? I heard about that one on the *Today* show. Celestial objects too small to get their nuclear fires started. They can't become true stars. Get it? The right sweet-faced musician gets hold of the right idea, and the Beatles happen all over again. My head is splitting. Have a nice evening, Laydelle. Your mother is going to bed."

She paused and remarked, almost appreciatively, "That skirt just barely covers your fanny."

Laydelle came into the kitchen and cracked her gum one more time for good measure, then tossed it in the trash. It had lost all its flavor.

"Where is everybody?"

Hubbell's fund-raising efforts for the navigation project kept his schedule erratic, now that he was finally working selflessly for Oklahoma. Civic saints could never be called to task. When Laydelle once griped to her mother that no one was ever home anymore, Mary sang a loud and off-key version of "I Gotta Be Me."

"Everybody is right here lookin' at you, even though it's four thirty-five and I'm gonna miss my bus."

"What's the deal, Aresta?"

"That's what I'd like to ask you. What's the deal? Looks like there's been a party here I didn't get invited to. Found this little-bitty balloon under your bed, child."

She turned and produced one of Mary Hanks' sweet pink dessert plates. But what lay in the middle of the plate was not a petit four or an iced cake. Aresta wasn't even offering her a Morton's honey bun, their usual afternoon snack. A used condom was pitifully displayed on Mary's favorite china.

"Sit there in that sorry chair and don't say a word till I'm done. Tone-A Chair, Tone-A Chair. My aching back. If I wanted to sit on a stick of wood, I'd be in a tree."

She lifted herself from the Thonet chair and threw the plate in the trash, then washed her hands with great ceremony. She took a long time wiping her hands on the dish towel.

"Cat got your tongue? Well, I've still got mine, so just sit there and listen. It's not enough I've got to find a sack of marijuana in the toe of a dress shoe, is it? You got to leave me *this* trick-or-treat under your bed. What kind of pig is it that leaves something like this under her bed for someone else to find?"

"Aresta, God! I thought I threw it away. I mean, I thought he took care of it or something. You act like I put it there just to insult you or something! God! It was an accident."

"This isn't my job! I am in charge of cleaning this house and taking my bus home. My job is not teaching a sixteen-year-old how to respect her own people and the place where she lives. My job is not teaching about female internal equipments and what a female's not supposed to do just because it all works! That's somebody else's job. *I am getting my hat.*"

But Aresta didn't get her hat or coat. She didn't move a muscle or bat an eye, because she was too busy thinking. She was thinking about love, about the special brand of love she suffered because of this damned family. It was love of the foolish and the weak, the kind her pastor talked about. Her feet hurt, but she didn't take off her shoes. She was too busy thinking about Mary Hanks, who would have a seizure if she knew. She thought about Hubbell, who would just blink and ask her to repeat the whole thing.

"Now then. Do you love him?"

"Kind of. A little."

"Enough to marry and make babies with if the balloon pops one day?"

"God, Aresta!"

"Answer me."

"No way! I'm too young to be a mother."

"Then you're too young to be having private parties in your bedroom, child. What if that gadget don't work?"

"Then I don't know. I get an abortion or something. Besides, they always work."

She stood up, banging her knee on the table as she did.

"Shit! Just because you found something in my room doesn't mean I have to listen to all this. I can't take this lecture."

"Siddown."

She did and began biting her thumbnail.

"Take your hand out of your mouth. Here's how I see it. The enemy in this house is time. You've got too much of it, and we're gonna fix that now."

Aresta folded her hands and appeared serene, though inside she was seething as she thought of the bus pulling up to her stop without her. The work that was waiting at home would still be waiting whenever she got there.

"Pick an activity out of a hat, so we can settle this."

"What do you mean?"

"I mean something you'd like to do after school. Some team, some club that meets in the afternoons."

"This is really dumb."

"Pick."

"I wanted to be on the newspaper staff, you know. I didn't get picked."

"I wanted to be the queen of England, but life is adjustments."

Aresta turned deep-brown, disparaging eyes toward Mary Hanks' kitchen window, filled with jars of salt and sugar crystals.

"Seem like your mama wants to be a rock scientist herself, but she isn't wasting time if it don't happen. I got an idea for you, honey."

She opened a section of the newspaper. A local department store was running a contest, and the winner would "flirt with fame" in an interview with the Ford Agency.

"Modeling, now, that's the thing for you. That way you could get your ticket out without spending a dime."

If anything hindered the sound advice Aresta had to offer, it was her prejudice that the best place was never where you were at the moment. The enemy was not only time but geography. Boys would not be pigs in Chicago or New York. Friends were truer elsewhere, and money—why, pots of it waited in any number of American cities.

"Why are you always talking about leaving home, Aresta? I don't want to go anywhere. I just want to be with my friends."

Aresta stood up now and did get her hat on. She picked up her coat and the pile of newspapers to line the cages of several pink and red songbirds, who needed her, too. This poor child wasn't the only one. She sighed.

"Don't tell me there's more than one. No. Don't tell me more than I've already heard with my ears and seen with my eyes. Tell me one thing, though, before I leave."

"What?"

"Was I here? Was that going on just over my head?"

Laydelle pressed a cuticle back. She had nearly lost sight of the pale white moon on her little finger. She didn't answer.

"Lord, Lord."

Laydelle made a face and watched Aresta walk heavily out the door.

"Your pop left you a note, but I must of washed it. Check the pants that's in the dryer. Never mind that newspaper staff. Nobody believes what they read anyhow."

Laydelle moved to the best part of the kitchen, the part filled with a pair of lumpy easy chairs, upholstered in a practical, Scotch-garded textile, and a wooden coffee table stained by years of dripping cups and sweating glasses. If she peered past the birdcage that hung in the window, Laydelle could manage the guarded river view she preferred. The calm and partial section of water stirred her more than the front-porch panorama. She took great comfort in the kitchen alcove, the screeching parrot that waited for peanuts and crackers just as she waited for the dishevelment of night and the reappearance of the two people who would soon fill the empty house.

c h a p t e r 3 7

1969

Laydelle watched her mother cry. Mary Hanks succumbed to the track of every tear that fell as if it were the tip of a lusty tongue sliding down her cheek. Her chest swelled as she took a deep breath. She shuddered slightly.

"I am so honored. It's a marvelous thing to receive a letter like this."

Another sigh. Mary folded the letter reverently and tucked it into the pocket of her jacket.

"We'll let them know this week."

"Let them know what, Mother?"

"Get on the train, Baby. We'll let them know you *accept* their acceptance. That you'll be going to Smith in the fall."

"Except that I'm not."

Mary banged her fist on the table.

"Lower your voice."

Hers had dropped to a whisper. It was as if the admissions committee had assembled just outside the kitchen door. Aresta scrubbed her copper even harder.

"We did not apply to Smith out of curiosity. We applied to the most prestigious women's college in the United States because we wanted to go. Or have you forgotten that, Laydelle? What has gotten into you lately?"

"All my friends are going to Norman."

" 'All my friends.' You can certainly make more friends where you're going. I have nothing against Sarah and Cindy, but they're settling for the state of Oklahoma when they could have so much more. If their parents tolerate that kind of parochialism, it's their business. This family is going to Smith."

"All of us? It might be a tight squeeze in that dormitory room."

Mary struck a match, hunched over and cupping her hand to protect the flame as if a strong wind were blowing. She got the cigarette lit, took a deep, short puff and pointed her finger at Laydelle.

"There, that's exactly what I mean! Where will you find what you need in Norman? Wit like that would float right over the heads assembled in Norman. Norman, Norman. Just listen to the sound of it. Does that make you think of a stimulating, intellectual college town? I think of a balding man with a can of beer in his hand. Now. Aren't you ashamed?"

Mary Hanks was backing out of the kitchen, with car keys in her hand.

"Laydelle, they offer fencing. I saw it in their catalogue—a picture of two women lunging at each other with masks. Stop thinking about missing Sarah and Cindy, why don't you, and think about that! Oh, they're sweet girls, but you're meant to outdistance them, and you might as well own up to your own qualities."

By now the tears had dried on Mary's cheeks, and Laydelle thought she might have imagined them.

"I've changed my mind about the time frame. I want a draft of the letter to Smith on my desk by tonight."

"Mom!"

"That's right. I am your mom, and one day you'll thank me for the little turning signal I've given you today. You'll meet the finest people up there, the very finest young people. Aresta, you talk sense to her. I'm late as it is."

Laydelle waited until the garage door had open and closed, her mother's tires had screeched off down the street. Aresta kept polishing, even though her arms ached. There was a little something she had to rub out completely before she could leave the pan in peace.

"Just sit. Don't say a word till I'm done."

She finished and sat down across from Laydelle.

"You go on and write that letter now, like she says. You'll be better off up there. Used to be you and me could just sit with a crossword and work things out that way. Well, you're big enough that I can talk straight, so listen. Ain't gonna be nuthin' left here in a few years. It won't stay like this forever, and I'll tell you why. Your daddy is busy spinnin' his wool, honey, and your mom's been spinnin' for years now. But they ain't spinnin' nuthin' together, not scarves, not shawls, not bed blankets for old age, and you'll just be stuck in the sadness if you don't git. Git on the train, like your mom says. She's right."

"I hate her. She's a bitch, and I hate her."

Aresta, rising slow as a loaf, stood over her.

"Hush! You talk about her like she's dirt on a shoe. Well, she's not; she's your mom. And she's lookin' to save your round behind some way, somethin' I don't see nobody else around here doin'. This ship's goin' down, and your mama's tossed you a life raff."

Aresta, strong arms crossed, waited for a retraction. There was none. "Smith. That anywhere near Saint Louis?"

Hubbell was happy, too. He thought it was a fine place to go to school, and he couldn't imagine his girl getting into much trouble that first tentative, hardworking year. He drove through the gates one afternoon in a red Mercedes, joyfully honking the horn. Aresta came out of the house first, thinking it was the yardman's wife blowing her horn again when Aresta had said don't. She pulled one of several dish towels out of the side pocket of her apron and mopped her face. The red meant trouble, but she didn't know yet what kind.

"Daddy, I love it! Can I take it for a drive?"

Laydelle was wearing very short cutoffs and the top of a bikini. She had been holding her face between the open sides of a tinfoil sun reflector, and a pair of almond-shaped metal sunglasses was poised on the tip of her pink nose.

"As soon as you put something on your feet. Congratulations, honey."

"You mean it's mine?"

Hopping on one foot and clapping her hands, Laydelle felt her shoulder caught suddenly in a firm grip.

"Hold it, Baby."

"Okay, okay. I'll change first, Mother. Oh, I'm so excited! Oooh, a shift. I always have trouble with reverse."

"I'll teach you to put it in reverse. It's nothing."

"Nobody's going anywhere in that car."

"Why, Mary? It's a graduation present for our daughter."

"Choose another. She is not driving to Smith in that car. Hubbell, I'm shocked. Your taste is still in your mouth, and after all these years."

Aresta could move fast when she had to. She disappeared inside, having been right about red. Laydelle's glasses slipped the tiniest bit farther down the end of her nose. She slid her hands into back pockets and looked at her mother's new navy-trimmed shoes to avoid her eyes.

"Smith is about battered family station wagons. It's about heirloom tablecloths and a string of good pearls and the slightly worn edge that is the *real* mark of confidence and breeding. Why, Smith is about summer jobs on the Cape and gardening gloves, houses that could stand a fresh coat of paint. Smith is about worn rugs and Baccarat crystal. Don't you see? Smith is about must!"

Hubbell looked completely stricken. Laydelle settled her feet into a pair of high-heeled, razzle-dazzle slings. She towered over her mother.

"You're the one who should go to Smith, Mom."

Laydelle's thick, matted hair was sliding out of its silver clasp. The white horizontal line across her sunburned nose showed it was allergy season.

"Smith, Smith, Smith! I'm sick and tired of hearing what I'm supposed to do when I get there, who I'm supposed to meet when I get there. You act like it's going to be a great big party, Mom! I'd like to know when I'm going to have time to party. I'm going to have to work like a dog so I don't flunk out. I'm going to be buried alive under a stack of books! Smith is about must, just like you said. The must in the stupid library. Daddy, give me the keys to my car."

She turned, and more hair fell. Mary grabbed the keys from Hubbell and dropped them into her purse.

"Laydelle, you're an honor student. You're going to flourish like a hothouse orchid finally transported to the jungle, right where it belonged in the first place."

She took her sunglasses all the way off, and even Mary became a little nervous at the sight of such eyes.

"The jungle. The horseshit you come up with, the total horseshit, is just unbelievable. But since we're talking geography, you might read *Newsweek* this week to bring yourself up to date. Ivy League schools want kids from places like Tulsa so they can brag about a cross-section."

She marched up the stairs, her strong back braced for her mother's retorts, her father's mumbled apologies and the sound of a Mercedes rolling out of the driveway to be returned as if it were a pair of gloves or a hat.

"Go on and belittle yourself, Laydelle. It doesn't matter. I know who you are. I know you're a bright, capable girl. You've just got the jitters is all."

"Why are you sending me to Siberia? What did I do to you? I'm going to freeze my ass off up there."

She continued to mount the stairs, slipping out of her high heels as she did. She hurled them to the top of the stairs.

"Plus it's a million miles away and I'll never get to see my friends, which probably suits you just fine."

"Laydelle, we will pretend this conversation never happened. You're not talking sense at all."

"And who would want to go to an all-girls school? They're probably all lesbians! It'll serve you right if I turn into a dyke!"

Laydelle slammed the door to her room. There was a moment of silence, then this floated in the open window so that Aresta, a black tower of sorrow for all this family could have been, heard:

"Get our child a Volvo, Hubbell. Dark green with tan interior and no electric windows. A bright-red Mercedes, what were you thinking of? Goddamn you for all the trouble you make in this house."

Her freshman adviser fought her emotions. This was her first year, too, at the august institution, and she was wise enough to understand that such fascination for the handsome girl and her dark, cluttered mind was inopportune and unwise. So she stifled what rose in her as she watched Laydelle's struggles that first year. But just barely. Mindy Adamson told her she might come to her office anytime with any problem, no matter what sort. Her door banged open at least twice a week. The fuming, confused beauty flopped down in the chair nearest hers, and Mindy stopped typing.

"Ever had anyone drop out the second month?"

"Hi, Laydelle. Oh, sure. At Cornell I even had a no-show. One girl just took the money and ran. Her clothes arrived, but she didn't. Her parents finally found her in Fort Lauderdale, and what a mess that was. You're not planning on going to the beach, are you, Laydelle?"

She looked just like a gypsy to Mindy Adamson. Laydelle, with glittering gold hoops in her ears and dark hair spouting fiercely from a knotted scarf at the top of her head, was not of her band. She had always thought the female world was divided into two categories, those who looked good in cheap clothing and those who didn't. If Mindy didn't wear a crisp, classic cut, she looked like a sow. And she thought that was a great shame, because it didn't match what ranted and raved inside her heart.

"No. But I don't understand a word in class or out of class. Linguistics, God!"

"I warned you about her. She's brilliant, and we're lucky to have her. But celebrity professors are sometimes difficult to follow. I know some of this must shock you. But only as much as it does me and not one bit more."

The girl was tapping her lips with a gold pen.

"What do you mean?"

"I mean I'm from Minnesota, and not Saint Paul, either. I got to Cornell by the skin of my teeth, and nothing has ever come easily to me. I have to work very, very hard here."

"Mindy, you don't understand."

"Then help me understand by talking."

"My roommate's father is a physicist. Her mother is a book editor! You people designed an independent study for her in something I can't even pronounce, and I want to know how I got into this place. I'm a national merit nothing, and I want to know!"

God, she had fallen in love. Mindy pulled out a roll of candy mints and offered her one. Laydelle crunched the mint loudly as she talked. Astonishingly, there were no tears. She even cracked up nicely, with new slashes of bright red across her cheeks and bright, bright eyes.

"Why do you distrust us so much?"

"Who said that?"

"You. You seem bent on proving how disqualified you are. How wrong we were to accept you in the first place. The oversight speaks out, or so it seems. You're a curious young woman, Laydelle. Have you never considered your own record?"

"My grades? Of course I have good grades! I'm from Oklahoma, and there's no reason why—"

"We should penalize you on the basis of geography. I've got my job cut out for me. I have to convince Laydelle Hanks that she was properly admitted to Smith, that she has something we want."

"What?!"

She spit the word out. For that was the issue. She looked at plodding, earnest Mindy Adamson and begged her to come clean.

"Your ferocity, for one thing."

They squared off for a minute to study each other. Laydelle thought of how her mother would melt at the sight of such fine, blond, carefully combed hair and such *appropriate* clothing, one of Mary Hanks' favorite words.

"You'll make a remarkable student, Laydelle, if you'll just let yourself. Smith is a fine haven for an oddball, believe me. You're looking at one."

Mindy Adamson saved her neck, and four years later, when Laydelle was finishing her senior year, when there was talk about Mindy and a young transfer from Idaho, she would race to her defense, saying in a final way that there could have been one million occasions for that kind of crap. One million, due to the kind of timid, insecure freshman she had been, and not a single impropriety had ever been uttered, no, nothing of the sort. Mindy had held a door wide open for her, and Laydelle's only disillusion, if it could have been called that, was that the door couldn't remain open forever and ever. That Smith, where ferocity was properly honored, offered only a temporary asylum.

chapter 38

1972

"What's that?"

A question she had asked over and over, in homes other than the one she was in. Something was tacked up everywhere in this one. A notice, a bulletin, a newspaper clipping. Information seemed to hold the bewitching little nest together.

"An oboe, goof. Mom plays for fun."

Mom plays for fun. It was a variation, but only one and on the same theme, which seemed to be ardor, for the sake of it, no holds barred. Laydelle Christmased and Thanksgivinged in places just like this, with pipe-smoking, bearded men peering solemnly through telescopes or doing experiments in basements they had paneled themselves the summer before they went to Rome or Sardinia or an island off the coast of Georgia to study the dialect. Laydelle, in velvet and close-collared, not Episcopalian but sympathetic to its canticles, held it all as tightly as she could. The passions of her friends' parents proved Mindy Adamson correct. Smith was a fine haven for oddballs. Oddballs that had sprung from oddballs. She crouched in marshes, accepting spyglasses with thanks, as she bird-watched with a full set of towheaded Brattons in Maine. Then Laydelle, no longer able to forestall the inevitable, invited a roommate home.

"All the way to Oklahoma? A houseboat? You must be kidding. Great! Oh, wait until I tell my brother. He loves navigation, and he'll be so jealous."

"My father's houseboat doesn't go anyplace."

"Oh, don't niggle. We'll have a great time. Of course I'll come!"

It became a way of seeing, and the first time Laydelle sensed that her very own life was vivid or remarkable was when a friend was injected into its midst. A friend from Montpelier or Framingham fed a fine spray of bubbles into something otherwise flat and full of unbearable grays and browns. Even Lovely became more so with an out-of-towner.

"You really *don't* get it, do you, Laydelle? Poor goof. Anybody would give their eyeteeth to be a part of this, and you hang your head when you talk about it. God, it's like a scene from *Giant* or something."

"What's *Giant?*"

"You are joking, aren't you? The movie? James Dean? Knock, knock."

Her friend Libby, a western buff who had never been West before, tapped the side of her skull.

"Want to trade, Lib? My life for yours, and I'll trade you any day."

"I really don't see what you're talking about. *This* was where you grew up?"

They arrived at The Dominion, now a museum, where Richard, an emissary from the foundation, waited. It was ordinarily closed on Monday afternoon, but he insisted that they drive over anyhow; he'd open up the place for Hubbell's visiting daughter. The Dominion was only the beginning of the grand tour. They'd "do" Buffabrook together afterward. Which meant buffalo burgers and, undoubtedly, Paddy Mahoney. Laydelle had paused to take a deep breath. She looked at her friend's wide, innocent eyes.

"Get ready, Libby, and don't say I didn't warn you."

"For this? Why, it's charming, and you're only the luckiest girl in the world."

Pretty little Libby tossed her curly hair behind her shoulders. Petite, the word, had been designed for her, Laydelle thought. Nothing caught or snagged or tore with Libby Sims. She was perfectly made for any space.

"Why on earth do you have that expression on your face? You look so gloomy."

"Take your time here and look all you like. Pick stuff up, even though the signs say not to. Let's linger as long as we can in the world of make-believe gentility. So I look gloomy, huh?"

"Morose, even."

"It's just that I hate to see my pretty little friend get so dirty. You're about to be showered by crude."

"Oh, God, how exciting. You mean we might see a well come in?"

"No, I mean Paddy Mahoney. I hear he's worse than ever. And he was so, so bad before."

Libby was having the most wonderful afternoon! In fact, she was having the time of her life at Buffabrook. Once they were inside the gates, Libby said so and said so and said so, exclaiming over a buffalo, its hide hung on bone angularity when seen this close, or a big yellow cat slinking over a rocky point they could barely see from the car.

"You don't mean it. A cougar? Is this a ranch or a stage set, Laydelle? This is all too wonderful."

By the time they reached the lodge, Libby's appreciation had reached its crescendo. She grabbed Mahoney's hand and pumped away.

"I've heard all about you, Mr. Mahoney."

"Is that so? And just what have you heard about Paddy Mahoney?"

"That you're a painter yourself. I'm studying art history at school and—"

"I'm merely mediocre, but I'm sure Laydelle told you."

Paddy slid a hand into his pocket and nibbled lightly on the end of his pipe.

"Laydelle also mentioned that you worked intimately with her grandfather to build the museum."

"Intimate. I wouldn't say the two of us were ever intimate. As crazy as I was about the old coot, I never—"

Richard leaped in.

"Paddy, time for that tour you promised."

"What he's really saying is am I drinking. Hell yes, I'm drinking.

The museum is closed to the public. I'm chez moi, and what I do on my own time is my own business."

"Why don't I just run the girls through and let you go on about your business, then? The keys, Paddy."

Paddy Mahoney held his nose.

" 'The keys, Paddy.' You and your lace doilies, Richard. They've got you talking like a girl. You ought to drive out here to boystown more often just to repair your diction. Keys, keys. Hang on a minute."

Paddy looked over his shoulder as he left.

"Now you be sure and apologize for my behavior while I'm looking, Rich. Tell Ms. Hanks' pretty visitor it's because I have a terrible self-image with my limp and all and how since Nelson died nobody's been able to do a thing with me. I'm like a cowlick nobody can control, Miss . . . what did you say your name was, honey?"

"Libby."

"Pleased to meet you, Lib. Now lemme just find those keys, so you girls can have a good look around. Laydelle, you're looking positively succulent, and Irishmen don't lie. Smith must agree with you."

"It does, Paddy. I like being away."

"I heard that. Your friend here strong enough to take a look at the entrails?"

Richard reached for a handkerchief and mopped at his neck.

"Tish, tish. Doing vivisection out here on your day off? Well, mum's the word. I won't let this get back to the board."

"That's very cute, Rich. Translate for him, honeybunch, while I go get you the keys."

She wondered if the limp had grown worse since the failed operation. She knew the invective had. Laydelle didn't rush to calm her friend or appease poor Richard. She felt the old stillness return, the calm that always infected her after a Paddy outburst. As long as Paddy's rage remained, something of her familiar world was still safe. She heard doors slamming open and closed. Something crashed to the floor and broke. They heard Paddy's voice, surrounded by a ring of echoes.

"Holy Mother of Jesus!"

Richard was a deep shade of red. Paddy was right about the lace doilies. The fussiness of his job had finally rubbed off on him. Too many receptions, too many teas. Laydelle shook her head, and Richard misunderstood.

"I know! Isn't it awful! We're going to have to do something about him. The board just has to act sooner or later. Paddy treats this place like his private palace and has since your grandfather died. Libby, excuse us for talking shop like this, but I so seldom see any member of the family. Why, with you off at school, Laydelle, and your parents so, uh, preoccupied with other things, there hardly seems a minute to just spout off."

He mopped his neck again and wondered why he had consented to wait outside for Mahoney in the first place.

"He has a complete disregard for things out here. I'm no more for unnecessary decorum than the next man, but we're not talking about that. We're talking about irresponsible behavior that could eventually . . . Why, Paddy acts on any fool notion, and he's all alone out here. Chez moi! He means that! He treats the museum like it's his bachelor pad."

Laydelle found a way to cut him off, flinging her arm around dear Libby.

"She's had an earful today, Richard—"

Libby, who was lapping it up, started to object.

"—so why don't we all just pretend to be visitors and see what there is to see? Oh, I forgot to tell you what he means by entrails. He just means the basement and the restoration area. Paddy used to take me down there when I was a child."

"So he could show you some of the restoration process? Why, I knew he was bluffing! He's got a heart of gold, and he's ashamed to show it."

"Wrong. The old goat did it to scare the pants off a little kid."

Richard swallowed hard. It really was hot, and he was sick and tired of waiting for Mahoney.

Paddy lived in a suite of rooms above the museum. He ignored the distinction between upstairs and downstairs. The whole damn museum was his, and that was that. Even in the glory days, when he and Nelson had been on the wildest spending spree imaginable, the museum was Paddy's. So that when he and Nelson collided on some issue and Nelson fired him, Paddy would just tell him he wasn't going anyplace and read books in his rooms until the oil

man stopped pouting and hired him back. The battle over owner-
ship never had changed, from Paddy's point of view. If it wasn't
Nelson thinking the place was his, then it was a newly appointed
chairman of the board, who couldn't see *how* he could justify such
an amount for a gun collection due to go on the market as early as
January when Paddy could. Paddy could! He threw the kind of fits
fitting to an ornery, iconoclastic museum director who didn't believe in his own vulnerability. He hurled phones across his office
and limped more, had even poured a drink on a disagreeable lady's
head at a fund-raising soiree. Now if you'll excuse me, he'd said,
wiping his face, not hers. So sorry you don't like my Winchesters.
Nelson Hanks had demanded that his young steward learn all he
could (fast), so the two could build their collection (fast), and a
brand of conduct had been not only authorized but encouraged.
And if Paddy had fallen under the spell of certain fables, it wasn't
pardoned, but it was understood.

Paddy ruled the roost with a strange mixture of passion and
detachment. Even when sober he would sometimes tumble into a
wheelchair at the entrance to watch visitors to the museum drift
in. He would wheel around for the hell of it, directing children to
his personal favorites, the exhibits that told the best stories. And if
he overheard any misinformation or pure bull in *his* museum, he
moved quickly to correct it, lancing the boil over the microphone in
the shadowy exhibit hall before it got any worse. "No, it is not true
that the Peruvian mummy was embalmed in the same fashion as
an Egyptian mummy, sir. The Egyptian method was to empty the
body and fill it with embalming fluids. Our Peruvian friend remains
preserved because of the soil content and the dry region where the
poor boy dropped dead." If visitors weren't frightened off, they
were mesmerized. Mahoney had knowledge and could even summon up a bit of charm if he was in the mood. He could talk about
a Choctaw burial or every delicate step that led to the acquisition
of a certain Zia pot or tell one more yarn about that son of a bitch
Nelson Hanks. He could also reach for the mike to berate visitors
over the public-address system, so that even the most intrepid
ticket holder to the Hanks Western Collection might clear his
throat and call for his hat or umbrella in the reception hall.

Paddy had returned with the keys. He jingled them lightly in the
air, teasing Richard.

"It's all so boring, Mahoney. Every time I drive out here, I'm struck by how tedious this act has become."

"Don't forget I come from a circus family. This kind of stuff's in my blood."

He'd gotten a little fat. Belly spilled over his belt buckle, eclipsing both turquoise and silver.

"The only thing that's in your blood at the moment is alcohol."

"Strike two, Richard. I certainly see how you got to where you are today. Give a holler when you're done. I'll be downstairs."

"Before you leave, Mr. Mahoney . . . ?"

She was a perfect, blushing pink foil for Laydelle. Of the two, he didn't know which he would choose.

". . . I'm having a little trouble characterizing your museum. Southwestern art and artifact, as it says here in the catalogue, but there's a hint of something so purely personal that I feel a little off course."

Paddy threw back his head and brayed.

"Darling, you've got Smith stamped right across your forehead! You're way off course. Buffabrook reflects whatever tickled the combined fantasies of Nelson Hanks and Paddy Mahoney. Oh, he tried to turn it into something more conventional when he sent me East, but it didn't work. Nelson Hanks couldn't ever convert this costly little warehouse into anything more than a hodgepodge, and let me tell you, it pained him more than any business bloop could have. He wanted to make this museum respectable, even academic. But Hanks didn't really have the stomach for it. I'd tell him about the importance of a particular serape . . ."

Paddy pointed to a Navajo blanket near where they stood. Light struck the center of the simple piece, a black-and-white diamond inside a field of nearly solid red.

"That old bastard would just get bored stiff looking at the very thing anybody else would have given their eyeteeth for. I'd watch his eyes glaze over as I told him about the importance of the piece, what made it special. How the Navajo took Spanish trade cloth and unraveled it, then wove it into their work. And why that made it extremely valuable and worth buying. He'd give in when I pushed hard enough, but what he really wanted, and what you'll see downstairs, where I've got it all massed together, was his own rumpus room. You can't miss it. Show saddles and Buffalo Bill's revolvers. You want stagecoaches, Lib? We got 'em, honey. So don't be too hard on yourself if you feel a little vertigo. You ought to be feeling dizzy. And you haven't seen anything yet. Wait until we go underground."

Paddy shuffled off. He belched as he left the room, and Libby covered her smile with her hand.

"He may be crude, but he's also brilliant."

"Brilliant? Libby, he's potted."

Richard sank onto a bench by the entrance, and they made their way to Laydelle's favorite Remington. There was nothing subtle about the bronze. The horses' raised hooves rattled her own rib cage every time she studied the sculpture.

"What's it like, Laydelle?"

"Listening to Paddy? Oh, just like old times. The world can turn all it wants to, but Paddy Mahoney will still be an embarrassment."

"No, no. I don't mean Paddy. I mean all this."

And Libby, exploiting her small size, did a neat three-quarter turn and seemed to get even smaller in the space emptied of other visitors.

"Having it and not having it at the same time."

Laydelle cleared her throat and looked her brainy friend over. Having it and not having it at the same time—that felt just like old times, too. She'd hit the nail on the head, and who'd asked in the first place?

"I don't know what you're talking about. C'mon."

"I mean, Paddy Mahoney seems to feel more entitled to this place than you do." She lowered her voice. "Even that wimp Richard."

Laydelle drifted toward the Spiro Collection and motioned for her to do the same. It worked. Libby got lost in another round of enthusiasm.

"Unbelievable! There's a passage in my textbook about LeFlore County. This is absolutely unreal!"

Mary Hanks accelerated as soon as her daughter left home. Traveling at high speed meant traveling light, and as Mary Hanks moved closer and closer toward a new self, she shucked, pared down and let go. Letter after letter floated to Smith as she avidly recorded her own transformation.

I feel like a million dollars. Speaking of a million dollars, your daddy has vehemently suggested that I drop a bundle on a brand-new outfit for a party he's throwing on that damn tugboat of his. Now I like spending money as well as the next person. Maybe even *better* than the next person. But if your daddy wants me to wear Bill Blass, he'll have to dream up something better than Catoosa, Oklahoma.

I've begun subscribing to a whole slew of California mags, even newspapers. I once objected to the West Coast! I wonder now what I objected to. Great weather, great people, great lives? Well, you won't hear any objections from yours truly now.

I sure like the sound of your new friend. Is that Standish as in Miles Standish?

Having it and not having it at the same time? Libby would have been better off asking Mary Hanks, who enjoyed the last word on that subject.

If Hubbell still doesn't see what those people have done to him, then God help him, because Mary sure can't. And don't bring up Nelson Hanks' dirty trick, that so-called contract; it's blackmail. All your father has to do is hire a lawyer, but oh no, your father won't hear of any more legal disputes. He's far too busy. So *Architectural Digest* is doing an article on his old houseboat. *So???* I know parents aren't supposed to burden their children with their own problems, but by now you're no child.

Not everything is bleak. I'm fusing a few ideas of mine and have recently had extremely positive feedback! Will tell all at Christmas. By the way, are you coming home at Christmas? I'm going to stuff a goose this year.

Laydelle leaned hard on a glass case and watched her friend pull out a notebook.

"I hope you're about done. We've still got the basement to do."

"Yeah, yeah. Just a sec. I've gotta take down this story about Tiffany's. I don't know how you can be so blasé about this place. It's almost sacrilegious."

"A museum's not exactly a church."

"I just don't think it's becoming, the way you behave. You treat it like it's nothing. Like it has nothing to do with you."

She'd never spent so much time with her friend outside of school and now remembered the little twinge she felt when Libby's face stiffened up under the strain of too much disapproval. She began to think that the basement tour was an excellent idea. Richard's chin rested on the top of his chest.

"Look! He's sound asleep."

"I guess I'd better wind this up, hadn't I? How are we going to wake him?"

"Like this."

She tiptoed, even though she didn't need to. He was fast asleep.

"Hey, what are you doing?"

"Calm down. This isn't Boston, it's Lovely."

Laydelle triggered the alarm, and his head popped up with a snap. The alarm blew and blew, filling the empty halls.

"It was just a joke. Plus I wanted to see if the system had been updated at all. Or if it still made that sound like a foghorn."

"You'll have some explaining to do to the police."

"No I won't. Paddy's already called the dispatcher, so you can calm down. Haven't you, Paddy?"

Mahoney pulled on his pipe. He had just appeared on the stairs.

"Yup. Told 'em I flipped it on by accident. If I don't call them, they call me. Frigging alarm goes off at least once a month out here. You girls ready? Come on downstairs for a grim fairy tale or two."

Richard lagged behind. He watched as Laydelle made her way down the stairs. Tight jeans and a man's T-shirt. He decided Smith had done absolutely nothing for her. She was the same wild-ass girl, with a string of pearls added, that was all. He smoothed his clothing and went outside to wait. It had cooled off some at least.

"Miss Libby, you hang on to your hat. You thought you had vertigo before, did you?"

He held a brass ring jammed with so many keys they didn't even rattle. They had gone down one flight of stairs and stood on a landing facing a red door.

"This is my home zone. Watch you don't step on anything that bites."

It was hot on the other side of the red door. Heat blasted their faces as he pushed through and switched on a light that led down one last set of stairs. Paddy stepped aside so that Libby could get a good look at his wild kingdom. He saw she was too proud to gasp or groan. Mahoney licked his lips at her combination of sugar and steel. Strewn with animal skins and heads, it was like the trophy room of a lousy hunter. Someone who could mow down a buffalo, but not without blasting away half the skull. Birdland was *triste*—headless eagles and one-winged owls hung suspended in the stuffy basement. Antlers lay piled in a corner, paws and hooves were heaped on a straw mat beside the furnace. The inventory was getting the best of Libby. She reached out for the railing.

"Ghoulish, isn't it? Careful, sweetie. It's hotter than blazes down here. I've got a practical reason for all this. Nothing is forever, not even taxidermy. Sometimes Nelson's beasties need sprucing up. When we've got to replace talons or a beak, even a patch of hide, we come down here to get it. The old man's animals are still dropping dead, and we're still finding uses for them. Hell, we even keep their peckers. This way; come follow me."

Paddy stopped to blow his nose.

"I've been doing charcoals these last few months. It's the damnedest thing, but I've lost my appetite for color. All I want is line and shadow now. Craziest thing."

"Stop locking yourself up in the basement to work, and your appetite for color will return. It's morbid down here."

"Upstairs they want to know if it's okay to give Alberta Stevens the senior-citizen rate or why don't I dim lights on the Spiro exhibit like they do in Tulsa so people won't keep thinking they're reproductions or what would I think about renting out Aviation Hall to a group from Tinker Air Force Base. See? I'm in the basement for a good reason. Here, we'll just let Libby have a look at a little overflow before you go."

And then down a hall of offices, with paintings leaning against the walls of the corridor and African masks lolling over the EXIT sign. He chose another key from the crowded ring. Paddy rubbed his hand over his forehead, and a look of pure confusion crossed his face.

"Bugs me. Bugs the hell out of me, but I don't know what else to do."

"About the mess?"

"No, I mean about the hoarding and about do I have the right to do this in the first place."

A moral sense? In Paddy Mahoney? Laydelle looked as worried as he did. The world was turning the wrong way.

"Look, nobody in his right mind is going to refuse these things.

This museum gets donations all the time. Things people have had in their family for years and years. See . . ."

They saw a knight's suit of armor, its legitimacy established by its small size, and a set of samurai swords. They saw a fabulous array of the mixed-up and the priceless, pottery and rugs and baskets filled with bright-blue trading stones. Weaving bags and mummy heads, brocade cut from Peruvian gauze cloth, occupied shelves sloping with erotic lamps of dark wood and effigy bowls. Stuff, and so much of it, that lay numbered, catalogued and contained by Paddy's lock and key.

"It's like my private peep show. And it worries me. Damn stuff is too expensive to insure at its real value and too motley to integrate into any exhibit upstairs. But it doesn't worry me enough to wreck what little order I've managed to establish. So this is the real answer to your question, Libby."

She looked at him blankly.

"You asked me about characterizing this museum. Well, that's just it. I still can't, after all this time. You're looking at an old man who was yanked out of class before he was ready and stuck quick into a job that was too big for him in many ways."

Laydelle stood near enough to realize that Richard's assessment was off. Paddy's breath was clean as a whistle. Clean and sober Paddy had been bluffing.

"Listen to me go on. You have to forgive me, but you're the two most erudite visitors I've entertained for a long time. You want to laugh, do you? Security system, hell. I don't even need the shoddy alarm I've got! I have had two burglaries over the past forty years. You know what for? A priceless gorget from the Spiro Collection? Twenty-five-thousand-year-old funerary urns or, hell, even Tom Mix's silver saddle? Those Lovely dumbshits broke in just to get my German Lugers. Twice! Ah, don't let me get started about the intelligence quotient around here. I start, and you'll never see samples of Paddy's blue period."

He took them into his office, a mess of books and papers, filing cabinets tipped and tilting with the weight of their contents. Paddy fumbled with a sheaf of papers that lay stacked on the floor and pulled out samples of his charcoals. They had no particular style, but Libby masked her disappointment with a competent stream of art talk. Laydelle had to hand it to her.

"You think so? Man, I struggled with this one. Fought like hell to get any depth at all."

He straightened his shoulders.

"The way I see it, the only thing I'm missing now is a decent nude."

He banged his pipe hard on the ashtray and fiddled with a bag of cherry-flavored tobacco.

"Which of you girlies wants to step out of her jeans for the sake of art?"

Libby looked a little peaked as Paddy Mahoney cackled rudely, but Laydelle's color was just fine. Paddy's improprieties sent the familiar earth spinning around and around as before.

Hussell's father was some big cheese, Hubbell.

chapter 39

1967

"Your father was some big cheese, Hubbell. I don't envy you, having those footsteps to follow. But this could be bigger than the discovery of oil, and you can play a hand in it."

The mayor of Tulsa had a fondness for Chevrolets. His first car had been a Chevy. He and Hubbell were heading east toward Catoosa in a tan coupe. Mayor Stone couldn't resist a comparison.

"You know what I'd be doing if I had my druthers, Hubbell?"

Hubbell shook his head. He had no idea, since he barely knew the mayor and had only the faintest notion of why they were barreling down these rude, rutted highways.

"I'd be running a Chevy dealership, that's what. Politics—why mess with the life in the first place? To tell you the truth, I'd have stayed cleaner working underneath a car. I'm no different than you, content to stay in the place I know best. But the point is, Hubbell, there's bigger things to work toward out there."

They pulled to a stop in front of a tangle of weeds. The mayor got out of the car quickly and went around to the back for a thermos of hot coffee. He poured Hubbell a cup, adding sugar without asking.

"Drink up, bub. We've still got a hike ahead of us. No way I'm going to let you miss first shot at this. No way. All the words in the dictionary wouldn't take the place of just seeing it, so I won't even try."

The mayor snapped his sunshades in place right on top of his glasses. Hubbell wished he could do the same. Maybe that way he could slide the mayor's vision of the future right on top of his own. His own vision led him to no particular conclusion, and he was having an awful struggle being enthusiastic. He slapped at a horsefly with his hat. The mayor had a long stride. He called back over his shoulder as he marched.

"Conceived in dust."

As he trudged along, Hubbell didn't think of the waterway that would one day cut through the surrounding fields. He didn't think of the Army Corps of Engineers and federal nitwits, as the mayor called them. They were still working on the project, though it had been years now. He thought about the high grass and the way it sprang back up after he walked, so that no path remained.

"Cradled in flood."

"What are you talking about, Ira? You've lost me completely."

"Cradled in flood. I'll never forget what my mother said when I told her I was running for mayor. Two words were all she had for me. Come to think of it, she never had much more than two words for any of us. Guess that's the way when you're raising four kids alone. I told her I was running for mayor, and all she finds to say about that is 'small potatoes.' "

Hubbell thought he glimpsed an arrowhead, but it was an ordinary stone. He spotted a blue jay, and that relieved him. His own theory about the birds, forged during expeditions he made before Mary, was that they didn't quite dare wilderness. They never strayed far from a human hub.

"Pretty lousy thing to say."

"That was just her way of keeping our accomplishments in perspective. Created by men. What do you think, Hubbell?"

Hubbell tripped lightly over a fallen tree limb.

"Conceived in dust. Cradled in flood. Created by men. Hell of a motto for our project, doncha think, Hubbell? I can see those words on a bronze plaque, can't you? You all right, fella?"

The port of the plains was subtle, Hubbell guessed. When they finally arrived at the site he was out of breath and out of patience, but that was why Ira Stone was mayor of Tulsa and Hubbell

Hanks wasn't. Ira knew this was the perfect position for the initial facility. Knowing, Hubbell saw, was what really separated the men from the boys, and Ira Stone knew plenty. He knew all about the Arkansas River, with its salty water, its erratic, trouble-causing flows. He understood an inland waterway for low-cost transportation would be hugely profitable. Hubbell was flattered and puzzled to be asked along for the ride. Ira Stone drew a great breath, and Hubbell found himself thinking of a toad's fat swell he'd recently seen on a *National Geographic* television special.

"Peru. Sardinia. Take it in, Hubbell. Dream notions can happen if you let them. Here, look what I've got in my back pocket. Whipped cheese and pimento. It's the wife's specialty."

The sandwich, wrapped in Saran, had molded to the exact impression of Ira's buttock, but Hubbell didn't mind. He was hungry, and the sandwich took his mind off the troublesome geography. He couldn't see what Ira Stone was asking him to see or understand why he was asked to think of those places at all. He bit into his sandwich and found Mrs. Stone had been liberal with the cheese. It spilled out the edges of the sandwich with his first bite. Ira talked faster now that his mouth was full.

"Barite from Sardinia, construction machinery to Peru. Peanuts to Rotterdam boggle my mind, and they'll boggle the minds of voters, too, if we don't spell it out. If you don't spell it out, Hubbell."

Hubbell almost raised his hand, as if he were in a classroom.

"Ira, I'd love to help, but I can't back you personally."

"I know that, and I don't want your money; I want theirs. People are blind, see. They don't understand how their lives and their state could be richer if they'd just vote in *the goddamn bonds*. That always gets me, how taxpayers can't see to the ends of their nose. They want everything for nothing. Oh, but they'll trust a Hanks once a Hanks gets on the bandwagon. Those federal clowns are creating twenty-five thousand miles of inland coastal waterways that connect us from the Great Lakes in the north to the Gulf of Mexico in the south. And we've gotta respond by turning Catoosa into a port city with those bonds! Two million dollars . . . hell, that's nothing when you think of the revenue it'll generate. What do you say, Hubbell? Are you getting on my bandwagon? You're looking at the maritime frontier, Mr. Hanks. You're looking at a project so grandiose that it will turn the whole nation's head. But who am I talking to? You love the water or you wouldn't live next to it on Riverview Road."

He did love it, and did you castrate the thing you loved, turn it into a house pet? Hubbell thought about that, the river he loved to watch rise and swell with sudden, slashing rain from his seat on the front porch. What would it become next, if all Ira said was true, and could he love that just as well? But another truth was that he needed to court Mary and Ira Stone had just shown him how. He would win back her love! He would wave his name in the air like a crazy banner and get her back.

"If I help you, how will you help me, Ira?"

Ira liked him asking, he saw that. He spread his legs stiffly apart and put his hands in the back pockets of his jeans, where the sandwiches had been.

"You know, that damn brother of mine keeps asking me about when I want my houseboat delivered. Did I say asking? I meant pestering. Keeps pestering me, since he plans to sell his business but not before he treats me to a custom houseboat. Oh, he does a hell of a business. . . . Sacramento and out in Arizona; don't even bring up the Northeast! What do I want with a houseboat? But you, Hubbell! Now that's another story."

"A houseboat? But where would I put her in?"

Ira arched his back and laughed.

"One thing I can do and do well is issue permits. You want to put her in here? Right here?"

Hubbell turned and blinked. There was nothing here but bleached grass and catbirds. The occasional jay remained to give hope.

"Unique. One of a kind. I can see it now. The only leisure craft in the entire turning basin at the Port of Catoosa. From where you sit on the houseboat, you can watch tugboats, barges. Hell, a freighter'll make it through here once we're done. A perfect spot for a man with dreams."

"You're the man with the dreams, Ira."

"My friend, I'll loan 'em to you if you help me out."

1971

Taxpayers called it the billion-dollar ditch. By the time the Army Corps of Engineers completed it, the nine-foot-deep navigation channel was 445 miles long. The appearance of an American President at the dedication ceremony boded well, at least for some. Mary Hanks talked and talked into the telephone at her desk.

"You *have* to come home, Laydelle. I won't take no for an answer."

"This is crazy. I have an important exam coming up, and I can't get away. Besides, I wouldn't be caught dead standing next to Richard Nixon."

"Aha, so that's it! Just who's paying your tuition for that fancy-schmancy girls' school? Remember, Laydelle, the Lord giveth and the Lord taketh away."

"That's a creepy analogy."

"It's no analogy at all. I am proud of your father, and I want us all out there together when they dedicate the project. It would mean so much to him. And here I thought college would help you think in larger terms. You still love democracy, don't you?"

"I'm nuts about it. Why?"

"Then all you have to do in that case is think past Dick and Pat."

"Pat Nixon is flying in, too? That does it. I'm not coming home, Mother. I do have some pride."

"Rather than focusing on Richard Nixon, concentrate on all the presidents who went before him, all those who will follow after. Think *continuum* and you'll get through it. Baby?"

"What?"

"Actually, I'm not asking, I'm telling. I want you home. It could be my last hurrah, and I want it pretty."

"What do you mean, your last hurrah? Mom?"

Mary's last hurrah was pretty. A cool breeze tousled her hair. She noted that Pat Nixon's didn't move, and imagined it was her slightly shorter cut. Hubbell looked twenty years younger as he locked hands with Ira Stone, who thanked him for his successful fund-raising efforts.

"We're landlocked no more. Which means we can anticipate fantastic revenue for this state. Once again, as before in Oklahoma's history, we have a Hanks to thank. Let's hear it, folks!"

They made quite a fuss over Hubbell, and somebody said later he got a louder round of applause than the President. Not that several hundred people weren't damned glad that Nixon had come to launch their project and offer his stamp of approval. But a collective relief was evident. Hubbell had done it, by God. All that public begging had come to something, after all. Most people thought it outrageous that his daughter had dressed in an orange and purple hippie costume for the afternoon ceremony, but maybe that was just college in Massachusetts. Anyway, there they all were, and how good it was to see a Hanks in public life again. And didn't Mary speak well, when she chose to speak? She'd kept so much to herself lately. The only meanness, if it could have been called that, took place when Sarah Moffett held a white patent handbag over the front of her mouth and whispered "Dale Carnegie Course" to her husband as Mary took up the microphone.

"Whiskey, sarsaparilla and mackerel, ladies and gentlemen."

Mary paused for a moment and locked eyes with an old man near the front of the crowd. She smiled sweetly and returned to her speech.

"That's what a bill of lading read in 1859. This old river highway has been a mean stretch of water, with quicksand and snags. Thirty-foot floods and channel changes that swept the Arkansas in a single night. One hundred and fifty-two riverboats sunk or destroyed in a sixty-year period. She has remained contentious and unpredictable until today."

Sarah Moffett slowly lowered her bag. She looked at her husband out of the corner of her eye. He was salivating like a dog, and Dale Carnegie had nothing to do with that. Mary Hanks was sexy. She went on to talk about the historical society she was president of. Sarah Moffett swallowed the wrong way and started coughing. She nearly choked to death before her husband turned his head to notice.

The afternoon ended with a spectacular storm nobody took particular notice of when it began building up along the eastern edge of the sky. The speeches, the sight of Pat Nixon smashing her bottle of champagne once, twice, over the prow of the little tugboat, had been so lively that no one even thought to roll up their car windows when they saw the dark clouds move in. Afterward, after everybody made a mad, laughing dash to their cars, it seemed the afternoon and the whole port operation itself were little more than a mirage. Inside closed automobiles, people shook damp heads and lifted off their shoes on sort of an individual basis. The rain fell so hard, whole families parked side by side were invisible to each other. An army of security guards couldn't shield a President from everything. Even Dick Nixon had to make a run for it, and seeing an American President run like hell from the rain seemed a sorry shame. Everybody just dispersed. Like that. Wham, as if nothing had happened at all.

Mary's flowers never did grow. Silver shells and cocklebells, to hell may you all go! she began to screech out the window at her English garden. But something was growing by 1971 in Mary Hanks' heart and mind. That kitchen window was later seen as a kind of document to her increasing unrest. Years later, when she had smoothed out a new life in California, she confided in her grown daughter.

"Okay, so there was Watergate. But you'd better know something, Baby, when you're busy criticizing poor old Dick Nixon. He kept me home a few more years. Just knowing he was coming to Oklahoma for that dedication ceremony helped me keep the lid on things a little while longer. And that much is good. Well, isn't it?"

Something had to grow under Mary's aegis, and if flowers didn't, she'd find something else that would. The something else had long been crystals. Salt and sugar, sprouted on strings that dangled for days in blue water, crystals soon threatened to overtake the entire kitchen. They were forming everywhere, everywhere. Hubbell took issue with it. He couldn't make himself a piece of toast, pour a cup of coffee, without having to move a cup of blue water to one side.

"If you were so unhappy about them, you should have spoken up long ago. Crystals have become the most important hobby I have."

"Not like this. I wouldn't mind if there weren't so many, hon."

"One is the loneliest number, or haven't you heard? Besides, I don't go out in the garage and root around, then tell you how to organize the place. I've got to belong somewhere, Hubbell, and if a woman doesn't belong in her own kitchen, then God help her."

Hubbell set his fork down quietly.

"But they started out just in the window. Now they're everywhere. Your crystals are like cancer. Plus there's nothing to eat. Do you ever go to the grocery store anymore?"

She weighed the charge. It was true. Meals had become more and more haphazard. Even creative leftovers and low-priced variety meats had lost their allure; she just couldn't summon the energy or interest.

"Mary, are you all right?"

She stared at him until he blushed. Really, he thought his wife had never looked at him so closely, so carefully. Under his hot skin he felt something else tingling and wondered if love couldn't erupt for the second time in their lives: if this terrible kitchen, sticky with spilled sugar, wasn't truly another kind of laboratory in which something new could form and spew in a hot, wet stream over both of them. As she looked, he fought down happiness, fearing that much hope.

"What a large question that is, Hubbell. I don't know. I don't know if I'm all right."

She carefully placed her face in her hands.

"Do you think I'm all right?"

"I'm not sure, Mary. I love you, and I'm just not sure."

The view from the house on Riverview Road had changed dramatically. About the time when the road had gotten to be a sort of expressway linking downtown with the quiet, residential south side of Tulsa, the city decided there was no good place to ride bikes. The river's edge remained, and it suited them just fine. A river park was soon erected, with trails looping in and out of the wild land on the edge of the water. Sculptures were dropped here and there, and city-commissioned pieces of steel and stone turned river-gazing from the roadside into something else. Hubbell and Mary sat out less and less, the automatic awning dropped rarely, if at all. Though the biggest front yard in town was still meticulously maintained, the green space seemed so austere and still, joggers and strollers barely turned their heads as they passed.

The houseboat arrived just in time, at a time when Hubbell felt ousted both from Mary's hectic kitchen and from his own front porch. At night he could no longer gaze undistractedly at the power company or the oil storage tanks or the line of shadows cast on the water by the brush. Even moonlight falling on the water lost its brilliant edge. One night, there was a performance at the Center Stage, built just downriver from his house. The crescent-shaped amphitheater floating on the water held only a hundred chairs, but screaming kids made the seating capacity seem much greater. Hubbell watched the concert begin as Al Jarreau parachuted out of the sky into an adjacent field. That summer nearly every performer in Tulsa had to jump out of a plane.

"Phone, Hubb. It's Ira Stone."

The screams increased as Al Jarreau stood up and brushed the seat of his pants. He waved and began to run toward his audience.

"Evening, Ira. What do you know?"

"Your houseboat arrives Thursday, and it's a beauty. Bernie sent me all the papers. You're gonna live like a king. Wait till you see it. My God, the details!"

Later, even seated as he was in a rotting canvas deck chair, Hubbell felt himself a king, just as Ira Stone had predicted. King of an imperfect realm but a king still. After the boat was delivered, hauled all the way up the channel from Chattanooga, and moored, after all the necessary inspections were completed and facility officials invited for a drink aboard the newest permanent installation, Hubbell wallowed in his new world. Hubbell was home. Improbable as that home was, it was the perfect place to rest. The houseboat would also become the perfect place to heal.

"Say that one more time, Hubbell. I don't believe my ears."

"I said I want you to find me a decorator. I don't want to just throw things together out there. Unless, of course, you want to help me."

"No, thank you. I'm afraid the Port of Catoosa doesn't have quite the same attraction for me as it does for you. Tell me, what do you see out there on your poop deck?"

"It's pretty calm. Oh, we did get a charge the other day, though. An ocean freighter, Mary! German. The *Frauke*, I believe she was called."

"Doesn't that sound divine! I'll track down a decorator for you. Why are you standing like that? You look like you're trying to straighten out an old injury."

Pain was reconstructing Hubbell Hanks, slowly but surely. He found his habitual backache let up a little if he shifted his shoulders back and up, as hard as doing that was. Though his new posture was rigid and unsure, Hubbell looked taller. He began to take up even more space in Mary's kitchen and seemed to require a brand-new clearance. He tipped over one cup of blue water, then another. He upset the crystals, and he upset Mary.

"Oh, there goes another. Can't you set them somewhere else, Mar? Yes, yes, I'm going."

He shopped for himself and loaded brown bags into the trunk of the errand car. Then he drove the fifteen miles to Catoosa in no time. He'd finally stumbled on a name for the boat that pleased him, and painters were scheduled that morning to tag it with identification, just like a newborn. The *Final Resort* would eventually be embellished with furniture and accessories that smacked of Hubbell before Mary, before he had suppressed a life filled with conga lines and broken soldiers. For now, though, cans of tinned meat and fish, stewed tomatoes, met and collided under scratched leather seats as he flew down bad roads toward home.

chapter 40

1988

As long as she stayed away, Laydelle sustained her belief in a confusing but benign world and promise that was just around the invisible bend in the road. Hubbell sent checks faithfully through her twenties. Checks were mailed when a roommate deserted through marriage or emotional breakdown, leaving Laydelle with both loneliness and a high overhead. Checks were mailed to cover what salaries or small business investments never quite did. They were mailed to cover moving expenses, as one fantastic lead led to another, necessitating a furnished apartment in still another city. They were mailed without complaint. They were mailed on time. They were mailed with a cheery enclosure plus a quote about courage right underneath Hubbell's own letterhead. But when she turned thirty they became not checks but loans. Cheery enclosures became admonishments, and by the time she hit thirty-two, Hubbell's letterhead had all but disappeared. He began protecting his checks with sturdy three-by-five cards, assigning each one a loan number, and strongly urging her to return to Oklahoma, where, Hubbell Hanks seemed to imagine, she had "contacts."

"Will you accept a collect call from Laydelle?"

There was a pause, then yes.

"Hey, it's me. What, are there small-craft warnings on the port or something? You sound funny."

"You've caught me at a funny time."

Hubbell was having a drink all alone on his beautiful boat, and that felt good and bad. He'd done the same thing three years ago, confessed immediately and been driven straight to an AA meeting by his sponsor. He thought he'd settled that old grief, but here it had come on its own two legs. He'd been missing Mary too, too much, and it came crashing down like a gathering wave. So he felt ashamed and titillated at the same time, knowing the furor a real bender would cause among his watchful friends. He would be the new focus at meetings for a while, there would be a solicitude and a renewed sense of risk for weeks and weeks. He wanted to think about these things, not talk to his daughter.

"Well, I'm nearly always having a funny time, and I need to talk, Daddy."

"Boy troubles, honey?"

"Boy . . . Daddy, I'm too old for boy troubles. I've got life troubles, the big ones. And they don't stop coming. I'm calling about this last check."

"What's wrong? I mailed it special delivery last week."

"I know; nothing's wrong. I got it and thanks, but something awful has come up."

The good thing about a martini was that it went straight to the heart and head. It was unadorned, and there was nothing remotely social about it. It both muddled the thought process and quickened it. For that Hubbell was grateful. He had long known that he was too impatient for hard thought. Too impatient and too frightened. Sometimes the outcome of actual thinking took him so far afield that he dared it rarely if at all. A martini, however, had that knack of flinging doors open quickly and then slamming them shut. He'd just seen his own father. He'd just heard a snip of that talk about river piss. Wait; rivers didn't piss. His father had said we pissed in rivers and then . . . what, what? He took another sip and forgot the whole thing. He was glad for the sharp and sudden chill.

"I've met someone. Someone extraordinary."

A marriage! Hubbell thought of Mary's face, all the expressions that would fly across it, as she rejoiced and planned and worried all at once.

"But that's wonderful, Laydelle. Meeting someone extraordinary is a marvelous thing. Why take that tone?"

"This someone is an extraordinary designer I found, who spent seven years in Paris. He actually worked for Chanel for a few months and just couldn't hack the hierarchy, you know. Daddy, are you there?"

"Yes, Laydelle, I'm still here."

"Well, the awful thing is that this man has so much talent. You can see it *dangling* from his earlobes, and I'm not kidding. My point is, I need to act fast before someone butts in front of me to do it. And I know this is a bad time. I mean, I just last week had to call you for money, and here I am with my hand out again. This time it's a shoo-in. I'm not talking about launching a line of clothing or anything. I mean, I am realistic. I just want to get him going on some fashion accessories. He makes the most unbelievable belts. And hats! Oh, the hats. He's shipped back boxes full of buttons and broaches, amazing feathers and antique lace, and you ought to see the concoctions he comes up with. Women down here will die for this stuff. He's an artist, so he's completely insolvent. I've got to seize this opportunity, Daddy."

Hubbell watched the street lights come on from his deck. He'd taken to wearing white again. White deck shoes, white slacks and a thick Irish sweater in the evening. He staved off delight with great effort, for delight wasn't required now. He needed something else. A firm hand and recall. If he couldn't quote his own father, maybe he could pull off a facsimile of his certitude. He thought not, but he could certainly try.

"I'm here, Laydelle. Look, honey, I might as well put it to you straight."

Hubbell took another quick sip of his martini, and the olive struck his nose.

"I think it's high time you took your situation seriously. And I don't see how you can do that if your father is always standing by with a safety net. Laydelle, how come you can't hang on to a job, honey? How come things always give way to other things that seem bigger and better and then never are? These last few years, honey . . . these last few years you've moved nine times. You've had . . . why, how many jobs have you had?"

He remembered the stream and his fear that Nelson would fall in it. That was it, a day of uncommon benediction, and Hubbell had gotten it all back. Now for the hard part. Hubbell finished the last of the martini and struggled to shape the blessing his own father had left him. To shape it so that it slipped over his sad daughter's head. It had felt like a blessing to him then. Would it feel like a blessing to her? He stammered in his excitement.

"Laydelle, dar-darling. I can't give you any more money."

"You what?"

"I said I can't give you any more money. At all. As of this minute. No, wait; in fairness . . . here's what I will do, in fairness. I'll move you and your things home. Are you listening, Laydelle?"

He could hear something in the background, some wild tapping as if she were standing on a construction site.

"I'll take care of all those expenses, and I'll even pay off any debts you owe, so you can have a fresh start. And I do mean for this to be a fresh start, Laydelle. It's important at a moment like this to look very hard at the facts."

"So what are the facts?"

"The fact is that you're almost forty, a wonderful time of life. But nothing has exactly taken wing, honey. I can't help but think of something I saw as a boy on one of my trips. I saw ptarmigan, honey, flightless birds, and so many they looked like fields. They're perfectly beautiful animals, but I felt so . . . why, they can't fly, and there they are, sad somehow. They seemed so helpless."

He heard someone, a man, call his daughter's name. The phone was muffled for a moment, and when she spoke her voice was tight and terrible. Not at all the voice that had called in the first place.

"Get to the point, Daddy. You're cutting me off, is that it?"

"Cutting you off? I'm your father!"

"Finish your nature story. Since the birds can't fly, the best thing is to herd them all up and stick them in a cage, where they'll be fed and protected."

"I didn't say that. I simply said they made me sad."

"That's marvelous. I love your little stories. You've forgotten I've heard them before. I can't tell you how much stronger I feel after hearing you go through your *National Geographic* bit. I've got problems, Daddy. I've got big money problems and things that can't wait; otherwise do you really think I'd be asking for another handout? Backing this guy is the only thing I can think of to make some money fast, which I happen to need. Do you have any idea how much money it takes just to live? What do you think this does to *me?*"

The phone was muffled again. Hubbell heard the man's voice, raised louder this time, and he got scared. Atlanta; that was so far away. He'd never even visited the city, and he had a daughter

living there. He would have made another martini in an instant if
the man hadn't taken the phone from his daughter's hand, or so he
imagined, and talked into it. He tried to imagine a face to go with
the voice but couldn't.

"I'm a friend of Laydelle's, and I've loaned her lots of money.
I'm like that. That's the kind of guy I am. I loaned her lots of
money, because I was crazy about her and figured if anybody could
pull these things off, she could. When I'm crazy for someone, I'm
crazy, and I don't refuse the basics. Only she didn't pull her ideas
off. It wasn't she didn't work or didn't try, only now we got two
problems."

"*Who* am I speaking with, if I may ask?"

"Oh, you want to know who this is. I gotcha. Well, *who* you are
speaking with is none of your business at the present time. Your
daughter's name is the only one that counts."

Some parts for a nuclear reactor had once passed down this
channel, and he'd seen the ordinary-looking barge with his very
own eyes. Why, the port had been packed with protesters! The
thought of something so mammoth and fearful had momentarily
erased everything else in Hubbell's world. Even losing Mary
seemed insignificant, an accountable loss. He wished he could see
that barge slowly chugging along right now.

"The first problem is my commercial space I got half-filled with
your daughter's stuff. But that's only my first problem. The second
problem is she's decided she's not so crazy about me as she
thought, so she'd like out. No problem; I'm like that. I don't get
insane like some guys, I just figure okay, but she's gotta square up
with me on this deal before she goes anyplace. I know she's telling
me the truth, that she doesn't have the money. But you, Mr.
Hanks. You gotta help your kid outa this one, 'at's all."

"Tell me, whoever you are. I'll get you your money. But tell me
if this is about drugs."

He didn't have a friendly laugh at all. There was nothing funny
about Hubbell's question.

"Drugs, okay! You wanna tell yourself and your friends your kid
is into drugs, it's okay by me. You wanna know? Your kid's into
peacock feathers and buttons, which is worse, if you ask me. She's
not telling the whole truth, either. She's got this little faggot design-
ing hats and belts already, only they're not selling. He wants to be
paid, and so do I, so with a little help from you she'll have both
monkeys off her back. She doesn't want to be my little friend any-

more? Fine, no hard feelings; I'm like that, you get me? But she's taking up commercial storage space, and it costs. That plus the loan at seven percent, and she won't hear a word from me. Not one word. Here, someone wants to talk to you."

"Laydelle."

He got some of it back. Some of that knowing his father had been so good at.

"Pay this gangster and the other one, the designer. If you own those feathers and buttons, why, bring them back here. You've got nothing but contacts, and you'll put them to some good use. You're in a bad jam, and I'm willing to help. But this time we're going to put you on your feet. Whoever this criminal is, he's right about one thing. You can't live with monkeys on your back. I know. I've had them. You've just got to come home, Laydelle."

Hubbell felt good. Now that night had actually fallen, it would be easier to phone his sponsor or mix another drink and another. All this shilly-shallying would be over because it was night. He had handled this thing with his daughter extremely well.

"One thing."

"Speak up, honey. I can barely hear you."

"Where's home?"

"What a question!"

"Well, answer it, then. The house is sold and Mary's gone Hollywood on us. You suggest I row, row, row the boat with you, maybe? Where's home, Daddy? Tell me what the ticket should read this time. I'm so tired."

She was tired. To regain her balance and lick her wounds, she didn't take an apartment right away. Instead, she spent several weeks aboard the *Final Resort*.

"The stench! You can't blame that on Aresta's housekeeping skills."

Aresta's voice rose from down below in the galley. *Damn straight you can't. Tell it, Laydelle, tell it.*

"What stench? It's all a matter of concentration. We smell what we want to smell, see what we want to see. Life is boundless that way, and we are free."

"Philosophy is fine, but I'm talking about something far more basic. What on earth is that smell?"

"That smell is commerce. That smell is success."

"Smells like shit to me."

She said it! Go on!

"Well, it's that, too. Aresta, could we have some privacy, or is that too much to ask?"

He pointed to a plant directly west of where his home was tethered. Laydelle squinted and read the sign for a fertilizer terminal. Hubbell was alone no more. Some forty-five industries had sprung up at the Port of Catoosa. He welcomed fishing rods and reels and liquid chemicals, household-bleach and windshield-wiper-fluid production plants. He welcomed trucks and stevedores and makers of ceramic tiles as creators of a new and better world. Hubbell also welcomed shit.

"Bravo. You've certainly carved out your own universe."

"I've had a hand in something very exciting. You want a refill, honey?"

He wanted to burnish his daughter into the old high shine. He wanted that laughter back, the spunk and the irreverence. His hands shook as he poured her coffee. Hubbell feared his own daughter, and his shipshape sense of things wobbled as she gazed at him with such slow, dark eyes. What all had she seen these past years? Whatever it was, she'd brought it on board with her. She admired his wonderful things, all the beautiful bric-a-brac that surrounded him, and her ardor accused him of everything and nothing. Now how was that? Hubbell wasn't drinking. He couldn't have borne her derision. But his heart and soul staggered, and that was just as bad. He pointed to the aging copy of *Architectural Digest*.

"You ought to try to put some more weight on, Laydelle. You're nothing but a sack of bones, and don't give me that stuff about too thin and too rich. Remember when this came out?"

He looked at her hands as she flipped through the pages. Mary had always been so careful about her hands, her nails. Why, the first thing she'd done after gardening was set upon her hands with glycerin soap and a nailbrush. The buffing, the polishing! Hubbell felt miffed as he studied his daughter's hands. Not a single nail was the same length as another, and her carelessness seemed deliberate. The backstroke in a pool full of swimmers going forward.

"Oughta take care of those hands before you set off on any job interviews, Laydelle. All part of that general-appearance factor."

Her eyes lifted up off the page, and she didn't need to say that he'd never interviewed for a job in his life. Hubbell cleared his throat and pointed a finger at the page.

"Look how they highlighted those jade bottles. Magnificent, eh?"

"Divine. Your things are divine, Daddy. You could renovate a toolshed and make it feel like a palace."

Her generosity turned him inside out, and why? She praised his taste, his "way with things." She had Hubbell scraping bottom, and he began to count the days before she left. She'd managed to set up that nice living arrangement with the Marbles and would start a new job in two weeks' time. His daughter was about to settle in and settle down, and all he felt was melancholy. Why? He'd been a real father, spent the time his own father had withheld. He'd given her a running start on her own life. Hadn't he? Hubbell watched her closely. Her breathing seemed so shallow; it must have been those damned cigarettes. She'd left the feature on his boat and lingered over other pictures, licking the tips of her finger to turn each page.

"Like the issue?"

"I hate the issue. I hate all the issues."

"You used to love this magazine."

"I used to *be* this magazine, Daddy. I used to be a person who could live in these rooms. I guess that's what you don't get."

"My home is in here, and how much closer can you get than that? Oh, I read you, all right. Maybe better than you think. Well, I believe a little self-sorrow is just fine after tough knocks. See how I call it self-sorrow and not self-pity? That happens to make all the difference in the world. Not only do I think it's fine. I think it's necessary and part of getting whole again."

She closed the magazine and put it firmly between her legs. Hubbell shifted his weight, and the wicker squeaked.

"Only I was never half, Daddy, so your theory doesn't really work. Would you like to know how to help me?"

"I am helping you! Good God, Laydelle. I've done nothing but help you for the last ten years. I've taken care of every bad debt you've ever had. I'm not a bank! I'm not Goodwill! Is that what's making you sore?"

"Help me more. Stop lying."

Hubbell gasped, but the wicker chair was so noisy, it didn't matter. He felt light and heat, soft breasts and hair. Mary! She was gone in the next instant, and he felt like crying. Could he? Hubbell wondered. Could he ever, ever stop lying?

"Nothing worked. You issued me a passport, and I blew it. Instead of boning up on the essential things at Smith, I studied women and rage, which is a pastime, not a profession. I'm back, and I'm not young. Cotillion's over, Daddy."

"I wish you could hear yourself talk. What about your mother? She's going great guns out there in California, and she wasn't exactly youthful when she left me. Your own mother, Laydelle. Think of that, why don't you?"

"I do think of that, and all the time, too. But you know what? She never stopped being a working girl, not even when she dropped everything to marry you. That's why your marriage blew up. Mom was a born scrapper who stumbled into a soft life, and it just didn't work."

"That's your version. And that's a pretty poor rationale. But here's one fact you can't talk away. You're forgetting a very important something."

"What?"

"You're a Hanks."

He damned the words as they slipped out of his mouth. If the rivers were full of piss, as his father had suggested, he had just entered the headwaters and was soaked to the skin. He was very, very frightened.

"Yeah, right. That's been a big, fat help. Want to know why I've never been able to hold down a job? Why I've quit or been fired so often? Because I never wanted those stupid jobs in the first place!"

"But that's where a little persistence would pay off for you, honey. Maybe staying somewhere for a while, even though it bores you, even though—"

"I am the *queen* of the entry-level job. I have answered more telephones for more pricks than you can even begin to dream of, Daddy. Brewed more cups of coffee, picked up stranded pets, stranded children, stranded mistresses, for the biggest, dumbest pricks in the universe. I've balanced checkbooks, scheduled meetings, scheduled manicures and masseuses. And I've done it with a poor attitude, Daddy. They've all claimed I've had a poor attitude. And you know what? They're absolutely right! I'd much sooner scrape some money together to get in on a big project that might carry me right over that whole lousy routine."

She was back! There was the old pluck, the old vim and vigor Hubbell missed most. Now they were getting someplace. He had gotten her to sound off, and that was important. Once they waded through that, through all the rage and phony-baloney excusing, they would arrive at the heart of the matter, whatever that was.

"Sound investments are always attractive. The trick is determining just what constitutes a sound investment, and frankly, Laydelle, some of your ideas . . . well, have been ill-advised."

"I'm a Hanks, like you said. So why should I have to work in the first place? How come I don't spend my time flying around to trunk shows and gallery openings? How come I don't have a publicist and a social secretary? *Why aren't I rich?*"

"You know full well what my father thought about inherited money."

"Oh, yeah? You're none the worse for wear."

Now Hubbell was hot. He wasn't to blame for this! Did she think for a minute that her lousy life was *his* fault?

"Poison, Laydelle. He actually called it poison. I'm interested in your character! These circumstances are fleeting. What matters is—"

She picked up the worn copy of *Architectural Digest* and shook it at her father.

"What matters is money. Why aren't *I* in here, Daddy? How come somebody isn't trying to copy my life style? How did I get so screwed up?"

"Now if this is all a talk about self-esteem, you've come to the right place. I've worked long and hard to feel—"

"Stop there. Don't give me any program crap, please. I am telling you that I'm too much of a Hanks and not enough of one. And that it's a horror, Daddy. So I'm back, but I'm not home. I am telling you that the world broke a long time ago."

chapter 41

1973

"This is a setup. Do you believe this?"

Laydelle looked at her father, whose mouth was full. He didn't nod or even chew. He just sat there, his mouth stuffed with hickory-grilled steak, and stared at his wife.

"She got us in here so we wouldn't scream and shout or throw things. Don't worry, Mom. I won't throw a fit. Your plan won't work, you know."

Mary Hanks patted the corners of her mouth with a napkin.

"I beg your pardon. This is the United States of America."

"You can't just up and decide to be somebody else, Mom."

"Millions of people do it. I'm more gracious than most. I'm saying here's where I'm going and here's who I'm going to be."

Hubbell began to chew his food, helping this along with a big swallow of minty iced tea. He could finally speak.

"It's nice you invited me along, Mary. Really. I'm pleased to be invited to your little press conference."

"What do you mean by that crack?"

"I mean you're one cold fish. What do you expect us to do? Give you a round of applause and wish you good luck out there in—where did you say you were going?"

"I'm going to California."

"Perfect. Home to loose ends and rolling stones. Well, I wish you all the luck in the world, and by the way, I've known this was coming."

"We've been unhappy for years, Hubb. I've been a witch, fussing and complaining, trying to get you to be a different man than the fine one you are. Don't think that's been a pleasure for me. I don't like who I've become any better than you do. This is my last chance."

"What does happiness have to do with this? Nothing, as far as I can see. No, you waited until our daughter was twenty-two years old. You waited until the business possibilities looked good. You're a pragmatic soul, Mary, and you always have been."

Juices from the steak were hardening on Laydelle's plate. She thought of them doing that in her stomach and turned up her mouth in disgust. Hubbell put his hand on top of hers.

"We'll do just fine, honey. Don't you worry."

Hubbell thought of his boat. He had been living on his boat, more or less, for months. Oh, he still *resided* on Riverview Road, but his living and dreaming had begun to take place in Catoosa. He would move everything onto the boat, since Mary had her mind made up. That's what he would do. Hubbell Hanks would sell the house and move. Lock, stock and barrel. She wasn't the only one who could pick up and change things. The worst thing he could do would be to stay in the empty house and mope. She would never come back to him that way. Because Mary would come back, he was sure of it. When she saw that he was getting along, that Laydelle was getting along. This was all some kind of bid for attention. Then the smoke cleared for one minute in Hubbell's mind. He thought about menopause. So that was it!

"What's the matter now, Hubb?"

"Daddy, you look like such a dope. What are you *doing?*"

Hubbell was weeping. From gladness, since it was all a hoax. Not a hoax exactly, because the body and its seasons were things to be taken seriously. But this was something Hubbell could fix. Hubbell and a doctor. He reached for Mary's hand, even though it now held a steak knife.

"Mar, darling. This is something a husband and wife go through together. I've stood by you all these years. Don't think just because you're going through this change of life I'm the kind of man who will run out on you."

"Will you all excuse me? I'm going to go to the bathroom and throw up."

Laydelle knocked over a glass as she was going and threw a napkin over the mess to hide the spreading stain.

"Hubbell, I have no idea what you're talking about."

"I just mean that if you think I'm going to abandon you because you're going through menopause, you've got another think coming."

She looked up at the ceiling and was quiet for a moment or two.

"You're forgetting I went through menopause two years ago. Remember? You took me to Mineral Wells before we figured out what was happening. Sorry, Hubb. I'm afraid I'm not going through menopause. I'm not cracking up, either. I'm just leaving you. Plain and simple."

"You bitch. You inhuman bitch."

She sat back in her chair and put both hands smoothly around the curve of its wooden arms. She shook her head at a waiter approaching with a dessert menu.

"Do you really believe that, Hubbell?"

"From the bottom of my heart. So the worst is true. You've had your eye on the door for years, just waiting for the moment when I would forget to close it."

"Only I'm not an animal. I'm a human being."

"You're a mongrel. That's what Mother thought from the very beginning, though she had the decency not to say it."

Diners at Emil's Steak House turned their heads. Conversations at neighboring tables subsided, then ended completely, the better to hear Mary and Hubbell, who were really letting it fly.

"I won't have you dragging the Hanks name through the mud out there in California. I want it back! Each and every letter, starting with *H*." Hubbell began to shout.

"I knew it would end this way, with yelling and screaming. You snake. You toad. I've got news, Hubbell. I plan to travel light. The houseboat is yours."

"You damn well bet it is."

"The house on Riverview is yours."

Hubbell's voice wobbled. "Not for long. I'm going to get hold of a broker tomorrow. It always boils down to money, doesn't it? Go on, Mary, get to the punch line. Say it, say it!"

"I'll only take what I need to get started and not a penny more. This old battle has never been about *money*, Hubbell. The name is *mine*. I've worked hard at being Mary Hanks, and I won't give that up now. I won't drag the Hanks name through the mud, but I will use it to build a new life. That's one hell of a settlement, if you ask me."

Laydelle had returned from the bathroom. She didn't sit down. Dinner was clearly over.

"Here. One for you and one for you. Laydelle, my love, my life . . ."

Mary slid off Lavinia's ill-fitting ruby ring and gave it to her daughter. She set her wedding ring on top of Hubbell's dirty napkin.

"I may be your love, but I'm sure not your life."

"You're right. Wear the ring wisely. I hope you have better luck with it than I did."

She studied her husband's face, tapping her fingers against the table as she added one last afterthought.

"You can keep this town, Hubbell. You can keep the whole bloody state, for all I care. This state was and still is nothing but a damn dust bowl, and it's no wonder. The earth is so clogged with dead oil men, nothing will ever grow. Paint me *g-o-n-e*. Gone."

She left the state in a red Chevrolet. The roof was shot, and bits of it flew up into the air as she drove. She traveled pell-mell and didn't stop until a tire blew in the desert. By the time she could smell salt water, she had sighted a tarantula, hit a stray dog on the highway and picked out its remains from the grille of her car with no help from anyone. When it got too hot to drive during the day, she bought an inflatable man in Phoenix, stuck a ten-gallon cowboy hat on his head and pressed him into the seat next to her. Armed with her bodyguard, she sailed fearlessly by cars full of rough characters on long, dark stretches of road, honking twice as she passed them. When they finally reached Santa Monica, she kissed the rubber man goodbye and pitched him out of the car. Months passed before she recognized the woman she had been all those years. Months went by, then years, before enterprising, tough and gritty Mary Hanks could afford so much as a glance over her shoulder. *I did what, Baby? You must be kidding. I don't remember any such thing. Gotta run. I'll be late for my two-o'clock. Of course I'll write, you goofball.*

. . .

Laydelle sat hunched over the phone. She found that by leaning way into her cubicle, she could partially block out the competing noise around her. She had Mrs. Dyer right where she wanted her.

"How on earth did your mama cook up an idea like that? Then to think she had the courage to hop on a train and march up those steps, with you in her arms! You could go on Merv Griffin with a story like that. I mean it. I would drop everything if I heard a story like that and just listen."

"I'm breaking all the rules today, Mrs. Dyer. My boss would kill me if he knew what all I was telling you."

Laydelle lowered her voice and hoped the woman on the line could still hear her. She held one hand over her ear as she talked on.

"I mean, here I am telling a perfect stranger my whole entire life story, and on company time, too. I've got to hang up now, Mrs. Dyer. I've got to just stop jabbering and hang up this telephone."

"Not before you sell me a subscription. What did you say you offer? *Redbook*, was it? What were some of the others?"

Laydelle's pencil was poised over an order form. The woman's voice made her sound so little, so helpless. Telling the Joy Baby story worked every time. Just feeding it into the conversation casually, as if she'd never meant to let it slip. She had been at this job, this mind-boggling, idiotic job, for three weeks, trying to make a little money before going on to something big. And she had been a real flop until she stumbled on the Joy Baby thing inadvertently. "Joy Roller, you say your name is Joy Roller? That's funny. Gee, that makes me think of something I haven't thought of for years." What people couldn't tolerate was a sales pitch. What they were starved for was conversation. The sales came if only she could provoke a nice friendly chat. She hoped Mrs. Dyer wasn't living on Social Security or something like that. That would be terrible.

"*Cosmopolitan, House and Garden*. Golly, Mrs. Dyer. I can sign you up for just about any magazine you're already buying on the newsstand, and I can do it for half the price."

"Gee, I don't know. Maybe that one about horticulture. My husband, now, he does love to poke around outside. Would it be okay by you if I just signed up for a year? Would that help you a'tall?"

She filled out the form, then noticed that Leo was standing above her, one hand holding his chin. She sat up straighter in her chair and repeated everything, pausing every so often to say okay. Leo insisted that the use of the word "okay" acted on a person's sub-conscious mind. That with persistent, intelligent use of this impor-tant word, the orders would just tumble in.

"And to think I've been using Joy for years and years without knowing. I'll tell you what. Every time I give that bottle a squeeze, I'm going to think of you and that wonderful little anecdote you just told me. You're some storyteller, young lady, and I still think you ought to go on TV. When did you say I'll get my first copy?"

She hung up and sealed the order form with her head bent, pretending she didn't know Leo was standing over her. She won-dered if he knew the guy selling in the booth next to hers was a felon. She had heard him on the phone. Fuckin' A, I'm out, man. Fuckin' A. He had heard plenty coming from her side. Laydelle was hardly in a position to tattle.

"Nice work, Laydelle Hanks. You're my most promising em-ployee. But that's probably not news, is it?"

His belly hung over the top of the wooden partition. When he was not prowling around the room, moving row by row past his telephone team, Leo was busy nibbling. He chomped and chewed on anything salty, purchased at the small grocery store under the offices. The belly wasn't going anywhere just at the moment.

"You're so full of promise, Miss Hanks, that I wonder why you're here in the first place."

He also read books; that was an astonishing thing. Not junk, either. He ate that and read quality. Dostoyevsky, Tolstoy. He didn't just haul them around for show. They had a nice talk during the job interview. He abandoned their conversation about the voice in *Mr. Sammler's Planet;* closing his dog-eared copy with great reluctance, and said yes, of course, she was hired.

"I think you will be gone in another month. Tish, tish. To think I ran an ad for a permanent position. Ah, well."

He looked at her, the belly unmoving. *No, Leo, I will not go to bed with you. I will not mix business with pleasure, and anyway, you're too fat.*

"Coffee? I'm going downstairs."

"No, thanks."

He went on. A nice man, she thought, but what a way to spend your life. He'd been in the business fifteen years, he claimed. She heard the man next to her start his pitch. It was pitiful; he could barely read. Laydelle dialed Libby's number in Cambridge. It didn't ring long. She always called her at the same hour, knowing her friend would be home. Libby's work-study routine didn't allow for much spontaneity. She could see her now, slipping on her uniform to go wait tables.

"So how is the brainiest lady in Cambridge?"

"Pooped. Better quit calling me. You're going to lose your very first job, Laydelle."

"I don't call that a great loss."

"Why aren't you out here in graduate school?"

"More women? More rage? Please."

"There are other subjects open to study, you know. A profession; heard of it?"

"I know, I know."

"So?"

"The idea of more school . . . it just turns me off. I'll go back at some point. I just needed a break. Hey, I'm seeing the world, after all."

"You're seeing the inside of a box, you bozo. Well, remember the invitation's always open. We could room together, you know. Have you fallen in love since last Thursday?"

She phoned Libby to be needled, she supposed. These conversations always left her feeling slightly uncomfortable. Libby dispensed adages as freely as her mother did. Though not lately, for Mary Hanks was going full tilt on her own plans and projects.

"Nah. This guy I'm seeing is fun and all, but I keep forgetting his last name."

"Bad sign, friend."

They laughed and reviewed all the old subjects. Love? No, but it's on the way. Money? Very little. Family?

"Dad's okay. At least Aresta's out there with him, so I don't worry. I mean, I suppose she would throw a life preserver his way if he went overboard."

"And since we're speaking of overboard . . ."

"Mom? Revved up all the time. If I didn't know her better, I'd swear she was on drugs or something. She says she has an office at long last. On a street called Cahuenga Boulevard."

"Cahuenga. What a strange name. Sounds like a kind of nut to me."

"You may be onto something there."

Laydelle, I'm in business! I found a place for a song! The Hollywood offices of Mary Hanks Alternative Promotion were perched over a tanning salon. Antoine, proprietor of the salon, owned the entire building and leased his shady courtyard to a portrait artist named Bettina. The scuttlebutt was that Antoine once wanted to be a painter himself. Until, undermined by his own lack of skill, he had dragged all his canvases into the same courtyard and destroyed them. He often brought the Scandinavian artist coffee while his clients basted. Bettina's portrait subjects were increasingly pale, wistful-looking young men who walked in straight off Cahuenga, without appointments. Alternative *Promotion. Emphasis on alternative. Anything, anything is grist for the mill. "Don't ever turn your back on occasion" is my motto.* Mary Hanks talked business to anyone who would listen. *Why do I always tell a potential client my story? Because they have no notion of time, that's why. If they can't see how one thing feeds into another, how everything, the blows and the getting ahead, is a preamble, I can't work with them. Life is successive.*

"She tells them she's no overnight success. That Hanks Promotion only appears to have come along from nowhere. She says, and I quote, 'A life's work crystallizes over time.' Do you believe it, Libby?"

"I see I was right about the nut part. Does it work?"

"Seems to. She's got a real client list. I have to hang up."

"Talk to you later. Remember, whenever you decide to get serious about your life, I'm here."

"Yeah, yeah."

Laydelle started dialing numbers again, but without enthusiasm. She didn't even have the heart to repeat the Joy Baby story, to let people know they weren't buying magazines from just anyone. To someone in Chico or Wichita, these exploits made her a celebrity.

"Big deal."

The ex-con tipped his chair back.

"Just what I say. Big effing deal."

Roses bloomed on his forearm. There was a garden in full, blue bloom that rambled right up to his shirt sleeve, perhaps beyond. Laydelle put a finger to her temple and wondered where the whole mess stopped.

"You're going to break the chair legs."

"So what?"

"So nothing. How are sales going tonight?"

"They're not. Quittin' time, Laydelle."

He stared at her breasts, just to annoy her. That routine had started when she turned down a dinner invitation. But dinner with

an ex-convict wasn't possible. Looking at that mutilated skin over
a meal was beyond what Laydelle could do, even though she had
done plenty since leaving Smith. This job was the dregs. But it took
four hours a day and didn't interfere with the rest of her life. This
guy was the dregs.

"What in the world are you looking at?"

He didn't blush or apologize or do anything but stop looking.
Then he put his jacket on and fished deep in a pocket for his car
keys. He drove a car that had flames painted on the sides. He
stood right above her, with his keys in her face. The room buzzed
with voices. There were eighteen members in all on Leo's telephone team. She could hear Betty, top saleswoman of the group,
booming out her closer. "Twenty-four issues for seventeen dollars.
Maxine, you can't beat that with a stick!"

"How about we grab something to eat?"

"Can't tonight. Sorry."

"When are you gonna soften up, Laydelle?"

"When you leave me alone."

She dialed a number in Washington State. She thought about
the Cascades, how pure and clean that mountain range sounded.
Maybe she would get there sometime to see them for herself. She
had some friends in Seattle. They were starting a vegetable co-op.
Why not? she thought as the number began to ring. Why not vegetables?

"We can either grab something to eat together or I can grab
something by myself. Then just eat it nice and slow."

He was staring at her again, and a woman was saying hello for
the third time, only Laydelle couldn't answer. She couldn't do anything at all except listen to the woman shouting, "Are you there? Is
anyone there?" and finally slam the receiver down. She stayed on
the phone after she hung up, listening to the buzz go on and on.
How had she been so stupid? She began to think of all the reasons
why a man might serve time, a man with tattoos up his arm and a
car in flames. It didn't take much thinking. He was still standing
there, still watching as she swam and swam in water that seemed
to be sucking her down. Her tongue felt thick as she answered. It
was as if someone had given her a shot of Novocain and she fought
a thick, unmoving tongue with all her might just to make words.

"Tomorrow night. How about tomorrow night after work?"

He put his hand on the back of her head and stroked it.

"That's nice. That's real nice. We'll have a good time. What do you like to drink?"

"Oh, gosh. Anything wet."

His hand pressed the back of her neck and gave it a little jiggle. She started dialing again and returned his wink. He finally left, just as Leo came struggling through the door balancing a cardboard tray filled with coffee for several members of the team. Bags of peanuts and popcorn were tucked under his arm. He frowned at the man who was holding the door for him.

"What's this? The night's still young."

"But I'm not. Bad karma tonight, but tomorrow'll be better. Tomorrow I'm gonna sell a million of these buggers, man."

Leo shrugged and began taking coffee around, offering peanuts and popcorn to whoever would have them. Laydelle kept on dialing, grateful when no one was home or when a man answered. She had less luck with men, Joy Baby story or not. She heard the engine on his car open up and roar. He always left the parking lot the same way, leaving skid marks or a chorus of angry honking horns. Leo prowled the aisles, listening in and peering at order forms and tally sheets. *Sorry, Leo. Sorry, sorry. I'll mail you back the copy of Hegel.* She planned the phone call she would make as soon as she got back to her apartment. She would be up all night packing her things, but it didn't matter. Lucky it was a furnished apartment, that most of her things were still in storage in Tulsa, right where they'd been since the house was sold. She would stay in a hotel for a while, that was what she would do. She would just stay in a hotel and not hurry, not rush into another bad situation. This all proved how a person could really get in trouble if great attention was not paid. If time wasn't taken. What had Libby just said? If a person didn't take life seriously. Well, she would, and starting this minute.

"Peanut?"

"Pass, thanks."

He smiled at her approvingly and continued his rounds. Despite all the mayhem, she had done a respectable night's work. Mayhem. She thought about Amos Sweet, Jr., now fishing alone off in Colorado after Mrs. Sweet's desertion. She had run off with not one but two younger men. The trio lit out for Las Vegas just as Amos took retirement. Her eyes began filling up slowly. For the first time in her life, she wished he were here, lumbering along after her as she pretended not to know who he was. Lingering in a doorway peeling a banana or reading *Motor Trends*. Laydelle had finally gotten just what she wanted. There was no safety net to-night, nor would there ever be. She began to plan her phone call to Hubbell, selecting a style as if she were reading a menu. Trem-ulous? "Daddy, I'm in an awful jam, and you've just got to help me." Businesslike? "Hello, Dad. Yes, it's me, and I know it's late, so I won't hem and haw." Simple and truthful? "God, he's got tattoos that go all the way up one arm, and don't tell Mom this part if you talk to her, but . . ."

But. It was going to be a long night and a long day, and, yes, she'd had a terrible scare, but if it all led to a good place on high, dry ground, then what did this difficulty matter? Mary Hanks was no fool. Life was successive—she could learn from this episode and discard it. Laydelle checked her face in the mirror Leo thought-fully included in each and every partitioned cabin.

"Try it, you'll like it. *Of course* we offer *Field and Stream*, Her-man!"

Betty was on a roll. Maybe there was even a twelve-step lesson in all this. She would ask Hubbell tonight. That would please him. He loved to adapt the twelve-step method to life, or was it the other way around? She could never remember.

"Okay."

She said that to trim the messy ends off the evening and stood up to go, deciding she really was okay. The guy was a creep, and she would never see him again. She waved so long to Leo, feeling pretty bad about that, but there was nothing she could do. He was beaming, having heard her utter his favorite four-letter word, the passport to success, the keys to San Francisco, a one-week stay for two, since even telephone teams, especially telephone teams, could use a little incentive. Okay. He had finally converted Lay-delle Hanks. The proof lay before him.

Nelson and Lavinia

chapter 42

1941

Surprise. That's what they called it: a surprise attack on Pearl Harbor that December 7. As if it were a birthday cake with pale, sputtering candles. Lavinia's feet were soaking in a tub of Epsom salts when the news broke on the radio. She fought the impulse to run to the window for a look at the sky. What would she see—whose warplanes? She tried to assemble her thoughts as the water cooled about her feet. She had concluded her grim civic address on a comic note, complaining of a woman's lot—high heels and aching feet. Better to discard them for the thick soles of practical shoes that would carry them to work. With enlistment figures on the rise, jobs would be vacated. Jobs that would need to be filled. Her thoughts broke off again as she looked about the room, seeking some change, some dislocation of objects, now that they were a nation at war. Joey's appearance at the door was disorienting, suddenly strange against the news announcer's sharp voice, denouncing the Japanese strike on the harbor. How many battleships damaged . . . ? The voice grew choppy with emotion. Ninety-four U.S. ships moored in the harbor, and now— She switched off the radio and lifted her dripping feet. Joey wrapped them in a towel and carried off the basin of water without a word.

She was left alone. Nelson flew out for Washington. The first

meeting of the Petroleum Industry Council for National Defense
was held that week. It was time to put into effect all the measures
he and the company men had been planning for weeks. There
would be major production increases, and the synthetic-rubber
venture Hanks mounted with another company would swell way
beyond its present capacity. Nelson advanced to a front line of
industry leaders and government officials, as eager to bring about
victory as a foot soldier. Lavinia stared out the window and envied
his departure, his bustle as he shouted orders, stomping up and
down the stairs as he prepared to leave.

She was hot first, then she was cold. There seemed no comfortable chair in the wide, empty house, and she passed from room to
room, agitated and anxious to light somewhere so she could cast
down an anchor, write the first entry in a journal she had been
unable to begin. How uncomfortable her house seemed. She
thought of the telephone, of how she must make calls. The first
thing to do was compare her version of events with others. But she
found after an hour of dialing familiar numbers that there wasn't
even this to do. An attack was unequivocal, and there was nothing
to do but quibble about the range of destruction and speculate
about the next few weeks and months. Hysterical Lorette phoned,
crying about the five thousand men lost in an instant. Worse than
the dead were the missing. Where were these missing men?
Trapped under the hull of a ship, drifting farther and farther out to
sea on a scrap of whatever would float after the chaos of fire and
bombs? Her voice trembled, and she said five thousand and one,
for her son had enlisted that morning. Put on his hat and coat,
drawn his mother up in his arms and kissed her like a lover, Lorette
said. On the lips to say goodbye forever in the way men and
women do. Lavinia could do little but set the record straight. She
did it even though her voice shook with reverence, for Lorette had
become holy with the possibility of such a huge loss. Not half that
many men are dead or missing, Lorette. They just said so on the
radio this morning. Not way that many men. She struggled to inject
this announcement with authority. After she hung up the phone
with her friend, there was little to do but fret and drink strong
drinks.

She surrendered to Scotch that afternoon. She drank it warm,
sipping with familiarity and affection. She let Scotch lead her to a
chaise longue, even though she longed for more drama than this
on the first day of war. She wasn't Lorette, she thought, nearly

asleep. The war had no face. She lay stretched on the chaise for nearly an hour, her dreams concocting a battalion of matrons. She and all the club women, their high heels properly discarded in favor of boots, took up wheelbarrows to search Hawaiian forests for the missing. They weren't missing at all! They lay sprawled in the forest, dangling from trees or crouched in the enormous fronds of a fern. The men were not missing but hiding, and it was up to her unit to fetch them from a forest blooming with bombs. For bombs were falling in Lavinia's dream. Falling to release a spray of red and violet. Their eyes strained with the work of finding men in such harsh, exploding country.

She woke up with a jerk. Joey stood over her with his old look of concern. He had prepared a tea tray, for it was late. Ordinarily the sight of finger sandwiches and the sugar cookies he rolled out himself in the shape of stars and hearts to please her would have happily bridged the two worlds of sleep and awakening.

"I didn't hear you come in."

"If you don't wake up now, there's no hope for you tonight."

She glanced at the bottle. How much had she drunk to achieve this? Her mouth was dry, and it was difficult to speak. So she didn't. She ate all her sandwiches. The tea was good, though she would have preferred sassafras. She took her usual long time chewing and swallowing, then allowed it had been a good idea to wake her and stoke the engine. She looked up to tell Joey something, but he had left the room.

There's no hope for you tonight. She played the phrase over and over again in her mind, wishing Nelson would be in his room down the hall from her own, like other nights. Though she never stopped to disturb him as she marched up and down those halls, she knew he was there, and she derived some comfort from his sleep, so unknotted and unlike her own. Only Joey knew how she paced the nights away. Her thoughts were slouching toward a bad place. She let them go there, and that was probably the Scotch tearing down the fences that ordinarily kept such thoughts contained.

"Damn it, Joey. Don't do that."

He lifted his eyebrows, the only form of arrogance he permitted himself.

"You startled me."

She stared at the man who had served her for eighteen years. He had seen her in bed more frequently than her own husband, and today he had multiplied to become a nation. She thought back to that letter of recommendation she had demanded years ago from a rasping old man in New York City. Where was he now, and could he still assure her that slipping, silent Joey Fujii wished her no harm? Lavinia was suddenly an old, enfeebled lady covered with a flimsy sheet of bleached white skin. She cast her eyes down, but not her thoughts, which spun off into nightfall and darkness, the terror suddenly come into her own house.

The nation steamed ahead into war, and Lovely mobilized, producing its own crop of healthy, living boys to be hacked down or split apart for a nation in need. Lavinia mobilized, too. Her war job was to remain in a vacant string of rooms unprotected by so much as a husband. She damned Hubbell, who seemed intent on making himself some kind of Red Cross unit for his fighting friends. What about his own mother? Lavinia Hanks would have to see about her own defense.

She set the stage carefully, pleased with her cunning. She felt a light twinge of regret, nearly imperceptible, at the crystal decanter and glasses, purchased in Venice, that were about to be sacrificed. It was nothing, a small loss. A large mirror hung over the table where the tray rested. She admonished the woman she saw reflected there to remain composed and keep her wits about her. Self-pity crept in as she memorized her own image. If I'd been one of those little women, one of those quaking creatures who never had a thought or a scheme, this wouldn't have happened. She saw breasts still proud as the hull of a ship and a strong though shifting face. She became so transfixed by her own image that her confusion was real when Joey appeared in the mirror beside her. Her hand swept across the top of the decanter, nicking the side of the first glass, which sent the others tumbling like a stack of dominoes. She carried out the act as planned. If it lacked concentration and was a split second late, she was the only one who knew. It all fell to the floor. Shattered glass fell to the floor as far as Nelson's wing-chair.

She turned to face him, arranging her features into an expression of wrath. There was no replacing the decanter, and that helped.

"See, Joey! Just look at what you've done with the way you go round this house like a fox. My nerves are on edge, and this isn't helping. It's worse than trapping a child in the dark."

She let her eyes drift down until they fell on the slippers, the house shoes replaced year after year by relatives in Kyoto.

"Nelson and I used to have our little cordials here by the fire with these. You know as well as I do how I love those little glasses, how perfect they were. All because of those dreadful things."

Not even Joey could mask his astonishment as she bent to her work, tapping the back of his leg lightly as if she were forcing the leg of a stubborn horse. She lifted Joey's leg up to remove the slipper. Then the other. He blanched and fought a nausea that resembled seasickness. The same seasickness he had felt as a young man who stood on the deck of a cargo ship for America. Only now he was floating on a real sea of despair, deeper than any he had crossed. He stood before his employer in white-stockinged feet. She examined his slippers briefly, the dreadful things, then tossed them in the fireplace.

"Take a match to them."

He supposed she had gone mad, but it was a supposition that carried little weight, so ill was he, so bent on reversing the waves of sickness and sending them away so he could stand without falling. She handed him a book of matches, not noting his pallor or the single vein that stood out on his temple. What else would she ask him to burn? Where would it end? He heard the flame snap alive and stared at his own fingers. They didn't shake, and that was strange, since he was shaking inside.

They both watched as the shoes burned. The tips of the toes curled up as soon as they caught. They took no time at all and soon became small and black as charred fishing boats. He looked out the window once. The ice on the streets would cut open the soles of his bare feet, tear at the skin until it detached reluctantly from bone like a piece of adhesive flypaper or the glossy drawer liner he inserted in kitchen drawers.

"Here. Do this for me."

Then he saw how it was all by design. How she had trapped him like a rabbit or a squirrel. What would a pair of Dutch clogs be doing in the drawing room in the first place? He knew where they belonged, in which box, in which corner of the vast closet. He saw she meant for him to step into them, so he did. Was this the last step or simply another? Now that she had her horse properly shod, would she slide a metal bit between his teeth? Would he munch oats from a feed bag and dip his face into a trough of water because a war had begun? At least he had his strength again. The sickness had passed, though he felt his head light and separate from the rest of him. He leaned forward, testing the clogs.

"This way I'll hear you coming, Joey. And there won't be any reason for me to startle. I need extra help now that there's a war on. Bad nerves splinter like bone if you don't take care. Why, you're as tall as I am now!"

The hate he felt for this woman grew great and fat as the tumbleweed he'd seen blowing across Texas. It caught hold of any debris along the way: thoughts and emotions that strayed were sucked up into this rough, ragged clump of hate. He regretted not having children. For this was his legacy, more than any sight and sound he ever noted swinging through America. The story of this blind fool was something to be passed on. In being handed over to another generation, the hate would not stay inside to poison him. The tumbleweed would unravel in the telling, until nothing remained but dry sticks and grasses, oddments of the American plain.

Nelson saved them both. He ditched Washington and the greater front to return to the skirmish at home. He burst out laughing when he saw Joey.

"Has she decided she wants a little Dutch boy to bring her morning tray? I guessed I heard a Clydesdale this morning, just like the one that pulled the milk truck through Creston. I never imagined it was you. Take off those ridiculous things."

It was the bare beginning.

"Dirty Jap!"

How many times can a man be wrong, he thought, as BB-gun bullets caught him on the back of his neck and shoulders. He had gone into town for oranges. Oranges, exotic now that there was a war on, had somehow gotten into the produce section, and the grocery store manager had telephoned with the news. Joey hadn't died by a single shot from a Colt or the thick blade of a tomahawk. Nor had he been taken in that fiery crash he'd foreseen behind the wheel of a Pierce-Arrow. He would be felled by these angry pellets, fired off by a tight-faced boy.

He turned to face his tormentor. The bag of groceries shielded his heart. His muscles tensed as he moved toward the boy.

"Put that thing away."

"Ugly Jap!"

But he was stepping back. Cautious and slow, but he had lowered the gun now. He was uncertain of what to do. His friends had abandoned him once he fired off the first shot. They'd run off, leaving him to figure things out. He thought of his father, what he'd do. He hadn't figured on the man speaking English or daring to turn after he screamed out the insult.

He decided to run for it, turning down an alley that ran alongside the market. He even dropped the gun, which Joey picked up to drop inside the bag of oranges. His neck stung, and one or two welts had begun to appear. Joey drove slowly. He thought of antidotes for the pain with disinterest.

The news of travel restrictions had grazed him just like this blast of birdshot. For a Japanese to board a train now required documentation from the district judge. What about California? he wondered, still stunned. What about the railroad I helped build? In the end, it was just as he suspected. It was the house that returned love, the house that gathered him in to hold him close.

For two days he lay inside the library walls. The chamber intended to protect Nelson Hanks and his family now protected him. He could hear the thunder and applause from where he lay on the chaise longue. The rally took place downtown, but it was being broadcast. Those without a radio had only to walk into the streets, for the addresses carried clearly over loudspeakers. They were instructed to remember Pearl Harbor, and Joey thought of the fool's notion from where he lay, growing stronger, less fearful inside the tight dimensions of the hidden room. One year later, who could forget? The rally was to offer veterans of older wars, men and women still raw with loss, some way to spoon off their anger and fear. He listened to the slogans. "Map our Japs," a woman repeated, until others joined her. "Know where our local Japanese are at all times." When the cries leveled off, another man took over, to reassure the crowds. He read aloud from an inventory list. He named and numbered all the items that had been rounded up from servants' quarters in those early months, more reasons for Lovely residents to feel safe and protected. Shortwave radios and flashlights. Knives and lanterns, typewriters and any garden tool that could be used to dig and bury important information. Joey held himself, his arms clasped tightly about his chest. He loved himself harder and better than ever, for that was important. Hanks could hide him until the ruckus was over, but who would love Joey Fujii through the debauch? He stroked his own face with a smooth hand and beat back the fever that had raged for two days. When Nelson came to get him, he emerged whole and healed. *Map our Japs!* His route ran to the center of this house, the place where its heartbeat lay.

Nelson called the two of them to the gazebo in back of the town house. Nothing was replanted in the spring of 1943, and what remained was a garden made up only of tough survivors. Some of the hardy plants had reseeded and burst through the packed soil. The expanse once given over to spring plantings now lay barren.

"With a yard like this, I'm walking around with my drawers down. You two get to work."

"On what? Planting tiger lilies, snapdragons, with the Germans rushing troops into Italy?"

"Not snapdragons. Snap beans! And sweet tomatoes! Squash will grow here, and don't tell me no. We need produce, and the two of you are letting precious land lie fallow. I'm telling Hanks customers to save their gas and leave their cars in the garage. To walk, not ride, for the sake of the rubber they'll be saving for the war effort. The least my wife and valet can do is start a victory garden."

She was grateful for her aching back, for hands that would shortly sport calluses. Her idle war was abandoned for this one. She pulled weeds and scattered seed to within an inch of her life. She smelled her own perspiration for the first time in years and was bleary with happiness for her body's energy. She inhaled pesticide as if it were lavender soap.

Order or chaos? Joey began his campaign of white cotton markers. He erected little fences barring peas from beans and beans from carrots. Potatoes inhabited a land of their own. Lavinia stood barefoot in their midst, planning to scallop them until she remembered the rich cream it required. She would make a warm potato salad, then. She would toss turnips together with sugar peas.

Joey kept his distance. It wasn't as easy as she had supposed. He didn't intend to forgive her for burning those shoes, and when her romance with pain ended and the summer sun continued to scorch the top of her aching forearms, she wanted to push him over into the pea patch he was tending. She had been shaken, and what was so hard about understanding that? Her folly became his fault.

Hot sun! They canned and preserved in the humid basement, sealing up their food and fuel with paraffin.

That fall they stood together facing a solid wall of mutual labor. The cruel sun had set, and Lavinia stared at the tapestry of fruit and vegetables, the rows and rows of summer fruit and vegetables, which would keep for months.

"Well, we've certainly done it."

Joey had a finer eye than she did. He spotted something high up. A jar of beans infiltrated his fruit section. He crawled up the ladder to put things in their proper order. That afternoon she planned another map. It wouldn't lead to further degradation, some version of Manzanar, the internment camp where Japanese immigrants would wait out the next few years. He stood high and still on the ladder until proof of their work appeared perfect and uniform. Lavinia planned that day to leave him fifty thousand dollars. She didn't realize Joey Fujii was already a wealthy man.

Joey had a stockbroker and a bank account in New York City. His net worth ensured a future that had nothing to do with Lavinia Hanks' temper tantrums or the proper segregation of summer fruit and vegetables. A separate career spanned nineteen years and at least one hundred poker games. As the country's leading industrialists shuffled and dealt their cards, emptied glasses and called for more whiskey and beer, Joey had served and listened. Scraps of the conversations he overheard were phoned in to a broker. Joey stood still under the shadows of a Texas longhorn head. A corn pone to the end, Nelson pushed a button to trigger his toy, and the eyes of the steer lit up. Smoke signals erupted from the nostrils as the voluble chairman of Chrysler laughed and laid down his cards for the rest of the table to see. Joey lit cigars and cigarettes, whisked off heaped ashtrays and retreated through the empty hallway as businessmen and politicians relaxed and gabbed in the fraternal atmosphere at Nelson's ranch. There were many reasons to remain in Nelson Hanks' service, even after love was lost and disaffection was complete. Joey worked two worlds assiduously. He bought stock in Japanese companies before the war broke out, and after it was over he reinvested dividends in companies formed to rebuild his country. The future of those companies would make Fujii a millionaire.

Laydelle

chapter 43

1989

"Let me get this straight. You can't afford a ticket to California? Even when you can write off the whole trip?"

"The Marbles are asking a lot for this place, I'm behind on some bills, and this job isn't exactly what I hoped it would be. Besides, I was just out there for my seminar. I'm kind of preoccupied at the moment, and it's not a great time, Mom."

"I will put a ticket in the mail for you, but I may as well be frank. It angers me. By now you ought to be . . . well, I don't know what. Plunging ahead. That's it! You ought to be surging on with things, too hot to stop. That I'm not reading all about my daughter in *Vanity Fair* is a mystery and a shame. I've got to put you on hold."

Mary was calling from her office. The up-and-at-'em philosophy was always more remarkable when it was being broadcast from Hanks Alternative Promotion. Laydelle squinted at the corners of the room and frowned. She'd vacuumed up there only a few days ago, though no one would have guessed it. Mary returned and told her to circle the fifteenth on her wall calendar.

"Fine. By the way, since when do people write off trips to visit their mothers?"

"Don't kid yourself, Baby. I'm flying you out business class. It's high time you learned how to capitalize on your talents. That's the kind of mother's milk I'm good for. You thought the Pedigree Protection seminar was great? Wait till I give you mine! I'll give you a seminar that'll knock your socks off, Baby."

She held her hand over the telephone for a moment, and when she spoke next her voice dropped a notch. They were conspirators again, and Laydelle assumed her assistant had left the room.

"There I go with all my bullshit, Laydelle. My infernal pitch."

What made the current Mary Hanks substantially different than the fussy old Mary Hanks she'd been was freedom of speech. Bullshit and balls, a string of undeleted expletives seemed to define her success as much as anything else. Her mother had become a very crass act to follow.

"I am doing great out here, just great. And sometimes I feel like crowing about it. And if you can't brag on yourself to your own daughter, then the world's gone to hell in a bucket."

"I've got the fifteenth circled, Mom. I'm coming out, don't worry."

"I've got it!"

Not even the hurly-burly of LAX diminished her mother. She produced quite a wake, but not because of clothing or cosmetic surgery. The kind of tan contracted on ski slopes or tropical beaches turned fewer heads than the sturdy, determined figure of Mary Hanks. Her oddball good looks and slightly metallic tone, that impregnable flip, all invited attention. Mary jawed, she prattled, with perfect strangers. Then offered her business card as intimately as if it were a secret handshake. "I've got it!" was an aside to a tall, silver-headed man Laydelle had never laid eyes on. Mary held up one thumb.

"Hi, Mom."

"I saw it there, right back there as you were turning your head. You're an artist, Laydelle."

"That's terrific, only I don't paint or sculpt. So how does that figure?"

"But let me finish. Don't you see? You're an artist without a palette. You have the temperament, the demeanor, certainly that slightly tarnished, tired air. . . . What do you think, Dave?"

"I think your daughter is perfectly charming whether she paints or not, and I think her mother is a blitzkrieg. Call my office on Monday, Mary."

"Will do."

He winked at Laydelle and moved off to greet someone across the crowded reception area.

"I see you're up to your old adventures."

"Dave's in aerospace. . . . Not that I know beans about it, but that's never stopped me. You look divine, and what we have to do now is flesh out that whole aspect. That whole je ne sais quoi. Love, love your hair, Baby. That wild look is very now. What's the scowl for?"

"My stomach's in knots. It's like I swallowed a hunk of ma-cramé."

Mary Hanks turned her head suddenly to stare at her daughter. She set her handbag on the floor and gently took hold of Laydelle's face. Tears welled up and spilled over, taking trails of black mascara with them.

"The worst part is over, Baby. I can help you now. I can help you because I'm finally better myself."

Laydelle could hear her talking to Nina behind the closed door of her bedroom.

"What can I tell you? My kid needs me, and I'm not coming in this week. Tell Russo the scumbag it'll have to wait until Thursday. I have a situation here, Nina, and I'm not coming in. I've got to rise to this occasion. Be sure to get the Stipley contract in the mail by this afternoon. Ciao."

Laydelle didn't have the energy to object, to ask what situation she was referring to or to correct her, saying that the occasion she was rising to was one Mary had created herself. It wasn't Laydelle who had cooked up this trip, after all. It was Mary. Life wasn't any more dramatic now than it had been at any point over the last decade.

Decade. The word smarted. It would soon be two decades since college, twin sets of years, since they so gloomily resembled each other. Phone calls continued, and Laydelle studied the room and thought of how appropriate "town house" seemed. A condominium was a flashy upstart beside this three-story, rather lugubrious relative. Mary's town house was all brick and ivy. Sunlight filtered in through carefully orchestrated plantings. Mature trees had been hauled in at rather alarming expense to frame the building, and the whole composition implied a stable, sturdy denizen of this Beverly

Hills P.O. Her mother's rooms were dripping with Ralph Lauren,
and knickknacks were provided by Pierre Deux. Laydelle studied
the paisley wool under her elbow. She would have been very happy
wearing her mother's fine and beautiful sofa. She might have argued with Mary, saying that she was no kid and that what she
needed wasn't mother's milk but a more lucrative job, if she hadn't
been busy with a cure of her own. Laydelle believed that grace was
a kind of good germ, that it could be absorbed by contact. That
grace and goodness and beauty could be stolen only from graceful,
good and beautiful things. She lay still with her eyes and self wide
open, filling up on all that Mary had wrought. On all that Mary
had bought.

"Like it? Like all my stuff?"

Her mother was off the phone, and the flip was momentarily
stuffed under a silk scarf. Her mother's face looked fuller without
the unmoving ridge of hair. She'd worn a collagen mask all morning, and her face shone now that it had been washed off.

"Yeah, I definitely like your stuff. You may have to pry me from
this couch."

"Sofa, my love. Nobody says couch out here. That's one of the
very first things I learned."

Something languorous and heavy seemed spread over the days,
and neither woman rushed to make a plan. Mary's seminar was
oddly low-key, for which Laydelle was thankful. They drank es-
presso until any ordinary mortal would sweat or shake, yet somehow they didn't. They eyed each other and idled, thumbed through
foreign magazines Mary subscribed to for "the visuals" or talked
in a very loose way about the theater piece they ought to see or a
screening at the Writers Guild they meant to attend. They didn't.
For a while it seemed their visit together would pass without a
tremor. It didn't.

"Up and at 'em, Baby. We're going limp, lying around this joint.
I told you I wanted to crow. I've made reservations for us at Oxy-
gène."

"What on earth is that?"

"It's my restaurant, my baby. One baby among many, I should
say. Don't get too impressed, though. I don't own it, I just dreamed
it up, and it's a dilly if I do say so myself."

The restaurant had become an overnight landmark on Melrose. There was valet parking. Three men rushed to the car, and both doors were jubilantly flung open. Smiles and French were ladled on thick as gravy.

"What are they saying, Mom?"

"Who knows? Who cares? This is bliss."

Mary rose from the car in a movement that suggested levitation. Laydelle was having a terrible time. She'd worn one of her perennial long skirts. The hem caught on the seat-adjustment lever, and she heard a loud rip. Her mother was already at the door. Laydelle forgot the torn skirt and the fluttering attendants as she stared at the structure. It suggested— No, that would be too weird. Her mother was being embraced by several people. She freed herself for a moment and waved her forward.

"Mother, is this place what I think it is?"

"People love sidewalk dining in L.A. Now they can have painless sidewalk dining. They're booked weeks in advance."

"But how did you rig this up? Aah. God, it's like taking a hit."

"I just hate that sixties talk. Always did."

They followed the maître d' to a table on the sidewalk. The dining area was sheathed in plastic. The appointments, the service, were all perfectly conventional. Menus opened to a respectable list of bistro selections. If it weren't for her spinning head, Laydelle might not have suspected she was eating in an oxygen tent.

"Their French fries are the real thing, cooked in lard. Want to know how I thought of it?"

"Not only that, but who bought such an idea."

"There's always someone to buy ideas, so there's nothing to be afraid of but the dearth of ideas. And that has never been a big problem of mine."

She poured from a bottle of Evian.

"I'm thinking of this photo of a bar in Japan where you can order oxygen, and suddenly I pull my car over."

"Why are you always pulling your car over?"

"I can't help it. Ideas come to me when I'm in motion; they always have. Once I'm parked, I think to myself, *Expand this thing, Mary.* At that point I looked out the car window and saw a smog ledge coming toward me, and I thought, Okay, go with this thing. So I went."

Laydelle's head was beginning to clear. It felt like one of those high-altitude moments when you could see forever and ever.

"How did you get city ordinances for this thing?"

"Tough, very tough. But I know people, Laydelle. Like you know people."

Mary was polite. She let her daughter eat in peace. She let her dawdle through green salad and suggested she order a slice of apple tart, knowing that would take forever, the way she ate.

"Slowpoke. Well, it's good to see you enjoy your food. You're too thin. It all comes off your chest."

Her mother tapped the table nervously, ready to spring.

"For you *do* know people. And how's your father?"

"Seems well. He's happy as long as he's afloat."

"Aren't we all? He's taken it to an extreme, though. I have a bone to pick with him, you know."

"You've had several."

"Do you wonder what I'm getting at when I say you know people?"

Laydelle's mouth was full, and her mother rushed on.

"Don't become a mascot, Laydelle. Don't make those mistakes your father has made. They want his presence at their goddamned balls?"

Here it came. The wall of bad words moved inexorably forward. When Mary was adamant, she was also profane.

"They want him there to preside over all that crap, they ought to make him the president. They should put him on salary. I'm for charity, Laydelle. Don't misconstrue what I'm saying. But let charity come from the proper source. Hubbell has been shrinking from his name for years. Shrinking! He pissed away all the authority his good name contained. He treated his last name like it was a hoax or a jinx or . . . something bad. And it's good! Laydelle, it's good! It's a commodity, and he's too blind to see that. But you, now, you're a different case."

She would have smoked, that was clear. All her gestures suggested an absent habit. A thing it would have been nice to do right now. She fussed with her flip until she got it. Mary fidgeted until all her notions congealed.

"You've had a hard time of it, Baby. It shows. Those beauty marks on your face mean you've been out there living. But I'm not talking about looks or youth, any of that crap. Go deeper, Laydelle. Make yourself go deeper. You're in a perfect position to draw upon your own good fortune."

"Right."

"You want to sell Pedigree Protection systems? Fine. But don't do it incognito. Let them know you're a Hanks. Let them know in subtle ways that you've grown up with beautiful things. That you've sat in rooms as fine or finer than theirs and that you *understand* just what it is they want to protect. Don't lord it over them. Just tell them your name and watch it pass for a secret handshake! You're a fellow clan member, and how will they know unless you tell them? I'm just suggesting that you use your own natural resources. You're a forest! You're a gold mine!"

"And you're a blitzkrieg. Dave was right. God, Mom, calm down. You're going to knock something over."

"You bet your sweet ass I am. I'm going to knock over this family's false pride. That little-old-me stuff is nothing but arrogance. Check, please."

Mary put an additional hundred miles on her car that week. She was famished for vistas, all the scenic drives she never took the time to enjoy. She hit an open stretch of Mulholland Drive and launched the last part of her offensive.

"So how's your love life?"

Laydelle was busy looking for coyotes. She'd read they came down out of the hills, that they raided garbage cans and doghouses and had even been seen eyeing babies from a safe distance. Safe for whom, she'd wondered when she read this. She thought if she concentrated hard enough, she could actually make one appear.

"I'm talking to you, Laydelle. Let me ask it another way, then. Who's the man in your life and do I know him? Or are there several? Are you stringing several fellows along, Baby?"

"When it's time to plan a wedding, I'll let you know."

"Aha!"

Mary pulled over. There was a fresh tightness around her mouth. She'd yanked her scarf off, and now her hair stood on end from the stiff wind.

"So you're in a serious romance and you haven't even told your own mother. You were always so furtive, but I guess it's too late to work on that. Just give me the basics. What's his name, what does he do, was his mother in the League with me? His mother didn't *make* the League, is that it? Go ahead, don't be afraid of hurting me. I must know his family."

"He's from Lovely."

Mary winced.

"When he's not in Lovely he's in Saint-Tropez."

She popped a stick of Juicy Fruit in her mouth and smiled at her daughter.

"I knew big things were in store for you. You'll forgive me for the *Vanity Fair* outburst, but this is exactly the kind of thing I mean. Saint-Tropez! Well, tell me his name."

"John Beaureve."

"Marvelous! The French make wonderful lovers."

"He's an Indian, Mother. He's an Osage Indian. Get it? I met him last year when I came out for the seminar."

Just then Mary was sideswiped, and not just by this revelation. A dark-green MG came careening around the curve and skimmed the side of her car, removing at once paint, a long strip of chrome and Mary's rearview mirror. The car stopped, and a tall blond boy leaped from the passenger seat, not bothering to open his door. The driver turned and studied the deep gash along the side of their car, then shut his eyes. He put his head on top of his hands.

"My God, ma'am. Are you hurt?"

"I'm not, but my car is."

Mary removed her sunglasses carefully and patted down her hair. She was shaken and gave herself a minute or two to gather some concentration. During that minute she sized up the British accent, the British plates and the military helmets and chains that both boys wore.

"Wait a minute. I know you. You boys were on the Carson show last week. In fact, it was Tuesday night. You boys caught my eye. Let me introduce myself."

She helped the blond to the car, for it turned out he was far more shaken than Mary Hanks. Luther and James were driving a friend's car, a friend who lived in Laurel Canyon. Insurance? Neither Luther nor James knew a thing about car insurance, and they were doubly glad to sit back and let Mary take care of all that. This was their first time to America. Los Angeles was so different from Manchester, and here was just one more example. Luther nodded and said that yes, sure, he would come to Mary's office on Thursday morning. It didn't seem possible they had just bashed up this woman's car.

"Good. You boys be off now. No more high jinks on these roads, do you hear? Yes, we can all thank our lucky stars. Until Thursday."

She trotted back to her car, not even glancing at the damage. Laydelle hummed the theme music from *Jaws*.

"Very funny. Never turn your back on occasion, as I've said more than once. Wring that fortune from misfortune. Now where were we? Ah, yes! How's your love life, Baby?"

chapter 44

1991

"What do you mean, you can't come? You have to come. It's *important* to me that you come."

Sally Marble refused to frown. She'd been reading up on Cher. It seemed that her fantastic appearance, cosmetic surgery aside, had to do with the fact that she never, ever frowned. The reporter in the article pointed out that Cher did not let her forehead crease, regardless of what she was feeling.

"Dougie Jameson is dying to meet you. He says your grandfather knew his. That they rode out to the Grand Canyon together once. He wants to talk all about that with you."

"Sally, please stop. I'm not coming to your party, and that's that."

She was in a nasty mood. In fact, she'd been in a nasty mood since seeing Johnny last month. She woke up each morning fully expecting to rise and shine, but she didn't. Getting up at all was like lifting herself out of a trench. Sally had redone the house for the umpteenth time, and that was another reason to growl. She had transformed good rooms simply because they no longer suited her, not because the chairs were worn, the satin ripped or the wool rugs stained by one of her dogs.

"Why? Give me a good reason and I'll stop badgering you."

"I know you better than that. You're prolonging your own misery, Sal. I'm not coming."

Sally pursed her lips. The article hadn't said anything about Cher's lips.

"I know what's eating you. I'll just bet I know."

She got up to walk the length of the room. She was wearing brand-new shoes, and the slick leather soles forced her to slow down.

"Larry raised the rent on you, didn't he?"

"Yes."

"Enough to make a difference?"

"Anything makes a difference."

"He's so cheap! He's been in therapy for years, and that's one of the things that's supposed to get better, only it hasn't. If you only knew how we talk about you around here. I'll tell you a secret. That week both girls were at cheerleading clinic and Cliffie managed to get himself invited to Denver, Larry and I had the nicest possible tête-à-tête. I cooked for once, and the whole thing was so cozy we even ate in the kitchen. We talked and talked! I don't know what got into us; we were like kids again. Well, your name came up, and do you know what happened?"

"I can't guess."

"We wound up praying for you. We bowed our heads and held hands and said a prayer that your life would change."

Laydelle examined a split end. She looked at her shoes and the new painting Sally had bought in Taos and all the folk art that now littered the mantel. Sally had taken down all the mirrors in the living room. But Laydelle knew the heat she felt on her face meant she was blushing. And not with a nice rosy tint that began in sweet blooms along her throat. Her cheeks were the color of blood.

"You are the two most manipulative people I've ever known."

Sally arched her back with a sigh.

"It's no wonder you live like you do. You spit on the very people who try to befriend you."

"How many times over the past year have I dashed to your rescue? Come upstairs and talked you down off the ledge or taken care of your own children when you were too busy with your show dogs? I have driven the twins to more lessons than I care to remember. Cliffie and his hormones, for God's sake. Sally, your son has a drinking problem, and I seem to be the only one around who's noticed."

"I guess that is the difference between us. I don't count. These are just the things friends do for each other."

"Friends? Friends!"

Sally Marble managed to work up the first tear, which was always the toughest. She couldn't do it without frowning. Screw Cher, she decided. Laydelle stood over her, and she was faced with an awful dangling silver pendant of some kind. Indian, probably. Yes, Indian. There were little turquoise chips all along the edge. Her voice was uneven when she spoke.

"I've invited a couple of judges to the party. Come on, Laydelle! I've bragged on you. They think it's *interesting* that you live here. I mean, our house has its little history, and they like that, but the fact that I've got a Hanks living here is truly, truly appealing. Are you going to make me beg, Laydelle? There's a name for this kind of behavior. You have some kind of sickness! I know that from the reading I've done. Laydelle, it's the last chance to do anything significant before the show at Madison Square Garden."

"I'll come."

"You will?"

"Yes. I wouldn't turn down something so important to you. I don't know why on earth I should be of so much interest to your friends, but that's not the issue. Yeah, I'll help you."

Sally was marching again. There was a light bounce to her step, and she snapped her fingers as she planned.

"But there's a problem."

"No, there's not. Not now that we agree."

"I don't have anything to wear."

"You big silly. You can borrow from me just like all the other times."

"I don't want to borrow from you, Sally."

She stopped pacing and looked at Laydelle, who needed to wash her hair. Sally noticed two blue cups under her eyes and wondered how many sleepless nights it took to put them there.

"I want a good dress and a pretty collar to go with it, just like the ones you buy for your doggy-woggies. I've got great legs, Sally, and I want to show them off for your judges. I'll come to your party and make chic, informed small talk with your guests. And I'll feel great because I look great. Clothes make the woman, isn't that it? Also—"

"There's more?"

"Uh huh. You'll get Larry to lower the rent and give me a two-year lease, which I can break if I want to. But only if I want to."

"I don't believe I am standing in the center of my living room listening to this."

"But you are. I think I can find just the right things for the party at Neiman's."

A squirrel was making the dogs frantic. They were being teased, and it was quite merciless. Sally Marble was too preoccupied to notice the commotion. Adobe Blue was scratching the fur behind one ear so fitfully, patches of it had come right off.

"I'm not as dumb as you think. I love my dogs and the show folderol dearly, but that's not my true passion, you know. And that's really why you're still here."

It was as if her insides were singing. Laydelle felt anger so pure it could have been strummed on a harp. She was definitely up from the trench.

"Why do you think I've been wading through dog shit all these years? To cuddle up to all those old ladies and freakies who come to the shows? Just to see my trophies and my ribbons in this house? Hell, no; they're in a box somewhere, God knows where. My fascination is with bloodlines, Laydelle. With what goes right and what goes wrong. I study my dogs and, honey, I study you. You're a mess. You're an insult to Nelson Hanks' memory, and genetic mishaps happen to be my hobby."

Sally turned casually to get her purse. She handed her a Neiman's card.

"Have them call me for an okay. Okay to the second thing, too. Who knows, maybe in two years I'll have an answer. Maybe I'll be the one to break the code and figure out why you're such a mess."

The howling of the dogs penetrated Sally's head, and she started out the door.

"By the way, I do know what's eating you, Laydelle. You're a whole lot more fun when Johnny Beaureve deigns to fuck you."

The saleswoman let her into the dressing room with a key. The pink and gold room contained a chaise longue. Laydelle removed her shoes and skirt and lay down, staring at the three black dresses that hung beside the mirror. She shifted to a more comfortable

position on the lounge and didn't rush to try them on. The saleswoman returned after several minutes and cleared her throat discreetly outside the slatted door.

"Doing okay in there?"

"Great, thanks."

She still hadn't gotten up.

"Can I bring you anything else?"

She doubted the dresses alone could transform what she saw in
the mirror, a lankiness that wasn't quite right. She didn't look lean;
she looked skinny. She didn't look stylish; she looked hungry and
underfed. She had anticipated this afternoon, and it was all going
wrong. She sighed and pulled a clasp out of her purse. With her
hair up off her shoulders, she stood a better chance of liking what
she saw. She pinched her cheeks several times.

The first dress flared out in all the wrong places, and the collar
on the second one was too tight. She was nearly into the last dress
when the saleswoman returned.

"Still there?"

"Can you get me into this thing?"

The woman let herself in, and as she worked the zipper up
slowly, she glanced over Laydelle's shoulder into the mirror.

"What kind of price tag are we looking at?"

Laydelle stared straight ahead.

"We aren't looking at price tags today."

The woman didn't miss a beat. She began unzipping.

"My name is Sadie, and I've been working here for seven and a
half years. I've been waiting for somebody to walk in here and
have the guts to say that. Do you need accessories? Shoes?"

"The works. I wear a seven and a half."

They parted fast friends three hours later. It developed that
Sadie was not only a saleswoman; she was a grandmother and a
psychic. So Laydelle wasn't ashamed when she didn't leave the
room to let her change clothes in peace. She stood in front of the
unlying mirror in underwear purchased long before at a lingerie
sidewalk sale. Sadie even translated various bras and silk che-
mises, showing what they were designed to do and how they could
be worn. At the end, when Laydelle had reached the summit of
the shopping spree and stood stock-still in deep-green silk and the
right necklace, indisputably beautiful, Sadie slipped away, to
return with a demitasse cup. Steam rolled off the top in little
bursts.

"Well, it's chicken consommé, so I won't be able to read your future in the coffee grounds. But it doesn't take a psychic to know you can get anything you want dressed like this. Here, drink. L'chaim."

And if it worked? If she could get anything she wanted dressed like this? She was almost at the door when the telephone rang. The lights were all on at the house, and the guests had begun arriving fifteen minutes earlier. She figured it was Sally, telling her to hurry up. Sally Marble had suggested they bury the hatchet, but she'd had such an unnatural gleam in her eye, Laydelle wondered where she intended the hatchet to be buried.

"It's me."

"Well, stranger."

She ran her free hand up and down her hip, loving the feel of the material. She blotted her lips carefully on a tissue.

"I'm in town. I want to see you."

"Mmmm. Me and who else? Sheila Langhurst called here for your number."

"I hope you didn't give it to her. Let's meet for drinks."

"Just like that? Why didn't you call earlier, Johnny? You never seem to think I have any plans, any life. I'm on my way out."

"Then see me after you go out. I'll wait up."

"You didn't answer my question."

"I don't operate like that, and you know it. I don't make dates and plans and maps for my life."

"You're out of luck, Beaureve. Call another number."

He didn't hang up and he didn't speak. She fingered silk and hated the way the palms of her hands had begun to sweat. She owned the dress she was wearing. It fit her and flattered her, and luck changed because of those things, didn't it? Shit. She bit her lip, marring the gleaming coat of Careless Crimson.

"Are you there, Johnny?"

"Of course."

"The party ought to be over by midnight. If it isn't, I'll leave. Don't come here, though."

"Meet me at the Orchard Bar, then."

"Johnny, I resent the hell out of you. I resent your confidence and your cruelty and your voice on the telephone when you call. You know what? I look great tonight."

"What do you have on?"

"It's expensive and it's clingy, and when I go to this party anything could happen. Someone could fall in love with me. Really in love with me. Not like you."

She waited for him to talk. The house was filling up fast, and she imagined Sally was beside herself, imagining she'd been cheated. That Laydelle would come really late or not at all.

"What do you have on underneath the dress?"

"It gets even better, Johnny. I treated myself real right this week. You dope. I hope you're in a state, thinking about me. And that you stay like that until you hit the Orchard. And then I'll either be there or I won't be."

"Now who's being cruel?"

"Me. It's high time, too."

Sally met her at the back door.

"Come on. Jerry Tibble is asking for you, and somebody else whose mother claims to have been your grandmother's fast friend way back in Creston."

"Oh, God."

"Oh, and an uninvited guest. Uninvited by me anyway. Larry told him to drop by without letting me know. Handsome. Real different. Give the bartender your order and circulate, circulate."

She moved listlessly around the room, surprised that owning the dress and jewelry didn't make her task any easier. She shook the hands of various strangers and tried to make small talk. The feasibility of ostrich breeding in Oklahoma? She nodded and waved at the waiter for a second drink. Screw ostriches! she wanted to shout. Laydelle found a judge, figuring that was her only real obligation to Sally Marble. She tried talking up the dogs, then she drew a blank on which one Sally hoped would take Best of Show. She dodged the elderly woman who tried to catch her eye, the woman whose mother recalled the Creston days. Jerry Tibble pursued her around the room.

"Hold it right there! Hanks, Laydelle Hanks. Isn't that your name?"

"That's me."

"I've been trying to get hold of you all night long."

"Well, now you have me."

He rubbed his chin and cheek ruminatively. What was it about men like him? she wondered. I bet he's a golfer. He pointed one finger at her suddenly.

"Stray fact."

She waited, but Jerry Tibble was biding his time. Laydelle thought of the debate team at Smith. The silent pause, most efficient of all forms of verbal punctuation.

"Your grandfather won a Daimler in a poker game. Chicago, am I right?"

"Right."

She sighed. He was showing off. She waited for the slew of facts that would follow. I Know Your Family Better Than You, most dreary of all parlor games.

"And your daddy up and lost his house in a poker game years later."

"What?"

"The Nelson Reeve story. The way Hubbell Hanks lost his house to some scoundrel named after his own father in a poker game. You look as if you don't believe a word I'm saying."

"I'm not sure I do."

"All those old title records are on microfilm now, you know. You mean you haven't heard this story?"

"But if that's true, how did my father get the house back?"

"Why, his daddy bought it back and then ran Nelson Reeve out of town. Seventy-five thousand dollars. Quite a lot of money back then."

And quite a lot now. Laydelle thought of Hair Apparent. She thought of rivers, of Hubbell's solemn address. Tibble was looking at her queerly.

"Do you play poker?"

"No. But maybe I should take it up, since it seems to run in the family."

"As long as you don't play with the pros." Tibble was laughing. At what? She looked down at her dress. Nothing was slopped or spilled. She looked fine, just fine.

"Thanks for the warning."

By the time she glanced at her watch, it was eleven-thirty. She retreated to a quiet corner of the study, sitting near a shelf that held the entire untouched Encyclopaedia Britannica. She stretched one leg at a time, examining her stockings for snags.

"Where'd she get off to? Dang, now I know you both would have a world of things to talk about. Laydelle? Anybody seen Laydelle Hanks?"

She stood up and wondered if standing up when a man entered the room was appropriate. Laydelle had no idea. She already knew this man. She felt her chest grow warm. Had she tried (and failed) to sell him a security system?

"There you are, you little devil. Got somebody here who wants to reintroduce himself. Seems he met you years ago, though he won't say more about it than that. I call him Pharaoh, but you can call him whatever you want. What do you say, Pharaoh? Has our little gal changed much?"

The man looked ill at ease. His suit was a poor fit, slightly short in the sleeve and tight across the shoulders. He moved as if he were unused to being indoors, as if the room itself held his stride in check. Laydelle glanced at the man's face, then down at her own hands. Nothing hid the hope that crossed his face. He drew one hand through thick, wavy hair going gray at the edges and leaned forward to brush his cheek with hers. Laydelle wondered if she was going crazy. The man smelled like bread.

"What's this about being a pharaoh?"

He grinned and motioned toward the sofa where she had just been sitting.

"Larry Marble likes to kid me. It's a nickname that has to do with my business."

"Which is?"

"Sales."

"Oh, I'm in sales, too. What's your product?"

"Vitamin tablets at the moment. But it could be anything. My real product is people."

She settled into his face, was listening and not listening at the same time. His face was welcoming. That was it. His face and, in fact, his whole person seemed to welcome her. He was tipping her way on the sofa but not too much. It wasn't impropriety but gladness. He mentioned pyramid sales, and she forced herself to a different kind of consciousness.

"But I've heard bad things about that."

Larry Marble was long gone, and she realized after the evening was over how remarkable that was. And how Sally must not have been lying about their little dinner in the kitchen. Maybe they did wish for her welfare in the only way they could.

"They'll be illegal in a year's time. But they're not now, and there's good money to be made. Real good money."

There was a small white nick under his left eye, and she thought about what a close call that had been. How whatever that nick represented had barely missed such a fine blue eye.

"You seem so familiar, but I can't remember meeting you. It must have been a very long time ago."

"The first time we met, you were seven years old, Lady. And I was seventeen. You took my hand and said you knew exactly where you were going. We caught fireflies and fished for shoes, and I thought you were the most beautiful thing I had ever seen in my life. I decided no matter how hard it would be to track you down one day, I would do it, just to find out if beautiful little girls turned into beautiful women. I promised I would come to see you and find out for myself. To do it I had to pretend I had an interest in distributing Larry Marble's fishing rods. But it worked."

She sat on the edge of the sofa, holding herself so rigidly she might as well have been perched on the edge of a precipice. She selected sensations from that important time. Her fear at seeing Mary's tight face, her sadness when the glass jar of fireflies shattered to set light loose for good, it had seemed then. She didn't actually remember the boy who stood at the center of sensation, but she remembered everything surrounding him.

"You've sure gone to an awful lot of trouble."

Laydelle put the tip of her finger on that nick. She felt its slight swell, its springiness under her touch.

"Your mother believed I had done something to you that night by the river. So did Father Ed, it turned out. He didn't give me that scar but he managed to work me over pretty good. I spoiled the picnic for him."

There was a deep, hushed space, wide enough to harbor them both. The party sounded far away, as if it were taking place on a different planet.

"Did your mother make you believe that, too? Or your father? You were a child! I didn't want to touch you. I just thought you were beautiful. Something I was lucky to watch for one night. And I forgot that nobody would buy that, coming from a seventeen-year-old delinquent."

She shook her head, which was ready to explode. She had to talk, otherwise the top of her skull would flip open, and she would burst with all this man made her feel.

"So why didn't you carry me off? Why didn't you just steal me away if you thought I was so beautiful? We could have . . ."

She turned, and the silk rode up her leg. She could see half of Sally Marble, who was split in two by the doorway. Cab Edwards took both her hands, which were fluttering like birds loosed in a closed room. He covered and stilled them with his own.

"We could have what? Children don't raise children. Don't make this a fairy tale."

She couldn't sit still. Why now? Why was everything heading straight at her right this minute? She thought of Johnny, who was waiting. She thought of the Orchard Bar and the wooden crates and barrels, all the phony plastic fruit that constituted decoration.

"You said that was the first time we met. Where else have I seen you?"

Cab turned his head to watch a waiter scurry past the doorway with a tray full of empty glasses.

"I talked my way into a fund-raiser out at Buffabrook, just like I talked my way into this party. You didn't give me the time of day, though. Guess you thought I was hired help the way you snubbed me."

He tilted her chin up with one finger, forcing her to look at him.

"Hey, it's not your fault I've got such lousy taste in clothes. I probably *did* look like a waiter."

"Sometimes I just want to lie down. I'm so tired I could curl up on the sofa and be dead to the world in a second."

He pulled one of her batting hands to the small of his back and then the other. She came so close, her bursting head didn't fly apart. Instead, it filled up with the improbable smell of sweet, warm bread.

"You can't lie down yet, Lady."

"Things aren't great for me at the moment. They haven't been great for a long time, and I'm scared to death. Every day it's worse, not better. What the hell am I telling you this for? You're a perfect stranger."

"Wrong on both counts. I'm not perfect and I'm no stranger. I've waited a long time for this. I won't let you lie down now."

Johnny Beaureve stayed at the Orchard Bar until one-fifteen. The bartender answered the phone and wrote something down on a

piece of paper. Slightly sheepish, he left his post behind the counter
to hand him a brief note.

Dear Johnny,
No more French postcards.
No more truck fucks.
You are one sweet dream I will never have again.

chapter 45

They couldn't find the old footpath by the river's edge. The only thing that remained the same was the second city of light and shadows, which leaned out into the river. There was nothing tranquil about the dark sweep of water. The illusory second city puffed and chugged even at midnight, magnifying all the power and energy of its neighbor along the banks. They could read the utility company's messages in the center of the Arkansas, could see the row of sanitation trucks farther down, where they appeared assembled on top of the water. Joggers and pedestrians still went through their paces. Children smoked dope under bridges and roared at the sight of slow carp, such funny fish. Laydelle saw something moving in the brush and caught at Cab's hand. It was nothing. There was nothing in that stand of untidy brush to cause her hand to be held in his. But she kept it there and wondered how long he would let her arm swing by his side before dropping it in forgetfulness or discomfort. They walked that way without speaking until they reached a second bridge.

"Had enough?"

"I think so. I never do this, even though crossing the road would be the simplest thing in the world."

They looked back together and could see the house, how it was set deep inside the grounds, finally achieving insignificance once night fell.

"What now?"

She couldn't read his face to see what he meant. There wasn't enough light for that. Laughter floated over the water like vapor. He looked away for a minute, wrestling with something he wanted to say. She spoke before he did.

"We could keep walking until we both get sleepy or bored. Or I could just cross the street and go back. But I don't want to do either of those things. I don't have the faintest idea who you are, but I'd sure like it if you took me back to your place."

Maybe her brusqueness frightened him. Watching her phone up the Orchard and say those things into the telephone might have dashed some version of her, some fiction he had held in his mind despite his distaste for fairy tales. Maybe he imagined she always spoke like this or felt like this. Maybe he thought she broke free of men easily. How could he know she was lurching toward new language and new acts with the cloudy consciousness of a drunk?

She didn't want to open her eyes. She was afraid the room would look cheap in the early light, that dusty venetian blinds and dirty ashtrays, an empty beer can or wastebaskets filled and overflowing, would make her forfeit part of the long, lush night with Cab Edwards. Her eyes opened reluctantly, and she thought of how little she knew, the risks she had taken on the suggestion of a perfect stranger. Was he a bachelor? She didn't even know that. She saw Cab before she saw the room. He was already awake, his chin cupped in his hand. She rubbed her eye with a closed fist and he smiled.

"You do that like a little kid."

"Mmmm. How did you sleep?"

"I didn't."

She drew the covers up to her chin.

"So if you didn't sleep, what did you do?"

"I was afraid I would wake up and find you gone. Besides, how could I sleep when I was so busy watching you?"

He touched the side of her head with his hand, and she lifted her head from the pillow, wide awake now.

"Did I snore?"

"Yeah. You tossed and turned, you sighed and said hello to someone. You're really something."

He traced the edge of her mouth with his finger.

"Thank you."

She scowled, and her eyes darkened at the words. She'd been thanked before. She'd been vaguely thanked on too many train platforms or badly lit stairwells to want to hear those words now.

"For what?"

"For being a beautiful child who grew into a beautiful woman. Turn over."

She rolled over on her stomach and turned her head away from Cab so that she could concentrate. She glanced at a table loaded with things not purchased in a sweep but collected and culled from the times of a life, and she would ask about that later. Right now she closed her eyes, appeased, to focus on the touch of his hand and the way her own skin felt. He was rubbing the small of her back, warming it with a slow, firm pressure that spread out from that center.

"I feel very guilty. I'm not doing much for you just lying here soaking this up."

"You're not just lying there. There's nothing passive about you, Lady Hanks."

Would he say it again? Turn her name into *that*? It sounded so beautiful the way he said it: Lady! His hand continued its circles, while the other ran up and down her back. He was on his knees, and when the sheet was lifted off, she forgot to be embarrassed about being seen. She forgot to consider how she looked, what the morning light did to her flesh, what seeing her unclothed meant to someone unused to the angles and planes she regretted. She was too happy to deduct anything from her own pleasure. For the first time, exposure relaxed her rather than the reverse. She lay thinking of gifts as his hands continued to move. Of all the gifts that had given her the greatest satisfaction. Red velvet valentines, a yellow duckling she once held under her chin, a piece of shiny quartz sliced from a mountain somewhere, and a brocade jacket with a mandarin collar. All these things were heaped around her as Cab Edwards pressed and stroked, spread his wide hands across her back. He turned her over gently.

"I can't believe I've really found you."

His exposure equaled hers. What had begun in a face seemingly unversed in disguise and concealment fanned out through broad shoulders and hands eager to give and receive pleasure. She would have supposed the opposite, that a hard life would have left its flinty deposit. She asked this as his hand stroked her face, brushed the hair from her eyes.

"You know all those stories you told me last night, Cab?"

"What about them?"

"Why don't all those hard times show?"

"They do. Take a look at this."

He pointed to the scar below his rib cage.

"I don't mean that."

Laydelle looked slightly uncomfortable.

"This is going to sound corny, but I'm talking about something else. Something kind of . . . spiritual. There, I spit it out."

He laughed and kissed her again, lightly on the cheek.

"Look. My idea is that fat people have no idea what they're eating; they just gorge and gorge, without any notion of a hunger pang. They've never let themselves feel real hunger, that stab in the gut. I have, over and over again, and I'll never forget it, but you get to a place where hunger doesn't affect you anymore. Once you've done that, outlived your own misery, you might be that one person in a million who can really feel joy. I'm not talking about happily ever after and cozy slippers, Lady. I'm talking about joy. Maybe that's what you mean."

The sound of the new name shot through her again. He pressed her mouth open gently. His tongue moved slowly back and forth over her palate, one hand still on the side of her mouth. Laydelle tipped her head back slightly, eager for him to run his tongue over her teeth and lips. She wanted Cab Edwards everywhere and fought her own impatience, which seemed greater than his. He paused to look at her, to plant deep kisses on her eyelids and her temples and retrace these spots with his warm tongue. Time passed without seeming to. He opened every square inch of her to love.

"Oh!"

It was a bare whisper of surprise. Laydelle reached down, and as she held him, lightly fingering the tip of him, she felt the small slip of wetness as it came. His skin began to glide under her fingers as he moved, and she stretched her legs wider still. He rubbed over and over the top of her, until the zone of her own pleasure lay wide as a cloth spread between her knees. His face held so many things that she looked away.

"You don't have to watch me if you're embarrassed. I love loving you, Lady."

She watched at first. She watched Cab Edwards lift her gently up with one hand and slide a pillow beneath her with the other. He began slowly to stroke her and part a clear path for his lips and tongue. Because she seemed much lower and farther away from the seat of such careful and deliberate lovemaking, she allowed herself to watch until the sight was too frightening. She held her eyes shut. That way she could memorize sensation. With her breath held, she could hold on tighter to the slip of his finger and his sliding tongue. She held his face in her hands, her eyes still closed. The sense of being coiled tighter and tighter inside finally hit its strange pitch.

He didn't stop. He entered her, and she grew both selfish and bold, leading him by tilts and turns, soft cries, to the seat of her greatest pleasure. The light changed, and the room warmed. Time slowed, then speeded up, spinning like a crazy wheel turning on its own.

Laydelle reached for her watch on the side table and frowned. There was a Pedigree Protection appointment that wouldn't wait. She cited this thing and others, wishing they would dissolve, and Cab Edwards warned her one last time about fairy tales.

"One thing I can say about Pleasant Hill. At least nobody insulted us with storybooks out there. The old s.o.b. banned novels. No Pleasant Hill boy ever believed a frog would turn into a prince, and maybe that's why I was content to just look at a little girl by the side of a river. Father Ed rocked his boys to sleep by reading them the state penal code. You want to know how many times you just used the word 'wish'? Four. You made four wishes right in a row. That's an awful lot of wishing for a grownup. Open your eyes."

They were open. She saw a man who'd spent a whole night just watching her sleep, who called her Lady Hanks without the slightest hint of irony. She saw a man who kept his peculiar appointments even after years had passed.

"What are you doing next Tuesday, Cab?"

"Nothing that can't be canceled."

"Will you run up to Lovely with me? I've got a meeting scheduled, but that won't take long. I'd really like you to go."

"On one condition."

"Okay."

He laughed.

"You're quick to concede. The condition is that I make us a
picnic lunch. That way we can avoid the Lovely Café."

"Come here, Cab."

He pressed her knees up and placed her feet on his chest as they
began to rock together. Shortly she turned on her belly and brought
his arms in front of her so she could lift up slightly off her chest.
Cab held her trapped close, and she hitched herself up high in back
to feel him. She fought for breath, and as she struggled she contracted, drawing him in deeper and deeper. He dove into her, not
letting up until he said her name one last time. Slowly, slowly she
let go of his hands.

Then, as if it were the most natural thing in the world, Cab
Edwards burrowed his face back into the pillow that was still damp
with her. He coiled himself into a round, breathing deeply in and
out. Her odors, her perfumes, seemed to send him straight off to
sleep.

They held their tailgate picnic on the leafy bluff where Indian coun-
cils had once sat. The shade and damp tricked them into thinking
the temperature had fallen or that there would be an early fall.
Everything smelled like earth and rot, dead and dying things allowed to accumulate and decompose into richness. Cab's station
wagon, rid of vitamin tablets for the moment, was stocked with
champagne and several jars of Beluga caviar. The present tense
was pleasantly muddied. They lounged on tree stumps and talked
of oil men and Osage, legacies left whole or squandered. The ice
chest was filled with smoked salmon and lobster salad. He'd
thrown in a pasta dish, thick with truffles. There was food for a
dozen people, and he didn't blink an eye at the excess.

"I didn't know if you liked seafood. There's filet, too. I sliced it
thin."

"I can't even make a dent in all this food."

"Don't try to. I just wanted you to have plenty to choose from."

"If you're trying to seduce me, it's working."

They were laughing, released from any restraint up there on the
bluffs. They could see the shoddy main street of Lovely and
the fields that lay about the town, dun-colored as the back of a
buckskin pony. The landscape was completely indifferent to
them.

Cab spread a blanket on the moist ground. It was so soft. Even
the colors were soft, light pinks and blues. A baby could have lain
there, perfectly soft and warm, with not a worry to sensitive skin.
It belonged on the end of a bed or folded inside a hand-painted
trunk belonging to someone's grandmother, not spread out over
muddy ground. Cab lounged near the edge. His shirt was open,
and he'd rolled up his sleeves. Laydelle felt her throat grow warm
and blamed it on the champagne and the excitement. There had
just been too much excitement today.

"Come lie down by me."

"No!"

Laydelle felt slapped, harmed by the question. She was surprised at how hard she snapped. But she was definitely done with
certain things. Love in the great outdoors just happened to be one
of them.

"I didn't mean to scream at you. God, look at the time! Paddy's
a stickler about punctuality."

He looked at her, puzzled, and she shrugged.

"I think I've had too much to drink. But that's one thing Paddy
won't mind."

"We've gone over this before."

"Hey. It's me, Paddy. You're not talking to a traveling salesman."

Mahoney had a bruised rib. Every breath he took caused
him trouble and pain. He wanted to yank it out like an ailing
tooth.

"Look, Laydelle. You know where I stand on this security
bullshit, and just because you're peddling high-tech padlocks
doesn't change my mind. You know what purchasing a new security system would mean?"

"I sure do. About fifteen thousand dollars and temporary peace
of mind."

"It would mean opening the books to dumbshit accountants and
a brand-new scuffle with the board of directors about expensive

appraisals and a huge increase in insurance premiums. And for what?"

"For me, Paddy! Christ, I'm asking you for a favor."

He drew a deep sigh and winced. He couldn't even remember the fall, but a bruised rib had resulted and a deep cut on the back of his head. He lifted himself heavily out of the chair and pulled a box down from a low shelf. The mindless task helped ease his foul mood.

"Have you even looked at the material I brought up here last week? I left you mounds of information, and I told you Jack Marsley himself would come down here from Houston. This installation is nothing to him, Paddy. Do you understand that? You're small potatoes compared to some of our clients."

"The VP of Pedigree. Sounds like a limerick. Don't try to shame me into buying your crap, honey. It won't work."

"What will, Paddy? Tell me what will. Speaking of crap, what is all that stuff?"

"This stuff, in part, is what you're trying to safeguard."

He held up a piece of bark, dropped it, and sifted through the box for something else. He held it up, a grin cracking over his face.

"It looks like an animal tooth."

"Walrus, to be exact. Let me read from this inventory sheet. 'Piece of elephant hide, fairy stones, piece of crude rubber.' Ah, now here's one. 'A piece of tile from the Emperor's Palace.' What emperor and what palace? Doesn't say. 'Pumice from Pompeii and a piece of bread.' I have to go to the board of directors for permission to destroy this crud. Do you believe that? Hubbell Hanks has to come all the way up here on official business, the business being do we trash water from the Ganges, water from the Sea of Galilee and the Dead Sea and water from Jacob's Well? Or do we keep filling these bitty bottles with tap water the way we've been doing for years and years? I'll take samurai swords and Anasazi pots with pleasure, but I'm also obliged to take any crap some descendant of a friend of Nelson Hanks wants to unload on me. And then you come. You arrive with a plan to make sure nobody makes off with anything from this pile or any other, and that plan is going to increase my woes about a hundredfold."

Paddy got up slowly, the grin gone.

"You're like a general who's massed his men on the wrong hill. You've been at the head of a stupid march for years. Think. Put your thinking cap on, and finish this small-time stuff."

She lit one of his cigarettes, though he thought she'd quit. She didn't bother to close the flap on the matches. Beauty! The kind that wasn't cultivated under glass lids in pale, precious sunshine. The other kind, her kind. Paddy thought about the book of matches catching fire. She would have tossed it in his face with no compunction.

"Who's the guy waiting upstairs?"

She remembered Cab, and the tightness in her shoulders melted. She unfolded the leg that was tucked underneath her. Unfolded it gently and let both legs sprawl open like a man.

"None of your fat business, Paddy."

"Easy. That's a man with something to say. That's a man who's been high and low, I'd guess, and all that altitude change is bound to give him an advantage that neither one of us has. We're all cooped up in our present lives, but not him. Not that one. I bet he can see for miles and miles. Backward and forward, up over our heads."

She blew smoke out lazily and tilted her head back, since it was done. Paddy had changed the subject, and there was no help for her here. She leaned forward and peered at a piece of paper next to Paddy's box of dusty junk. *Destroy.* She counted twenty typewritten orders to destroy. Five gifts were to be made to a service league. She chuckled and stood up to go.

"Just who's at the head of a stupid march? So this is where you carry out your military assignments, General. In a dark basement. You know where the rest of us have to operate, Paddy? Outdoors, where there's wind and rain. So what if you don't *really* need a security system? So what if it causes you a little more paperwork? You're a sorry, pompous bastard, Paddy, posing as bad boy all these years. All that stuff about new insurance premiums and opening the books is just stuff. You don't want to be accused of favoritism. What I'm proposing is an unnecessary expense that means pocket money for Laydelle Hanks, and you don't want to get your hands dirty. I'll let you get back to your work."

She took a second look at a charcoal propped against the wall.

"Stinky. No life."

"You're telling me. That's why I'm going to a workshop in Chicago next month, to try to resuscitate my charcoals. Appeal to the man upstairs, Laydelle. He's got the power, not me."

"Screw you, Paddy."

Jeans, God love them. He watched her walk slowly from his office. He succumbed to very private thoughts and was both lost and redeemed by the beautiful, vanishing sight of her.

chapter 46

"I'm sorry."

She didn't think Cab heard or, if he had heard, cared that she was sorry. She'd forgotten about this, fear disguised as sleepiness, which snared her at the worst moments. She could have curled up anywhere just then and slept for hours. Even movement was difficult, like pushing through thick paste. She looked at his shoulders as he worked, realizing that she no longer knew him, if, in fact, she ever had. He was all tight concentration, focused on tools and metal, entering a room on a soundless shaft. Cab Edwards was primed for this, but she wasn't. This was his vein of gold ore. Here, in the foyer of the Buffabrook Museum, he turned pure professional.

"Flip it the other way."

He put his fingers to her lips and was firm, not unkind. This evening, this nine o'clock evening, Lady Hanks was strictly decoration. In her somnambulant state, she would settle for that. She stood by his side and watched his hands, strange and gone from her forever, it seemed, in leather gloves. She watched the butt of a .38 revolver, where it poked out from his waist, still not understanding how he had let that get in the way. Because it had gotten between them, shown up clear misunderstanding of an event that had less to do with robbery than with reclamation. "What are you doing with that?" He didn't bother with an answer. For a horrible moment that seemed as opaque as the surface of his eyes, she saw herself as she must have seemed: a fool who concluded that armed robbery was nothing more than a kind of retrieval.

The power went off suddenly, and the sleepiness was gone. A single thread of terror went straight from the back of her head to her heels, snapping her upright.

"Cab? Hey, where are you?"

She heard him fumble for something in the suitcase that lay by his feet and then saw the beam from a flashlight. It struck the sides of the room where they stood, and she followed the light, not Cab, as it seemed to lead her into the first exhibit hall.

"Well, here we are at last. I've pulled off worse than this and lived, but I want you to remember this was your idea, not mine. It's your score to settle, and I'm happy to help because I'm nuts about you. But remember this is your gig. Dig in, Lady. Take what you believe belongs to you, and no stories, please. You seem to think you're robbing your own house, and it can't be done. If you're caught, they'll nail you like any other criminal. All the sophisticated rationale in the world doesn't change the fact that you're crossing over, Lady, and faster than you think."

It was terrible to hear him and not see his face. It wasn't just how he moved; his voice was new, deep and rough, full of messages she didn't want to hear. She was alone in dark rooms, and she saw how all the other bad places in her life had been nothing next to this. He facilitated nothing. He was nothing. He was a silent passenger in a car she drove by herself. He handed her a suitcase without touching her.

"Go on. The system's shut off. You can help yourself to whatever you want. Point me in any direction, and I'll bust open the cases."

If I have to wake up, she thought, let it be far from here. I don't want to remember any of this. She couldn't recall plans, if she'd had them, or motives, if they existed. She was carrying out orders, whether Cab believed it or not. He had said to help herself, and that was a command. She moved toward a case that held Billy the Kid's guns. She hadn't realized he would break the glass. That there would be that mess the following day, like the aftermath of a domestic scene. Shattered glass felt like that to her. Horrible. A whole house collapsing.

"Don't waste your time. Collectors know there's nowhere to go with this stuff if you don't accept their offers. Try over there. That stuff from Spiro."

When she had presented the idea to him, he'd disappeared for two weeks. He hadn't telephoned, hadn't said where he was going, but he came back with a more precise idea of what needed to be done than she had. The flashlight's beam trembled slightly and fell on red glazed bowls with feminine, scalloped edges, effigy pipes and a gorget traced with imagery that shocked her now in the dark museum. She hadn't ever assumed that these things could be touched. She gritted her teeth, for a length of black metal was coming down. Glass was flying now, with the second and third blow. Amazed, she saw up and down the length of Cab Edwards' whole life as he broke open the top of the case.

It got easier. She began the work of forgetting. If what they were doing took place at a certain hour on a certain day, she forgot it. She was movement and action; reflection seemed to occupy insignificant space somewhere else. She saw something gold, something that glittered under the dancing light, and moved toward it. There was glass, lots of it, which littered the first room and then the second. As she lifted up jewelry and beadwork, shawls centuries old, she set them on her own neck and shoulders. She filled the suitcase and felt it bump along her leg as she moved forward. Soon (was it soon?) all sense of desecration was lost. She was a child again, loosed in a room full of heirlooms she could touch at last. It was a dress-up party for her own pleasure. She could see her reflection occasionally, and because the image made her sad, she averted her eyes. She didn't follow Cab's voice or even, after a while, the thin rod of light. She vanquished everything, the present, past and future, as she rolled through the rooms, riding on sensation. The suitcases were nearly full. They were difficult to carry.

"Now what?"

But it wasn't Cab talking. She smelled the odor of cherry tobacco and saw the beam of the flashlight as it skimmed walls and doorways, faltering as it fell on Paddy Mahoney's face where he lounged inside an alcove.

"If you're carrying a gun you can forget it. I'm not armed. Well, don't talk at once. Now what?"

He sucked on his pipe, squinting his eyes under the strong light.

"Paddy, you're supposed to be in Chicago."

"No, I'm not. I'm supposed to be right here, waiting for you and your buddy-o. In the future you shouldn't take anybody's word for it. You should have nonchalantly asked me where I was staying in Chicago, who was running the workshop anyhow. Then called to find out I was lying through my teeth. That's what separates the men from the boys in this business, my darling, though your friend here should know this already. By the way . . ."

Paddy smirked under the light and took the pipe out of his teeth.

"I don't think we've been properly introduced."

He extended his hand in their direction. Laydelle lost the sense that anything in particular had happened. Here they were, standing in her grandfather's museum and talking, that was all. And Paddy, who had known her forever, was chiding her for not introducing him properly to a new friend. The edge in Cab's voice awakened her to a gun in the room held by a man she didn't know, since new men kept emerging from him like eggs from the belly of a live trout.

"Shut up. Take the pipe out of his mouth, Lady."

"It's just Paddy. We don't have to—"

"Shut up."

She threw her head back and opened her throat, releasing a bloody yell. When she opened her eyes, coming to, she saw that she held the gun now, even though it still rested in Cab Edwards' hand. She reached up into his hair, her nails scraping his scalp. She grabbed as much hair as she could find, both to hold her steady and to hold him still. Her voice came between clenched teeth, and she wondered where power came from, power and a fury it had taken this night to release.

"Put that away and talk to Paddy. That man knew me before I could walk. That man is me."

Paddy jerked his head and motioned for them to follow. There was the red glow from the pipe and the sound of his echoing steps through the halls and downstairs. He threw a switch at the top of the stairs, stairs she knew by heart. She still carried the suitcases, though they were headed toward the basement.

"Independent power system, in case the big one fails. Follow me, children."

Her back was cold. She was thinking not of the treasures in the suitcases, nor of any outcome in particular, because the two of them had lost. They had turned on each other, pivoting on fear and rage, and lost. She remembered their first encounter, along the river. No messenger of light stood beside her tonight.

"C'mon in and sit."

They did. Like two exhausted travelers done in by their journey. He poured them both a drink, waited, and filled Cab's glass a second time.

"Will someone at last answer my question. Now what?"

"Now you call the cops, and each of us will be slapped with a hefty sentence by some redneck judge in a few weeks. And the national press will have a helluva time with the added twist. Heiress robs own museum."

"I'm no heiress."

"To them you are."

"Well . . ."

Paddy drank deeply, with pleasure. Laydelle noticed he was fully dressed. No pajamas, no tousled hair.

"Is that the only scenario you two bozos can come up with?"

"What if you just talked, you know? This question-and-answer routine might amuse you, but you're the only one laughing. Just talk, Mahoney. And pick up the phone, so we can get this over with."

"I'm surprised at you, lowering the gun like that. There's a lot at stake."

"Look, will you just make the goddamned phone call?"

Paddy stood up and began to pace. His limp was more pronounced, and watching him became grotesque. Laydelle looked at her hands and thought, for once, they looked pretty. They looked like hands that had never touched a dish or a patch of dirt.

"So come on. Why did you tell me the story about Chicago?"

He came around to the back of the chair and put a moist hand on her neck.

"To trap you, darling. You may think you cooked up your little plan for this evening, but you're wrong. I planted the seeds, I prepared the earth and watered it liberally. You're here tonight because I set you up for it. Oh, I don't mean to rob you of all the glory. I could only prepare and suggest. You couldn't come here before you were ready. Pedigree Protection . . . your innocence, child! It was all I could do to smother my laughter that day."

Cab watched him carefully, rubbing his chin. He rested more comfortably in his chair.

"You're a Hanks, all right, but diluted. Third generation! Your grandfather would have hooted and howled at this—Lord, I wish he were sitting here now to take it all in. Your hesitant proposal that I install a system I *didn't really need.* I know what that cost your honest little soul. You're a Scout; not as bad as your father, but a Scout all the same. I've watched you grow up, don't forget, watched you manage to elude one opportunity after another, even though your mother fussed and fussed at you. Now this probably isn't exactly what Mary Hanks had in mind for you, but hell, I'm doing what I can. I told you to appeal to this con man sitting next to you, if you'll remember, because I knew you'd need him to get here at all. Well."

He put his hand on the telephone and lifted the receiver. Then he dropped it lightly back into the cradle.

"Sorry, couldn't resist. Nothing went wrong tonight, and I do wish you'd both wipe those frowns off your foreheads. Didn't have time to read the notice outside the entrance, I suppose? No? The museum is not only closed tomorrow, as it always is. It's closed for the entire week, because we're working on the north exhibit hall. You left me a pretty mess to clean up, but I counted on a little housekeeping, so it doesn't matter. When the staff returns day after tomorrow, they'll assume I've been on another toot and look the other way, like they've done for years. When I return all the pretties you removed from my displays, life will settle right down around here."

Cab clinched a fist, turning the knuckles white.

"What if it doesn't go back?"

"But it will. I've set aside all kinds of things for you two. In the end we'll all be happier. Come this way."

Down, down past the animal graveyard and into the room that held all the cast-off richness that couldn't be worked into the exhibits upstairs. But a new order had emerged since the last time Laydelle had visited. Objects were grouped, and the whole area seemed more spacious, less a minefield of unwanted art.

"Gave me a dandy excuse to inflict a little order on this place. My last hurrah, if I may say so. Aah."

He groaned as he bent to two low shelves at the very back of the room and reached behind a row of basketry.

"Cleaned up my files and worked nights on computer entries. I've done a shitload of work for the two of you, fool that I am. Most of what you're walking away with tonight has never been entered in any inventory sheet. The other stuff I've eliminated or reordered, so that this little absence will never be remarked. This is my baby, and everybody who works here knows to keep their hands to themselves. Here."

He put his fist in the pocket of Laydelle's jacket and pulled it out quickly. She reached in and felt pearls.

"These damn Spiro pearls. I can't just throw them out, and how many stickpins can a man wear? Sell them, why don't you? I've got the address of a plant in Tennessee that'll take 'em off your hands. They process them and send them to Japan. One small fragment set into a farmed oyster creates a whole new pearl. Or use 'em like worry beads, like Nelson used to. He just liked to touch them. Crazy. I can think of a hundred things I'd rather touch."

He looked rakishly at Laydelle.

"Ah, lighten up. I've been dipping into this museum for years, and it's time I retired from that, too. I don't mean to sound officious, but this is some night. I'm doing for you, Laydelle, in the only way a mediocre man can. I've been wanting to do something for you for years. Watching you tread water has just about made me a madman. You, I've got business to talk over with you. You can't just rush out of here with this stuff. Wait here, honey. We're going to talk things over for a little bit. You want something else to drink?"

It was four o'clock in the morning, and she wished she were asleep. She felt bad; crossing over felt bad. She regretted the shattered glass, the broken things and the mess. Paddy was mistaken, for something had gone wrong. The night had tipped over like a porcelain cup and burst into fragments, with all its contents revealed. She hadn't planned a thing, she had only stepped into a trap, a velvet trap, and she couldn't imagine what the new confinement meant. She freed a strand of Cab Edwards' hair from the dull copper bracelet that was supposed to ward off pain and didn't.

She could only see their silhouettes when they appeared in the doorway. Soon it wouldn't matter. The blazing sun would creep up through the sky before too long. Her knees ached as Cab helped her to her feet.

"I gave you a pretty bad time in there. Guess my nerves are shot." He pulled her closer and laid his cheek against hers for a moment. Paddy spoke up.

"Beat it, you two lovebirds."

She got behind the wheel as Cab loaded the suitcases in the trunk. He closed it gently, not slamming it. She supposed all his gestures would be like that for a while, self-conscious and tender, so she wouldn't explode or bolt or whatever he imagined she might do.

"You don't want to use the main exit?"

"There's something I want to see first."

She turned the car out of the parking lot toward the mausoleum, the real safe-deposit box at Buffabrook. She gunned the motor, and they headed slowly up the dirt road that led to the patchy clearing above. In a minute, with light just now squeezing into the sky, they would see all of it—the land laced with lakes and rivers, gullies and gulches. They would see the darkened museum and imagine *that* spectacle: kids, moms and pops come to Buffabrook on a Wild West pilgrimage.

Laydelle hit the brights, and a raccoon froze in her path for a second, then scuttled away. She could see the mausoleum ahead on the bluff, which was more overgrown than ever. They placated Nelson Hanks to this day. He wanted it wild. He wanted to rest under dry leaves and bramble. She cut the motor and rolled down her window.

"What's in there?"

"My grandfather. Let's sit for a moment, so I can catch my breath. If we take the road behind this building, it'll put us right onto the interstate. Fastest way of all to leave Buffabrook. He made sure of that."

At first she wasn't certain. She wouldn't have sworn she heard it, until it grew too distinct to ignore. It was Nelson, all right. Laughter, a round of soft laughter, rippled through the building. Laydelle leaned forward over the steering wheel and arched her back as she turned the key in the ignition. It was finally okay to leave.

About the Author

Linda Phillips Ashour is a native of Oklahoma. She is the great-granddaughter of Frank Phillips, founder of Phillips Petroleum. A graduate of Denison University, she is the author of *Speaking in Tongues*. Her short fiction has appeared in the *North American Review* and the *Paris Review*. She has received a fellowship at Yaddo.